P. 48
   61
   113
   125
   131
   241
   356
   559 St Martin's summer

Joseph A. DeBlase, M.D.

THE SPOILS OF WAR

THE
SPOILS
OF WAR

Thomas Fleming

G. P. PUTNAM'S SONS   NEW YORK

G. P. Putnam's Sons
Publishers Since 1838
200 Madison Avenue
New York, NY 10016

To John J. O'Connell

The will, that never can relent—
The aim, survivor of the bafflement—

HERMAN MELVILLE
Memorials of the slain
at Chickamauga

For we are bound where mariner has not yet dared to go
And we will risk the ship, ourselves and all

WALT WHITMAN
Leaves of Grass

I shall always reign through the intellect, but
the life! the life! Oh my God! shall that never
be sweet?

MARGARET FULLER
Journals

PROLOGUE

Clay Pendleton stood at one of the windows in the circular room beneath the golden dome of America's most successful newspaper, looking down on New York City. Below him, crowds were already gathering to celebrate the beginning of the twentieth century. They were in a self-congratulatory mood. In the last one hundred years Americans had laid more railroad track, built more factories, mined more metals and more coal, poured more steel, stretched more telegraph wire, launched more ships and—with the possible exception of old Mother England—made more money than any other nation in the world. Best of all, they had just won a war and acquired an overseas empire, proving that they were now a world power.

Tonight, stupendous fireworks would burst above the city. Boozy cheers would soar from hundreds of thousands of throats. From his lofty vantage point, Pendleton would watch his fellow Americans with a wary mixture of affection and apprehension. He would be there on the street with them, sharing their pride and optimism. But he would also be above them, not with a sense of superiority—far from it—but with a knowledge born of twenty-five years as a newspaperman. He knew how easy it was to play on the American people's hopes and fears. He knew how difficult it was to tell them the truth.

The truth was on Pendleton's mind tonight. He had been thinking about it, one way or another, for a long time. It had begun with a faded editorial he had once carried in his wallet, as a traveler to a foreign country might bring a letter of introduction. The editorial had been written by a newspaperman he barely knew, a one-man band who had printed his truths on a tiny flatbed press with the same ink-stained hands that had scribbled them on the back of old bills of sale. Pendleton had traveled long and far from his father's tiny two-room newspaper in South Carolina. Deep in the basement, eleven stories below the golden dome, the *New York World*'s stupendous steam-driven presses were spewing a million copies of tomorrow's paper into waiting trucks and wagons.

The truth. He heard it as mockery on the lips of another man, a swaggering golden youth who had given Pendleton the courage—the swagger too, for a while—to see the American world as something they would master, rule, on their own revolutionary terms, indifferent to the nostrums and prohibitions of tyrannical fathers and stultifying mothers. But the truth had shattered the bonds of friendship, broken both their hearts and hopes.

The truth, insisted another man, wandering the world like the mythical Jew of the nightmare fable, connected to the newspaper beneath Pendleton by telegraph and cable wires that carried his snarls and curses, his praise and his passion under oceans and over continents. The Jew tormented by history, by his sometimes hysterical hopes and fears. But linked to Pendleton by that maddening mystical word.

The truth, sighed another man, respecting the word, yet bitterly aware of the distance between inner and outer truths, between history's secrets and its myths. He had fought for the truth in its most elusive form, the chiaroscuro world of politics, driven by a dream of justice and peace burned into his soul by the staring eyes of the dead. He had sacrificed an extraordinary woman's love for it.

The women, the women. They had their own truths concealed in their intricate hearts. Failed truths, many of them. Lost causes. But also secret triumphs, surprising victories of the spirit. Over the last year, as the nineteenth century dwindled into months, weeks, days and now, finally, hours, Pendleton had tried to assemble all the truths that had come his way. The truths of the heart and the truths of the mind. Women as well as men possessed both kinds now.

At least, one woman in his life possessed both truths. From a nearby window, Pendleton could see the twisting miles of track in the railyards across the river in Jersey City where her train would soon arrive. His eyes followed the main line, the double set of gleaming steel rails that ran west into the heart of the continent, where Genevieve was arguing, cajoling, organizing other women into joining the struggle to make the mind and the heart equally important in their own lives and in the lives of their daughters and granddaughters.

Tomorrow, in his apartment overlooking the Central Park, Pendleton decided he would begin trying to shape the truths he wanted to remember. At the moment they were only a large dark object, gleaming like malachite in his mind. He wanted to carve memory into a thousand facets. Some day perhaps its blend of public and personal history might help others understand the old century that was passing and the new century that was coming toward them. If that happened, well and good. Pendleton was not writing it for that reason. He wanted to honor the truthtellers of his time—the men and the women.

BOOK I
1866–1872

ONE

The Legrands were born to sing, the Knowles to sigh.

The words echoed through Cynthia Legrand Stapleton's mind as she laid the last flowers of the season on her father's grave. Beneath the branches of the ancient cypress tree slept a dozen other Legrands, their tombstones dating back to the days when Louisiana belonged to France. She took a sprig of white aster from the bouquet and laid it on her brother Lancombe's grave. He had been a Knowles, sensitive and brooding like their mother, troubled by questions of honor and conscience, like so many of the earnest Protestants who had floated down the rivers to Louisiana after the purchase that made it part of the United States of America. Lancombe had been killed by a Yankee shell at the siege of Vicksburg.

But you never thought the last song would be so sad, did you, Father?

Cynthia looked across the two thousand acres of Bralston Plantation to the dun slopes of the levee and the mud-brown Mississippi beyond it. A cold wind whirled out of the gray sky, raising little dust storms in the weedy furrows. Not a single white bud, not a trace of a cotton plant. For over a year now the black earth had been untouched by grubbing hoe or rake. First in a trickle, then in a rush, like the Mississippi pouring through a crevasse in the levee, their slaves had run away. Victor Conté Legrand had sat on the veranda, drinking brandy, letting them go.

For a moment, Cynthia saw beyond the river, saw the whole South, prostrate in the debris and flotsam of the lost war, saw the deserted battlefields and the graves where so many thousands of young men like Lancombe lay, saw the shattered cities and the bands of vagabond ex-slaves and the endless acres of untilled land like Bralston's. "Sad" had become a hopelessly inadequate word for Victor Conté Legrand's last song. It was a dirge, a *Dies Irae* thundering across the desolated land.

"Cyntie."

It was her sister Jeannie. Her flower-petal mouth was troubled. Her brown Knowles eyes were sad. She was wearing Cynthia's last decent dress. Without its magnificent hoop, the yellow damask hung on her, a shapeless mass. "I hope you don't mind. I borrowed your dress. Frank and I are going to Baton Rouge to see if we can raise some money to put in a crop. He wanted me to look prosperous."

"I trust you're not going to see anyone who knows what's in style."

"Probably not," Jeannie said, gazing down at the collapsed skirt.

After decades of supremacy, the hoop had vanished from women's dresses. It had been replaced by something called the bustle. "Try to keep it clean," Cynthia said. "If our damned New Orleans cousins ever get around to sending me a magazine or two with some patterns in them, I have hopes of altering that dress into something approximating the latest fashion."

Around Concordia Bend churned a huge white steamboat, heading downriver toward New Orleans. More than once in the past year, Cynthia had thought of hoisting the signal at Bralston's dock and boarding one of these boats, with her yellow dress in her portmanteau. She had no doubt that she could fine some new-rich cotton speculator who would be eager to buy her the gowns and jewels and champagne a Legrand woman expected from life. While Cynthia rewarded her benefactor in the expected way, she imagined herself carrying on a savage dialogue with her father. *Are you happy now? Am I fulfilling my destiny?*

"I wish you wouldn't spend so much time out here. It can only make you morbid."

"I know," Cynthia said.

She could not possibly explain to Jeannie the bitter thoughts she flung at Victor Conté Legrand's grave. They were what he deserved for his arrogant assumption that he controlled his children's destiny.

"It's so quiet all the time. I think that's the strangest part of it, don't you?"

"Yes."

Once these fields had resounded to the shouts and songs of one hundred and fifty pickers, plowmen, drivers. Almost every morning when she awoke, Cynthia had to look out her bedroom window at the empty shacks in the slave quarters, to remind herself that it had really happened. The South had been defeated. The war was lost. It had been lost for over a year now. On the steamboats, on the road that ran parallel to the levee, you no longer saw returning veterans, so many with missing hands or arms or eyes, or legs shattered by Yankee metal. The war had ended, but the paralysis, the grief, the desolation of defeat continued to trap her at Bralston.

Other men and women were trying, however pathetically, to free themselves from the paralysis, to resume some semblance of a life. Her sister Jeannie had married a man whom Cynthia found repellent. But at least he had enough money to pay off the most voracious of Bralston's creditors. Cynthia's best friend Nelly Ames had married Walter Howie, her girlhood sweetheart, even though he had come home from the war with a bullet in his spine and would be confined to a wheelchair for the rest of his days. But Cynthia could not free herself from the tangle of love and loss and disappointment that Victor Conté Legrand had woven around her.

"Mama and I can't get over the way you've been mourning Papa," Jeannie said. "We never thought of you as a grieving type."

"I'm not mourning him," Cynthia said. "I come here to think."

"About what?"

"The lies he told us. All of them told us. About the war and the South's glorious empire."

Jeannie released a baffled Knowles sigh. She could only dimly understand her sister's feelings. It was with Cynthia, not his wife or Jeannie, that Victor Conté Legrand shared the fabulous dreams he and his friends concocted in their meetings at the St. Charles Hotel in New Orleans with Senator John Slidell and the coterie of lesser politicians who swarmed around him. They had envisioned a southern empire stretching from Kentucky to the equator, with all the riches of the Caribbean islands included in its sway. The silver mines of Mexico, the sugar plantations of Cuba and Jamaica would pour money into their laps.

John Slidell was to be the ruler of this empire. They might allow some fire-breathing Mississippian such as Jefferson Davis to sit in the president's chair to keep the North at bay. But Slidell would rule behind the scenes, as he had run the entire country in the administration of the last Democratic President, James Buchanan. At his right hand would be Victor Conté Legrand. He was to be the South's Talleyrand. His cool French brain would provide the intelligence, the diplomacy that would make the Southern Confederacy acceptable in the capitals of Europe, above all France, which was yearning for an ally to challenge England's arrogant empire.

Cynthia, his Legrand daughter, was destined to join him in this historic drama. She would be a courtesan in the French tradition of Madame de Maintenon and Madame de Barry—a courtesan in the service of the South. In exchange for her love—or the desire for it—men of wealth and power would become the South's passionate partisans. How fantastically exciting he had made it all seem on Bralston's veranda in the twilight.

"They weren't lies, Cyntie. He believed in them," Jeannie said. "They all did."

"Then they were damn fools. That's an even worse thought."

"Oh Cyntie. If you'd only be reasonable and consider marrying again. Frank's brother—"

"No."

"George Lucas—"

"I told you. I couldn't marry a one-arm man. Even if he was a hero in the war."

"Someone like Charlie Stapleton only comes along once, Cyntie."

"I know that."

Her marriage to Charles Gifford Stapleton in 1858 had seemed to be the first spectacular step to the fulfillment of her courtesan's destiny. His father was the U.S. Senator from New Jersey, one of the most powerful and influential politicians in the country. Charlie was incredibly handsome and just wild enough, blasé enough, to soothe her Knowles conscience whenever it accused her of not loving him. Courtesans, women of the world, were not supposed to love anyone. They kept their hearts at a cool, careful distance from love.

Cynthia did not dislike Charlie. No one did. It was hard to dislike someone who had a rakish smile on his face and a reckless gleam in his eye and expected to inherit four or five million dollars' worth of stock in one of the most profitable railroads in the country.

Best of all, Charlie was as entranced by Victor Conté Legrand's fabulous dreams as Cynthia was. He sat beside her on Bralston's veranda and agreed that it would be ridiculously easy for a few hundred well-armed determined men to capture Cuba. All they had to do was land on its long, undefended coast and the oppressed Cubans would rise as one man to drive the hated Spaniards into the sea.

In the U.S. Congress, Senators John Slidell and George Stapleton had a bill ready to be introduced, accepting Cuba into the Union. Charlie was going to be the Sam Houston of Cuba, a legendary hero in his time. They would have their pick of palaces in Havana and thousands of acres of prime sugarcane to put diamonds on Cynthia's fingers and power in Charlie's hands.

Instead of splendor, glory, there was only a column in the *New Orleans Picayune*, telling how Charlie and his men were all killed or captured and executed by the Spaniards within a week of their landing on New Year's Day, 1859. The Cuban peasants were not enthusiastic about joining the United States of America after all. Cynthia Legrand Stapleton was a widow—and a penniless one at that. Every cent of the $100,000 Charlie's father had given him as a wedding present had been spent in outfitting the expedition.

"Have you written to the Stapletons about Charlie's estate—to see if there's any money left?" Jeannie asked.

"No."

"Frank still thinks you should write. Papa told him before he died there might be some."

"I doubt it. The Senator died years ago. His wife's probably dead, too. That would leave the older brother, Jonathan, in charge. He became a Yankee general. I'd hate to beg from someone like him."

"Cyntie—you've got to face the truth. That's what we're reduced to. We'll all become beggars in fact if Frank loses this plantation. He's put every cent he's got into it and it still isn't enough."

Cynthia continued to brood. Jeannie fiddled with the dress. "He's not the best-tempered husband in the world, Cyntie. It would make things a little easier for me."

Cynthia could not endure the pain in her sister's eyes. She looked down at Victor Conté Legrand's gravestone, thinking of the man Jeannie would have married if it were not for the politicians and their deluded drunken visions of empire. Jeff Forsyth had been their local Bayard, their knight without fear, beyond reproach. As handsome as Charles Gifford Stapleton, but infinitely more serious. He had died at Gettysburg.

Two shrill hoots from an impatient steamboat captain drifted toward them on the wind. Out of the slave quarters wobbled spindly-shanked Cleopatra, their childhood nurse. "Miz Jeannie," she screeched across a half mile of empty fields, "your husband says to get down to the levee. That steamboat ain't goin' to wait."

"Oh dear," Jeannie said, and ran across the fields, the yellow dress hiked above her ankles. Once she stumbled in a furrow and almost fell. Cleopatra scolded her. She still talked to Jeannie and Cynthia as if they were six years old. Cynthia turned away and pressed her forehead against the cold trunk of the cypress tree. Jeannie was right. She had to stop coming out here. She had to stop thinking about the past. She had to think about her future.

Her brother Robert regularly urged her to join him in Galveston, where he was making a precarious living as a cotton broker. With typical Legrand ebullience, Bob described his fellow brokers, all ex-soldiers like himself, as panting for the sight of a young widow as pretty as Cynthia Legrand Stapleton. She was quite certain their panting would cease at the mere mention of marriage. Better New Orleans, where there were still a few cousins to give her a semblance of respectability while she displayed herself on the auction block.

She hated the idea, because she knew the sort of man she would attract. Even if she could inveigle him into a church, there was about as much chance of him remaining faithful as there had been of Charlie Stapleton performing that feat. Her father had explained it to her: women like her, beautiful Legrand women, should not expect faithful husbands, because they invariably attracted men who were buccaneers, men who took life's pleasures and prizes wherever their animal courage and luck led them.

During the past year of desolation and defeat, Cynthia had discovered an angry despairing wish to defy this destiny. She wanted to turn her back once and for all on the Legrands and their lying dreams. She wanted to elicit from a man the kind of devotion her sister Jeannie had won from Jeff Forsyth. She wanted a man for whom love was an ideal, a spiritual quest. But she did not have the slightest hope of finding him.

"Miz Cynthia? What the devil you doin' with your face pressed up against that old tree? I hope you ain't tryin' to conjure your father's spirit."

It was Cleopatra. She had labored across the fields to the graveyard, a long walk for an old woman who regularly claimed that she expected to die tomorrow. "You got a letter," she said. "You got a letter off that steamboat."

Cleopatra stood about ten feet away from the graveyard wall, waving a white envelope in her yellow hand. "Well, give it to me," Cynthia said.

"No, you got to come out here and get it. I ain't goin' into that place. I tol' you not to go in there you'self. There's evil spirits loose in that place ready to steal your soul."

Cynthia opened the rusty gate and walked over to Cleopatra. It was probably another invitation from her brother Robert to risk—or sell—her virtue in Galveston.

This letter was not from Robert. The return address was 217 East Seventeenth Street, New York, New York. Cynthia tore open the envelope wondering whom in the world it could be from. She did not know a soul in New York City.

> Dear Mrs. Stapleton:
>
> I expect to be in your vicinity sometime during the first week in November. I feel it would be unseemly not to call on the only member of the Stapleton family south of the Mason-Dixon line. There will be no need to entertain me. I can only stay an hour or two. I will be en route to visit an old friend from New York who is trying his hand at raising cotton in Mississippi about 25 miles down the river from Bralston. I hope you and your family have survived the terrible trial our country has undergone and are in reasonably good health and spirits.
>
> Very truly yours,
> Jonathan R. Stapleton

Her Yankee brother-in-law. Saving her the trouble of writing to him. He had been best man at her wedding. She remembered how surprised she had been by his looks. He was so different from Charlie, she found it hard to believe they were members of the same family. Jonathan Stapleton was immensely tall. His long narrow face had a proud Roman nose and a confusingly soft, sensitive mouth. He had been almost as shy as the homely Pennsylvania wife who was clinging to his arm. Cynthia had not been surprised by the shyness, or the homely wife. Charlie frequently made fun of his older brother, calling him Brother Jonathan, the family Puritan. Not that she cared at the time. Brother Jonathan's height and bearing had added dignity to the wedding. The defects of his personality had been irrelevant to Cynthia Legrand in 1858, on the first step of her supposed ascent to splendor.

Cynthia read the letter again and realized they were already in the middle of the first week in November. It had taken three weeks for the letter to reach Bralston. Jonathan Stapleton could step off the next steamboat, and here she stood in a filthy calico housedress.

What did it matter? Why should she try to look any better than the rest of Bralston? Jonathan Stapleton must have shaken off his shyness, to become a Yankee general. She could picture him striding up the path from the levee to the house, contemptuously noticing the grass growing between the bricks on the veranda, the chunks missing from the paint-peeling pillars. She would have to invite this cold Yankee conqueror into Bralston's looted wrecked interior, with the smashed chandeliers and mirrors and the claptrap furniture Jeannie's husband had bought from a local carpenter. The General's wife might well be with him. Cynthia could already see the condescension on her smug pudding face. She might even pretend to be sympathetic. Defeat, the bitter desolation of defeat, engulfed Cynthia once more.

"Who's it from?" Cleopatra demanded. "Jack Chambrun? I tol' you not to let him get away to Oregon. He was pretty close to your last chance in this neighborhood."

"I don't want to go to Oregon. I wasn't born to live in the woods."

Cleopatra clucked like a stupid hen. "That's them high ideas your daddy put in your head. All that man ever done for you is spoil you. You're twenty-seven years old and ain't gettin' no younger. Or prettier."

"Shut up," Cynthia said.

Cynthia strode across the field toward the garden in the rear of the house. Cleopatra labored after her. "Who's the letter from anyway?"

"My brother-in-law, the Yankee General. He's coming to visit."

"Oh my goodness. He bringin' his army with him?" Cleopatra asked, remembering what the last contingent of visiting Yankee soldiers had done to Bralston.

"No. He's not in the army anymore."

In the center of the ruined garden the shattered sundial lay in the uncut grass beside its bullet-chipped column. The once precisely trimmed hedges bulged in every direction. The cork tree her father had planted with so much fanfare stood among the weeds and wayward shrubs like a dismayed foreign aristocrat in a slum. Cynthia walked around the veranda, ascended one of the two winding staircases to the second-floor gallery, and entered her mother's bedroom through the open French door.

Blanche Knowles Legrand was sitting up in her canopied bed, reading a novel while Livia, Cleopatra's sister, combed her gray hair. Cynthia's mother was wearing one of the embroidered pink night robes and nightcaps that she had brought to Bralston in her trousseau forty years ago. She seldom wore anything else. She had spent most of the last fifteen years in the bedroom, safe from Victor Conté Legrand's cruel tongue and the disasters that had overtaken her family and the South.

"A bit of news, Mama," Cynthia said. "My brother-in-law, General Stapleton, is going to pay us a visit."

Blanche Knowles Legrand clapped her hands. Her lined face came aglow with an ethereal smile. "I knew my prayers would be answered. I'm sure he'll loan us the money to save Bralston," she said. "I told your father to write to him the moment the war ended. But he was too bitter, too proud."

Cynthia looked around the half-furnished bedroom. The red damask curtains, the blue-cushioned French Empire loveseat and the dressers with their sensuous curves and inlays had been sold soon after the war ended. The ribbonette wallpaper was faded and splotched by stains from the leaky roof. Yet her mother transcended these tawdry surroundings. Wrapped in her silk night robes, enjoying the novels she had read as a girl, she managed to retain some of the dignity of their life before the war. This was the one room in Bralston where Cynthia could bear to entertain Jonathan Stapleton.

"I don't want you to say one word about money, Mama. We're not going to beg from this man. There's a good chance that Frank Powers may raise enough cash from his friends in Baton Rouge to make it unnecessary. General Stapleton's coming to visit a Yankee friend who's bought up someone's land across the river in Mississippi. How do we know he isn't stopping here hoping to get Bralston cheap?"

"He seemed like such a nice young man at your wedding, Cyntie. And his little wife was so sweet."

"Mama, he became a general in the war. He didn't do that by being nice. Especially in the Yankee army."

For the rest of the day her mother talked incessantly about borrowing money from Jonathan Stapleton. She would hastily promise when Cynthia glared at her that she would not say a word about it when he arrived. The next morning, there was all sorts of fussing to get Mother ready for the day. She insisted on taking a bath, which left Livia and Cleopatra exhausted from lugging gallons of hot water up the stairs. She lamented that they had run out of Mr. Massey's Potpourri, a fragrant jar of which she had always kept open on her night table. She tried on and took off a dozen different nightdresses before settling on a pale-blue one trimmed with point lace.

Cynthia put on a clean calico housedress and confronted herself in the cracked mirror in her bedroom. She pushed her thick dark curls into passable order and told herself it would do. She was not interested in charming General Stapleton, and there was no hope of impressing his wife.

At about eleven-thirty she was in her mother's room listening to the usual prattle about her marvelous days as a belle on the Cane River when Cleopatra came panting to the door. "He's here. The General's here. He's got a boy with him."

"Remember, Mama. Not one word about money," Cynthia said.

She went out on the gallery and began descending the south staircase. Jonathan Stapleton and the boy were standing on the veranda just below her. Each, for a very different reason, was a startling sight.

Jonathan Stapleton's russet hair had turned snowy white. His face had been transformed. Gone was the bland shyness. The sensitive mouth had been replaced by a hard compressed line. The once diffident eyes had become a penetrating gaze that struck her with almost physical force. Cynthia summoned her Legrand boldness to meet it. She had never let a man stare her down and she was not going to start now, no matter how wretched she looked.

Formidable, that was the first word that came to her mind as she returned his gaze. This was a formidable man. A bullet or saber had left a livid white scar on one cheek. The complacent flesh that had filled out his face had vanished, to be replaced by intriguing hollows and shadows. Yet it was not an old man's face. In the gray November light the white hair cast a glow across the craggy features, suggesting vigor as well as determination. As their eyes met, she caught a puzzling hint of sadness. Why should a Yankee general be sad? Especially when he was as rich as this man?

"Brother Jonathan?" she said. "Or should I say General Stapleton?"

"Jonathan, by all means," he said. "This is my son, Rawdon."

"How do you do," Cynthia said, descending the rest of the stairs.

Rawdon had an amazing resemblance to Charlie Stapleton. The same wavy dark hair, defiant green eyes and arrogant mouth. She wondered if he had Charlie's laugh, that mocking, rippling sound that had made her flesh shiver.

"I almost can't believe it," Cynthia said. "If he were a little taller, I'd swear it was Charlie."

"Everyone notices the resemblance," Jonathan Stapleton said in a curt, rather impatient way, as if he had heard it mentioned too often.

"I wish we could offer you dinner," Cynthia said. "But we only have two house servants left, my mother's maid and my old nurse. You'd have to depend on me as a cook, which might prove fatal."

"I wouldn't dream of imposing on you," Jonathan said. "As I said in my letter, I just thought I should call . . ."

"It's very kind of you. Has your friend who's growing cotton in Mississippi given you thoughts of investing in a plantation down here?"

"Not really," he said.

"He's lost his shirt—or Father's shirt," Rawdon said.

The General gave his son an annoyed glance. "That's more or less the truth," he admitted. "I loaned him some of the money. He's run into all sorts of problems."

Hurrah, Cynthia thought. "What a pity," she said.

She invited the Stapletons upstairs to see her mother. On the way she gave them a brief history of what the war had done to the Legrands. She told them of Lancombe's death and her father's death (omitting the brandy and the despair), the purchase of Bralston by Jeannie's husband. She explained their absence in Baton Rouge.

Blanche Legrand welcomed her daughter's Yankee relations with queenly dignity. She urged them to stay for the night, for the week, if they chose, as if Bralston were still swarming with servants, the smokehouse were crammed with meat and the wine cellar stocked with her connoisseur husband's favorite vintages. Jonathan Stapleton politely declined.

"Doesn't Rawdon remind you of Charlie, Mama?" Cynthia said.

"Remarkably," her mother said. "Oh General, I think you should know, among all our other griefs we've never ceased to mourn your brother. He was such a gentleman. I've wept for him as much as I have for my son or my nephews, my sister's boys. We lost two of them on the Red River defending their ancestral lands."

"Thank you," Jonathan Stapleton said. "I'm glad to hear Charlie is remembered that way."

His voice was flat, empty. Alas poor Charlie, Cynthia thought. No one, including your widow, seems to have grieved for you. Genuine emotion returned to Jonathan Stapleton's voice as he talked of how much the war had cost everyone, North and South. "My youngest brother, George, was killed in Tennessee."

"Oh how sad," Cynthia said. She remembered George at her wedding. He had some of Charlie's good looks, but he seemed to have inherited his oldest brother's seriousness.

"We were hoping you might bring your wife with you, General," her mother said. "I remember her with such pleasure. She was so sweet, so well bred, the way she put up with our southern hilarity. Perhaps she couldn't face another visit . . ."

Jonathan Stapleton's eyes flickered toward Rawdon. "My wife died in childbirth, three years ago."

"Oh I'm so sorry." Her mother's eyes drifted toward Cynthia as she asked, "Did the baby live?"

"Yes. A boy."

"Two sons and no mother. I don't envy you, General. No doubt you've thought of marrying again."

Once more her mother's eyes sought Cynthia. *NO.* The word exploded in her mind. She could never marry a Yankee. Above all a Yankee general. No matter how rich he must be, as the only surviving Stapleton son.

"I'm certainly not opposed to the idea," Jonathan said. "But I can't imagine what woman would want the job, especially if I gave her an honest estimate of this young hellion's character."

He nodded toward Rawdon, who smiled in an odd surly way, as if he more or less liked his father's opinion of him.

"And all I could offer her by way of consolation," Jonathan continued, "is a shot-up old wreck of a husband."

Cleopatra served coffee and bread with butter that was starting to turn rancid. Rawdon wolfed down four slices of bread without the butter and Cynthia pretended to regret they were sending away guests who were obviously on the brink of starvation. Her mother began to ramble. The strain of not asking for money was beginning to show. She chattered about Cynthia's wedding and her husband's gambling and Bralston's debts. Cynthia stopped her in midsentence by announcing that the Stapletons had to resume their journey. Downstairs, she sent Cleopatra out to the levee to hoist the signal for the next steamboat.

"They come past two or three an hour these days," she said. "I love to watch them, especially when two of them are racing. I sometimes think I hated the war most because it drove the boats off the river."

"They're magnificent, but I fear their days are numbered," Jonathan Stapleton said. "They can't compete with railroads."

A typical Yankee notion, Cynthia thought. Replacing something as splendid as a steamboat with a sooty clanking uncomfortable train. As they talked, they strolled along the veranda, which encircled the house. She noticed that General Stapleton limped as badly as any southern veteran she had seen struggling along the levee road. "I hope the Confederates are not responsible for that ailing leg," she said.

"I'm afraid they are," Jonathan said. "There wasn't much left of my knee after Chancellorsville."

On the rear veranda, Cynthia pointed across the ruined garden at the sundial. "The officers of a Massachusetts regiment spent a week here when General Banks made his foray up the Red River in 'Sixty-four. They amused themselves by shooting at the dial. The man who knocked it off won a cash prize. They absolutely terrified us with their gunnery. They were drunk most of the time on the contents of our wine cellar."

"If they'd been in my division, I would have cashiered their colonel and fined every one of them three months' pay."

A surprising reaction. Was he telling the truth?

"Didn't you shoot a few, Father?" Rawdon asked.

"Yes," Jonathan Stapleton said. "For more serious crimes." A nerve twitched in his scarred cheek. He was obviously displeased by his son's question.

Rawdon asked if he could look around the slave quarters. His father warned him not to disturb anything. "That's hardly a worry," Cynthia said. "They've been swept bare."

The boy dashed toward the double row of dilapidated frame cabins. Jonathan Stapleton pondered the shattered sundial. "You were here throughout the war?"

"There was no place else to go. There still isn't."

She asked him why he had moved from New Jersey to New York. "Mostly to get away from my mother," he said. "She insists on treating me as if I were still sixteen years old."

"I know what you mean. My mother has tried to push me into the arms of every returning Confederate veteran who's come along the levee road."

"It sounds as if we've learned the same lesson. Parents must be resisted at all costs."

The remark was so close to her own feelings, she was momentarily stunned into silence. "Yes," she finally said, adding mournfully in her mind, It's so much easier for a man to say that and do something about it.

Jonathan Stapleton began talking about New York. He told her how much he enjoyed the theaters, the restaurants, the opera. He had gone to Columbia College and had many friends and several relatives living in the city. A cousin, Katherine Kemble, had married into one of the oldest and best Knickerbocker families. "You'd be surprised by how many southerners live in New York," he added.

"How interesting," Cynthia said.

There was a pause. Was he expecting her to say something more enthusiastic? Did he want her to sigh like a Knowles and pathetically wish she could visit this Yankee metropolis?

A hoot from a steamboat vibrated in the distance. Jonathan called Rawdon out of the slave quarters and they walked toward the river beneath the gray sky. "Could I trouble you to make an inquiry for me?" Cynthia said. "I'd like to know if there's any money left in Charlie's estate. It was tied up in that dreadful litigation with those ship owners in New Orleans when the war began. We're desperate for cash to pay some of my father's more pressing debts and get a crop in the ground. It would make me feel a little less superfluous here if I could contribute something."

"I'll look into it the moment I get back to New York."

"I was going to write you about it. But I wasn't sure, after all that happened, if you cared to hear from a southern relation."

"Nothing could be farther from the truth," Jonathan Stapleton said. "What I want—the only thing I ever wanted, the only reason I went to war —is to see us one country again."

He said this with an absolutely amazing fervor. There was no question that he meant it. Cynthia managed to conceal her confusion. "What a lovely thought," she said.

They were on the levee. The steamboat was snuffling and bumping against the dirt wall. The usual string of bored passengers lined the railing of the upper deck studying them. Jonathan Stapleton told her he would write from New York about Charlie's estate. If there was no money left, he would be happy to loan her—or her brother-in-law—whatever Bralston needed.

For reasons she did not entirely understand, Cynthia burst into tears. Perhaps it was pain at the thought of a man having so much money that he could casually offer a loan without even inquiring into the amount. Or maybe it was the humiliation of having to feel grateful to this puzzling Yankee after all, when she had gone to such lengths to avoid it.

With a struggle, she put a good face on her tears. "I can't tell you how much this will relieve us of the most awful worry. Relieve me above all."

Jonathan pressed her hand. He seemed to be struggling with some deep emotion of his own. "That alone," he said, "that alone will make this visit worthwhile."

She wiped her eyes and kissed Rawdon on the cheek. "Goodbye, Nephew," she said. "I hope we meet again someday."

"I hope so, too," he said.

The Stapletons seized their bags and climbed up the steep gangplank. The captain gave another tremendous toot on his whistle and headed for the center of the river. General Stapleton's visit was over and she was never going to see him again. Maybe that was why she was weeping. When they were alone on the rear veranda, the right words, the right emotion in her voice, might have won her an invitation to New York.

But she could not find the words, the feelings. They were sealed in her barren heart, not by the bitterness of defeat, she saw now, not by patriotic antagonism toward Yankee generals, but by her rage at the whole male sex, who required her to play the dissembling seductive female if she was to have any hope of happiness.

Goddamn them all. Fathers, brothers, husbands, sons, nephews, brothers-in-law. Goddamn them all.

TWO

Forlorn, Jonathan Stapleton thought, standing on the top deck as the steamboat churned toward the middle of the river. There was no other word for Cynthia Legrand Stapleton.

His emotion was sharpened by the memory of the woman he had met on Bralston's veranda when he arrived for his brother's wedding in 1858. That day, Cynthia Legrand had been wearing a beribboned yellow dress with an enormous hoop and a matching bonnet, which did not entirely conceal a mass of luxuriously curled black hair. She had twirled a yellow parasol and said, "So this is Brother Jonathan. You don't look nearly as *puritanical* as Charlie says you are."

He had been prepared for the gleaming black hair, the green eyes under long black lashes, the ripe figure. Charlie had detailed these attractions in more than one gloating letter. It was the voice that momentarily demoralized him. Its dark liquid croon had stirred a response deep in his body, like a bow drawn across a bass violin. Unfair, he had thought sullenly, unfair that Charlie, who had broken all the moral rules, should have this woman as his wholly undeserved reward. While he was tied for life to the dull creature clinging timidly to his arm.

"I can see why Uncle Charlie married her," Rawdon said, bringing his father back to the present. "She's a looker."

"Rawdon—she's your aunt," Jonathan said. "You don't call your aunt names like that."

"Why not?"

"It makes her sound cheap."

"What does that mean, exactly—when you say a woman is cheap?"

"It means she'll . . . do things for money."

"Instead of for love?"

"Yes."

"Why did Uncle Charlie come down here in the first place?"

"Your grandfather Stapleton wanted him to learn the cotton business."

That was about ten percent of the truth. Senator George Stapleton had shipped Charlie south in 1857 largely to escape a lawsuit from the outraged parents of a girl who had yielded too much to his powers of persuasion. As usual, Caroline Stapleton, the Senator's wife, had deeper political motives. Already it was evident that the South was either going to rule or ruin the Union. If it came to ruin, it would do Stapletons no harm to have a son connected to one of the more politically potent families in the South.

The Legrands qualified on several counts. Victor Conté Legrand had distinguished himself as a colonel of volunteers in the war with Mexico. He had met Senator Stapleton, who had been a brigadier general in that unsavory conflict, and they had been mutually charmed. Charlie had arrived in Louisiana with a letter of introduction that made him more than welcome at Bralston.

Charlie, of course, paid very little attention to these intricate political plans. He had concentrated on enjoying the quadroons and octoroons for whom New Orleans was famous. He sent his older brother a steady stream of reports about his conquests.

"Do you think she loved Uncle Charlie?"

Every woman he ever met loved Charlie. The bitter words leaped to his lips, but Jonathan suppressed them. The envy would be too obvious, even to a thirteen-year-old. "Most women love the men they marry," he said.

"She barely said a word about him. She let her mother do the talking."

Jonathan was frequently startled by how perceptive Rawdon was about adult relationships. It was quite possible that he was right about Cynthia Legrand. The defiant way she had met his eyes when she paused on the stairs, the delicately edged use of Charlie's nickname for him, Brother Jonathan, suggested she was not a woman who gave love first priority in her life. That did not jibe with those sympathy-stirring tears on the levee. Perhaps there were two women struggling for control of that beautiful body. Which one would you prefer, General?

A man could not share such steamy thoughts with his thirteen-year-old son. "It's been almost seven years since your uncle died," Jonathan said. "We've been through a war. That makes it seem twice as far back. You can't expect people to mourn the dead indefinitely."

The furtive hostility in Rawdon's eyes suggested that he had not stopped mourning his mother—or blaming his father for her death. A half-dozen times in the course of the past four days Jonathan had yearned to explain it to him. *Your mother stopped loving me because I went into the war. But that wasn't my fault. It didn't kill her. Women don't die of unhappiness.*

Was any of that true? Didn't the unhappiness, the unloving, begin long before the first shot was fired at the flag? Was it on the plantation that you just visited, face to face with the woman you just saw, that your dwindling affection reached a bitter conclusion? Wasn't that the moment when Jonathan Stapleton, president of the Camden & Amboy Railroad, decided that he deserved something more exciting in the way of a wife than prim, pious Laura Kemble?

"Why did Uncle Charlie invade Cuba? Was it his idea?"

"I doubt it. The idea was in the air down here in Louisiana. They called it filibustering. There were a half-dozen expeditions launched from New Orleans in the 1850s. One almost conquered Nicaragua."

"Did you know he was going to Cuba?"

"No."

Cynthia Legrand had seemed more a delectable climax to Charlie's seemingly endless sexual banquet than a political portent when Jonathan met her on that April day in 1858. But politics of the darkest, most dangerous sort lurked just beyond her bedroom. Nine months later, Jonathan had rushed to Bowood, the Stapleton's New Jersey home, to find his father weeping on the couch in the parlor, clutching the telegram informing him that Charlie had died on a bullet-swept Cuban beach. While his dry-eyed mother paced the Persian carpet saying over and over, "I don't believe it."

"Would you have gone with Uncle Charlie if you'd known about it?"

"No. I wouldn't have risked my life to make Cuba another slave state."

"Could we get something to eat?" Rawdon said. "I'm still pretty hungry."

Jonathan barely managed to conceal his exasperation. He had brought Rawdon along on this trip because he thought they badly needed some time together. He had come home from four years of war to find his older son a surly antagonist. Jonathan had seen this trip as a chance to explain himself, the Stapletons, the war. He had imagined himself telling Rawdon how much his grandfather, Rawdon's great-grandfather, had influenced him, how the old man, who had served in the Continental Congress and the first federal Congress under Washington, who had known all the founders, Hamilton, Jefferson, Madison, added a sacred aura, a mystical vibration, to the word "Union."

He had hoped to talk frankly about Ben Dall, his closest friend, whom they were going to visit in Mississippi, how he had influenced the way Jonathan thought and felt about slavery. En route they could visit battlefields, talk even more frankly about the way the war had been fought; he could explain how and why it had lasted four horrendous years, instead of the three glorious months that everyone had expected in 1861.

Nothing had gone right. To Rawdon, his great-grandfather was a painting on a wall in Bowood. The founders and their struggle to create a nation had no mystical vibrations for him. Their history seemed quaint, remote, boring, compared to the stupendous events of the past five years. The word "Union," the idea it embodied, seemed a pale compensation for the anguish and rage and hatred that the war had sent coruscating through the Stapleton family. Jonathan's attempts to explain Ben Dall had been met with something worse than indifference. Rawdon's mother and grandmother had poisoned his mind against poor Ben so thoroughly, he took advantage of Jonathan's frankness to sneer at his old friend for going broke.

Visiting the battlefields was the one idea that had stirred Rawdon's enthusiasm. Here Jonathan's plan had collided with a totally unexpected obstacle. From Washington they had ridden the Orange & Alexandria Railroad through northern Virginia to Manassas Junction. The moment they stepped off the cars and began walking across the Bull Run battlefield toward Henry House Hill, where the Sixth New Jersey had encountered a hitherto obscure Confederate general named Thomas Jackson, strange things began happening to Jonathan Stapleton's mind and body.

Needles of sweat burned beneath his shirt, although it was a relatively cool November day. His heart began to pound in his chest, his mouth was as dry as it had been beneath the scorching July sun in 1861, when the raw colonel marshaled his regiment of friends and neighbors and gave them a speech about patriotism before leading them up the slope of Henry House Hill. Now the dead seemed to rise out of the lush grass to stare accusingly at him. All he could remember was the blood, the confusion, the colonel making a fool of himself, trying to carry off the wounded, discovering later he was considered one of the few Union heroes of that disastrous day because he had somehow survived blasts of Confederate musketry.

That had been the end of battlefield visits. It was really the end of his attempts to talk to Rawdon about the war. He had decided it was too soon, his nerves were not ready for it, Rawdon was not ready. Peace was what they needed, at least five years of tranquility in the restored Union, to give the wounds of the spirit and the flesh time to heal. Jonathan Stapleton had turned most of his attention to their southern fellow passengers on the railroads and steamboats, listening, hoping, for evidence of reconciliation. Perhaps that was the chief reason he had decided to visit Bralston. To see how his only southern relations received him.

Two hours later, with at least a pound of beefsteak in Rawdon's stomach to make him a little less surly, they debarked on the Mississippi side of the river. A Negro with an almost unintelligible drawl pointed them toward the headquarters of New Destiny Plantation. They trudged up a winding road to the porch of a white clapboard house without any of Bralston's architectural distinction.

Margaret Dall flung open the door, gave a little cry and threw her arms around him. "Oh what a joy to see a friendly face," she said.

He was shocked by her appearance. Margaret had aged ten years since she had left New York fourteen months ago; she looked closer to forty-seven than thirty-seven. Her face was lined and drawn, her red hair had thinned alarmingly; she had lost at least twenty pounds. Emphasizing the change was the child clinging to her skirts. Eight-year-old Eleanor Dall was a miniature of her mother's rosy-cheeked Dutch beauty in its prewar prime.

Dressed in the same cheap country calico that Cynthia Legrand Stapleton had worn, Margaret was only a remnant of the aristocratic New York beauty who had defiantly married Ben Dall, practitioner of the dubious profession of journalism, fifteen years ago. She knew it, too. Her hands fussed with her lank hair. "I hope you're not as horrified with me as I am every time I look in the mirror," she said. "Mississippi's gift to American civilization, breakbone fever, did this to me. I've had it twice. I was in bed a month each time. Ben has had it four times. He practically lives on quinine."

"I had—no idea," Jonathan murmured.

"The children seem immune to it. So you don't have to worry about this young man. What a handsome fellow you've turned out to be, Rawdon! You're going to break a thousand hearts."

Margaret bussed Rawdon on the cheek. "Genevieve will be so glad to see you. She doesn't have a single friend her age down here."

"Where is Genevieve?" Jonathan asked.

"Out in the schoolroom with her father. He's made her his assistant teacher."

Margaret Dall led them through the sparsely furnished house into a big vegetable garden. In the nearby Negro quarters, only old men and old women and a few babies were in sight. Margaret explained that the hands—men and women—worked in the fields until sundown.

The schoolroom was in a sagging barn just beyond the Negro quarters. Ben Dall stood before a blackboard, writing words on it. He wore a loose tan suit, with the empty sleeve of the right arm he had lost at Chancellorsville pinned across his chest. Ben was never a muscular man. Now he looked like one of the half-starved victims of Confederate cruelty in the prison camp at Andersonville. His face was a skull. His neck had shriveled. Only his eyes were unchanged. They still had their transcendental glow. But the incandescence was dimmed by a haunted sadness that made Jonathan almost flinch.

Jonathan ordered himself to remember the Ben Dall of 1846—the slim, remarkably handsome eighteen-year-old in a droopy home-sewn suit whom he had encountered in his room at Columbia College.

"Stapleton?" Ben had said. "Is your father the U.S. Senator from New Jersey?"

"Yes," Jonathan said.

"How do you explain his vote to admit Texas into the Union as a slave state?"

Before they went to bed at four o'clock the next morning, Jonathan Stapleton had admitted that his father's politics were singularly lacking in moral force and there were even worse things to be said about the monopolistic stranglehold the Camden & Amboy Railroad had on transportation in New Jersey. There was nothing personal about Ben's assault. As he saw it, the Stapletons were no worse—just a little more successful—than the rest of America at asserting their individual greed and self-importance at the expense of the moral tone, the spiritual condition, of the republic. Proof, if it was needed, was the indifference they shared with a majority of their fellow Americans to the agony of four million black men and women toiling under the lash in the South.

Winner of a scholarship set up for New Englanders by some quirky fellow Yankee who had made money in New York banking, Ben had come to Columbia equipped with a headful of outrageous ideas. He scoffed at organized religion, thought workmen had a perfect right to form unions and favored the sensuous waltz for two over the sedate cotillion for ten. With his mane of chestnut hair, his vivid talk and enormous self-confidence, he was fascinating to men and women alike. When he descanted on the power, the importance, of the ideal, the sacrifices that Americans must make to achieve it, New York beauties like Margaret Van Vorst practically swooned into his arms.

It was Jonathan who introduced them. He brought Ben along to balls and parties on Bleecker Street and Astor Place, ignoring social New York's dislike of opinionated New Englanders. He gave Ben a few of his castoff suits and took him to his tailor to have them refitted. At times he felt like Barnum displaying a new species of aborigine, at times like the Roman millionaire Maecenas supporting a philosopher-poet.

But they never lost sight of the more serious side of their friendship. More and more, Ben's eloquence forced Jonathan to confront what his father's generation of Stapletons had conveniently ignored; the moral content of the word, the name, the title, American.

Now that feeling, like most other good feelings, was only a memory, as remote as everything else in America before the war. Like a great smoking chasm, the war had divided their lives into a past seemingly as distant as the days of the founders and the wounded diminished present.

"Hello, Ben," Jonathan said.

"Hello, Jonathan."

The voice was flat, empty. It reminded Jonathan of the voices of men who had been in combat too long, men who were spiritually as well as physically exhausted. The living dead, he used to call them.

"Where's Genevieve?"

"There."

He nodded toward the back of the barn. Thirteen-year-old Genevieve was bending over the desk of a Negro boy, helping him spell out a word. She looked up at them, and Jonathan Stapleton was struck by the resemblance to her father. She had his angular body, his chestnut hair and luminous eyes.

For a moment Jonathan found himself wishing he had fathered this sweet intelligent girl instead of his surly, rebellious son. During the war, when he and Ben regularly exchanged their letters from home, all he ever read were reports of Genevieve's high marks in school, her intense affection for her father, which gave her nightmares about his death in battle. While from New Jersey came nothing but stories of Rawdon's latest escapade at home or in school, and his deplorable marks. All blamed on the absence of his father.

Ben spoke to the twenty or so black faces gazing up at them. "We have a very famous visitor to our school, children. Major General Jonathan Stapleton. One of the men who won the war and set you free."

Only Jonathan heard the sarcasm in those words. Only he was saddened by them, because they meant that the war was still poisoning his friendship with Ben Dall.

After a brief demonstration of their reading ability, Ben dismissed the class and they began walking back to the house. A rawboned bearded man on a worn-out-looking white horse rode up to them.

"Colonel Dall," he said, "I can't get another lick of work out of them niggers without whiskey. They say Fred Stowe gives his niggers whiskey and they don't see why they can't have some."

"Tell them that there is no whiskey on this plantation and there never will be," Ben Dall said. "Tell them that it's in their contract that they will work six days a week until sundown. If they break their contract, I'll have the Freedman's Bureau arrest them!"

The overseer rode off across a wide furrowed field. In the distance, about fifty or sixty tiny black figures leaned on hoes and rakes, waiting for him.

On the porch of the house, Margaret Dall served lemonade and Ben explained that Fred Stowe was Harriet Beecher Stowe's son. She had spent some of the thousands of dollars she had made from *Uncle Tom's Cabin* to buy him a plantation a few miles down the river. Fred had gotten a severe head wound at Gettysburg and spent most of his time drunk. He shared his whiskey with his field hands, and now half the Negroes in the country were refusing to work unless they got some, too.

"Mrs. Stowe paid us a visit last month," Margaret said. "I thought she was insufferable, bragging about meeting Queen Victoria and Louis Napoleon and the Duke of Marlborough."

"She has swelled a bit," Ben said.

"It was the first time she'd actually seen a plantation," Margaret Dall said. "So much for the truth of *Uncle Tom's Cabin.*"

"The book told an essential truth, even if the details were wrong," Ben said.

Margaret Dall had never been happy with her husband's decision to join the abolitionist crusade. Jonathan could understand why. Ben had quit his job at the *New York Times* and spent almost every cent of the $200,000 dowry Margaret had brought to their marriage to launch an abolitionist newspaper in New York City. All her aristocratic Van Vorst relatives had stopped speaking to her. Rocks had been flung through the windows of their house in Stuyvesant Square. Abolitionists had not been popular in New York.

They had not been popular with Jonathan Stapleton either. From New Jersey he had written his ex-roommate a scorching letter, asking him how he could join a group of maniacs who called for a civil war to end slavery. Ben had written him a strident reply, arguing out of all sides of his mouth, denying that he favored a war, but admitting that he was willing to risk one. A year later, Ben's name appeared on the list of abolitionists who had given money and guns to the Kansas madman John Brown and encouraged him to launch a guerrilla war in West Virginia.

Probably none of it mattered, Jonathan told himself now. They had all been sliding toward the precipice, the earth was shuddering beneath their feet, the chasm was about to open. The fanatics of the North and the wild men of the South were swarming toward it from opposite directions.

"Genevieve," Ben said, "why don't you show Rawdon around the farm? Start with the cotton gin. That should interest him if he's inherited his father's fascination with machines."

"Take Eleanor with you," Margaret said.

As the children departed, Ben looked after them with a reflective smile. "Remember how we used to talk about Rawdon and Genevieve when they were in their cradles, Jonathan?" he said.

"Of course," Jonathan said. "We looked forward to being joint fathers-in-law. It could still happen."

"Not likely. Rawdon will have the pick of the herd. He won't settle for my scrawny little doe."

"I *wish* you wouldn't talk about her that way," Margaret snapped. "She'd be an attractive girl for her age if she lived someplace where there was a reason for putting on a decent dress and tying a ribbon in her hair."

"She has a remarkable mind," Ben said, ignoring his wife's comment. "Really extraordinary, Jonathan."

"It isn't her mind I'm worried about," Margaret said. "It's her sensibility. I don't think it's healthy for a young girl to see no one, day in, day out, but her parents and little sister."

"If it's a sacrifice she's perfectly willing to make, I see no reason for you to carp at it," Ben said.

"How does a girl of thirteen know what she wants when her heroic father urges sacrifice on her as a way of life?" Margaret said.

Jonathan shifted uneasily in his chair and tried to change the subject. He began telling the Dalls about the trip from Washington, D.C., on the South's battered railroads.

"No doubt all the trains had separate cars for Negroes?" Ben asked.

"Ben—you can't expect people to change their minds about blacks over-night after having them as slaves for two hundred years."

"That's what I told him," Margaret said. "I saw absolutely no need to get into this schoolteaching business. It's turned our neighbors into enemies."

"She means the threats," Ben said offhandedly. "We've gotten several tossed through our windows on recent nights. I have one here."

He fished a dirty crumpled piece of paper from his pocket and handed it to Jonathan.

> You abolitionist son of a bitch you are teaching niggers to read if you keep it up we will burn your cotton gin and if you still keep it up we will burn your house and if you persist we will kill you.
>
> THE COMMITTEE

"I'm not worried about them," Ben said. "I've bought a shotgun and a good watchdog."

"Every time I hear that dog bark I'm awake for the rest of the night," Margaret said.

"I'm awake most of the night anyway. I think it's the quinine."

Margaret's expression, the remark about sleeplessness, made Jonathan wonder if Ben's casual air was a pose. The haggard face, the haunted eyes that had confronted him in the schoolroom suggested the worst possibilities.

"I'd better see to supper," Margaret said.

General Stapleton and Colonel Dall sat on the porch in the late-afternoon sunlight, looking across the half mile of fields to the Mississippi. Conquerors, in the heart of the South. Possessors of the land and its richest product, the fiber that had enmeshed them all, white and black, in a century-long muddle of anger and greed and idealism that had left a million men in graves from the Ohio River to the Gulf of Mexico.

"What happened to your crop, Ben?" Jonathan asked. "We were all a little baffled by your somewhat cryptic note, asking us for an extension of the loan, and another twenty-five thousand into the bargain, with no explanation of what happened."

Jonathan had loaned Ben $50,000 of the $100,000 he had needed to buy and farm New Destiny Plantation. The rest of the money had come from three other Columbia College classmates. Jonathan had urged them to contribute to the experiment, which seemed to have a reasonable chance of making a profit when Ben went south last year. The war had created a worldwide shortage of cotton. The price per bale was at an all-time high.

Ben put down his lemonade and squeezed the bridge of his nose like a man trying to relieve a severe headache. "Just as we were about to pick, out of the swamps slithered thousands of army worms. They were ankle deep in some places. They feasted on our cotton. All we could do was stand there and watch them."

"Good God. Is that likely to happen again?"

"The overseer thinks not. They only appear about once every five years."

"No wonder that Confederate brigadier was so eager to sell this farm. Any business that loses a whole year's investment every fifth year is perpetually on the brink of bankruptcy."

"Don't talk to me like a goddamned accountant, Jonathan. You know I didn't come down here to make money."

"You borrowed money from me and three other friends on that basis. You have no worries about my reaction, but I'm not sure about the other fellows."

Little Eleanor came scampering up the path to the porch, her dress hiked above her knees. "Rawdon let Caesar out and he bit Genevieve," she cried.

Ben led the race around the house through the garden to the barn. Inside they found Rawdon using a rake to defend himself against a huge snarling mastiff. Genevieve was cowering against the wall, blood streaming from a gash on her arm.

"Caesar!" Ben shouted. He grabbed a piece of kindling and whacked the dog on the nose. Caesar slunk to Ben's feet and crouched there.

"Don't you have any sense at all, Rawdon?" Jonathan snapped. "What did you think you were doing, letting an animal like that loose?"

"He's trained to obey no one but me," Ben Dall said. "The boy didn't know that, Jonathan."

"I didn't," Rawdon said. "He seemed to want to play."

"It's partly my fault," Genevieve said. "I thought he'd obey me. He does when I'm with you, Father."

"Oh my Lord," Margaret Dall cried, charging into the barn. "Look at that girl's arm! I told you I didn't want that bloodthirsty animal on this farm."

"It's only a scratch, Mother. It doesn't hurt at all," Genevieve said.

Back in the house they cleaned the wound and bandaged it. Only then did Genevieve confess that she felt a little faint and thought it might be better if she went to bed. Ben felt so guilty, he let Jonathan violate the teetotal tenets of the house and give her a small drink of whiskey from his traveler's flask to soothe the pain.

Supper was a sketchy meal. Growing up in a mansion on Bleecker Street with ten or fifteen servants, Margaret Dall had never set foot in the kitchen. She served overdone fried chicken and underdone fried potatoes and talked about how impossible it had been to train any of their Negroes to cook. "I don't know what happened to those famous house servants you always heard about. I'm the only northern wife still on duty in this country. All the others gave up and went home."

"The southerners aren't much better off," Jonathan said. He described his visit to his brother Charlie's widow at Bralston.

"I hope you're not thinking of indulging in some spoils of war, Jonathan," Ben said.

For a moment Jonathan almost lost his temper. Ben was assuming his old authority to pass moral judgment on his opinions and actions. "Nothing of the sort," he snapped. "I consider her part of the family."

Ben persisted. "Is she still as pretty as you described her in 1858?"

"Hardly. She hasn't got a decent dress to her name. I suspect they don't have enough to eat."

"It's what they deserve," Ben said. "The dresses and the jewels, the liquor and the ten-course dinners were all purchased from the sweat and blood of black men and women."

"I really think it's time for an end to those sentiments, Ben," Jonathan said. He was reminding Ben that he had seen too many of the million corpses that the abolitionist crusade had produced.

"I think the sentiments are more apropos than ever," Ben said. "The women spent most of the money made from driving the slaves. Now they're the ones who refuse to admit they've lost the war."

"I didn't see a trace of bitterness when I visited Bralston," Jonathan said. "In spite of what a regiment of your fellow Yankees from Massachusetts did to the place."

For a moment the casual mask dropped from Ben's fleshless face. Jonathan glimpsed what he was thinking. Alien, they were alien to him, this best friend from New Jersey and his wife from New York. "Excuse me," Ben said. "I want to see how Genevieve is feeling."

They finished their almost inedible supper, and Margaret Dall put Eleanor to bed. Jonathan suggested that Rawdon might want to retire early and for once his son agreed with him. Margaret served coffee in the living room and they waited for Ben to join them. Instead, he came downstairs and went out the front door without saying a word.

Jonathan struggled to converse with Margaret. He told her about his move to New York, trying to make it sound amusing. The hapless male trying to organize a household for his two sons. His cousin Katherine Kemble Brown, one of Margaret's closest friends, took pity on him and rushed to Stuyvesant Square with a cook and two servants to rescue him. "Katherine's back from Paris with all kinds of notions. She's building a mansion in the wilds of Fifty-seventh Street. Poor Brownie is paying out the money as usual. She's got him terrorized."

It was a mistake, this evocation of New York places and names. Tears began to ooze from Margaret's eyes. "Oh Jonathan," she said. "I'm so miserable. You know I love Ben and I've tried—I've tried so hard to follow him. But this time I think he's led me—led us all—too far."

It poured out, a Mississippi-sized flood of resentment and unhappiness and anguish. "No northerner can live in this climate. The air in the summer makes you feel as if you've taken a bath in warm glue. The freedmen are almost impossible to discipline. Ben began by being too easy with them, and now when he tries to enforce the rules they call him a Yankee Simon Legree. That monster of a dog is to guard us from them as much as from the southerners who are against Ben's school."

"What can I do or say, Margaret? This means so much to him."

"Don't give him any more money. Make him go back to New York."

"Let me talk to him. Where's he gone?" Jonathan said.

"Probably down to the levee. He goes down there almost every night and doesn't come back until I've gone to bed. That solves the problem of talking to me."

The wind had turned warm, almost tropical in its softness, as Jonathan walked through the starry darkness to the river. He found Ben sitting on the levee, his legs hunched against his chest, the way soldiers often sat when they fell out for a few minutes' rest on a march. Officers, of course, never sat that way. They strode around looking authoritative, or leaned against a tree.

Ben had been a good officer. Jonathan had had no hesitation about recommending him for command of the Sixth New Jersey when Abraham Lincoln made Colonel Stapleton a brigadier general. Now this hunched position seemed to emphasize Ben's vulnerability. It recalled the memory of that awful day in the trenches before Cold Harbor, when Jonathan had been forced to relieve Ben Dall of his command.

The Sixth New Jersey had charged the Confederate trenches twice and taken appalling casualties. When General Stapleton ordered another attack, Colonel Dall came apart. "You're trying to rub my face in it," he had screamed. "Rub my face in the blood!"

Privates who refused to attack were shot; colonels were cashiered. Jonathan had shielded Ben from that disgrace. He had gone to Ulysses Grant and pleaded Ben's case in person. He had persuaded the commander in chief to transfer Ben to a desk job in Washington for the rest of the war.

Jonathan sat down beside Ben and took out his tobacco pouch and pipe. "What's this?" Ben said as he lit up.

"One of my father's old pipes. I started smoking it when I came home. You ought to try it."

"You know my opinion of liquor and tobacco."

"Think of it as a pipe of peace, Ben. The old Indian idea. It might incline you to ask yourself an important question."

"What?"

"How long a man can expect himself—and his family—to live in a state of war."

"I can see you've gotten a full bill of particulars from my wife."

"She doesn't have to say anything, Ben. I've got eyes and ears."

Silence. The stars glinted in the swirling river.

"Ben. We've given four years of our lives to saving the damn country. We deserve a little peace, a chance to live as civilized human beings again. Don't you want that for Margaret's sake—for the sake of Genevieve and little Eleanor?"

"Of course I want it. But what if the war hasn't ended? What if the cause —the cause that so many men died for—still needs us? The South hasn't surrendered. They have no intention of surrendering. They're going back to half slave, half free under another name."

Jonathan Stapleton shook his head. "I talked to fifty men coming down here. Ex-soldiers, most of them. Not one mentioned such an idea. They admit that slavery is finished. They don't like the idea of giving the freedman the vote. But neither do a lot of Republicans I know. I'm not sure Lincoln was in favor of it."

Was it only eighteen months ago—it seemed like eighteen years—that General Stapleton and his headquarters staff had escorted Abraham Lincoln into captured Richmond? Negroes had leaped and danced around them, comparing the exhausted President to Moses and Jesus. Lincoln had turned to Jonathan and said, "There are times, General, when the thought of peace terrifies me almost as much as continuing the war. What are we to do with four millions of these people?"

Ten days later he was dead, a southern bullet in his brain.

"You know how little I thought of Lincoln," Ben Dall said. "He was a politician first, last and always. Without the vote the Negroes might as well become slaves again. At least they'd be sure of regular meals."

"There's no point in arguing about Lincoln anymore. No one is looking for an argument, Ben. All everyone wants is peace."

"What if the price is too high?"

Jonathan sighed. Inwardly it was a groan that permeated his spirit. "Ben," he said. "Can't we forgive—or at least forget—things that were said at the worst of times? Why can't we remember the good times?"

Ben's head only seemed to sink a little lower. "Lately all I think about are the dead," he muttered. "How lucky they are, how peaceful it must be there in the dark."

Land of milk and honey, whispered an ancient sheltering voice in Jonathan's head. He felt pinpoints of sweat burning on his chest. His heart began to pound. It was as bad as the visit to Bull Run with Rawdon.

"Ben—I went through that, too, when I first came home. It hasn't been easy for me either. They've run me out of New Jersey, that's the truth of it. My own mother at the head of the pack. When I first came home, and people spit at me in the street and sent me vicious notes calling me the butcher, more than one night I sat there with a loaded pistol on my night table. The only thing that kept me going was little George, my three-year-old. I'd hold him in my lap for hours."

Ben said nothing. Was he thinking, It's just what you deserve? Jonathan stared into the starry darkness, pondering the gulf that had opened between him and his old friend.

"Let's go to bed and talk this whole thing over tomorrow morning, with clear heads."

"I'm going to sit here a while longer."

Jonathan lay in bed thinking of the day. Cynthia Legrand Stapleton in calico on the levee, weeping tears of gratitude for his gesture of reconciliation, Margaret Dall's tears of desperation.

The sultry wind ruffled the cheap muslin curtains. The watchdog barked somewhere out in the darkness. Then another sound, a *crack*, such as a man might make stepping on a dead branch in a thicket or snapping a stick of kindling wood, building a fire.

But there was no thicket near the house and no one in the house building a fire. That was a pistol shot. *Crack*—another one. Jonathan fumbled through the darkness to his portmanteau and found his long-barreled army pistol. He shoved six bullets into the chamber and tiptoed to the window.

A man came running up the path to the house and crouched in front of the porch. The starlight picked up the gleam of a gun barrel in his hand. It was Ben. A dozen details fell into place in Jonathan's mind. The haggard face, the exhausted voice, the comments about sleeplessness, the dog who obeyed only him, the retreat to the levee after supper. New Destiny Plantation was under siege and Ben patrolled it all night with his guard dog and shotgun.

Jonathan pulled on his pants and started downstairs. As he reached the landing, Ben's shotgun boomed outside. Instantly, *crack crack crack*, there was a volley of answering shots from pistols and muskets. Bullets smashed the parlor windows. Jonathan dashed downstairs, flung open the front door and fired six shots into the darkness. He did not expect to hit anything. He just wanted to let the attackers know there was another gun in the house.

"Get in here, Ben," he called as he reloaded the pistol. "I'll cover you."

Ben scuttled up the steps into the house. For a moment he was visible against the white paint, and *crack crack* two bullets bit into the wood only inches from Jonathan's head. He emptied his gun into the darkness again.

"My God, what's happening?" Margaret Dall cried from the stairs.

"Take the girls into your room and lie down on the floor," Jonathan said. "Send Rawdon downstairs."

Rawdon joined them in his nightshirt. "Have you got a gun for him?" Jonathan asked.

"My pistol," Ben said, handing it to Jonathan.

"Hold this in both hands," Jonathan said. "And shoot anyone who tries to get in the kitchen door."

Rawdon took a deep breath. "I'll try," he said, and disappeared down the dark hall.

"What happened out there, Ben?"

"They killed Caesar. I think I winged one of them with my pistol."

"Can you really fire that shotgun with one arm?"

"Not very well."

"Let me take it."

They exchanged weapons and ammunition. Jonathan crouched at the shattered parlor window. Ben positioned himself in the dining room, so they could enfilade the path.

"Hey, you abolitionist fucker," called a voice from the darkness. "We only come to kill your goddamn dog. But you put a bullet in a good man. You better plan to go back to New York real quick."

Crack crack crack. Another volley of shots smashed into the house.

"Where are the nearest federal troops?" Jonathan called to Ben.

"At Ford Adams, twenty miles away."

"Where's the overseer?"

"Probably hiding under his bed."

"Jesus Christ."

For a moment Jonathan was thoroughly exasperated with his old friend. It was typical of Ben's idiotic unrealism to provoke a war with his neighbors without any hope of winning it.

"Ben," he said. "I'm going to knock out windows all over the house. Make them think we've got a half dozen men in here."

He moved swiftly through the darkened house, smashing the windows with the butt of the shotgun. In the kitchen he whispered to Rawdon, "When you hear me start yelling, you yell, too. As loud as you can."

Back in the parlor, Jonathan lay flat on the floor and roared, "Hey, you shitkickers. You picked the wrong night to call. The colonel's got six of his old friends from the Army of the Potomac in here wide awake and ready to put some lead in your gutless bellies."

"Come on, you sons of bitches," Rawdon howled in the kitchen.

Silence in the darkness. Jonathan was betting that some of the bushwhackers were ex-soldiers who had seen enough men die in frontal assaults. A half hour passed without an attack. An hour. Two hours. Jonathan lit an oil lamp. They waited another half hour without a sound or a shot from the darkness. "I think they're gone," he called.

Footsteps on the stairs. Margaret Dall appeared in her night robe, holding another oil lamp high. She looked into the parlor, where shattered glass covered the rug and bullets had smashed lamps and pictures and gouged holes in the furniture. Turning, she spoke to her husband in the dining room. "Do you still think this is a place to raise two daughters?" she asked.

Another sound, strange, unidentifiable at first. Abandoning the shotgun, Jonathan walked into the hall. Ben Dall sat at the dining-room table, weeping. He kept rubbing his fist into his streaming eyes. Margaret Dall watched him without an iota of affection on her face.

Appalling, the way time, history, eroded, corroded love. While it remained so umblemished, so scarifyingly pure, in the memory. Jonathan would never forget the radiance on Margaret Van Vorst's face as she gazed at her husband on their wedding day. They had been lightbearers, witnesses to love's transcendence. Within a month, Jonathan had proposed to Laura Kemble.

"You'd better talk to him," Margaret said, and went back upstairs.

Jonathan stood in the doorway, watching Ben weep. What was there to say? *You've done everything a man could expect of himself down here. We'll go back to New York and let you get your nerves together. All we need is a little time, a little peace, Ben.*

Better to say nothing.

"I'm afraid . . . it's time . . . to relieve me of another command, Jonathan," Ben sobbed.

Pathetic mockery in the Mississippi night, spoken by the ghost of a friendship. He had hoped that this trip south might restore that friendship. Now Jonathan saw that it was another casualty of the war. He would continue to honor the friendship. He would continue to try to help this wounded exhausted man. But it would be the gesture of a survivor laying flowers on a grave.

For a moment the dead clutched at him. He felt their ghastly fingers tugging at his sleeve. His whole body, his spirit trembled with an enormous echoing wish for sympathy, affection, that would help him resist their staring eyes and gaping mouths, their blind blundering claim on his soul. He realized how foolish he had been to hope that this man, who had also experienced the holocaust, could help him. The wounded cannot heal the wounded any more than the blind can lead the blind. It had to be someone who had somehow escaped the nightmare, whose spirit was unblemished by its ugliness and anguish, someone who could summon hope, affirmation from his battered heart.

Suddenly he was back twenty-four hours, hearing himself proclaim a noble purpose for the nightmare, remembering Cynthia Legrand Stapleton's green eyes skeptically searching his face for sincerity. Was that place, the place where naïve first love had finally expired, where a different kind of love might begin?

Perhaps love was not possible. Charlie's ghost would always be there, mocking him. Perhaps that other woman, the bold sensual beauty he had glimpsed on Bralston's stairs, was all he could win. Perhaps sensuality was all that the iron general, with those thousands of staring eyes and slack mouths accusing him, could expect. So be it. He was pretty sure the general could keep Cynthia Legrand Stapleton happy, with or without love.

He could almost swear that he heard a sinuous southern voice crooning assent, either way: *What a lovely thought.*

THREE

Dark-gray snow clouds loomed over New York as the S.S. *Minerva* steamed through the Narrows. An icy northeast wind whipped across the great harbor, churning it to gray foam. Huge chunks of Hudson River ice, mute messengers from an even colder climate, swirled past the bow. Cynthia Legrand Stapleton retreated to the coastal steamer's shabby saloon, trembling from her first encounter with Yankee winter.

The weather was not her only reason for tremors. She was about to confront the elite of the wealthiest, most sophisticated city on the continent, after six years of isolation at Bralston, six years of seeing no one but relatives and a handful of old friends. She stood in front of the wall mirror in the saloon, trying to decide how she looked.

She was wearing a gray cashmere walking dress, a new idea in women's clothes. It disposed of the clumsy train and gathered the skirt about three inches above the floor, revealing her two dark-blue petticoats and her red boots. The Irish dressmaker in New Orleans had assured her the dress was in style in New York, but dressmakers always pretended to know the latest fashion, even when their pattern books were years out of date. Cynthia trembled at the possibility that she might look like a country clown the moment she stepped off the boat. She wanted to show these Yankee women, she wanted so badly to show them that southern women could rise from defeat if given a chance.

"I told you not to go out there," Hayne Butler said. He grinned over her shoulder in the mirror. He was one of those handsome amoral men who seemed to gravitate to New Orleans. Originally from Charleston, he bragged about a brother who had made a fortune in blockade running during the war and was now doubling his money in Atlanta real estate. He reminded Cynthia too much of Charlie Stapleton and a dozen other buccaneers before whom her father had dangled her at Mardi Gras balls while they talked about millions to be made in Mexico or Brazil.

"I'm going out again, directly," Cynthia said. "I don't want to miss *anything.*"

Clutching her wool paletot to her throat, she braved the freezing wind once more. New York was much closer now. It looked huge and vaguely menacing in the gray light, like a mythical monster, a gigantic whale or sea dragon, floating somnolently in the dark water. The Great Metropolis, everyone called it, with a million people, a million arrogant, victorious Yankees at work there. It was ten times bigger than New Orleans—and ten times more exciting, according to Charles Gifford Stapleton. He had promised to take her there the moment he finished conquering Cuba. He had assured her that she would love the city and the city would love her.

But that had been before the war, before four years of killing. Cynthia did not expect New York to love her now. She expected snubs and even insults from its women the moment they heard her Louisiana drawl.

Snowflakes began whirling past the steamer's smokestacks. Bells rang and the ship slowed down. They were passing the tip of Manhattan Island now. A half-dozen ferries, great, broad-beamed vessels, bigger than Mississippi steamboats, were plodding between New York and the New Jersey shore. One passed close enough for her to see hundreds of faces peering from the cabin windows. Then they were edging into the dock. Snow swirled in her face. Cynthia's hands and feet were numb, she was sure her ears had turned to ice.

On the pier, a craggy-faced man in a black fur-collared coat waved to her. He stood head and shoulders above the rest of the crowd. It was her brother-in-law, Jonathan Stapleton. For a moment, Cynthia could not breathe. It was really happening. It was not a dream.

Early in December, she had received a letter from Brother Jonathan telling her that he had made the promised inquiry into Charlie's estate. Senator Stapleton's death in 1861 had entangled his estate with Charlie's; both had been sued for large sums by shippers and arms merchants after the failure of Charlie's expedition to Cuba. Jonathan had discovered that a remnant of Charlie's money still survived: $11,000. He had put it into New York Central & Hudson Railroad stock, which would pay her at least six percent a year. If she wanted to loan money to Bralston, she could borrow against it or borrow directly from him.

As things turned out, she did not need to loan Bralston money. Jeannie's husband, Frank Powers, had managed to hornswoggle or intimidate most of her father's creditors for a year. Cynthia assumed this was the end of her correspondence with Brother Jonathan.

Late in January, another letter arrived, the most astonishing letter she had ever received in her life. As casually as if he were discussing the weather, Jonathan Stapleton informed her that there had been a remarkable "bull movement" in New York Central stock, and her $11,000 was now worth $110,000!

Cynthia remembered walking into the garden with the letter in her hand and standing there for an hour, staring at the wrecked sundial. Magic. It was magic. That was how the Yankees had won the war, she thought. They had won it with their magical power to multiply money.

She finally read the last part of the letter, in which Jonathan Stapleton suggested that she come to New York and discuss what she might do with this "comfortable little fortune." If she needed money for the journey, he would wire funds to a New Orleans bank. His cousin, Katherine Kemble Brown, would be delighted to have her as a house guest for as long as she wanted to stay.

Cynthia was not so simpleminded that she believed Brother Jonathan was inviting her to New York simply to discuss the money. She was perfectly aware that she was a twenty-seven-year-old widow and Jonathan Stapleton was thirty-nine and wifeless. But she doubted very much whether the General would succeed in marching her up the aisle, now that the marvelous vagaries of the stock market had made her independent.

Independent. Cynthia would never forget the moment in Bralston's garden, staring at the smashed bullet-chipped sundial, when that incredible word penetrated her mind. Life, hope, joy stirred in her flesh for the first time in years. She understood why the Negroes talked of freedom as a resurrection from the grave. She had been lying in the grave of her father's hopes and dreams—a two-thousand-acre grave, with a crumbling mansion in the center of it. Suddenly, miraculously, she was free.

She had decided to go to New York. She told herself she would experience the exhilarating sensation of meeting Jonathan Stapleton, his Yankee friends, his relations, as an independent woman. She would be as defiantly southern as she chose to be, as headstrong and opinionated as her Legrand blood inclined her to be, without the least compulsion to flatter, dissemble, conceal her true feelings. She would not be impolite. She owed her tall Yankee brother-in-law a debt of gratitude. She was quite sure her feelings for him would never go beyond that tepid emotion. She was almost as sure that when he saw the real Cynthia Legrand he would be glad to escape her.

A smiling Jonathan Stapleton, unaware of the volatile creature he was greeting, awaited her at the bottom of the gangplank. "You must be frozen, standing out there on deck," he said. "Why didn't you wait in the main cabin?"

"Because there was a man in there who made it his business to tell me I would get pneumonia if I dared go out."

Her impudence only broadened his smile. "Oliver, will you look after Mrs. Stapleton's luggage?"

Jonathan introduced Oliver Cromwell, a gigantic Negro, as tall as his employer and twice as wide. While Oliver went in search of her trunk, General Stapleton escorted her through the crowd on the pier to a street that was jammed with a thousand different wagons and carriages. There he helped her into a big maroon coach which was as warm and dry as a parlor. A small stove full of glowing charcoal was built into the floor. He drew a furry lap robe around her and from a compartment beside the stove produced a silver jug full of hot toddy.

"In spite of our abominable weather," he said, "we're determined to give you a warm welcome."

Once more she marveled at the transformation the war had wrought in the shy gawky young railroad executive whom she had met in 1858. Was it the result of being a conqueror, one of the architects of the South's defeat? She told herself not to think that way. She reminded herself of his apparent sincerity when he said he wanted America to be one country again.

Oliver Cromwell appeared with her trunk, and they rode uptown through streets jammed with private carriages, hacks, wagons, omnibuses. The sidewalks were almost as crowded, with thousands of pedestrians trudging along, their heads bent against the blowing snow. Jonathan assured her it was just an ordinary business day in New York. Soon they were on Broadway, inching past the great department stores with their plate-glass windows full of beautiful dresses, bonnets, furs. "I'm sure you'll be spending a lot of time down here," he said. "We call it the Ladies' Mile."

At Fourteenth Street they abandoned Broadway for Fifth Avenue, and their pace improved. Cynthia was fascinated by the solid blocks of looming brownstone houses with their elaborate Italianate façades, their silvered door handles, plates and bell pulls. She could see why Fifth Avenue was called the street of palaces. But Jonathan Stapleton talked it down. He pointed out one house built by a man who had made a million dollars selling a patent medicine that cured nothing, another belonging to a man who had gotten even richer selling rotten meat and moldy bread to the Union Army. Shoddies, he called them, introducing Cynthia to a key phrase in the vocabulary of the New York aristocracy. She had no difficulty grasping the idea, because the Legrands and their fellow Creoles had been equally disdainful of the hustling Americans who had made fortunes in Louisiana.

The epitome of nouveau-riche ostentation, in Jonathan Stapleton's opinion, was department-store tycoon A. T. Stewart's white marble mansion on the northwest corner of Thirty-fourth Street. Almost as bad was the brownstone pile of John Jacob Astor III across the street. "In this country—and especially in this city—money should be heard but not seen," he said.

On Fifty-seventh Street, Katherine Kemble Brown's cut-stone five-story French town house was a lonely tower of elegance in a street of vacant lots. The trees of the Central Park, visible through the whirling snow a few blocks away, added to the rustic atmosphere. Jonathan assured Cynthia that within five minutes of meeting his cousin she would understand why she had been the first member of New York society to move so far uptown.

A blond, pink-cheeked mountain of a woman, Mrs. Brown had the coldest, shrewdest eyes and the most determined jaw Cynthia had ever seen. Cynthia suspected she was one of those northern women who were waiting for a chance to demolish her. She was sure of it when they sat down to tea in a parlor full of French Renaissance Revival furniture and Mrs. Brown announced that a dinner in her honor was scheduled for tomorrow night.

"But I have nothing to wear," Cynthia cried. "I only bought traveling clothes in New Orleans."

"My dressmaker is waiting upstairs," Katherine Kemble Brown said.

By 5 P.M. the next day, Cynthia had an evening toilette of pink coral grosgrain, with an overskirt of point lace, and a cluster of pink roses at the waist. She had also learned a good deal about Mrs. Brown, Jonathan Stapleton and New York City. Far from conforming to Cynthia's stereotype of the flinthearted Yankee woman exulting in the North's triumph, Mrs. Brown had apparently considered the war a seizure of national insanity and ordered her husband to take her and their two daughters to Paris, where they stayed until the conflict was over. When Cynthia mentioned that her father's best friend, Senator John Slidell, had been the Confederate ambassador to Paris, there was an instant bond. Mrs. Brown had found him one of the most charming, most cultured, most delightful gentlemen she had ever met.

On the subject of Jonathan Stapleton, Mrs. Brown displayed an interesting combination of pride and affection that went considerably beyond cousinhood. Blithely ignoring her previous denunciation of the war, she boasted about General Stapleton's reputation for never retreating in the face of the most ferocious Confederate attacks. His men had nicknamed him "Old Steady."

"I must confess I never imagined him as a general when I knew him best, during his college years," she said. "I was more than a little interested in him in those days. His height—those marvelous shoulders! And so tractable, so agreeable. He actually seemed to like women, instead of merely tolerating them the way so many men do. But it would have taken a female with nerves of steel to marry him without his mother's approval. I knew I never had any hope of getting that. Caroline Stapleton was my mother's half sister and they'd hated each other from birth. So all of us New York girls had to watch and weep while he married that Philadelphia frump Laura Kemble."

"I trust he loved her."

Katherine Kemble Brown sniffed skeptically. "She was a pathetic little thing. I think she appealed to his protective instinct. Men crumble before those whining women. I've never understood why."

If there was any whining in the Brown marriage, it was on the male side. Cynthia had met Blackwell Brown, a pale, muted balding man obviously dominated by his formidable wife.

"Are you going to settle in New York, Mrs. Stapleton?" Mrs. Brown asked. "Jonathan seemed to think there was some chance of it."

Cynthia fumbled out phrases about her southern feelings and her doubts about living in the North.

"But New York isn't the North, my dear. New York is, well, New York. I think you'd be perfectly comfortable here."

Mrs. Brown's dinner party in Cynthia's honor was virtually a fulfillment of this prophecy. Not a single man or woman among the dozen guests at the table betrayed a glimmer of hostility to her Louisiana accent. On the contrary, several of them managed to convey their sympathy for the South and its sufferings. But Cynthia's most stunning discovery was a woman as southern by blood, instinct and breeding as anyone she had ever met, bearing the name of one of New York's oldest and wealthiest families.

A delicate, dark-haired cameo, Martha Bulloch Roosevelt, whom everyone called Mittie, was from Georgia. Just before dinner was announced, Katherine Kemble Brown, perhaps noticing Cynthia's bafflement, drew her aside and explained that Mittie had married tall bearded Theodore Roosevelt in 1854. "She lived in New York throughout the war while her two brothers fought for the Confederacy. I don't know how she *endured* it," Katherine whispered.

After dinner, when they left the men to their port and cigars, Mittie sat down next to Cynthia on the drawing-room couch. "Katherine tells me you have an independent fortune, Mrs. Stapleton," she said. "What a wonderful sensation that must be."

"I'm told it's the quickest way to attract men," Cynthia said. "But so far I haven't received a single offer."

"I'm sure that's never been a worry for you," Mittie said. "Will you be staying in New York for a while?"

"That depends on a good many things."

"I'm perfectly at home here, but it would be a joy to have a true *Confederate* among my friends."

"That" offer alone is enough to tempt me to stay," Cynthia said.

Mittie glanced over her shoulder to make sure no one was listening. "Between us," she said, "Yankee men are much easier to manage. They have the most surprising notions. They actually *want* to be good. It must have something to do with the way their mothers raised them."

Cynthia laughed. She assumed Mittie was being facetious. Would any woman want to manage her husband? Only pale limp men like Blackwell Brown were manageable. On the other hand, she had no desire for a husband who managed her. Surely there must be a happy middle ground where love made management unnecessary.

Over the next two weeks it became quite clear that Jonathan Stapleton did not intend to give Cynthia a chance to meet any other prospective husbands, manageable or unmanageable. He had something planned for every night, tickets to the opera, a play, a minstrel show, a visit to Tony Pastor's theater on the Bowery, which featured a random collection of skits and songs: a new idea called "vaudeville." There were additional dinner parties at houses even more splendidly furnished than Katherine Kemble Brown's. On another night, the most exciting yet, Jonathan took her to a lavish banquet in honor of General Ulysses S. Grant at Delmonico's Restaurant. People were beginning to push the conquering hero as a presidential candidate. Jonathan introduced her to Yankee senators, congressmen, ex-generals, including the hero himself. There was not a word, not a hint, of hostility.

Once or twice, to keep up the pretense, Jonathan went through the motions of discussing her comfortable little fortune. He took her downtown to the gilded headquarters of the Stock Exchange on Broad Street. From the visitors' gallery she watched brokers shouting orders on the trading floor. He explained the magical way stocks could rise—and fall. If she wanted to speculate in new railroads or steel mills, she might multiply her $110,000 to a million—or lose it all. She decided to leave her little fortune where it was, in the hands of the New York Central & Hudson Railroad.

Cynthia was not sure she liked the way Jonathan Stapleton was wooing her. It was a little too understated, too Yankeeish. There were no books of poetry delivered with verses ringed in red, no letters or speeches full of passionate praise of her beauty, no extravagant gifts. But Jonathan was not dull. Behind his serious mien he had a delightful eye for gossip and scandal. He knew who had jilted whom and how much money had changed hands in each marriage.

He wryly gave her the insider's view of Katherine Brown's union. Blackwell Brown had been one of the city's most brilliant bankers and a confirmed bachelor. Katherine had pursued him from New York to Newport to London and back and finally drove him to his knees—a position from which he had yet to rise. "People call it the taming of the shrewd," Jonathan said.

Marriage was clearly on Jonathan Stapleton's mind, but Cynthia found herself more interested in enjoying her independence. How she savored the word as she wandered the Ladies' Mile, exploring Arnold Constable, Lord & Taylor, A. T. Stewart's and the other great department stores. She found Stewart's block-long seven-story emporium on Broadway from Ninth to Tenth Street particularly enchanting. Beneath a great glass dome was an arcade like something out of the *Arabian Nights,* counter after counter loaded with beautiful things, mounting floor after floor to the glowing roof. It was so delicious to feel free to buy, buy, buy, whatever pleased the eye or hand, lacy peignoirs, silk scarves from Italy and India, perfume from Paris.

Independence, I love you.

Other afternoons were absorbed by fittings for more dresses at a shop on Twenty-third Street that Mittie Roosevelt had recommended. A woman needed an amazing number of dresses if she was to hold her own in New York society. There were morning gowns and visiting gowns and tea gowns as well as walking dresses and evening toilettes.

By now Cynthia had been in New York over a month. Blustery snowy March was dwindling into a last drizzly week, previewing April. General Stapleton continued to occupy her evenings with remarkable, no longer subtle persistence. One rainy night as they rode downtown to the home of Delancey Apthorpe, a Columbia College classmate, Jonathan cleared his throat and said, "Please don't construe this as a lecture. But I've been getting your bills from the department stores and from your dressmaker. I'm afraid you're in danger of invading your principal."

She did not know what he was talking about. He patiently explained that her income, if the New York Central & Hudson Railroad remained profitable, would be about $6,000 a year. Since she had come to New York a month ago, she had already spent $5,000. She had charged everything to Jonathan Stapleton. He had suggested the arrangement so there would be no delay in establishing her credit. She was to settle her account with him when she received the dividend on her stock. But now it seemed that with a few more bills she would have to sell some of her stock to pay up. That would reduce her income and begin a downward spiral into that familiar Legrand condition, debt.

Independence. It was dissolving in front of her eyes. For a moment she felt angry. She found herself wishing she had put her $110,000 into some new railroad's booming stock. Then came a twisting spear of doubt. She was still her father's daughter. Like all Legrands—or maybe all southerners—she knew nothing about money except ways to lose it or spend it.

No, wait. She was no longer Cynthia Legrand, daughter of the reckless gambler-dreamer-schemer. The new Cynthia, the woman resurrected from her two-thousand-acre Louisiana grave, had command of her own destiny. She could choose to take the advice of this earnest Yankee without cringing or groveling. "I should have warned you, Brother Jonathan, we Legrands have never been strong on principles," she drawled.

He smiled. But he seemed to have sensed the play of her previous emotions. Those gray eyes could deliver the most penetrating gaze she had ever encountered. "I wish I could arrange matters so that you'd never have to worry about money again," he said. "But that's the last reason in the world why I'd ask you to consider me as a husband."

Cynthia was startled to discover that this conqueror was shy, almost timid, about his appeal to women. It was her turn to say something significant, but her usually glib tongue deserted her. "I . . . I agree—other reasons are far more . . . important," she murmured.

The following Sunday she and Jonathan rode the New Jersey Railroad's cars out to Hamilton, the northernmost town in the Passaic River Valley, to call on his mother. Charlie had referred to Caroline Rawdon Stapleton as "the dragon." She lived up to the name. Cold, imperious, she served them tea and talked exclusively about Charlie—his charm, his wit, his gifts as a leader of men. When Jonathan excused himself to get a book from the study, Mrs. Stapleton put down her teacup and said, "My friends in New York tell me he has hopes of marrying you. I hope it isn't true."

"We haven't discussed the subject," Cynthia lied.

"He has money—if that's all you're looking for. But after Charlie you'd be bored to death, my dear. Dullness aside, Jonathan has become a very insensitive, stubborn man. I don't know where he got such traits. Certainly not from my side of the family."

Caroline Stapleton refilled Cynthia's teacup and passed her the cream and sugar. Then she resumed her demolition of her son. "The Senator and I begged Jonathan to stay out of the war. It was the only honorable thing to do, considering his father's position as a spokesman for a peaceful solution. But nothing we could say—or poor Laura, his wife, who was in complete agreement with us, could say—moved him. He was totally under the influence of that obnoxious abolitionist he took up with in college, Ben Dall.

Have you met him? I'm sure you'll find him even more insufferable than we did."

On the way back to New York, Jonathan lamented his mother's hostility. "She blames me for my father's death and my brother George's. I did everything in my power to keep George out of the fighting. I got him assigned to hunting deserters in Indiana. But he transferred to some local regiment . . ."

Cynthia saw how defenseless he was against the old woman's malice. Would another woman's love heal the wound? Cynthia wondered if the capacity for such a love existed in her elusive courtesan's heart. She had never seen herself offering a man spiritual sustenance. She realized how poetic, how girlish her ideas about love had been, how self-centered.

A few days later, Cynthia expressed an interest in meeting Ben Dall. Jonathan was evasive. He said he was ill. Katherine Kemble Brown bristled when she asked her about him. She told Cynthia how little she thought of this arrogant idealist who had spent the dowry of one of her closest friends on an abolitionist newspaper. He was back in New York, recovering from his attempt to prove his ridiculous theories about Negroes, living on money Jonathan had loaned him out of pity for his wife and daughters.

Spring breezes sighed through the Central Park. Trees began to leaf, flowers to bud, and still General Stapleton persisted in his gentle siege. Cynthia visited his house on Stuyvesant Square with Katherine Kemble Brown and saw at a glance how desperately he needed a woman to run it. The draperies were faded, the prewar furniture poorly arranged and the carpets badly in need of a good beating. (Mrs. Brown thought it was the lazy Irish housemaids who needed the beating.) A virago of a Scottish governess tyrannized his younger son, four-year-old George; the older one, Rawdon, seemed more sullen and defiant than she remembered him at Bralston. Again the word "need" stirred in Cynthia's mind. But she thrust it away. It was still too strange, too threatening to her.

To preserve her principal, Cynthia had declared her determination to shun the Ladies' Mile. Worried that she might grow bored, General Stapleton was now at her door almost every afternoon to take her for a ride through the park in his phaeton. Two lean long-legged black trotters named Castor and Pollux guaranteed that the pace was lively.

"Do you ever race these creatures on Harlem Lane?" Cynthia asked one day as they headed up Fifth Avenue.

She had heard about this road in northern Manhattan from several dinner partners. It was a favorite raceway for amateur sportsmen.

"I took a hundred dollars away from Commodore Vanderbilt up there last Saturday," Jonathan said.

At the entrance to the park, whom should they encounter but the legendary old man himself, the titan of the New York Central & Hudson Railroad, driving two muscular bays. "If you didn't have that lady with you, General Stapleton, I'd get my money back today," he called.

"I only weigh a hundred and nine pounds," Cynthia called back. "Give us a quarter of a mile advantage and I'll bet a hundred dollars on these horses."

"Done," roared the Commodore. "To the 110th Street gate."

"It's too dangerous," Jonathan said. "Racing in the park—"

"It's my money—and there is *nothing* in this world I love more than fast horses," Cynthia said.

"Now I know why you married Charlie," he said.

No you don't, she thought. But this was not the time or the place to attempt that explanation. He handed her his high black hat and they were off. It was early afternoon and the park was relatively deserted. After a quarter of a mile the phaeton's wheels barely seemed to be touching the ground. They careened past gigs and victorias and thundered around the numerous curves. A sudden lurch almost sent Cynthia flying out of the seat. A long Stapleton arm encircled her waist and drew her firmly against him while he drove the horses with one hand. She clutched his hat and laughed in delight at the danger—and simultaneously thrilled at his white hair streaming in the wind, the fierce combative glow on his craggy face.

As they passed the boat lake, the Commodore was only twenty yards behind them, and gaining fast. "Give me your whip," Cynthia shouted.

He handed it to her. "All they need is a touch," he said.

She flicked it expertly against those gleaming black rumps, and Castor and Pollux added twenty paces to their gaits. They pulled away from the Commodore and beat him to the 110th Street gate by at least six lengths. Vanderbilt paid Cynthia the hundred dollars, growling all the while that she must have lied about her weight. He was slightly less disgruntled when Jonathan introduced her as one of the New York Central's stockholders.

That night Cynthia and Jonathan drank champagne in the sky parlor of the Metropolitan Hotel on Broadway before going to the theater. Six floors below them, the usual mass of vehicles, horses and people on Broadway flung a faint roar against the windows. Cynthia felt her flesh tingle. New York was so bursting with energy, excitement. It was impossible to think of going back to Bralston's dullness; even New Orleans now seemed drab.

"Are we celebrating our victory over the Commodore?" Cynthia asked.

"Why not?" Jonathan said.

"Then I should pay—from my winnings."

"Out of the question."

"You can't appreciate how thrilling it is for a woman to have her own money to spend. Instead of being a mere wife spending her husband's."

"You must know you would never be a mere wife—to any man."

"I have no idea what I might be. I have very little experience of wifehood. Charlie and I were together for such a short time. He used to say we were perfectly matched—both hopelessly spoiled from birth."

Cynthia was dazed, astonished by this outburst. What was wrong with her? Was it instinct, woman's intuition, warning him—and her—that they were not a good match? Was it a lurking remnant of rebel defiance? Or an equally southern wish to be wooed with less patience and more passion? Or was it an inside-out omission that something remarkable had happened on that wild ride through Central Park? That fierce, daring man who exulted in the danger and the speed—that man could have her. Perhaps he could toler-ate the possibility, the very real possibility, that she might fail any man who truly needed her.

To Cynthia's dismay Jonathan abandoned the subject and did not bring it up for the rest of the evening.

The next day, Katherine Kemble Brown began dropping hints as heavy as cannon balls. A woman could keep a man dangling only so long. Then it became cruelty. She knew that southern women were mistresses of the art, but she hated to see it practiced on such an undeserving victim.

"I thought Old Steady was famous for never retreating," Cynthia said. "Last night, when I performed a few evasive maneuvers, he fled the field, horse, foot and cannon."

Two nights later, Jonathan took Cynthia to dinner at the Maison Dorée. They sat in a secluded corner, with a view of Union Square. Jonathan pointed to a newly erected bronze statue of Abraham Lincoln across the street. "There's another southerner who settled in the North," he said. Dam-ask draperies framed the window, gaslight glowed softly in the crystal chande-liers. From a nearby table, Henry Raymond, editor of the *New York Times*, greeted them. Jonathan told her the story of Raymond's long-running affair with the red-haired woman he was escorting, the actress Rose Ettynge.

The casual boldness with which Jonathan stated the erotic facts stirred a flush of warmth, excitement, in Cynthia's body. A man did not mention such things to a woman without a presumption—or an expectation—of intimacy. Jonathan never seemed more masterful, more in command, as he ordered the wine, repeated her dinner selections to the hovering headwaiter. He looked young in the yellow gaslight, the craggy face full of good humor and confi-dent vitality. This was a *man*. He had a place in this awesome opulent complicated city, a place he occupied without boasts or brags because such histrionics were unnecessary.

Their conversation rambled, but Cynthia had a feeling that none of it was as careless or as casual as it seemed. He talked frankly about his friend Ben Dall, who seemed to be recovering from his nervous collapse. He told her about their bitter disagreement over abolitionism, Ben's hostility to southerners. He was warning her that this man was going to be part of their lives, that she would have to deal with him. They talked about his sons. He had decided to send Rawdon to St. Paul's School in New Hampshire, where he hoped the boy would acquire some study habits. As for little George, only this morning he had asked if the pretty lady who said his name in such a funny way—"Jaw-gie"—was going to visit them again. "I told him I hoped so," Jonathan said.

As the carriage jounced over the cobblestones on the way back to Katherine Kemble Brown's townhouse, Jonathan took Cynthia's left hand and said, "I have something I want to put on one of those fingers." From his pocket he drew a small box. As they passed a yellow streetlamp she caught the unmistakable flash of a diamond.

"I know I can never take Charlie's place," he said. "I don't have his looks, his wit, his spirit. But if you can find even a tiny corner in your heart for me . . ."

Cynthia was momentarily speechless. Someday she would tell him the truth about Charlie. "A tiny corner?" she said. "There's no room for anyone else. There hasn't been—for months."

That was almost a lie. That was Cynthia Legrand, the courtesan, saying the seductive, romantic thing. But the impact of her declaration on Jonathan was so magical, she abandoned all thought of amending it.

Within a month they were married, in a small, almost private ceremony at Grace Church. Cynthia asked Mittie Roosevelt to be her attendant. Jonathan's best man was his Columbia classmate Delancey Apthorpe.

They spent their wedding night in the bridal suite of the new Fifth Avenue Hotel, a block-long marble palace overlooking Madison Square Park. Cynthia had no idea what to expect from this serious unromantic Yankee. Charlie, after seeming so southern, so passionate in his talk about adoration and rapture, had been a disappointment. Perhaps part of the failure had been her fault. She had been all courtesan that night, determined to withhold her heart, her deepest feelings, from her husband's reach. Not that Charlie seemed particularly interested in reaching them. He did not even use the word "love." Instead he talked to her as if she were a new item on the menu at the St. Charles Hotel. "Delicious," "rare," "luscious" were among his adjectives.

Jonathan said very little as they prepared for bed. But when he began caressing her, his hands did the most remarkable things. Exquisite waves of warmth flowed up through her body. Next those long arms enfolded her, and deep deliberate kisses left her breathless. Then he was above her, within her, and the sensations were even more remarkable. The strokes, like his kisses, were incredibly deep and full and deliberate. Slow, steady, rising now to a gentle crescendo, those immensely strong arms still wrapped completely around her. Cynthia felt self, independence, careening away from her, she was lost in a flood of maleness, Yankee mastery, abandoned by father, brothers, sisters.

Oh. He was there in the darkness whispering *I love you I love you* and she could not answer him, but she promised herself, almost promised him, she might say it soon.

She was horribly seasick on the voyage to Europe. But Paris restored her. Her father's favorite city filled Cynthia with a near-delirium of happiness. She adored the magnificent boulevards and squares and vistas created by Emperor Napoleon III, who had ripped down most of the old medieval city. She exulted in the wild music of Offenbach resounding in the cafés and theaters. She could not wait to join the gorgeously dressed women strolling in the Tuileries Garden.

Within twenty-four hours, young men in bright cravats and skin-tight frock coats were greeting her at the shrine of haute couture, the House of Worth on the Rue de la Paix, and escorting her up the winding staircase to the Salon de Lumière, where the windows were sealed and the walls mirrored from floor to ceiling and a hundred gas jets burned, so that you could see exactly how your gown was going to look in the Tuileries Palace when you were presented to Napoleon III and his incomparably beautiful Spanish-born empress, Eugénie.

For a month Cynthia persuaded Jonathan to like Paris for her sake, even though the rich sauces troubled his stomach, which had been ruined by the tensions of the war. He was almost as unenthused by the blatant decadence of the Second Empire. The streets swarmed with gaudily dressed prostitutes. The comic newspapers were filled with nude drawings and endless jokes about adultery. For a few days he seemed to be reverting to Brother Jonathan, the family Puritan that Charlie had mocked.

Cynthia teased him out of his American propriety. She urged him to regard the comic newspapers as anatomy lessons. She reminded him that he had a wife who was fifty percent French, which meant that in Paris he should consider himself half a Frenchman and act accordingly. Before their first week was over, he abandoned his puritanism and took her to see the can-can danced in its red-damasked shrine, the Bal Mabille.

Paris was full of Americans. They dined with former Union generals and wandering congressmen. The American ambassador invited them to receptions and dinners at the embassy. They picnicked *à deux* in the Bois de Boulogne and enjoyed the races at Longchamps. Touring the art galleries, Cynthia fell in love with a new school of painters, called the Impressionists, who maintained that in painting—and in life—moments were more precious than hours. "If I'd heard that six months ago, I would have disagreed," Jonathan said. "It's amazing how fast I'm turning into a Frenchman."

One morning, after a particularly amorous night, Cynthia was at the dressing table, combing her hair, when a note arrived via a bellman. It was from Louisiana's ex-Senator, her father's dear friend, John Slidell. He had heard they were in Paris and was inviting them to dinner. Cynthia was delighted and assumed Jonathan would feel the same way.

Her husband was paying a visit to the barber. When he returned, looking extraordinarily attractive in a newly purchased gray Parisian suit, she handed the letter to him and casually suggested next Saturday as a possible date.

"We're not going near that man," Jonathan growled. The tone of his voice was bad enough. Even more appalling was the way he was glaring at her, as if she were responsible for the invitation.

"Why in the world do you say such a thing?" she said.

"John Slidell is one of those people who cooked up the purple dream of a slave empire. I can remember him at your wedding in 1858 holding forth about the South's destiny while your father and your brothers and cousins stood around agreeing with him. He's responsible for killing Charlie and a million other good men, North and South. He's never gone home to get a pardon, which proves he has no regrets. I'd rather shake hands with a murderer."

"I thought he was one of your father's best friends. They worked together in the Senate—"

"I don't care what they did together. When it came to politics, my father was a gullible fool. He let southerners like Slidell lead him around by the ear."

Cynthia struggled to control chaotic feelings. Jonathan was perfectly right about the South's purple dream. But it was one thing for her to pronounce that judgment in her mind, and quite another matter to hear her father, her brothers and her cousins condemned in this harsh Yankee voice with the arrogant clang of the conqueror.

"Would you object to my meeting him for an apéritif one day while you're busy elsewhere?"

"I'd find it objectionable—but I wouldn't . . . object," he said.

"Thank you," she said, staring into the dressing-table mirror, refusing to look at him.

That night, after a dinner filled with stilted attempts at conversation on Jonathan's part, they prepared for bed in icy silence. He turned out the gaslight and settled on the thick pillows beside her. "I'm sorry I snapped and snarled that way this afternoon," he said. "I'm afraid I've spent too much time in the last several years giving orders to people."

"But you won't come to dinner with him?"

The Yankee voice clanged in the darkness. "No."

The chill persisted until she met ex-Senator Slidell at a café on the

Champs-Élysées two days later. He seemed a smaller man than she remembered him. Time, or grief, had etched deep lines in his once handsome face. Cynthia told him that she and Jonathan were leaving for Italy in a few days and they did not have a single night left for him.

"I understand," he said, nodding his gray head, letting the word cover all possible meanings. He seemed so sad, so weary, Cynthia almost wept.

She listened to him talk about ruined hopes, lost opportunities. One of the South's many mistakes was Jefferson Davis' refusal to send Victor Conté Legrand to France. Davis had forced Slidell to undertake the mission, to get his rival out of the country and enable him to rule the Confederacy unchallenged.

I would have gone with him, Cynthia thought. I might be one of Louis Napoleon's mistresses now. He reportedly had about a dozen. No matter how repulsive the prospect, she would have given herself to that potbellied tyrant or one of his strutting gorgeously uniformed marshals, she would have done anything to prevent that moment in the Hotel Splendide when she heard her Yankee husband use the word "southerners" with undisguised loathing.

Maybe her marriage was a horrible mistake. Maybe this visit to Paris only underscored the inevitability of her destiny. What else explained the cold rage engulfing her heart? How could she feel that way only twenty-four hours after giving herself to Jonathan Stapleton with every appearance—even to herself—of love?

Meanwhile, at their café table on the Champs-Élysées, John Slidell drifted ever deeper into the past, all the way back to his student days in New York. "It's a good omen, I feel, you and Jonathan Stapleton coming together this way. I loved his mother and father and I loved your mother and father. Tell him I just wanted to bestow whatever blessing that sort of thing has to offer. Nothing but an old man's wish."

Back at the Splendide, Jonathan was writing a letter. "Oh," Cynthia cried, "he's so pathetic. How could you be so cruel to him?"

The mouth compressed to a harsh line. "Did he explain why he's never come home?"

"No. But isn't it obvious? He's a proud man. Why do you want him to grovel? We're never going to do that."

The "we" simply flew from her lips. Jonathan studied the tops of his shoes. For an instant his face was convulsed by the angriest imaginable frown. Then it passed. He looked up at her, surly but penitent. "You're right," he said. "Perhaps I should have gone. Can you forgive me?"

Forgiveness. What a delicious idea. This majestic Yankee, this conqueror, asking for her forgiveness. Looking so sad, so humbled, by her southern pride. She kissed him on the lips. "I won't even impose a penance, much as you deserve one."

They left Paris, lovers once more. But, for Cynthia, the city, France itself, had become a kind of threat. She was fleeing that cold rage she had felt on the Champs-Élysées. She recognized it as an enemy of love, a part of the past she was trying to escape.

Italy rescued them from the decadence and doubts of the modern world. For them it was a peninsula drifting between centuries and eras, a land, a people, a language rich in beauty and tenderness, as yet unburdened by the agonies of modern nationhood. Italy seemed to exist solely for lovers who wanted, needed, to deepen their love, to arm it against future dangers.

Had Jonathan known how she would be stirred by Tuscany's sensuous landscapes, by the magnificent male bodies of Michelangelo, the exquisite contours of Canova's nudes, the glowing skin of Titian's women? After weeks in Rome and Florence, they rented the Palazzo Rospigliosi, just beyond the sudden bend in Venice's Grand Canal, within sight of the scrolled storm-white dome of the Church of Santa Maria della Salute.

The owners, suave Count Vittorio Rospigliosi and his petite pretty young wife, welcomed them as if they were guests of the family. They showed them through the forty rooms crammed with fifteenth-century inlaid furniture and priceless paintings and cloth-of-gold tapestries, the Count explaining where this or that famous ancestor had acquired a particular treasure.

At last the Rospigliosis departed, urging the Stapletons to visit them in their villa in Florence before they left Italy. The palazzo's *maggiordomo*, Fabrizio, a tall spectral man with as much dignity as the Count, served them cakes and wine in their bedroom. They fell asleep in a massive fourposter bed that had belonged to a doge of Venice in its days of glory.

The next morning, with sunlight streaming in the open French windows, it did not seem in the least embarrassing when Jonathan gently lifted Cynthia's nightgown over her head and began making love to her. His hands on her breasts, her thighs, aroused her in a way that she had previously only imagined.

She had never thought she would see a man's face as he entered her. She had imagined Charlie's handsome face glowing there in the dark, she had even touched it once, but it was impossible to learn from it. That morning in the Palazzo Rospigliosi she saw Jonathan's face, that serious, scarred face transformed by her giving into something beautiful, joyous. For the first time she believed in love as something more than a word. For the first time she believed in her power to create it.

As a daring quid pro quo, she insisted on touching, examining his naked body. It was a tremendous physique, still amazingly youthful, the muscles of his arms and chest especially developed from horseback riding. She had cried out at the wounds, the shattered, shrunken right knee, a raw gash along his right side, a red splotch on his left shoulder. A wound for each year of the war, he had said. She had wept at the thought of so much pain inflicted on someone she loved.

That night they went to hear Verdi's *La Traviata* at La Fenice, Venice's magnificent opera house. Again and again, the composer and his librettist seemed to be speaking directly to her. Especially in the first act, when the noble Alfredo offers the courtesan Violetta his devotion and sings of love's meaning and power.

> *O amore misterioso,*   O mysterious love,
> *Misterioso, altero,*   Baffling, aloof,
> *Croce e delizia al cor.*   The heart's cross and delight.

The last line sent a shivering, soaring mixture of fear and wonder through Cynthia's body. *Croce e delizia al cor.* The music swept her back to New Orleans, where she had seen this opera with her father beside her. Afterward he had wryly assured her that not all courtesans died in misery like foolish Violetta. Her mistake had been to lose control of her heart, to give it to Alfredo.

Croce e delizia al cor. The line resounded through the opera, echoed again and again in voice and music with Verdi's imcomparable sweetness. Was it happening to her, that kind of love, with its threat of pain, its dream of rare delight?

Later that night, Cynthia stood arm in arm with Jonathan at the window of the Palazzo Rospigliosi, looking down on the moonlit Grand Canal. Ripples of laughter drifted from passing gondolas; in the distance a guitar strummed. Now, she thought, now was the time to tell him everything— about her father, Charlie, the new meaning, the fresh hope Jonathan had infused into her life, and the fearful love that was stirring in her uncertain heart in response to it.

But the words remained locked in her throat by another fear—that the truth might destroy the love she had created in him. She struggled for words that would avert this calamity. "Those gondolas remind me of nights at Bralston," she said. "We used to sit on the veranda and watch the steamboats glide past on the river like great ghostly creatures. I used to imagine them taking me away to someplace like this, escaping my destiny."

He said nothing. Did he hear the anxiety in her voice?

"My father had some strange ideas about my destiny."

"I'm in charge of your destiny now."

She did not like the way he said it. She told herself it was only male pride, husbandly protectiveness speaking. But there was an echo, perhaps more than an echo, of the conqueror. Cynthia Legrand did not want anyone, southern father or Yankee husband, in charge of her destiny.

She let the moment of truth drift away into the murmuring Venetian night.

FOUR

"I wonder what he'd think about it all if he came back for a look," Ben Dall said.

He pointed to the statue of George Washington on horseback, in the southwest corner of Union Square Park.

"He'd probably buy some real estate a little farther uptown," Jonathan Stapleton said. "My grandfather told me he was the shrewdest man with a dollar he'd ever met."

Their hack was stuck in the traffic pouring out of Broadway into Union Square. It was a beautiful late-September day. The sky above New York was just beginning to lose its bright blue luster. The sidewalks swarmed with men and women hurrying home from jobs and shopping expeditions. By and large they were well-dressed, cheerful, contented-looking Americans. Many people stopped to buy papers from the newsboys hawking them at every corner.

"Look at them," Ben Dall said. "Perfectly satisfied with our wonderful country. They read the newspapers as if the reporters were writing fiction. As if everything were happening on the moon."

Jonathan sighed. There were times when he shared Ben's exasperation with the great American public in the year 1869. But most of the time he tried to understand them. For the first five years of the decade they had been pounded with history. Crucial elections, murderous battles, meddling foreign powers had menaced their safety and peace of mind. Casualty lists thrust grief and anguish at them. Was it any wonder that four years of peace and prosperity had seen them grow indifferent to burning political issues, more absorbed in their private lives? These days, Jonathan Stapleton too had a private life that absorbed him.

"I think I'll get out here," Jonathan said. "I have to pick up Cynthia's present at Tiffany's. I'll see you at the Roosevelts' around eight."

Ben nodded. Jonathan climbed out of the hack feeling a sense of relief, escape. The ride up Broadway with his old friend had been an excursion into nostalgia at first. They had looked down Park Place at the building Columbia College had occupied until it moved uptown in 1855, and reminisced about their student days. They had laughed about the time President Charles King had tried to stir an interest in boxing as a sport and found it impossible to lure their classmates out of Phelan's Billiard Room on the corner of Murray Street. Passing Bleecker Street, they could see the old Van Vorst mansion and the other houses on that once fashionable thoroughfare where they had danced away more than one winter night. The well-to-do families had long since fled north before the city's relentless commercial advance. The houses had been chopped into studios and flats rented by reporters, actors and similar bohemians.

Instead of cheering Ben up, these memories only made him gloomy. He began lamenting the demise of the easygoing city of their youth and bemoaning the frenzied commercial capital it had become. New York—and by implication the rest of the country—was in thrall to the power of the dollar. "Eat thy neighbor"—that was the city's motto, Ben declared.

Jonathan wondered if his old friend was about to succumb to another bout of indigo. This was what Margaret Dall called the melancholy that had periodically descended on Ben since his return from Mississippi. The moods were frequently preceded by this sort of lamentation about the moral condition of the city and the country. Not that Jonathan thought the country's moral condition was marvelous. He simply did not think it was bad enough to render a person incapable of living a normal life.

Jonathan had persuaded Delancey Apthorpe to make Ben a partner in his brokerage firm. Jonathan had loaned Ben enough money to carry some weight, and things had gone beautifully at first. Once Ben had recovered from his ordeal in Mississippi, he seemed to be his cheerful prewar self. He attracted new customers, and the booming stock market soon enabled him to repay Jonathan everything he owed him.

Then came these crippling bouts of indigo. He would not appear at work for a week, sometimes for two weeks. Customers wondered if he had taken to drink or embezzled their money. It was driving Delancey Apthorpe crazy.

Jonathan hurried across Union Square to the ugly cast-iron building on West Fifteenth Street where Charles Louis Tiffany sold his expensive jewelry and silver. The smiling manager led him to a rear counter and unwrapped a brooch, cut from glowing pink onyx in the outline of a tiara and set in colored gold enameled with miniature flowers. "Direct from Mr. Pugin's workshop in Paris," he said.

"Splendid," Jonathan said. "Charge it to my account."

He headed east on Fifteenth Street, past Dr. Cheever's white marble Congregational Church, where Ben Dall, like many New Englanders who migrated to New York, had worshiped until he argued himself and his room-mate out of Christianity into "creative doubt." Three more blocks and Jonathan reached Stuyvesant Square. The lamentations of his old friend, the newsboys' screeches, ceased to gnaw at his nerves.

Between Fifteenth and Seventeenth Streets, on both sides of Second Avenue, stretched a lovely green park. The crowds and commerce of Broadway and Union Square seemed as irrelevant here as the brawling Irish "bhoys" and strolling prostitutes of the Bowery, also only a few blocks away. On the sunswept green lawns, beneath noble old elms still rich in red and gold fall colors, mothers and governesses chatted or read novels while laughing children played marbles or hopscotch, rolled hoops or tossed balls, as if the disciples of commerce and vice were a thousand miles away. Order, permanence, privacy, but above all peace—that was what Stuyvesant Square seemed to guarantee.

Jonathan had hoped that Ben Dall would return here when he abandoned Mississippi. But Ben had found the war-inflated prices outrageous and had chosen a more modest house on East Twenty-sixth Street, next door to the novelist Herman Melville. Ben could certainly afford to live here now, Jonathan thought as he crossed the square to Seventeenth Street. He would have to twist his arm a little. It would not be difficult to change his mind. He knew Margaret Dall was unhappy with Twenty-sixth Street.

Jonathan mounted the steps of 217 East Seventeenth Street and unlocked the polished walnut door, with its embossed brass bell pull. In the front hall he paused to inhale the scent of fresh flowers. On the massive Gothic side table, some of the two dozen yellow roses he had ordered to be delivered at noon were arranged in the great silver bowl he had inherited from his grandfather the Continental Congressman. On its side were the magnificently scrolled words INDEPENDENCE FOREVER.

Cousteau, the mulatto butler Cynthia had imported from New Orleans, emerged from the shadows at the end of the hall. There were times when Jonathan swore the fellow's feet did not touch the floor, he moved so silently. Jonathan handed him his hat and cane.

"Is Mrs. Stapleton in her room?"

"Yes, General. Dressing for dinner, I believe. You're dining out tonight?"

"Yes."

"I told Muzzey to lay out your evening clothes."

"Thank you."

Cynthia's door was open a crack. He peered into the room. She was sitting at her ribbon-festooned dressing table in a lacy peignoir, humming a song. He tiptoed across the green Axminster carpet, approaching so she could not see his image in the mirror until the last moment. He bent down and kissed the curve of that supple neck just where it met her shoulder.

She gave a little cry. "Now I know I shouldn't have settled in this dreadful city. A lady isn't safe from assault in her own boudoir."

He took the pink onyx brooch out of his pocket, stripped away the tissue paper and placed it on the dressing table. "Happy birthday," he said.

"Ohhhhh," she sighed, picking it up. "This may go a long way toward excusing your indecency, General. It's by Pugin, I'm sure of it."

"So Tiffany tells me."

Her knowledge and taste in jewelry, furniture, painting constantly amazed him. His mother and his first wife had been utilitarian in their approach to such things. They bought whatever was in style, whatever would "do." Cynthia was familiar with the workmanship of all the famous designers of London and Paris and had her own very strong opinions about them. Pugin was one of her favorites.

She leaped up and clung to him, pressing her dark scented head against his chest. "How can I be so happy when I'm growing older by the second? In a year I'll be thirty. You'll be ready to discard me for some nineteen-year-old mistress."

"You talk the damndest, most delightful nonsense," he said, kissing her on the lips. "What have you done with yourself today?"

"I took Georgie shopping and bought him the most darling little sailor suit. I hope it's not a violation of the family's military tradition."

"Of course not. We've had a few Stapletons in the navy. Not that it matters."

He frequently missed the signal when she teased him about the Stapletons' tendency to regard themselves as an American institution. Cynthia called Bowood, his family home, with its ancestral portraits and cabinets full of Revolutionary War memorabilia and gifts from presidents, "the museum." He could not quite bring himself to laugh at the Stapletons, though he was ready enough to admit their shortcomings.

There were other times when she teased him a little beyond the bounds of his toleration. She ridiculed the small study he had set up on one side of his bedroom, with battlefield photographs and the bullet-shredded flag of his old regiment on the wall, beside a captured Confederate flag. She called it his "war corner," and when he spent too much time there she gave him mock salutes and called him "General" for the rest of the day.

There were other moments of irritation that had nothing to do with their different pasts. When he sat down at his desk to pay the bills and saw "Two evening toilettes—$8,000" from Maison Worth, he was tempted to modify his promise that his wife would never have to worry about money. But these minor imperfections did not really trouble him. He could still affirm without qualification that the past two years had been the happiest of his life.

Lately, happiest had become an inadequate word. Stirring in him was a hope he usually managed to conceal, even from himself—for a love that spoke coded words such as forgiveness, peace, trust to his guarded soul; spiritual gifts that the iron general did not think he deserved. He had begun to wonder if they might be within his grasp after all. More than once he thought he saw them standing just outside the barred windows, hooded figures, bearing gifts which only she, this quick-tempered, teasing, passionate woman, could smuggle into the fortress.

Good God. He would be writing poetry if he kept thinking that way. The simple, unadorned fact was enough. He had somehow persuaded a beautiful woman to love him, to be as enthusiastic about being his wife as he was about being her husband. For a man who had spent the early years of his life thinking of himself as unattractive to women, this was vintage contentment.

"Do we have time for a glass of sherry?" Cynthia asked, after another kiss.

"Of course. I told the Roosevelts we'd pick them up at eight."

Cousteau served the sherry, and Cynthia began telling him about her search for a suitable school for George. Well-to-do New York families like the Roosevelts favored private tutors, but Jonathan wanted his sons to share a common experience with other children their age. Cynthia had discovered that one of the younger ministers at St. George's Church, only a few doors away on the west side of the square, was teaching a group of boys. She had visited the class and liked the warm cheerful atmosphere. "I don't want to see Georgie thrust into the hands of some snarling old schoolmaster," she said. "He has such a sweet nature."

Jonathan was not sure he wanted a sweet-natured son. But it was a difficult point to argue. Cynthia's enthusiasm for motherhood had been a complete surprise to him. She had fired George's sour Scottish governess and brought Cleopatra, her girlhood nurse at Bralston, to New York. Cleo made sure George's clothes were clean and his face and hands washed, but Cynthia appointed herself his governess for most of each day. She read to him for an hour each morning and evening—poems and stories and essays on natural history. To these she added a seemingly endless supply of tales about sometimes mysterious, sometimes comical happenings on the bayous and rivers of Louisiana. She had heard them all from a personage named Mammy George, and as Cynthia told them her eyes widened, her voice deepened and shifted to a Negro dialect in which every second word was marvelously mispronounced. George now refused to go to bed without a Mammy George story.

Equally amazing was Cynthia's supply of singing and chasing games such as Who Stole the Cardinal's Hat? and Walking on the Levee. Often, she romped around the house with George and Lucy, their upstairs maid, another import from Louisiana, as if they were all five years old. Just when he began to worry that she was making George a mama's boy, she thrust him into the hurly-burly of the Roosevelt household, where he quickly became the devoted friend of Mittie's rambunctious younger son Elliott. If Cynthia had done nothing else, the transformation of George from whining waif to cheerful child would have won Jonathan's eternal gratitude.

She was less successful with Rawdon. He made a point of calling her "Stepmother" and stonily resisted her attempts to ingratiate him. Jonathan was inclined to lose his temper and issue orders, but Cynthia counseled patience. Rawdon spent most of his time at St. Paul's School in New Hampshire; they saw him only on holidays, and for a few weeks during the summer.

Jonathan found himself agreeing to let George try Mr. Davidson's classes. Cynthia promptly turned the conversation in an entirely new direction. "I saw the most wonderful painting by Frederick Church at the Düsseldorf Gallery this afternoon. A temple in some ancient Arabian city called Petra. It would go so beautifully in the front hall. But I almost shudder to tell you the price."

"How much?"

"Five thousand dollars."

The cost of outfitting a New York house to suit a wife with impeccable taste frequently amazed him. Cynthia had discarded almost every piece of the humdrum old-fashioned furniture his first wife had bought in slavish imitation of her mother-in-law. Each room had become a separate harmony of taste and beauty, French Renaissance Revival furniture in the parlors, Elizabethan Renaissance in the dining room. Paintings by the French Impressionists, by George Inness, William Page and other American artists blossomed on the walls, Persian and Turkish carpets in red and gold and blue and silver on the floors.

"It's one of the best things Church has ever done," Cynthia said when he hesitated. "Better than his Andes paintings. It has such a spiritual quality. I'll pay for it out of my money . . ."

He had made an elaborate pretense of keeping her comfortable little fortune in a separate account at his office. Legally, of course, it was now his money—or, to put it more precisely, again.

"Don't be silly."

She clapped her hands like a delighted child. With a rustle of silk, she crossed the room to kiss him on the mouth. "You are a dear," she said. "Now leave me so I can suitably adorn myself for such a paragon of a husband."

At seven-fifty, Oliver Cromwell had the coach waiting for them at the door. Cynthia was wearing a purple gown embroidered with blue orchids that had to be one of Worth's checkbook-boggling creations. They rumbled toward the Roosevelt brownstone on Twentieth Street. Cynthia talked about Mittie's desire to move uptown. "I'll miss her so. I almost wish Theodore would forbid it," she said. "But I don't have much hope. I don't think he ever says no to her."

"You make it sound as though your monster of a husband growls that word all the time," he said.

"I know you're *capable* of doing it," she said, tilting her chin defiantly at him. "But I must confess I haven't heard it lately."

He smiled and said nothing.

"I wish you liked Theodore more," Cynthia said as they turned into Twentieth Street.

"I like him well enough," Jonathan said.

"I adore Mittie so."

"Everyone does. Theodore and I share a similar fate. Dull men overshadowed by scintillating wives."

"Now who's talking nonsense?"

Jonathan thought he was reasonably friendly with Theodore Roosevelt, considering the way he (and his three brawny brothers) had managed to avoid going near a battlefield during the war. At the Roosevelt house, Jonathan got out and turned the bell. A servant answered the door.

Mittie came halfway down the front stairs in a filmy white gown, smiling excitedly. "Does she suspect?"

"Not a bit," Jonathan said.

"Bring her in."

Back at the carriage, Jonathan said offhandedly, "Would you come in for a moment, dear? Mittie has something she wants to show you."

Cynthia allowed him to lead her upstairs to the Roosevelts' Rococo Revival parlor. A dozen men in evening clothes and women in silk and taffeta gowns raised champagne glasses and chorused, "Happy birthday!"

Cynthia's eyes filled with tears. Jonathan felt a rush of endearment, tenderness. How much this seemingly confident, carefree, impudent woman needed and wanted affection!

"You are a devil," she cried, and embraced Mittie.

"And you," she said, turning to Jonathan. "You charlatan of a husband with your mythical theater tickets. I'll never believe another word you say."

"We decided this was a perfect opportunity to testify to our universal delight in your migration from Louisiana," Mittie said.

"No one is happier about it than I am," said a short husky young man with a black handlebar mustache. "Without her encouragement I'd never have found the nerve to leave Galveston." Cynthia's brother Robert Legrand gave her a kiss. He had arrived in New York about a month ago. Jonathan had gotten him a job with Apthorpe, Dall and Company.

"I'm afraid I can't let you get away with that claim, Major," Jonathan said, using the rank Legrand had won as a Confederate cavalryman. "But I'm perfectly willing to let you be the second happiest."

"I accept your offer, General," Robert said, shaking his hand. "Starting a war over that point would be almost as stupid as the reason we started shooting at each other the first time."

Jonathan forced a smile, even though he disliked this tendency to dismiss the war as a tragic mistake caused by the blunders of both sides. He looked around the crowded parlor. Schermerhorns, Jays, Gansevoorts were among the familiar faces he saw. Katherine Kemble Brown chatted with Ward McAllister, Virginia-born gourmet and aesthete. Jonathan had known most of these people before his marriage, but always as an outsider, a New Jerseyan. It pleased him enormously to see them here in the Roosevelt parlor, offering toasts to his wife.

But there was one face—no, two faces—missing. The Dalls. Had Ben surrendered to indigo and retreated to his room for another week? He broke social engagements as well as business appointments when he was in one of his moods. Jonathan was about to confer with Delancey Apthorpe when a hand tapped his shoulder. Ben smiled up at him, Margaret on his arm in a lovely ruby satin gown. The gloom that had enveloped Ben this afternoon in the hack seemed to have vanished. "Where is this sorceress who's almost changed my opinion of southern women?" he said.

Jonathan led him across the room to Cynthia. "Here's another admirer," he said.

"Two admirers," Margaret said, and kissed Cynthia on the cheek. "What a marvelous gown."

"Thank you," Cynthia said. "Your dress is lovely, too. Did you have it made here in New York?"

"Yes. I've managed to persuade my mother's old dressmaker to take pity on me and remodel some of my prewar gowns."

Ben listened to this exchange with a sardonic expression on his face, then stepped forward and kissed Cynthia's hand. "You are looking magnificent, Mrs. Stapleton," he said. "It's hard to believe it's your forty-second birthday. You're living proof that the malaria of the Mississippi Valley does wonders for the complexion."

"It's the contrast to my eighty-two-year-old husband that sets me off, Colonel," Cynthia replied.

Jonathan laughed and plucked a glass of bourbon from a passing tray. He had taken a calculated risk, telling Cynthia about Ben's extreme opinions, and asking her to try to like him for his sake. She had done more than that. She had charmed Ben into liking her.

This raillery set the tone for the dinner conversation. Jonathan could not remember a more cheerful party. Cynthia responded to the numerous toasts with a marvelous combination of wit and charm. Mittie climaxed the good cheer with a birthday cake decorated with a vivid Confederate flag.

"I never thought I'd see the day when you saluted the Stars and Bars, Jonathan," Ben Dall said.

Jonathan heard an edge of sarcasm in his voice, but everyone else thought the remark was amusing.

"You underestimate the power of love, Colonel Dall," Mittie said.

"A failing my wife has pointed out to me more than once," Ben said.

When the ladies left the men to their cigars and brandy, the talk rambled casually for a few minutes, then veered to the topic that was uppermost in every male mind. "Do you think Jay Gould can pull off this corner in gold, General?" Theodore Roosevelt asked.

"I hope not. I think the fellow ought to be in jail," Jonathan said.

"It's a perfectly legitimate speculation," Jefferson Gansevoort said.

A short, dandyish man with a waxed mustache and goatee, Gansevoort had been a highly successful broker since the late fifties. He had been one of the first to make a market in gold stocks, a new idea in America. Before the war, all United States currency had been redeemable in gold. But the government had been forced to finance its fleets and armies with paper money, which it printed in abundance and promised to redeem in gold at some later date.

Congress was still debating the problem of redeeming the greenbacks. This indecision left speculators with a volatile market, which the government had attempted to regulate by releasing gold from the Treasury periodically to keep the price reasonably steady. But in the past week the price had soared as Jay Gould, a Massachusetts-born speculator who was rapidly emerging as a power on Wall Street, began buying gold at a tremendous rate. It soon became apparent that Gould was out to corner the market, which would enable him to charge whatever he pleased for the precious metal.

"Is it true what I heard on the Street today, that Gould has President Grant in his pocket?" Ben Dall asked.

For a moment Gansevoort's eyes glittered mockingly. Jonathan thought he was about to say, "What of it?" Instead, he tapped the ash off his cigar and said, "That's a bit of an exaggeration. I think Mr. Gould has persuaded the President that the government should stay out of the market and let gold find its own price."

"Did this persuasion have anything to do with the two-million-dollar account Mr. Gould is carrying for the President's brother-in-law?" Ben asked.

There was shock and dismay on almost every face in the room. Most of these men had voted for Grant when he ran for president last year. Jonathan had given over $20,000 to various state and national committees and had joined other ex-soldiers in statements proclaiming the candidate's virtues and abilities.

"Gould *is* carrying such an account?" Delancey Apthorpe asked.

"Yes, of course," Gansevoort replied. "But I don't think the President is aware of it. Mr. Corbin is simply getting into a good thing. A sure thing, gentlemen, in case any of you are interested," Gansevoort said. "Gold will go to two hundred by the end of tomorrow's trading day, I can guarantee it."

Gansevoort's words only increased everyone's consternation. It was hard to believe that Jefferson Gansevoort, from one of New York's oldest and best families, was asking them to trust a man with Jay Gould's reputation. Last year Gould and his fat buffoon of a partner, Jim Fisk, had looted $10 million from the Erie Railroad by watering stock, bribing judges and reporters and corrupting the entire legislature of the state of New York.

"Three cheers for the Flash Age," Ben Dall said.

Jonathan winced at the bitterness on his friend's face. The phrase had become a favorite newspaper term. It encapsulated the emergence of amoral Wall Street operators like Gould and shoddy millionaires who competed to see how much money they could spend on banquets at Delmonico's.

Everyone was relieved to have the conversation interrupted by a knock on the door. The knob turned and Cynthia stood there, smiling, waving aside the cloud of cigar smoke. "Since it is my birthday party and I am presumably immune from male retaliation, I've been sent to warn you that you're exceeding all reasonable limits for this deplorable custom. What are you doing? Trying to solve all the problems of the world or just brazenly guzzling poor Theodore's brandy?"

"The latter, I assure you," Jonathan said.

They rejoined the ladies, and the party wound down. Jonathan noticed that Ben Dall had little to say in the half hour or so they lingered. A grimness seemed to sharpen his features. The mood of the hack ride uptown was returning, intensified by their after-dinner conversation and brandy. The Dalls left without saying goodbye to Cynthia or Mittie.

Riding home, Jonathan felt an impulse to apologize to Cynthia for Ben, to share his worries about him. But Cynthia wanted to talk only about the surprise party, how much it had meant to her to receive such a tribute of affection. The tenderness stirred by the tears he had seen in her eyes reawakened. Ben Dall would have to make his own way. This beautiful woman had the first, the only claim on Jonathan Stapleton's affection.

In the hall outside her bedroom, Cynthia whispered, "There is one more thing that will make this the happiest birthday of my life."

They made ardent love in her canopied bed, with the gas lamp glowing on the opposite wall, creating a chiaroscuro of white skin and black hair and shadowed eyes and lips. *Happiness*, Jonathan thought, it was amazing to find it in his arms, as palpable as breath, as real as flesh, as warm as the voice murmuring, "Oh my dearest friend, I'm amazed at the way my love for you keeps growing every day."

The next morning, Jonathan decided to walk to work. A New York doctor with some mechanical ability had devised a brace for his knee, which freed him from pain and almost eliminated his limp. His mind and body still vibrated with the memory of last night's lovemaking. He felt simultaneously animal and spiritual, as if part of him was a great cat, stretching electric muscles and sinew, and part was a winged creature, angel or eagle, soaring above the city. As he walked through Printing House Square, the City Hall Park fountain leaped above the surrounding trees. Everywhere he looked he saw magical symbols of his happiness, with his sorceress wife at the center of it all.

"Jonathan."

Ben Dall came out of the New York Times Building, a copy of the paper under his arm. He looked weary, diminished; as if he had spent a sleepless night.

"I hope you went up there to tell your old friends to tear Gould apart," Jonathan said.

"Hardly," Ben said. "I wanted to check out Gansevoort's prediction that gold will hit two hundred today. Cal Norvell says he thinks it will go to two ten."

Norvell was the *Times*'s financial editor. "That stuff about Grant and his brother-in-law is true?"

"Absolutely. I got it from Cal when we had lunch yesterday."

"I can't believe the whole federal government is going to sit on the sidelines and let these fellows make a killing that could ruin the value of the dollar."

"You can't believe it because you don't want to believe it," Ben said as they walked down Park Row past the other newspapers. "You don't want to believe anything is wrong with our wonderful country these days. Look at this." He pointed to a story in the center of the *Times*'s front page. "They've shot another justice of the peace in Louisiana. He's the fifth Republican murdered in that state this year. They've killed ten in Mississippi. Have you so much as mentioned them? You'd rather listen to that southern siren you've got murmuring in your ear every night."

"You're talking horseshit," Jonathan snapped. "I have mentioned those murders. I've deplored them. I'm sure Grant will do something about the situation, once he gets acclimated to the job."

"I made a rough count last night when I couldn't sleep. About sixty southern Republicans, white and black, have died waiting for Grant and people like you to say something. The truth is, Jonathan, you're like the rest of our noble Republican Party. The election results have turned your blood to water."

Ben was talking about the stunning narrowness of Ulysses Grant's victory last November. A shift of only 27,000 votes would have put a Democrat in the White House. Without the 800,000 Negro Republican votes cast in the South, the party would have been swamped. It was suddenly clear that the Republicans and their policy of equal rights for the Negro did not command a majority of the white voters of the United States.

In New York State elections, Republicans had been drubbed. The gleeful Democrats called it "running against the nigger." Jonathan began arguing that the party could not be expected to commit political suicide over the Negro question. But he—and every prominent Republican he knew—would stand firm if it came to a wholesale suppression of the Negro's rights.

At Broad Street they stopped before the gilded cast-iron portico of the Stock Exchange. "Prove it to me, Jonathan," Ben said, pointing into the building. "Come in here now and join me in putting every cent you've got into gold. It's going to hit two hundred. I'm going to risk my piddling hundred thousand. Let me take the profits and go south again—not by myself, this time. But with enough money and guns to create a Negro army that will defend Republican voters everywhere in the South."

"Ben—that's insanity."

Ben glared at the stream of men in black high hats hurrying into the Stock Exchange. "No," he said. "This is insanity. This whole repulsive city, with its stock swindles and its worship of the dollar, is morally insane, Jonathan. But you can't believe it because she won't let you. You might stop buying her those Worth gowns and give some money to a good cause."

"Ben—"

He was gone, swallowed by the shadowy interior of the Stock Exchange. Jonathan rushed down Wall Street to William Street, where Apthorpe, Dall and Company had offices in a narrow old-fashioned brownstone. He told Delancey Apthorpe what Ben was doing. Delancey swore like a cavalryman— he had been colonel in Custer's division—for a full minute.

"Jonathan, I'm afraid I'm reaching the end of the line with our friend. I need a partner. I don't need a patient."

"I know, Del. Let's discuss that some other day. Go down to the exchange and try to talk sense to Ben. I'm going over to the *Times* to see Jack Reid."

Jonathan caught a hack on William Street that deposited him in front of the Times Building in a matter of minutes. In the city room he found squat managing editor John Reid conferring with a reporter. Reid had covered New Jersey during the secession crisis of 1861, and they had become friends. The reporter was dismissed and Jonathan sat down beside Reid's desk. "What's the straight story, Jack? Is Grant really in bed with Jay Gould?"

"Cal Norvell thinks so, but I won't let him print it," Reid said. "I finally talked George Jones into sending Grant a telegram urging him to do something before his reputation is ruined. I wish to God Raymond was here. This would never have happened."

George Jones was the publisher of the *Times*, more a businessman than an editor. Three months ago, Henry Raymond, the editor who had built the *Times* into the most influential Republican paper in the nation, had been carried home from his mistress Rose Ettynge's house and left dying in his hallway. Bizarre, the way a man's private life intersected with history. Jonathan remembered Raymond and the actress tête-à-tête in the Maison Dorée the night he proposed to Cynthia. They had been lovebirds at the time. But rage, not love's excesses, had killed Raymond. He had been trying to buy back some letters he had written to the actress when he collapsed with a fatal stroke.

"Where is Grant? I'll send him another telegram," Jonathan said.

"He's visiting relatives in western Pennsylvania," Reid said. "He doesn't have any idea what's happening here."

Jonathan composed his own telegram urging the President to act decisively to rebut the rumors and stabilize the price of gold. Reid bellowed for a copy boy and told him to rush the message to Western Union. Jonathan sat with the managing editor for another ten minutes talking politics. Reid was worried about the Republican Party's divided uncertain policy toward the growing number of political murders in the South. He showed Jonathan an editorial he had written urging Grant to commit more troops to keep order. George Jones hesitated to print it. Jonathan could see why. Reid was practically urging Grant to start another war. Until Raymond's death the *Times* had been a moderate voice, urging patience, opposing the extremists in Congress who called for a punitive policy toward the South. Reid was obviously ready to move in this ugly direction. He had a very poor opinion of southerners. He had been captured in 1863 and spent a nightmarish year in Richmond's Libby Prison, under constant threat of being shot as a spy.

Jonathan hurried back down Broad Street to the Stock Exchange. He found Delancey Apthorpe waiting for him on the steps. "Did you get anywhere?" he asked.

"I got this," Apthorpe said, handing Jonathan a letter. "He just stuck it in my pocket when I started talking."

The letter was Ben's resignation from the firm. "Jesus Christ," Jonathan said, and rushed into the Stock Exchange. He charged across the floor and out a rear door which led to the Gold Exchange, in an adjacent building on New Street. At least two thousand men were jammed together on the ornate trading floor of the Gold Room, with its gilded ceiling and central fountain featuring a cherubic bronze cupid holding a dolphin in his arms. The silence in the room was virtually absolute as the secretary wrote the latest bids on an oversized board. Every eye in the room was fastened on that board, where 162 marked a new, unprecedented high.

Jonathan found Ben Dall on the outer edge of the crowd and tapped him on the shoulder. "Ben," he said, "it's not going to last. Jack Reid just told me that the *Times* has sent Grant a telegram, urging him to stop this madness. I sent him another one. I'm sure other people are doing the same thing."

Ben's eyes remained on the board. "Everyone's still buying," he said. "As long as Corbin sticks, Gould's got the President in his pocket."

He pointed across the room to the diminutive Gould and Grant's brother-in-law, Abel Corbin, a tall sallow old man with a nervous look on his face. What Gould was thinking or feeling was as usual masked by his full beard.

A moment later, a massive intake of breath swept the Gold Room, followed by an emotion that Jonathan Stapleton instantly recognized: panic. He had breathed its rank air more than once during the war, when one of his regiments broke under fire.

Up on the board, the price of gold was faltering. The bids clung at 162 for another sixty seconds, then fell to 160, 158. Someone was selling large amounts of the precious metal, someone who had already bought a great deal of it. Jonathan looked across the room and saw that Jay Gould had vanished. In Abel Corbin's trembling hand was a telegram. "The President's ordered the Treasury to release four million dollars in gold," he cried.

On the board, gold had already plummeted past 150. Jonathan instantly divined what was happening. Gould had been in on the secret. He had begun selling his gold stocks early. He had bribed Corbin to come to the Gold Room to lull everyone's suspicions.

In sixty seconds, the Gold Room became a pit of frenzy that exceeded anything Jonathan had seen on a battlefield. Men clawed and trampled each other to sell their certificates. Fistfights broke out. Men staggered past with hysterical tears running down their faces. One man wandered around dazedly, babbling nursery rhymes.

Jonathan turned to say something consoling to Ben Dall. He was not there. Gold plummeted down, down, past 140. The frenzy soon spilled over to the trading floor of the Stock Exchange, where frantic brokers tried to raise money to support gold by selling other stocks, driving their prices down almost as rapidly as the falling numbers on gold. Jonathan watched the chaos for a while, glumly noting a half-dozen railroad stocks on which he was losing several hundred thousand dollars, and finally retreated to his office on Wall Street.

He sat at his desk for a long time, staring at a miniature of Cynthia, painted in Venice during their honeymoon. He tried to regain the contentment that had suffused his body and soul as he walked downtown this morning. But all he could see was the frenzy in the Gold Room, all he could hear were Ben's vicious words about his southern siren, John Reid's heavy voice lamenting indecision in high places. A shadow had fallen on his happiness, a fear that history might invade it like a heavy ugly careless beast.

Land of milk and honey, murmured the comforting voice that had gotten him through the worst moments of the war. He looked up at a portrait of his grandfather Hugh Stapleton, the Continental Congressman, above the door. In the last year of his life, when Jonathan was ten years old, the old man's mind had frequently wandered back to the Revolution. Jonathan had often heard him murmuring the phrase. During the war it seemed to tell him that there was a purpose, a meaning, to the endless slaughter, that someday, somehow, America would become the land the Founders envisioned.

About two-thirty, Jonathan walked over to William Street and asked Delancey Apthorpe if he had seen Ben Dall. Delancey shook his head, his hands full of stock ticker tape. "How do you like this panic? Isn't it a hell of a mess? People are selling the New York Central short, believe it or not."

Delancey was not an imaginative man. He had no idea what might be happening in Ben Dall's soul. Nor did he particularly care. They had never been close friends. Right now, Delancey was busy trying to keep his own little canoe afloat.

Where would Ben go, what would he do for consolation? Jonathan wondered. He would not get much sympathy from Margaret Dall, especially if he confessed that he had lost all the money he had saved in the last two years.

Back in his office, Jonathan scribbled a brief note: "Ben—Come see me tonight. Let's talk things over." He sent it uptown by messenger and walked home along New York's crowded sidewalks. In Union Square, the newsboys screamed about "Black Friday" on Wall Street. He looked up at George Washington's statue and remembered Ben's question yesterday. He heard himself confidently assuring Rawdon, Cynthia, a dozen other people, that Ulysses Grant was the man who could solve America's problems. He saw Abel Corbin's corrupt sallow face.

He quickened his steps, as if he thought—or hoped—he could escape the heavy tread of the beast that was pursuing him. Stuyvesant Square seemed to promise the possibility. It was full of golden sunshine. The brownstone fronts, St. George's Church, still seemed to be ramparts behind which peace, love, could prosper.

"Father," called a voice. "Father." It was George racing toward him across the park. Elliott Roosevelt followed him.

"Look what Mother bought me today," George said.

He held up a brown leather mitt on his left hand. "It's a second baseman's glove," George said.

"I'm getting one tomorrow," Elliott said. New York and several other cities had recently spawned professional baseball teams. George and Elliott followed their fortunes with passionate interest.

"Isn't that nice."

Jonathan struggled to find hope, reassurance, in those innocent boyish faces. His personal world was still intact no matter what was happening to the public one.

He strolled across the square and up the steps of 217 East Seventeenth Street. In the dim front hall, his yellow birthday roses still stood in the big silver bowl. But they were fading fast.

Cynthia parted the portieres of the parlor and stood there all in white, smiling at him. She kissed him boldly, tenderly, on the lips and he breathed her violet perfume. "How's my magnate?" she said. "How many new railroads did you launch today?"

"None," he said.

He did not expect her to know or understand what had just happened on Wall Street. But her ignorance subtly irritated him.

"What's wrong?" she said as they sat down in the parlor.

"The market collapsed. There was a panic. Hundreds of men are bankrupt. Ben Dall is one of them."

"Oh, how sad."

"It's worse than sad. He got into a quarrel with Delancey Apthorpe and resigned from the firm. I don't know how he's going to make a living."

"Why did he do such a thing?"

"I'm afraid he's having another breakdown."

It was easier to tell her this. Yet his conscience somehow bothered him that he did not tell her the whole story.

"I feel so sorry for Margaret and those two sweet girls," Cynthia said. "It's losing his arm in the war, don't you think? It's affected his whole nervous system."

"Probably," Jonathan said, dismayed that he was getting farther and farther from the truth.

Cynthia poured him a glass of sherry. He wanted to drop the subject, but it was impossible. "It's not just Ben," he said. "It's the whole disgusting mess." He told her about Gould's conspiracy with Grant's brother-in-law.

"Husband dear," Cynthia said, springing up to kiss him on the forehead. "Don't let it upset you so. None of it—not even poor Ben—is your fault."

"It's my country! That's why I'm upset!"

"Must you tell me in such an unpleasant tone?"

Cynthia returned to her seat on the sofa. He realized that she had no reason to grieve over corruption smearing the name of Ulysses S. Grant. She might even be secretly rejoicing at the fall from virtue of the hero of Appomattox.

"I had another letter from my sister Jeannie today. She says the situation in Louisiana is just dreadful. The carpetbaggers and scalawags have passed a whole new set of taxes that will bankrupt every farmer in the state."

There were times when Jonathan wished the restoration of the Union did not include the regular delivery of mail from Louisiana. The smear terms which the southern Democrats had devised for northern-born Republicans and their southern allies were often on Cynthia's lips after she received a letter from home. Fortunately, the letters were sporadic. Most of the time he and Cynthia avoided the subject. Was she bringing it up now to point out that she had just received some bad news about her part of the country but she was not snapping at him?

For a moment he heard himself giving her a crushing answer: I find it hard to feel sorry for your countrymen when they murder innocent men in cold blood just because they're Republicans.

Before he could decide whether to say these brutal words there was a clatter in the hall. "Oh, there's Georgie," Cynthia said.

George and Elliott surged into the parlor, creating a small maelstrom peculiar to seven-year-old boys. Any moment, Jonathan was sure, a porcelain vase or an expensive lamp was going to end up in pieces on the rug. But Cynthia ordered an instant stop to the shoving and pushing and they were soon sitting on the couch drinking cups of tea. The conversation collapsed to the seven-year-old level. Baseball, school. Jonathan felt slightly bewildered. A few moments ago history seemed about to shoulder its ugly snout into the parlor.

George and Elliott went off to eat their supper. Jonathan and Cynthia dressed for dinner. In the dining room they chatted about people they had gotten to know on their second visit to Italy last summer. Their return to Venice had won them acceptance in the Anglo-American society of the pleasure capital. It was surprising how many Americans had settled there permanently, preferring exile amid beauty to the commercial and political hurly-burly of the United States. Cynthia enjoyed their arty talk, but he found it difficult to respect anyone who turned his back on his country. He preferred the Italian nobility to whom the Rospigliosis introduced them.

Their conversation turned to their Venetian hosts. They were far from a loving couple. The Count was pursuing a French actress. The Contessa was having an affair with an English painter. It was all very European and reminded Cynthia of similar arrangements in New Orleans. "I once thought that would be my fate, to marry that kind of husband," she said.

"Are you sorry you surrendered to a puritanical Yankee?"

"If last night was a sample of your puritanism, General, I fear you've abandoned your faith."

Two circles of color glowed in her cheeks. Warmth, desire, surged through his entire body. It was amazing how she could arouse him with that crooning southern voice. For a moment he was upstairs with his hands on her breasts, his tongue deep in her mouth.

By the time they finished a feast of crab cayenne and shrimp Creole—with their New Orleans butler had come his wife, Annette, one of the best cooks on Royal Street—Jonathan felt more like the man he had become in the last twenty-four months. He almost forgot that he had urged Ben Dall to come see him for a talk. When he remembered it, he hoped Ben would put it off until tomorrow at the office.

After supper he sat down on the couch and began reading an article on the New Jersey shore in *Scribner's Magazine*. Cynthia was playing some Gottschalk waltzes on the piano when the doorbell rang. "Who in the world can that be?" Cynthia said, without stopping her music.

Cousteau peered into the parlor. "General. It's for you."

Jonathan assumed it was Ben Dall and called from the sofa, "Come in, Ben."

Instead of his friend, a heavyset gray-bearded man, who might have stepped out of a Bible illustration of the Lord Jehovah, appeared in the doorway. "General," he said in a deep rumbling voice, "I'm Herman Melville."

"Yes of course," Jonathan said, instinctively responding to the name of one of his favorite writers.

"I'm afraid I have sad news. Your friend Colonel Dall has shot himself."

"Oh Jesus," Jonathan gasped. For a moment he felt the impact of the bullet in his own brain.

"I gather he lost a good deal of money in the gold panic today," Melville said. "According to the evening papers a half-dozen other men have chosen the same regrettable solution."

"Oh Jonathan!"

It was Cynthia, beside him on the sofa, her arms around him, offering him the redemptive power of her love. But he sat there, frozen, unable to touch her, appalled by the emotion that was ripping through him. He blamed her. It was bizarre, insane, absurd. But he could not, he would not let her comfort him. It would be the ultimate betrayal. Perhaps later he could tolerate it. But for now only Ben claimed his lacerated heart.

"He's joined them," he said. "The dead."

She sensed, she knew, with that uncanny gift women possessed, that her sympathy was being refused. She moved away from him. "What in the world are you saying?" she sobbed.

Not even her grief moved him. "The dead," he rasped. "He's wanted to join them for a long time. I should have known—should have seen . . ."

Cynthia's lips trembled. She did not know how to cope with a man who had these faceless voiceless legions clutching at his mind and heart. Jonathan saw her confusion, her fear, but he could not stop himself. He almost rejoiced to inflict his dark anguish on her.

In the doorway, Melville spoke. "Mrs. Dall was hoping you could come directly, General."

"Of course."

He pulled a garment off the rack in the hall. It was his old army cloak. He kept it there to wear on rainy days. He stepped back into the parlor doorway. Cynthia still sat on the yellow sofa, one white arm across the back of it, staring after him, seemingly dazed by what she had just seen. "Go to bed," he said. "I may be hours."

He was appalled by how flat, how curt the words sounded. "Forgive me," he said.

"I never realized you loved him so," Cynthia said.

FIVE

"I can't believe it," gushed Eleanor Dall as the train chugged south from Jersey City. "A whole summer with Rawdon Stapleton. I may die of adoration."

Eleanor bounced all over the wooden seat, almost knocking *Middlemarch*, the new novel by George Eliot, out of her sister Genevieve's hands.

Genevieve was not looking forward to another summer at Kemble Manor, the Stapleton summer home on Raritan Bay. She was glad to escape New York's ferocious heat and humidity. But this summer her best friend, Alice Gansevoort, would not be in nearby Long Branch to keep her company. Alice was sailing for Europe tomorrow with her parents.

Much as she loved Alice, there were times when Genevieve envied her. Alice's father, the enormously successful Wall Street broker Jefferson Gansevoort, doted on her. She had looks that attracted men in swarms and the aplomb to deal casually with their panting pursuit. While Genevieve, if she managed to capture the attention of one of the blasé heirs who frequented the Junior Assembly balls, invariably seemed to say something argumentative or intelligent which caused him to flee.

In their two previous summers at Kemble Manor, the Dalls had had the place to themselves. General Stapleton and his wife had gone to Europe. Their sons Rawdon and George vacationed at the summer homes of friends and spent only a week or so at the manor when their parents returned in late

August. But the summer of 1872 promised to be different. In April Mrs. Stapleton had given birth to a baby girl, who had lived only a day. The doctor had decreed she was not well enough to face the rigors of transatlantic travel. For reasons unexplained, Rawdon was also said to be spending the summer in New Jersey.

"Aren't you even a little excited?" Eleanor demanded. "What's wrong with you, Gen? Isn't he the most handsome creature you've ever seen?"

"I don't happen to like Rawdon Stapleton very much," Genevieve said, doggedly pursuing the misery of *Middlemarch*'s heroine on her catastrophic honeymoon with her pedant husband.

"That remark is a perfect explanation of why you spend most of the time at the Junior Assembly balls watching while your friend Alice Gansevoort is dancing," her mother said.

Genevieve felt the sting of a well-aimed dart. Her mother had an uncanny ability to inflict verbal wounds. "What do you mean?" she said.

"I mean you're in no position to be so fussy about the opposite sex," her mother said.

Genevieve retreated to *Middlemarch*. "I've told you before, Mother, I'm perfectly resigned to remaining single."

"And I've told you to stop thinking such nonsense. You're no beauty, but you could attract men if you'd get your nose out of your books and dress with a little more style."

"And stop expecting men to be a combination of Ralph Waldo Emerson and Henry Ward Beecher," Eleanor said.

"And your father," her mother said.

Genevieve's head snapped up. She glared at her mother. That was more than a dart. It was a spear. Genevieve remained stubbornly, sadly loyal to her father's memory even though she could not deny the wound he had inflicted on the family, on her above all, by his suicide. Her mother retaliated by repeatedly reminding her that thanks to her father she had no dowry and therefore no hope of a decent marriage if she did not flatter some wealthy male, however witless, into proposing. This tactic only redoubled Genevieve's determination to remain single for life.

"I sometimes think I made a mistake giving you permission to go to Vassar," her mother said. "Maria Gansevoort is furious that you've talked Alice into going with you. It's given you both grandiose, unrealistic ideas. Four years from now, when you get your marvelous degrees, you'll find the most eligible young men, the really good catches, married."

This time Genevieve did not try to fight back. She kept her eyes on her book, hoping her mother's spasm of antagonism to Vassar would pass. Margaret Dall could still change her mind and revoke her permission.

Eleanor resumed mooning over Rawdon. "I know he'll never think of me as anything but a child," she said, fluffing her glistening red curls. "But that won't quench my love for him. Nothing ever will."

Eleanor had been entranced with Rawdon ever since he visited them in Mississippi in 1866. He had made her into a kind of pet, carrying her around on his shoulders, telling her stories, playing hide-and-seek with her. Their games and jokes had continued every time they met over the past six years. Rawdon called Eleanor his little sister and sent her Christmas and birthday gifts. Even General Stapleton, who did not approve of much that Rawdon did, seemed to find it charming.

Genevieve was willing to admit that Rawdon Stapleton was incredibly handsome. But he was much too arrogant for her taste.

No. Reacting to the assault her mother and Eleanor had just made on her, she struggled to be fair. In Mississippi, her first impression of Rawdon had justified the word arrogant. He had astonished her by bragging about his flirtations with various women on trains and steamboats. More recently, it was his enormous self-assurance that irritated her.

Although they had been born only a few days apart, Rawdon now seemed years older to Genevieve. He talked casually of escapades at boarding school, making life there sound as daring and dangerous as infantry combat. He was captain of the St. Paul's crew, star of their baseball team. His athletic ability and his looks and charm made him tremendously popular.

While Genevieve, like most girls her age, remained severely within the family circle, Rawdon spent his summers traveling up and down the eastern seaboard, visiting St. Paul's classmates. Sailing the Maine coast, playing tennis at Newport, betting on the races at Saratoga were as routine to him as strolling in the Central Park. It made Genevieve more than a little resentful of the freedom Americans gave their sons and denied their daughters.

"Middletown!" bawled the conductor.

They descended from the hot sooty little three-car train and watched the railwaymen wrestle their trunks out of the baggage car. Blinking into the bright sunshine, they searched for the carriage that General Stapleton had said would meet them.

"Greetings, Dalls," said a masculine voice.

Wearing white flannels and a yellow striped shirt, Rawdon Stapleton leaned nonchalantly against the small wooden station. He *was* handsome, Genevieve admitted grudgingly as she studied the gleaming dark hair, the perfectly proportioned tanned face. But there was something trite, almost artificial about such good looks. It was hard to believe there was a real person behind them.

"Oh my beloved!" Eleanor cried, and hurled herself into Rawdon's arms. She gave him such a resounding kiss, her mother exclaimed, "I begin to think you're getting too old for that sort of nonsense, Eleanor."

She was right. Eleanor's white muslin suit featured a cuirass basque, a long tight bodice that revealed a startlingly mature figure for a fourteen-year-old.

"No, Mrs. Dall, please," Rawdon said, throwing his hand against his forehead like Edwin Booth playing Hamlet, "don't destroy the only love in my life."

"There, you see," Eleanor giggled. "I'm only being kind to him. I know how dreadfully unattractive he is to most women."

"That's true," Rawdon said as he hoisted their bags into the victoria. "Your sister has convinced me of that sad fact. How long have I known her? I think we first met when we were seven. I've yet to win a smile from her."

"There's only one way to do it," Eleanor said. "You'll have to burn all her books."

"A marvelous idea," Rawdon said, smiling at Genevieve in his most arrogant manner. "How is the studious Miss Dall?"

"I'm perfectly fine," she said. "How are you, Mr. Stapleton?"

"For a condemned man, I'm not bad."

He helped them into the carriage, and her mother asked him why he was a condemned man. "I took Jupiter, my father's favorite riding horse, out for a canter," he said. "It occurred to me that he ought to be taught to jump fences. He didn't agree and we wound up splattered all over the landscape. Jupiter broke his leg and had to be shot. I believe the General has scheduled my execution for tomorrow morning at sunrise. Just put a little cotton in your ears when you retire tonight so the noise won't interrupt your sleep."

"Oh Rawdon. You have the most awful luck with horses," Eleanor said.

Last summer Rawdon had caused a minor scandal by riding a horse into the foyer of the casino at Newport. Some people said he had been drunk. He said the horse had bolted. Genevieve wondered if the escapade explained why he was spending this summer at Kemble Manor.

"Almost as bad as my luck with women."

"I don't believe that for one moment, Rawdon," her mother said.

"It's true, Mrs. Dall. My four years of exile in the snowdrifts of New Hampshire have left me out of touch with the fair sex. They find me rude and crude. Their mothers view me with alarm because of my past sins."

"Oh bosh," Eleanor said, resting her head against his shoulder. "Women like men who misbehave. At least they do in the novels I read."

"You think if I persevere in degeneracy I may get a smile from the studious Miss Dall?"

"I know a better way," Eleanor said. "Sing 'Sweet Genevieve' to her."

"You know I hate that song," Genevieve snapped. When it came out last year, Eleanor had played and sung it by the hour.

By now they had emerged from the pine woods and were riding across a vast meadow of salt hay. A soft wind wafted a tangy marshy smell off Raritan

Bay. On the shore, outlined against the dark-blue water, was a rose-red brick house, built in the severe geometric style of the eighteenth century. It stood in a park surrounded by a brick wall of the same color. Passing through a gilt-tipped gate, they rode up a lane of ancient oaks toward a white-pillared portico.

"How is your stepmother feeling, Rawdon?" Mrs. Dall asked.

"She seems to have made a complete recovery. She and the General spend most of their time in Long Branch, kowtowing to President Grant. That's where they are at the moment."

Kemble Manor was only a half hour's carriage ride from Long Branch. Since Ulysses Grant began spending his summers there in 1869, the little seaside town had become the most popular resort in the country.

In the manor's center hall, Rawdon gestured to the portraits on the green-and-gold papered walls. "Captain Gifford and his lady fair are still on duty," he said. The captain wore a blue frock coat and knee breeches of 1776, the lady a lace-fringed red dress of the same era. According to Rawdon's irreverent version of the Stapletons' family history, the lady had seduced the captain and persuaded him to abandon the British Army and join the rebels.

"Here's a newcomer," Rawdon said, gesturing to a portrait of a thin, intense-looking young man with a long lean sharply defined face. Rawdon said he was Kemble Stapleton, Captain Gifford's stepson, who had died heroically in the Revolution. "I found him in the attic, covered with dust," Rawdon said. "He was the family's only idealist. When they saw what happened to him, the Stapletons concentrated on making money."

"Rawdon," Genevieve's mother said. "Your father is one of the most idealistic men I've ever met."

"Why is he hanging around with President Grant?"

Rawdon deposited their traveling bags in their bedrooms. Genevieve was not thrilled to discover she was sharing a room with Eleanor. Downstairs, Cousteau, the Stapletons' butler, served them a cold lunch of crab and lobster salad. Afterward Eleanor went down the beach to visit her friend Dolly Bradford, who was also fourteen and had her head stuffed with romantic novels. Margaret Dall decided she needed a nap, and Genevieve retreated to the rear terrace with *Middlemarch*.

She had barely finished a page when Rawdon Stapleton peered over her shoulder. "What are you reading?"

She showed him. "Good God," he said, "that will give you a terrible headache. And it's too thick to burn."

He slouched into a chair opposite her. "Isn't Alice Gansevoort a friend of yours?"

"Yes."

"Bradford tells me she's become the best-looking girl in New York."

Hal Bradford was the leader of the horde of males who had pursued Alice at the Junior Assembly balls. He was Dolly Bradford's older brother. The family owned a big rambling shingled house about a half mile down the shore from Kemble Manor. Their father was a Wall Street speculator.

"Hal says she's an iceberg. But I could thaw her."

"Alice doesn't need thawing. She's a perfectly normal woman. But she's going to spend four years at Vassar. She feels it would be cruel to encourage anyone for the present."

"Vassar. That must be your influence."

"Not really. Alice has an excellent mind."

Already, this was a longer conversation than she had ever had with Rawdon Stapleton. But its object was clearly an introduction to Alice Gansevoort. Rawdon and his friend Hal Bradford were presuming Alice would spend the summer in Long Branch again this year. Genevieve decided to dispel this illusion and watch Mr. Stapleton vanish.

"You'll have to wait a few months to meet Alice. She's sailing for Europe tomorrow with her mother and father."

Rawdon surprised her by laughing. The news did not seem to bother him in the least. "I can't wait to tell Bradford. He may drown himself. I've never seen anything like the case he has on her."

Silence. Mr. Stapleton lounged in his chair. He did not seem inclined to vanish. "One of the shining ones," he said.

"I beg your pardon?"

"That's what my father said about you last night. It's the first time I've agreed with him in about ten years."

"What does it mean?"

"He was explaining to my stepmother why you remind him of your father. He said certain people—extraordinary people—had a kind of incandescence. You had it the first time I saw you, really saw you, down in Mississippi. Now there's a lot more . . . added."

The pause after "more" intimated he was not talking about more incandescence. It was the first time a man had told Genevieve that she was attractive. It created the most peculiar sensation in her body. An odd mixture of heat and cold. Her face was flushing and her hands were icy.

Rawdon sighed. "It's too bad you're so determined to give us the freeze in the name of higher education."

"I'm perfectly willing to be friendly with men. So is Alice. It's the serious feelings we want to avoid."

"Do you think they can be avoided—when they start to happen?"

Rawdon's voice seemed to darken as he said this. He was looking boldly at her. For an incredible moment, Genevieve thought she heard him saying, *If I fell in love with you, could you resist me?*

"I—I don't know," she floundered. "I've never been . . . in love."

"Neither have I," Rawdon said.

"Really?" Genevieve said. "I heard you broke at least three hearts in Newport last summer."

"Some women like to have their hearts broken," Rawdon said. "It makes marvelous conversation. It's about as serious as my romance with your sister Eleanor. I'm talking about something happening down deep. Something real."

The way he said "real" sent a shiver through Genevieve. "Aren't you . . . going to college?" she asked.

"Oh yes. Having completed my four-year sentence in New Hampshire's worst penitentiary, I've been rewarded with four more years in another prison. It's called the College of New Jersey, sometimes known as Princeton."

"Why in the world are you so hostile to education?"

"Because it doesn't have anything to do with the real world." Rawdon leaned toward her in an aggressive, almost menacing way, although his expression remained friendly. "How much is Jay Gould worth?"

"I have no idea."

"Fifty million dollars. Who's the leader of the Cuban Revolution?"

"Campañeros?"

"Maximos Campos." He smiled triumphantly at her. "You may know what's in a few books. But you don't know much about the real world. I'll bet you never read a newspaper."

"I certainly do!"

"How many?"

"How many do you have to read? The *New York Times* is the most reliable paper in the city."

"Bosh. The *Times* would never print anything even faintly critical of the Republican Party. When I'm in New York I read all ten major newspapers every day. It's the only way you can hope to find out what's really happening in this crazy country. I've thought about becoming a newspaperman. Didn't your father work for the *Times* before the war? Why did he quit?"

"Because he thought the cause, freeing the slaves, was more important, and no one was really fighting for it in New York."

"He should have stayed on the paper. He might be editor by now. One of the most powerful men in New York. That's what makes a newspaper so exciting. The power. Look what the *Times* just did to Boss Tweed."

During the past year, the *New York Times* had exposed the depredations of William Marcy Tweed, boss of Tammany Hall, the Democratic political machine that ruled New York City. Tweed and his henchmen had been revealed as looters of the public treasury on a titanic scale. But Genevieve was not thinking about these greasy revelations. Her thoughts, her feelings, were arrested by Rawdon's careless description of her father as a man who had blundered. Tears began trickling down her cheeks.

"What's the matter?" Rawdon said.

"Nothing," Genevieve said, wiping her eyes as the tears kept oozing. "It's just . . . that I've been thinking about my father today. Coming down here. Expecting to see your father."

"I'm sorry," Rawdon said. He thrust a handkerchief into her hand. "It's one of the worst Stapleton traits. We don't give a damn for other people's feelings. I've been trying to overcome it."

It was a surprise to discover that this seemingly self-satisfied young man was trying to reform himself in such an insightful way.

"I've got a date to go sailing with Bradford. Would you like to come?"

Of course she would like to come. But Genevieve simultaneously felt an overwhelming wish to avoid Rawdon Stapleton's company for a while.

"I think I'd rather get into this book."

Rawdon stood up and stretched. It was the most interesting motion Genevieve had ever seen a human make. She had spent so little time with males. They were amazingly animal-like. "I don't blame you," Rawdon said. "When Bradford isn't talking about horses he talks about baseball. When he isn't talking about baseball he talks about horses. I was hoping you'd break the monotony."

"Some other time, maybe," she said.

"It's a date," Rawdon said. "I'll get rid of Bradford and we'll brave the high seas together."

He left her struggling to regain her absorption in the marital travails of *Middlemarch*'s heroine. But George Eliot's somber prose kept drifting away from her, while words like *real* and *together* and phrases like *down deep* surged through her mind.

Suddenly a large figure loomed over her. "Genevieve! How long have you been here? Where are your mother and sister?"

It was General Stapleton, looking remarkably elegant in a tan summer suit and tall tan hat. Beside him was his wife, wearing an elaborate Swiss muslin dress with a heart-shaped neck and a series of dramatic bows on the skirt.

Genevieve explained the whereabouts of the other Dalls and said hello to Mrs. Stapleton, who smiled and drawled in her extravagant—and, to Genevieve, insincere—southern way, "It's so *delightful* to have you with us, dear."

"Where's Rawdon? Why has he left you here by yourself?" the General growled. "I told him to consider himself your host."

"He went sailing with his friend Hal Bradford."

"He didn't invite you?"

"Oh he did. But I . . . felt too tired."

"Was it a polite invitation?"

"Jonathan. Why can't you accept Genevieve's perfectly straightforward explanation? Aren't you angry enough at Rawdon?" Mrs. Stapleton said.

The General glowered. For a moment he resembled the man her father had described on the battlefields. His gray eyes flashed darkness, his mouth became a menacing slit. He reminded Genevieve of the angry eagle on the United States seal.

"Every time I think of that horse. He knew it was my favorite. Why would he do such a thing?"

"Because he's eighteen years old and loves to take chances."

"Rawdon told me what happened," Genevieve said.

"No doubt making it sound like a joke."

"Oh no, not at all," she said, amazed that she was more or less telling a lie on Rawdon's behalf.

"I'm glad to hear he's capable of a little contrition."

"The railwayman just delivered your trunks, Genevieve," Mrs. Stapleton said. "I hope you brought lots of party dresses. It's simply amazing how many people have rented houses in the vicinity this summer. No one believes Paris or the rest of Europe is safe."

Mrs. Stapleton was talking about the abortive revolution that had followed the collapse of Napoleon III's regime in France last year. Anarchists and Communists had seized control of Paris, burned the Tuileries Palace and the City Hall and fought pitched battles with the French Army on the boulevards. But Genevieve was more interested in the personal implication. Lots of parties would mean lots of girls, most of whom would be prettier and better dressed than Genevieve Dall.

Rawdon did not show up for dinner. He sent a message via a servant that he was dining at the Bradfords'. Jonathan Stapleton discussed an article he had read in *Scribner's Magazine* about Vassar College. It seemed to remove his greatest worry about Genevieve's going there: the widespread opinion that a woman could not survive the rigors of a college education—she would break down mentally or physically.

"They've had very few withdrawals, fewer than West Point or Harvard, for that matter."

"I hope the reporting is accurate," Mrs. Dall said. "Genevieve has a tendency to overdo things. Too much intensity, like her father."

Genevieve felt an almost suffocating surge of anger. Her father had promised to send her to Vassar. He had apparently discussed it with Jonathan Stapleton, because the General had spontaneously offered to pay her tuition. He seemed to regard it as part of the promise he had made to them the night of her father's death: "From this moment I consider you members of my own family. You'll never want for money, for anything I can do for your happiness."

Genevieve would never forget the grief that convulsed Jonathan Stapleton's huge frame as he clutched the baffling one-line note her father had left for him: *"The price is too high."* He had talked incoherently about Ben Dall's courage in battle. He said he had loved America so much he had let it break his heart. He abjured them never to mention how he had died. He assured them that he would keep it out of the newspapers.

Going to bed, Genevieve had to listen to Eleanor describe the dozen new dresses Dolly Bradford had acquired for the summer. "While I've got two. It's so humiliating to be poor. Sometimes I really hate Father for spending mother's money to free those stupid niggers."

Genevieve said nothing. She had given up trying to defend their father against Eleanor's greedy regret. But her sister's diatribe, her mother's remark at dinner, made it impossible for her to sleep. She began to remember it again. She no longer wanted to remember it. But she could not stop the memory once it began to flood her mind.

Her father had come home late that fatal night and had another quarrel with her mother. She did not know what it was about. She only heard the angry words drifting up the stairs. He had retreated to his study. Genevieve had lain in her bed, wishing she could find the courage to tiptoe into his study and kiss him on the cheek. "I love you," she had wanted to whisper.

Would it have made any difference if she had gone downstairs that night? Would Ben Dall have flung that huge black army pistol into the alley? Or would she only have reminded him of the three helpless women he had on his hands? All she knew was what she remembered, the crash of the gun drifting up through the house, an ominous sound, different from anything she had ever heard in the city. Ominous, evil, she thought as she heard her mother running down the hall, then the screams, her own trembling rush to the door of the study, the slumped figure in the chair, blood trickling from a corner of his mouth.

Oh. Oh. Oh. Father, forgive me.

She did not know why, but those words always whispered in her mind at the end of the memory.

Finally asleep, Genevieve dreamed of Mississippi. Pompous Harriet Beecher Stowe seemed to be her mother. She was telling her what to read, what to eat, what to wear. A group of Negroes kept running in and out with books in their hands, asking her to spell out words for them. One word especially baffled them: "swoon." Harriet Beecher Stowe pointed to Genevieve and triumphantly declared, "No one's ever going to swoon over you."

Something woke her. A wind, much too soft to disturb a sleeper, sighed in the trees. She heard it again. "Genevieve. Sweet Genevieve!" Someone was under the window calling her name.

She peered out. A white half moon filled the rear garden with vanilla light. A squat, long-armed young man with a wide thick-lipped vulgar mouth leered up at her. "Genevieve. Give us a hand. Open the back door."

"Why?"

"Stapleton's passed out. Got to get him to bed or his old man will order up a firing squad for sure."

"Who are you?"

"Hal Bradford."

She recognized him now. Three A.M. bonged in the hall. She put on a night robe, lit a candle and tiptoed down the back stairs into the kitchen. Hal was waiting at the door.

"Is this your idea of a joke?"

"I should say not. You've got to help me. I'm seven seas over myself and Stapleton weighs a ton." He led her into the garden. Rawdon lay on his back behind the first row of box hedges. His arms were flung out, making him look like pictures she had seen of the battlefield dead in the war. Hal sat him up and patted his face. "Come on, Rawdie. We're going to bed. Sweet Genevieve's going to help us."

He hauled Rawdon erect, put one arm over his shoulder and told Genevieve to take the other arm. They half carried, half dragged him toward the house. "How in the world did he get so disgustingly drunk?" Genevieve asked. With every step she inhaled the smell of liquor.

"Stole a bottle of the General's Havana rum. It's the ninetieth anniversary of his great-granduncle Kemble's death at the hands of the redcoats."

That made no sense whatsoever. Genevieve concentrated on getting Rawdon up the narrow stairs and into his bedroom, which was across the hall from hers.

"Liberty or death," Rawdon said as they lowered him onto the bed.

Hal Bradford jammed a hand over his mouth. "Not a sound until I get out of this house."

Back in her room, Genevieve lay awake for an hour. Rawdon's conduct was appalling. How did it jibe with the young man who said he was trying to make himself more sensitive to other people's feelings?

Genevieve slept late and discovered when she came down to breakfast that General and Mrs. Stapleton had gone to the races at Monmouth Park and taken her mother with them. Eleanor had departed to Dolly Bradford's house. Rawdon appeared as Cousteau was pouring her coffee.

"I just saw Bradford down at the dock," he said. "He came over in his catboat to see if I was still alive. He tells me you saved my neck last night. Thanks."

"Do you often get that drunk?"

He stared at her for a moment, as if he were choosing among a half-dozen possible answers. "No," he said.

He poured himself some coffee and heaped his plate with oysters and scrambled eggs and chops from the sideboard. "I dimly recall Bradford calling you Sweet Genevieve last night. I apologize."

"That's all right."

"There's a solution to your dilemma. Take a summer name."

"A summer name?"

"It's a game invented by my late Uncle Charlie. You take the name of someone you want to be—perhaps don't dare to be."

Genevieve hesitated. Was he serious? "Do you have one?"

"Diarmuid."

"What does that stand for?"

"He was a Celtic hero. My great-grandfather Rawdon was a Welshman. Diarmuid was a famous lover, like Don Juan. He wandered the world, seducing just about every woman he met."

This only increased her hesitation.

"Come on," Rawdon said. "You're not supposed to think about it too much."

"Antiope."

"Some Greek goddess?"

"No. She's the leading character in my favorite novel, *A Woman's Quest*. She had a passionate nature—but she learned to control it. She turned down offers of marriage from two men to remain true to herself, her talent as a painter."

"What, may I ask, is your talent?"

"I'd like to be a writer. I hope to find out if I have the talent at Vassar."

"What do you want to write?"

"Novels, poems, about people who live—and sometimes die—for great ideals."

"I'm awed."

Throughout this conversation, Rawdon was consuming an astonishing amount of food. Finished with this masculine breakfast, he leaned back in his chair and smiled mockingly at her. "I hope you realize what you risked last night, my dear Antiope. The loss of the great man's favor. I'm sure he has a comfortable sum for you in his will. It would be gone with a stroke of his pen if he found out you've been helping his renegade son sink a little deeper into debauchery."

He was playing Diarmuid. Genevieve sipped her coffee and remembered the masterful way the fictional Antiope had dealt with one of her suitors who claimed she was driving him to drink.

"I'm more concerned about why a man who claims to live for love would yield to such animal excess."

"There are several possible explanations. A, he has failed to find true love in his long quest. B, when he gets enraged at his father for cutting off his allowance for the entire summer, he tends to do reckless things. C, it's a marvelous way to escape being a Stapleton, with all those famous ancestors breathing down your neck."

"Oh," she said. She was amazed to discover that she understood all three reasons.

"While I decide which explanation is correct," Rawdon said, "let's go for a swim. That will cure my headache and then I'll take you for that sail I promised you yesterday."

Genevieve got her bathing dress and they strolled down the hill to the cove. This placid oval body of water, sheltered on three sides by huge gnarled maples and oaks, was a perfect swimming pool. General Stapleton had constructed a bathhouse on the sandy shore. In the dim interior, Genevieve put on her bathing dress and studied the results in the shadowy mirror. Of course decorum required that almost every inch of the female body be covered. But Genevieve could see a woman's curves there in the mirror. Not the wasp-waisted high-bosomed splendor of Cynthia Stapleton or her mother in her days of debutante glory. Her curves were more subtle—more in proportion, in Genevieve's defiant opinion.

Incandescence—with a lot more added. It was amazing how much encouragement Genevieve found in those rather shocking words. Maybe she was not a great beauty. Her snub nose alone was enough to disqualify her in any contest for that title—which as an intelligent woman she scorned in the first place. But she was still a woman and it was pleasant—even a little thrilling—to think that she might be able to attract a man without flattering and groveling to him. Pinning up her hair, Genevieve perched her lace-trimmed bathing cap on the back of her head at a decidedly rakish angle and stepped into the bright July sunshine.

Rawdon was waiting for her at the water's edge. The sunlight pouring through the trees created a kind of aureole around his dark head. His bathing suit was red on top; the pants, which ended above his knee, were blue with white stripes.

Something extraordinary began happening. The red top seemed to concentrate the rays of the sun and glow with unbelievable intensity. The glare made Genevieve close her eyes for a moment. When she looked again, she saw something new on the shore of the cove: a beautiful man.

Genevieve had thought only women, women like Alice Gansevoort and

Cynthia Stapleton, were beautiful. But this was another kind of beauty, this masculine purity of bone and muscle.

"You have the most remarkable hair," Rawdon said. "The way it catches the sunlight. It turns the sunlight to burnt gold."

Antiope, what would Antiope say? Genevieve thought wildly. How would she deal with this dissolution that seemed to be occurring in the center of her body and spreading outward until she was afraid she was going to faint or become hysterical? To her amazement, she heard the needed words on her lips, crisp and apparently calm: "What a patriotic bathing suit."

Rawdon dove into the water and disappeared for what seemed like a full minute. Genevieve was beginning to grow panicky when he surfaced at least a hundred feet out in the cove. "Come on," he called.

"I'm afraid I can't swim that far," Genevieve said.

Rawdon swam to shore with a tremendously powerful stroke, backed by a furious kick. He plowed through the water like a racing steamboat. He asked Genevieve to swim a few feet. She took a half-dozen flailing strokes and stopped, gasping. "Stretch out more, relax," Rawdon said. He put his arms beneath her waist to support her and she began to improve.

As he crouched in the shallow water, Rawdon's face was only inches from hers. What would Diarmuid do if Antiope suddenly kissed him? Was it the summer names? Was there something supernatural in the air at Kemble Manor, a distillation of the passions of earlier lovers? Or was she simply losing her mind?

Genevieve concentrated fiercely on staying afloat and before the end of the hour struggled about twenty-five feet. Rawdon predicted she would be swimming like a lifesaving guard within the week.

By the time Rawdon hoisted the single sail of the catboat tied up next to the Stapletons' broad-beamed schooner, Genevieve had regained her self-possession. They bounded over the whitecapped bay, admiring the marvelous view. To the south loomed the great cliffs of the Atlantic Highlands. To the north were the wooded hills of Staten Island. The coast around Kemble Manor was dotted with splendid houses.

"Do you respond passionately to the beauties of nature, Antiope?"

"Yes."

"So do I. My favorite times out here are dawn and sunset. Sometimes the water is so still you feel you're floating in the middle of the sky. It's enough to make you believe in God."

"You don't?"

"Most of the time I don't. How about you?"

"The same way."

"What's your reason?"

"The churches tell you God is love. But He doesn't seem to help people who need Him. People you love, who've done . . . nothing wrong."

"Uncanny. That's my reason, too."

He began telling her how his mother had died. "She begged my father to quit the war, she was so miserable. He'd done more than his share. Instead, he came home and insisted on having another child, because he was sure he was going to get killed and if I died—I'd come close a few times during an asthma attack—there wouldn't be anybody left to carry on the family name. She died giving birth to my brother George."

Rawdon looked away from her, at the green shore. "It was so . . . rotten. I've never been able to forgive God—or my father—for it."

"I know what you mean," Genevieve said. "I've never been able to forgive God—or my mother—for the way my father died."

"Why? I thought your father died of heart failure. I remember my father blaming it on that fever in Mississippi. He said it weakened his heart."

For a moment there was no breath in Genevieve's lungs. Was she really going to share the secret that General Stapleton had ordered them to conceal? *No one must ever know about this. Ben's reputation must be preserved unspotted.* She could see him pacing before the windows in their parlor the morning after her father's death.

"My father shot himself."

"Oh no."

Sympathy, there was nothing but sympathy, no trace of arrogance on that handsome face. Genevieve told Rawdon the worst, the darkest part of the secret, the part that no one, not even General Stapleton, knew.

"It was my mother's fault. My father failed—his spiritual strength failed— because she didn't believe in him."

They began exchanging the bitter details of their parents' unhappy marriages. Genevieve told how her father used to retreat to his study to escape her mother's sharp tongue. Rawdon recalled the way his mother would come home weeping from an insult she had received on the street, perhaps a "cut" from a former friend whose husband or brother had been wounded or killed in the war. She would write to her husband at the front telling him the story and he would ignore it. Or he would curtly tell her to stop bothering him with such trivial matters.

"Yet I'm sure . . . they loved each other once, don't you think?" Genevieve said. "They look so happy in their wedding photographs."

There was a long sad silence which seemed to confess or reveal their wariness of love, having seen how it could deteriorate.

Back at Kemble Manor, they found Hal Bradford on the lawn with a half-dozen other young men and women. The men were in sporting clothes, the women in expensive silk or organdy walking dresses and pert bonnets. "We've come to take your last dollar in croquet, Stapleton," Bradford roared in his oafish way. "After that gallon of rum you drank last night you'll be seeing two wickets every time you look and I'm betting you'll aim for the wrong one."

Now it begins, Genevieve thought as Rawdon exuberantly accepted the challenge and introduced Genevieve to the rest of the party. Yesterday and today had been an odd interlude, in which Rawdon Stapleton, having nothing better to do, had paid an extraordinary amount of attention to her. Now there was statuesque Florence King in a sky-blue silk dress studded with lace flowers reminding him that they had met last summer at Newport. Red-headed Florence was an incontestable beauty—and her dowry was reputed to be a million dollars. At least three other young women in the group were almost as pretty and as rich.

To her amazement, Rawdon announced that he and Genevieve would play as a team and bet Bradford ten dollars they could beat all comers. For the next two hours they pursued the orange and blue and red balls around the green lawn. Genevieve had played last summer with Alice Gansevoort and was fairly good. But Rawdon was the acknowledged champion. He regularly ran three and four wickets at a turn and rocketed males and females indiscriminately, without mercy. By the end of the morning, she and Rawdon had won forty dollars from the groaning Bradford.

Hal invited everyone back to his house for lunch. They piled into a big open carriage, the girls sitting on the men's laps. Hal entertained everyone with the story of carrying Rawdon home last night and made Genevieve the heroine. After lunch they went for a sail on the Bradfords' forty-foot sloop. Rawdon circulated casually among the group, but he did not ignore Genevieve. She found that her mere association with him made her a sort of celebrity among the women. "How can you stand to be in the same house with him?" Florence King said. "I couldn't take my eyes off him last summer at Newport."

Over the next two weeks, Rawdon's interest in her seemed to grow rather than diminish. Antiope and Diarmuid conversed in their arch way, which they both knew was silly. There were more lessons at the cove, which soon fulfilled Rawdon's prophecy that Genevieve could become a good swimmer. Then there was Rawdon's newest enthusiasm, photography.

His grandmother had given him a tripod camera for his birthday, and he had built a darkroom in a woodshed. He took pictures of Genevieve hefting a croquet mallet, riding a horse, standing at the water's edge; always he insisted that she smile. In the hot close darkroom, she would stand beside him while he dipped the plate into the foul-smelling developer fluid and waited until the image took shape on the glass negative. Finally he would make a print, dip the paper photograph into another chemical bath, and there was the studious Miss Dall, smiling beatifically.

Every two or three days there was an invitation for a sail in the catboat. Gradually, these voyages became a kind of journey into their private selves. It was amazing how often their experiences coincided. Genevieve revealed her suspicion that her mother disliked her because she resembled her father. Rawdon was even more certain that his father disliked him because he resembled his Uncle Charles. "He doesn't want me around because he knows I remind my stepmother of the man she really loved," he said.

They discussed the future as often as the past. General Stapleton had definite plans for both his sons. He wanted Rawdon to join him as a partner in his investment company on Wall Street after he finished Princeton. George (who was spending the summer with the Roosevelts on Long Island) was to take charge of the family textile company, Principia Mills. Rawdon detested the idea of working on Wall Street.

"What do you really want to do?" Genevieve asked.

She asked that question one sunny afternoon in late July as the catboat glided across a glassy bay in the lightest imaginable wind. "I don't know," Rawdon said.

They sailed in silence for almost five minutes. She had learned that Rawdon disliked women who chattered.

"I know this much. I'd like to do something that made a contribution to this country, improved it in some way."

More silence. "I suppose that sounds ridiculous coming from me."

"Not in the least."

They tacked upwind. Kemble Manor was a rose-red toy on the bluff. "I'd like to show you something I wrote at St. Paul's one night when I was especially miserable. Can I trust you never to mention it to anyone—above all to Bradford?"

Trust. The word stirred Genevieve the way *real* had made her shiver the day she arrived from New York. "Of course."

Ashore, he led her upstairs to his bedroom. She stood in the doorway while he extracted a piece of paper from a scrapbook hidden in the back of his closet. He told her that he had kept a scrapbook for each year of his life since he was seven. Thrusting the paper at her, he said, "Remember your promise."

> *There is a longing that was born with me*
> *And makes continual unrest in my mind;*
> *And though each man for his felicity*
> *Must suffer and must labor, mine would be*
> *To leave a single noble thought behind.*
> *And I have hoped and do at times believe*
> *That once while I keep watch in doubt and pain*

The angel will appear with my reprieve,
Stand by my side just long enough to leave
His shining message and depart again.

She saw the yearning for the ideal, corrupted by doubt and loneliness and the failures of others. She saw his need, his hunger for meaning and direction. "Oh Diarmuid," she said, "that is such a lovely poem. I never suspected that your friend Rawdon Stapleton had such a beautiful soul."

"He hasn't—really," he said. "There are times when he thinks he was born without a soul. Maybe he's been waiting—hoping—for a woman like you to help him create one."

She kissed him there in the hot still upstairs hall, astonished by her boldness. Yielding finally to the wish that had been growing in her ever since the moment in the cove. Kissed him with the possibility of seduction, ruin, only a few feet away. But she had confidence in the power of the word that soon became a living presence between them: trust.

"I never thought I could mean so much to a man," she whispered. "Or a man could mean so much to me."

Day by day, over the next two weeks, the idea of trust expanded until it became a separate country, with a language which only they understood. Genevieve and Rawdon peopled it with promises, vows, pledges. They would face the future together, man and woman, husband and wife. She would become the woman her mother had failed to be, the sustainer of the spiritual quest, the restorer of male strength in the struggle for the ideal.

Externally, the summer continued. The Stapletons often invited friends to dinner. Rawdon and Genevieve were required to sit and solemnly discuss fashion and education and yachting and foreign travel with boring bankers and railroad executives and their wives, all the while exchanging delicious, coded messages with their eyes. They went to parties at Hal Bradford's house and the houses of other young people along the bay. They watched the casual flirting and cavorting with the eyes of lovers. Genevieve complacently permitted a half-dozen girls such as Florence King to send Rawdon amorous signals, knowing they would be ignored.

The summer ripened into the blazing heat of August. Genevieve turned photographer and took dozens of pictures of Rawdon. She called them "character studies." Instead of smiles, she sought brooding profiles, angles of vision that captured the nobility she saw lurking just beneath the surface of that handsome face.

The cove remained the center of the enchantment. It was there that Genevieve frequently yielded to her dangerous wish to kiss Rawdon's inviting mouth, to press her body against his, the kisses sliding wildly down necks, arms. A dozen times in her spirit Genevieve surrendered to him. She wanted him in the center of her body, longed to be possessed and possessor, to become one sighing murmuring self. The wish, the idea, surged in her soul with unimaginable sweetness. It had a power, an intensity that overwhelmed conscience, prudence, all the ideas mind and morality ever invented to resist the ultimate temptation.

But Rawdon never took advantage of her willingness. He freely admitted the torment this denial caused him. Diarmuid, that arrogant Celtic seducer of women, had been abandoned. Rawdon Stapleton, undisguised, told her how precious her purity was to him.

By midsummer Eleanor became aware of what was happening. She noticed how much time Genevieve and Rawdon spent together, how little time Genevieve spent with her books. One day she caught them kissing at the cove. That night she lay in bed, wide-eyed, while Genevieve combed her hair before the mirror. "I can't believe it," Eleanor said. "Tell me what you've done. Have you given yourself to him?"

"I'll explain it to you someday, when you're old enough to understand," Genevieve said. "For the time being, would you please do your best to say as little as possible about it?"

Eleanor receded to a figure in the middle distance. The enchantment remained; it grew more powerful each day. Soon it became impossible to think that it would not always be summer, an eternal season there beside the shining bay.

But the summer began to end. General Stapleton and his wife talked about coming dinner parties in New York. Genevieve's mother began worrying about the clothes she would need for Vassar. Suddenly Rawdon was declaring that there was only one way to guarantee their happiness. They had to elope. He had a story concocted to wangle a thousand dollars from his grandmother —a tale of gambling debts in Long Branch. He wanted to use the money to flee to Chicago or San Francisco and get a job on a newspaper. He was ready to discard four years at Princeton; was Genevieve willing to abandon Vassar?

The question broke the enchantment. For Genevieve, Vassar was not the four years of boredom that Rawdon anticipated at Princeton. Vassar was still unique, the only authentic college for women in the entire world. Rawdon saw his college years as a repetition of the subjects his father had studied, none of which had prevented him and his generation from making a mess of the country. Genevieve had no idea what Vassar would do for her and the other pioneer women who were exposing their minds to four years of rigorous mental effort. She could not surrender the opportunity to find out, not even for Rawdon Stapleton.

Genevieve tried to explain this to Rawdon. He seemed peculiarly unimpressed. "What if you discover you're a literary genius?" he said. "Will you still want to marry a lunk like me?"

"Do you think I could possibly take back the promises we've exchanged?"

"I think a great many things can happen in four years to someone who sits around listening to a lot of man-hating old maids fill her head with diatribes about women's right to vote and wear trousers and smoke cigars in public."

"Rawdon, that is a completely erroneous idea of Vassar's purpose. They have no interest in the woman suffrage movement. Their purpose is education. Training women's minds. Nothing else."

"You're only convincing me all over again that you know nothing about the real world."

Furious, almost weeping, Genevieve stormed up to her room and found Vassar's catalogue in the bottom of her trunk. She forced Rawdon to read the statement of the college's purpose—"the creation of educated wives and mothers."

"No sane man would send his daughter there if they said anything else," Rawdon retorted.

For two days they barely spoke to each other. Genevieve could not believe the devastation, the loss, she felt. She barely slept or ate. She never stopped talking to Rawdon in her mind, alternating between rage and pleas for forgiveness. She catalogued his faults, mocked his sincerity. At supper on the second night, when their eyes met, he was obviously so miserable she was overwhelmed by guilt. That night she lay in bed, staring into the darkness, telling herself that if Rawdon made it a condition of their love, she would elope. She would give up Vassar. Even though the idea desolated her almost as much as her father's death.

The third day was engulfed by politics. President Grant, who had recently become a candidate for a second term, paid a call. General Stapleton gathered his wealthy and influential summer neighbors for a reception. Genevieve was introduced to the famous man and his smiling dark-haired cross-eyed wife. She found him dumpy and distinctly unheroic, even though he seemed impressed when General Stapleton said her father was the man who had stopped Stonewall Jackson at Chancellorsville. Later, Rawdon stood beside her on the lawn acerbically annotating the frauds and follies of Grant's administration. She barely listened, certain he was only trying to avoid a serious conversation about their quarrel. He was determined to make her surrender. Desolation swelled in her throat.

Suddenly Rawdon took her by the arm and walked away from the rich and powerful swarming around the President. "I have something I'd like you to take to Vassar with you," he said. "I hope you'll read it now and then."

He handed her a folded piece of paper. It was a kind of poem. But it was more than a poem. It was a testament.

A TRUE MAN

Asks only for trust
And vows to merit love
Knowing it is a gift
That he can never deserve.
He seeks in woman what the world
Cannot give him, a Tahiti
Full of peace and joy
To which he can return
For refreshment, renewed hope.
His faith is in her love and with her love
World without end.

"I'll read it every night," she whispered. "But you must have something to read at Princeton, too."

They walked through the chattering crowd into the empty house. At a slim Sheraton desk where another woman might have sat, scribbling a note to her British lover, Genevieve composed her testament.

A TRUE WOMAN

Feels what her beloved feels
She thinks his thoughts
She dares his faith
Breathes his breath
Lives his life.
She glories in his victories
Grieves in his defeats.
She holds in her heart
Like a relic in a shrine
The ideals for which he strives
World without end.

"Maybe you are a literary genius," Rawdon said. "It took me most of last night to write mine."

He kissed her gently, tenderly, at first. But as she responded, Genevieve felt a surge of terrific longing, a kind of sympathetic fire flowing through both their bodies. "Four years," Rawdon whispered. "Oh Jesus, Gen, I don't know whether I can stay true that long."

"You can. You will," she said. "Oh! I feel the pain, too, my dearest dearest love."

This time the kiss was wild with yearning, with regret. Upstairs, Genevieve thought. She would lead him upstairs to her bedroom now. She would risk Vassar, risk desolation, disgrace. She would let him drink the sweetness that was surging in her thighs, her breasts. She would be woman, mindless, idealess, she would be love and nothing else. What else mattered?

Behind them there was a polite cough. They turned to find Cynthia Stapleton smiling in the doorway. "Careful, you two," Cynthia said. "There are newspaper reporters all over the place. You may find yourselves on the front page of the *Herald* or the *Times.*"

Enormously flustered, Genevieve fussed with her dress. Rawdon glared defiantly at his stepmother.

"Don't be embarrassed on my account," Cynthia drawled. "I'm young enough to appreciate a kiss like that. We've all been watching and hoping it's as serious between you as Eleanor and other spies report."

Why can't they leave us alone? Genevieve wondered angrily. The knowledge that the smiling superior adults had been watching them somehow violated, soiled, the enchantment of the summer of love. Perhaps Rawdon had been right about eloping.

No. Genevieve's mind was in control again. Eloping would mean the extinction of a wish, a hope, that was intimately connected to her four years at Vassar. What was it? Why was she afraid to put it into words? Did she sense that the wish was as dangerous as the smiling adults to the happiness first love had created at Kemble Manor?

BOOK II
1876

ONE

"Mistress, you 'wake? Listen to me, now. Master George say he was too sick to go to school. But I just caught him downstairs in his nightshirt puttin' a message for that scamp Elliott Roos'velt in the telegraph box."

Cleopatra's wrinkled yellow face hovered over Cynthia Stapleton's bed like some evil bird. The telegraph box, which enabled homeowners to send messages all over New York, was made to order for evaders of parental authority like George Stapleton and Elliott Roosevelt.

"Oh, let him be," Cynthia said sleepily. "There's only a few days of school left and there's no hope of him improving his marks."

"Mistress, you spoilin' that boy. You makin' a mess of him, just the way your daddy made of you."

"My father did *not* make a mess of me. If I hear you insult me—and him —that way, I swear I'll send you back to Louisiana on the next train."

Cleopatra's eyes brimmed with tears; her withered lips trembled. Cynthia reminded herself of how much she had loved this old woman once. "I'm sorry, Cleo. You know I didn't mean that. What time is it?"

"Ten o'clock," Cleopatra said, drawing the blue velvet draperies. May sunlight burst into the room, setting the yellow wallpaper aglow. Cynthia had ransacked Paris to find that wallpaper, with its groups of eighteenth-century figures dancing grave minuets. It was identical to the wallpaper in her childhood bedroom at Bralston.

Cleopatra put the breakfast tray on Cynthia's bed. A single slice of toast and weak tea. Cynthia yearned for some grits, a little ham. But she had to stay on her diet if she had any hope of getting into the summer dresses Worth had designed for her.

Outside in Stuyvesant Square, an organ grinder began cranking out "O

Sole Mio." In the hall, Lucy, the upstairs maid, was humming "Toucoutou," an old Creole song. Cynthia began to feel better. She leaned back against the pillows for a moment and thought about her house.

She began in the sunny front parlor, with its red flocked Lincrustra wallpaper and its yellow-cushioned French Renaissance couches and chairs, its Japanese corner, its Italian statuary and Impressionist paintings she had bought on her honeymoon in Paris. She crossed the hall to the dining room, where her Tiffany silver lay in the massive Elizabethan Renaissance mahogany sideboard and pieces of her Sardinian green Copeland china were displayed in a shining breakfront. She ascended the curving staircase, with its Louis XVI lion-head brass sconces and its stained-glass oval window on the landing.

Everything gleamed, furniture, floors, the sinuous walnut balustrade. Bowls and vases of cut flowers brightened the hall and both parlors. She insisted on fresh flowers, replacing them three times a week when they wilted from the illuminating gas. It was not a great plantation, with an army of servants and guests perpetually coming and going. But it was hers. She had chosen the furniture, the wallpaper, the paintings.

There was only one thing wrong. The house was on Stuyvesant Square. Jonathan's decision to buy here after the war had been a mistake, an indication of how out of touch he was with New York. During his college days in the 1840s, the square had undoubtedly been a bastion of aristocratic wealth and fashion. But nothing remained fashionable in New York for very long. Three years ago, Mittie Roosevelt had persuaded Theodore to build her a splendid mansion not far from Katherine Kemble Brown's town house on Fifty-seventh Street. Many other New Yorkers with impeccable social credentials had decided it was ridiculous to surrender Fifth Avenue and its side streets to the shoddies. But Jonathan Stapleton still clung to Stuyvesant Square and dismissed the Fifth Avenue world as ostentatious.

Husbands. She was *married* to this complicated stubborn man. A month ago they had celebrated their ninth wedding anniversary. She was a *wife.* A rather successful one, if the extravagant gifts Jonathan gave her on her birthdays and anniversaries and Christmas were any indication. For nine years she had confounded her father's prophecy that she was destined to be a courtesan. For nine years she seemed to have discovered that rare happy medium between a dictatorial husband and a manageering wife.

But now . . .

On the wall opposite her bed hung a painting of a man and a woman picnicking in the Bois de Boulogne. Shafts of sunlight slanted through the shade, turning the grass aglow, brightening the woman's white dress. The man, his back turned, was an ominous chunk of darkness in his black coat.

He seemed to contradict the natural beauty of the sun and the grass, the promise of pleasure from the lounging woman in white.

On their honeymoon she and Jonathan had often picnicked like that in the Bois. She had not thought of him as an ominous chunk of darkness then, or in the happy years that followed. They had had a quarrel or two about the severe way he dealt with Rawdon, about her tendency to spoil George, her repeated pleas to help her brother Robert find another job. Such minor disagreements were hardly the stuff of darkness. Those emanations were coming from another source, Jonathan's involvement with the odious Republican Party.

This year, with the presidential election looming in November, he had agreed to serve as their national treasurer. Three times last week he had not arrived home for dinner until eight o'clock, and then he sat there, so exhausted he could barely converse. Next week he was going to New Jersey for Decoration Day, an occasion invented by some midwest Republican supposedly to mourn the war's dead. It was really an excuse to give political speeches slandering the South. Jonathan was going to put on that hateful blue uniform again, the uniform worn by the men who had looted and wrecked Bralston, and march behind bands playing songs that accused southerners of being traitors. He seemed indifferent to the effect this might have on her feelings.

A knock on the door. George Stapleton peered into the room. At fifteen he was a pimply-faced mess, with a voice that screeched one moment and at the next breath rumbled in his chest. "I need some money," he said. "Nell says he'll go to Niblo's Garden with me."

Nell was the odd nickname that Elliott Roosevelt had given himself. He had taken it from the heroine in Dickens' *Old Curiosity Shop*. It always made Cynthia uncomfortable.

"I told you not to use the telegraph for such silly messages."

"It's the only gram I've sent all week."

"And it's to no purpose. If you're too sick to go to school, you're too sick to go to Niblo's Garden. Or Barnum's Museum. Or the Central Park. You will stay home and study your Greek."

"Oh Mother, please. There's no point to it. Only three people passed the last examination. Everybody hates Greek."

"In England, boys your age speak it fluently."

"The English are a bunch of nancys. You only need Greek to get into St. Paul's. You won't let Father send me to freeze in the New Hampshire snowdrifts, will you? Rawdon says it's the worst place he's ever been in his life."

"I have no control over your father."

"Liarrrr," George said, with his infectious grin. "Look, I'll spend four hours on the Greek tonight. I swear it. Now can I have a dollar for Niblo's? Nell is waiting for me on Broadway."

"Oh, all right," Cynthia said. "Take it out of my purse."

He took the money and hurled himself on the bed to give her a kiss on the cheek. "You're the best mother in New York," he said, and went bounding down the stairs.

Cynthia's eyes misted. Her fingers strayed to her cheek. She loved the boy.

Cynthia wondered if she would feel so strongly about George if she had a child of her own. In the spring of 1872, after eighteen hours in labor, she had given birth to a baby girl who had lived only a day. That fall, when she was strong enough to travel, Jonathan had taken her to Europe and consulted the best physicians in Paris. They had recommended a new device, a diaphragm, which was guaranteed to prevent future conceptions. At the time she had rejoiced to escape the threat of another pregnancy. It had enabled her to continue to welcome Jonathan wholeheartedly whenever he was inclined to visit her bedroom. But lately Cynthia had felt a sense of loss, a vague, drifting wish to be able to talk about *my* son or *my* daughter, the way other women chattered so incessantly.

Cousteau peered into the bedroom to announce that her brother Robert was downstairs. Cynthia groaned inwardly. What was she going to do with Robert?

"Tell him he'll have to wait."

Robert had lost several jobs Jonathan had gotten for him, usually, he claimed, because he found Jonathan's friends full of ill-concealed hostility to southerners. Cynthia could readily believe that such animosity still existed between men who had repeatedly tried to kill each other during the war. Jonathan barely managed to conceal his own dislike of Robert, even though he had tried to help him for her sake. But jobs on Wall Street had grown scarce since the catastrophic collapse of the stock market in 1873. For the past year Robert had been living hand to mouth, with much of his cash coming from her hand.

Lucy helped Cynthia comb out her hair, freeing the dark curls that Henri, her French hairdresser, had toiled to create in the true, thick Cadogan style. Next came the careful application of the eyebrow pencil, a touch of powder and the tiniest hint of rouge on her cheeks and lips. She studied the result in the tilted mirror. At thirty-six there was not a sign of a wrinkle. It was the same face that had smiled up at Charles Gifford Stapleton when he stepped off the steamboat at the dock of Bralston Plantation in Louisiana eighteen years ago.

Where was Charlie? She kept a tiny daguerreotype of him and one of her father on her dressing table. They were always getting lost behind jars of cream or perfume bottles. Her mother-in-law had given her Charlie's picture two years ago. Jonathan had said nothing, but she knew he was certain to notice what she did with it. At first she considered stuffing it in a drawer and finally telling him the truth about Charlie.

She still remembered—and sometimes regretted—that missed opportunity on their honeymoon in Venice. Lately there were times when she wondered if Jonathan's feelings for her were affected by his assumption that Charlie was the great love of her life. Did he feel it entitled him to treat her with a certain indifference when it suited him? When, for instance, the sacred Republican Party demanded his time and attention? Perhaps this neglect was also the reason why Charlie had remained on her dressing table beside her father.

Robert came charging into the bedroom with his usual ebullience. No matter how many disappointments he suffered, his Legrand high spirits remained intact. It was one among several reasons why Cynthia found him hard to resist. He was wearing a mauve sack coat with satin facing on the lapels and a stiff turn-down collar, pinstriped trousers and fashionably pointed black patent-leather shoes. He could have stepped off—or onto—a Paris boulevard. No matter how acute his poverty became, Bob always managed to dress in style.

"Darling little sister," he drawled, kissing her hand. "How do you stay so beautiful?"

"Magic," she said, gesturing to the bottles on the dresser. "Imported from Paris."

"Have you heard about Jimmy Fish?" he asked. "One of our southern adventuresses has taken him for at least a million. The story will be in the papers in a day or two. He stole the money from his father's bank."

Robert seldom failed to bring her one of these delicious stories, well in advance of the newspapers. She sometimes suspected he knew some of these southern adventuresses—there seemed to be squadrons of them in New York. But it was better not to ask.

"Hey, there's old Charlie," he said, picking up the daguerreotype from the dressing table. "Just between us, Cyntie, how can you stand that Yankee icicle you're married to now when you once had a man like Charlie in your bed? He wasn't southern born or bred—but he was southern in every other way."

"Robert, I've told you before, I don't appreciate that kind of remark. Jonathan has been very good to me—and to you too."

"Okay, okay, he's the perfect husband. You are not bored for one second while he sits around telling you about how many shares he bought in the Nashville and Cincinnati Railroad and what his friend Senator Conkling said about the South when they huddled at Republican headquarters. By the way, have you heard about the Senator's latest speech?"

Roscoe Conkling was the Republican boss of New York State and its U.S. Senator. Cynthia had sat next to him several times at dinners in New York and Long Branch. He was everything she disliked in a man, arrogant, overbearing and overdressed. If the *New York Herald* was to be believed, he was a crook in the bargain.

Robert took the *Herald* off Cynthia's breakfast tray and spread its pages on her bed. "Here it is." He began reading from the paper.

> "Every State that seceded from the Union was a Democratic State. . . . Every man that endeavored to tear the old flag from the heaven it enriches was a Democrat. . . . Every man that shot down Union soldiers was a Democrat. The man that assassinated Abraham Lincoln was a Democrat. . . . Every man that clutched babes from the breasts of shrinking, shuddering, crouching mothers and sold them into slavery was a Democrat. . . . Every soldier's scar, every arm that is missing, every limb that is gone is the souvenir of a Democrat. . . . Shall the solid South with the aid of a divided North control this great and splendid country?"

"Dear—God," Cynthia said.

"The bloody shirt," Robert said. "That's the only argument the Republicans have left, after eight years of Ulysses Grant."

Cleo appeared with coffee.

"Would you like some brandy?" Cynthia asked.

"I got it right outside on the hall table, Miz Cynthia," Cleo said, with her yellow-toothed smile. "Whenever I see Mister Robert, I say to myself, 'Get out the brandy.' He's his daddy's son, no question."

"I'm trying, Cleo, I'm trying," Robert said, letting her pour a generous splash into his cup.

"What's on your mind, besides trying to wreck my marriage by reading me Senator Conkling's speeches?" Cynthia asked.

Robert gulped his coffee. "Little sister," he said. "How would you like to help me raise an army?"

"Robert, please, not another expedition!"

For a while, Robert had tried to raise money for an army of American volunteers to help the sputtering Cuban revolution. Then he began coming to Cynthia with wild schemes for conquering Puerto Rico or some other island or Central American country. All she had to do was persuade Jonathan to get President Grant's cooperation. She had declined to try, having no desire to re-ignite the quarrel about the South's purple dreams that had almost ruined her honeymoon.

Robert hurtled across the room and dropped to his knees in front of her chair. "No, not another expedition," he said, seizing both her hands. "An army to redeem Louisiana. And this time make sure it stays redeemed."

Redeeming the southern states was a struggle that had been filling the columns of the New York newspapers for several years now. It consisted of agitating until the federal government withdrew its troops, then electing redeemer legislatures and governors to replace the Republican Negroes, carpetbaggers and scalawags. Republican papers such as the *New York Times* insisted that redemption was achieved by terror and assassination. Democratic newspapers such as the *Herald* praised the redeemers as honest men who were fighting to oust an unholy league of ignoramuses and plunderers.

So far, seven of the ten Confederate states had been redeemed. Last year everyone thought Louisiana had joined them. But the local Republicans had claimed fraud and President Grant had nullified the election and ordered federal troops to oust the new Democratic governor.

"I've just spent ten days in New Orleans," Robert said. "We've got it all figured out. We need two hundred and fifty thousand dollars to raise ten thousand men."

"Where in the world do you expect me to get that kind of money?"

"Didn't you tell me your comfortable little fortune had grown to over three hundred thousand dollars?"

"Yes, but I certainly wouldn't give you nine tenths of it. Anyway it's completely in Jonathan's hands."

Cynthia had liked the idea of keeping the money that had brought them together in a separate account at Jonathan's office. Until recently she had used it to tease him when he spent too much time fretting over a sick railroad. "Remember you have an independent woman at home, General." But she had not played the virago about his recent plunge into politics. He was so gloomy, so tired, most of the time.

"Some fortune. If you can't use it when and as you please."

"I can do anything I want with it. But I'm a *married* woman, Robert. A wife has a responsibility to act in some accordance with her husband's opinions and wishes."

"Why? He sure as hell isn't acting in accordance with yours. Do you really like him working hand in glove with people like Roscoe Conkling? People who want to keep the South enslaved for another hundred years?"

"I don't believe Jonathan has any such desire. He has his reasons—his memories of the damned war, just as you do."

She was back seven years, seeing the awful expression on Jonathan's face the night Ben Dall died, feeling his inner withdrawal from her sympathy, her touch. She had sensed something ghostly, ghastly emanating from or surrounding him: a musty coldness that one might find in an abandoned house in winter. For a frightening moment she had thought he hated her. But the following night Jonathan had made love to her with unforgettable tenderness. He had talked about his need for her. She had sensed his wounded spirit reaching out across geography and time to an idea, a dream of healing love.

That was real. That had actually happened. Yet his present neglect of her, his indifference to her feelings, was also real. Marriage was a strange business.

"Cyntie, this is the opportunity of my life," Robert said. "If I can pull this off, bring back this money, it'll be one continuous bowl of cherries for me—and for you too if you ever need any. The people who redeem Louisiana will own that whole big beautiful state. Where can I get the money?"

The Legrands were born to dance.

No, Cynthia told herself. Don't listen to that voice. You owe it nothing. It almost buried you in that two-thousand-acre grave down there on the Mississippi.

"This doesn't have anything to do with the presidential election, Cyntie. The Republicans are going to get whomped anyway. It's strictly personal, a chance to get into this redeemer business. All I need is one rich Democrat who'll do Brother Bob a favor for your sake. Come on!"

"I do know one. But I couldn't ask him directly."

"Why not?"

"I'm afraid any woman, however well married, who asked Lionel Bradford for that kind of money might be expected to return the favor."

"Bradford," Robert said. "He's big money. How well do you know him?"

"We used to see him and his wife regularly at Monmouth Park. They rented a house not far from Kemble Manor for several years. Then his wife left him—for good and sufficient reasons, I gather."

"Cyntie—all I need's an introduction to him. I'll do my own talking."

"I could invite him to a dinner party I'm giving a week from Saturday. I could also invite you—if you promise to be discreet and reasonably well behaved."

The last dinner party Robert had attended, a year and a half ago, he and his actress of the moment had gotten disgracefully drunk.

"I swear by all the saints and sinners of the Mardi Gras," Robert said, raising his hand in a mock oath.

"Discreet, Robert. Please concentrate on that word. I don't want my husband to have the slightest idea that I am in any way connected with this scheme."

Robert kissed her exultantly on the cheek. "Don't worry. Diplomacy's my middle name. Remember Daddy making me read the life of Metternich and all those other European slickers? You and I were supposed to be political confederates."

For a moment Cynthia felt a current of grief, of sadness, flowing between them almost as palpable as breath.

"This is going to work, Cyntie. The timing, everything about it is right."

Robert kissed her again, gently, tenderly. He headed for the door, then abruptly stopped, snapped his fingers and turned to face her with the most awful hangdog expression. "Damn. I forgot to ask you something else. I was playing cards last night and my luck was rotten . . ."

"There's money in my purse," she said, turning away from him. In her dressing-table mirror she saw him, reduced to one-fifth his size, rummaging in her purse on the bureau. She bowed her head and heard him scuttle to the door.

"God bless you, little sister," he said.

For the rest of the day, Cynthia vacillated between caution and daring, the past and the present, pity for Robert and loyalty to Jonathan. She wrote out an invitation to Lionel Bradford, but she did not mail it. She went to a luncheon at Katherine Kemble Brown's house and played duplicate whist with her and Mittie Roosevelt and one of Mrs. Brown's married daughters, Clara Livingston. Clara talked of nothing but Madeline Terhune, the English actress, and the daring play in which she was appearing, *Gallantry*. It apparently recommended a shocking idea—a wife should forgive her husband for adultery.

Clara Livingston thought Mrs. Terhune should be banned from the city. Her mother and Mittie agreed with her. Cynthia disagreed. "I haven't seen the play. We have tickets for tomorrow night. But the alternative, separation and a life of miserable antagonism, surely can't be worse than forgiveness."

"That's easy for you to say," Clara said with a bluntness that she had obviously inherited from her mother. "You're married to a man who adores you."

Rather than argue, Cynthia turned to a far more interesting aspect of the subject—whose husbands were wandering. If rumors were fact, the number was astonishing. That reminded Katherine Kemble Brown of another reason to ban Mrs. Terhune and her play. "Speaking of husbands who've been caught in adultery, that scoundrel Lionel Bradford is squiring her around town. I always said poor Milly Pell would rue the day she married that European man of mystery."

Milly Pell was the homeliest woman Cynthia had ever seen. A great clod of a creature. Lionel Bradford had unquestionably married her for her aristocratic name and whacking dowry. Cynthia was more interested in learning that he was escorting Madeline Terhune. She would add some spice to her last dinner party of the season, which was in danger of being dominated by dreary Knickerbocker friends of Jonathan's youth such as Collie and Cecilia Schermerhorn.

At home, Cynthia discovered a message that had grown familiar. General Stapleton would be late for dinner. By the time he arrived, it was eight o'clock, and she had read every copy of *Godey's Lady's Book* in the house. Sharp words rushed to her lips, until she saw how tired he looked.

"Have mercy on a starving man," he said. "Can we have dinner right away? I never did get any lunch again today."

"I am going to sue the Republican Party for depriving me of a husband," Cynthia said. "Day after day, I send a healthy, contented man off to work and get back an exhausted, grouchy wreck."

She rang for Cousteau and told him to serve the first course. They sat down before savory plates of chicken gumbo soup.

"I saw your friend Senator Conkling today," Jonathan said. "He sends you his warmest regards. He still says you're the best-looking woman in New York."

Senator Conkling liked pretty women. He always fussed over her when they met.

"I wish I could return the compliment—but I read the report of his speech in the *Herald* today. It's not the sort of thing a person with any southern feelings could read with equanimity."

Jonathan put down his spoon. "Dearest," he said in a sad weary voice. "I come home to escape this kind of discussion. There's no reason in the world for you to burden your mind with the woes and antagonisms of our politics. It will do nothing but sour your disposition and put wrinkles on your lovely face. Leave politics to us males. We deserve all the headaches we get from it."

You and I were going to be political confederates, Robert said. Instead she was a wife, a creature who was apparently not supposed to have political thoughts.

They finished the soup in silence. Jonathan tried to change the subject. He talked about Princeton's chances of winning the intercollegiate regatta on Lake George. Rowing was the only thing at Princeton that had stirred Rawdon's enthusiasm. "I still wish we could go," Cynthia said.

They had had a rather tense discussion about this a week ago. It was Rawdon's last race. But Jonathan had decided he could not spare the time to go to it. A Republican victory in November was more important than his son's feelings.

"I know I'm being a deplorable husband and father," Jonathan said. "Be patient for a few more months. It will all be over in November."

November was five months away. Half a year. Politics, about which she was forbidden to think, would spoil the spring and the summer and the best part of the fall social season. But Jonathan was trying to apologize, in his clumsy way. Sometimes she wished he was not always so serious. A different, perhaps wiser man would have teased and joshed her into a better humor.

In the morning, when Cynthia sat down at her dressing table, she saw her dinner invitation to Lionel Bradford propped against Charlie's picture. Should she send it?

Cousteau knocked at the door. "Madam," he said. "General Stapleton left a message. He does not think he'll be able to join you at the theater tonight. He has a pressing engagement in New Jersey."

What a cowardly way for the conqueror to deliver his latest piece of bad news. He did not have the courage to tell her last night. She picked up the invitation and handed it to Cousteau. "Have Muzzey take that to Mr. Bradford's house this morning. And send this telegram to Mrs. Roosevelt."

She scribbled the message: WILL YOU COME WITH ME TO GALLANTRY TONIGHT IN PLACE OF A WANDERING HUSBAND?

TWO

The color bearer came pounding out of the dark trees of Chancellorsville into the campfire's circle of light, the rest of the Sixth New Jersey behind him. Shells were exploding everywhere. The *yi-yi-yi* of the rebel yell mingled with the crash of musketry, the lowing cattlelike groan of panic that he had heard at Bull Run and other battles when men broke and ran. He shot the color bearer in the heart. He could see his frantic boy's face, swaying there in the firelight, the shock on the other faces as they recoiled from his pistol. He stood there, the flag in his hand, roaring, "Who will take this back to meet the enemy?"

Suddenly all the faces turned to fleshless skulls. They grinned insanely at him. He was shouting at an army of dead men.

Jonathan Stapleton swung his long legs out of his boyhood bed and sat there, listening to his heart pound. His nightshirt was soaked with sweat. The clock in the hall bonged four. *Land of milk and honey,* the sheltering voice whispered in his mind. It was Decoration Day, 1876, and he was back in New Jersey to honor the dead. All night they had been blundering through his mind.

He went downstairs in search of some whiskey. In the center hall he paused to confront his father in the family portrait gallery. The painting portrayed George Stapleton in the Senate, blithely holding out the hand of friendship to the South. Behind him on his desk was the Compromise of

1850 and the other measures that had been supposed to placate the slaveowners. The confidence, the complacency on the handsome genial face made him wince.

The whiskey only gave him a stomachache. He lay there, watching dawn gray the windows. When he heard movement downstairs, he got up and put on his full-dress blue uniform. A ridiculous rig, he thought, adjusting the gold-braided epaulettes.

Unable to think of a reason for delay, he went downstairs to breakfast with his mother. Dinner last night had been an ordeal. He did not expect this meal to be an improvement.

She was sitting at the dining-room table in her inevitable black dress, her face the same emotionless mask. Instead of withering her, age seemed to be turning her into stone.

"Good morning," he said, and kissed her on the forehead. That was the only kiss she tolerated. The kiss on the lips, the tender kiss of love that she had once given him almost too freely, was forbidden.

"Good morning," she said. "Did you sleep well?"

"No."

"Why not?"

"Too much on my mind, I suppose."

"The election?"

"Among other things."

"I think we Democrats are going to win this time."

"I hope not."

"How can you defend your friend Grant? He's been an abomination."

"He's been a disappointment, I admit. His family, some of his friends, have had an unfortunate influence on him. But he's not going to run again."

Walter Jackson, the ancient Negro butler, placed before him the sort of breakfast he had eaten at the age of twenty-one: a platter laden with lobster Newburgh, steak, fried potatoes and fried eggs.

"You have the gall to defend the Republican Party—after the Whiskey Ring, the Indian-trading-post scandals?"

"May I remind you that I live in New York, Mother, where the courts are finally getting around to trying that Democratic hero, Bill Tweed, for stealing two hundred million dollars from the city? Neither party has a monopoly on virtue. You above all should be aware of that."

He was reminding her of how often she had seen Senator George Stapleton walk out of this house carrying a carpetbag crammed with money to make sure that the state legislature preserved the Camden & Amboy Railroad's monopoly in New Jersey.

"I've never had the slightest illusion about the necessity, the inevitability, of corruption in politics. I'm thinking of the way you once declared the

Republicans the saviors of the country. The awful things you said to your father in front of his followers and friends that night in 1861. Does your conscience ever trouble you?"

"Yes," he said.

Because I really wanted to say those things to you.

"But never enough to make even a gesture of repentance."

"Mother, I thought we agreed years ago that this argument does neither of us any good."

There were times when his stomach ached with the wish to tell her how much he knew. Senator George Stapleton seldom had a political idea that his wife had not put into his head. She had pushed him into politics and ultimately into waters utterly beyond his depth. When the Mexican War broke out, she had persuaded her husband to volunteer and spend a hundred thousand dollars to raise a brigade. Ben Dall, in the first flower of their friendship, had helped Jonathan see the conflict as a southern plundering expedition, an unsavory, barely concealed plot to extend the arc of slavery to the equator.

After the war, Senator Stapleton, with a prescience that could only have come from his wife, abandoned the Whig Party, inheritor of the tradition of reason and responsibility that came down from Washington and Hamilton, and joined the Democrats, the party of the slaveowners and race-hate mongers. As managers of a winning war, they were enormously popular. Under his leadership, New Jersey virtually became a southern state.

In Congress, Senator Stapleton was the South's best friend. He spoke for compromise and conciliation on every issue, from gutting the Fugitive Slave Act to repealing the neutrality laws that prevented filibustering expeditions. When the South finally seceded, the Senator was in a perfect position to urge the North to let their erring brothers go in peace.

The move was enormously daring, supremely ambitious. It was aimed at making Senator George Stapleton president of the northern confederacy that would emerge from the shattered Union. But the monster, history, had declined to cooperate. The southern ultras had fired on the flag at Fort Sumter before Senator Stapleton's plea for peace could resound through the land. And in New Jersey his oldest son had declared that he was raising a regiment to fight for the Union.

No, Jonathan Stapleton had done much more than that. He might as well face the whole thing one more time, as his mother was daring him to do. He had strode into Bowood's parlor, where every important Democratic politician in New Jersey had gathered on that April night in 1861 to hear Senator George Stapleton urge them to remain neutral in the great crisis, assuring them that there were other states—Delaware, Pennsylvania, Indiana, Kentucky—that would follow their lead. Jonathan had interrupted his father in midsentence to snarl, "Sir. You're talking like a fool."

He could still see the trembling wattles under his father's stringy old man's neck, the soft subtle mouth collapsing under the impact of those words. His son had made his first and last political speech. He had said that secession was treason and there was only one choice: war.

"How is Cynthia?"

"What? Oh—fine."

His mother was attacking from the opposite flank. "When she was here at Christmastime, I got the distinct impression she was less than happy with all the time you devote to the Republican Party."

"She may fret a little. But there's no conflict of *opinion.* She doesn't have your jugular interest in politics, Mother."

The rebuke only drew another thrust. "Does she ever mention Charlie?"

"She keeps that photograph you gave her on her dressing table."

"You don't mind?"

"Why should I mind? I loved him, too," he lied.

Lying to her stirred a sullen satisfaction in his soul. It was a kind of revenge for the lies she had once told him, to inveigle him into a marriage to a woman he did not love. She had spent most of their dinner last night talking about Laura Kemble, recalling his pity for her pathetic plight as the supposed victim of a hostile stepmother, her shyness and timidity, all part of the bait they had dangled in front of the poor oversized fish who had promised Mother to stay pure until his wedding day.

Jonathan sat there savoring a memory that he often wanted to tell her, whenever his mother combined Charlie and Laura in her repertoire of assaults on him. That spring afternoon in 1850, in his senior year at Columbia, when he and Ben Dall strolled up Broadway toward the Astor House and saw Senator George Stapleton emerge from the hotel with a woman beside him. Not his wife Caroline, walking in her tippety-toe, pouter-pigeon Queen Victoria way, but a woman twenty or thirty years younger, a swarthy spectacular creature who walked with a bold stride that matched the mane of black hair streaming shamelessly down her back.

The Senator had seen them and decided to brazen it out—typical of the man. He introduced them to Mrs. Maria Theresa Galvez, widow of a Mexican officer who had been killed in the battle of Palo Alto. They had met in Mexico City. She was in New York visiting friends. One smooth lie after another had flowed from the Senator's lips. While his virtuous son stood there, fixing him in a frozen glare. As the guilty pair stepped into a carriage and rode away, Ben Dall had given a low whistle. "Spoils of war," he had said.

"Jonathan!" His mother was frowning at him. "You're unusually dull this morning. I don't believe you've heard a word I just said."

"I'm sorry."

"I was warning you to be careful. You can't neglect a woman like Cynthia. Not when she has a man like Charlie in her past."

"You're sure you won't come to the cemetery? You could lay some flowers on Charlie's grave. You always said he died in the service of his country."

She shook her head, her eyes icy. She knew what her absence would communicate to New Jerseyans. Senator George Stapleton's widow considered Decoration Day a Republican publicity stunt.

Weariness overwhelmed Jonathan. Was there no end to this woman's hatred? "Mother, it's over," he said. "It's been over for eleven years. Why can't you accept it?"

All pretense of calm, dignity, reserve, vanished. The once lovely mouth twisted into a snarl: "If it's over," she hissed, "what are you doing here? Why are you going out there, pretending to mourn the dead, soliciting votes?"

Outside on the boulevard, a military band began playing "The Battle Hymn of the Republic." Jonathan abandoned his mostly uneaten breakfast, took a sip of coffee, and went out to the kitchen to say goodbye to Walter Jackson and his wife, Bertha. Jackson's back was bent with arthritis; white hair crowned his lined black face. Bertha trembled with some kind of palsy. Time was eating away at them, at the whole house, abandoning it on one of history's side streets.

Outside, three bands were playing war songs before the bronze statue of the charging infantrymen in the center of Stapleton Square. The blue ranks filled the intersection, a solid reassuring mass, standing at parade rest. They burst into a long ragged cheer as their old commander mounted the reviewing stand. He waved to them and shook hands with the governor and a half-dozen other dignitaries in swallowtail coats. Among them was his cousin, Mortimer Stapleton, now the Democratic mayor of Hamilton. During the war, in which he had scrupulously avoided serving, Mortimer had made a habit of calling Lincoln "the brainless bob-o-link of the prairies." His growing political power—he was a probable candidate for governor—was dismaying evidence of the Democratic Party's revival.

They listened to an hour of predictably boring speeches, which put wings of heroism and sanctity on the dead. After the oratory, Jonathan strode across the circle to join the troops. The bands struck up "Marching Through Georgia" and the blue ranks swung down the street in the morning sunlight. Spectators on the sidewalk cheered and waved.

Woodlawn Cemetery was on the brow of a hill overlooking the Passaic River. It offered a spectacular view across the broad stream and the coastal plain to New York. At the foot of the hill on the riverbank clustered the dozen red-brick buildings of Principia Mills which his father had inherited from a bachelor brother in the late fifties. The clattering looms were silent today. Jonathan had authorized a holiday with pay for the work force to add marchers and spectators to the parade.

As the regiments disbanded at the end of the march, hundreds of veterans came ambling over to shake Jonathan's hand. Then they scattered through the cemetery, joining wives and friends to lay flowers on graves of dead comrades. Jonathan walked back to the gate, where he had arranged with a local florist to have two wreaths of white roses waiting for him. He put one wreath on his brother George's grave, in their family plot near the gate. Then he walked down the carriage road and laid the other one on Ben Dall's grave. He had persuaded Margaret to bury him here, where many of the Sixth New Jersey lay.

He paused for a moment, pondering the inscription he had chosen for Ben's headstone: SELDOM THE LAUREL WREATH IS SEEN.

It was from an unpublished poem by Herman Melville. The aging writer, a forgotten failure who now worked in the Federal Custom House, had given Jonathan a copy of it on the day of Ben's funeral. The stanza whispered in his mind.

> *But seldom the laurel wreath is seen*
> *Unmixed with pensive pansies dark.*
> *There's a light and a shadow on every man*
> *Who at last attains his lifted mark.*

A few feet away, a voice began screeching very different sentiments: "THERE HE IS, THE BUTCHER, WEEPING HIS HYPOCRITE'S TEARS OVER ONE OF HIS ASSISTANT BUTCHERS. YOU'LL END LIKE HIM OR THERE'S NO GOD IN HEAVEN."

The woman stood a few dozen feet above him on the sloping hill, pointing her finger at him. She had a round red face that glared at him beneath a cheap black hat. She was dressed entirely in black, down to her gloves, shoes and stockings.

Jonathan turned his back on the woman and stalked to the carriage road. She followed him, screaming more abuse. "What's the matter, butcher? Can't you stand the sight of a widow? Haven't you made enough of them to get used to it?"

Dozens of blue-coated veterans surrounded Jonathan Stapleton. "Don't worry, General, we'll get rid of that harpy," one of them snarled.

"No, let her alone. I have to leave anyway to catch my train."

"It's a cheap election trick, General," someone else shouted. "She ain't worn them widow's weeds for ten years."

The woman had a circle of men around her now. "Lay a hand on her and you'll find enough trouble to make you wish you were back fighting Robert E. Lee," one of them called.

"Are you going to let them traitor Democrats get away with that, General?" another veteran asked.

Jonathan struggled to answer him calmly. "I don't want this day disturbed by a riot. Let the Democrats rave. We know—we know we saw the right and did it."

"What about tomorrow or the next day, General?" asked a big man with a red mustache. "If we see one of them, can we give him a kick?"

Jonathan looked across the two dozen yards of tombstones and statuary at the Democrats. "By all means," he said, with a small smile. "Give it to him with my compliments."

The veterans burst into a loud reckless laugh. Their civilian faces had vanished. In their eyes and on their mouths was nostalgic ferocity. Jonathan Stapleton found himself wishing it away. Once he had exulted in that ferocity. Now he felt uneasy about arousing it. What was happening to him?

"Let's give the General three cheers," shouted the big man.

"Hurrah! Hurrah! Hurray for Old Steady!"

"Thank you," Jonathan Stapleton said. "Let me give you one more order to be passed through the ranks. Vote this November. Vote for the Union. For peace with justice. Do everything you can to dissuade your friends and neighbors from voting for disunion, disloyalty, disorder."

"You can depend on us, General," someone bellowed.

It was disgusting. He had fulfilled his mother's prophecy and turned the salute to the dead into an election rally. But what else could he do in the face of such low Democratic tactics?

The bands playing near the cemetery gate had marched to their support. The musicians wheeled and led them back up the road, blaring the favorite song of the war. Behind them, the men roared out the words.

> *"The Union forever,*
> > *Hurrah! Boys, hurrah!*
> *Down with the traitor,*
> > *Up with the star,*
> *While we rally round the flag, boys,*
> > *Rally once again,*
> *Shouting the battle cry of freedom!"*

From all parts of the cemetery the veterans rushed to the carriage road to cheer and wave. At the gate, the bands opened ranks and blasted out the final chorus while Jonathan Stapleton climbed into the victoria that would take him to the railroad station. As the music died away, some Democrat lurking in the bushes got in the last word: "Go back to New York, butcher!"

THREE

Legs folded, head bent, Genevieve Dall sat in the dome room of Vassar College's observatory, operating the fourth-largest equatorial telescope in America. The gleaming brass-and-steel cylinder rose from the huge stone piers in front of her to the opening in the roof. Next door in the clock and chronograph room she could hear Professor Maria Mitchell taking the other six members of the class on a voyage toward infinite space.

". . . Beyond the Milky Way, the very tiara of the skies—where minute points of light seen with a small telescope burst into stars and where other white spots defy all power of vision and science . . ."

Genevieve followed Maria Mitchell's words with the lens of the great telescope. She shivered in near-rapture at the colors of the double stars, their subtle shades of red and green and blue. Slowly she guided the telescope across the sky from the Great Orion to the magnificent Corona Borealis to the horizon, where fiery Antares shone.

Suddenly, five degrees above Antares, a glow of incredible brilliance filled the lens. Was it possible? Had she discovered a new star? Was she about to be catapulted into world fame, as Maria Mitchell had been in her youth when she became the first American astronomer to sight a new comet?

"Miss Mitchell, Miss Mitchell," Genevieve called.

In a moment, gray sausage curls flapping, her astronomy professor was beside her peering into the telescope. "Silly girl," she said, "thee is looking at thy engagement ring!"

With a clanging clattering crash, the ten strokes of the electromagnetic bells that began the Vassar day resounded through Genevieve's confusion. She was lying face down, her left hand only inches from her eyes. In the gray light the hand looked huge and strange—a moonscape. There was no engagement ring on her hand now. But in exactly three weeks a diamond solitaire would be glinting on her third finger, replacing Antares as the dominant glow on her horizon.

Genevieve closed her eyes again, annihilating time and space. Now there was only darkness through which names drifted: Rawdon Stapleton. Genevieve Dall Stapleton. Mrs. Rawdon Stapleton.

Names can never hurt me, whispered a childish voice.

Are you sure? asked an adult voice.

"Gen!"

Across the moonscape of her hand Genevieve saw her roommate, Alice Gansevoort, combing her blond hair before the mirror above the bureau. With Spartan intensity, Alice poured cold water into the washbasin and flung it into her face.

Alice saw herself as the realist of their suite, the practical spirit. Without her housekeeping abilities, Alice maintained, Genevieve and her fellow honors student, Elizabeth Wellcombe, would disappear in a chaos of unmade beds and unsorted laundry, piled-up books and newspapers and magazines. There were times when Genevieve suspected Alice was right.

"Why did we stay up so late last night?" Genevieve asked, rubbing her eyes.

"We were discussing fundamentals," Alice said. "People always stay up late when they discuss fundamentals."

"When I graduate I'm going to write an article," Genevieve said. "I'm going to tell the world that college is dangerous to a woman's health not because it strains her delicate constitution but because she's liable to get idiotic opinionated roommates who spend half the night arguing with each other."

"It was a very important argument," Alice said. "Now get up. Rawdon and his crew will be arriving right after chapel. We won't have time to come back here and change."

"I see no need to wear anything extraordinary," Genevieve said. "They've invited themselves, after all."

"Sometimes your attitude toward that man is incomprehensible," Alice said. "On your feet or I'll open the door and let Wellcombe talk you into old maidenhood."

"You're too hard on her," Genevieve said. "She's not completely opposed to marriage."

"She's spiritually warped," Alice said. "She hates men. I sometimes think she's infected you."

"She's critical of them. Which is better than adoring them."

"I don't adore men. I'm realistic about them. Now get out of that bed. We don't have time to start the argument all over again."

Genevieve brushed mechanically at her hair and stared at the photograph of Rawdon Stapleton on her desk. It was the last picture she had taken in their summer of love four years ago. Wearing an open-necked yachting shirt,

Rawdon stood on the bluff at Kemble Manor, gazing into the distance. There was a brooding sadness in his expression, but it did not detract from the perfection of that supremely masculine face.

In two or three hours—less if Alice was correct—she would be kissing that mouth. For some reason, Genevieve found herself wishing Rawdon had not decided to visit Vassar on the way back from the intercollegiate regatta on Lake George. She did not want to deal with Rawdon in this last month of her college career.

She wished she could spend the day at the observatory studying sunspots with Maria Mitchell. Together she and her astronomy professor would ponder these immense explosions on the star that gave their solar system light and warmth. They would discuss the differences in shape and color and frequency. No one at Vassar had done more work on sunspots than Genevieve. She had fallen in love with astronomy—or perhaps with Maria Mitchell—in sophomore year, that bitter year when she realized that she did not have the talent to be a great writer.

"Gen! For someone who says we shouldn't adore men . . ."

Snap! went a blanket as Alice made the bed. There was no time, no reason, to explain to Alice what she was really thinking. In ten minutes Genevieve was dressed in a trim dark-blue walking suit with a small stylish bustle.

In the sitting room, Elizabeth Wellcombe sat on the couch, her straight brown hair twisted into the usual efficient bun, wearing her usual black dress without a bustle or a ruffle or even a single attractive button.

"Good heavens!" Alice said, glaring at Wellcombe. "Are you going to wear that outfit to lunch with our Princeton guests? Genevieve has spent four years trying to convince Rawdon that Vassar isn't an old-maid factory. You'll undo her arguments in five seconds."

"Genevieve knows I can't afford to own a different dress for every hour of the day," Wellcombe said.

"I'll bet you're not even wearing a corset," Alice said, ignoring Wellcombe's plea of poverty. There were times when Alice could be cruel.

"I'm not wearing one, either," Genevieve said. "Rawdon says he doesn't care if I ever wear one."

"Really, Gen. How can you discuss a thing like that with your fiancé?" Alice said.

"I think most men know about the existence of corsets. They're advertised on signboards along the Hudson twenty feet high."

Alice was not usually so prudish. She was really protesting Genevieve's alliance with Wellcombe on the much debated issue of the corset and its evil effects on women's health. In spite of Wellcombe's acerbic Boston personality, Genevieve's relationship to her was basically friendly. She rather liked

Wellcombe's habit of calling their classmates by their last names, the way men referred to each other. She liked her instinct for equality.

Unlike most of their class, Wellcombe was not at Vassar because she had a rich father. Wellcombe had saved the money for her Vassar tuition by working for two years as a clerk in a Boston department store, living on bread and water half the time, going without a fire through two New England winters. When she talked about "work" and "earning a living" she surrounded these ordinary words with an aura of significance that Genevieve found intriguing.

The three suitemates settled down to wait for the eight bells that would summon them to breakfast at 6:45. "What did you think of that article by Antoinette Brown Blackwell in *The Woman's Journal?*" Wellcombe asked Genevieve.

"Very interesting," Genevieve said, avoiding Alice's glare. Alice did not think that Genevieve should even read the *Journal,* which was the guiding light of the women's movement. In the article Mrs. Brown maintained that a modern woman could combine marriage with a career.

"I should have mentioned it during our argument last night," Wellcombe said. "But I'm not sure, given the limitations of the modern American male, whether it's practical advice."

Last night's argument had begun when Wellcombe declared that Vassar should be doing more to support the faltering women's movement. Twenty-eight years after Susan B. Anthony had issued her call for the vote and equal economic rights at Seneca Falls, New York, the movement had been deserted by most of its male allies and now seemed in danger of splitting into factions. Alice had retorted by saying good riddance to the movement. As far as she could see, it did nothing but strain relationships between the sexes. Once and for all, Alice maintained, women should accept the existence of a man's sphere and a woman's sphere and agree that neither sex should trespass on the other's territory.

"Vassar's whole plan of education assumes this arrangement," Alice argued. "It's aimed at giving a woman a healthy body and a well-trained mind. A Vassar graduate is ideally prepared to achieve the cornerstone of a happy marriage—rational love."

Alice spoke with the aggressive assurance that most of the women in Vassar agreed with her. Genevieve was one of them. She and Rawdon had discussed rational love and its importance. He had resisted the idea at first; for Rawdon the essence of love was the enchantment that had consumed them at Kemble Manor. Only after strenuous explanation did he reluctantly accept this vital concept. Perhaps that was why Genevieve listened with a certain undercurrent of sympathy to Wellcombe's rebuttal.

"Rational love is a beautiful idea that isn't going to work because the two spheres are hopelessly unequal," Wellcombe said. With rhetoric worthy of

Susan B. Anthony at her most scathing, Wellcombe maintained that contemporary marriage swallowed a woman as totally as it obliterated her surname, and the only thing that would alter this fate was the achievement of "genuine independence"—the right to vote and work at a paying job.

Out in the corridor, the electromagnetic bells clanged for breakfast. They went down the three broad flights of stairs to the ground floor. Standing in the hall in her familiar white shirtwaist and straight black skirt was Maria Mitchell.

"Genevieve," she said, tossing her gray curls and allowing a glow of affection to kindle in her severe, deep-socketed dark eyes, "I almost woke thee last night. There was a perfect shower of meteors about three-thirty A.M. But I remembered just in time that thee would be occupied today with the visit of thy beloved. So I got Helena Gordon to stand an extra watch instead. She's still at it, tracking a large one that looks a good deal like a comet."

"Fascinating," Genevieve murmured. Why did that word "beloved," which came so naturally to Professor Mitchell's lips from her Nantucket Quaker girlhood, make her feel uncomfortable?

"Helena tells me she's decided to accept the offer from Harvard. I still wish thee were going. I'd have no doubts about thy performance there."

Last month, in an unparalleled gesture, the Harvard School of Astronomy had offered a one-year appointment to a Vassar graduate to assist in the study of sunspots. The seven astronomy majors had spent much of their time wondering whom Miss Mitchell would nominate. Genevieve had thought she was almost certain to win the contest. A year at Harvard gradually became a very exciting idea to her.

There was only one problem. It would require her to postpone her wedding, which was planned for December 21st. She realized this might make Rawdon unhappy. For three weeks she had oscillated between defiantly insisting on her right to accept the opportunity and making a tender plea for patience, forbearance.

Two nights ago, while she was standing her regular meteor watch, Maria Mitchell had told her she was selecting Helena Gordon, a tall solemn girl from Delaware, to go to Harvard. The astronomer said that Genevieve's imminent engagement and December wedding had been the reason she eliminated her. Genevieve had gone back to her room in the dawn and wept bitter confused tears.

"Why didn't you get that Harvard appointment?" Wellcombe asked as they sat down to breakfast. "I thought you were the school's leading authority on sunspots."

Genevieve explained. "What a shame," Wellcombe said. "It seems to me astronomy is a profession a married woman could pursue, assuming her husband was willing to cooperate and live near an observatory."

"You make that sound so simple," Alice said. "Genevieve's fiancé is going to work for the *New York Times.* I don't believe there are any observatories in the middle of Manhattan Island."

"Further proof of Gotham's primitive cultural and scientific state," Wellcombe said. "All you know how to do in the great metropolis is make money and spend it."

"Rawdon plans to start his own newspaper eventually," Genevieve said. "I think it will do a great deal to change the moral atmosphere of New York."

"A rather breathtaking ambition," Wellcombe said.

"Rawdon is breathtaking in more ways than one," Alice said.

"He is incredibly good-looking," Wellcombe admitted. "I can see how Genevieve found him irresistible."

For some reason, that compliment induced a strange gloom in Genevieve's mind. What was wrong with her today? First the weird dream, now an inability to accept this perfectly straightforward compliment from someone who was seldom inclined to have a good word to say for any man.

Alice's prediction of an early arrival was soon punctured. There was no sign of Princeton's colors on Vassar's green lawn either before or after chapel. Genevieve teased Alice about her premature expectations. "I think you're the one who wants a certain oarsman to go weak in the pectoral muscles at the sight of you."

She was talking about Isaac Mayer, the bow oar in Rawdon's crew. He was the fifth member of the crew to pursue Alice. The other four had retired with badly bruised hearts and egos. Isaac was unusual. Short, burly, intense, he was the only Jew in the Princeton class of 1876. His father was a wealthy cotton broker and banker. There was more than enough money to support Alice in the style to which Jefferson Gansevoort's daughter had grown accustomed. But Genevieve had always imagined Alice marrying into one of the old New York families.

"He's interesting," Alice said, coloring prettily. "He can make almost anything sound interesting. European politics. Even American politics. He's made an awful lot of men I once found rather attractive seem boring."

Genevieve glanced through a copy of the *New York Times.* On the front page was the story of an "enormous" turnout of Union veterans for a Decoration Day parade in New Jersey, led by Major General Jonathan Stapleton. The reporter declared it was a good omen for the Republicans' chance of carrying the state.

"Here they come!" cried Alice, who was playing sentinel at the window.

Even Wellcombe abandoned *The Woman's Journal* for a look. Up the drive between the sheltering oaks thundered half the Princeton crew in an old victoria pulled by two skinny horses. Rawdon had dismissed the hackman and was holding the reins, urging the horses to do their utmost. Behind him sat Isaac Mayer, holding a large silver cup in his lap, and Clay Pendleton, Rawdon's dissolute South Carolina roommate, strumming a mandolin. They were all wearing their orange-and-black sweaters, which alone would have won the attention of every stroller on the lawn.

"They must have won the race," Alice cried.

A dash to the mirror for a quick touch of the comb by Alice, a hasty smoothing of skirts by Genevieve, while Wellcombe watched tolerantly. They rushed down the first two flights of stairs, then paused and sedately descended the last flight with Wellcombe trailing diffidently in their wake.

They found their three visitors grouped before the faculty member on duty at the reception desk, a tiny shriveled professor of French named Dorcas Watson. Clay Pendleton began strumming "Genevieve, Sweet Genevieve" on his mandolin the moment he saw her. Miss Watson started violently and glared at him. He went right on playing. "Ah Miss Dall," she said. "I was about to send someone up to notify you. These—er—gentlemen just arrived. You may entertain them in the north parlor."

"Hello, darling," Rawdon said, striding toward her. He had grown two or three inches during his four years at Princeton. He was now almost as tall as his father. His body had added flesh. There was new breadth, new solidity to his shoulders. All traces of boyishness had vanished. For a moment, Genevieve wondered if she saw a disturbing new sensuality in the contour of his mouth. Then he had both her hands, he was kissing her firmly, confidently on the lips.

Impossible, she thought. It was impossible to resist the feeling of being absorbed, consumed, engulfed. Rawdon held the kiss much longer than decorum recommended. In fact, decorum frowned on such liberties in public. But Rawdon was indifferent to etiquette books. He spun Genevieve around, his arm pressing her against him, and pointed to the cup Isaac Mayer was holding. "Second prize," he said. "The best piece of silver Princeton's ever won on the water."

"Marvelous," Genevieve murmured.

"Is that all? Don't I get another kiss? We want kisses from every one of you. We're ready to kiss the whole school."

Miss Watson looked as though she might explode—or have a nervous collapse. Genevieve extricated herself from the encircling arm and told Rawdon to behave himself. She introduced Wellcombe and led them to the north parlor.

There, Alice coquettishly kissed Rawdon on the cheek. "Does that make you feel better?" she said. He seized her in a pseudopassionate embrace and groaned, "Oh why why why didn't I meet you before I fell in love with the cold brilliant Miss Dall?" Rawdon frequently pretended that a single glance at Alice drove him berserk.

With a flourish he took a flask from his back pocket and emptied it into the trophy cup. He swirled the liquor around and offered the cup to Genevieve. "Have some champagne and brandy punch," he said.

"Rawdon, you'll get us expelled," Genevieve said. "Didn't I tell you about those sophomores who were sent home last year for drinking wine in their rooms?"

"Pendleton," Rawdon said, "stand sentry duty until each of us has a drink to celebrate."

"All clear," Pendleton called from the door. Genevieve took a swallow of the punch. The champagne had gone flat. It did not taste very good, but it was strong. A single mouthful made her head swim.

Alice took a hearty swig and pronounced it delicious. Alarming hypocrisy, Genevieve thought.

Wellcombe declined the cup. "I don't drink alcohol," she said.

"Ah, that's why we brought Pendleton along," Rawdon said. "He never touches the stuff either unless we force it down his throat."

"Lately, I've been able to manage it on my own," Pendleton said, deserting his post at the door. "Will one of you ladies take over as sentinel?"

Alice volunteered and the three men quickly finished the contents of the cup. Genevieve frowned as Pendleton drained the dregs. His lipsmacking enjoyment only reinforced her conviction that he was a very bad influence on Rawdon. As a student of physiognomy, she saw nothing but moral weakness in the burly southerner's heavy jaw, his beetling brow, his thick-lipped mocking mouth. She had been dismayed when Rawdon told her that Clay was planning to stay in the North after graduation and had also gotten a job on the *New York Times*.

The punch increased the oarsmen's already high spirits. Rawdon hiccupped extravagantly. "We've come to Vassar to get smashed. Isn't this the place for it? Your secret's out, ladies; everyone at Princeton has been reading that article in *The Yale Literary Magazine*. Is it true?"

He took Genevieve by both arms and studied her intently. "Has my beloved been smashed? She looks perfectly sound to me. But you women are geniuses at hiding things from men."

Everyone at Vassar had seen the article, too. It described a custom that was already flourishing when Genevieve and Alice arrived in 1872. They had awakened one morning in the fall of that year to find a bouquet of flowers and a note with a love poem in it, addressed to Alice. They were baffled until a New Yorker in one of the upper classes explained that this was the first step in the process known as "smashing." Usually the object of the smasher's affection resisted for a while. Eventually, most of them collapsed and surrendered to days and nights of intense confessions and tender professions of affection. But this intimacy was usually brief, their New York friend warned them. After two or three weeks, the smasher went in search of another quarry.

"That article was full of vicious exaggerations, Rawdon," Genevieve said.

"Oh?" Rawdon said. "You've never been smashed?"

"Never."

"How about you, ladies?" he said, turning to Alice and Wellcombe. They shook their heads, but Wellcombe looked uncomfortable. She was one of Vassar's preeminent smashers. Alice frequently claimed that Wellcombe yearned to smash Genevieve.

Although it was clearly time to drop the subject, Rawdon persisted, like a prosecuting attorney. "You mean the article is a complete fabrication? Such things never go on here?"

"It does happen occasionally, but there's a perfectly simple explanation for it," Genevieve said. "When you come here at the age of seventeen or eighteen, you're away from home for the first time. You're lonely. You're grateful for any show of affection. Sometimes it gets out of hand."

"I've indulged in a few of these friendships," Wellcombe said. "They're pretty much as Genevieve describes them. We all need some affection in our lives. Women simply express it more freely than men."

"I've got a better explanation," Rawdon said. "It's part of the old-maid machinery. Part of the modern woman's plan to eliminate men completely from her life. From the country, if she can get away with it."

"Rawdon," Isaac Mayer said, "did it ever occur to you that we've got a few customs at Princeton that are pretty bizarre? The freshman rush, for instance."

"Yes," Wellcombe said, "how many arms and legs got broken this year?"

The freshman rush was an annual melee in which the Princeton sophomore class tried to prevent the freshman class from organizing and electing its officers. Bones were frequently broken, and for the next week Old Nassau was full of black eyes and split lips.

"I think he just enjoys arousing the Amazon in Genevieve," Clay Pendleton drawled.

"If he doesn't shut up," Isaac Mayer said, nervously noting the storm gathering in Alice's blue eyes, "he'll arouse the whole tribe."

"Personally, I think the only thing that needs smashing is Stapleton's ego," Clay Pendleton said.

"I agree most heartily," Genevieve said.

"I surrender," Rawdon said, throwing up his hands. "Are we going to be allowed to explore this magnificent institution? Or are we quarantined here for the rest of the day because we're carrriers of that awful disease husbanditis?"

"We can go anywhere on the campus that we please," Genevieve said.

"Amazing," Rawdon said. "The first place I want to see is this famous observatory which has absorbed so many of your daytime and nighttime hours."

"I'd rather show Isaac the gymnasium and riding academy," Alice said. She had won a number of prizes in gymnastics. "We'll meet you down at the baseball field. I think the Giants are playing the Orioles."

"You have a baseball team?" Clay Pendleton asked, frankly amazed.

"We have six of them, organized in a league," Alice said.

"All part of the master plan to eliminate men," Rawdon said, smiling triumphantly.

"Perhaps you'd like to see our natural-history museum, Mr. Pendleton," Wellcombe said.

At the observatory, Genevieve showed Rawdon how they moved the ton-and-a-half dome on its circular iron track, using pulleys that required only ten pounds of pressure. Positioning one of the three smaller telescopes, she inserted a smoked-glass cap on the lens and let Rawdon study the sun until he saw one of the dark irregularly shaped explosions known as sunspots emerge on the surface. "What does it mean?" he asked skeptically.

"You have to study hundreds of them to find out," she said. "We know they come in eleven-year cycles and we think they may affect the weather on earth. They definitely disturb magnetic compasses."

"Fascinating," he said grudgingly.

"I wish you could stay for the evening, so we could look at the stars together," she said. "They're so beautiful. You'd be thrilled, Rawdon, I know you would."

"I'll buy you a telescope and we'll look at them together from our parlor window in New York."

She shook her head. "You can't use a telescope in the middle of a city. Too much ground light. Anyway, an amateur's telescope would be an awful come-down after using this." She gave the huge brass-and-steel equatorial an affectionate pat.

As they left the observatory, Professor Mitchell came striding up the path toward them. "Ah, Genevieve," she said with a warm smile. "Is this thy beloved?"

Genevieve introduced Rawdon, and Maria Mitchell shook his hand. "Thee art one of the most fortunate young men in America," she said. "Thee art getting a wife with one of the finest minds I have encountered. I hope thee will give her a chance to use it."

"Oh, I will," Rawdon said, smiling at Genevieve. "I've already learned I can't stop her from using it. She has her own opinions about everything under the sun and on it."

"He's just been looking at sunspots," Genevieve said.

"I understand thee hopes to publish a newspaper someday. That would be an admirable project on which a husband and an intelligent wife could work together."

Genevieve told Professor Mitchell they were on their way to the baseball game. The astronomer pulled a large gold watch from the pocket of her skirt. "Thee have exactly two minutes and forty seconds to get there."

As they walked toward the baseball field, Rawdon chuckled over Maria Mitchell's precision. "She should work for a railroad," he said.

"The astronomy department sets all the clocks in the school," Genevieve said. "We check the time against the meridian each night."

"I give up," Rawdon said. "That's enough astronomical mumbo-jumbo."

They watched five innings of the baseball game. The Giants were the leaders of the league, and at the end of the fifth inning they were ahead by ten runs. The three Princetonians were impressed by the hitting, but thought the fielding could use some improvement. "It's those straight skirts," Clay Pendleton said. "Why don't you wear knickers?"

"We haven't advanced quite that far," Wellcombe said. "But we'll get there eventually."

At lunch, Rawdon dominated the conversation, discussing the war that the Turks and the Russians were fighting in the Balkans. The conflict had been started by an American reporter, Aloysius MacGahan, who had exposed Turkish brutality in rebellious Bulgaria and thrown all Europe into an uproar. Russia had intervened to protect the hapless Bulgar Slavs, England had rushed a fleet to the Bosporus to support the reeling Turks, and Europe trembled on the brink of a gigantic explosion. "All because one reporter told the truth," Rawdon said.

This was the Rawdon that Genevieve loved. She took quiet credit for his decision to become a journalist. They had thought there would be opposition from his father. Reporters were considered bohemians, only a narrow notch above actors and actresses in their manners and morals, and a gaping notch below the sort of respectability that families like the Stapletons expected from their sons. But her father's career as a newspaperman made it difficult for the General to object. He had even helped Rawdon get a job on the *New York Times*.

"Are you going to go with him, Gen, when he roams the world in search of a war to start?" Isaac asked.

"Why not?" Clay Pendleton said. "If that Harvard doctor is right, they won't have any children to worry about."

"Are you talking about Dr. William Clark?" Genevieve asked.

"Rawdon was quoting him on the train. He says higher education lowers a woman's fertility."

"The man's an idiot," Wellcombe said.

"Whether he's right or wrong doesn't worry me in the least," Rawdon said.

"Well, it worries me," Genevieve said. "His book is nothing but a slander designed to keep women in subjection."

"Why did you bring up Dr. Clark? You've awakened the Amazon again, Pendleton," Rawdon said.

"I'm beginning to think this is no ordinary Amazon you've got on your hands," Clay drawled. "She may well be the reincarnation of Antiope, their famous Queen."

This intrusion of her old summer name blurred Genevieve's anger, even though Clay was talking about a different Antiope. Rawdon did not seem to notice the coincidence. He smiled complacently at her. "Oh, I think I'll keep her busy at home with a brat or two. I have confidence in my virility no matter how much damage Vassar may have done to her."

"Vassar has not done any damage to me in any way," Genevieve said.

"Mayer," Clay Pendleton said, in a pseudo-stern voice, "this is all your fault." He smiled cheerfully at Alice. "Mayer reads everything in print. Two illiterates like Stapleton and me would never have discovered Dr. Clark's existence."

"Is that true?" Alice said, turning her bold blue eyes on Isaac.

"It's a gross—an absolutely gross—slander. The doctor was quoted at length in the *New York Herald*," Isaac spluttered, disintegrating beneath Alice's glare.

"You obviously need further training in the art and science of Amazonian warfare, Mayer," Rawdon said. "Meanwhile, I think we have established one scientific fact: a college education does not improve a woman's disposition."

After lunch, they went for a row on Mill Cove Lake. Rawdon immediately organized a race. He and Genevieve competed against Alice and Isaac and Clay Pendleton and Wellcombe. The Massachusetts–South Carolina team won by two lengths. Wellcombe turned out to be an expert oarswoman. She matched Pendleton's stroke perfectly in strength and timing. Genevieve repeatedly missed Rawdon's beat and he kept pulling much too hard, veering them off at a disastrous angle. Alice and Isaac had a similar problem.

"If we had you with us at Lake George, we would have beaten Harvard," Rawdon called to Wellcombe. To Genevieve he muttered, "If she cut her hair, no one would have noticed the difference, even in a rowing suit."

Genevieve forced a smile. It was cruel, but true. She often smiled at the cruel things Alice said about Wellcombe. Why should she object to Rawdon's cruelty? Perhaps it bothered her because it was so gratuitous. Wellcombe had done her best to be pleasant all day.

The June sun beat down. Mill Cove Lake acquired some of the characteristics of a steam bath. Rawdon suggested a stroll in the grove of huge old oaks along the brook that fed the lake. By mutual consent, they split into couples in the cool shadows. Everyone assumed that the lovers, Rawdon and Genevieve, wanted to be alone.

As soon as they were at a discreet distance, Rawdon drew Genevieve to him for a long, passionate kiss. Now it begins, Genevieve thought, as those muscular oarsman's arms pressed her against his big masculine body. She closed her eyes, expecting to find in the darkness the familiar sense of being overwhelmed, consumed. But all she felt was refusal, resistance, a silent angry *no* that stiffened her mind and body.

Rawdon's hands were in her hair. He pressed her head against his chest. "Gen, Gen," he said. "It's still there. The first love. After four years. I'd thought we'd lost it once or twice. Did you?"

"Yes," she said.

For a moment she remembered the guilt she had felt during her second term at Vassar, when she realized she had stopped reading Rawdon's testament. Her life as a thinking, learning woman had engulfed her. There were times when she had thought Rawdon himself no longer mattered. But a letter from him, full of good humor and affection, followed by seeing him during a weekend in New York, would change her mind. Rawdon remained part of her life.

"I . . . even tried to lose it more than once. Did you?"

"No," she said.

But she had lost something else—the vague expectation that Vassar might somehow transform her into an extraordinary being with a preordained task, a burning commitment to science or art that would give her life irresistible purpose and meaning. Instead, she had discovered she was merely intelligent. She could master almost any subject, from English literature to astronomy. But this ability shed no special light on Genevieve Dall's future. If anything, it became more opaque.

"Even when I was trying to lose it, I was struggling to keep it at the same time. I was like the man in the Bible saying, 'Oh Lord, I believe. Help Thou my unbelief.' Do you understand?"

"Yes," she said.

That was a lie. She did not understand what had happened to her four years ago. She did not really understand what was happening now. She only knew that the anxiety mounting in her had nothing to do with the old fearful delight Rawdon had evoked at Kemble Manor.

Rawdon's lips brushed her neck. "All year I've felt the need for you grow in me, Gen. Now it's beginning to flower. It's taken root in me. It's the old need and something stronger, finer. Have you felt the same way?"

"Sometimes," she said, as his hands moved up and down her back. He used to fondle her that way at Kemble Manor. Now his touch stirred only fragments of the desire she had felt four years ago. She was no longer that demoralized female yearning for surrender. She was a thinking woman now, a being with a mind.

Were the yearning female and the thinking woman irreconcilable opposites? All day, Rawdon had stirred antagonism, disagreement in her mind. These negative reactions had seeped into her feelings, her flesh. Was that a minor or a possibly major discovery?

"When I was in New York a few weeks ago, I looked through my scrapbooks. I came across our testaments. Do you remember any of yours?"

"Rawdon—it's been four years."

He kissed her again. His hands moved up her body to her breasts. Oh. She was there in the hot still upper hall at Kemble Manor with his arms around her. She remembered the wish to be engulfed, consumed. But now she resisted, disliked the idea.

" 'A true man,' " Rawdon whispered, " 'asks only for trust. He vows to merit love, knowing it is a gift he can never deserve . . .' "

" 'A true woman . . . feels what her beloved feels. She thinks his thoughts . . . she lives his life . . .' "

It was amazing. Another person seemed to be reciting those extravagant words while Genevieve Dall listened, appalled by her spiritual distance from them.

"I hated the idea of rational love at first," Rawdon said. "I thought it was going to ruin everything we had. Now I think we can blend the two loves into something better than either of them."

They walked through the trees until they reached Sunset Hill, eighty feet above the rest of Vassar's grounds. Around them glowed a green countryside with brooks and groves and well-tended farms, redolent with peace and happiness. "Unreal," Rawdon said. "They shouldn't put colleges out in the country."

For Rawdon New York was the real world. The great metropolis with its roaring elevated trains and packed streets and fetid slums. It was his latest reason for disliking Princeton—and, presumably, Vassar.

"I wish Harvard was in New York," Genevieve said. "Maria Mitchell wanted to send me there to work in their graduate program on sunspots."

"What the hell did she mean by that?" Rawdon snarled. It was hard to believe it was the same voice that had been talking about blending loves a few minutes ago.

"She would have proposed me for a fellowship Harvard's offering—if we weren't going to be married."

"I didn't like the way that old Quaker bat looked at you when she was talking about your wonderful mind. She's trying to lure you back into the old-maid machinery."

"Rawdon, once and for all, Vassar is *not* an old-maid factory! A woman doesn't have to be an old maid to have a career. She can combine it with marriage if her husband cooperates. I read an article on it by Antoinette Brown Blackwell in *The Woman's Journal* yesterday."

"Gen—I'm getting damn sick of these opinionated three-name women messing up our lives. I'm hoping I'll have heard the last of them when I put that ring on your finger."

"Well, you won't! I intend to go right on reading them. I intend to go right on using my mind."

"Are you trying to tell me that you want to go to Harvard? Does that mean I'm expected to give up my job on the *New York Times* and work for the *Boston Evening Transcript* reporting what doddering Ralph Waldo Emerson said to senile Henry Wadsworth Longfellow?"

"Of course not. I was only trying to tell you that I felt a little sad about it, that's all. I wish I could become two women, and one could go to Harvard and the other could walk up the aisle of Grace Church next December. That's all I was trying to say."

"And what was I supposed to say?"

"Just that . . . you understood. You sympathize."

"I understand. I sympathize," Rawdon said.

"I hate to interrupt the course of true love," Clay Pendleton called from several dozen feet back in the trees at the bottom of the hill. "But we have a five-o'clock train to catch."

"We're coming," Rawdon said.

He took both of Genevieve's hands and glared at her with a strange smile on his lips. Was it a mixture of anger and tenderness? "If Antoinette Brown Blackwell can change your mind, maybe I can change it back," he said.

There it was, the voice of the husband, confident of his coming ascendancy. In spite of their midnight discussions at Vassar, the calm, thorough analysis of human sexuality in their physiology course, Genevieve realized that she knew pathetically little about how love and marriage actually worked. Did Rawdon really want a wife who stayed home with a brat or two, thinking his thoughts, living his life? Could rational love speak or act in such an atmosphere?

His final kiss was fierce, full of anger. Genevieve's response was resistance, nothing but resistance. Her arms dangled, refusing to return the embrace. Rawdon stepped back, baffled, bewildered. "I love you so much," he said.

Genevieve flung her arms around him, overwhelmed by contrition, by remembered sweetness. "It's all right," she said. "Everything will be all right . . . in New York."

A half hour later she and Alice and Wellcombe stood on the steps and

BOOK II / 125

watched their guests ride down the lane of oaks and vanish between the two small stone houses that flanked the gate.

"I never thought I could fall in love with someone who's shorter than I am," Alice said. "But I think it's happening."

"Dear, dear," Wellcombe said, "it makes me wonder if Rawdon is right—they were carrying the germs of husbanditis. I'm sure I haven't contracted it, but I did find Mr. Pendleton surprisingly intelligent for a southerner. I suspect his claim to being a know-nothing is a pose."

Upstairs in their rooms, Genevieve picked up the copy of *The Woman's Journal* and opened it to Antoinette Brown Blackwell's article. She stared at the opening sentence: "Marriage for a modern woman will be an incident in her life—a grand experience, a solemn relation, but it will not be the purpose of her existence."

Genevieve flipped the pages of the journal. Familiar names flickered past: Anna Brackett, Eliza Duffey, Caroline Dall. Genevieve was not related to this famous Dall, a Bostonian who was in her fifties. But she read almost everything Caroline Dall wrote. It pleased her to see the name Dall on calls for "sexual equivalency," the reform of divorce and inheritance laws and the correction of other "dysfunctions" between men and women. Rawdon liked to make fun of her. He called her Caroline Dull. Unfortunately he was half right. Caroline Dall's prose was often labored. But there were plenty of dull male writers around. Why didn't Rawdon ridicule them?

After supper, Alice went off to converse with one of her fellow French majors. Genevieve retreated to her room. But studying was out of the question. She did not even open a book. She sat at her desk and stared at the photograph of Rawdon on the bluff at Kemble Manor. How could she fail to respond to the need on that noble, beautiful face? It was essentially the same face that she had seen here at Vassar a few hours ago. The added flesh, the increased self-assurance, even the disturbing, possibly imaginary sensuality she saw on his mouth changed nothing essential. He was still Rawdon. She sat there, feeling his lips on her throat, hearing bits and pieces of the day's conversation.

Keep her at home with a brat or two.

A true woman.

The old-maid machinery.

The need for you growing in me.

Someone was knocking on the door. "Dall—are you all right?" Wellcombe called.

Genevieve opened the door. Wellcombe was in her dark blue night robe. Hours must have passed. "I—I heard you crying," she said.

Only then did Genevieve realize her face was wet with tears. She heard someone speaking from a great distance. It took a moment for her to realize it was her own voice saying, "I can't marry Rawdon. I love him, but I can't marry him. I don't know what to do."

FOUR

It was almost eight o'clock by the time Jonathan Stapleton escaped from Republican headquarters at the Fifth Avenue Hotel. The streetlamps glowed in Madison Square, casting weird shadows on the arm of the proposed statue of the Goddess of Liberty, which was being constructed in Paris as a gift to the United States on its hundredth birthday. The arm was being displayed to encourage donations for the pedestal. So far the response had been unenthusiastic. Most New Yorkers were wary of importing French ideas about liberty only five years after the Paris Commune had defied the elected government of France, shot the Archbishop of Paris and other hostages and started a civil war in the city's streets that led to the slaughter of thousands.

Jonathan climbed into a hack and told the driver to get him to Stuyvesant Square as quickly as possible. He was already half an hour late for Cynthia's last dinner party of the season.

More than once he had damned himself for letting Ulysses Grant talk him into becoming national treasurer of the Republican Party. But it was hard to say no to a President. The Republicans desperately needed a new face, a man with no previous political scars, to shake money out of the faithful if they were going to avert disaster in November.

It was eight-thirty when he debarked before his brownstone house. The parlor was aglow. He could see figures moving behind the lace curtains. Whom had Cynthia invited? The Roosevelts. He could not remember the others. He had too many names wandering through his tired brain. In the hall, Cousteau took his hat and cane and spoke in the weary tones of a man whose patience was all but exhausted by his employer's unpredictability. "Everything's ready for you, General. I gave Muzzey orders to draw your bath and lay out your clothes an hour ago."

Washington Muzzey, his Negro valet, was waiting for him when he emerged from his bath. He spoke to Jonathan with his usual familiarity. His father and his grandfather had been Stapleton servants. "That damned New

Orleans nigger was up here at seven o'clock telling me to do this and that, as if I didn't know what had to be done to get a gentleman ready for dinner. But I was politeness itself to him."

"I'll bet you were."

Jonathan had tried, without much success, to bridle Muzzey's loose tongue. His habit of looking down on the blacks Cynthia had imported from Louisiana infuriated her. She frequently urged Jonathan to get rid of him. He resisted the idea. Muzzey had followed him into the army and lost his right foot to an exploding shell in the Wilderness.

Jonathan descended the stairs with his usual caution; the knee brace made it a tricky business. As he reached the doorway of the parlor, he heard Cynthia say, "Well, I prefer my women polite and my men passionate!"

That marvelous voice still stirred something primary deep in his body, a unique blend of the spiritual and the physical. Cynthia was in the center of the room, her head thrown back, her face in profile. Her emerald-green silk gown revealed her lovely white shoulders, the graceful neck. The diamond tiara he had given her for their last wedding anniversary glittered in her gleaming black hair. It was amazing the way she seemed immune to time. She was more beautiful at thirty-six than she had been when he married her.

On Cynthia's right stood a tall red-haired woman in an elaborate mauve dress. Jonathan's weary brain began to function. That must be the English actress, Madeline Terhune. Cynthia had asked him if he minded having her among the guests. Influenced, he suspected, by her brother Robert, Cynthia had begun mixing writers and theater people with members of old New York society at her dinner parties.

Jonathan had expressed some doubts about inviting bohemians into their house. Although he admitted that the Knickerbockers tended to be dull, there was something to be said for their determination to keep the amoral side of New York at bay. But Madeline Terhune was famous enough, fascinating enough, to transcend this objection. Recently she had created a newspaper furor by refusing to go to dinner—and, everyone presumed, to bed— with the Prince of Wales.

On Cynthia's left, Martha Bulloch Roosevelt was dressed in her usual white, with yards of lace on her skirt. She was a delicate contrast to her hostess's vibrant colors. Jonathan wondered if Mittie consciously cultivated the sibyllike pose she struck in public. He often felt as if he were watching an actress in a play whose plot remained obscure to him.

Jonathan strode across the room and touched Cynthia's arm. *"Meglio tardi che mai,"* he said, putting his hand on his heart. He hoped the Italian would be a reminder of their days and nights of love in Venice last summer, and other summers, back to the golden moments of their honeymoon.

Cynthia coolly, curtly, ignored his appeal. "You may think you're better late, General. But these poor starving people may never accept another invitation to this house. What's the excuse this time?"

"The usual. Another summons from Senator Conkling and the other panjandrums of the Republican Party, to discuss how we can raise a few more million to prevent the world from coming to an end."

Cynthia sighed explosively. "You have not been on time for dinner one night this week. I have to endure it. But you shouldn't expect our guests to go hungry to reelect General Grant."

"I agree with everything you say, my dear," Jonathan said. "You have carte blanche to abuse me all day tomorrow. But for the moment allow me to throw myself on the mercy of our guests."

"Has Mrs. Stapleton let us in on a secret, General?" asked the dapper mustached man on Madeline Terhune's right. "Are the Republicans going to nominate Grant for a third term?"

Lionel Bradford was obviously looking for a hint that would signal a rise in the market. Quick killings were his speciality. Cynthia liked Bradford for his Parisian style and charm. But Jonathan was wary of a man whose reputation on Wall Street had earned him the nickname the Wandering Wolf. To this day no one knew what country Bradford came from. He had arrived in New York in the late 1850s, his pockets full of money that was said to belong to the Rothschilds and other European bankers. Like Jay Gould, he had made millions speculating in gold, wheat and other commodities whose prices had soared during the war. Beneath the suavity Jonathan sensed something slimy about Bradford, but he had to be polite to him as long as he was a guest in his house.

"I'm told Grant's chances are fading. He's planning to take a trip around the world."

"Maybe they'll make him president of the Sandwich Islands. That would be about the right-size country for a man of his intelligence."

The speaker was Robert Legrand, Cynthia's brother, another unwelcome guest.

"Major," Jonathan said, "the spirit of Appomattox is already dying. There's no need to stomp on it."

"Have you heard the awful new song about Grant?" Mittie Roosevelt asked. She knew Jonathan was incapable of objecting to her smiling support of a fellow southerner.

"No matter how awful it is, if you sing it for me, Mittie, I'm sure I'll enjoy it," Jonathan said.

"A *total* capitulation," Cynthia said. "I wish I could manage that now and then."

Mittie Roosevelt twisted her lovely face into a caricature of Uncle Tom and sang:

> "Gone am de days
> When Grant was young and gay,
> Gone am his friends
> From de Old White House away.
> Gone am de thieves,
> All der heads are bendin' low,
> And now I hear de people calling,
> Go, Grant, go."

"Oh that's splendid. Politics aside, don't you think so, Jonathan?" Cynthia said.

"I can't stand it when you crinkle up your face that way, Mittie," Theodore Roosevelt said.

"I'm tempted to call for another chorus," chortled pudgy William Colford Schermerhorn. "But the General looks as though he may not tolerate it."

For a moment, a blaze of anger almost consumed Jonathan Stapleton's carefully maintained smile. He wanted to say something outrageous about mindless northern Democrats like Collie Schermerhorn and spineless liberal Republicans like Theodore Roosevelt. But these people were his guests. His wife was watching him, expecting his good-humored acquiescence.

"No, no," he said. "I wouldn't be surprised if Grant himself would get a laugh from it."

"I saw Jay Gould on the way down here," Bradford said. "He was still in a state of shock. He said you'd asked him for a million dollars this morning."

"I'm going to get it, too. I got it from Vanderbilt yesterday."

"I wish we Democrats had a few people we could ask for that kind of money."

Bradford had suddenly discovered an enthusiasm for the Democrats. He and his fellow European-born man of mystery, August Belmont, were raising money for the party of the people. No one had quite figured out what Bradford hoped to get out of it.

"What a marvelous scene," Madeline Terhune said. "To ask a man for a million dollars—in so many words. You Americans are the most astounding people."

The real scene had been considerably less than marvelous. Gould had kept Jonathan waiting for an hour and a half. Then he had sat there, the Mephistophelian eyes glittering in his bearded face, occasionally consulting the stock ticker beside his desk, while Jonathan made his plea. Gould had contemptuously refused to give him a cent until he saw whom the Republicans nominated for the presidency later this month. "I only give money to individuals, not to parties, Stapleton," he declared, implying that anyone who failed to follow this rule should be confined to an asylum.

When Jonathan said that a Democratic victory would nullify the sacrifices of the war and condemn the Negro to virtual slavery, Gould had sneered, "Nobody gives a damn for the war—or for Sambo—anymore, Stapleton."

"It's high drama for you, Miss Terhune," Cynthia said. "But I'm the one who has to sit home in utter boredom while he collects money to bushwhack the poor Democrats."

"This year the bushwhacking is going to be mutual," Robert said. "Would you care to make a bet on the election, General?"

"I only bet on horses, Major," Jonathan said. "Anyway, I think your crowing is a bit premature. I was talking to my friend Jack Reid, the managing editor of the *New York Times,* the other day. He's got a couple of file drawers full of ammunition that's going to make you Democrats pretty uncomfortable before November."

"I just came back from Louisiana, General," Robert said. "We're collecting the kind of ammunition down there that redeemed Mississippi last year."

Jonathan struggled to control his temper. It was infuriating to find himself face to face with revived southern arrogance in his own house. Ulysses Grant and his divided administration had never dealt effectively with the guerrilla terror that lay behind that hypocritical term "redemption." Grant's Missouri-born wife and her family of former slaveowners had a lot to do with it. One of Julia Grant's brothers was the most outspoken white supremacist in Mississippi.

"I'm surprised it hasn't occurred to you, Major, that we can use that kind of ammunition, too," he said.

Cousteau rescued them by announcing dinner. Jonathan offered William Colford Schermerhorn's wife, Cecilia, his arm and they strolled into the dining room. "That was nobly said, Jonathan," she whispered. He remembered for the first time in years that Cecilia's father had been one of New York's few Republicans.

In the dining room, Jonathan found that Madeline Terhune was seated on his right, Mittie on his left, and Cecilia was halfway down the table. It was another tiny *touché* in the invisible duel that Cynthia and Cecilia had been fighting for years. Cecilia had been one of the belles of his youth, with whom he had danced many a night away. Whether Cecilia disliked Cynthia for snaring him or Cynthia disliked Cecilia for once coveting him, Jonathan had no idea. But the two women had become instant enemies and seldom missed a chance to inflict small wounds. Yet they continued to invite each other to dinner and tea; a less astute observer would consider them friends. It was an aspect of the feminine personality that Jonathan could not comprehend. If a man disliked another man, he simply avoided him.

The Negro maids began serving oysters in Bearnaise sauce while Cousteau poured a golden Pouligny Montrachet 1869 into their glasses.

"Can we look forward to seeing you in Italy this summer, my dear?" Cecilia Schermerhorn asked Cynthia.

"I fear not," Cynthia said with another sigh. "The call of the Republican Party takes precedence over pleasure."

"Then you and Georgie must spend at least a month with us at Oyster Bay," Mittie Roosevelt said.

"I accept—with eternal gratitude," Cynthia said.

"Perhaps we can return your hospitality and lure you to New Jersey for a few weeks," Jonathan said.

"Out of the question, husband dear," Cynthia said. "I wouldn't inflict Kemble Manor's miserable heat and mosquitos on anyone—above all someone whose health is as delicate as Mittie's."

This was the first time Jonathan had heard Kemble Manor described as if it were in Mississippi. He stared down the table at Cynthia. What was happening? She had not said a single affectionate word to him since he came home.

"I'll strike a bargain with you, General," Theodore Roosevelt said. "I'll swap you a good-sized check for the Republican Party in return for the same amount for my Newsboys' Lodging House."

"Done," he said.

As far as Jonathan could tell, Roosevelt spent most of his time collecting money for various charities such as the newsboys and high schools for Italians. He had retired from his family's importing business several years ago. Jonathan was sometimes tempted to ask him what he did with himself all day. No, that was too cruel. God knows, the poor needed men like Roosevelt. For three years now, ever since the stock market crashed in 1873, the desperation in New York's slums had grown increasingly acute each winter. Jonathan donated to all the charitable appeals that came his way.

At the other end of the table, Collie Schermerhorn was explaining why he did not vote. Thanks to the Fifteenth Amendment, his Democratic ballot would be nullified by the Republican vote of some illiterate Negro sharecropper in South Carolina.

"Careful, Collie," Lionel Bradford said. "We Democrats depend a good deal on a lot of Irishmen on the Lower East Side who can't read or write either."

"That's more than enough of your nonsensical politics," Cynthia said. "I would like to offer a toast to Miss Terhune for her recent refusal of a dinner invitation from the Prince of Wales. She's won the admiration of women around the world."

The toast was promptly drunk with a murmured chorus of "Hear, hear."

"Was it morality or fear of damaging your career that prompted you to say no?" Cecilia Schermerhorn said.

Madeline Terhune flushed slightly. For a moment Jonathan thought she was going to make Cecilia look silly by curtly explaining that acceptance would have helped her theatrical career. "You might say it was the morality of an independent woman," Madeline said.

"Exactly," Cynthia said. "Miss Terhune made it plain that not every woman was at the Prince's beck and call. I think we all enjoyed seeing an arrogant male get his comeuppance."

"I agree," Mittie Roosevelt said.

Cecilia Schermerhorn was looking discomfited. Madeline Terhune sipped her wine and smiled contentedly. "Now, General," she said, "you must tell me the whole truth and nothing but about the presidential election. My British friends are depending on me to bring back inside information. Do you really think the Republicans have a chance in November?"

Madeline Terhune was not referring to women friends. Most English-women were as uninterested in politics as their American counterparts. He was talking to a courtesan, a woman who was proud of her ability to deal with men as more or less an equal.

"If I didn't think we had a chance, my dear Mrs. Terhune, I'd have steamship tickets to Italy in my pocket instead of train tickets to Buffalo."

He looked down the table at Cynthia as he said this. Did she understand his regret, his yearning to escape this never-shredding political warfare, the voice that compelled him to continue it? He could only hope.

"If the Republicans win, will you keep the South in utter subjection? It seems to me you've treated them worse than the British have treated Ireland," Madeline Terhune said.

"The South is a little more complicated than Ireland," Jonathan said. "We all want to welcome them back into the Union. But we can't agree on the terms. Perhaps you know the aphorism by Clausewitz—'War is a continuation of politics by another means'? In America, it's just the opposite. Politics has become a continuation of war by other means."

"I met Clausewitz in Italy years ago," Collie Schermerhorn said. "He was studying Napoleon's campaigns. A bore, I thought. Most Germans are bores."

"Who is this dreadful Prussian?" Cynthia asked.

"A practitioner of total war," Robert Legrand said. "He maintained that war should be waged against an enemy's men, women and children."

"Just like General Sherman and his bummers in Georgia," Mittie Roosevelt said.

"This turtle soup is superb," Theodore Roosevelt said. "Don't you think so, Mittie dear?"

The anxiety in his voice was unmistakable. So was the rage and, yes, loathing that momentarily suffused Mittie Roosevelt's delicate face as she looked across the table at her husband. For a split second, Jonathan Stapleton glimpsed the reality behind the part that Mittie Roosevelt was playing. He saw what was happening inside the Roosevelt marriage. He understood the offhand remarks he had heard from Cynthia about Mittie's languor, her habit of eating dinner alone in her bedroom, of frequently spending most of the day there. Theodore Roosevelt had had to quit his job to become both father and mother to their children. Mittie was a southern irreconcilable. She had all but withdrawn from the northern family in which she had found herself trapped by marriage.

"I find myself yearning for the minestrone in that restaurant on the Via Condotti," Cecilia Schermerhorn said. "What's the name of it, Collie?"

"Luciano's."

They were obeying their instincts, the good manners inculcated by mothers and governesses. Jonathan Stapleton did not blame them. He had seen the conversation go through similar contortions at a dozen dinner parties lately. Politics had become as explosive a topic as it had been before the war, when the mere mention of the word "abolition" at a New York dinner table inspired dismay.

At the other end of the table, Robert Legrand, apparently oblivious to this taboo, began discussing the South's preparation for the coming presidential election. Phrases like "White League" and "rifle clubs" sent prickly sensations across Jonathan Stapleton's scalp.

"I begin to see what you mean about a continuing war, General," Madeline Terhune said. "What happened to the good faith and mutual forgiveness President Lincoln urged on both sides?"

"It got used up," Robert Legrand said. "When southerners saw Yankees buying their land for a dollar an acre and illiterate niggers getting elected to state legislatures with the help of northern bayonets. That's when we decided to fight again."

Jonathan felt something loosen in his chest. Politeness, sophistication, good humor vanished. He was face to face with the ugly lying southern arrogance he had fought a war to destroy. "It's the way you fight that disgusts a real soldier, Major Legrand. Shooting unarmed men from ambush, massacring defenseless Negroes. Terrorizing men into giving up the vote."

"I'll admit it's disgusting, General," Robert Legrand said. "But it's less disgusting than the alternative—nigger government."

"That was never the alternative. There were white men, honest men, in the reconstruction governments until you smeared them with terms like carpetbaggers and scalawags."

"I never saw any difference between one of them and a nigger," Robert said.

"If that's your opinion, sir, I regret to say I can't see any difference between you and a piece of scum."

"Jonathan! Robert! Please!" Cynthia said.

The Negro maids began serving broiled Spanish mackerel, and Cousteau refilled the wineglasses with the last of the Montrachet. After several minutes of strained silence, couples began exchanging inconsequential small talk. It looked as if Jonathan had dealt a death blow to the party, until Lionel Bradford raised his glass. "May I propose a toast to the two daughters of the South we have with us tonight? No matter how much we may disagree about the South's politics, I'm sure we admire their ability to create bewitching women."

"With all our hearts," Jonathan said as the men raised their glasses.

"Jonathan," Cecilia Schermerhorn said. "After all the longing looks I gave you twenty-five years ago, have you nothing to say for New York femininity?"

"Of course," he said, mechanically raising his glass. His mind was still paralyzed with rage at Robert Legrand.

Cecilia sighed. "Your cousin Katherine Kemble used to compare the Stapletons to mules. She said you had to hit them on the head with a sledge-hammer to get their attention."

"Cousteau," Cynthia said. "Put 'one sledgehammer' at the top of the shopping list for tomorrow."

Everyone laughed. Good humor seemed restored. A roast pheasant in truffle sauce soon absorbed the company's attention. Collie Schermerhorn went into raptures over the wine, a Lafite-Rothschild '45. After a dessert of marvelously fragile floating island, the ladies withdrew and Cousteau served coffee, cordials and cigars.

"Fate cannot harm me, after a dinner like that," Theodore Roosevelt said, sipping chartreuse.

Jonathan looked down the table toward Robert Legrand and wished he could echo the casual contentment of that familiar aphorism. "Major Legrand," he said. "I want to apologize for losing my temper a few minutes ago. Will you shake my hand?"

Robert ignored him and went on talking to Lionel Bradford.

"Major Legrand—" Jonathan said.

Robert stared contemptuously at him. "I wish we were in New Orleans, General. You'd be looking down the wrong end of a pistol before the night was over."

Robert exchanged a glance with Bradford that suggested there was some sort of arrangement between them. Was it to make him look like an idiot in his own house?

"If you weren't my wife's brother," Jonathan snarled, "I'd go upstairs and get the pair of dueling pistols that belonged to my father and invite you to leave for Staten Island with me right now."

"If you're implying that I'm hiding behind my sister," Robert Legrand snarled in return, "I'll insist on a challenge."

"Gentlemen," Theodore Roosevelt said, "I've never heard such intemperate talk. Major Legrand, you are now as much to blame as General Stapleton. His apology was as full and forthright as a man could make it. I urge you to shake his hand."

Robert Legrand ignored him. He poured himself two fingers of brandy. Jonathan realized he was drunk.

"I don't think you're much of a duelist, General," Robert said. "Didn't you usually depend on a regiment of riflemen to kill a man?"

"We had a saying in the infantry: 'Have you ever seen a dead cavalryman?' I didn't share the men's prejudice until I met you, Major. Now I see what they meant."

Theodore Roosevelt, Collie Schermerhorn, even Lionel Bradford were looking appalled. They did not matter. They were all noncombatants. Roosevelt seemed crushed by how totally irrelevant they had become. Was he regretting that he had allowed his southern wife to keep him out of the battle fury? Or was it dismay at seeing before his eyes the hatred that still festered between the two sections?

"Perhaps we should join the ladies," Roosevelt said.

They trooped into the drawing room, where the women were listening to Cynthia discuss the engagement party she was planning to give for Rawdon and Genevieve. "I'm only worried about one thing," she said. "What the dear girl will *wear*. She's so full of modern notions, after four years at Vassar, I'm afraid she may choose to appear in bloomers. She's absolutely convinced that a corset is fatal to a woman's health. She gave me a lecture on it only a few months ago."

Jonathan Stapleton struggled to conceal renewed irritation. He himself was worried about some of the ideas Genevieve seemed to have picked up at Vassar. But such feelings should be kept within the family circle. He heard in Cynthia's mocking tone a renewal of the hostility he had sensed in her manner all night.

Cynthia broke off her monologue and turned to them. "I hope the two ex-warriors shook hands and regained the spirit of Appomattox."

"I made a feeble gesture in that direction," Jonathan said, trying to make his tone jocular. "But Robert said he'd rather fight a duel."

Cynthia whirled on her brother. "Bob," she said, "you will shake General Stapleton's hand or leave this house immediately!"

Robert Legrand held out his hand. The hostility on his face made the gesture meaningless. But everyone applauded it.

"I love happy endings," Madeline Terhune said.

In five minutes, the guests were calling for their wraps and carriages. Cynthia summoned Cousteau and his wife Annette and the two maids to receive the thanks of the well-fed diners as they departed. A little touch of old plantation life, and an excellent way to flatter Annette to ever higher levels of culinary achievement.

Jonathan said goodbye to the Roosevelts, the last to go, and turned to discover that Cynthia was already mounting the stairs. After most parties, they had a glass of port in the parlor and discussed the guests, the conversation.

"No port tonight?" he said.

"No," Cynthia said, in a cold curt voice. "I'm too tired."

She continued up the stairs without looking back. He poured himself a glass and followed her, hoping the bedroom door might be open. But the blank panels of black walnut confronted him. He trudged down the hall to his own room. In his war corner opposite the bed, Ben Dall's haunted eyes looked down on him from a dozen pictures.

He drank his port and thought about the faces, the voices, of the evening. Above all what he had seen on Cynthia's face as he shook Robert Legrand's hand—a strange, alarming mixture of anger and grief.

FIVE

"Define love—for me—Pendleton," Rawdon Stapleton said.

"It's a transaction—that can cost a man—anywhere from five to five million—dollars."

"I knew I could—depend on you—for enlightenment."

They were rowing up the Delaware River against its formidable current. The temperature was in the nineties; the June sun glared from the smooth dark-gray water. Waves of heat rose from the baked green fields on either side of the river. Past Washington's Crossing, where the Continental Army had braved ice floes and sleet on Christmas night in 1776, the long, slim racing shell glided, the six oars pulling in rhythmic unison. Rawdon Stapleton was at the stroke oar. Behind him sat Clay Pendleton at the first oar. Behind him, red-haired Rufus Goodman, almost as tall as Rawdon, hauled his starboard water and gasped, "What's he—saying?"

"Raise it to fifty," Pendleton said.

"Fifty?" groaned Hal Bradford, behind him on the third oar. "Fifty—in this—bloody heat? I thought—this was—for fun."

"Whoa," roared brawny Mitch Collins as he caught a crab, spraying everyone with icy water. The shell slewed into the current and almost capsized.

"Jesus Christ," snarled Rawdon. "You slimy water rats still haven't learned to row!"

"It's over, Cap," Rufus Goodman said in his Ohio twang. "From now on you'll have to content yourself with abusing that poor girl you're going to marry."

"How'd he get someone as smart as Genevieve to consent?" Mitch Collins asked no one in particular.

They drifted downstream with the current. It was a sentimental outing, their last foray to the river before graduation.

"Why did he consent? That's a better question," Pendleton asked. "Why does Stapleton, the world's best-known self-advertised foe of the modern woman, want to marry the queen of the Amazons?"

"Shut up," Rawdon said.

"Say, Stapleton, tell us about your ancestor Kemble who dodged the ice floes hereabouts with Old George Washer," Hal Bradford said. "Was he like you, ready to stick his oar into anything that came along for a stroke or two?"

General laughter.

"You're being unfair to him, Bradford," Pendleton said. "That was the Stapleton of freshman, sophomore and junior years. This year he's reformed. He hasn't gone elephant hunting once, as far as I know, since September."

"The question is, how far do you know, Pendleton?" Mitch Collins said.

"He tells us he's going to see sweet Genevieve on those weekends in New York. He could do a lot of elephant hunting on the side," Hal Bradford said.

"Maybe the elephant's been hunting him and he's finally seen it," Pendleton said.

"Shut up," Rawdon snarled far more menacingly.

"Elephant hunting" was slang for the pursuit of illicit sex. "Seeing the elephant" meant that a man had finally admitted the astonishing or dismaying truth about a person or a situation.

Yesterday, Rawdon had received a telegram from Genevieve Dall.

DEAREST: AFTER MUCH ANGUISH OF MIND I HAVE DECIDED TO POSTPONE OUR ENGAGEMENT. MY LOVE FOR YOU REMAINS UNALTERED. I WILL EXPLAIN MYSELF MORE FULLY WHEN WE MEET. FORGIVE ME FORGIVE ME AND BE PATIENT I BEG YOU.

Four years ago Rawdon had arrived at Princeton angry at Genevieve for choosing virginal Vassar over erotic elopement. Now he was leaving in the same—or a worse—state of mind.

This impromptu farewell row on the river was Rawdon's attempt to escape his anger. He had found the river a better escape than elephant hunting or alcohol. The power emanating from the unison of each stroke, the salt taste of sweat as the beat was raised, its hot drool on legs, chest, thighs, the raw taste of gulped air in the throat, had obliterated everything except the fundamentals of breath, rhythm, muscle. But today Pendleton could see that the river's magic was not working.

So much for the soothing, beneficent effects of the love of woman. For four years Pendleton had been waiting for Rawdon to discover the idiocy of this idea—especially when it involved an attempt to love a Yankee female in evolution from woman to Amazon.

Pendleton studied a stain of sweat on the back of Rawdon's shirt. It was shaped vaguely like his native state of South Carolina. That reminded Pendleton of his state of mind when he arrived at Princeton four years ago, the lone representative of the fifth generation of Pendletons to enroll there. He had stepped off the train clutching his ragged carpetbag, his mother's farewell words echoing in his ears: "Remember what you stand for, Clay, Jesus and the honor of the South." His mother frequently confused her religion and her devotion to the lost cause.

Pendleton had actually planned to find some equally pious southern friend. They would sing hymns in the evening and perhaps a southern song or two. "Maryland, My Maryland" was one of Pendleton's favorites. He had been hoping he would get a roommate from Maryland. Surely Princeton, with its long tradition of southern students, would not expect him to room with a Yankee!

Imagine Pendleton's consternation when he discovered that his roommate was not merely a Yankee but the son of a Yankee general. Rawdon Stapleton had looked him over like a prime buck at a slave auction. "I think you'll do, he said. "I need a good first oar."

Then he had taken a bottle of bourbon out of his trunk and poured Pendleton half a tumbler. "I presume as a son of the South you prefer this to water," he said.

Pendleton had promised his mother that his Presbyterian lips would never touch liquor in his four years at Old Nassau. For a moment he stood there, paralyzed by dread and confusion.

Rawdon knocked down his half a tumbler and sprawled on his bed. "Tell me about the whorehouses in Charleston," he said. "I've heard they were as good as New Orleans before the war."

"Oh," Pendleton said, "they're not what they used to be. But a man can still have a good time in them." A moment later the bourbon was burning in his stomach and swimming in his head. The prim Presbyterian South of Spartanburg was dismissed as forever irrelevant.

That unforgettable night, Rawdon had revealed to Pendleton the philosophy that made him the leader of the class of 1876. He regarded the adult world with a marvelous combination of defiance and contempt. The gospel according to Stapleton dismissed everyone over the age of forty, from the simpering moralists on the Princeton faculty to the pompous tycoons and strutting politicians in the real world. They were all venal hypocrites like his father, claiming the right to run the country because they had butchered a million men in a war that never should have happened.

For Pendleton the proto-newspaperman, this was particularly electrifying stuff. The secret inner life of the Stapletons which Rawdon shared with him revealed that the victors were almost as divided and demoralized by the war as the beaten bedraggled South. Exultantly, Pendleton confessed his secret ambition to undo both sides, the princes and poltroons of Yankeedom and the bourbon-swilling slave-fucking pseudo-aristocrats of the South, by telling the truth about them in the most scathing newspaper the world had ever seen.

When Rawdon expressed astonished delight in such an enterprise, Pendleton told him the story of his own family. His newspaper-editor father had never been a Democrat. Edmund Pendleton IV was proud of his descent from the Virginian of the same name who had opposed and ultimately defeated most of Thomas Jefferson's program to level all distinctions and turn Virginia and the rest of America into a mobocracy. His father had belonged to the now extinct Whig Party, which had once numbered among its leaders a midwest politician named Abraham Lincoln.

Pendleton's mother was from Charleston, headquarters of flaming Democrats and bellicose bellowers for secession. When the war started, his father had written an editorial in the *Spartanburg Gazette* damning secession as folly and slavery as a moral blot that would ruin the South's cause. Then, to prove his courage to his berserk Charleston wife, whose nine hundred and ninety-nine cousins had all enlisted, he had recruited a company of infantrymen and marched to war. "Eighteen months later the stupid bastard was killed at Antietam," Pendleton said.

Those words were the only thing Pendleton had said or done in four years of outrageous behavior at Princeton that bothered his conscience. They were not his final judgment on his father. No, not by any means. The world would discover that final judgment when Henry Clay Pendleton used Rawdon Stapleton's money to found a newspaper that would rule or ruin this excuse for a country laughingly known as the United States.

They were both wholeheartedly committed to the enterprise now. Rawdon had persuaded his father to get Pendleton a job on the *New York Times* where they would learn the big-city newspaper business together. Only one thing marred this bravado future from Pendleton's viewpoint—Rawdon's involvement with Genevieve Dall. Having watched her correct Rawdon's faulty knowledge of Greek, Roman and even American history and argue him into futility about everything from politics to rational love, he had an alarming premonition that she would undertake to edit their newspaper.

"I think she's turned you into a nancy, Cap," Hal Bradford boomed, returning Pendleton to the watery present. "I was down to Aunt Molly's last week and there wasn't a girl in the place who remembered what you looked like."

They were gliding toward the boathouse dock two miles below Washington's Crossing. Rawdon sprang out and glared down at his crew. "Maybe a farewell visit to Molly is in order."

"I think I'll lie low and pound a few Greek verbs into my skull," Isaac Mayer said.

"What the hell are you talking about, Mayer? You've gotten an order from the captain," Bradford shouted.

"He's promised Alice to renounce Satan and all his works," Mitch Collins, Isaac's roommate, explained.

"I've promised her nothing. I just expect better of myself since I met her," Isaac said.

"Jesus Christ, Mayer," Rawdon said, "if I may invoke a false god, of course you expect better of yourself. But that doesn't mean immediate results. Alice doesn't expect it, Mayer. Her father gets a new mistress every year the way other men get new hats."

This was the Rawdon Stapleton who had led them on orgiastic tours of New York and London and Paris, who knew all the dirty secrets of the older generation, who regarded rules and regulations and moral laws as challenges to be smashed. Pendleton and everyone else rejoiced in his restoration.

"I'll drink with you. But no girls," Isaac Mayer said.

"We'll see about that," Rawdon said.

In the humid boathouse, they changed into the high silk hats and black coats they wore as part of their senior privileges. Pendleton thumbed his mandolin and they began the ride back to Princeton roaring out their favorite boating songs. Rawdon drove the two-horse team down the dusty back road at his usual headlong pace. Old men in sulkies, farmers in carts loaded with hay hastily retreated to ditches and fields.

By the time they cantered down Nassau Street to hand the wagon and the blowing horses over to the hostler at the University Hotel, Pendleton saw that Rawdon was feeling much better about life. He had convinced himself that all he needed was a taste of speed on the road and a visit to Aunt Molly to restore his confidence.

Over an alcoholic dinner in their club room at the University Hotel, Rawdon discussed tactics for the expedition to Aunt Molly's. Usually, they left their horses and wagon with a friendly neighboring farmer when they traveled to Trenton by night. But the horses would not be in shape to make another long trip after the punishment Rawdon had just given them. The captain decided they would go by train.

This raised the problem of gimlet-eyed Matthew Goldie, the head proctor. Goldie met every train that stopped in Princeton after dark to make sure no students got on it. "We'll just give Matty something else to worry about—the biggest horn spree of the decade," Rawdon said.

A horn spree was one of the few Princeton traditions that Rawdon endorsed. Distributing horns to the freshman and junior varsity crews, he ordered them to strike Nassau Street precisely at nine o'clock. The senior crew dispersed to their rooms in Nassau Hall to prepare for the evening.

Pouring an after-dinner drink, Pendleton found himself in a reflective mood. He pondered the trophies, the paintings, the photographs on the walls, which were a sort of history of their four years at Princeton. There were headlines and sketches from the illustrated newspapers of 1873 recalling the rally organized by Rawdon to protest Spain's execution of fifty-three Americans for running guns to the Cuban rebels. The rally had turned into a riot that smashed half the windows on Nassau Street. Rawdon had come within a whisker of expulsion.

Nearby was a drawing of a large ape in a cocked hat under which Rawdon had lettered: GREAT-GREAT-GRANDFATHER. For four years the faculty had denied that Darwin's *Origin of Species* proved religion was irrelevant. With gleeful perversity, the class of '76 had declared survival of the fittest the motto of the era—a moral as well as a biological principle.

The centerpiece of the room was a group of photographs of Genevieve Dall. The more recent ones Rawdon called "mood pictures," taken at twilight, in which Genevieve's delicately boned sensitive face assumed a mournful ethereal quality. This was the Genevieve that Rawdon loved, the wounded one, the woman who needed his strength, his defiance of a brutal world. This was the woman he saw—or thought he had seen—at Kemble Manor the year he fell in love with her.

Picking up his mandolin, Pendleton began strumming "Sweet Genevieve." He had been playing and singing it as parody for some time.

"It isn't funny, Pendleton," Rawdon said.

"Why don't you take a train up to Amazon headquarters in Poughkeepsie and dare her to say no to your face?"

"I'm not going to plead. I'm going to get her back on my terms. The same terms Grant gave the South at Vicksburg."

"Unconditional surrender? I believe the penalty for rape is twenty years pounding rocks in Sing Sing."

"I'm not talking about rape. I'm talking about surrender, Pendleton. Voluntary unconditional surrender."

A strange darkness could gather on Rawdon's handsome face when he talked about Genevieve Dall. It was enough to make a man worry about his roommate. When Pendleton was somewhat drunk, as he happened to be at the moment, he could regard Rawdon Stapleton with dangerous affection. It went back to the first term of sophomore year when his mother informed Pendleton that he would have to withdraw from Princeton. The Panic of 1873 had reduced the South, along with much of the rest of the nation, to beggary. Rawdon had sent a telegram to his father, and the money for Pendleton's tuition arrived the next day. As he handed him the check, Rawdon said, "I don't let misfortune befall people I love, Pendleton."

The intensity of Pendleton's reaction had momentarily alarmed him. It was one thing to admire Rawdon Stapleton, to be fascinated by him, to accept his headlong cynicism as a way of life. But love? Pendleton had seen what that emotion could do to a man. He had told himself he was synchronous to Rawdon, as a good first oar should be to a lead oar. But men did not love each other. A wise man did not love anyone, if he could avoid it.

The payment of his tuition had also exposed Pendleton to some curious emotions about Rawdon's father. At first, he had totally agreed with Rawdon's antagonistic estimate of the General. He seemed to pursue Rawdon like an avenging angel or a prosecuting attorney, always presuming the worst. Whenever Rawdon got into trouble at school, he could look forward to a withering letter or a ferocious lecture from his father.

Against this record had to be set the times when General Stapleton invited Rawdon and Pendleton duck hunting on Barnegat Bay. They stayed in a collection of shacks he owned down there, called Camp Scruffy. Pendleton had loved the barren chilly solitude of the salt marshes, broken only by the sighing wind and distant bird calls. He enjoyed even more the evening hours around the campfire, pungent with roasting duck, everyone in mackintoshes and boots, ignoring the wind and drizzle. The General's friend Delancey Apthorpe had a knack for getting him to talk about the war. Jonathan Stapleton spoke with amazing candor of the corruption, the confusion, the irresolution that had hamstrung the North until Ulysses Grant took charge.

Pendleton had returned from those Barnegat weekends in an odd state of mind—exhilaration mingled with a puzzling sadness. Gradually he understood his feelings. South Carolina had marshes and winging ducks above the Pee Dee and a dozen other rivers, but there was no father with whom to share an evening campfire, to talk about the war with the tough careless honesty of a man who had earned the right to tell bitter truths.

For a few days, Pendleton was tempted to give his roommate a lecture on sonship. Rawdon had persistently refused to enjoy himself on these expeditions. When his father began talking about the war he had contemptuously gone to bed. But such noble thoughts and feelings hardly fitted the persona of the bourbon-swilling southern cynic who called his father a stupid bastard for forgetting to duck at Antietam.

For a moment Pendleton wondered if both he and Rawdon had been wearing cynics' masks for the past four years, each trying to outdo the other in disillusion and dissipation. He wished that instead of going to Aunt Molly's he could sit down and have a serious talk with his friend about Genevieve Dall. Before he could even suggest such a novel idea, a swirl of horns rose through the darkness. Uproar engulfed the campus as the undergraduate oarsmen's cacophony swept down Nassau Street. "It's a spree, a spree!" echoed through the night, followed by the thunder of hundreds of feet in the halls and on the stairs.

The crew mustered in Rawdon's room and headed for the train station, where they boarded the 9:05 for Trenton unchallenged. In a half hour they were knocking on Aunt Molly Carpenter's door on a dim sidestreet only a few blocks from the State Capitol.

Resplendent in yards of purple satin, Molly had a belly as wide as a Dutch barn and the face of a leftover Halloween pumpkin. She greeted Rawdon with a disbelieving cry. "Mr. Stapleton! I thought you was dead!"

"We've all come to kiss you goodbye, Molly," Rawdon said. "We want the third-floor parlor and the best girls in the house."

"Listen. You come at the right time. I just got a coupla girls from New York. Knockouts. I telegraphed a friend I got up there and he sent me his best. Then there's Daisy, a local girl. Looks like she just finished milkin' the cows. And Estelle, from New Orleans. She's French and she knows it. Coupla Irish girls from Philly. Real colleens."

"Irish. I go for Irish," Hal Bradford said, practically slavering.

"What will you gentlemen be drinking?" Aunt Molly asked.

"Champagne, of course," Rawdon said. "And cocaine on the side."

"No coke," Molly said. "I don't like what it does. Some guys've gone nuts and hurt my girls."

"Doctors recommend it for headaches. Women put it in their hair," Rawdon protested.

"When you put it up your nose, it's a different story," Molly insisted. "You got money? I never give credit to no one this close to graduation."

"Of course I've got money," Rawdon said, and handed her a hundred-dollar bill. Aunt Molly led them into her gaudy parlor. The girls were sitting around in nightdresses. Daisy and Estelle were introduced. Daisy was rosy-cheeked, thanks to chemistry, but the last cow she had milked had long since died of old age. Estelle had probably left New Orleans because her profession embarrassed her grandchildren. The two Irish girls from Philadelphia were younger, but that was about all that could be said for them.

The New York girls, Carrie and Charlotte, were a distinct improvement. Carrie was blond, with a button nose and a southern accent that echoed in Pendleton's ears like a voice from home. "A perfect match," Rawdon said, practically shoving her into Pendleton's arms. The second New York girl Rawdon appropriated for himself. She had an interesting resemblance to Genevieve Dall—the same chestnut hair and somewhat haughty gray-blue eyes. Bradford and Chapman took the Irish girls, and Mayer and Collins settled for Estelle and Daisy.

They ascended to the third-floor parlor, Pendleton lugging a case of champagne. "Do my ears deceive me or are you a fellow rebel?" Carrie asked as Pendleton opened the wine that guaranteed their authenticity as gentlemen.

"A halfhearted rebel, Carrie," Rawdon said. "You've got to sing 'For Southern Rights Hurrah' to him while he's making love to you. For an encore try 'The Bonnie Blue Flag.' "

"I know every word of both of them," Carrie said.

"I'll secede," Pendleton said. His mother and his sister had forced him to sing both songs interminably throughout the war.

Rawdon began giving Charlotte one of his lines. "You remind me of a girl I used to love," he said. "She was worth twenty million dollars—ten times more than my skinflint of a father is going to leave me. One night I had her panting in my arms. Naked. But the thought of all that money . . ."

"He couldn't do a thing," Hal Bradford chortled. "He told me right after it happened."

"Is that the level?" Charlotte asked Pendleton. In the shadowy parlor, her resemblance to Genevieve was even more pronounced, until she opened her mouth. Then a hard New England accent tinged her lower-class slang.

"I haven't been near a woman since. I hope you can cure me tonight," Rawdon continued.

Charlotte began eying Rawdon hungrily. She was wondering if she saw more than a night's pay; she was hoping, or half hoping—Pendleton suspected Charlotte had long since taught herself not to hope too recklessly—that rescue, at least temporary salvation, might be within reach if she somehow managed to please this wild wealthy bohemian.

The champagne flowed. Mitch Collins, Pendleton, Isaac Mayer recited comic poems. Aunt Molly sang "Oh You Naughty Naughty Men," one of the hits of the 1860s, which made them feel almost as old as their fathers.

Carrie sat on Pendleton's lap and nuzzled him. "Listen," she whispered. "You'd better protect yourself."

"Why?"

"I've got something. I don't know what it is. Probably the syph. I never tell Yankees. I figure the more of them bastards get it, the better. But I wouldn't want to give it to a fellow rebel."

For a moment, Pendleton heard the Reverend Daniel Gladstone, pastor of the First Presbyterian Church of Spartanburg, fulminating against the sins of the flesh. Carrie was his first southern whore. What did that mean, in the Darwinian march of American history? Pendleton decided it was better not to think about it. It was better to consider himself a man without a country.

"I've got protection," he said. "Dr. Condom is an old friend."

"Oh gooood," Carrie said, evoking a dozen of his mother's Charleston cousins. Pendleton suddenly had a vision of all of them wrapping their arms around him, clinging like tendrils of an enormous vine, smothering him with their elegiac voices and perfumed melancholy. Here was the real reason he was never going back to South Carolina.

"Where you from?" he asked.

"Georgia."

He did not want to hear the rest of it. She probably had a brother or a father who was killed in the war. A Union officer or sergeant had wronged her, diseased her. She surprised him by not bothering to tell it. Georgia was supposed to be enough for a fellow southerner. Sherman's march, the bummers fanning out from the immense snakelike column to burn and rob and rape. Georgia said it all.

"Gentlemen!" Rawdon roared, swaying back into the parlor after a half-hour interlude with Charlotte. "I've been cured. Your captain has been restored to you."

Drunken cheers and yawps. Charlotte clung to Rawdon, telling everyone how wonderful he had been. Her cascade of chestnut hair was a tangled mess now, some of it spilling over her shoulders and breasts. It increased the wildness or desperation Pendleton sensed beneath her haughty manner.

"Now," Rawdon said, "one last time, let's follow the old stroke's lead. Take your girls, adjust Dr. Condom's invention and leave your doors open so you can hear the beat. That includes you, Bow Oar."

"No," Mayer said. "Said . . . drink. No girls."

"Estelle, take charge of Mayer. His father is the richest Jew in New York. If you make his son happy, he'll shower you with diamonds."

"Come on, Ike," roared Bradford and Collins. Followed by Estelle, they dragged Mayer down the hall to a bedroom and returned with his trousers, which they carefully folded over the back of one of the parlor chairs before disappearing with the two Irish girls.

"Carrie," Pendleton said. "May I have the honor of this fuck?" He bowed low and almost fell on his face, while Carrie giggled.

"What's the position tonight, Cap?" Hal Bradford shouted. "Roman or romantic?"

"Roman," Rawdon said.

On their tour of Europe during the summer of sophomore year, Rawdon had made a close study of the wall paintings of Pompeii, especially the ones that women were not permitted to see. He had been fascinated by the Roman custom of taking females from behind. He saw it as the opposite of the romantic American way.

Without her perfume-drenched nightdress, Carrie smelled like a moldy sofa. It was about 110 degrees on the third floor, under the hot roof of the old house. The windows were shut and covered with heavy draperies to muffle the sound of gentlemen at their revels. "Get ready for an historic experience," Pendleton said, positioning Carrie on the bed. "This is the way Antony did it to Cleopatra."

"Are you ready?" Rawdon boomed from the next room.

"Ready," came the voices in chorus.

"Is Mayer ready, Estelle?"

"He's ready," Estelle cried.

"Stroke," Rawdon roared. He was inside Charlotte, and Pendleton was inside Carrie. Was Rawdon having a better time because Charlotte was pseudo-Genevieve? Perhaps he should convert Carrie into someone or something. The personification of the South? Then who was he? The rapacious North? No, maybe his disgusted conscience saying with each stroke, Fuck you.

"Raise it to ten," Rawdon bellowed.

"Ten," returned the shout.

"Twenty," commanded the captain, after a suitable interval.

"Twenty," shouted the crew.

"Thirty," boomed the captain.

Carrie began shaking her head back and forth like a rebellious horse. "What the hell—is this?" she muttered.

In the next room, Charlotte was making little wailing sounds. Was she pretending, as an ambitious whore should? Or was it genuine? Rawdon's effect on women was invariably remarkable. Stroking away, his hands disdaining Carrie's floppy breasts, Pendleton reflected on the Roman method. It was ideal for whores, but he suspected there would be disadvantages with a wife or mistress. It was a bit too detached, impersonal, like the imperious old Romans themselves. He could see Marcus Cato slipping it to his wife while dictating to a secretary, *Carthago delenda est.*

"Forty," chanted the captain, returning Pendleton to the business at hand.

Rawdon was having a wonderful time. He bellowed the chorus of their boating song:

> *"Steady boys, swing to it!*
> *Lift her as you spring to it!*
> *Now now you're fairly driving her,*
> *   by Jupiter she jumps!"*

"Jesus—Christ . . ." Carrie gasped. "I knew we shouldna come down here—and fooled around—with a lot of rich college—*bastards.*"

Alas for Carrie, for southern honor, for the voices of home. Pendleton's sentimental shackles were shattered, thanks to Rawdon Stapleton. He was free to be a Darwinian American male of the year 1876 getting close now to the moment when their frantic gulping breaths and pounding hearts and exploding pulses united in one glorious ecstatic SHOUT.

They were there, all of them, swollen flesh, gathered wish, irresistible pleasure erupting in the sweaty darkness. It was a penultimate of male excess, of imperial lust. They would guffaw over it at class reunions for the next fifty years. Only Pendleton knew that for Rawdon it was also an angry parody of the act of love he had hoped to perform with Genevieve Dall.

SIX

DEAREST CYNTIE:

I wanted you to be the first to know. I've gotten the swag from Bradford and I'm catching the next train to New Orleans.

Kisses,
Bob

Cynthia crumpled the note in her hand and thrust it into her wastebasket, wishing she could dispose of her brother the same way. For a week she had fluctuated between guilt for inviting Robert to her dinner party and wrath at her husband for collaborating with him to wreck it.

Thank God for Mittie. Cynthia had poured out the behind-the-scenes story of the dinner party—the plan to introduce Robert to Lionel Bradford—to her the following day. Mittie had counseled patience and fortitude. Admit nothing about her brother and Bradford. A twinge or two of guilt was a small price to pay for redeeming another southern state. As for Jonathan's prejudices, Mittie offered a dictum that was obviously drawn from experience. A wife cannot change her husband's political opinions. But in time she can moderate them.

Cynthia took a green bottle from her dressing table and poured two or three drops of heavy liquid into a glass of water. Her doctor had prescribed Balm of Gilead four years ago after she lost her baby. She had probably taken more of it than he would approve—the mixture was mostly opium—in the past week.

Jonathan's knuckles rapped on her bedroom door. "Are you almost ready, dear? That train isn't going to wait for us."

"Five more minutes," she said. She added another touch of powder to her face and turned slowly before the pier mirror to make sure the organ-pipe pleats on the train of her sapphire-blue traveling dress were in place.

"Perfect, Missus," her maid Lucy assured her as Cynthia adjusted the mandarin satin ribbon of her Tuscan straw bonnet. For a moment she heard her father's voice urging her to aim at perfection. *Never be satisfied with being merely beautiful.*

Downstairs, Jonathan said nothing about her dress, her hair, her bonnet. He had his big gold watch in his hand. Even George, standing beside his father in an identical gray suit, had a disapproving frown on his face. Men, Cynthia thought. There were times when she felt beleaguered, as the only woman in the Stapleton ménage. "It will be a miracle if we catch that train," Jonathan fumed.

Outside, Cynthia told Oliver Cromwell that if he did not get them to the Cortlandt Street ferry in fifteen minutes her husband was going to divorce her. Oliver performed heroic feats, charging through the traffic on Broadway and on Sixth Avenue. They caught the train with five minutes to spare and were on their way to Rawdon's graduation at Princeton.

Cynthia was grateful for the two hours of tranquility in the comfortable parlor car. She was glad they had taken Rawdon's advice and skipped the three-day round of graduation festivities at Princeton—although she thought Jonathan had accepted the idea with too much alacrity. June of the year 1876 was turning into a frantic month. Between Rawdon's graduation from Princeton and Genevieve Dall's from Vassar and the round of parties that their engagement would entail, the Stapletons would scarcely have time to catch their breath before July Fourth, the great Centennial Day, would be upon them. Jonathan, along with the other High Mightinesses of the Republican Party, had been invited to the ceremonies in Philadelphia.

The graduation was a pleasant if boring ceremony. Clay Pendleton, generally acknowledged to be the best orator if not the best student in the class, gave the valedictory address: "Am I for the World or Is It for Me?" Cynthia did not really listen to it. Men seemed to enjoy this sort of soul searching. Women had to accept the world as they found it. She spent the time contemplating the young masculine faces on the platform behind the speaker, Rawdon's in particular.

His resemblance to Charlie was now almost uncanny. He had acquired the same cocky tilt to his head, the same bold curling smile on the wide sensual mouth. At the moment the smile was not there and the face was strangely blank, almost sad. That too reminded her of Charlie. Without his smile, his face could relapse into surprising gloom.

There were times—this was one of them—when Cynthia felt sorry for Rawdon. She sympathized with the confused anger behind his swagger. The war had filled her with similar bitterness against her father, for different reasons. She could only hope that Genevieve's love would soothe and eventually eliminate Rawdon's resentment. He was young enough—they were all so heartbreakingly young—to outlive the ugly past in which she and Jonathan were still dismayingly entangled.

After the ceremony, the graduates joined their parents and friends on the lawn. Cynthia kissed Rawdon and whispered in his ear, "Right up to the very last minute, I was afraid you were going to get yourself expelled."

"I did my best, Stepmother. But you never taught me how to be wicked." He was making a sentimental reference to a game they used to play when she first married Jonathan. She had tried to make light of his hostility by calling herself his wicked stepmother. As a riposte, he used to demand lessons in wickedness.

"I'm so proud of you, Clay," she said, kissing him too. She had grown fond of this bulky bearlike fellow southerner with the bulldog face. "Such a profound address. I'm sure it cured a few Yankee prejudices."

"Not if they ask me for a character reference," Rawdon said.

Everyone retreated from the sunbaked lawn to the relative coolness of Nassau Hall, where a reception was in progress. Cynthia met Clay's mother, a sweet gushy woman who had once been a beauty and still displayed tattered remnants of regality. Clay's sister and her husband had also come; the husband was a rather pompous man who pretended to blame Jonathan for getting Clay a job on the *New York Times*, depriving him of an assistant editor on the *Spartanburg Gazette*. But Cynthia sensed it was all talk for the benefit of his in-laws.

From Clay's relations they progressed to Isaac Mayer's parents. The father, Adolph, was almost spherical; his round beaming face seemed more suited for a shopkeeper than an investment banker, until you encountered his shrewd eyes. Mrs. Mayer was slim and quite pretty but she spoke only German. Jonathan left Cynthia to cope with this problem and edged away to confer with Adolph Mayer about a railroad in which they had apparently invested several hundred thousand dollars. Cynthia tried to explain to Mrs. Mayer that she was thirsty and went in search of some punch.

"I can't believe you have a son graduating, madam," said a voice behind her. "It must be a younger brother."

She turned to discover Lionel Bradford in a light-blue French-cut suit with braided cuffs and collar. It was a touch garish for sedate Princeton. "Where's Hal?" Cynthia asked. "I want to give him a graduation kiss."

"Why not deposit it with me?"

"I'm afraid you might speculate with it."

He laughed. "After your dinner party last week, Mrs. Stapleton, I began to think you ought to change your name to Desdemona. But in this modern version of *Othello* she's the plotter and poor Iago and her black Republican general are mere tools of her clever brain."

"What in the world are you talking about?" Cynthia said, glancing nervously past him at Jonathan, who was still conferring with Adolph Mayer.

"I'm talking about the coming redemption of Louisiana," Lionel Bradford said in the same low, measured voice. "It's been handled with such a consummate combination of boldness and subtlety, it's won my awed respect. Now, if I may speak as Iago, I wonder what the second and third acts of our play will bring."

"I have no idea, Mr. Bradford. I'm not an actress," Cynthia said, growing more and more flustered.

"Madeline Terhune thinks you could be a superb one. She said you were the only American woman she's met who has the imagination to become another self."

"Ah, Bradford," Jonathan said, towering over them. "I suppose we should exchange congratulations for getting our two hell-raisers through four years of college."

"I'm as amazed by it as you are, General," Bradford said, shaking hands.

After an hour of similar pleasantries with parents of other graduates, they caught a four-o'clock train back to New York. "How is Genevieve?" Cynthia asked Rawdon, once they had settled into their seats in the parlor car. "Did you pay Vassar a visit after the Lake George regatta?"

"Genevieve is fine, I presume. I saw her at the old-maid factory and got this telegram for my reward a few days later."

He handed Cynthia a piece of crumpled yellow paper. "My God," Cynthia said to Jonathan. "She's putting off their engagement."

"What?" Jonathan growled, snatching the telegram out of her hands. He glared at Rawdon. "What did you do to bring this on?"

"I knew you were going to say that. I even predicted the exact words to Pendleton." He mimicked his father's growl. " 'What did you do to bring this on?' "

"Answer my question, dammit," Jonathan snapped.

Heads were turning in the parlor car. It was hardly the place to have a family quarrel.

"I did nothing, as far as I know, General," Rawdon said. "I think you yourself will be the first to admit that women are difficult, unpredictable creatures. Don't you agree, Stepmother?"

"Only when they're dealing with difficult, unpredictable men," she said. "Be serious, Rawdon. This isn't a joke to us. I can't believe it is to you either."

The raillery drained from Rawdon's face. "It isn't."

The rest of the trip home was pure gloom. The moment they reached Stuyvesant Square Jonathan went after Rawdon again. He could not believe that a young woman as intelligent as Genevieve Dall would do such a thing without provocation. Rawdon's replies grew more and more obnoxious. Jonathan finally ordered him out of the parlor. Instead, he stormed out of the house.

George had long since fled to his room. Cynthia was left alone with her overwrought husband. The more she listened to Rawdon, the more convinced she became that he was telling the truth. Whatever had happened at Vassar, Rawdon had no idea that he had said or done anything that justified Genevieve's telegram. Jonathan was giving all the benefit of the doubt to a cold overeducated girl and denouncing his own son without a speck of evidence to justify it.

"This is a perfect example of the way you've mishandled Rawdon practically from birth," Cynthia said.

"Oh? Now it's become my fault?"

"I'm merely trying to tell you for the fortieth time that you're too severe with the boy."

"And I presume that George, whom you have assiduously shielded from this so-called severity—I call it discipline—is offered as a shining example of success?"

"Surely you must admit he doesn't defy you and mock you to your face."

"Judging from his last report card, he prefers to defy me behind my back —which some people might consider a worse flaw. It suggests cowardice, underhandedness."

"There is nothing underhanded about George. He is the most honest openhearted boy I have ever seen!"

All Cynthia's love for George rushed into that endorsement. Jonathan dismissed it with a snide curl of his lip. "Muzzey says he saw him and Elliott Roosevelt talking to streetwalkers on the Bowery the other day."

"I don't believe anything that damn troublemaker says!"

Jonathan sat there, his arms folded across his chest, staring down his patrician nose at her, apparently amused at her distress. Cynthia lost all control of her temper.

"Instead of trying to blame me for George's flaws, you might examine your own conscience. If you devoted less time to the godalmighty Republican Party, I think both your sons would be better behaved—and I know your wife would be a great deal happier."

"If that's the most helpful thing you have to say, let's end this discussion here and now."

Slam, slam went the bedroom doors, and Cynthia found herself in her room, staring at the painting of the picnic in the Bois. The darkness emanating from the man in the black coat seemed to devour the entire picture.

For the next two days, Jonathan maintained a cold surly silence that Cynthia found enormously unnerving. It was such a Yankee tactic, to stalk through the very house in which you lived and supposedly loved a person, without speaking. Even in the worst years of her parents' marriage, they had spoken when her mother came to the dinner table. They discussed the weather, the crops, the family news.

At supper, their only meal together, Cynthia talked to George. Rawdon ate elsewhere. From what the servants told her, his meals were largely alcohol. He was taking the disappointment very badly. She could understand why. Cynthia felt almost as embarrassed, as she rushed off telegrams to friends and relations, canceling the engagement party she had planned to give for the happy couple at Kemble Manor.

On the third night of their uncivil war, Jonathan joined Rawdon in absenting himself from the dinner table. About ten-thirty, as Cynthia was preparing for bed, there was a familiar rap on her door. Jonathan came into the room in a dressing robe. He gazed mournfully at her for a long moment, then walked across the room and clipped an emerald bracelet on her wrist. "A peace offering," he said. He frowned down at his slippers and blurted out the next words in a rush that reminded her of his apology about John Slidell on their honeymoon in Paris. "It doesn't matter which of us is right about Rawdon. What can we do to rescue the situation?"

Cynthia was so touched by his tacit admission of error, so flattered by his confession that he needed her help, all her resentment vanished. She unclipped the bracelet and stood on her tiptoes to kiss him. "You didn't need to bring me anything," she said.

They sat down in shell chairs by the open window overlooking Stuyvesant Square and Jonathan asked her if she thought postponing the engagement was a prelude to cancellation. Cynthia was inclined to say yes—and add that she thought the cancellation should come from Rawdon. But the pain on Jonathan's face, the awareness that this difficult, proud, short-tempered man was asking her help, restrained her instinct to be blunt. She listened patiently as Jonathan told her that Genevieve had the strenth of character, the intelligence, to give Rawdon the stability he so badly needed. A wife, Cynthia thought, he is talking to you as his wife, the mother of his son. Even if she did not agree with him, she had to try to help him.

"I'll speak to Rawdon," she said. "That's the first step."

He sighed with relief, as if she had already produced the miracle and Genevieve had been delivered (bound and gagged?) in her wedding dress. Cynthia asked Cousteau to bring them some sherry. Jonathan remarked that he had seen Lionel Bradford at the Stock Exchange today and he had invited them to join him and Madeline Terhune for the closing day of the races at Jerome Park. "I begged off for the usual political reasons, but I told him you'd be delighted to go."

It was another peace offering—one that she did not particularly want. She would enjoy seeing Madeline Terhune again, but she was inclined to keep Lionel Bradford at a distance for a while. "Are you sure you can't come?" she said.

"I'm afraid not. I have four bank presidents on my calendar for that afternoon."

They chatted about summer plans. He said he had no objection to her spending a few weeks with the Roosevelts but he hoped she would give him some time at Kemble Manor. She declared she was glad they were not going to Italy now that she had learned Cecilia Schermerhorn would be there. She gave a wicked imitation of Cecilia laboriously describing sunset on the Bay of Naples. In a half hour she had kindled a glow of laughter, affection, on Jonathan's scarred face. Their quarrel was over.

When they said goodnight, his kiss was no ordinary peck on the lips; her response was far from perfunctory. If she was being seduced, Cynthia thought as he led her toward the bed, she was being extraordinarily cooperative. Rather than mar the moment, she even lied and told him her diaphragm was already in place—no doubt making him think seduction had been on her mind all along.

Why did nakedness seem more daring, almost wicked, here in New York, and in Italy simply natural, innocent? It was Italy he was trying to evoke. She surrendered to those insistent male hands, that demanding mouth, his thrusting maleness that aroused such inexplicable surges of sweetness, tenderness in her.

In the morning, Cynthia found her conscience bothering her. Had she surrendered too easily on all fronts? Did men, because they had the power to elicit that primary surrender, presume that a wife had no opinions worth listening to? She wished she had talked more frankly to Jonathan about Genevieve Dall. She could think of a half-dozen girls who would make Rawdon happier. She suspected that Jonathan's plea was not based on simple fondness for Genevieve or admiration for her character. It was because she was Ben Dall's daughter. He saw the marriage as somehow expiating or at least mitigating the guilt he still felt over Ben's death.

If Genevieve had remained the shy, vaguely pathetic creature of her first visits to Kemble Manor, Cynthia might have been able to share some of Jonathan's wish to see her happy. She might even be able to believe Rawdon would be moderately happy with her. Some men liked helpless women. But four years at Vassar had transformed Genevieve. The girl had theories on everything, and most of them could not be mentioned in mixed company. Corsets were evil, women should exercise with dumbbells and Indian clubs, rational love, not passion, was the key to a happy marriage.

How could any sane woman let theories get in the way of marrying Rawdon Stapleton? He had looks, charm, and every chance of inheriting not only half his father's fortune, but his grandmother's money in the bargain. Sixteen, perhaps twenty million dollars! The girl was either a damn fool or the most independent woman alive. Either way, Rawdon was probably better off without her.

But she had promised Jonathan.

Cynthia spent the next two days in fuming indecision. Jonathan asked her once if she had spoken to Rawdon, and he got such an abrupt no he did not mention it again. She slept badly Wednesday night and awoke late. It was eleven o'clock before she began combing her hair and putting on her face powder and rouge. Cleopatra came in to get her breakfast tray and hovered by the door in a way that signified she had something to report.

"What do you want?" Cynthia said to Cleo's image in the mirror.

"That girl drivin' poor Master Rawdon crazy. Muzzey say he come home last night so drunk you could smell him all the way to the roof."

"Tell Muzzey that if he so much as mentions that to General Stapleton, I'll roast him alive. Is Mr. Rawdon awake?"

"I just saw Muzzey bringin' him his breakfast."

"Tell him I'd like to see him."

Cynthia finished powdering her face and called Lucy to comb out her hair. She had better talk to Rawdon now. Lionel Bradford was arriving in an hour to take her to Jerome Park. He might have heard about the postponed engagement from his son Hal. It would be far less embarrassing to her, and perhaps to Rawdon, if she could tell him something definite, one way or the other. Cynthia spilled some Balm of Gilead in a water glass and drank it down.

As Lucy finished combing out her hair, Rawdon called from the doorway, "May I come in, Stepmother?"

He had never abandoned that unpleasant word. Cynthia made wry humor out of it by replying in kind. "You're just in time, Stepson. I've finished putting on my face."

Cynthia sat down in one of the shell chairs by the window and gestured to a chair opposite her. Rawdon glowed with health and apparent good humor. It was hard to believe that he had reeled into bed a drunken mess a few hours ago. Ah youth, indestructible youth, she thought, remembering dusk-to-dawn dances at Bralston.

"I've heard from the servants that you were in a state some people would call wicked when you came home last night."

"Just getting ready for my job at the *New York Times*, Stepmother. You have to know how to drink hard to succeed as a newspaperman."

"It's very painful when someone you love disappoints you."

She let the words linger in the quiet bedroom for a moment. They took Rawdon by surprise. They also took her by surprise—there were layers of meaning in them beyond the one she had intended them to have.

"Is this the voice of experience speaking, Stepmother?"

She thanked God for the Gilead drops. "I'm trying to tell you, Stepson, that I'm aware of your disappointment with Genevieve."

"You've got it all wrong, Stepmother," Rawdon snapped. "I'm not in the least disappointed with Genevieve Dall. She's done exactly what I thought she'd do from the day she headed for Poughkeepsie to matriculate in manhating."

"Rawdon—don't lie to yourself. Or to me. Have you answered her telegram?"

He shook his head.

"Do you think that's sensible?"

"At this point, I have no idea what's sensible," Rawdon said, lowering his head to avoid her eyes.

"Stepson, take some advice from your old stepmother. When a woman sends you a message that includes the words 'my love for you remains unaltered,' she wants a response."

Rawdon began strolling around the room, studying the paintings. "She may get one, someday."

"Perhaps your love for her has altered. You should ask yourself that question."

Rawdon scrutinized the painting of the picnic in the Bois. "What if it hasn't?"

"I advise you to answer that telegram as soon as possible. The Vassar graduation is a week from today. You should go, and assure Genevieve that your feelings haven't changed, either. Then I think you should bide your time. Genevieve has spent four years at Vassar thinking about being an independent woman. You must give those feelings time to subside a little. Don't challenge her. Be subtle, indirect. We'll try to help. Let's begin with the Centennial weekend. Your father can get all the tickets he wants to the celebration in Philadelphia. We'll spend the first two days at Kemble Manor—"

"Is this going to be your summer amusement, Stepmother? Pasting my Humpty-Dumpty romance back together?"

"Can you possibly believe that a wicked stepmother is sincerely concerned for your happiness?"

For a moment he glared over his shoulder, then looked away, down the room in the direction of her unmade bed. "It has nothing to do with happiness," he said. "She still . . . has a meaning for me. A meaning I don't want to lose."

"What is it?"

"I can't put it into words. But it's there. She made me believe my life could be different. I think we all have meanings for each other, don't you?"

"I must confess I haven't truly thought of it before," Cynthia said. "What meaning do I have for you?"

"The spoils of war."

"Rawdon! What a cruel, a terrible thing to say. It reflects on me—on your father."

"I heard Genevieve's father call you that one day."

"Where, when?"

"In Mississippi, when my father and I went down there to visit him. I've never been able to get the idea out of my head."

"I wish you'd get it out, as soon as possible!"

Rawdon's remorse seemed genuine. "I'm sorry," he said. He glanced at the shell chair, as if he wanted to stay longer, then decided against it and walked to the door. "I'll write to Genevieve," he said.

He left her in turmoil. Creating an uproar sometimes seemed to be Rawdon's only gift. The spoils of war. What a vicious, ugly idea. It stirred all Cynthia's latent antagonism to Ben Dall—and, by descent, to his opinionated daughter. Did Genevieve think the same thing of her? Was that why she often detected hostility in her manner?

Did it also explain Jonathan's visit to Bralston ten years ago? He was the only Yankee who knew that Cynthia Legrand was marooned there, waiting to be rescued—or abducted.

No, it was ridiculous. Nine years of affection barred such a conclusion.

Cousteau spoke from the doorway. "Mr. Bradford is downstairs, madam."

"Oh dear God. And I'm not even dressed. Get Cleo and Lucy up here. Serve Mr. Bradford some coffee."

Last night Cynthia had mentally chosen her cream-colored faille promenade outfit. It had a dramatic overdress of red-and-white striped India silk, with numerous cardinal-red bows. Now, after getting every button into place, she studied it in the mirror and decided it was too gaudy for the impression she wanted to make on Lionel Bradford. While Cleo groaned, she changed to her white Victoria lawn suit trimmed with black grosgrain ribbons. It was what an attractive wife—in contrast to an actress or woman of fashion— might wear.

Lucy buttoned the back of her skirt. Cynthia shook out the flounces, adjusted the huge black bow at the waist, and studied the net effect. Yes. She chose an Italian straw bonnet trimmed with cream-colored serge ribbon and a black ostrich feather. Yes. To make sure, she tried on her Brussels straw, with is streaming ruby serge ribbon. She went back to the Italian straw, pleased by the way the black feather and the black bow complemented each other in that indefinable way that evoked approval.

By now Lionel Bradford had been waiting a full half hour. Cynthia went down the stairs expecting the glare that her lateness often drew from Jonathan. Instead, there was a small anticipatory smile on the financier's smooth face. As usual, she found herself guessing his age. His bottle-green cutaway coat was a perfect fit on his trim body. Only the hint of a wattle beneath his chin suggested he might be well past forty.

"My dear Desdemona," Bradford said, kissing her hand, "you must have been up at six to achieve such an effect."

"On the contrary, I wasn't even dressed when you arrived," Cynthia said.

"If I had known that, I might have stormed your bedroom."

"That would have been out of character, my dear Iago."

"Getting out of character is the heart of our play. I have an interesting suggestion for a second act. Desdemona elopes with Iago, when she discovers beneath his treacherous reputation a generous heart."

"It lacks believability, I fear."

"Ask what they think of Iago in that distant land with the romantic name —Louisiana."

It was all tossed at her in such an offhand way, she found it easy to believe he was not serious. As she started past him toward the door he caught her wrist. "You will ask them, won't you?" he said.

Turning her back on him, she selected a small corsage from the white roses in the silver bowl Jonathan had inherited from his grandfather, with the words INDEPENDENCE FOREVER on its side. A dangerous motto, she thought as she descended the steps into the hot June sunshine.

Hal Bradford and Grace Schermerhorn, Cecilia Schermerhorn's homely daughter, sat on top of the coach, drinking champagne from stirrup cups. Why was Cecilia permitting Grace to go to the races with Lionel Bradford's dissolute son? It revealed either how rapidly moral standards were collapsing or how much money Collie Schermerhorn had lost in the Panic of 1873.

"It was worth the wait, Mrs. Stapleton," Hal said, doffing his gray hat. He too was wearing the bottle-green coat of the coaching fraternity.

Four footmen in buckskin top boots and red livery waited beside the coach. One of them opened the door, and Madeline Terhune descended to give Cynthia a cheery hello. She was wearing a cream-and-white striped India-silk dress that was a virtual copy of the one Cynthia had almost worn. The narrow escape convinced her that this was one of her lucky days.

"I'm the chaperone," Madeline Terhune said.

"In that case, you should have stood guard at my bedroom door," Cynthia said. "This man was threatening to batter it down."

"He tends to be outrageous. But you'd be surprised how a touch of the whip makes him behave."

She smiled mockingly at Lionel Bradford. Cynthia sensed a strange current of feeling flowing between them. It was definitely not affection.

The four jet-black horses tossed their blinkered heads and twitched their muscular rumps as one of the footmen blew a blast on his coaching horn. Another footman propped a ladder against the side of the coach and handed Cynthia and Madeline Terhune up. Bradford joined them on the box and took the reins. In coaching-club etiquette, the owner and his guests sat on top and the servants rode inside.

Another blast on the horn and they were off. In five minutes they were pounding up Third Avenue, the horses stepping in perfect rhythm, the crowds on the sidewalk stopping to point and gape. Cynthia felt perfect delight course through her body. This was life as a Legrand was meant to live it, on the peaks of happiness, rather than in the dull lowlands of everyday humdrum. She told herself not to worry about Lionel Bradford, no matter how alarming his lechery became. Keeping men simultaneously entranced and at bay was one of the inherited gifts of a Louisiana girl.

For a moment, the words *spoils of war* swooped across her mind like the shadow of a bird of prey. She banished it and found her Legrand exhilaration again. Ahead lay a champagne lunch at Jerome Park, an afternoon of bets and banter. She turned to Madeline Terhune and said, "Isn't it the most glorious day—for people without a care in the world?"

SEVEN

"All aboard for the big birthday," Clay Pendleton bawled in the doorway of the Stapletons' private railroad car. Somewhere Clay had found a conductor's shiny peaked hat. He twanged the strings of his mandolin dramatically and bowed from the waist as Genevieve mounted the steps. "How good of the Amazons to send their Queen to our humble celebration," he drawled.

Clay greeted Alice Gansevoort in the same absurd way, pretending she was the Queen's lady in waiting. Rawdon and Isaac Mayer, just behind them, got leers and a guffaw. "You've brought along two of your slaves. That's what I call traveling in style. My granddaddy always brought along a few of his bodyservants when he went abroad."

If looks could kill, Pendleton would have become an instantaneous corpse. Inside the car, which had just been delivered to General Stapleton by the Pullman Company, everyone was admiring the brass chandeliers, the luxurious red velvet upholstered seats, the walnut paneling with scenes of sporting life painted in ovals above the windows. The older generation was sitting in the front of the car. General Stapleton and Cynthia greeted Rawdon's guests with warm smiles, and the General introduced them to rotund Zachariah Chandler, the chairman of the Republican National Committee, and his thin rather frosty-looking blond wife. The young people proceeded through the dining area to the rear, where Genevieve's sister Eleanor and Hal Bradford and his girl of the moment, Grace Schermerhorn, greeted them boisterously.

It was exciting to be among the select few thousand with grandstand seats for America's hundredth birthday party. Excitement, significance, seemed to be permeating Genevieve Dall's life these days. She had the heady sense of being part of something new and momentous. America was beginning its second century as a nation and she was beginning her life as a woman with a college degree. She had a job that was opening horizons in all directions.

Only one thing was wrong. She had made Rawdon Stapleton unhappy. The evidence confronted her now in Rawdon's mournful eyes and morose mouth as the locomotive expelled its first chugs and the train lurched into motion.

Clay Pendleton began telling them about the interview he and Rawdon had had yesterday with John Reid, the managing editor of the *New York Times*. "He's not too fond of southerners," Clay said. "First he made me take an oath of allegiance to the flag. Then he searched me to make sure I wasn't carrying any concealed weapons."

"He didn't treat me much better," Rawdon said.

"That's true," Clay said. "He told Stapleton cub reporters were as useless as Croton bugs for their first year on the paper."

That was New York slang for water bugs—cockroaches.

"How awful," Genevieve said. "Doesn't he know you're college graduates?"

For a split second, her eyes met Rawdon's. He seemed to be asking, *What do you care?*

"I read Mr. Reid the entire Latin text of our Princeton diplomas," Clay said. "He claimed that made us semi-educated Croton bugs. You should have seen Stapleton when he heard that one. He worked himself into a tremendous rage. He swelled his chest and asked, 'What about my great-grandfather, the Continental Congressman?' Reid said that made him a Continental Croton bug."

"Enough of this idiocy," Isaac Mayer said. "Tell us about your job, Genevieve. I gather you're doing something important."

"Not really," Genevieve said, carefully avoiding Rawdon's eyes. "But it is a job. I'm working as secretary to the president of the American Association for the Advancement of Women."

The variety of expressions on the faces of her audience momentarily bewildered Genevieve. Disapproval was all too visible on her sister Eleanor's face. Rawdon wore a mournful frown, Clay Pendleton his usual mockery; Alice and Isaac looked worried, Hal Bradford and Grace Schermerhorn seemed amused. Genevieve struggled through her explanation, wishing she did not sound so defensive. The AAAW had been founded by her astronomy professor, Maria Mitchell, several years ago. It was dedicated to expanding job opportunities for educated women in the professions and business.

"What do you *wear* to work?" Grace Schermerhorn asked, seeming to imply that the costume might be anything from indecent to bizarre.

"Bloomers, I'll bet," Rawdon said.

"Nothing of the sort," Genevieve said. "The AAAW is a very moderate organization. It has no use for extremists like Amelia Bloomer. I wear plain sensible dresses, with tight sleeves that won't pick up dirt and dust and without ribbons or bows to get caught in the typewriter."

"You're working as a typewriter?" Grace said. "I thought only men could do that."

"Oh no," Genevieve said. "I predict that machine will do more for equality than the vote. It's going to give thousands of women a chance to work at clean safe jobs."

"Would you wear such sensible dresses if you worked in an office with men?" Eleanor asked.

"A good point," Grace Schermerhorn said. "Men don't like sensible dresses any more than they like sensible women."

"A working woman is lucky if she makes seven dollars a week," Genevieve said. "She can't afford gowns covered with three or four hundred dollars' worth of silk ruching and ribbons."

She looked around the semicircle of listening faces and tried to say the next words only for Rawdon. "I haven't had many paydays so far. But I can tell you this much. It's a wonderful feeling to have money in your purse that you've earned, even if it's only a few dollars."

She was dismayed by the disapproval on Rawdon's face. Did she sound as though she was bragging? She only wanted him to know how important the feeling was to her.

"I'm meeting a lot of interesting women," Genevieve went on. "Jane Croly was in the office the other day. I talked with her about getting a job on a newspaper."

Jane Croly, or Jenny June, as she was known to her readers, was married to a newspaper editor. Her essays on topics of interest to women appeared in the *New York Tribune* and other papers around the country.

"What did she say?" Rawdon asked, glaring at Genevieve as if she had just insulted him.

"She said it would be very difficult."

"What are we going to do," Clay Pendleton asked, "if the women of America take Susan B. Anthony seriously and join her call to celebrate the Centennial by declaring their independence of men?"

"Negotiate a treaty of alliance," Isaac Mayer said, smiling at Alice.

"You're hopeless, Mayer," Rawdon said. "There'd only be one answer. A declaration of war."

"I'm afraid no one takes Susan B. Anthony seriously anymore," Genevieve said.

She was trying to tell Rawdon that she had not become a wild-eyed extreme feminist. But he did not seem inclined to listen. Genevieve's eyes drifted to Alice Gansevoort. She seemed to be saying, *I told you so.*

Alice had warned Genevieve that her telegram was an act of madness. She had listed a dozen young women, from regal Florence King to lumpy Grace Schermerhorn, who were going to rejoice when they heard the news and immediately start inviting Rawdon to parties, balls, summer weekends. Her sister Eleanor had been even more critical. She had accused Genevieve of barbarously mistreating the noblest, kindest, most patient young man in America.

Her mother had bluntly questioned her sanity. Even Maria Mitchell had deserted her. "To pledge thy love and then renounce it is no small matter, Genevieve," she said. "I hope it was not out of ambition for that Harvard appointment. It's beyond thy reach now." Elizabeth Wellcombe was the only friend who had supported her. She guaranteed Genevieve that twelve months in a job would give her a new perspective. If she decided to marry Rawdon then, it would be the choice of a mature woman, not a schoolgirl.

By now the train was clipping along at about forty miles an hour. They were beyond the cities and their fringes of Irish shantytowns, rolling through the green fields of rural New Jersey. Rawdon began telling the group about the tradition of summer names at Kemble Manor, making it sound like a joke.

"What was yours, Cap?" Hal Bradford asked.

"It used to be Diarmuid, after an ancient Celtic hero. But I've been thinking of changing it to Cato, my favorite Roman. Have you read what he said about the female sex? 'Woman is a headstrong and uncontrolled animal, and you can't give her the reins and expect her not to kick over the traces.' "

There was an embarrassed silence. Genevieve realized that everyone was waiting for her reaction. "Now we know why Rome fell," Genevieve said.

For a moment, gazing at Rawdon's surly face, Genevieve had a panicky suspicion that love was dead. She did not want that to happen. Above all, she did not want to be responsible for it. Somewhere, sometime during this weekend she had to explain herself to Rawdon. She had made an attempt at it when he came to her graduation. But it was the wrong time and place.

At Kemble manor, they got settled in their various rooms and the party reformed on the rear terrace for conversation and drinks before dinner. General Stapleton mixed a champagne punch for an apéritif. Rawdon took a taste and pronounced it much too weak for Princeton men. He casually added an entire bottle of rum to it.

"Couldn't you at least wait until we served the ladies?" his father growled. Cynthia soothed the General by sending a servant to fetch another punch bowl. He mixed a separate punch for the ladies, and the men made numerous trips to Rawdon's "Princeton Special," as Zachariah Chandler called it. The Republican national chairman liked his liquor and drank as much as Rawdon and Clay Pendleton.

Vulgar was the word that best described this professional politician. Listening to his breezy, chuckling geniality, Genevieve understood what her father had meant when she asked him why he was no longer active in the Republican Party and he had replied, "It's not my party anymore. It belongs to a new breed." Genevieve wondered how General Stapleton could stand this porcine jokester with a diamond stickpin in his loud tie and the manners of a traveling salesman.

On the terrace Zachariah Chandler had learned that Rawdon and Clay Pendleton were going to become reporters for the *New York Times*. When they sat down to dinner Chandler gave them an astonishing discourse on newspapers around the nation. He knew the leading dailies in every city in the country, exactly who controlled each paper, how influential it was in its city and state. "Of course, none of them can match the New York press when it comes to influence," he said. "Remember what they did after Bull Run, Jonathan?"

"I'll never forget it," Jonathan Stapleton said.

The young people did not know what they were talking about and begged them to explain.

"I don't think I'm exaggerating when I say that those papers saved the country," Zachariah Chandler said.

"The government, the army were demoralized," Jonathan Stapleton said. "There was talk of surrender, a negotiated peace. Then the *Times*, the *Tribune*, the *Sun* arrived, telling us the rest of the country wasn't ready to quit. Their editorial pages called for an army of a million men if necessary. They changed the atmosphere in Washington overnight."

"That's what a newspaper should do—lead public opinion," Rawdon said. "Why don't they do it today?"

"I blame it all on the Democrats," the Republican national chairman said with a wry grin. "They're like the proverbial horse that won't drink the water. We print the truth every day in the *Times*, but they won't read it."

"I don't think the *New York Times* or any other newspaper is dealing with the fundamental problem of this country," Rawdon said.

"What might that be?" Chandler asked goodhumoredly.

"Our failure to live up to the promises America made to its citizens exactly one hundred years ago. The promises of the Declaration of Independence."

Genevieve felt her pulse leap at these defiant words. Rawdon was speaking for their generation, who were determined to search for the shining message America had lost in the smoking factories and screeching railroads of the North and the slavery-fouled cotton fields of the South. The search, the quest which she had vowed to share as Rawdon's true woman.

"By God, General," Chandler said. "I think you've got a radical Democrat on your hands."

"Everyone's a radical at twenty-two," General Stapleton said. "If he's still got those opinions at thirty, I'll start to worry."

"Then I take it you don't believe in the Declaration of Independence, Father?" Rawdon said.

"I don't believe the Declaration was ever intended to be a guide to the government of this country. Not even Thomas Jefferson in his most demagogic moments claimed that much for it."

No one was taking the argument seriously except Rawdon and his father. They were glaring at each other. "Personally," Rawdon said, "I think we need a new political party in this country. One that takes ideals seriously."

"I agree completely," Chandler said. "That's the way we felt when we started the Republican Party twenty-five years ago. Just remember you've got to beat the fellows who are running for office. Lose a few elections and your political party becomes a tea party."

"That's when realism takes charge of things," General Stapleton said.

"Who's going to be the backbone of your new party, Rawdon?" Isaac Mayer asked. "The Democrats have the Irish, the Republicans, the Negro."

"The women," Clay Pendleton said. "That's his secret. He's got it all figured out. When the women get the vote, the handsomest candidate will be elected, nine times out of ten."

"Not just the handsomest," Cynthia said. "But the most courageous, the most honorable candidate. That's why Rawdon will get our vote. Don't you agree, Genevieve?"

"What? Oh . . . yes," Genevieve said.

Mrs. Stapleton's remark took her by surprise. She found herself wishing she had said something like that instead of sitting silently, a mere spectator.

The ladies retreated to the parlor while the men continued the discussion over port and cigars. This segregation always irritated Genevieve. She happened to like port. She might even like cigars. She resented the implication that the presence of women somehow interfered with the men having a really serious conversation.

Genevieve brooded in Kemble Manor's drawing room while Mrs. Chandler entertained them with stories of Mary Lincoln's peculiar ways. Through the closed doors of the dining room they heard voices suddenly raised. Jonathan Stapleton distinctly said, "Your goddamn opinions." The door flew open and Rawdon appeared in the center hall, his face flushed. He glared in at them briefly and rushed out on the lawn.

"Excuse me," Genevieve said, and followed him.

She found Rawdon on the bluff above the darkening bay. "What happened?" she asked.

"Nothing important. We just finished our little discussion, that's all. I told Father I thought the Republican Party deserved to lose this election. He thought I was being impolite to that fat slob, Chandler, and he lost his temper."

"Rawdon. You started the argument."

"How long am I supposed to sit there, nodding like a dutiful son, while the great man pontificates? Do you expect me to do it for the rest of my life?"

"Of course not. I agree that your father is partly to blame. But you seem to go out of your way to provoke him."

"He provokes me just as much as I provoke him. I want to get him out of my life. I thought I was going to do that, with your help. But you seem to have lost interest in my wants."

"Rawdon, that isn't true. I've tried to explain to you how I feel. Not rushing into marriage is important to me. I'll be a better woman, a better wife. I'm sure of it."

"A better wife? You expect me to nod my head in agreement when you said on the train that you want to become a newspaperwoman?"

"I haven't decided to do that. But it does seem like a perfect job for a year, if I could get it."

"No wife of mine will ever work on a newspaper. Reporters spend half their time in a city's sewers. What man wants a wife who's spent a year in a sewer?"

"Rawdon! Don't talk to me as if I were fifteen—or five—years old. Why can't we discuss this problem like mature, rational people?"

He kissed her. She was staggered by the ferocity, the intensity of his embrace. His arms crushed the breath from her lungs. It lasted only an instant. Then he let her go and became a blur in the starlit night again. But now she could see him. She could see the clean-limbed body, the paradigmatic male face beside the sunny cove. Desire—was it fact or memory?—the old yearning to hold and be held made Genevieve tremble.

"How do we discuss that?" Rawdon said. "How do we discuss your presumed right to turn your back on that—as if it never existed, as if it was something trivial, childish?"

"I haven't turned my back on it. I said in the telegram that my love remains unaltered."

"That's a lie. Why don't you admit that before we go a step further? If it was the same love we had here four years ago—you couldn't have sent that telegram."

"Rawdon—my love hasn't changed. But I have."

He laughed, a bitter nasty sound. "Neat," he said. "Very neat." He turned away from her to stare out at the murmuring bay. She felt the meaning of the movement, the physical and spiritual withdrawal from her, as pain, a kind of amputation.

"Was it the way I acted at Vassar? I know I was obnoxious. I should never have gone near the place. I felt I was confronting . . . an enemy. That stuff about going to Harvard was the last straw."

She wanted to touch him. Her throat, her whole body ached with the wish to put her arms around him, to let him feel her pain and simultaneously soothe his grief. But first she had to explain.

"Rawdon—it was something that was growing in me, a need. That day just forced me to face it."

"A need." The word withered on Rawdon's tongue. He still stared away from her into the dark watery distance.

"I'm aware that you have needs. I know they're not easy to control. I know I'm asking you to do something difficult—for my sake."

"I presume you're talking about physical needs."

"Yes."

"Ah. Three cheers for the Vassar physiology course."

What would he do if she told him it was almost as difficult for her? If she confessed the wish that was swelling in her body and mind now, this moment, in the summer night? Would he call her a hypocrite? Would it be tantamount to surrender?

He was silent again. She wished she could see his face. It was unnerving to have words flung at her out of the darkness.

"I see that your tiny rational mind has reduced the word 'need' to its minimum physical meaning. Would you like to know what I think about you now?"

"Rawdon—you've been drinking. Don't say something we'll both regret—"

"You enjoy the thought of keeping me dangling for a year or two or three on the hook of desire while you poke around New York in search of your destiny."

"I don't enjoy it. I told you—I recognize the cruelty, I regret it!"

"No, you like it. All the things you told me four years ago, our testaments, everything was so much posturing. You're one of those women who want to make men grovel. Well let me tell you something. I'm in no danger of going insane with desire. There are too many women available to a man with money in his pocket. Women a damn sight more physically desirable than you."

"You go to them? To prostitutes?"

There was a long ominous silence. "You make me think about it."

Tears of rage—or shame, she could not identify them—rushed down Genevieve's cheeks. "Rawdon, I won't let you threaten me this way."

"A true woman," Rawdon said, "feels what her beloved feels. She thinks his thoughts, she dares his faith, breathes his breath, lives his life."

There was no sleep for Genevieve that night. While Alice Gansevoort murmured dreamily beside her, Genevieve stared up at the dark ceiling and tried to weep. But no tears came. She wanted to grieve for the death of love, she wanted tears to flow. But anger was the only emotion that surged in her mind and body. Love was unquestionably, irretrievably dead. But it was not her fault. The murderer was Rawdon's male arrogance.

The next morning after church, General Stapleton announced that he and Mrs. Stapleton and the Chandlers were going down to Long Branch to visit President Grant. He and Zachariah Chandler had some rather urgent political problems to discuss with him. Margaret Dall was going to stay at Kemble Manor and "matronize" the younger generation. The term had recently replaced "chaperone" in the etiquette books; it seemed to amuse General Stapleton.

Rawdon promptly undermined Mrs. Dall's matronizing by proposing a sail to Sandy Hook on the eastern side of the bay and a picnic there. Genevieve said she had a headache, which she was sure several hours in the sun would not improve. Rawdon threw surly looks in her direction; she avoided them.

The sailors departed, laden with picnic baskets, blankets, beach umbrellas. Hal Bradford was paying a great deal of attention to Eleanor, whose blue-trimmed piqué sailing outfit emphasized her ever more spectacular figure. Alice Gansevoort and Isaac Mayer held hands and smiled beatifically at each other. Grace Schermerhorn said something to Rawdon and he whispered a reply in her ear. Genevieve watched, bitterly indifferent to love and pseudo-love.

In the cool dim tranquility of Kemble Manor's library, she found a half shelf of books by Herman Melville. She had been promising herself to read more of their neighbor's works. So far, she had struggled through *Moby-Dick* and found it boring. She chose *The Confidence Man* and spent the morning with it on the rear terrace. It was not a very good novel, but she liked its bitter tone.

It was well past noon when her mother sat down beside her. "Lunch is almost ready."

Genevieve did not look up from *The Confidence Man.*

"What did you and Rawdon quarrel about?"

Genevieve shook her head.

"He has some right to be angry with you, Genevieve."

"Does he have a right to . . ."

"What?"

"Say hateful things. Absolutely hateful things."

"That's what people do when they quarrel."

"Did Father ever say hateful things to you?"

"Yes. And I said more than a few to him. People in love often quarrel."

"I'm no longer in love with Rawdon. I despise him."

"I've never seen you so irrational."

As usual, her mother's verbal aim was deadly. Genevieve writhed at the thrust and began to lose her precarious self-control. "I'm merely responding to his beastliness."

"What in the world did he say?"

"He said he didn't need me. There were other women he could go to—prostitutes."

She was weeping. *The Confidence Man* vanished in a glaze of hot tears. "Let's have lunch."

They ate cold lobster in Kemble Manor's formal dining room. Sunlight glinted from the cut-glass chandelier above them. The delicate lines of the Sheraton sideboard and chests gave the room a quaint, timeless quality. Her mother talked about Rawdon's sad childhood, his lost mother, his difficulties with his father. "In some ways he's never known love, Genevieve. Until he met you. The difference it made in him was extraordinary."

"Are you telling me I should forgive him?" She almost hissed the words.

"You're too young to understand the ways a man needs a woman—besides the obvious one. When your father came home from the war, there were nights when he couldn't sleep, when he'd just lie there, weeping. I'd hold him in my arms until dawn, sometimes. But when we came back from Mississippi, I couldn't comfort him. No one could comfort him—"

Please don't weep. Please don't reveal your regret at your failure. Can't you see that will destroy me?

As her mother wept, Genevieve groped for an answer and found only sacrilege. Rawdon Stapleton and her father both made woman's love meaningless. One in an obnoxious way, the other in a pathetic way, declared that woman's love could be purchased or ignored as a man chose. The idea was so appalling she instantly thrust it out of her mind and sat there, defenseless, while her mother talked through her tears.

"Rawdon needs you so much, Gen. If you could only see it as clearly as we all see it. The General was talking about it to me yesterday coming down on the train."

After lunch, Genevieve returned to the terrace, and *The Confidence Man.* Her mind, her body were full of unnameable pain. She heard a chair scrape and found Clay Pendleton sitting beside her.

"Back so soon?" she said.

"Very hot out there. The sand practically burned our feet off."

"I'm glad I didn't go."

"Rawdon would like to see you down at the cove. I'll keep the others entertained." Clay strummed a chord on his mandolin. "I don't know what you two argued about last night, but it's put him in a worse funk than your telegram. Why are you torturing him, Antiope? Why don't you just finish off the poor gink and get it over with?"

Genevieve sprang to her feet, trembling. This surely was the ultimate outrage: Clay Pendleton lecturing her! "You—are talking obnoxious nonsense," she said.

Her first inclination was to ignore the summons. Upstairs, she found Alice putting on a tennis dress. Her ex-roommate talked ecstatically about Isaac Mayer. She was obviously falling in love. Genevieve decided to put on a bathing dress and find out what, if anything, Rawdon Stapleton had left to say to her.

At the cove, there was no sign of Rawdon. Genevieve plunged into the deliciously cool water and swam a hundred yards as if a sea serpent were pursuing her. She pulled up, gasping for breath, and Rawdon suddenly surfaced beside her. He must have swum underwater all the way from the shore, an awesome feat.

"Your headache's gone?"

"Yes."

"We had a great sail. A great picnic. We had the beach to ourselves."

"How nice."

Rawdon treaded water a few feet away from her. It was like a dream in which their bodies had been amputated and all that was left were their heads confronting each other on this shining sheet of water: antagonists more in spirit than in flesh.

"I'm sorry about last night. The threat. The other things I said. I didn't mean any of them. Part of it was liquor, the argument with my father. Part of it was that interview with Reid at the *Times*. He treated us with such . . . contempt, Gen. That's the only word for it."

"Why does that give you a license to abuse me?"

"It doesn't. It just made me realize—next week I'm entering the real world. It made me realize how much I wanted you beside me."

No. Wait. Stop. Let me explain how deep my need is, how much I want that year of freedom and independence.

Rawdon talked on. "Four years ago, Gen, I gave you part of my soul. A part I wanted you to protect, guard. Because I wasn't sure I could go it myself. Maybe I haven't trusted you enough to admit this. Even to myself."

It was the word "trusted." Genevieve did not know, she would never know, whether she kissed him or Rawdon kissed her. All she knew was movement, union, his mouth on hers, his arms around her, while they sank down down into the cold dark water. It was more than a kiss, more than an embrace. He was devouring, consuming her. His legs, his arms, were around her. There seemed to be no part of his body that was not touching her. She began to struggle for breath, wondering if he was going to drown her in his frenzy, if this was a kiss of death.

A terrific pain throbbed in her chest. Darkness began to gather in her throat. She struggled feebly against him, wishing not so much for life as for a chance to speak, to let Rawdon know the irresistible undeniable power of her love for him.

Sunlight exploded against her eyes. They were on the surface, gasping air.

"Love you—"

"Always—"

"Marry me?"

"Tomorrow if you—"

"Nothing matters, without you."

One arm still around her waist, he paddled them slowly to shore. They stumbled up the beach and fell onto the sand and lay there, gazing dazedly at each other. Rawdon reached out and touched her face. "Don't say anything," he whispered. "Let's forget words for a while."

He began kissing her in a new way, his tongue roving deep into her mouth. Wild amazing wishes bounded through Genevieve's mind. She wanted him to strip away the wet bathing suit, to touch her everywhere with his hands, his arms, his lips. She wanted to prove to herself and to him her absolute pledge, her abandonment of egotism and selfish so-called needs.

His hands were on her breasts, her thighs. Each kiss was like a descent into the dark depths of the cove. Eyes closed, she blended with him, with his needful desire, confessing her own blind yearning. Somehow he unbuttoned the front of her bathing dress and his fingers found her nipples. Incredible surges of sweetness swept her body, a different deeper surrender from the primary gift she had been ready to make to Rawdon four years ago, a dark blend of remorse and abandonment of her thinking self, the woman she had become at Vassar.

"Oh Rawdon take me, take me now. In the bathhouse," Genevieve whispered.

There was a bench built into the wall beside the shower in the bathhouse. It was as long and almost as wide as a bed.

"No," Rawdon said, his words almost a groan. "I want you as—my wife. Nothing else."

"Oh my love my love," Genevieve said. "You have me. I belong to you forever."

Another kiss, a wild ultimate embrace. Genevieve did not know how long it lasted. She all but vanished into the darkness behind her eyes, a kind of underworld in which only primary words like *love* and *trust* existed. Finally they sat apart, allowing some semblance of civilized, ordinary feelings to return.

"Would you mind if I told everyone before we went back to New York?" Rawdon asked. "Clay saw the telegram and told the rest of the crew. It was a little humiliating."

"You can tell the whole world whenever you choose."

Genevieve expected Rawdon to announce their renewed engagement at the dinner table that evening. But he never mentioned it. In fact, before and after dinner, he kept a rather cool casual distance from her. Perhaps he felt they could not compete with the nation's hundredth birthday. That was the main topic of conversation all evening. They went to bed early, after General Stapleton sternly warned everyone that reveille was at 6 A.M. and no stragglers would be tolerated.

They arose in the dawn and hurried to the railroad station. While a locomotive hauled them to New Brunswick, they breakfasted in their private car. Before they finished their coffee, they were whizzing down the main line to Philadelphia at the rear of an express. By 10 A.M. they were in their seats in Independence Square, in the grandstand behind the speaker's platform. An immense crowd jammed every inch of the ground in front of them. On the opposite side of the square loomed the graceful red brick and white trim of Independence Hall, where the Declaration of Independence and the Constitution had been signed.

The program began with music: a chorus sang a hymn by Oliver Wendell Holmes. Vice-President Thomas Ferry apologized for President Grant's absence and read a brief speech. Then the mayor of Philadelphia invited a grandson of Richard Henry Lee of Virginia, the man who had introduced the motion for independence in the Continental Congress, to read the Declaration of Independence.

"How nice of them to admit it was the South's idea," Cynthia Stapleton said, *sotto voce.* Genevieve thought she saw General Stapleton twitch. It was astonishing, the impudence Cynthia displayed to her formidable husband.

As Lee drawled the final words of the famous document, Genevieve saw five women charge down the aisle toward the speaker's platform. They were dressed in black and carried thick bundles of paper in their hands. She recognized the Roman nose and masculine profile of Susan B. Anthony in the lead. At the platform, Miss Anthony thrust a piece of paper into the hand of Vice-President Ferry and turned to the crowd. "Ladies and gentlemen," she cried. "We have with us copies of a new declaration of independence, written by and for American women."

Astonishing. Everyone had read in the papers that the suffragists were going to issue this document. But no one dreamed they would do it right here in the middle of the Centennial ceremony. Genevieve stared at them in amazement, like everyone else. But she found herself thinking, exactly right. What better place to issue this call? She heard Grace Schermerhorn say, "Horrible woman" as Miss Anthony's cohorts began throwing copies of the declaration to the honored guests on the speakers' platform and into the crowd in front of it. In little more than sixty seconds they completed their task and left the platform.

As the perspiring chairman introduced the next speaker, Genevieve's eyes were on the black dresses of the suffragists appearing and disappearing as they struggled through the packed crowd. New York's favorite poet, bearded, noble-browed Bayard Taylor, began reciting his sonorous Centennial ode to "Liberty's Latest Daughter."

On the far side of the square, the suffragists mounted the platform where the musicians were sitting. One of the women opened an umbrella and held it over Susan B. Anthony's head. She began to read her declaration. But it was a dumb show; no one on their side of the square could hear her. Nor did they even try. Their attention was focused on the famous poet.

Again and again the crowd burst into tremendous applause for a passage that pleased them. Genevieve writhed at the futility, the absurdity, of those figures in black on the other side of the square, mouthing their unheard defiance. This humiliation was all they had to show for twenty-eight years of agitation and controversy.

There were more speeches, hymns, cheers, prayers. Finally they were back in General Stapleton's private car, returning to New York. Clay Pendleton had found a copy of the Women's Declaration of Independence, crumpled and dirt-smeared by indifferent feet, on the ground in Independence Square. He read it, with mock heroic vigor, as they sped across New Jersey.

" 'The history of our country for the past one hundred years has been a series of assumptions and usurpations of power over women in direct opposition to the principles enunciated by the United States at its foundation . . .' "

"Hang your heads, you tyrants," Alice Gansevoort said. She was smiling. It was clear that she did not really mean it.

Isaac Mayer threw himself at her feet. "Is this low enough?"

"Yes," Alice said. "If you promise to stay that way for the next fifty years."

"I bet Genevieve agrees with every word of it," her sister Eleanor said.

"I've told you a dozen times I'm not a suffragist," Genevieve snapped.

"Division in the ranks. That's why you women never get anywhere!" Hal Bradford said. "When men want to fight for something, we organize into an army or a political party."

"Who's going to see that your shirts are washed and your children are civilized if we start doing that?" Alice said.

Rawdon rose to his feet. "Quiet, please," he said. "I have an announcement to make." At both ends of the car, conversation came to a halt. "Now that we've finished one celebration, I have news that I hope will start another one. Miss Dall has agreed to marry me as soon as my duties at the *New York Times* give me a free day to arrange the ceremony."

Cries of delight and amazement from everyone. Rawdon held up his hand for another moment of silence. "Because certain doubts have circulated about this happy event, I want to *prove* its certainty."

All in one smooth motion, so it seemed to Genevieve, he drew her to her feet and slipped a diamond ring on the third finger of her left hand.

Applause. Alice leaped up and kissed her. Eleanor jumped up and down with excitement like a three-year-old. The crew surrounded Rawdon, pounding him on the back and shoulders, pumping his arm. Genevieve's mother embraced her with almost hysterical fervor. Cynthia Stapleton bestowed an enthusiastic kiss. General Stapleton did likewise and ordered Cousteau to see if there was any champagne on board.

A few minutes later, the General stood in the center of the car, a smile wreathing his scarred face. He raised his glass. "To the pursuit of happiness," he said.

A perfect American toast for July 4, 1876. Rawdon put his free arm around Genevieve's waist and gave her a quick, fierce kiss. Everyone applauded and Hal Bradford shouted, "They'd better get married as soon as possible."

Laughter. A little embarrassed, Genevieve lowered her eyes. On the floor beneath Rawdon's foot was the dirt-smeared copy of the Women's Declaration of Independence. Suddenly, unaccountably, she was empty of faith and hope and love. She gazed into Rawdon's handsome face and was rescued by the happiness, the confidence, she saw there. She had sacrificed her little experiment in independence for something infinitely finer, nobler, more enduring.

She was a true woman after all.

EIGHT

"It's the mollycoddles around Hayes that worry me. The idiots who talk about extending the hand of friendship to the South!"

Jonathan Stapleton sat in the ornate main dining room of Delmonico's downtown restaurant, at Broadway and Pine Street, listening to James Fish, president of the Marine National Bank, tell him what was wrong with the Republican candidate for president, the honest but colorless governor of Ohio, Rutherford B. Hayes. Fish's diatribe was mostly a reprise of countless lamentations and complaints Jonathan had heard in the past two months from railroad presidents, factory owners, shippers and oil men from New York to San Francisco.

Outside, a cold September rain pelted down, turning Broadway's gutters into miniature rivers. If it rained that way on Election Day, the Republicans would lose New York, the state they had to carry to win the election. Respectable people, citizens who did not take money to vote, were chary about getting wet. Incredible, the trivial details on which the fate of the republic depended.

If it rained this way tomorrow Jonathan Stapleton would have a morose wife and a distraught daughter-in-law on his hands. There were times in the last few frantic weeks, as the presidential campaign gathered momentum, when he was afraid he might forget the day, even forget the fact, that his son Rawdon was marrying Genevieve Dall.

"I presume you read in the papers what that southern trollop did to my son?" James Fish asked.

Jonathan nodded. Fish had gone into seclusion after the *Herald* reported that his son had embezzled four million dollars from the Marine National Bank to silence a blackmailing southern adventuress. Fish had promptly repaid the money—the actual figure was less than a million—from his personal funds. But the impact of the scandal was visible on the lean old man. His skin was papery, his hand trembled as he picked at his roast beef.

"I sometimes think we should have let the rebel bastards go in 1861. Maybe we should have built a wall around the goddamned Confederacy and let them wallow in their women and liquor and slaves until they reverted to the jungle."

Inwardly, Jonathan flinched from Fish's raw hatred. But he had been pursuing the banker for a major contribution and he did not want to endanger it. Fish finally handed over a check for $50,000. But there was a catch to it. He wanted a job in the Custom House for his son. "He can't work in the bank and no one will give him a job anywhere else," he snarled, implying that he did not blame the reluctant employers.

It was a paradigm of why the Republican Party was in trouble. Powerful men like James Fish used political jobs as a dumping ground for drunken, corrupt, incompetent relatives. But Jonathan could identify with the pain and grief behind the old man's bitter disposal of his ruined son. Too often he had imagined Rawdon disgracing the Stapletons in a similar way.

He thanked Fish and trudged back to his Wall Street office beneath his black umbrella.

"Hello, General." It was John Reid, the managing editor of the *New York Times*, under another umbrella.

"Hello, Jack. You're doing a hell of a job on the Democrats."

From the day Rutherford B. Hayes had been nominated with fulsome acclaim on the *Times*'s front page, Reid had seized the initiative from the Democrats. Instead of trying to defend the Republican Party, he had been pounding away at the enemy's numerous flaws. He was applying the fundamental lesson of the war: victory favored the attacker.

"Thanks," Reid said. He looked haggard. There were splotches of raw red skin on his cheeks and nose. He was obviously drinking as hard as he was working.

"How do things look from where you sit?"

"Pennsylvania's improving all the time. But I'm worried about New York. We're unlimbering some heavy ammunition on Tilden's connections with Tweed. Maybe that can turn things around."

Jonathan nodded approvingly. The Democratic candidate, Samuel Tilden, the governor of New York, liked to portray himself as the man who had put Boss Tweed in jail. Actually, he had ignored Tammany Hall's corruption until the *Times* exposed it.

"How are your two Princeton reporters getting along?"

Reid hesitated. "The rebel kid, Pendleton, is first rate. A born newspaperman. Gets the story, puts it together just the way you want it. Your boy, Rawdon—I'm not so sure if he's in the right business. A newspaperman is a team effort, Jonathan. Rawdon wants to do everything his way."

Jonathan trudged the rest of the way to his office feeling depressed. He sat at his desk staring at a daguerreotype of Rawdon on a rocking horse at the age of seven. Even then he seemed to look out on the world with a hauteur that was subtly irritating. *A prince*, he seemed to be saying. *I am a disinherited prince.* In the same frame was a picture of George at the age of five. His round earnest face gazed plaintively out at him. *Just a boy, a good boy*, he seemed to be saying. *Why don't you love me?*

An hour later Jonathan took a hack uptown through the continuing downpour to the Union League Club at Madison Avenue and Twenty-sixth Street, where he had an appointment with the owner of a Trenton steel mill. In the club's deserted lobby he met Theodore Roosevelt.

"Friend Stapleton," Roosevelt said in his cheery way. "How are you on this miserable day?"

"Busy," Jonathan said.

"I'm sure the wedding has the whole family doing flips. I hear the bride-to-be is something of a genius. You can look forward to brilliant grandsons."

"A frightening thought."

"My older fellow, Theodore, is turning into quite a scholar. He must have inherited Mittie's brains. No one in the Roosevelt family ever went near a college before, but I've decided to send him to Harvard."

"Wonderful."

Roosevelt obviously had nothing to do for the rest of the day. He blithely ignored Jonathan's unresponsiveness and began talking about the election. "I hope the new President, whoever he is, will take a more reasonable approach to the South."

"You don't care whether it's Hayes or Tilden?"

"I like Hayes well enough, but Mittie's convinced me that Tilden is a good man, too. Anyway, those Indian trading-post scandals made me think it might be better for the party and the country if the Republicans lost this election."

For a moment Jonathan was tempted to tell Theodore what he thought of a man who let a woman change his mind about the most important election of the century. But he did not have time to argue with this cheerful well-intentioned man, whom everyone in New York regarded as a model citizen. That was the trouble with the liberal Republicans. They were hard to criticize because they were all paragons of morality and civic virtue. But their ideas about political power and what men could do with it were unbelievably naïve.

"I wish I had time to debate with you. But I have a man upstairs who's waiting to give me twenty-five thousand dollars to keep the Rebellion out of the White House."

Jonathan strode toward the elevator. "See you at the wedding," Roosevelt called in a curiously forlorn voice.

Jonathan talked the steel mill owner into giving him $40,000 by pointing out that the other major steel producer in Trenton, Abram Hewitt, was the chairman of the Democratic National Committee and would do everything in his power to put his competition out of business if Tilden won. With $90,000 in his pocket, Jonathan walked across Madison Square to Republican headquarters at the Fifth Avenue Hotel.

In the French Directoire sitting room on the second floor, chairman Zachariah Chandler sat with Senator Roscoe Conkling of New York. The Senator's hyacinthine curl fell picturesquely down his noble brow. Chandler had his inevitable glass of bourbon on the desk and his perpetual cigar in his hand.

"General," Chandler said. "Thank Christ you've finally arrived." He mashed Stapleton's hand in his rugged grip. "I've been sitting here listening to this fellow tell me we're licked for want of a few thousand dollars."

"Why are we licked?" Jonathan Stapleton said. The mere phrase knotted his stomach.

"If we don't find a half-million dollars by the day after tomorrow, General," Conkling boomed, "we're going to lose the Empire State—and the election. Our Democratic candidate Mr. Tilden, the heroic prosecutor of Bill Tweed, has gotten back in bed with Tammany Hall. If he ever got out. We need the money to hire an extra ten thousand poll watchers here in the city and upstate."

Jonathan was perfectly aware that hiring poll watchers was a euphemism for buying votes. There was little alternative in New York's big cities, where the Democrats had made vote selling a habit among the poor.

"Here's a ninety-thousand-dollar down payment," Jonathan said, handing the checks to Chandler. He told Conkling, who doubled as boss of the New York Republican Party, about James Fish's request for a job for his disgraced son.

"Tell him to write me a letter. We'll do everything possible," Conkling said.

"For another fifty thousand we'll do the impossible," Chandler said.

Jonathan forced a smile, remembering Theodore Roosevelt's disdain for Republican corruption. He wondered what Ben Dall would think of these politicians—and of him, consorting with them, raising millions for them, asking no questions of any of them.

Ben would be heaping moral obloquy on him, far more cutting than Theodore Roosevelt's plaintive disapproval of selling Indian trading posts in Washington, D.C.

Remember what happened at Cold Harbor, Ben, Jonathan said to the accusatory ghost. Remember the day you found out that once you start a war it is too late for second thoughts. It was still too late. Bitter fanatics like James Fish, corrupt realists like Zachariah Chandler, orotund egotists like Roscoe Conkling, were far from perfect allies. But you did not win an election by demanding character references from everyone, any more than you won a war. The main point, the only point as far as he was concerned, was to stop the South from proving that the bullet could triumph over the ballot after all.

Jonathan went over their New York contributors' list to see where they could find another $400,000 for Conkling. "Gould still hasn't given a cent," Jonathan said.

"I'm going to be head of the Interstate Commerce Committee next year," Conkling said. "You tell that little bastard if he doesn't come through with the cash I'll investigate the way he's running the Union Pacific until he's in jail."

"That's a message I'll be delighted to deliver," Jonathan said.

"We've got to carry New York," Zachariah Chandler said. "From everything I hear, Indiana's gone, New Jersey's going. If we lose New York the game's over."

Jonathan rode home to Stuyvesant Square through a dwindling drizzle and found himself engulfed by domestic chaos. Two dressmakers were at work in the back parlor, frantically sewing and snipping. A rabbit-eyed little man scurried upstairs carrying a tray of hot towels. Cousteau identified him as Henri, Cynthia's hairdresser. Jonathan asked what the dressmakers were doing. "Making a new gown for your mother, General," Cousteau said, with a sigh.

A short squat German rushed into the hall with a veritable garden of flowers in his arms. "Where do these go?" he cried.

Jonathan retreated upstairs, where he encountered George, on his way down. "Careful what you say," George whispered, nodding toward Cynthia's door. "You can get your head taken off."

Jonathan peered warily into Cynthia's room. She was sitting in front of her dressing table, a sheet draped around her. Henri was creating a series of tiny curls across her forehead.

"Everything under control?" Jonathan asked.

"Rawdon arrived with your mother about noon. She decided after seeing my gown that hers was too old-fashioned. So we had to send out an emergency call to my dressmaker. I spent half the afternoon at Delmonico's working out the seating with Margaret Dall. It's appalling how many of our friends aren't speaking to each other or would rather not sit at the same table because of your damn election. I spent the rest of the afternoon at the church seeing to the flowers. Poor Margaret is exhausted and Genevieve is worse than useless. She keeps saying she doesn't care, there's no need for everything to be perfect. Rawdon is no better. They both keep saying they wish they'd eloped. I told them I concurred heartily."

For a moment Jonathan was tempted to point out that Cynthia had joined Margaret Dall in persuading Rawdon and Genevieve to postpone their wedding from July to this more socially acceptable September date. In the meantime, the wedding had swelled from the small private affair the young people had planned to a major social event, with Van Vorsts and Roosevelts and Schermerhorns and Browns on the ever lengthening guest list. When Jonathan wondered what had happened to the smaller wedding, he was told that this elaborate ceremony was for Genevieve's sake. The girl had to be made aware that as Mrs. Rawdon Stapleton she was a member of society.

"Where's Rawdon?"

"In his room, I think. His bachelor dinner last night seems to have tested even his powers of recuperation."

Jonathan climbed to the fourth floor and knocked on Rawdon's door.

"Come in," Rawdon said. He was sprawled on the bed, turning the pages of the *New York Herald*. "Now what have I done?" he asked.

"Not a thing, not a thing," Jonathan said. "I've been looking for a chance to talk to you. But between politics and your newspaperman's hours, the days have just slipped away."

"What do you want to talk about?" Rawdon said, continuing to scan the *Herald*, a paper that vituperatively supported the Democrats. During the war it had tirelessly slandered Lincoln and the Union Army.

"A couple of things," Jonathan said, closing the door. He pulled a chair away from the wall and straddled it. "A father's supposed to make sure that his son knows the basic facts about sexual intercourse, that sort of thing. We discussed it in a sort of fundamental way when you were sixteen or so. I just thought you might have some specific questions."

Rawdon turned to another page in the *Herald*. "I don't think there's anything you can tell me on that subject."

"Maybe I can still give you some *advice*," Jonathan said. "Genevieve's a very sweet, sensitive, innocent girl. Don't rush things. Be as gentle as you possibly can."

"Father. She's taken a course in physiology. She knows as much about it as I do."

"All right, all right," Jonathan said. "There's something else I want to say. I know you and Genevieve are determined to live on your salary. An admirable idea. But there are bound to be extra expenses in setting up a household. When I got married, my father gave me a hundred thousand dollars. Not to spend, but to invest and use the income. Prices are a lot higher since the war. I'd like to give you two hundred thousand."

"No thanks," Rawdon said, perusing the *Herald*'s editorial page.

"Would you mind telling me why?"

"Grandmother's giving me five thousand dollars for a wedding present. That will take care of setting up a household. I don't want any money from you because I don't want any more orders or advice from you for the rest of my life. That's going to stop, tomorrow, when I walk out of this house."

For a moment Jonathan was back thirteen years, on his first furlough from the front, discovering what his wife and mother had done to his son, confronting the enmity on Rawdon's eight-year-old face. He was filled with remembered pain—and a renewed rage at the mindless malice that caused it.

"Rawdon, I was hoping—I always thought there'd come a time when this thing between us would end. It was started by women. I hoped another woman from a different background might help you understand—"

"I know all about what you think Genevieve might do for me. Grandmother's told me. She's supposed to give me stability. In other words, make me a nice obedient boy, a worshiper of my noble father. I won't even try to explain why I'm marrying her. You wouldn't even begin to understand it."

"Perhaps not. But you are marrying her. I would think you might reconsider my offer—for her sake."

"I'm perfectly capable of taking care of my wife without any help from you."

"That's not what John Reid tells me," Jonathan snarled. "I gather you're close to getting fired from the *Times*. Are you hoping to get a job on the scummy sheet you're reading?"

Rawdon flung the *Herald* aside and thrust himself to the edge of the bed, the green eyes glowing with defiance. "I should have known you were getting regular reports on me."

"I happened to meet Reid on the street today—"

"Bullshit."

Jonathan's hand leaped from the back of the chair, his body lunging after it. There was a crack like a distant rifle shot. He had smashed his twenty-two-year-old son in the face.

Rawdon rubbed his cheek. "That's the last time you'll ever do that to me," he said.

At eight o'clock the Stapletons, including George, who was one of the ushers, rode down to Grace Church for the rehearsal. Genevieve had asked Jonathan to give her away—a request that had renewed his vision of her as a bridge of understanding between him and Rawdon. How pathetic that idea seemed now. But the rehearsal went smoothly, with Eleanor Dall standing in for the bride while Genevieve, as was the custom, watched. Rawdon ignored him and talked almost exclusively to his best man, Clay Pendleton.

Going up the aisle, Eleanor Dall whispered kittenishly to Jonathan, "How I wish I were doing this tomorrow." He assured her she would be making the journey soon enough. "But Rawdon won't be there waiting for me," she sighed.

There was simply no limit to women's susceptibility to a handsome face, Jonathan thought gloomily. He found himself wondering whether Rawdon would remain faithful to Genevieve. Within a month of his wedding, Charlie had been back in New Orleans chasing quadroons and telling his brother about it. Sometimes Jonathan wondered how Cynthia, who was usually so discerning about people, had not seen the real Charlie. Another proof of the power of the handsome face, alas.

The rehearsal dinner went smoothly, too, thanks in large part to his mother's decision to remain in her room. Only Jonathan, Cynthia and Margaret Dall represented the older generation, and they were soon made to feel superfluous. Clay Pendleton predicted ten children; one would succeed Rawdon as president, the other nine would become justices of the Supreme Court. Rawdon's decision to live in a new "French flat," as they were called, on West Forty-third Street, was grist for more extensive joking. Both Jonathan and Margaret Dall had been dismayed but thought it best to say nothing. At least they were not going to live in a hotel, another choice that was becoming popular among young people.

Rawdon entertained the party with unflattering stories about the *New York Times*. He told them about covering the death of an out-of-work porter on the Lower East Side. When the man was evicted from his tenement he put a rifle in his mouth and pulled the trigger. As a head, Managing Editor Reid had written: A COWARDLY SUICIDE. When Rawdon protested, he was told the *Times* did not make heroes of the unemployed.

Rawdon discoursed at even more cynical length on another newspaper tradition: faking it. Few people outside the profession were aware of it. Jonathan himself had never heard the term, although he had long since learned to be skeptical about most newspapers' claims to the truth. Apparently it was a common practice for reporters to invent facts wholesale in their stories. Sometimes they were out to prove a point about an ethnic group or a political party. Often it was simply a device to pad the story and make more money for the reporter, who was paid by the word—in the jargon of the business, "on space."

As Jonathan listened his eyes sought out Genevieve. He pondered the sensitive mouth—a feminine replica of her father's—the thoughtful gaze, the touching way she allowed Rawdon to cover her hand with his while he talked. Had he made a horrendous mistake encouraging this match?

The next morning saw a brief reprise of chaos as his mother and Cynthia got combed and dressed in their finery. Downstairs the sight of Rawdon in his cutaway made Jonathan's chest tighten. He looked so much like Charlie, all they needed was the Mississippi flowing outside the door to make him believe that time had reversed itself overnight and the year was 1858.

Rawdon, I'm sorry about what happened last night. Can we at least shake hands? The words were on his lips. But he could not say them. He could not risk another rebuff. A renewed quarrel might disrupt the wedding.

Instead, he found himself watching Cynthia as she came downstairs to say good morning to Rawdon. There was no perceptible change in her smile, her good cheer. Then his mother descended and proclaimed, "Oh Cynthia, Rawdon looks so much like Charlie. I'm afraid this is going to be a heartbreaking day for you."

"You're the one I'm worried about, Mother," Cynthia said. "You mustn't get overwrought."

His mother seized Rawdon with one of her clawlike arthritic hands. "Oh Rawdie," she quavered. "You're the only reason I've lived so long. To see you settled, happy, in spite of everything."

"I am, Gammy, thanks mostly to you," Rawdon said.

In crisp cool air, rich with sunshine, they rode to Grace Church through the rainwashed streets. Rawdon and Clay Pendleton went off to the sacristy. Ushers led Cynthia and his mother to their seats. Jonathan paced the vestibule. The bride arrived exactly at eleven. In the nave, the organ boomed some music he did not recognize. Margaret Dall led Genevieve over to him. She was spectral beneath her white veil. She carried a bouquet of orange blossoms. Her dress was corded silk with satin bows and a wide band of lace and an enormous bustle and train.

"I'm so pleased—that you asked me to give you away, Genevieve," Jonathan said.

"You've been a father to me in so many ways," Genevieve said.

Pain throbbed in Jonathan's chest. He was gaining a daughter—and simultaneously losing one. She was marrying a son who would turn her against him.

For the rest of the day Jonathan felt as if he were riding a merry-go-round that was tipped at a crazy angle, leaving him in constant danger of sliding off. Everyone kept telling him the wedding was a huge success. Lorenzo Delmonico himself said that he had seldom seen such a cheerful party. All Jonathan saw and heard were danger signals. Before they sat down to eat, his mother ensconced herself in a corner of the ballroom and received callers as if she were at a separate party. Rawdon brought Genevieve over to her, and Caroline Stapleton launched into a long frowning monologue. Then Cecilia Schermerhorn and Margaret Dall and Katherine Kemble Brown swirled around her, as if she were still the great lady of yore.

Waiters passed through the crowd, bonging chimes to announce that the wedding breakfast was being served. Cynthia took Jonathan's arm as he walked to the head table. "Why in the world are you looking so gloomy, Husband dear?" she asked. "Last week you were telling me that this was going to be one of the happiest days of your life."

"It is," Jonathan said, forcing a smile.

His mother was the last to join them at the long table, which seated the entire wedding party. She hobbled toward them on her cane, while Rawdon hovered beside her. No doubt people wondered why her son was not performing this tender task. She sat down next to him and immediately took over the conversation. "I'm so disappointed to hear that Rawdon and Genevieve are not going to Havana. A week at Kemble Manor is hardly a honeymoon."

"I agree," Cynthia said. "If Rawdon turns out to be a typical Stapleton with politics on his mind twenty-four hours a day, their honeymoon may be Genevieve's last chance to get his attention for the rest of her life."

"I'm as interested in politics as he is," Genevieve said. "Besides, the *New York Times* wouldn't let one of its best reporters take thirty days off in the middle of the presidential election."

"A good sign, as far as it goes," Caroline Stapleton said in a more private tone to Jonathan. "But I wonder if her politics will ever agree with Rawdon's. I presume she inclines to her father's fanaticism."

Rawdon leaned forward to call down the table, "We'll go to Havana on our first wedding anniversary, presuming you'll loan me the money, Gammy."

"Of course I will. If you need money for any reason, let me know."

After a series of toasts to the bride and groom, the orchestra began playing. Rawdon led Genevieve out on the floor for the first dance. Jonathan, as the substitute father of the bride, volunteered for the second one. He warned Genevieve that his damaged knee made him an awkward partner and swung her into a passable waltz.

"What was my mother saying to you before we sat down?" he asked.

"She told me she hoped I wouldn't make Rawdon unhappy."

"Why should you? Don't let that woman intimidate you, Genevieve. Rawdon badly needs your influence in his life. Your positive influence."

Dismay was all he could see on Genevieve's face. "What do you mean?"

He was close to doing what he had vowed to avoid: ruining Genevieve's wedding day. "Maybe I worry about him too much," he said. "I've always felt responsible for leaving him at my mother's mercy during the war." He blundered out a sketchy explanation of his mother's antipathy to him.

"I wish you'd all leave us alone," Genevieve said. "Rawdon and I have our own ideas about the kind of life we want to live. You probably won't approve of it any more than your mother will."

For a moment he was tempted to be blunt: to warn her that he was afraid Caroline Stapleton might turn Rawdon against his wife as she had turned him against his father. He wanted her to realize that poison still festered in the primary wound and could menace her happiness. But it was impossible to explain.

"I'm beginning to think you've found out how to get a Stapleton's attention, Genevieve," said a southern voice behind them. "You must tell me your secret."

Cynthia drifted past in Lionel Bradford's arms. He had been invited because his son Hal was one of Rawdon's ushers. Jonathan returned Genevieve to Rawdon's side and spent the rest of the afternoon watching the young people enjoy themselves. He was somewhat alarmed by how much they drank. He was particularly upset to discover George and Elliott Roosevelt in the men's room swigging from a bottle of champagne. Elliott was already drunk and George was well on his way.

Jonathan took the bottle away from them and told them to go back to their respective tables and stay there. He was hoping that the Roosevelts would take Elliott home, but Theodore was dancing with Cynthia, and Mittie seemed oblivious to the cockeyed grin on her fifteen-year-old son's face. Jonathan grimly vowed to send George to St. Paul's School in January no matter what Cynthia said against it. Another year of Elliott's company and George would turn into a charming wastrel.

That night, back home on Stuyvesant Square, the newlyweds on their way to Kemble Manor, his mother on her way back to Bowood, there stirred in Jonathan feelings that reminded him of the war. Those times, after a battle, especially after one of those blunderous defeats such as Fredericksburg, when he wanted a woman. When he needed to touch the transforming power of female flesh, to hear the voice of another spiritual dimension in his soul.

Now he wanted a specific woman. He wanted Cynthia's languorous voice murmuring against his throat. He wanted to dismiss all the ugly thoughts and memories of the last two days, from Rawdon's defiance to his mother's vicious evocation of Charlie to Genevieve's rejection of his fatherly advice. He wanted to reclaim his wife, to reassert his love before another week of nerve-shredding politics began.

I don't know about you, but a wedding stimulates certain ideas in me that I would like to discuss with you later tonight. He waited for a chance to say something like that, while he listened to Cynthia tell him how much youthful romance had been swirling around him at the wedding. Isaac Mayer had proposed to Alice Gansevoort and she had accepted him. Hal Bradford had ignored Grace Schermerhorn and spent most of the day on the dance floor with Eleanor Dall.

"Good God," Jonathan said. "I'm not sure I like that idea."

"Jonathan. Hal's going to inherit three or four million dollars from his mother alone."

"I don't want to be connected to Lionel Bradford, no matter how much money is at stake."

"You won't be. You're not related to the Dalls, even though you act as though you are."

"That's a rather strange thing to say."

"I happen to find the way you moon over Genevieve a trifle exasperating."

"I don't recall doing anything that deserves the word 'moon.' I'll admit to a very sentimental affection for her. She's the daughter of my oldest friend—"

"I know, I know."

No you don't. You don't have the slightest idea what Ben Dall meant to me. Nor do you realize or care how much that meaning grows each day as everything Ben predicted about the South and the Negro and the war comes true.

The words blazed in his mind. He had absolutely no control over them. He did not want them or welcome them. They were simply there.

Cynthia was changing the subject, talking about a party at Cecilia Schermerhorn's. "It's in honor of Governor Tilden. The Roosevelts are going. I hope you don't mind. You'll be away all week—"

"I'm afraid I do mind. There'll be reporters around, I'm sure. I don't want your name appearing on a guest list. How do you expect me to explain that to Zachariah Chandler and Roscoe Conkling?"

Cynthia sat up very straight in her yellow wing chair. "Really, Jonathan. Am I to have no social life whatsoever while this madness persists?"

"May I remind you that you've just enjoyed an entire day of social life?"

"That was not *my* social life. That was my contribution to your—machinations. Which I hope and pray will not prove fatal to Rawdon's happiness."

"Good God. Now you sound like my mother."

"Your mother is not a stupid woman, Jonathan. She's an acute judge of human nature."

"Does that mean you agree with her judgment of me?"

Cynthia did not speak for a full minute. Did she know how awesomely beautiful she was, with every dark curl gleaming, the green eyes flashing?

"I've been thinking for several days now that this might be a good time to pay my mother a duty visit. I gather from Jeannie's last letter that she may not live much longer. I would hope, when I return after the election, I will have a loving husband again. Instead of a worn-out nervous wreck of a man who asks me ridiculous, quarrelsome questions."

She stood up, shook out the flounces and folds of her pale-blue gown, and kissed him on the forehead. "Good night," she said.

He sat there, breathing her violet perfume, while her footsteps mounted the stairs. *A wedding stimulates certain ideas.* But there was obviously no hope of discussing them tonight. Tomorrow night he would be on a train to Buffalo.

Suddenly there was another voice, an alien voice, whispering in the parlor.

The spoils of war.

Is the price too high?

NINE

The city room of the *New York Times* boiled with an explosive mixture of fear and rancor. The burden of portraying the scandal-smeared Republican Party as the nation's saviors had left Managing Editor John Reid in a state of nervous exhaustion. The walls shook as he excoriated reporters for everything from bad grammar to lack of zeal. In the airless corner where Croton bugs toiled, Clay Pendleton's stomach somersaulted when he heard Reid snarl, "Dixie!"

"Yes, Mr. Reid," he said, hurrying to the elevated desk from which Reid abused his harried minions.

"Get your rebel ass up to the American Association for the Advancement of Women. The husband of the dame that runs it told somebody she'd give us a statement endorsing Hayes. We might pick up a few votes from the pinheads who believe the garbage Henry Ward Beecher spouts about the new woman."

"Yes, Mr. Reid," Pendleton said, concealing his chagrin.

The wildest, most important election of the century was roaring to a climax and he was being sent to interview someone who could not even vote in it. Was it the fate of a Croton bug or an assignment reserved for a man from South Carolina? Pendleton inclined to the latter more vicious conclusion.

General Stapleton had apparently told Reid that Pendleton's father had been a newspaper editor. When Reid mentioned it one day, Pendleton had showed him the copy of his father's last editorial which he carried in his wallet. It had given him a sort of bona fides with this terrible-tempered, foul-tongued man. Reid sometimes praised Pendleton's work and occasionally gave him challenging assignments.

When the presidential campaign began in September, the managing editor's attitude underwent a dismaying change. "Dixie" seemed to regain the sneer Reid had injected into it on Pendleton's first day on the job, and his assignments became preponderantly trivial.

Still, he was doing better than Rawdon Stapleton, Pendleton consoled himself as he rode uptown on the ear-shattering Ninth Avenue elevated train. Thanks to his determination to disagree with Reid about everything from the *Times*'s political policy to the clothes a Croton bug should wear to work, Rawdon seldom wrote anything but obituaries and five-line reports of suicides.

Looking at the managing editor as a newspaperman rather than as a human being, Pendleton stubbornly maintained in the teeth of Rawdon's sneers that Reid was a genius. With an absolute minimum of faking it, as far as Pendleton could tell, the *Times* had maintained a slashing offensive against the overconfident Democrats. Urbanely, derisively, Reid had skewered the party of the people for its tacit endorsement of terror in the South and its loose talk about making the federal government pay off the Confederate war debt. Almost singlehanded, Reid had transformed the election. The campaign was ending with the Democrats on the defensive, frantically trying to remind the voters of the scandals that had made the Republicans look like certain losers in July.

A half hour later, with his ears still ringing from the elevated's clangor, Pendleton skirted a dead dray horse lying in the gutter and knocked on the door of a brownstone house on West Nineteeth Street. This was the home of Mrs. Charles Edwin Wilbour, president of the American Association for the Advancement of Women. A servant led him to a rear parlor which had been converted into a study. There, in a pristine white blouse and a straight black skirt, sat Mrs. Rawdon Stapleton operating one of those unwieldy collections of keys, wires and bars known as a typewriter. The working woman had become a working wife. As Rawdon casually explained it to Pendleton, he had agreed to let Genevieve stay on the job until she became pregnant.

"Clay," she said. "What a pleasant surprise."

"I'm from the district attorney's office, Mrs. Stapleton," he growled. "I understand you plan to put on a pair of trousers and try to vote tomorrow. Confess to me and I'll get you off with a twenty-year sentence. I've got influence in this town."

"I wish I had the courage," she said. "I'd love to cancel my husband's Democratic ballot."

Pendleton's friendship with Mrs. Rawdon Stapleton had become one of the few consoling aspects of his life since the presidential campaign began. Genevieve's disapproval of him, which she had made little effort to conceal, seemed to have vanished with her marriage. Perhaps it was part of a beatific resolution to like all Rawdon's friends. But Pendleton also suspected that closer, more continuous contact with Rawdon made Genevieve realize that a degenerate mandolin-playing southerner was not the cause of all her beloved's flaws. At any rate, Pendleton was a frequent dinner guest in the Stapleton flat on West Forty-third Street, where he soon became Genevieve's ally in her polite, oh-so-loving but also very determined disagreement with her husband's politics.

In the past, Genevieve had been content to let Rawdon denounce both parties. But when he decided to gall both his father and John Reid by espousing the Democrats, his wife remembered that her father had been one of the founders of the Republican Party. As an educated woman, married to a man who had acceded, however insincerely, to the tenets of rational love and equal marriage, she felt she had a perfect right to express her disagreement. As the son of a man who had devoted his editorial page to exposing Democratic excesses, Pendleton could not resist joining her. Between them they frequently reduced Rawdon to furious incoherence.

"Who's going to win this crazy election?" Genevieve asked.

"If I knew that, I could get rich. The city is full of bozos betting two to one on Tilden."

"I don't really *care*," Genevieve said with a sigh. "Except that Rawdon is so involved. I'm beginning to think it might be better for him if the Republicans won. He'd be so disgusted, it might inoculate him against future frenzy."

The sigh made Pendleton wonder if she was unhappy. Could such an ordinary, humdrum thing happen to the new woman? She would have to resign as queen of the Amazons. Pendleton got down to business and told Genevieve why he was there. He was awarded with a stunning smile.

"We can use some newspaper publicity," she said. "Let me tell Mrs. Wilbour."

Genevieve hurried upstairs and Pendleton strolled around her office, which contained a remarkable collection of ancient Egyptian art. Mrs. Wilbour was married to New York's leading Egyptologist. Pendleton peered at the letter in Genevieve's typewriter. It was to none other than Susan B. Anthony.

After a few minutes, he heard Genevieve inviting him upstairs. He followed her into a room that was the opposite of every study he had ever visited. The dominant color here was pale rose, and the landscapes on the walls were equally cheerful in color and scene. Chintz draperies, a flowered rug, added to the brightness.

Mrs. Wilbour, a petite dark-haired woman of about forty with a humorous slant to her mouth, sat on a rose sofa awaiting him. "Mrs. Stapleton tells me you'd like a comment on the election," she said.

Clay nodded, took out his notebook and pencil, and Mrs. Wilbour began.

"The executive committee of the American Association for the Advancement of Women has authorized me to say that we favor the election of Mr. Hayes. We believe he is an honest man and will bring an honest administration to Washington. We support the Republican Party because we feel that by extending the vote to the Negro it has at least accepted the principle that the vote can be extended to other members of our society—in particular, women."

"I seem to recall Mrs. Stapleton telling me that you weren't interested in the vote," Pendleton said.

"The AAAW doesn't believe the vote is the main issue for women at this time. We want to see the new woman given an opportunity to use her mind, her talent, for the improvement of our country. When this happens, we believe the vote will come as a matter of course."

Like hell it will, Pendleton thought as he scribbled notes on Mrs. Wilbour's sweetly reasonable optimism. Why couldn't these moderate sensible women see the fatal flaw in their program? Men were not rational about women. Any more than women were rational about men.

Pendleton found himself studying Genevieve Dall Stapleton as Mrs. Wilbour lectured him on the coming age of equality. Genevieve's nose had a slight snub to it, which gave her a somewhat impudent expression. The effect was softened by the mouth, which had a charming purity, an almost childish innocence, to it. There was a small cleft in the upper lip that hinted at erotic possibilities. But the blue-gray eyes seemed to cancel this congery of opposites. They existed in a world of their own, a strange mingling of mood and mystery.

Genevieve's trim tight-waisted blouse recalled the slim firm figure Pendleton had seen in a bathing dress at Kemble Manor. What a lucky son of a bitch Rawdon Stapleton was, to go home each night to explore the various fascinating combinations this woman emanated. While Pendleton trailed back to his furnished rooms on Bleecker Street, picking up a Broadway street-walker when he was in the mood, which was seldom these days.

Did Rawdon appreciate his good fortune? Not as far as Pendleton could see. Rawdon seemed more interested in dueling his father and John Reid for some sort of supremacy that would guarantee him a niche in the Stapleton pantheon.

Mrs. Wilbour was telling Pendleton how glad she was that Genevieve had persuaded Rawdon to let her work until she was "expecting." When the newlyweds came to supper a few nights ago, Mrs. Wilbour had informed Rawdon that there was no reason in the world why a healthy young woman could not work right up until her confinement. "That's what I did," she said.

"I'm afraid that's too much for Rawdon to handle at the moment," Genevieve said. "I had enough trouble getting him to agree to let me come back to work after the wedding."

The things you learn while chasing a story, Pendleton thought. Between the day Miss Dall surrendered unconditionally at Kemble Manor and the wedding, there must have been some negotiations that the conqueror, Rawdon Stapleton, never mentioned to his aide-de-camp. More negotiations were obviously scheduled.

Was it like the South, struggling, underhandedly and overhandedly, back to some semblance of independence after Appomattox? No. Genevieve would not ambush Rawdon in the dark. Or would she? There were times when the blue faded from those eyes and only awesome gray depths were visible.

Downstairs, Genevieve gave Clay a brief demonstration of the typewriter. It was impressive the way it multiplied writing speed. "I'm surprised they haven't sold some to the newspapers," she said.

"A reporter suggested it to Reid and almost got fired. He said a pencil was good enough for him when he wrote ten thousand words on Lincoln's funeral."

"You make him sound almost as bad as Rawdon does. What assignment did he get today?"

"I think it was the morgue again. The cops fished about six bodies out of the rivers last night."

"Oh dear."

"We're starting to call him Suicide Stapleton."

"I wish he could see the humor of it," Genevieve said, with another alarming sigh.

Back in the city room Pendleton concentrated on reporting why the American Association for the Advancement of Women was endorsing Rutherford

B. Hayes. They were turning on the gaslamps as he laid his copy on John Reid's big desk.

The managing editor reacted as if Pendleton had dropped a bomb in his lap. "Where the hell have you been?"

Pendleton pointed to the story and started to stutter an explanation.

"That shouldn't have taken a half hour!" Reid shouted. "Look at this!" He whipped a red ballot out of his desk and thrust it at Pendleton.

Republican ballots were red, Democratic ballots were blue. The colors helped the numerous citizens who could not read, and simplified counting the votes. But this red ballot had the names of the Democratic candidates, from Samuel Tilden down to the lowliest alderman, printed on it.

"A federal marshal just caught some fucking Irish printer turning out a couple of hundred thousand of these," Reid thundered. "Get your lazy rebel ass out of here and don't come back until you find some Democratic son of a bitch foisting one of these on an honest Republican tomorrow. Tell your friend Stapleton to do the same thing."

Pendleton slogged across City Hall Park to Mouquin's, the restaurant on Chambers Street where many of the city's newspapermen congregated. He found Rawdon finishing off a steak and told him what they are going to do on Election Day.

"Pretend you never located me," Rawdon said. "I'm working on a much bigger story. If the *Times* won't print it, the *Herald* will."

Rawdon had been making a lot of remarks about switching to the *Herald* lately. He had met the debonair owner, James Gordon Bennett, Jr., at the Hoffman House Bar, favorite rendezvous of the city's wealthier Democrats. They had managed to impress each other as the two hardest drinkers in the city. Pendleton found himself wishing Rawdon would make the break. Being known as Rawdon Stapleton's best friend was not making his life any easier at the *Times*.

Pendleton interviewed the federal marshal and the printer, who said he had been paid in cash to print the ballots. He did not know the name of the man who had paid him and saw no reason to doubt his story that the ballots were "a joke" to be used at a party after the election. "A party for two hundred thousand people?" Pendleton asked. The printer had nothing more to say. Pendleton spent the rest of the night prowling the saloons on the Lower East Side, talking to an assortment of Tammany Hall politicians, all of whom expressed profound ignorance of such a shocking thing as a phony ballot, then slapped their thighs and pounded the bar in hysterical hilarity when he showed them his sample.

Pendleton finally got Big John Morrissey, massive boss of the Fourth Assembly District, to tell him a semblance of the truth. "We don't need dem ballots here in d'city. We put a million a dem on an Albany train for d'hayseeds upstate." The authoritative "we" had the thud of authenticity that Pendleton wanted to hear. It signified a meeting of the sachems of Tammany Hall, the machine that confidently expected to grind out 300,000 Democratic votes tomorrow.

Although it was 3 A.M., Pendleton decided to go back to the *Times* and write his story before going to bed. In the city room the gas lamps were glowing but all the desks were empty—except one. Managing Editor John Reid was snoring away on his imperial platform, his head on a pile of copy paper, an empty bottle of bourbon beside him. Pendleton finished his story and, not without some trepidation, woke him.

The managing editor rubbed the sleep out of his eyes and read the copy, occasionally stabbing at it with his pencil as if he wanted to impale it. By the time he got to the last paragraph, Reid was awake. "Jesus Christ," he snarled. "Did you take this to headquarters?"

"The police?" Pendleton asked.

"Republican headquarters, you fucking idiot," Reid roared. "Take it down to the composing room and have a copy run off. Get it up to the Fifth Avenue Hotel as fast as your rebel ass can travel." In Reid's brain, the line between the Republican Party and the *New York Times* had obviously ceased to exist.

"Yes sir," Pendleton said, and headed for the door.

"Dixie!" The rasping voice caught him in midstride.

"Yes, Mr. Reid?"

The splotched, exhausted face, the red-veined eyes glared at him. "That's a damn good story. Did you fake any of it?"

"No."

"That makes it even better. Tell them downstairs to hold it for the front page."

At the Fifth Avenue Hotel, a sleepy desk clerk directed Pendleton to the gilded second-floor rooms where the Republican National Committee was ensconced. He handed the page proof to a big bejowled man with a derby tipped on the back of his head.

"Holy shit," the man gasped, leaping to his feet, the derby bouncing across the room.

Five hours later, in his bachelor rooms on Bleecker Street, Pendleton awoke from a dream of Genevieve Dall Stapleton pressing that erotic upper lip against his mouth. Rain drummed on the roof above his head and sloshed against his windowpane. At the *Times* city room, the atmosphere was grim. The Weather Bureau reported it was raining in New York State from Buffalo to Montauk Point. Beefy Joe Sullivan, the *Times* police reporter, explained to Pendleton what the rain meant.

"In New York, Dixie," he said, simultaneously writing a story (a trick he had learned as a telegraph operator), "the Republicans have got the hayseeds and the millionaires. The Democrats have got the slumbums and the crooks. Up in the Genesee Valley a lot of farmers are going to decide it ain't worth struggling four or five miles through the mud to vote. But down on the Lower East Side and over in Hell's Kitchen, they'll stand in the rain all day for the two bucks they get from their local Tammany leader. Two bucks will put meat on a man's table for a week—or, more likely, beer in his belly for a month."

That was not the only Republican worry. As stories flowed into the city room from reporters around town, it was evident that Tammany's bruisers were also taking a toll. Five, six, seven Republican election workers had been rushed to Bellevue Hospital with broken jaws or cracked skulls. The city's Negro voters were staying home virtually en masse. They were always a favorite target of the "bhoys." A furious Reid sent Pendleton racing up to Republican headquarters again with this information. "Give it to Jonathan Stapleton," he snarled. "He's the one guy who can talk turkey to the cops."

The resplendent lobby of the Fifth Avenue Hotel was now jammed with politicians. Upstairs, the gilded sitting room where the lone derby wearer had been on duty last night was equally crowded. Pendleton was directed down the hall to the suite reserved for the chairman of the Republican National Committee. Zachariah Chandler was sitting at a white-and-gold Directoire writing table, surrounded by aides. Jonathan Stapleton was standing behind him, staring gloomily out the window at the rain. The General was looking haggard. His cheeks were dark hollows, there were puffy circles of exhaustion under his eyes.

A flush of anger replaced the weariness as he read the stories. "I'll see what I can do," he said. "Come on. I'll give you a ride downtown."

In the hack, the General contributed to Pendleton's continuing education in New York politics. "This wouldn't be happening," he said, tapping the envelope containing the stories, "if Grant had been able to give us the troops we wanted." In 1872, he explained, they had persuaded the President to assign two regiments of regulars to New York City. The troops had guarded the polling places with fixed bayonets and New York had had its most honest election of the century. This year, thanks to reckless slashes of the army budget in the Democratic-controlled House of Representatives, there were no troops available. Neither for New York City nor to protect the terrorized Republicans of the south. The tiny regular army was badly overcommitted in its on-again-off-again war with the Plains Indians. The massacre of George Armstrong Custer and his cavalry regiment last July made that all too clear.

"Aren't half the city's cops on the take from Tammany?" Pendleton asked.

"The top people are fairly honest. The superintendent, Walling, is a pretty good friend of mine."

Pendleton had covered police headquarters while Joe Sullivan was on vacation. He had met the tall jut-jawed superintendent. "I gather he's a pretty tough character. Did you get to know him in the army?"

A remarkable change took place on the General's face. His anger at vote fraud seemed to travel into a new wintry dimension. Pendleton could almost feel the chill, although the General's words remained casual: "In a way. Walling and I got pretty friendly during the Draft Riots in 'Sixty-three."

Whether the General's intercession at police headquarters was effective or the rain made Tammany's bruisers superfluous remained an open question. But the number of battered Republicans fell off dramatically in the late afternoon and early evening. Reid gave Pendleton a collection of violent incidents and told him to write a roundup. "Cut loose on it," he growled. "Make those Tammany bastards sound like descendants of Attila the Hun."

As Pendleton finished this job, Rawdon Stapleton sat down at the next desk and gave him a preview of his mystery story. "I've got the dope on how the Republicans slipped two double-dealing Tammany district leaders a hundred thousand bucks to buy votes for them," he whispered.

"Good luck," Pendleton said.

Rawdon handed in the story and sat around cleaning his fingernails, waiting for Reid's reaction. But Reid had stopped editing copy. He had vanished into Editor in Chief John Foord's office. Rawdon buttonholed Reid's assistant, a little Irishman named Lynch, and found out that they were conferring with the Republican national chairman, Zachariah Chandler. "Lynch says they all look worried," Rawdon gleefully reported.

Outside, the rain came down hard for a while, then slowed to a drizzle. Ignoring the danger of pneumonia, a huge crowd gathered in City Hall Park. Here and there bonfires began to glow. Along Broadway near Fulton Street new electric arc lights added some weird illumination.

"Stapleton!"

A roar of rage from John Reid. Rawdon strolled across the city room past the scribbling reporters to the managing editor's desk.

"Is this a joke?" Reid asked, waving the story about Republican vote buying.

"It happens to be the truth."

"The truth! Jesus Christ, the Bible is the truth, but we don't print that. We're a newspaper, Stapleton. A newspaper that supports the Republican Party, that fights for honor and decency and order in this country. Do you know what this city was like before we cleaned it up? Tweed and his Irish scum making us the laughingstock of the western world? I've only kept you on this paper out of friendship for your father, hoping by some miracle you'd straighten yourself out. One more story like this one and I'll decide you're hopeless."

Slowly, contemptuously, Reid ripped Rawdon's copy into pieces and threw it into his wastebasket. "Now go down to Western Union and pick up the latest wires."

He had demoted Rawdon to copyboy. In ten minutes he was back with a sackful of telegrams. The *Times*'s special correspondents around the country were hard at work. Rawdon distributed their bulletins to various reporters and sat down next to Pendleton again. "Indiana's gone Democratic," he whispered.

Pendleton only nodded, determined to maintain his neutrality. He had wavered a few times during the campaign when he read the vicious broadsides the *Times* flung against southern influence in the Democratic Party. But he was rescued from partisanship by his mother, who regularly sent him copies of the repulsive editorials written in the *Spartanburg Gazette* by his Democratic brother-in-law. They were clotted with standard rhetoric about scalawags and carpetbaggers and nigger rule.

Did you really expect me to go home and try to save the South from itself, Father? Pendleton asked the darkness outside the window. *Would you enjoy seeing me with my face pulverized by buckshot?*

Silence. The dead had a bad habit of not answering questions.

Rawdon made several more sullen sodden trips to Western Union. The telegrams he brought back and the stories they produced did not enthuse Managing Editor Reid. He snarled at reporters who were too blunt in describing Democratic gains. He was in the midst of one of these tirades when a fat man with a dripping umbrella approached his desk.

"I'm from the Democratic National Committee. Congressman Hewitt wants to know how much of a majority you're conceding to Tilden."

"None," Reid snarled.

The night trickled away with nothing but bad news for the Republicans. First New Jersey, then Connecticut and finally New York slid into the Democratic column. Outside, the crowd became more and more excited. Rawdon, returning from still another visit to Western Union, reported that the popular vote was bulging in Samuel Tilden's favor. He was outrunning Rutherford B. Hayes by 250,000 votes.

Rawdon was looking weary. His trousers and shoes were soaked. Pendleton borrowed his umbrella and volunteered to make the next trip to Western Union. As he came out on the street the crowd in City Hall Park exploded into tremendous cheers. The *Sun* had posted a bulletin announcing: TILDEN VICTORY. "Oh boys, we're up to our asses in honey," howled a skinny Irishman.

At the Broadway end of Park Row, Pendleton paused to check the bulletins in front of the *Herald*'s marble palace. To his surprise, a copy boy was posting a sheet which read: JURY STILL OUT. In the Western Union office, he met a reporter from the *Herald,* a southerner named Tracy. "What's wrong with you fellows?" Pendleton asked. "Why haven't you joined the victory chorus?"

"No one's heard a word from Florida, South Carolina or Louisiana," Tracy said. These were three southern states still controlled by the Republicans with the help of federal troops.

Back at the *Times,* Pendleton reported the *Herald*'s wariness to Reid. The editor's saturnine expression brightened slightly. He roared for the reporters who were covering the South. They rushed to the desk with the information they had received so far.

"It's a standoff," said the man who was assigned to Louisiana. "The Republicans say they carried the state by ten thousand, the Democrats say the same thing by twenty thousand." The telegrams from Florida and South Carolina reported virtually identical claims.

Reid looked around the circle of reporters at the desk. "Get me that goddamned electoral-vote chart."

On a piece of white cardboard someone had listed the thirty-eight states beside two columns in which their electoral votes were recorded as the returns came in. Reid shifted the electoral votes of Florida, South Carolina and Louisiana to the Republican column and added them to the votes of Illinois, Ohio, Massachusetts, Pennsylvania and other Republican bastions. A gasp ran through the circle of watching reporters. The total was 185 for Rutherford B. Hayes, 184 for Samuel Tilden. In spite of the mounting Democratic majority in the popular vote, the Republicans might still win.

"There's our lead story," Reid said.

"But we don't have the facts," one reporter protested.

"All right," Reid conceded. "We'll say Florida's still doubtful. Here's your head." He scribbled on top of the column: RESULTS STILL UNCERTAIN.

Reid snatched up the cardboard and disappeared into the office of his editor in chief. The managing editor came back in five minutes with a triumphant smile. "Print it," he said.

Shouting, snarling, cursing, Reid assembled the first edition. As dawn grayed the windows, he strode down the newsroom to Rawdon's desk. "Go find your father and tell him to get over to Zach Chandler's suite at the Fifth Avenue Hotel. We'll meet you there." Reid's bloodshot eyes strayed to Pendleton. "You come with me, Dixie," he said. "I may need a messenger."

Outside the rain had stopped. The crowd in City Hall Park was still huge, and more visible now. They were dancing around the bonfires shouting Democratic slogans. Reid finally found a hack in Chatham Square and they headed uptown. The managing editor offered Pendleton a drink from a silver flask and told him he liked his roundup on Election Day violence. "That was a good touch, working in Stapleton's trip to police headquarters to protest the beatings," Reid said. "Readers still remember him as the guy who saved this city from the mob during the draft riots in 1863. That's exactly the way I want people to think—connecting the Democrats to mob rule."

In the Fifth Avenue Hotel, the splendid lobby looked dim and tawdry. The glowing chandeliers were extinguished and the dawn's early light failed to capture the color of the expensive carpets, the gleam of the marble walls. The floor and the furniture were littered with the debris from the Election Day crowd. Reid asked a sleepy desk clerk if General Stapleton and his son had arrived. The answer was no and they sat down in easy chairs to await them.

Reid swigged from his flask and handed it to Pendleton. "Let me see that editorial your father wrote," he said. Pendleton fished the faded piece of newsprint out of his wallet. Reid glanced at it and shook his head. "He must have been a hell of a guy, to stand up to the Democrats that way."

Jonathan Stapleton strode toward them looking more haggard than ever under his high black hat. Beside him, Rawdon had changed from his rain-soaked suit into a pair of old college trousers and a black coat.

"I hope this is important," the General said. "I'd gotten about a half hour's sleep when this fellow arrived."

"It couldn't be more important, General," Reid said. "For the party and the country. Let's go find Zach Chandler."

Entering the suite with a passkey, Reid shook the Republican national chairman awake. An empty bottle of whiskey stood on the night table. The room smelled like a saloon. On the floor were a half-dozen crumpled telegrams that had obviously brought only more bad news.

Reid pulled a proof of page one of the *Times* out of his pocket and showed it to Chandler and Stapleton. "It says here that we carried South Carolina and Louisiana and all we need is Florida to win," he said. "Actually, we don't have the facts about any of the three. Do you, Zach?"

Chandler blinked his sleep-heavy eyes, trying to remember. "I only know I went to bed sure we were up Salt Creek," he said.

Reid seemed to make some sort of inner decision. Jonathan Stapleton was making it, too. That was all Pendleton could read in the look that passed between them. The managing editor turned to Rawdon and Pendleton. "You two young fellows wait in the sitting room. We're going to have a powwow."

In the sitting room, Pendleton sank into an easy chair. He was never able to handle a sleepless night. His head felt like a hot-air balloon. Any moment he expected to find it bobbing against the ceiling. Rawdon, as he had demonstrated on more than one college foray to New York, seemed immune to sleeplessness. He paced the carpet, picking up random pieces of paper, telegrams, notes, reading them, throwing them aside.

"What the hell's going on, Pendleton?" he asked.

"How do I know?"

Rawdon tiptoed over to the bedroom door and pressed his ear against it. But the walnut was too thick, or the voices too low. He made a disgusted face and peered through the keyhole.

"Rawdon, for Christ's sake," Pendleton gasped.

"Shut up," Rawdon hissed.

Frustrated again, Rawdon retreated from the keyhole—just in time. Reid flung the door open. "Okay, boys," he said in his managing editor's bark.

In the bedroom, Zachariah Chandler was writing a telegram. Beside it was a list of names to whom it was to be sent. Jonathan Stapleton was watching the Republican chairman's hand as it formed the block letters. The General looked up as Rawdon and Pendleton walked into the room. Pendleton was struck by the expression on his face. It was the wintry look he had seen yesterday, mingled with something else: sadness—extraordinary sadness. Pendleton began to suspect that something momentous was happening.

Reid handed Pendleton the list of names and the telegram. "Take this to the nearest Western Union office. There's one on the corner of Twenty-third Street and Sixth Avenue. Charge it to the *Times.*"

"Yes sir," Pendleton said, reading the telegram in a quick glance.

HAYES IS ELECTED IF WE HAVE CARRIED SOUTH CAROLINA, FLORIDA AND LOUISIANA. CAN YOU HOLD YOUR STATE? ANSWER AT ONCE.

"Is there anything I can do?" Rawdon asked in a tone that was much too humble for him.

"Should we discuss this with Conkling or anyone else?" Reid asked.

"Not necessary," Chandler growled.

As they left the bedroom, Chandler was saying, "Louisiana will be the biggest problem. We'll send Garfield down to handle the reporters . . ."

Rawdon did not speak until they were outside the Fifth Avenue Hotel, on the sidewalk opposite Madison Square Park. "Pendleton," he said. "I think we've just been handed the story of the century."

"What the hell are you talking about?"

"All we've got to do is take that telegram and list of names to the *Herald,* and the Republican Party and the *New York Times* will both cease to exist tomorrow morning."

"Why?"

"Don't you realize what they're doing up there? They're planning to steal the goddamn election. Steal the presidency."

"How can they do that?"

"Pendleton. Put that feeble brain of yours into locomotion. Each one of those states has something called a Returning Board that certifies the votes.

They can throw out the vote of a whole county if they find evidence of corruption. I guarantee you that for the right amount of money they're going to find enough corrupt counties to elect Rutherford B. Hayes."

Pendleton stared at the telegram in his hand. Was it possible? He was appalled at the fierce delight on Rawdon's face.

"The paragon of rectitude, General Jonathan Stapleton, stealing the presidency. It's too rich," Rawdon said.

"This telegram doesn't say anything about stealing the presidency."

"They're not that stupid. Give me the telegram and the names, Pendleton. We can fake the rest of the story. You can swear I was listening at the door. I'll make up the dialogue between the General and his cronies."

Pendleton had only enough mental energy to focus on the figure in front of him. If Rawdon was right, the Republicans were stealing the presidency. But if he gave Rawdon this telegram, Jonathan Stapleton would be his enemy forever. Somehow he found this idea unacceptable.

"Rawdon," he said, "I don't think either one of us has lived long enough to judge what those men are doing up there."

"Give me that telegram and that list of names," Rawdon said, holding out his hand.

"That's your father up there. Do you want him to hate you?"

"Let me worry about that."

For a moment Pendleton saw himself pulling his father's last editorial out of his wallet, thrusting it in Rawdon's face and snarling, *Look at that. That's all I've got left of my father, you arrogant son of a bitch.*

"Believe it or not," he said, "I won't give it to you for another reason: it would kill Johnny Reid. I don't like the son of a bitch. But he's been square with me. He's made me think I might be a real newspaperman—"

"You're selling out your own state, your people, the South. You're turning yourself into a man without a country," Rawdon shouted.

"I think I've been one of those characters for quite a while."

Rawdon stepped back. He saw that he was not going to get the telegram or the names. "The hell with it," he said. "I don't need them. I'm going home and write the story and give it to the *Herald.*"

"Jesus Christ, Rawdon, take some advice for once in your life. Don't do that."

"Your moral cowardice, your utter gutlessness, dismays me, Pendleton. How did I ever choose you for a friend?"

Pendleton watched Rawdon board an uptown red Broadway stage on the corner of Twenty-third Street. He dashed over to the Western Union office on Sixth Avenue and handed the telegram to a thin elderly clerk with a gray mustache. First the Florida names, then the Louisiana names, then the South Carolina names. His hand trembled as he slid these across the plate glass. Rawdon was right. He really was a man without a country now. But there were other ideas, other values, to which a man could be loyal.

"Charge them to the *New York Times*," he said, and dashed out and caught a hack up Sixth Avenue to Rawdon's flat on Forty-third Street. He raced up the stairs to the sixth floor. Genevieve, dressed in her black-and-white working outfit, answered the door.

"Where's Rawdon?" Pendleton gasped.

"He isn't home yet."

It was the answer Pendleton wanted to hear. He had been pretty sure the hack would outpace the plodding Broadway stage. Quickly, while Genevieve served him a cup of coffee, he told her the story. "We can't let him do it," he said. "We can't let him do that to his father."

"No," she said. "We can't." There was nothing but gray in those wide determined eyes.

They heard a key in the lock. In a moment, Rawdon was in the kitchen. "What the hell are you doing here?" he snarled at Pendleton.

"Clay came up here to stop you from doing a terrible thing, Rawdon," Genevieve said. "He's told me about it."

"*He's* told you about it?" Rawdon roared. "Let *me* tell you about it. Let your husband tell you."

The gray eyes only grew more opaque. "Tell me."

She listened while Rawdon expounded his conviction that the telegrams were a first step to stealing the presidency. "Before the day is over, they'll have men with bags full of money on trains heading south to make sure every election official in those three states sticks with them."

"Rawdon, it's all supposition," Genevieve said. "All part of this hatred of your father that's disfiguring you."

"Oh? I'm disfigured now? I've passed beyond being merely repellent? I'm permanently repulsive?"

"I didn't say that." Genevieve clenched both her hands into fists; her eyes almost closed. Pendleton sensed that she was seeing an inner reality that neither of them understood. "You can't do something like this to your father without proof. I don't believe, I will never believe that Jonathan Stapleton would participate in such a vile immoral conspiracy."

No, Pendleton thought. Take that back, Genevieve. Don't stake your judgment, your reputation as an intelligent woman, on those words. Something I saw on Jonathan Stapleton's face yesterday and today, that wintry look, evoking scenes, memories, unimaginable to you or even to me, makes me think you should take back those words.

"You don't believe it," Rawdon said. Pendleton looked up at him and was amazed to discover that he could see what Genevieve saw: ugliness. The once generous mouth was twisted, mean; the once open, supremely handsome face had become crafty, sly, unbalanced. "You don't believe it," he said again.

"No, I don't," Genevieve said.

Suddenly Pendleton wanted to shift the argument. Even if the General was involved in stealing the election, Rawdon could not expose him. But it was too late. He was a spectator to the primary clash he had created between husband and wife.

"It seems to me there's only one thing to do," Rawdon said. "Let's go down to Stuyvesant Square and ask the great man, point-blank, Is the election being stolen? Don't you agree, Pendleton?"

Pendleton nodded. There was no other answer. He was a reporter, after all.

"Do you want to come, dearest?" Rawdon asked, with ravenous sarcasm.

"No. I have to go to work," Genevieve said.

"Oh yes. Work, wonderful work. It's much more important than the fate of the republic."

They left Genevieve sitting in the kitchen, her hands still clenched on the tabletop. Rawdon did not say one word to Pendleton all the way down to Stuyvesant Square. His silence was the best—or worst—possible expression of what he thought of Pendleton's attempt to enlist Genevieve's support.

But it would all be solved, peace would descend, peace in which friendship, love, could be repaired, if Jonathan Stapleton appeared in the parlor and calmly, persuasively assured them that there was not the slightest intention on anyone's part to steal the election. Almost frantically, Pendleton reminded himself that the telegrams only informed the Republicans in the contested states that an exact count of their votes was crucial.

The hack clopped into deserted Stuyvesant Square. Up the steps they went to twist the bell. Cousteau answered the door.

"I'd like to speak to my father," Rawdon said. "It's quite urgent. Even if he's asleep, I'd like you to wake him up—"

"I'm afraid that's out of the question, Mr. Stapleton," Cousteau said in his calm magisterial way. "Your father left ten minutes ago for the Fulton Street ferry. He's on his way to Louisiana."

TEN

The river was rising. The dark heaving water was lapping at the very top of the levee. Any moment, it would be swirling around Cynthia's green silk dancing slippers, soiling her white ball gown. But Charlie was oblivious. Or drunk. "Play something from the Côte Joyeuse," he bellowed. Blind Tom, the old Negro fiddler, began hacking away at one of the waltzes of the fifties, dedicated to *les belles de la Côte Joyeuse*, the girls of the Joyous Coast, a name that Charlie found amusing.

"The river, Charlie," Cynthia said. "The river is rising." But Charlie only laughed and kept on dancing.

A wave broke onto the levee, splattering her with mud. The old Negro was still playing, but she could not see him. Out of the night exploded a tremendous whistle. Bearing down on them was an enormous white steamboat. It was dark except for a single light in the pilothouse. Its paddlewheels were beating the river into foam. "Charlie," Cynthia cried, but he kept on dancing. She tried to tear herself free from his arms. The boat's huge prow loomed over them. In the pilothouse she saw Jonathan's glaring face.

Cynthia awoke to the sound of a steamboat's whistle out on the Mississippi. It was another gray, gloomy day. Northern Louisiana in November could be as dismal and almost as cold as New York.

Her maid, Lucy, heard Cynthia stirring and came in with her breakfast. "That steamboat brought you a letter from home," she said. "I hope it's got some news about Cleo and the other folks downstairs."

"I'm sure it does," Cynthia said. "I'll let you know."

Lucy missed New York acutely. After nine years up north, she had nothing but scorn for the "country niggers" of her native Louisiana, who had never seen an elevated railroad or a vaudeville show. Cynthia sampled her grits and ham and fingered the thick envelope. It looked like a real letter, instead of the curt scribbles from hotel rooms in the Midwest and New England that Jonathan had been sending her since her retreat to Bralston.

The first page was devoted to home news. All the servants, including Cleopatra, who had been ill when she left, were well. Ditto for George and the newlyweds; at least, Jonathan presumed they were well. He had heard nothing from them. Next came news that Cynthia especially wanted to hear. Their invitation to the Patriarchs, the series of balls arranged by Mrs. William Astor and her foppish friend Ward McAllister, had arrived, assuring them that they were still ranked among the elite of New York society.

Jonathan maintained that these affairs were the ultimate in boredom. There was no doubt that McAllister was a pompous ass and Caroline Astor was an equally pompous frump. But they had succeeded in making Mrs. Astor's guest list the test of social standing in New York, and Cynthia wanted to be on it.

The rest of the first page was full of fresh gossip. Lionel Bradford was looking rather silly. When Madeline Terhune's play closed, she had instantly abandoned him and decamped for London and, according to the rumor, the arms of Joseph Chamberlain, one of England's political titans. Alice Gansevoort was in a decline. Her father refused to let her marry Isaac Mayer because he was Jewish. Jonathan thought this was outrageous and urged Cynthia to strike the senior Gansevoorts from her guest list.

Cynthia was charmed by the social news. Jonathan must have taken the trouble to consult Katherine Kemble Brown or Margaret Dall to get it. There was not a word, not even a hint, of reproach for his wife's abrupt departure for Louisiana. She read quickly through a discussion of George's latest awful report card and Jonathan's growing conviction that only a few years of St. Paul's School would give him some sense of direction and purpose.

Then came an astonishing last paragraph.

> How I miss you! The house seems a tomb without your smile, your laugh. I hear the sound of your voice in every shadowy corner. The other night when I could not sleep I stood in your bedroom for ten minutes, breathing a last lingering scent of your perfume. I really begin to hate this political maelstrom that keeps swallowing me, just when I think I have crawled out of it. Two weeks ago I did not think we had a chance of electing a president. Now I begin to think if we get a fair count in New York, there will be four years of stable government. I promise you, if that happens, I will stop worrying about politics and spend three months in Italy and France with you every summer and at least one winter sailing up the Nile. Is this sufficient penance or must I wear sackcloth and ashes and stand in front of St. George's Church for a month with a candle in my hand like a medieval sinner?

The words stirred warmth deep in her body. He loved her. He was apologizing, insofar as a proud man could apologize. He was still hoping for a Republican victory, of course. But did she really care? She had no particular affection for the Democratic Party. She still wanted to see Louisiana redeemed, but that was a trivial emotion compared to her affection for that sometimes endearing, sometimes infuriating, frequently contradictory tangle of generosity and bad temper, contentious pride and puzzling humility known as Jonathan Stapleton.

It was time to go home. It was the day after the great election. She would get a telegram off to him on the first passing steamboat. She took paper and pencil from the drawer of her night table and scribbled: "Starting for home tomorrow. No election news here in the wilderness. Don't worry about lengthy penitence. Love, Cynthia."

She threw on a dressing gown and went down the hall to her mother's room. Her mother was being fluffed and combed by Cleopatra's sister, Livia, the only house servant left from prewar days. Blanche Knowles Legrand never left her bed now. Her fragile wrinkled face was like a dried leaf that a chance wind might blow away at any moment. Cynthia inhaled the familiar odor of Mr. Massey's Potpourri, a jar of which sat open on her mother's night table. She sent her a case of it every Christmas.

"Good morning, Mama."

"Good morning. How's my Yankee daughter this morning?"

"I just got a letter from my Yankee husband, telling me I ought to come home."

"You don't dare disobey him?"

"Oh—I dare a good deal with him, Mama. He's not nearly as fierce as he looks."

"Then why can't you get money from him for Bralston?"

This was the only more or less contemporary thought that persisted in her mother's head. She regularly wrote letters to Cynthia asking her to beg money from Jonathan.

"Bralston doesn't need any money, Mama. Bralston's doing fine these days."

For a moment her mother looked blank. Then an angry light crept into her eyes. "But the price, Cyntie. To sell my daughter to a man like Frank Powers. I wanted your father to write to General Stapleton. But he wouldn't listen to me. No matter what I said, he never listened."

Cynthia suddenly remembered an encounter on Bralston's veranda when she was eight or nine. A steamboat snuffled at the levee. Her father appeared with a portmanteau in his hand. Behind him came her mother, crying, "You will not go to New Orleans. You will not." Her father had turned with the weary air of a grand seigneur, and said, "Madam, I will do as I please. Go to your room." That had been the beginning of her mother's retreat to her bedroom. She had stayed in it more and more with each succeeding year, serenely claiming "indisposition" as the reason.

A question trembled on Cynthia's lips. *Did you love him, Mama? If so, what sort of love would you call it?* For a long time she had accepted the sensible answer. Of course Blanche Louise Knowles had loved Victor Conté Legrand in those fabulous flush 1840s, when all Louisiana was awash in cash, and a Creole, a young handsome Creole, was an exotic creature, with his Paris clothes, his Continental manners, his Gallic wit.

Maybe there was a time limit to it. Maybe after a few more years Jonathan would start treating her the way Victor Legrand had treated Blanche Knowles.

She did not really believe that.

Back in her own room, Cynthia changed to a dark-green riding outfit and went downstairs. In the dining room she found her brother-in-law, Frank Powers, at the table eating breakfast. The sight of him in a workshirt and dusty overalls was bad enough; the way he shoveled down his ham and grits, like cotton going down a gin, was repulsive.

She remembered her father sitting in this room at one end of a magnificent mahogany table. On the walls were scenes of Paris in the 1830s, when he had studied there. A silver coffee service glistened in a dim corner. On the table were hot waffles, buttermilk biscuits, broiled chicken, cane syrup, scrambled eggs and hominy. Now a rickety table and a half-dozen cheap chairs were the only furniture in the room. The wallpaper still had splattered stains where drunken Yankee officers had thrown wine bottles against it.

"Good morning," Cynthia said, determined to be polite to her brother-in-law for Jeannie's sake.

"Morning," Frank said, and kept shoveling away.

"Any news of the election?"

Frank shook his head. "All I can tell you is what I told you last night. The Democrats carried Concordia Parish by about seven to one." Frank Powers smiled at Cynthia. At least, his lips curled back. All he needed was a forked tongue to complete his resemblance to a rattlesnake.

"I wouldn't go out riding today," he said, eying Cynthia's costume while still shoveling down his grits. "Roads ain't likely to be safe."

"You said that yesterday. If I don't ride there's absolutely nothing for me to do around this place."

Coolly deserting her irritable, irritating husband for her southern homeland had seemed like a marvelous idea in New York. But the reality had been somewhat less than thrilling. Five weeks at Bralston had left her so bored, Cynthia often had to force herself to get out of bed in the morning. Only a long ride each day—she frequently went twenty or thirty miles—enabled her to sleep at night.

"Our nigger sheriff might grab that horse for the taxes I ain't paid," Frank Powers said. "Today's the last day he might try it."

"Yellow George's son wouldn't do that to me," Cynthia said. "He was born right out back. I promised Nelly Ames I'd ride down to see her once more before I went home."

"Home?" her sister Jeannie said, coming into the dining room with a big tin coffeepot in her hand. She set the monstrosity on a white plate, and Frank Powers stopped shoveling and filled his cup. "How can you call New York home as long as Bralston is standing?" The more obvious it became that Cynthia did not feel at home in Bralston, the more Jeannie insisted on the word in this heavy-handed way.

"I'm afraid the time has come, Jeannie," Cynthia said, her eyes drifting from the coffeepot to her sister's raw red hands. It was easier to look at the hands than it was to look at the rest of Jeannie, with her sallow face and bulging body. She was pregnant again, the fifth or sixth time in the last ten years. Three children had survived.

Along with perpetual motherhood, Jeannie ran the house without servants. Last night Cynthia had seen her on her knees scrubbing the kitchen floor. Frank Powers claimed they could not afford servants if Bralston was going to pay its way. He also said he did not like niggers in his house. Only old Livia was retained at Cynthia's insistence for her mother's comfort. She sent Frank five hundred dollars a year for her wages.

Looking at her older sister as she joined them at the table, Cynthia thought she saw a further coarsening of her features. She was becoming, she had become, Frank Powers' wife. Even her voice had acquired the nasal twang of Frank's people, the northern-Louisiana dirt farmers who lived in the flat harsh country west of the river.

"I had the strangest dream," Cynthia said. "I woke up fairly shaking all over. I dreamt the river was coming right over the levee, but Charlie was out there dancing with me, and old Tom the fiddler was playing away and neither one of them was paying the least mind to the water."

"That reminds me of the time we had that awful crevasse. I think it was in 'Fifty-one," her sister said. "Do you remember? We got up and found three feet of water over everything! The house was completely marooned."

"Of course I remember," Cynthia said. "Bob and Lancombe kept falling into the water until they used up every piece of dry clothes they owned. I got Little Oscar to paddle me around in the old pirogue and we hit a sunken tree and went right over and I would have drowned with my dress all wet if Oscar hadn't found bottom and held me up."

"Do you know what I believe?" her sister said. "The niggers dug out the levee to make that crevasse. We never knew how close we were to destruction from them in the old days."

"Do you really think so?" Cynthia said. She was baffled by the way her sister talked about Negroes—as if they were evil creatures who did nothing but scheme to ruin or murder whites. She got it from her husband, who ranted on the subject by the hour.

"If we win this election," Frank Powers said, "we ain't going to have to worry about niggers destroying us. This state's going to be redeemed."

Frank Powers was always talking about redeeming Louisiana. He was the commander of the local branch of the White League. Two weeks ago, her brother Robert had visited Bralston to confer with him. After Bob's second or third drink he gave Cynthia credit for the creation of the league. He swore that he never would have gotten the money from that slippery Wall Street millionaire Lionel Bradford without her intercession. This extravagance had won a glimmer of admiration from her usually surly brother-in-law. But it made Cynthia worry about what Bob was telling other people in Louisiana— and New York.

"Would you give this to the first steamboat that comes by and ask the captain to send it from Baton Rouge?" Cynthia said. She handed Frank Powers her telegram and a dollar bill.

After a hasty cup of bitter coffee, Cynthia hurried through the kitchen to the garden. Where box hedges had once pleased the eye and bougainvillea had filled the air with fragrance, there was nothing but rows of cabbage and lettuce and tomato plants that her sister labored over for several hours every day.

At the stable, Cynthia saddled a placid, sturdy roan named Zephyr. She cantered out of the barnyard and along the path through the fields to the levee road. Nelly Ames lived at Ormond, about five miles down the river. She was almost the only old friend Cynthia had left in the vicinity. Most of the others had lost their lands or followed husbands to Texas or California.

About a mile away, the village of Lincoln clustered around a post office. The town had been created by the Freedman's Bureau after the war as a place for ex-slaves to live. Wherever possible, the bureau did not want the Negroes to stay on the plantations, lest their old masters browbeat them back into slavery or something very like it. Cynthia planned to stop at the general store and buy some candy for Nelly Ames's children.

As she approached, she noticed that the main street was strangely deserted. Usually there were a dozen Negro men and women strolling or lounging in the shade of a big old sycamore that the Freedman's Bureau's engineers had spared.

Little Oscar was the owner of the general store. But he was not called Little Oscar anymore. Now it was Oscar Legrand. His brother, Little George, was the sheriff. They were sons of Yellow George, the Negro headman at Bralston. He had ruled the men, and his wife, Mammy George, had ruled the women.

The sons had taken the Legrand name when they were freed. Her sister

Jeannie seemed to think it was a reflection on the family's virtue. From what Cynthia knew of Grandfather Legrand's morals, it was all too probable that they were related. Yellow George, who had died five years ago, certainly had white blood in him. Grandfather Legrand had been furious with his son for marrying a Protestant, but he had never had much compunction about cohabiting with his prettier women slaves.

Cynthia dismounted in front of the store, still wondering where all the Negroes were. Inside, she was surprised to find not one black face. A half-dozen white men were sitting around the potbellied stove; each had a breech-loading shotgun on his lap.

Behind the counter was the only person she recognized, pathetic shambling Fred Stowe. Little Oscar had given him a job after Fred went broke as a plantation owner across the river in Mississippi. He was ashamed to go home to face his mother and used the pittance Little Oscar paid him to stay drunk most of the time.

"How are you today?" Cynthia asked.

Fred simply nodded. When he did not talk, that usually meant he was drunk. But today something else seemed to be bothering him. His eyes rolled in his head and he kept glancing at the men with the shotguns.

Cynthia bought two dozen peppermint sticks and turned to go. "Give my regards to Little Oscar. Tell him I'm going back to New York."

"Fred don't work for Little Oscar no more," one of the men with the shotguns said. "Ain't that right, Fred?"

Fred nodded. Cynthia realized he was frightened.

"Tell the lady what happened to Little Oscar, Fred," the same man said. He was short and bald, with a hard, nasty mouth. Cynthia recognized him as a friend of her brother-in-law's. He had visited Bralston several times.

"He . . . sold . . . out," Fred Stowe said.

"Sold out? Why in the world?" Cynthia asked.

"Here's the bill of sale," the baldheaded man said, waving a piece of paper. "I'm the new owner. Fred works for me now. Ain't that right, Fred?"

Fred nodded frantically.

"Fred—tell Mrs. Stapleton what you really thought of Little Oscar."

"He was . . . a no-good nigger."

"Now that you've been South, Fred, what do you think of your mama's famous book?"

"A pack . . . of lies."

"Ain't that something, Mrs. Stapleton?" the baldheaded man said. "Now that Louisiana's almost redeemed, Fred ain't afraid to tell the truth. Sure hope you let your friends up North hear about it."

Like all southerners, Cynthia believed that *Uncle Tom's Cabin* was a farrago of outrageous lies and slanders. But she did not like the cruel game these men were playing with Fred Stowe. She decided silence was her best answer and turned to leave.

The baldheaded man's voice followed her to the door. "Where you going, Mrs. Stapleton?"

"To Ormond."

"If I was you, I'd just take them peppermints and go home."

Cynthia slammed the door, making it a statement of her opinion of the baldheaded man and his friends. Stuffing the peppermint sticks into a saddle pocket, she rode south through the flat bare countryside, under a gray sky. A November wind whipped off the river and rattled the branches of random trees along the muddy road. About a mile from Lincoln there was a junction with a road from Wakefield. As she approached it, Cynthia saw something dark in the branches of a big cypress tree that stood in the southeast angle of the crossroads. A dozen feet from the tree, Zephyr skittered and she had to struggle to keep him under control. The dark thing was a man—what was left of him.

There was a rope around his neck, but his face, even with the popping eyes, the twisted mouth caused by the noose, was easily identifiable. It was Little Oscar Legrand. Someone had hung him there and fired buckshot into his body. Blood oozed through his shredded white shirt and dripped onto the dirt beneath him. Tied to his foot was a sign: THIS NIGGER TRIED TO VOTE.

Cynthia clutched Zephyr's mane to stay on the horse. *You are not the fainting type,* she told herself. But it was too gruesome. A swirl of blackness swept over her, like a crevasse from an evil river beneath the ground.

When she awoke she thought she was still in a nightmare. She was surrounded by blue uniforms; Yankee blue. She heard a deep voice saying, "You can't patrol five hundred square miles of Louisiana with fifty troopers."

She sat up and faced a detachment of federal cavalry. The boyish lieutenant in command took off his cap. "We cut the poor nigger down, ma'am. You don't have to worry about looking at him anymore."

The lieutenant helped her onto her horse and she rode numbly back to Bralston. It was true, what Jonathan had told her about the White League massacring defenseless Negroes. Now she knew where all the blacks had gone. They were cowering in their homes; Frank Powers and his friends had used their shotguns to make sure that no black man in Concordia Parish ventured out of doors to vote.

The closer she drew to Bralston, the angrier she became. "Jeannie!" Cynthia shouted at the foot of the big stairs down which she had come to marry Charlie Stapleton. Paint peeled from the steps, and the bannister was missing a dozen posts. "Jeannie!"

Silence, then some stumbling footsteps. Jeannie appeared at the head of the stairs in her petticoat. "What in the world is the matter? Your brother is trying to get some sleep."

"Don't call him my brother. He's a murderer!"

"Don't say another word. I'll be right down."

Cynthia realized that her sister had been giving herself to Frank Powers. Opening her body to that repulsive man. It only deepened her anger. By the time Jeannie came down the stairs, straightening the skirt of her calico dress, Cynthia was almost berserk. "I just saw Little Oscar Legrand at the crossroads, hanging from a tree, dripping blood. He did it. Your husband killed him. He and his friends—"

"Shut up," Jeannie said, opening and closing her raw red hands. "Shut up about something that's none of your business. He told you not to go riding. Why didn't you listen to him?"

"Jeannie—how can you ever look Mammy George in the face again?"

"It's none of your business. You don't live here anymore."

There was the truth, the brutal truth, at last. They had been sliding toward those words ever since Cynthia arrived. For a moment she felt bereft, betrayed, deserted. Not because she had lost Bralston. It was the loss of Jeannie that she was mourning. Her wise serene older sister had become this bitter ugly stranger.

There was nothing to bring her back to Louisiana again. Her mother was already living in another world. New York was Cynthia Legrand Stapleton's only home now. The friends, the relations, she had there were the only ones that mattered. Home. The word had come naturally to her mind as she read Jonathan's letter. *It was time to go home.*

Suddenly the bitterness fled from Jeannie's eyes. "Oh Cyntie," she whispered. "Please don't hate me. I only married him because Daddy asked me and it didn't seem to make any difference after . . ."

Cynthia opened her arms, and they clung together, weeping, sisters again. They went out on the veranda and sat on the steps holding hands. She knew what Jeannie was doing. She was taking them back to that terrible July day when the news from Vicksburg and Gettysburg had arrived: their brother Lancombe was dead and Jeff Forsyth, Jeannie's fiancé, was dying of wounds. They had sat there, holding hands, staring out at the relentless Mississippi, as silent as they sat now. It was a bond between them, a bond of sorrow that could never be broken.

Finally Jeannie spoke in her old voice, the soft gentle croon of the past. "There are some things it's better for a woman not to know, Cyntie. Let the men solve this mess their way. They got us into it."

"I suppose you're right," Cynthia said.

Later in the afternoon, Cynthia was on the lawn playing ball with Jeannie's youngest child, a sweet little blond three-year-old named Susannah, when Frank Powers emerged from the house.

"I hear you come back early from your ride," he said. He drew back his lips into his rattlesnake smile.

"Yes," she said, and tossed the ball to Susannah.

Powers scooped up the little girl as she ran after it. "I didn't have nothing to do with killing Oscar Legrand," he said.

"Oh?"

Susannah squirmed in her father's arms. "I want to play with Aunt Cynthia," she cried.

"I didn't have no cause to kill him. I didn't owe him a dime. But there was lots of others who owed him. That nigger was trying to become king of this parish. He was in with his brother the sheriff, buying up all the land they could grab. His brother'd tell him whenever a farm was being condemned—"

"Would you please hoist the signal at the dock tonight? I'd like to take an early steamboat to New Orleans."

"Why, sure," Powers said. "I'll do it the minute the sun goes down."

Except for the children's chatter, dinner and supper were silent affairs. Cynthia went to bed early but found sleep eluding her. For a while she read Mark Twain's silly novel, *The Gilded Age*. Finally, around midnight, she got up and wandered around Bralston in her dressing gown. She was saying farewell. To youth, the South, Jeannie, her mother's pathetic daydreams— above all to her father.

Let it come, she thought, let it come one last time—the love she had felt for Victor Conté Legrand. It rushed through her body, full of bittersweet regret.

On the veranda, the wind from the river had a November chill. Not like the summer nights when you could put your hand on the pillars and they would still be warm from the day-long sun. How many of those nights she had spent here with Jeannie and Jeff Forsyth and her brother Lancombe singing songs, chanting poems such as *The Lady of the Lake*. When the Mississippi lapped the top of the levee, the steamboats would glide past, higher than their heads, dream ships on dream voyages down a river that seemed to be flowing toward the stars.

Oh Jeff, Lancombe, Jeannie, Father, swallowed by the river, by time, by night. Cynthia crept back to her bed feeling sadness clinging to her dressing gown like tendrils of Spanish moss. For an hour she felt overwhelmed by the power of fate. She wept and wept and wept. Finally she lit a candle and reread Jonathan's letter and told herself she had chosen a different destiny, to be the wife of a serious man who loved her in spite of her quick temper and frivolous nature.

At seven in the morning, a steamboat hooted at the levee. Fortunately,

Lucy had packed before they went to bed. With some scrambling and the assistance of several field hands, Cynthia got her luggage aboard the *General Beauregard*. Only Jeannie came down to the levee to say goodbye. They embraced without words. Jeannie seemed to know this was Cynthia's last visit to Bralston.

Picking her way through the assorted laborers and Negroes and riffraff on the main deck, Cynthia ascended to the ladies' cabins at the rear of the second deck. She was delighted to find them practically deserted. She wanted to be alone for a while.

Later in the day, she went out on deck as they rounded College Point above Baton Rouge. A few miles away were the shaded walks and ivy-covered buildings of the Convent of the Sacred Heart, where she had spent two happy years studying French, needlework and music. Her Protestant mother had been opposed to sending her there. For reasons he did not explain, her father had insisted. Not until she was leaving did Cynthia discover his motive. The mother superior had reproached him for not raising his daughter as a Catholic. "I sent her to make sure she would never succumb to that superstition," Victor Legrand had replied. "She has been raised—and will continue to be raised—as a child of this world."

The next morning, as the *General Beauregard* rounded the huge bend below Carrollton, Cynthia repeated a youthful ritual. She ascended to the hurricane deck and watched New Orleans take shape in the distance. First the churches, in particular the Gothic spire of St. Patrick's, and the triple crown of the St. Louis Cathedral; then the majestic Egyptian bulk of the Custom House and the magnificent classic front of the block-long St. Charles Hotel. Missing from the scene as she remembered it in girlhood was the hotel's triumphant dome. When the original St. Charles burned in the late 1850s, the owners had decided not to rebuild the dome.

A mistake, Cynthia thought. It deprived New Orleans of a splendor, a grandeur, it badly needed.

Suddenly she was standing with her father in the colonnade at the top of the dome. His smile was cold, wry; he gestured to the city below them, and spoke to her in French—always a sign that it was a special conversation. "Take your choice, my darling," he said. "Save your soul or possess the world." Then he told her they were going downstairs to meet the man he wanted her to marry. Her career as a courtesan was about to begin. Five minutes later, on the floor of the rotunda, Charles Gifford Stapleton was kissing her hand.

Stop, Cynthia told herself. It was better not to think about it. Bury it with the dead.

Disembarking, Cynthia and Lucy faced the usual chaos in Jackson Square: gesticulating hack drivers, shouting wagoners hauling loads of cotton, peddlers selling fruit or oysters. The buildings that enclosed the square, the ancient cathedral, the Pontalba apartments, the frowning bulk of the old Spanish Cabildo, all looked dirty and tired.

On Canal Street, the dividing line between the French and American sections of the city, Cynthia noticed an extraordinary number of men standing or strolling with rifles or shotguns on their shoulders. She asked the Irish hack driver who they were.

" 'Tis the White League, madam," he said. "The Demmycrats. They've redeemed the state and they don't intend to let the Raypublicans and the niggers steal it from them again. There's five thousand of them in the city."

"Have the Democrats won the presidency?"

"No one seems to know for sure. But they say Tilden's got to hold Louisiana or he's sunk and so are we. It'll be another four years of nigger rule."

Cynthia shivered at the way some of the White Leaguers eyed her as she rode past them. Did her expensive clothes make her look like a Yankee? Or were they ready to rob anyone? "Where are the federal troops?" she asked.

"Oh they never come into town. They generally let the Raypublicans and the Demmycrats fight it out among themselves, then come sweep up the corpses."

Cynthia sighed with relief when she finally saw the majestic Corinthian columns of the St. Charles Hotel. Once inside that granite fortress, she and Lucy would be safe.

As she stepped out of the hack, a gun boomed on the street behind her. Lucy screamed and plunged to the floor of the carriage, her hands over her ears. *Crack*, another gun with a sharper sound. People scurried past her. Cynthia turned to see two middle-aged men in the street, blasting shots at each other. One had a black beard, the other wore a wide-brimmed western hat.

The bearded man was having trouble with his gun. He spun the cylinder, then took aim, but it failed to fire. A bullet struck him in the shoulder and he staggered back, steadied himself, and shook the gun. The man in the western hat fired again and the bearded man toppled into the muddy street.

The victor strode toward him, reloading his gun. Her back pressed against one of the hotel's pillars, Cynthia watched, horrified. He was going to execute the wounded man, who was groaning in agony.

"Hold your fire," said a voice on the other side of the pillar. A gaunt, grim-eyed man stepped into the street, a pistol in his hand, a ferocious scowl on his angular face. "Who in hell are you, and who is he?" he asked.

"He's Gus Chandler, a Republican son of a bitch," the man in the western hat replied. "Run against me for the legislature and put some lying stories in the newspapers about me."

"You may be a good Democrat, but you're also a damn fool. Get yourself out of town before we apply some hemp to your neck for disturbing the peace."

The victor spat on the wounded man and sauntered up St. Charles Street toward Gravier Street. Still scowling, the peacemaker, who wore his brown hair in long flowing prewar style, turned to someone in the St. Charles arcade and said, "Get this fellow to a doctor."

As he spoke he saw Cynthia backed against the pillar. He shoved his pistol into the holster that he wore under his black frock coat and walked over to her. "I apologize for the fright that must have given you, madam," he said. "My name is Edgar Calhoun. I'm the commander of the White League."

"I've heard about you, Colonel Calhoun. I'm Cynthia Stapleton—Robert Legrand's sister."

"I'm doubly regretful for the ugly quarrel you just encountered. Your brother is in Baton Rouge." He hesitated; for a moment the angry scowl almost reappeared on his face. "I suppose your husband advised you to join him here."

"My husband? He's in New York."

"I wish that were true, madam. He arrived an hour ago, with a carpetbag full of money. I wish I could soften my language a little, but the truth is, he's come to steal the election from us."

"I find that hard to believe."

"Perhaps you should ask him rather than argue with me, madam. I regret, truly regret, meeting you under such circumstances. I'm not at all sure we can control our men if they see General Stapleton on the street. His Republican friends are holed up in the St. Louis Hotel. I can assure you they won't have the courage to defend him."

"Where is General Stapleton?"

"Upstairs having dinner." He smiled briefly. "We have him under rather continuous surveillance."

"Would you take me to him?"

Calhoun helped Lucy out of the carriage and assured her that she was safe. He instructed the driver to leave the luggage at the desk and led Cynthia through the hotel's immense circular lobby. On the second floor, in a corner of the huge otherwise empty dining room, sat Jonathan Stapleton. He looked weary and disheveled. His black suit was a mass of wrinkles and his shirt cuffs were sooty. He had obviously spent the last thirty-six hours sitting up on a train.

"General Stapleton?" Edgar Calhoun introduced himself. "I just encountered this lady coming into the hotel. I hope you don't mind my escorting her here."

Jonathan seemed more dazed or confused than Cynthia had ever seen him. "Thank you. I had no idea . . ."

"General. Let me take this opportunity to repeat a concern I've already stated to Mrs. Stapleton. I'm the commander of the militia the Democratic Party has brought into New Orleans. As you probably know, we control all the principal government buildings. We're determined to keep the peace, so no one can claim we've resorted to force to win this election. But I'm very much afraid that one of my men might lose control of himself if he saw you leaving this hotel with the carpetbag you brought in here this morning."

"Colonel Calhoun," Jonathan snapped, "my luggage is none of your business. As for my freedom to go where I please in an American city that is presumably governed by law, I resent and will ignore any attempt to limit it."

"You'll excuse me, then, General?"

"Most definitely."

"I'll see that your servant is settled and your luggage delivered to the General's room, Mrs. Stapleton."

"Thank you, Colonel Calhoun."

Edgar Calhoun withdrew. Cynthia sat down. Jonathan sat down more slowly, gazing at her.

"Did they send you—bring you here?" he said.

"What are you talking about? I'm on my way to New York. I got your letter—urging me to come home."

"Oh . . . yes. Would you like something to eat?"

She nodded. He summoned a waiter. She ordered gumbo filé and king crab. He poured her a glass of white wine. She had never seen him so uneasy. He could not keep his hands still. He brushed at his wrinkled coat, his dirty cuffs, thrust at his uncombed hair.

"Colonel Calhoun says you're here to steal the election."

"He would say that. I see it somewhat differently. I'm here to stop them from stealing it—and the presidency of the United States into the bargain."

"How can you do that—all by yourself?"

"There are ways. Disagreeable ways, I'm afraid. I see no need to explain them to you."

His curt tone chilled her impulse to tell him what she had seen at the crossroads on her horseback ride yesterday. Suddenly she could see nothing but Jeannie's red hands. Did they somehow balance out Little Oscar Legrand dangling from that cypress tree?

Jonathan shook his head in an abrupt ferocious way, as if he wished he could banish her from his sight. "I'd give a million dollars to get you out of this city."

"Why?"

"It's dangerous. Those five thousand rebels out there are under no discipline. All we need are a few random shots to start a massacre."

He was lying now. She knew why he wanted her out of the city. So she could not witness his shame. He was here to commit a crime, to bribe election officials. Jonathan Stapleton, who never missed a chance to sneer at crooked Democrats—and living in New York gave him endless opportunities —was about to imitate them. He was here with the power of his money and the implied threat in the word "General" to keep Louisiana—her people—in subjection.

The waiters brought their food. They ate. He asked for her mother and sister. She said they were fine.

The waiters brought coffee flavored with chicory. Cynthia heard Mittie Roosevelt warning her, *The most a wife can hope to do is moderate her husband's opinions.* But this man resisted even a modicum of moderation. What did love mean, if a husband persisted in a course of action that he knew—he had to know—would desolate his wife's feelings?

"French coffee," Jonathan said. "That brings back memories." He was trying to escape this ugliness, remind her of their honeymoon days in Paris.

"What if they kill you?"

The words burst from her, a mixture of reproach and love. He sat back in his chair, his face rigid, eyes glaring. "You've been a widow before," he said. "You'll be a lot richer this time."

It was a horrible, hateful thing to say. It seemed to imply that he thought she had married him and his brother for their money, that she was incapable of being a loving wife. She was about to answer him with the hottest angriest words imaginable when a husky black-bearded man rushed up to the table.

"General," he said. "I've been talking to our friends at Western Union. They tell me there are telegrams arriving from Democratic headquarters in New York. You'd better talk to those people at the St. Louis Hotel as soon as possible."

Jonathan introduced Cynthia to Congressman James Garfield of Ohio. "My wife has been visiting her mother up the river. She's on her way back to New York," he explained.

The Congressman produced a sparkling smile. "I'm charmed. I wish the circumstances were happier."

"So do I," Cynthia said.

"Sit down, Congressman," Jonathan said. "Have you talked to the reporters?"

"Yes. I think it went pretty well," Garfield said. He began recapitulating his interview with the newspapermen. In a few sentences the Congressman slipped into the indignant tone he had adopted for public consumption. Phrases like "theft of the presidency" applied to the Democrats flowed effortlessly from his lips.

Jonathan finally interrupted the Congressman's performance. "I'd better take Mrs. Stapleton up to our room. She's had a trying journey down the river."

"Of course," Garfield said. "I hope you'll join us for supper." The man was incredible. He was pretending they were at a resort.

As they climbed the stairs to the third floor, Jonathan took her arm and said, "Now you know what they mean by 'gifted politician.' "

She freed her arm and stalked silently ahead of him down the hall to their room. Jonathan unlocked the door. Cynthia hurried past him and stood at the window, her back to him. After a moment, Jonathan touched her on the shoulder. "My dearest, I am so tired—and disgusted—by this whole business. I'm sorry."

She shook her head. Footsteps. The door closed.

Below her, St. Charles Street was empty. But in the windows of the business buildings across the street Cynthia saw one, two, three, a dozen men with rifles. More riflemen lounged on the second-floor galleries of a three-story brick building on the next block. My God, they were going to kill him. Did she want it to happen?

No. She thought of his longing letter, of her sadness last night as she surrendered her last ties to Louisiana, accepted her destiny as his wife. She still loved him. But she loved Jeannie, she loved her dead, too.

There he was. Jonathan Stapleton had emerged from the hotel and stopped in the middle of St. Charles Street. He glared up at the riflemen in the windows of the building across the street. One of them raised his gun and drew a bead on him. "No!" Cynthia cried.

They could not hear her through the closed window. Calmly, contemptuously, Jonathan turned his back on the rifleman and stalked down the street toward the French Quarter. Cynthia closed her eyes, waiting for the crash of the gun.

It never came. When she opened her eyes, Jonathan was gone. The empty street, the riflemen, confronted her. She began to tremble and weep. How could Jonathan subject her to such torment?

An urgent knock on the door. Edgar Calhoun stood there, a frown on his tanned face. "Mrs. Stapleton," he said, "I hope you'll excuse this somewhat indelicate intrusion. But I wanted to tell you, I've issued orders to my men. No one will harm your husband in any way. You can at least rest easy on that score."

He stopped, noticing the tears on her face. "I wish I could have given you that assurance earlier. Let me say again how much it grieves me that a lady of your breeding and beauty should be exposed to such controversy."

It was almost quaint—the courtly language, this southern voice uttering sentiments she had not heard in such a long time. What a contrast to the contempt her Yankee husband had just flung in her face.

"Thank you, Colonel Calhoun," she said. "I hope someday I'll have an opportunity to repay your kindness."

BOOK III
1877–1878

ONE

Control your temper.

For the twenty-fifth time, Jonathan Stapleton issued this order to himself while he paced restlessly around the sitting room of their suite in the Willard Hotel. He was waiting for his wife to finish dressing for a state dinner at the White House, at which the outgoing President, Ulysses S. Grant, and other luminaries of the Republican Party would greet the new leader of the nation, Rutherford B. Hayes.

The festivity was to serve as a substitute for the inaugural ball, which the President-elect had decided to cancel. The decision was only a straw in the violent political wind that was blowing through Washington, but it suggested a timidity that made Jonathan uneasy. He wanted desperately to believe that the ordeal he had undergone in the past four months had put a courageous leader in the White House. Hayes had been a brave man on a battlefield, with five wounds and a brigadier's star to prove it. But political courage and military courage seemed to be two very different things, as Ulysses S. Grant had dolorously demonstrated.

Jonathan consulted his watch. They were already a half hour late. He looked morosely around the sitting room, with its frayed damask drapes, its worn saffron-cushioned French furniture. The Willard was showing its age. He had planned to stay at the Arlington, in Lafayette Square just across from the White House. It was Washington's newest and best hotel. But the Arlington had been full—reportedly jammed to the roof with liberal Republicans from all parts of the country panting for a chance to shake the new President's hand and recommend themselves or a relative for a federal job.

Jonathan wanted nothing from Rutherford B. Hayes, so the loss of proximity meant little. Hayes's tilt toward the liberal wing of the party had grown more and more obvious since the election. According to Zach Chandler, the new President had all but put a notice in the window of his house in Fremont, Ohio, announcing, "No regular Republicans need apply." This was irritating because it suggested that Hayes was embarrassed by the way the regulars had won the election for him. It was alarming because Jonathan had no confidence in the liberals as politicians.

Perhaps the Willard sharpened his antipathy to liberal Republicans, Jonathan mused. It was full of wartime memories. Generals and their staffs stayed here when they retreated to Washington to fight the political side of the war. He kept seeing himself and other grim-jawed men in blue uniforms striding down the carpeted corridors on their way to testify before congressional committees, where they frequently had to take abuse about their casualties and incompetence from politicians who could not understand why a noble cause and a few stirring slogans did not guarantee instant victory.

Not all the Willard's memories were political. Late at night, many of those blue-uniformed ghosts in the corridors—himself among them—had their arms around laughing, careless-eyed women. No question, this was the wrong hotel for an ex-soldier trying to soothe an angry wife.

A great many Americans, most of them Democrats, had not accepted amicably the mathematical rearrangements Jonathan and his fellow Republican emissaries had purchased in Louisiana, South Carolina and Florida, making Rutherford B. Hayes president of the United States by one electoral vote.

Democratic newspapers, led by the *New York Herald*, had assailed General Stapleton and everyone else involved in the operation with an apparently endless supply of epithets. Rocks had been flung through the windows of his house on Stuyvesant Square. Death threats arrived regularly in the mail, many supposedly from relatives of "victims" his troops had "murdered" in the Draft Riots of 1863. For a few weeks his friend Police Superintendent Walling had stationed a patrolman in front of his door. In the office, Jonathan worked with a loaded pistol in his desk. He slept with another one on his night table.

The personal turmoil was bad enough. It was worsened by the threat of national violence. On the blue Empire couch lay a copy of *Harper's Weekly* which Jonathan had just finished reading. Its entire front page was devoted to a drawing of a Democratic hand reaching for a pistol. A Republican foot was stamping on the hand. Beneath the pistol was a poster with the cry TILDEN OR BLOOD.

Democratic politicians, in particular the governor of New York, had been making speeches practically urging their followers to augment their ballots with bullets. Democratic newspapers encouraged this idea by constantly calling the President-elect "Rutherfraud" B. Hayes. Not all the madmen were Democrats. An ex-general from Illinois had been caught writing letters to congressmen, offering to raise 100,000 men and march on Washington to install the Republican candidate.

After weeks of wrangling, Congress had created an electoral commission composed of eight Republicans and seven Democrats to resolve the crisis. After more weeks of wordy pointless hearings, they had voted along party lines to accept the returns from Florida, South Carolina and Louisiana that made Hayes president by a single electoral vote. The decision had done nothing to mollify the enraged Democrats. A final battle had erupted in the House of Representatives, which the Democrats still controlled. For a few days last week, it looked as if the nation would have no President on March 4th. Democratic newspapers and politicians talked ominously of an "interregnum" in which lawful authority would cease to exist and almost anything, including insurrection, could happen.

Instead, secret negotiations had ensued between Hayes's spokesman, his fellow Ohioan James Garfield, and the southern congressmen. A day or two later the southerners had abruptly deserted their northern Democratic colleagues and certified Hayes's election.

No one knew what Hayes had promised, but the negotiations had made many Republicans nervous. In the telegram that invited Jonathan and Cynthia to the state dinner at the White House, Zachariah Chandler had written: "I WISH I COULD TELL YOU WHAT'S GOING ON. ALL I HEAR ARE RUMORS ABOUT CERTAIN PUSILLANIMOUS PUKES NEGOTIATING AS IF WE HAD SOMETHING TO FEAR."

"I'm ready at last," Cynthia said.

Her maid, Lucy, stood beaming in the doorway of the bedroom, as if the spectacle were her creation.

Color was obviously the word of the year among the high priests of fashion on the Rue de la Paix. Cynthia's gown was a blaze of coral and ivory climaxed by a great swatch of green chenille fastened at the waist and train by red poppies. With diamonds sparkling in her dark hair and pearls glistening on her white throat and massive gold bands on her wrists, she was womanhood personified, in all its splendor and beauty.

But there was no sparkle of delight in those green eyes, welcoming his admiration, no amorous promise in the rise of that coral bodice. She was not Cynthia Legrand, dressed for his delectation. She was Mrs. Jonathan Stapleton, wife of the more or less notorious Republican politician, gowned and coiffed for public display.

"You look lovely," he said.

Cynthia smiled at him in a polite way, as if she had received a compliment from a stranger. Jonathan helped his wife into the fur-trimmed Siberian cloak he had given her for Christmas and they went out to the elevator. The Negro operator stared at the wall. General Stapleton stared at his wife. His wife stared at him.

"Almost over," he said.

The words stirred warmth in Cynthia's green eyes—warmth that Jonathan hoped to increase before the weekend ended. "I can hardly believe it," she said.

"It's true."

In New York, confronting Cynthia's wrath, Jonathan's first instinct had been to summon that stoic public figure he thought he had left behind in Virginia, the iron general. He had tried to invoke the general's old friend, necessity, to explain his trip to Louisiana, but Cynthia found the argument unconvincing and the character who emerged from it loathsome.

Jonathan had banished the general and tried to think like a loving husband. He had inflicted a wound on their marriage by his mere presence in Louisiana. It had been compounded by encountering Cynthia in New Orleans. But he had infinitely worsened the hurt by his vicious remark about making her a rich widow.

He had been sure the White League militiamen would not shoot a former Union general and personal friend of President Grant. That would have brought a division of federal troops down on their rebel necks. Why hadn't he explained that to Cynthia instead of snarling those cruel words about money?

A few nights later, Jonathan had visited Cynthia in her bedroom and apologized for those words. He carefully excluded any regret for going to Louisiana. The emphasis was on his remorse at meeting her there and allowing exhaustion and bad temper to control his tongue. To his surprise and delight she accepted the apology—accepted him as a husband once more. But the moment they began to make love, he sensed her reluctance, perhaps her inability, to surrender to him. Only at the climax did emotion break through. Cynthia had cried out and clung to him—a strange mingling of passion and pain.

"Oh Jonathan—I *want* to go on loving you . . ." she had murmured.

"You will—you must—" he whispered.

With an honesty and sincerity that left him feeling humbled and ashamed, she told him of the lynched Negro she had seen the day before she left for New Orleans, ugly proof of the White League's terror in Bralston's neighborhood. For a few minutes he thought she was about to praise him for his Republican courage and fortitude. But it was much more complicated. She talked about her love for her sister Jeannie, her memory of the July night in 1863 when they had sat on Bralston's veranda mourning the deaths of her brother and Jeannie's fiancé. She told him what the war had meant to her: losses and more losses unto desolation.

He gradually perceived that she was trying to make him see that she could not bear this new war, uglier in some ways than the old one. His first wife had made a similar plea to the iron general, and he had ignored her. The loving husband could not ignore this woman. But all he could offer her was penitence, a renewed promise that the nightmare would end when Rutherford B. Hayes entered the White House.

Cynthia had responded with a bold proposal. "Why don't we go to Europe now?" she had whispered, her arms still wrapped around him in the bed of love. "Turn our backs on the whole disgusting business. Spend a year loving each other, enjoying life in Paris, Florence, Venice."

For a moment, the loving husband almost said yes. But the iron general was standing in the shadows, watching. "I'm afraid that would look as though I was running away," he said.

The iron general, famous for never retreating, quietly applauded. But Cynthia did not applaud. Although she said she understood his feelings, she soon acquired a melancholy stoicism of her own. Henceforth their lovemaking seldom achieved more than physical warmth.

Outside the Willard, a chilly March wind whistled down Pennsylvania Avenue as the doorman signaled for a hack. Cynthia shivered and wrapped herself more tightly in her Siberian cloak. "That wind makes me think of poor Georgie in New Hampshire," she said. "His last letter said there was still five or six feet of snow on the ground. He's had one cold after another . . ."

Dear lazy Georgie had tried in vain to procure his stepmother's intervention to suspend his sentence to St. Paul's School, several hundred snowy miles away from Elliott Roosevelt and the charms of Bowery streetwalkers.

"He'll survive. It'll make a man out of him."

Silence. That had become his wife's favorite tactic when she disagreed with him. Patience, Jonathan told himself. Wait until Italy. In his wallet were two tickets on the Cunard Line's *Melbourne* for May 1st. He had cabled their agent in Venice, reserving the Palazzo Rospigliosi for two months. Later tonight, he planned to produce the tickets. He hoped they would restore warmth, begin to heal wounds.

"Who'll be there tonight, besides the old President and the new one?" Cynthia asked.

"Your admirer Senator Conkling will be hurling compliments at you."

"How can any woman stand that man?"

"Some women apparently like compliments."

"All women do, if they're sincere."

"So do men."

"I sometimes wonder if men care a speck about sincerity. They abuse it so regularly."

Irritation prickled his skin. Was she suggesting that he had abused her sincerity by not yielding to her plea for an immediate retreat to Europe?

That thought started him brooding about a woman who had abused his sincerity. Jonathan had heard nothing from Rawdon or Genevieve after he returned from New Orleans. He did not expect anything but sneers from Rawdon, who had quit the *Times* to go to work for the *Herald,* where he undoubtedly supplied them with some of the inside information they used with devastating effect in their stories on the election crisis. Cynthia, determined to preserve some family feeling, invited the newlyweds to dinner and an exchange of presents on Christmas Eve. Jonathan sensed something was wrong with his daughter-in-law the moment he saw her. Sullen reproach clouded her transcendental eyes. She said almost nothing throughout dinner while her husband blithely told them how much he enjoyed working for his father's chief abuser, James Gordon Bennett, Jr.

On January 1st, when Jonathan and all the other men in New York set out to make their traditional New Year's Day calls, he put Genevieve first on his list. As he had expected, he found her alone, and lost no time getting to the point. "I hope you don't believe everything you read about me in the papers," he said.

"How could you do such a despicable thing?" Genevieve had hissed.

Yes, hissed, with a rage that exceeded anything Cynthia had displayed. Raw pain had run through his body. Rawdon had obviously convinced her that Jonathan Stapleton was as low as the *Herald* portrayed him. He responded with a cold anger of his own and they parted without a single conciliatory word.

What did he expect? he asked himself bitterly as the hack swung through the White House gate and approached the lighted portico. The election was a war. There had to be casualties in a war. There had to be losses. He had lost the love of two women, his wife and his mother, in the last war and survived.

No. Jonathan's hand went to his wallet, to the Cunard Line tickets to Italy. That was the iron general talking. He had heard his ghost whispering malicious thoughts several times lately when he came home to a stoic wife.

As they mounted the steps of the White House portico, a figure emerged from a crowd of newspapermen. It was Clay Pendleton, covering the story for the *Times.* "General," Clay said. "I'm supposed to get a statement from you. Do you feel this evening is a vindication of your efforts?"

"I most certainly do."

In a much lower voice, Clay added, "If you pick up anything inside about the secret negotiations with the southern Democrats, I'd appreciate hearing about it."

"Come see me tomorrow. I'm at the Willard."

Vindication. He could see the impact of the word in Cynthia's disconsolate eyes as he joined her at the White House door. Maybe there was no end to this mess.

"Stapleton. How good to see you!"

In the doorway of the East Room, President Ulysses S. Grant seized his hand in a soldier's grip. "And Mrs. Stapleton," he added. "Now I know the evening will be a success."

"My husband is much too partial to your wife, General," Julia Grant said in her merry way.

"General Hayes, I'm sure you remember General Stapleton," Grant said, introducing him to the tall bearded Ohioan.

"Of course. We met in Columbus after the nominating convention. How good to see you again."

That's all? Jonathan thought. Not a word about the ten million dollars I raised to make you president? He nodded and smiled as Hayes introduced him to his plain firm-jawed wife, Lucy. He introduced Cynthia and took some satisfaction in the awed look Mrs. Hayes bestowed on her gown.

They strolled into the East Room, taking champagne from a passing tray, nodding to familiar faces, members of Grant's cabinet, General Sheridan, the army's corpulent commander. An elbow nudged his ribs. Zach Chandler, side whiskers bristling, grimaced up at him. "What'd our hero say?"

" 'How good to see you,' " Jonathan said.

"That's the last good thing you're going to hear from him. Leave Mrs. Stapleton with my wife. Conkling wants to talk to you."

"Look who's here, Cynthia," Jonathan said.

She greeted the Chandlers warmly. Letitia was wearing a gown almost as splendid as Cynthia's. Twenty years in Washington had made her a sophisticated amusing woman. Jonathan's conscience did not bother him too acutely when he excused himself and followed Chandler through the crowd to the other side of the room, where Roscoe Conkling was standing alone.

"I was finally granted an interview by the two-faced bastard you sojourned with in New Orleans," Conkling said.

"Garfield?"

"Right. He and our heroic candidate both wet their pants when the rebels threatened to filibuster in the House until June and create that terrible Democratic spook, an interregnum. They made a deal. They're going to withdraw the troops. Let the Confederates redeem Louisiana, Florida, South Carolina."

Withdraw the troops. The unthinkable words reverberated in Jonathan Stapleton's mind. *Withdraw the troops?* He had rescued Louisiana, ruined his reputation, soiled his conscience, endangered his marriage—to abandon the Negro and white Republicans of the South without a fight? A Republican President was going to do such a thing?

"Didn't anyone consult you? Or Zach? Or Grant?" he asked.

Chandler shook his head. "We're unclean. We got a little mud on us putting the son of a bitch in the White House."

Jonathan still could not believe it. "Down in New Orleans Garfield told me what Hayes said to him on the day after the election, when he thought he'd lost. He said he only felt sorry for the poor Negroes."

"He decided he feels sorrier for the fucking Confederates," Conkling snarled. "He couldn't bear the thought of them filibustering their balls off."

Something about being in the White House made Conkling's scatology doubly obscene. But it was justified. A man had to be obscene to describe an obscenity.

"Garfield says they got assurances that the Negroes' civil rights will be protected," Chandler growled. "He's sold out to the fucking liberals. I almost think he believes that shit about the hand of friendship."

"Wait—you haven't heard the best part," Conkling said. "To make sure the Confederate fuckers are happy, we're going to build them a railroad. A transcontinental railroad with federal money, the way we built the Union Pacific."

"Good God! What can we do about this?" Jonathan said.

"We're going to fight," Conkling said, smacking fist against palm. "This is a fight for control of the Republican Party, for the destiny of the goddamn country. I hope you're with us, General. The first thing we've got to do is stop this Texas Pacific Railroad. No one knows the railroad men of this country better than you. I hope you'll organize a goddamn avalanche of letters and telegrams from them, condemning it as the most outrageous giveaway of federal money in the country's history."

"Consider it done," Jonathan said.

He glanced over his shoulder at Cynthia. She was still chatting with Letitia Chandler. He thought she was looking bored. He shuddered to think of how she would look if she could overhear this conversation.

Zach Chandler started naming Hayes's cabinet choices. They were all liberal Republicans or political allies from Ohio. Hayes obviously wanted to distance himself from most of the regular Republicans. "It's a goddamn coup d'état," Chandler fumed. "But if you stick with us, General, they'll never take over the party. You can block them on the money side. They've got to deal with us as long as we control the big contributors."

"Let's start lining up votes against that railroad here and now," Conkling rumbled. "Right under Rutherfraud's nose."

The two politicians began buttonholing nearby senators and congressmen. Jonathan began edging his way back to Cynthia through the packed room.

"General!" called a familiar voice.

He found himself face to face with smiling James Garfield and sleek Tom

Scott, president of the Pennsylvania Railroad. Scott shook his hand with the special vigor railroad presidents reserved for members of their board of directors. Jonathan had acquired the seat when the Pennsylvania bought the Camden & Amboy in 1866.

"I just saw you with Conkling, General," Garfield said. "No doubt he filled your ears with his version of our negotiations. I hope you'll give us a chance to explain our side. You've read the newspapers. You know the state of nerves the country is in. I'm sure the thought of another war—the kind of war that might have started in cities and towns across the nation—fills you with horror, as it did us."

"You really think those promises to protect the Negroes' voting rights mean anything?"

"They were given by honorable men," Garfield said in his most unctuous tone. "Anyway, we can't build a party on Negro rights. There are more important issues. Civil-service reform, redemption of the greenbacks, reviving prosperity in the South. This railroad we're proposing to build will do far more to restore the Union and build a Republican Party in the South."

Tom Scott was nodding eagerly, agreeing with every word. "The Pennsylvania's going to operate the railroad, General. It can be the nucleus of the Republican Party in the South."

Bullshit, whispered an inner voice which might have belonged to Ben Dall. Tom Scott's greedy smile only embellished the manure. Scott could hardly wait to get his hands on a railroad that the government was going to finance for him. He did not care whether it was staffed by Republicans or Democrats or Hottentots.

"Very interesting. But I must get back to my wife before she secedes."

"Oh!" Garfield cried, rolling his eyes like a third-rate vaudeville comedian. "We wouldn't want to be responsible for that!"

Jonathan progressed another twenty feet in his struggle to regain his wife when a hand caught his arm. He stared into the bearded face and glittering eyes of Jay Gould. It was hardly surprising to see him here. He had given the Republican Party a check for a million dollars—even if Jonathan had had to wring it out of him by threatening to put him in jail with Roscoe Conkling's help.

"General," Gould said, "I'm sure you were talking about that new transcontinental railroad just now with Garfield and Scott. It would compete with my Union Pacific and Missouri Pacific. I don't like competition."

"So?"

"I didn't give you and Roscoe Conkling a million dollars just to put this Ohio chucklehead in the White House. I expect a healthy return on all my investments. I want to build that railroad, Stapleton, and run it."

Gould's arrogance left Jonathan momentarily speechless. The diminutive financier complacently continued:

"I'll cut you and Conkling into it. You could be very useful, Stapleton. Railroad men respect you. I'll give you twenty percent of the preferred stock and another twenty percent of the construction company. That's where we'll make the real money. I would say that's thirty million dollars I'm offering you."

Jonathan's mind churned into motion as Gould talked. Here was a perfect opportunity to sabotage the Texas Pacific before it even reached the floor of Congress. Tomorrow he would give Clay Pendleton the whole story of the secret negotiations and link this slimy creature confronting him to Hayes. In politics, ugly suggestions frequently became facts. Meanwhile, he would dispose of Jay Gould.

"Did you ever read a story by Melville called 'Bartleby the Scrivener'?"

Gould shook his head. "I collect books, but I never have time to read them," he said. "Melville's a has-been anyway."

"Bartleby is a clerk who refused to do certain kinds of work. He just says, 'I prefer not to.' That's the way a real railroad man feels about going into business with you, Gould. He prefers not to."

"You're going to be sorry you said that, Stapleton," Gould murmured. He vanished almost magically into the crowd. The titan was so tiny, when he stepped behind the person nearest him he disappeared.

Jonathan resumed his difficult progress toward Cynthia, wondering if he had just made a mistake. A man with a hundred million dollars could make things uncomfortable on Wall Street for a man with only five million. The hell with it, he thought. He felt cleansed. Here in this sacred building he had announced to himself, if not to the world, that he was still an honest man. Somehow Gould balanced the other memory that kept haunting him, the image of himself in the St. Louis Hotel in New Orleans, handing wads of greenbacks to the four members of the Returning Board.

Cynthia. There she was at last. Not chatting languidly with Letitia Chandler but cheerfully with a tall dark-haired man whose back was turned to him.

It was Theodore Roosevelt. Cynthia said he had appeared like a knight errant to rescue her, just as she was about to expire from thirst. "My champagne glass had been empty for a half hour. My husband was indifferent to the fact. Thank God there's one gentleman left in the Republican Party."

Roosevelt cheerfully shook Jonathan's hand. "You arrived just in time, General," he said. "I'm masquerading as a bachelor tonight. I was invited at the very last moment by my friend Evarts. Mittie said she had nothing to wear."

William Evarts was the distinguished New York lawyer who had pleaded Hayes's case before the Electoral Commission. "Evarts is going to be secretary of state," Roosevelt continued in his amiable way. "He wanted me to meet the new President."

In his dazed state of mind, Jonathan could only nod. Evarts and his fellow liberal Republicans had not wasted an invitation on smiling Theodore simply to give President-elect Hayes the pleasure of shaking his hand. Roosevelt fitted into their political plans. They were probably going to offer him a job that would help them take over the Republican Party in New York. Did he know it? Or was he as naïve as he seemed to be?

All through dinner Jonathan's rage simmered as he endured the innumerable toasts and speeches of the victory celebration. Jollity was the prevailing mood in spite of the thunderclouds on the faces of Conkling, Chandler and a half-dozen Republican senators to whom they had revealed the secret deal. It was the Grant Administration's last crack at the White House wine cellar, and vintage reds and whites, sauternes and champagne and brandy, flowed freely.

Cynthia was seated next to James Garfield. Jonathan watched her pretending to enjoy his hearty good humor. She was charming him in spite of the loathing she felt for his smiling hypocrisy, which she had seen in action in New Orleans. It was somewhat unnerving to have a wife with such a remarkable ability to deceive people about her true feelings.

By the time the guzzling, gorging and oratory ended at 1 A.M., Jonathan's rage had subsided to weary disgust. His head ached, his stomach throbbed. He was puzzled, almost irritated, by the smiling wife who joined him outside the cloakroom. He had to remind himself that Cynthia had not been exposed to the ugly truths behind the charade of amity and good cheer.

In the hack, Cynthia turned to Jonathan, her eyes aglow. "Congressman Garfield tells me that President Hayes is determined to prove himself a friend of the South. He wants to put the war behind us. Isn't that wonderful?"

Jonathan had never dreamed Garfield would talk politics to his wife. "There's nothing wonderful about it," he growled.

"What do you mean?"

"I mean I'm appalled at what Hayes is going to do. Withdraw the troops from Louisiana and South Carolina and Florida. Let the redeemers take over with the shotgun and the noose. Then, to make sure everyone is happy, he's going to give the South a transcontinental railroad. Build it with public money."

"Is that so . . . awful?" Cynthia said.

"We think it is." He heard the snarl in his voice. Heard it and regretted it. But he could not control it.

They rode in silence for a half block. He seized Cynthia's white-gloved hand. "Darling, it doesn't have anything to do with us."

"Yes it does," she said. "You must stop telling yourself that lie, Jonathan."

More silence, broken by shouts of revelers on the sidewalks. The party faithful had insisted on an inaugural parade. They were crowding into the city for a triumphant strut up Pennsylvania Avenue.

"I thought it was over," Cynthia said.

It was almost unbearable, the sadness in her voice. Was it pretended or genuine? Either possibility was infuriating because it threatened to unman him.

"Garfield's a liar. A damned double-dealing liar," he growled.

Cynthia's lovely head drooped, her lips trembled. They were at the hotel. Conversation was safely avoided until they reached their suite. He had hoped they would come back here tonight flushed with wine and mutual forgiveness. He had imagined himself whispering, "Over, it really is over," and producing the tickets on the *Melbourne.* Instead it was a repetition of the last five months—the melancholy, accusatory eyes, the stoic mouth. For some reason he found himself less able to tolerate it. Did she really think he should let those two-faced Ohio bastards make a fool of him?

From the sitting room of their suite he could see the double bed, its pillows banked, the covers turned down. He still wanted her, with or without her forgiveness. The iron general would be satisfied, either way.

No. He would be tender. But he would be insistent. He would make her accept him as the man he was, with all the visible scars and secret wounds and bitter memories, a man with metal in his body and in his soul.

Lucy tottered to the door of the bedroom, yawning sleepily. They exchanged the usual small talk. It was a lovely party. They had a wonderful time. Cynthia retreated into the bedroom to undress with Lucy's help. Jonathan ordered a brandy and soda from the hall porter and sat there, remembering long-vanished nights when the iron general had sat in a similar suite, waiting for a tap on the door, for a brief, perfume-scented escape from mud and guns and the staring eyes of the dead.

A half hour later, beside Cynthia in bed, he kissed her tenderly on the throat. She trembled slightly but did not turn to him with the warm welcoming embrace of other nights. Slowly, deliberately, he lifted her against him and kissed her on the mouth. He held the kiss a long time, feeling the resistance slowly dwindle as his right hand drifted along the curve of her breasts and moved beneath the silk nightgown, to the place that made every woman surrender.

Somewhere in the recesses of his mind a voice warned him he was making a terrible mistake, it was wrong to abuse this woman's wish to love him, to force her to convert wish into fact with the power that was in his hands and lips, with his claims to her gratitude, affection, loyalty.

There he was, sliding into the magic place, that silk-lined darkness, the liquid world of love that Mother had once forbidden him to enter without her approval.

Yes, General, in the saddle, a conquering hero, possessor, ruler of your piece of rebel gash—

No! Husband, lover, needy, hungry, desperate, pathetic lover. If only he could tell the truth . . .

Ahhhhh. There you have it, General. Surrender, gasping trembling surrender. Wasn't that what you wanted? You have it have it have it.

Not with the lovely face turned away from his lips. Not with tears oozing down those curved cheeks. Did she know? Did that uncanny sensitivity with which women are gifted or cursed divine the truth? Did she *see* the iron general there in the bed beside her, above her in triumph?

No. He had been tender. He had been crafty in his disguise. He would admit nothing. "I love you," he whispered. "I'll never stop. Never."

Silence. Did it mean what he feared? He padded across the room and found his wallet in the semidarkness. Returning, he showed her the tickets on the *Melbourne*. "For June first," he said. "We'll be in Italy by June twentieth."

Was that true? June 1st was less than three months away. Did that give him time to whip up a newspaper frenzy against the Texas Pacific and rally major Republican contributors all over the country? Perhaps more to the point, could he help start a war and then sail away from it?

Instead of creating delight, the tickets only seemed to increase the sadness on Cynthia's tear-stained face. She touched them with her fingertips, as if she did not believe they were real. Then tears came in a gush. "Oh Jonathan. We could be so happy!"

She clung to him, sobbing. She wept and wept while he frantically tried to soothe her. She knew—without the words, she had not found the awful words, the desolating image. But she knew what he had just done. Jesus, what was he becoming?

TWO

Snowflakes swirled out of the gray March sky past the window of the kitchen where Genevieve Dall Stapleton was cooking her husband's breakfast. Standing at the stove, she could see nothing but snow and clouds. Living six floors above the ground was still a strange sensation. Often she felt as if she was in one of Jules Verne's airships.

It was 9 A.M. Most New Yorkers had long since finished their breakfasts and gone to work. But reporters for morning papers seldom came home before midnight. Genevieve had arranged with her employer to work from ten until six. This theoretically gave her daring young journalist eight hours of sleep before his nine-o'clock breakfast. If, as frequently happened, Rawdon wandered home several hours past midnight, he still had to get up at the agreed-upon time. A fair compromise between competing needs was the essence of rational love.

Rawdon's first course, a green salad, was already on the dining-room table. Genevieve was cooking a Havana omelet, a dish Rawdon had discovered in a Lower East Side restaurant run by a refugee Cuban revolutionist. It was a complicated recipe, involving chicken livers, mushrooms, port wine and Espagnole sauce. In another pan a small steak was frying beside some sliced potatoes and onions.

Rawdon insisted on a big breakfast. The dread of not getting one had been one of his major objections to a working wife. Genevieve had vowed to supply him with a banquet every morning. So far she had kept her promise. But it was irritating, in a subtle persistent way, to awaken to the clanging alarm an hour before her husband and stumble out to the cold kitchen while he continued to enjoy their warm bed.

The Espagnole sauce bubbled and oozed around the omelet. Whenever she cooked one of these spicy things, she found herself thinking about the month-long honeymoon they had planned to spend in Havana, before she sent Rawdon that disastrous telegram. Rawdon sometimes lamented their failure to begin their marriage in the so-called Paris of the New World.

Yet in many ways Kemble Manor had been the perfect place to begin. It had not been very warm in late September, but they had had the beach, the bay, to themselves. There was no older generation frowning—or smiling—in the distance. At last they had faced each other, true man and true woman, ready to launch their great experiment in blending the real and the ideal.

Genevieve almost smiled remembering the terror that had raged in her mind and heart on her wedding night. Extinction, that was what she had feared, remembering the wild wish to surrender, to abandon her egotistic thinking self, that had engulfed her at Kemble Manor. A summer of association with educated women such as her employer, Mrs. Wilbour, had made her doubt the wisdom of that wish. She had gone to bed with her husband hoping to find some middle way, to escape obliteration and yet give herself to Rawdon, to love that would incarnate the ideal.

But her mind refused to stop working. Even while Rawdon was kissing and caressing her, while his hands were producing remarkably pleasant sensations in the most intimate parts of her body, she found herself wondering how he knew exactly what to do. There was no hesitation, none of the fumbling that the Vassar physiology professor had warned them to expect when both partners were virgins. She remembered Rawdon's ugly remark about prostitutes and wondered if he had made a habit of visiting them after all.

Then the brief tearing pain of the broken hymen and Rawdon was there, within her. Thought vanished, obliteration, extinction became mere words that meant nothing compared to the surges of sweetness that swept through her.

Then it was over. Rawdon did not stay long enough. It was over in a few brief strokes. She lay there, dazed, full of disappointed longing, like a gift-laden birthday or Christmas caller who discovers that the object of her affections is not at home. Rawdon confused her by telling her how marvelous it had been for him.

In the morning she had awakened wondering what she would think, feel, now. Would she hurl herself at the feet of her master? Would she hang on his every word? Would he coolly decree this and announce that, expecting absolute submission? *I've changed my mind, I don't think I'll let you keep your job after all. From now on, I want you to address me as Mr. Stapleton.*

What an idiot she had been. Rawdon had become more considerate, more affectionate. But he never stayed inside long enough, on the following nights, to bring Genevieve to that much-discussed climax known as orgasm. Doctors and other self-appointed experts frequently debated its importance. In one part of her mind Genevieve was pleased. It removed the fear of becoming a love slave, as the feminists called women who gave their husbands mindless adoration. But another part of her self, the daring woman who wanted to test her strength against experience, wondered what was on the other side of that plunge into pure feeling.

Back in New York after the honeymoon, Genevieve found herself siding with the thinking woman. She felt compelled to disagree with Rawdon when he revealed his mindless infatuation with the worst elements in the Democratic Party. Behind her on the kitchen table lay the copy of the *New York Herald* that Rawdon had brought home last night. In the left-hand column, the lead story's headlines were readable from the stove.

GOULD AND THE TEXAS PACIFIC

NEW REVELATIONS

PROOF OF REPUBLICAN PERFIDY

THE PRICE OF A PRESIDENCY

There it was, the latest development in the ugly quarrel that seemed to infect their marriage like the malaria that had ruined her parents' health in Mississippi: subsiding, seeming to disappear, then flaring up with a fresh headline or a new personal disagreement. The theft of the presidency and his father's role in it had become the ultimate proof of Rawdon's knowledge of the male world of politics and power—and his wife's ignorance of this supreme reality.

That was one among several reasons why Genevieve took a sullen satisfaction in today's headlines. The *Herald* was only echoing a sensational story Clay Pendleton had broken last week, tying President Hayes and his supposed fellow reformers to Jay Gould and a sordid scheme to loot the Treasury while building a transcontinental railroad in the South. Rawdon had gloatingly maintained that the truth about the stolen presidency proved Clay was as ignorant about the real American world as Genevieve. He had christened them "the dull-witted duo." There was nothing dull-witted about this story, which had apparently come from a source deep in the confidence of the new President's administration. It had enabled Clay to move to the New York *Sun* and double his salary.

"Sire," Genevieve called down the dim hall, "your breakfast is ready."

This second notice produced a thud of bare feet on the floor. In five minutes Rawdon appeared, wearing a robe over his nightshirt. He did a jig in the doorway and declaimed, "The top of St. Patrick's Day morning to ye, Mrs. Stapleton. Here's your favorite Celt, ready and eager to bestow a smack upon your cherry-red lips." He kissed her and gazed into the frying pan. "A Havana omelet. I must have smelled it in my dreams. I was making love to you under a palm tree when your dulcet sarcasm interrupted me."

"You'd better start eating," she said. In five minutes she brought the steak and the omelet and a side dish of fried potatoes into the dining room and joined Rawdon at the table. He was demolishing the salad. "Will you be home for supper?" she asked.

Rawdon shook his head. "Bennett is taking me to the Friendly Sons of St. Patrick dinner."

Genevieve grimaced. "Don't drink too much."

"No more than necessary to uphold my reputation as a gentleman."

Genevieve poured herself a cup of tea and began buttering a slice of bread.

"Is that all you're eating?" Rawdon said, slicing into the omelet.

"I don't *like* a big breakfast."

"You could be eating for two."

"You'll be the first to hear about it, don't worry."

Rawdon could not understand why she had yet to conceive. He had begun reading books on the subject, wondering aloud if Dr. Clark of Harvard was right after all, college did lower a woman's fertility. He had found some other idiot who reported that women who worked in factories had fewer children—and wondered if her job was the reason. Fretting over her diet was his latest attempt to solve the problem.

"Eat some of this. It's delicious, incidentally." He dumped half of the Havana omelet on her plate.

"I'm not hungry in the morning, Rawdon," Genevieve said.

"Eat it. Your lord and master commands it. Eat for the sake of generations yet unborn."

She picked at the omelet. It did not taste very delicious. Something had gone wrong with the Espagnole sauce. She had no enthusiasm for cooking complicated sauces over a low flame, as the cookbook always suggested. They invariably came out either half blended or burned.

Rawdon began discussing the continuing turmoil about the stolen presidency. He could not understand how Clay Pendleton had gotten hold of the tremendous beat on President Hayes's secret deal with the southerners and Jay Gould. Clay was not telling anyone, especially Rawdon, who was on a rival paper, the name of the "prominent Republican" he kept quoting.

"How the hell did old Pendleton get close enough to a big shot Republican to pry that stuff out of him?" Rawdon wondered.

"He knows how to ingratiate himself with all sorts of people. He doesn't have any pretensions to being important."

"Oh? Do I hear an implied criticism?"

"I think you've let your friendship with the great James Gordon Bennett, Jr., go to your head a little."

"My friendship with Bennett is based on my ability as a reporter. He thought those stories I did on the Communists on the Lower East Side were tremendous."

Rawdon had published a series of stories reporting that Irish labor union leaders and politicians were conferring with refugees from the Paris Commune and other European revolutionaries. The stories implied that the Democrats were going to launch a violent protest against the installation of Ruth-erford B. Hayes as president. Genevieve thought Rawdon's hostility to Hayes made him too eager to believe tall tales told in smoky Lower East Side saloons.

"Bennett's a social climber first and a newspaperman second. If your name wasn't Rawdon Stapleton you'd still be writing obituaries."

Rawdon shoved his supposedly delicious Havana omelet aside. "Learn how to cook one of those before you try it again."

Genevieve took the mostly uneaten omelet out to the kitchen and stood there, staring at the dirty pots and pans on the stove. For a moment she was swept by a terrible desire to weep. Instead, she talked calmly to herself. Tit for tat, that was how Rawdon's mind worked. You criticize me, I'll criticize you.

Seeing your spouse realistically was part of rational love. You also had to see yourself realistically. She had just said a rather obnoxious thing to her hus-band. Why? Because she was concealing a secret from him. A secret which she knew was going to start a quarrel. Maybe it was better to have the quarrel now.

She returned to the dining room and sat down in front of her cooling tea. "Rawdon," she said. "Clay's gotten me an assignment from the *Sun*. I'm going to work on it today."

Rawdon chewed on his steak. "So the star reporter has finally come through. What's it going to be? A murder on Baxter Street? An interview with Rutherfraud B. Hayes?"

"No. The House of the Good Shepherd—a Catholic home for wayward girls—is celebrating its twenty-fifth anniversary. I'm supposed to interview the mother superior."

"Big deal. That's the sort of story the *Sun* doesn't want to waste a real reporter on. It's not going to get you any closer to a job."

"It's a start. We don't all have fathers who can arrange things with a managing editor."

Rawdon slammed down his fork. "I remember once, down at Kemble Manor, you spent an hour telling me all the rotten things your mother used to say to your father. It's a talent you've inherited, in spades."

They glared at each other. Rawdon shoved the steak aside. "This is too well done, as usual. Have you ever thought of staying home and learning to cook?"

"Rawdon, I don't see why you won't encourage me—just a little. If you're right and I have no hope of getting a job on a paper, what harm is there in a few assignments like this one? Won't it make me a more helpful partner when you start your own paper?"

"I suppose so," Rawdon said. He grabbed his coffee cup and retreated into the bedroom. He often stalked out of the room when they argued, leaving her feeling simultaneously victorious and defeated.

Genevieve washed the dishes and left the dirty pots and pans to soak in the sink until she came back from work. In the bedroom, Rawdon stared gloomily out the window. His face in profile was such a heartbreaking reminder of the photographs she had taken of him at Kemble Manor, Genevieve was undone. She put on her business skirt and blouse and kissed him on the cheek. "I'm sorry," she said.

Rawdon did not return the gesture of affection.

"I was hoping you'd coach me a little," she said. "I've never interviewed anyone before."

"I thought you'd get a full course of instructions from your favorite reporter, Pendleton."

"He's not my favorite reporter. Don't be silly. Rawdon—I wish you'd understand how important this is to me."

Rawdon whirled and faced her, glowering. "It's St. Patrick's Day. You may recall, in the stories I wrote about the insurrection I'm convinced is coming, that I predicted St. Patrick's Day was a likely day for it to start. There'll be fifty thousand disgruntled Irish Democrats marching up Broadway today and another hundred thousand watching them. All they need is one incident, one cop swinging a club, to start a war. I don't even think you should go out on the street today, much less go to a place that could be involved in the violence. You know what those wayward girls are, don't you? Prostitutes, most of them, tied up with the worst Irish gangsters in the city."

"Rawdon, I won't be intimidated by your fondness for sensational stories without three facts in them!"

Genevieve jounced uptown in a Fifth Avenue omnibus, brooding over Rawdon's hostility to her attempt to become a reporter. She had begun thinking about changing jobs soon after he switched to the *Herald*. She was already bored with being a secretary. When she cautiously raised the possibility of joining him in journalism, Rawdon had displayed the same negative attitude he had revealed at Kemble Manor before their engagement. He compounded her irritation by telling her it was out of the question, in the first place, because no newspaper would hire a woman.

Genevieve stubbornly declared she would find out for herself if Rawdon was right. She wrote long earnest letters of application to the editors in chief of all the major dailies except the *Herald* and got nothing but polite—sometimes barely polite—refusals.

Shortly after she got her last rejection, Clay Pendleton had come to Sunday dinner. Seeing her disappointment—and perhaps resenting Rawdon's habit of linking him and Genevieve as a duo of dullards—Clay suggested another approach. The managing editor of the *Sun*, Amos Cummings, had served in General Stapleton's division during the war. A mention of her father might evoke a sentimental response from him. Instead of asking for a reporter's job, Clay advised her to suggest "contributing" to the paper on topics that a woman would be especially qualified to discuss.

The contributor approach disarmed most of Rawdon's objections. Cummings had responded favorably, saying kind words about Colonel Dall's courage and consideration for his men.

At Ninetieth Street Genevieve pulled the rope attached to the driver's foot and descended from the Fifth Avenue omnibus. She gazed across vacant lots and unpaved streets dotted by an occasional shack or isolated frame house to a rectangular prisonlike brick building on the shore of the East River. It was a long walk from Fifth Avenue through the blowing snow. She saw only a few people, most of them Irish squatters living in the shacks. Bottles in hand, they waved cheerily to her; their St. Patrick's Day celebration had already started.

At the House of the Good Shepherd, an old nun in a black habit, her wrinkled face framed by a white coif, answered the door. Genevieve introduced herself, and the nun led her down a corridor to a small office where an angular-faced woman in an identical habit sat at a desk. For some absurd reason, she reminded Genevieve of General Stapleton. She had the same gray eyes and penetrating stare. "Why'd they send a woman?" she snapped. "Are they going to print this?"

"I—I hope so. I think the managing editor thought I'd be . . . more understanding—have more appreciation of your achievements."

"Do you?"

"I don't know. I'm not sure . . . what you've achieved. I know you deal with . . . fallen women."

"Prostitutes," the nun said. "We deal with prostitutes. I'm Mother Aloysius McGovern. I've been here twenty-five years. What do you want to know?"

Genevieve struggled through a series of basic questions. She found out that the House of the Good Shepherd had about a hundred inmates. They were sent to the nuns by the city courts after they had been arrested for prostitution or for theft or drunkenness—frequently related offenses. They spent from sixty to ninety days in the institution.

"And in that time you convert them?"

"They're all Catholics to begin with. The Magdalen Home gets the Protestant girls." Mother Aloysius McGovern drummed her fingers on her desk. "So far, Mrs. Stapleton, you've asked me the same questions male reporters asked on our tenth, fifteenth and twentieth anniversaries. I've given you the same standard answers. Is that what you want? Is that what you call understanding?"

"Not really. To tell you the truth, I don't think I've ever even seen a prostitute."

"How many do you think there are in New York?"

"Perhaps three, possibly even four thousand?"

"Fifty thousand."

"You can't be serious," Genevieve said. "That would mean one prostitute for every ten men in the city."

"New York is the pleasure capital of this whole region," Mother Aloysius said. "Fifty thousand is not an exaggeration, I assure you. I've gotten the figure from friends on the police force."

"I've never seen it published in a newspaper."

"It never has, and probably never will be. It would make our great city, our modern age, blush if the truth were told."

"I'll certainly try to tell it," Genevieve said, scribbling notes.

"Good luck," Mother Aloysius said, intimating that she had tried and failed in the past.

They went for a walk around the institution. Genevieve had envisioned prostitutes as rouged, gaudy, vulgar women. Instead she saw scrubbed faces, sad, subdued eyes.

"They're all so young," Genevieve exclaimed.

"We never take anyone over twenty. Above that age it's practically impossible to help them."

In the kitchen, where about two dozen girls were preparing dinner, Mother Aloysius pointed to a pretty freckle-faced redhead shelling peas. "That's Mary Walsh," she said. "Her brother's a member of the Whyos, the most vicious bunch of gangsters in the city. One of his friends, Piker Ryan, took Mary out on her fourteenth birthday and got her drunk. When she woke up she was naked and Ryan was telling her she was his favorite girl. When she said she wanted to go home, he beat her up, told her she was a whore and sent her out on the street. Her father wouldn't let her back in the house. So she became one of Ryan's stable. He's a very gifted pimp."

"Why didn't she go to the police?"

"Ryan or some other Whyo would kill her. You can't believe the power the pimp has over a prostitute. An awful combination of love and fear. He beats them—and flatters them. We haven't been able to reach Mary. She'll go back on the street when she leaves here."

In the next two hours, Genevieve heard more about the ugly underside of women's lives in New York than she had heard in the previous twenty-two years of her life. Mother Aloysius described the "parlor houses" on grimy Baxter Street where prostitutes saw as many as thirty men a night, the upper-class brothels in elegant brownstones on West Twenty-sixth Street where gentlemen arrived in evening clothes.

Mary Walsh's seduction by a gangster was not the only route into prostitution. Other inmates had worked in factories and been seduced by a foreman who passed them on to a pimp. One girl had worked in a department store; she had been seduced by a floorwalker who doubled as a pimp for friends with pretensions to being gentlemen.

Back in her office, Mother Aloysius admitted that seventy percent of the women the courts sent to them went back into "the life," as they called it. Good Shepherd tried to teach them the rudiments of a trade—sewing, baby nursing, cooking—in the ninety days they were permitted to hold them. But jobs for women were scarce and most people were frightened by the girls' previous reputation. "In short, Mrs. Stapleton," Mother Aloysius said, "I find very little to celebrate on our twenty-fifth anniversary."

Genevieve rode back downtown through the continuing snowstorm feeling dazed. This obscenity was happening to women in New York City while men quarreled over which politician should sit in the White House!

In the parlor of her apartment on Forty-third Street, Genevieve wrote page after furious page, informing the readers of the *Sun* that the twenty-fifth anniversary of the House of the Good Shepherd revealed that a crime against women was being perpetrated in their midst. She included capsule biographies of a half-dozen young women she had interviewed, a ferocious attack on pimps such as Piker Ryan and copious quotes from Mother Aloysius.

Genevieve rode a Broadway stage downtown to Park Row through a chaos of celebrating Celts. The annual St. Patrick's Day parade was over, but hundreds of police were still on duty, making sure that Rawdon's prediction of an insurrection did not come true. After delivering the story to a clerk at the *Sun*'s shabby headquarters, Genevieve decided to visit Alice Gansevoort at her home on Gramercy Square. She had to tell someone! She was almost exploding with excitement and pride.

Tomorrow her story would be on the front page of the *New York Sun*. It would shock the city into action. Even if Genevieve Dall Stapleton got pregnant tomorrow or the next day, she would have accomplished something. Two women, a Catholic nun and a Vassar graduate, the most improbable imaginable collaboration, working and talking woman to woman, would have taken a giant step toward rescuing thousands of women from humiliation, shame, death.

Genevieve was stunned by Alice's tepid reception. "Really Gen," she said, "aren't you getting a bit carried away? We've always had prostitutes in New York. We probably always will. It's a seaport, after all."

Before Genevieve could reply, Alice shifted to her favorite topic—in fact her only topic—of conversation these days. "If even half of what Isaac tells me about New Orleans is true, New York is a model of civic virtue."

In the hope of cooling Isaac Mayer's passion for Alice, his father had shipped him to New Orleans to work as a cotton broker. Distance had only enhanced Alice's charms. Isaac filled the mails with anguished longing, and Alice responded in kind, in spite of her father's wrath. Jefferson Gansevoort still opposed a marriage because Isaac was Jewish.

"If it lasts much longer, I think you and Isaac should take matters into your own hands."

"I suppose you're right," Alice said. "But Father still says he won't come to the wedding."

"Maybe it's the last stage of growing up—learning to disagree with Father," Genevieve said, thinking of her angry blast at General Stapleton when he visited her on New Year's Day.

"It's not easy, Gen. When you've loved someone so long."

As the oldest child, Alice had always been her father's favorite. He had seemed to be the most progressive of fathers, delighted to send her to Vassar, proud of her athletic prowess. Now, with no warning, he had turned into an anachronism, issuing orders, insisting that he had the right to decide her destiny.

"I know it isn't easy. But I have confidence in you."

"I wish I did," Alice said, with a wan smile. "I hope the *Sun* puts your story on the front page, even if I don't entirely agree with it."

They kissed with some of the fervor of their high-school days, as if each wanted to assure the other that their feelings had not changed. At home Genevieve ate a hasty supper and spent five hours cleaning her apartment. Her mother and Eleanor were coming to tea on Sunday, and Genevieve was determined to have everything in a state of shining spotlessness that would meet or surpass Margaret Van Vorst Dall's Dutch standards of cleanliness.

At midnight she crawled into bed and managed to summon the strength to write a letter to Elizabeth Wellcombe. Her former Vassar suitemate was living in Boston, struggling to become a lawyer despite the armored prejudices of the city's bar. Naturally Genevieve filled her letter with the story she had just written. She asked Wellcombe if the Hub of the Universe tolerated such a heinous crime as prostitution. Perhaps a book needed to be written on the subject, attacking it as a national problem.

Within seconds of putting down her pen Genevieve was asleep. It had been an exhausting day, traipsing up and down Manhattan Island, putting so much fervent emotion on paper.

Suddenly her blank peaceful dreamlessness was demolished by a hand on her breast. "It's your favorite Celt, Diarmuid," Rawdon whispered, "in search of a partner to help him celebrate the day after St. Patrick's Day."

She did not like it. She did not like being awakened this way in the middle of the night. She needed time to prepare her mind, her feelings, for love. She especially disliked it if Rawdon had been drinking.

"Come on," Rawdon whispered, his hand traveling to her other breast. "It's been five or six days."

"I'm awfully sleepy, Rawdon."

"You'll wake up soon enough."

The hand was pulling up her nightgown, traveling up her legs. Another hand, or arm, sat her up in bed, and presto the nightgown was over her head, her arms, and she was naked. Now the hands were everywhere in the darkness, the mouth was on her mouth, the tongue moving against her lips, forcing them open. One of Rawdon's hands was between her legs, touching the place or places that made her heart pound, even though her mind still said no, no.

Everything about this was wrong. They had not made up since this morning's quarrel. Yet he expected her to celebrate with him. Or let him celebrate with her. That was what drunken sailors did when they went to brothels.

"Maybe we ought to try something new," Rawdon whispered. "The Roman position. Maybe they had the right idea about conception. Maybe this is how they conquered the world."

He was standing beside the bed. She felt his bulk looming over her. His hands were around her waist, flipping her on her face, then drawing her up until she put out her arms to lift her face off the mattress. "That's the idea," he whispered, and entered her from behind.

"Ohhhh. How's that?" Rawdon whispered. "How's that for penetration? That's what Dr. Clark says you need for conception. That's how old Marcus Cato and Julius used to do it. Does that conquer your gall, Mrs. Stapleton?"

No, raged the voice in Genevieve's head. No. How could Rawdon mention loathsome Dr. Clark and remind her of his ugly quotation from Marcus Cato about woman being a wild animal while he was inside her, even this way?

"You may not—have tits—worth mentioning—but the rest of you—is first rate—Mrs. Stapleton." He stroked her with each phrase. "How's the *Sun's* hot new reporter—like that? Hot—enough? You're not—the hot type—but I'm going to heat you up—before we're through."

"Rawdon, I don't like this!" She tore herself free and turned to face him, still on her hands and knees.

"You don't like it?" he said. "You don't like it?"

He crashed into the bed beside her, and one outflung arm hauled her down on top of him. "Okay," he said, rolling over and entering her in one amazing motion. "Okay. We'll do it the other way. It all—comes down—to the same thing—Mrs. Stapleton."

He was stroking her again. It was not loving, there was none of the gentleness or tenderness of the honeymoon about it. Yet she wanted him. She wanted him to come in her. She wanted him in spite of her anger and disgust.

His hands grasped clumps of her hair. "Not the sort of thing—you'd expect—from an obituary reporter—is it, Mrs. Stapleton? This sort of talent is strictly star quality . . .

"Ahhh. There we are, Mrs. Stapleton."

In two minutes Rawdon was snoring beside her. Genevieve lay awake watching dawn gray the windows, struggling against inner chaos. She had to keep her head, her heart, under control. Why had Rawdon treated her that way? Was he jealous of her story in the *Sun?*

Her story! Was that it? Was that the real reason? Perhaps he had seen it. Perhaps it was so sensational it had aroused the worst imaginable hostility.

Genevieve's hands shook as she buttoned her winter coat and hurried into the cold. On the corner of Forty-second Street, an urchin hawked the *Sun*. "Hey, d'latest on Gould's grab!" he shrieked.

The story was not on the first page. Nothing there but presidential politics, the sinking of another steamship in an Atlantic storm, the final collapse of the ten-year revolution in Cuba. It was not on the second page, the third page, the fourth. Finally, on the back page—there it was: a pathetic ten lines in the lower right-hand corner.

It was incredible. There was not a word about Mary Walsh. Only the merest hint of Mother Aloysius' despair. Most of it was devoted to a dull summary of the purpose of the home and how many inmates they treated each year. Genevieve walked downtown to Nineteenth Street in a fog of misery. In Mrs. Wilbour's back parlor she sat down and began typing letters like a machine. She did not want to think about supper with Rawdon tonight, listening to him sneer at her tiny story.

The doorbell rang. Mrs. Wilbour's maid answered it. A moment later, a smiling Clay Pendleton stuck his head in the door. "I'm interviewing someone in the neighborhood. I thought I'd drop in and offer congratulations."

"What for?"

"Your story. Didn't you see it?"

"That's not the story I wrote! It's a—a perversion of it."

Clay rolled his eyes heavenward. "Calm down. The *Sun*'s a Democratic paper. It's never going to publish an exposé of prostitution in New York and make the mayor and his Tammany friends look bad. But Cummings was impressed with your copy. He wants to see you and give you more work."

"Maybe I don't want to see him. I begin to think this whole thing is a conspiracy between you and Rawdon to discourage me."

She was surprised by how much this accusation upset Clay. His squarish face flushed, he stared down at the rug and mumbled, "I thought your opinion of me was a little better than that."

"Did you *read* my story?"

"Yes. I thought it was first rate. But much too long."

"Didn't it mean anything to you? Didn't it make you want to stop what's happening? Stop women from being destroyed?"

"Sure. But I don't have the faintest idea how to go about it. The *Times* won't publish it because it's a family newspaper. It would be a waste of space in the *Tribune*. They've squawked for moral reform so much, no one listens to them anymore."

"Oh you're all so—so detestable!"

Clay was growing more and more dismayed. "You and Rawdon are a pair," he said. "He did the same thing at the *Times*. He wrote two thousand words on that unemployed Dutchman who killed himself and then got insulted when Reid cut it to a paragraph."

"He did?" Genevieve said.

"I can see why he never mentioned it to you. He made a fool of himself."

It was amazing how that seemingly irrelevant piece of information calmed her. Rawdon, who never stopped portraying himself as the star reporter, telling off John Reid, swaggering around town with James Gordon Bennett, Jr., Rawdon had made a fool of himself.

"Gen," Clay said. "We're only twenty-two or twenty-three years old. We don't run this country. There are powerful men out there who do. You're never going to help women, help yourself, if you pull this prima-donna act. Do you or don't you want to see Cummings?"

Genevieve stared at the opening sentence of a letter from Mrs. Wilbour to Caroline Dall in her typewriter: *"I could not agree with you more when you say, to have the strength of a man without losing the delicacy and sensitiveness of a woman would be to conquer the world."* "Yes," she said sullenly.

"Okay. We'll have lunch at Mouquin's Restaurant tomorrow at one o'clock."

"Okay," she said, half mocking him. She was still angry.

Clay walked toward the door. Something about the droop of his head, the slump of his shoulders, made Genevieve feel guilty.

"Clay," she said. "I didn't mean any of that—personally. I appreciate everything you've done."

He nodded and thickened his Carolina accent. "Old Mose Pendleton, at yo' service, Missus Stapleton."

For the rest of the day, while she typed letters, even while she told Mrs. Wilbour about her visit to the House of the Good Shepherd (she was as unmoved by the statistics and anecdotes as Alice Gansevoort) Genevieve kept thinking about Rawdon's first story. Somehow it made the ugly feelings he had displayed last night more tolerable.

On the way home she stopped at the Franklin Market and bought a lobster, one of Rawdon's favorite foods. She imagined herself telling him the story of her disappointment and then persuading him to tell her about his first story. Then she would talk to him about her dislike of the Roman position, how much it upset her to make love to him when he was drunk. She would tell him some of the cruel things he had said. It would be a triumph of rational love over instinct and resentment.

About ten-thirty she started cooking Rawdon's supper. She filled her biggest pot with water for the lobster and decided she would add liver and bacon, another favorite dish. She shelled some peas to go with it, and washed lettuce for a salad.

Suddenly Rawdon was behind her in the kitchen, kissing her on the neck. In his hand was a bouquet of yellow roses. "To make up for last night," he whispered.

"How—nice," Genevieve said, thrown off balance by his penitence. Rawdon frequently confused her by abrupt shifts of emotion. They could go from quarreling furiously over her desire for a newspaper career to declarations that she was the perfect wife an hour later. Or vice versa.

"I don't remember the details. But I think I was abominable," Rawdon said.

"You were drunk," Genevieve said. "I wish you'd promise never to come home that way again."

"I promise," Rawdon said, putting his hand on his heart. The extravagance suggested he did not mean it, but Genevieve accepted it as a step in the right direction. They kissed and she arranged the roses in a bowl.

"I saw your story in the *Sun*," Rawdon said. "Not bad."

"I know it sounds silly, but I was disappointed. They cut it to almost nothing. Has that ever happened to you?"

Rawdon shrugged. "You've got to expect the editors to do some trimming."

"I mean—with your first story?"

"No. My first story was a silly little thing about a suicide."

He was lying to her. She understood why, but it still wounded her. She retreated to the kitchen and began cooking the liver and bacon. The lobster's water was boiling. She popped him into it and watched him turn rosy red.

It was all wrong. She had made it too easy for Rawdon to say he was sorry. She had let him lie to her. It was all a disastrous failure, not a soaring success, of rational love.

Suddenly the various smells, the pungent liver, the greasy bacon, the salty steamy odor of the lobster seemed to be creating a very unpleasant combination—

Oh God. She was running down the hall toward the bathroom. She did not reach it. She vomited part of her lunch, mixed in a strange filmy mucus, on the floor.

Rawdon came rushing from the parlor. "Gen . . ." he said anxiously.

She stumbled past him into the bathroom, where he held her head while she vomited into the toilet bowl. Vomited and retched and retched after there was nothing left in her stomach.

Rawdon picked her up and carried her into the bedroom and laid her down gently on the bed. "Gen," Rawdon said, holding her hand, "this isn't the most pleasant way to get the news. But you know what it might mean. Have you missed a menstrual period?"

"Yes. I mean, I'm two weeks late. But I've been late before. I told you—I'm irregular."

"But the two things together." He lifted her against him and murmured, "I know it sounds crazy, but I feel as if this is the first day of our lives together. I really do."

Her promise to quit her job and stay home was still part of their understanding. The lost argument over the stolen presidency had made it impossible to alter that agreement. There would be no point in having lunch with Managing Editor Amos Cummings tomorrow.

"It's for the best, Gen. We'll have so much more time together. We won't be fighting about stupid trivial things like working for a newspaper."

Oh yes. Very stupid, very trivial, if you are a female.

What a horrible thought. What a horrible feeling. What was wrong with the true woman?

THREE

"It's flush times, little sister, flush times for Louisiana again," Robert Legrand said, doing a Mardi Gras strut up and down Cynthia's sitting room.

"I swear, you sound like you've just won the war," Cynthia said.

"We have, just about," Robert chortled. "Wait'll you see the money we make from this lottery."

The redeemed state of Louisiana had launched a lottery to rebuild its finances, supposedly ruined by a decade of carpetbagger and scalawag swindling. Robert was in charge of selling the tickets in New York. The lottery office had been open only a month and already the dollars were pouring in from Democrats eager to help their needy southern friends—and perhaps make a fortune for themselves. The winners got stupendous sums.

"What do you think of it all, Colonel Calhoun?"

Edgar Calhoun had sat there, coffee cup in hand, barely saying a word while Robert talked and talked. Cynthia had been more than a little startled to discover that he was in New York, working with Robert in the lottery office. She felt compelled to return a modicum of the kindness Calhoun had shown her on that grisly day in New Orleans, eight months ago. But she was sure that Jonathan had no desire to see him again. This invitation to morning coffee was a discreet compromise between gratitude and prudence.

Edgar Calhoun mused for a moment, a shy smile on his lean face, as if he was both surprised and pleased by her attention. "To tell you the truth, I thought I'd rather lead a charge against a full division of Yankees than live in New York. But I'm beginning to change my mind. The hospitality has been so warm, so . . . southern, I may never go back to Cane River."

"Everybody loves a hero," Robert said, beaming at Edgar.

In the newspaper stories announcing the lottery, Colonel Calhoun had been described as the manager of the ticket office. Vivid anecdotes of his military career had been included, especially his exploits in the Red River campaign, where his regiment had routed an entire Yankee brigade.

"Slow down that hero stuff, will you, Bob?" Calhoun said. He smiled ruefully at Cynthia. "He's a genius at publicity. If half those stories were true, I would have had General Lee's job."

"Did I hear you mention the Cane River?" Cynthia said. "We have scores of cousins in that valley. My mother came from there."

"His middle name is Knowles," Robert said.

"Dear God, I sometimes think everyone in the South is related," Cynthia said.

"That's why southern blood is warmer—and thicker—than the icewater in most Yankee veins," Robert said. "Speaking of relations, how is your husband?"

"Fine, as far as I can tell from the little I see of him. He's out of town these days more often than he was before the election, rallying the true-blue Stalwarts against the traitor in the White House."

"Stalwarts" was a term Senator Roscoe Conkling had coined to describe the regular Republicans, who opposed Rutherford B. Hayes's conciliatory policy toward the South. Cynthia instantly regretted her sarcastic tone, which encouraged Robert's inclination to gloat. "I would have loved to see the expression on his long Yankee face when he heard the news about withdrawing the federal troops."

For Cynthia the words recalled the night of the pre-inaugural dinner in Washington. The expression on Jonathan's face that Cynthia remembered was not the one Robert imagined. It was not even an expression; it was closer to an emptiness, a blank mask of a face with agate eyes in the shadowy gaslight of the Willard Hotel bedroom.

It was only a glimpse, like a face in a dream. Then her husband was there again, whispering words of love. But Cynthia recognized that alien spirit. She had met him once before: the night Ben Dall killed himself. Seeing him in her bed had been far more demoralizing.

"I'm only expressing my impatience with his absence," Cynthia said. "I've told you before, I have no desire to get involved in this political vendetta." She turned to Calhoun. "Do you think there'll ever be an end to this eternal quarrel, Colonel?"

"As far as the South is concerned, it's over," he said. "We've finally gotten back what we had before 1861—our right to rule ourselves as free Americans."

Then why in God's name did you go to war and kill a million men? Cynthia wondered.

"Your friend Lionel Bradford still thinks we should fight for a southern transcontinental railroad," Robert said.

"I'd say Senator Conkling has made that another lost cause," Calhoun said, with a mournful smile. "But that's all right. It won't hurt us to stay poor for a while."

"I thought it was flush times?" Cynthia said.

"That's only for the stockholders of the lottery," Calhoun said.

"I hope you're among them," Cynthia said.

"So far, all we've gotten from Lionel Bradford are promises that we'll be first in line when they issue more stock," Calhoun said.

"He's a stockholder?"

"One of the principals," Robert said. "He put up the money to get us started. We're having dinner with him tonight at Delmonico's to celebrate our first glorious month. It's going to be a party, let me tell you. We gave Del twenty thousand and told him to spend it all. Why don't you join us? The mayor'll be there. Half of Tammany Hall."

"Thank you. But I'm expecting my husband to join me for dinner here, if the Pennsylvania Railroad maintains its reputation for being on time."

Edgar Calhoun rose and kissed Cynthia's hand. "In the midst of our revels, there will be one soldier envying General Stapleton the privilege of your company," he said.

"How sweet," Cynthia said. "You must join us for some revels here in Stuyvesant Square when we return from Europe, Colonel. I wish I could invite your confrere Major Legrand. But his last visit to my dinner table almost resulted in a duel."

"I heard about that," Calhoun said, smiling at Bob. "I told him he deserved to be court-martialed for distressing you that way. Though I must confess, in the Confederate Army we had a tendency to acquit fighting sons of guns like him."

Southern, Cynthia thought, feeling the warmth, the camaraderie passing between the two men. But she was not southern anymore. Or northern. She was simply a woman trying to cope with men who could not get war out of their blood.

Her visitors departed and Cynthia finished dressing. In thirty days she and Jonathan would be on the Atlantic, with politics behind them for three months. Perhaps for six months, if she could persuade him. Thirty more days of tension and bouts of melancholy, and they would be on their way to Italy.

She was going to buy an entire new summer wardrobe. She had decided it was necessary to guarantee Italy's enchantment. If Jonathan groaned even once at the cost, she would insist on taking the money out of her comfortable little fortune, which continued to grow if newspaper reports of the New York Central's prosperity were true.

"The mail, madam," Cousteau said in the doorway.

Cynthia gestured to a side table and finished adjusting the flounces of her navy-blue walking dress. She riffled through the envelopes; she was already in danger of being late for her doctor's appointment. There was only time to open the most important letter: the one with 350 Fifth Avenue, the Astor mansion, as the return address. It undoubtedly contained their invitations to the last Patriarchs' Ball of the season. Yesterday she had had the final fitting for the new damassé silk dress she planned to wear.

What in the world? Instead of the engraved invitations, there was a hand-written note.

DEAR MRS. STAPLETON:

As you know, our balls are organized on the basis of each patriarch inviting four ladies and five gentlemen. The patriarch who has named you and your husband to our previous fetes has inexplicably withdrawn your name from his list. Believe me, my dear lady, when I say I personally disapprove of politics intruding into our little band of devotees. But I am a mere vizier in this business, helpless to object. I trust we shall meet on other occasions in the season and I may be the beneficiary of your wit and beauty.

Very truly yours,
WARD McALLISTER

Cynthia did not know how long she stood there, the letter in her hand. Rage mingled with a furious desire for revenge. But against whom? No one believed in the fiction of the patriarchs' invitations. Everyone knew that admission to this social Olympus was controlled by Caroline Schermerhorn Astor and a handful of people who spent their time flattering the ugly boring old Dutch harridan. The more Cynthia thought about it, the more convinced she became that her enemy was Cecilia Schermerhorn. For a decade now she had been waiting and watching for a chance to strike a blow at Mrs. Jonathan Stapleton.

But the reason. *Politics.* It was not that anyone in the Astor circle disapproved of Jonathan's foray to New Orleans. They had no political opinions; politics was never mentioned at a Patriarchs' Ball. They objected to the notoriety her husband had acquired. They considered becoming a politician on a par with going on the stage or getting divorced.

Cynthia splashed several drops of Balm of Gilead into a glass of water and drank it almost greedily. She was taking too much of this dangerous medicine again. Perhaps it would turn her into an opium addict, a gaunt skeleton. That would be just what Jonathan Stapleton deserved. An ugly invalid for a wife. But the violent pains she had had during her last two menstrual periods were unbearable without the drug.

Lean beak-nosed Warren Bayley welcomed her in his Twenty-eighth Street examining room with his usual minimal cordiality. He listened carefully to her symptoms, noting them on a sheet of paper. "I'll have to make an examination," he said.

There were some doctors in New York who required women to lie down on an examining table, where they lifted their skirts. Cynthia had even heard of a few who used a new instrument, the speculum, that examined the most private place of all. Madeline Terhune had written her a very racy letter from London, telling her tales of women who had purportedly been driven mad with passion and disgraced themselves with their doctors as a result of this scientific advance.

Dr. Bayley was a member of the older, more modest school of physicians. He looked out the window while Cynthia stepped behind a screen and removed her underdrawers. When she told him she was ready, he knelt in front of her and put his hand under her skirts. He pressed and poked all over her lower abdomen for five minutes, then told her to dress again.

"I find no evidence of a tumor," he said when she was seated beside his desk once more. He fiddled with his pen for a moment. "Are you continuing to have intercourse with your husband more or less regularly?"

"No."

"Why not?"

"He's out of town a good deal. When he's home . . . there's been a certain distance—a kind of estrangement—between us."

More fiddling with the pen, frowns at the symptoms on the sheet of paper. "Were you . . . content with your physical relations with your husband?"

"Yes."

"Not many women who come into this examining room say that, Mrs. Stapleton."

"Really."

Dr. Bayley cleared his throat. This conversation was obviously difficult for him. "You grew up on a southern plantation, as I recall."

"Yes. In Louisiana."

"You saw animals in heat, then?"

"Yes. Many times."

"We're animals, Mrs. Stapleton. We have the same desires. Male and female. Make peace with your husband, Mrs. Stapleton, and your symptoms will disappear."

What about him making peace with me? Cynthia thought as she climbed into the Stapleton coach. It was infuriating the way Dr. Bayley assumed that the estrangement was her fault.

Cynthia told Oliver Cromwell to take her to Mittie Roosevelt's house. Dressed in her usual white muslin, Mittie welcomed her southern sister in her pristine bedroom overlooking Fifty-seventh Street. Cynthia was sometimes puzzled by how much time Mittie spent in her room. Her marriage to Theodore seemed more than happy. He adored her, and why not? Although she was at least eight years older than Cynthia, Mittie's skin still had the moonlight white of youth. There was not a trace of gray in her silky black hair.

Mittie's blue eyes glowed with outrage when Cynthia told her about the Patriarchs. "That proves Ward McAllister is the ultimate toady," she said. "No true southerner would allow a fellow southerner—above all, a woman— to be treated that way." For a moment Mittie looked positively fierce. "I begin to think Mrs. Astor needs to be taught a few social lessons. By happy chance we have someone in our midst who's eager to do it. Have you met Alva Vanderbilt?"

"No."

"She's from Mobile. She and her husband are determined to enter society, and they have about twenty million dollars to spend on the task. She called on me last week."

"Tell her she has another confederate eager to meet her."

"We'll have tea here one of these days. What will the General think of this business with the Patriarchs? Will it inspire penitence?"

"Oh of course. He'll tell me how sorry he is. But it's all words. Honestly, Mittie, I begin to despair of moderating his opinion of anything. This trip to Italy is my last hope."

"You're just feeling discouraged. What did Dr. Bayley say about your pains?"

Cynthia told her Dr. Bayley's diagnosis. Mittie wrinkled her lovely nose. "My doctor told me that women don't have sexual desires." She put her teacup down on a barrel table. "I know I've never had any of the purely animal variety. Have you?"

"I suppose not," Cynthia said. "But I'm not sure how . . . you identify them."

Wasn't it all one thing? Cynthia wondered. The desire for pleasure and affection and the wish to give him as much of those elusive but oh-so-real feelings as he gave you. Cynthia resisted separating pleasure and affection. That led to *Madam, I will do what I please* and pathetic retreats to bedrooms.

"If our higher natures are in control of our lower natures, which we believe as Christians," Mittie said, "then it isn't possible for a respectable woman to have animal desires."

Cynthia nodded automatically. She would not dream of disagreeing with Mittie. But for the first time she felt a stir of resentment against the way Mittie perpetually treated her as the younger sister. She found herself wondering if Mittie and Theodore had sexual intercourse at all. They had had four children in six years. Then the war started and the babies stopped. Had everything stopped?

Mittie began rejoicing over the final redemption of the South. The last federal troops were to be withdrawn from Louisiana and South Carolina in less than a week. "I hope General Stapleton is resigned to it by now," she said.

"He still looks as though he just swallowed a quart of vinegar every time he hears the name Rutherford B. Hayes."

"That's too bad. I wish you could change his mind on that point above all. I must confess he disappointed me when he became a Stalwart. I never thought of him as a vindictive man."

"Mittie, he's not. But his feelings about the war are so strong. When he talks about his dead soldiers you're ready to believe he still sees them before his eyes, as if it all happened yesterday."

Mittie pursed her lips as if she did not entirely believe her. Or did she dislike being reminded that the Yankees too had their dead to mourn?

Cynthia rode home brooding over the differences she had begun to discover between herself and Mittie. Did it mean that this incessant political quarrel was taking both her husband and her best friend away from her? Anxiety mingled with her anger as the coach crept down Fifth Avenue in heavy traffic. She passed Lionel Bradford's turreted mansion on Forty-seventh Street, next door to Jay Gould's equally opulent pile. Bradford was still pursuing her, murmuring about Louisiana every time they met, joking about an erotic second act for their unfinished play.

Remember who you are, Cynthia told herself bitterly. Cynthia Legrand.

There was always that heritage for a final resort. She was still one of the more beautiful women in New York. She did not have to depend absolutely on her fanatical Yankee husband for the pursuit of happiness.

The five-o'clock bells were bonging in St. George's Church as Cynthia entered the house. In fifteen minutes she was in her bathtub, rubbing creamy fragrant Violette de Toulouse soap on her face, her breasts, her thighs. She always bathed naked, unlike many women, who were so prudish they wore chemises in the tub so that the sight of their own bodies would not shock them. Animal, she thought, contemplating the soft curve of her belly, the hairy black triangle of love. Her fingers strayed to the magical place that she used to touch in the hot Louisiana night, imagining a man's—any man's—hand there, his lips on her mouth. Maybe she was a courtesan after all, destined to give and receive animal pleasure.

No. She was a *wife*. She had devoted ten years of her life to becoming a wife. She could not deny the satisfaction, the pride, the happiness she had known as Mrs. Jonathan Stapleton. How could her husband betray that happiness, threaten that satisfaction, undermine that pride with his fanatic politics?

She had just finished dressing when the front door slammed. Was it Jonathan? She waited for his footsteps on the stairs. Instead Cousteau appeared, a telegram in his hand. "TRAIN DELAYED IN HAMILTON. I WILL BE LATE FOR DINNER. PROCEED WITHOUT ME IF YOU WISH."

Cynthia crumpled the telegram into a ball. Jonathan was on his way home from Washington, where he had spent most of the week. The mention of Hamilton meant he had taken a detour to visit his mother.

Caroline Stapleton always put her son in a vile mood. Tonight he would find a wife in a similar mood. She told Cousteau to delay the dinner and thumbed the new fashion magazine, *Harper's Bazaar*.

Seven, then eight bells tolled in St. George's steeple. Cynthia was reduced to reading the personals in the *Herald*. It was a naughty habit she had acquired when she began taking the *Herald*—over Jonathan's objections. Everyone in society now read this paper, which they had once scorned, because it reported almost every ball and dinner in the city with assiduous detail. Cynthia wondered if other women also secretly enjoyed the personals. They were amazingly salacious, full of messages between clandestine lovers, erotic advertisements from women who were obviously prostitutes, attempts to arrange a meeting by a salivating man who had seen a pretty woman on a street corner the previous day.

Stomp. Stomp. Jonathan Stapleton always came up the stairs like a whole army on the march. He knocked on her door and peered in. "I'll be ready as soon as I wash off the soot," he said.

In a half hour they sat at opposite ends of the candlelit dining-room table.

The swan-shaped épergne that Katherine Kemble Brown had given them for a wedding present glowed in the center, surrounded by camelias. Cousteau poured them each a glass of Amontillado sherry.

"I like that dress," he said.

"Thank you," she said. "How is your mother?"

"Not well at all. But she never tells me anything. I have to find out the truth from the servants."

He fretted for several minutes about his conviction that his mother was going to leave most of her money to Rawdon and George. Cynthia only half listened, waiting for the chance to tell him about Cecilia Schermerhorn, the Patriarchs. But he went from his mother to complaining about the situation in Washington without taking a breath. All the regular Republicans, the Stalwarts, were being ignored by the new President.

Jonathan fingered a silver salt cellar. "That brings me to something I've been hoping I wouldn't have to tell you. But this visit to Washington has convinced me it's an absolute necessity. I'm afraid we'll have to cancel our trip to Europe."

"Jonathan! You promised me. That night at the Willard Hotel—you showed me the tickets!"

"I know I promised," Jonathan said, head down, an image of dogged determination. "It breaks my heart as much as yours, believe me. But this Texas Pacific Railroad has turned half the businessmen in the country insane. I thought when Congress voted down the subsidies that would be the end of the idea. Instead, Jay Gould announced he'd finance it without any help from the government, and the Pennsylvania Railroad decided to fight him. They plan to raise the money by cutting the salaries of their entire work force ten percent. Tom Scott has persuaded the other major carriers to imitate him, on the idiotic premise that it will keep the Pennsylvania's workers quiet. It's liable to start a revolution."

"Where?" she said, frankly incredulous.

"Everywhere. But this city will be the prime target. There are mobs on the Lower East Side, on the West Side, just waiting for an excuse to erupt."

"Why can't the police deal with them?"

"The police can't handle a *mob*. It will take troops to restore order."

"You're not in the army."

"I may be, before it's over. Anyone who's had some experience, who has a military reputation, may be needed."

"I don't believe a word of it! On the mere chance, the possibility of trouble—"

"It isn't a possibility. It's a certainty. I've been talking to railroad men in Pittsburgh, Baltimore, Jersey City. We've got a President that half the country detests . . ."

"And why shouldn't they?" she said.

Jonathan stared at her for a moment, then drained his already empty glass. "Yes, why shouldn't they," he muttered, and added a sound that resembled a sigh.

"You have chosen the perfect day to announce this," Cynthia said as Cousteau served consommé carème. She told Jonathan about their exclusion from the Patriarchs.

"What can I say?" Jonathan murmured. "It's regrettable—deplorable. But our happiness doesn't depend on those boring people."

"Your *dear* friend Cecilia Schermerhorn is behind it, I'm absolutely certain of it. Venting her spleen against me. She's waited years for an opportunity. To think my own husband gave it to her."

"You haven't been terribly nice to Cecilia. But I thought women enjoyed that sort of cat-fighting."

"Women! Jonathan Stapleton, you know as well as I do the reason for this humiliation. It's your political fanaticism. If you value my affection, you will *not* abandon me to another summer as a house guest at the Roosevelts' while you perpetrate more enormities in the name of the Republican Party."

Jonathan put down his soup spoon. "I'm not worried about the Republican Party. I'm worried about the United States of America. Its survival as a nation!"

"As far as I can see, that's synonymous in your mind with the greater glory and power of the Republican Party. In the name of that dreadful entity, you are ready to besmirch your reputation, our standing in this community, to make us social outcasts."

"My dear," he said, leaning forward now, gripping the table with both hands, "I—and you—we are not besmirched by anything I've done, no matter what small minds like Cecilia Schermerhorn may think or do. Her husband was one of those Democratic cowards who sat out the war here in New York. He paid a substitute to do his fighting for him. Some poor Irishman, who's probably feeding worms down in Virginia right now."

"The bloody shirt. You'll wave it even here, in your own dining room. Wave it in your wife's face."

"What in God's name are you talking about?"

"Isn't that what they call this endless invoking of the war as the reason for doing everything, from glorifying niggers to stealing the presidency?"

"I am not invoking the war. But by Christ you'll never get me to deny it! There are too many dead men. Too many." His fist came crashing down on the table. "And I did not steal the presidency. I regained it from two-faced traitors who were trying to steal it."

"You bought it," Cynthia said. "That carpetbag was crammed with money. You bought the presidency."

The word "bought" seemed to strike him in the face. He slumped in his chair. "Yes," he said. "I bought it. I bought your noble Louisianans. It was nauseating. But there was no other choice."

He tried to resume drinking his soup. The spoon slipped from his fingers and clattered on the floor. Cousteau peered nervously from the kitchen and thought better of trying to retrieve it.

For the first time Cynthia seemed to be winning a political argument with her husband. She pressed on, although she was no longer sure precisely what she wanted to win. The war, the South, the bribe, the Patriarchs, their lost summer in Italy—everything blended and blurred in her angry mind. "You won't turn your back on the war. But you'll turn your back on your wife. You'll sacrifice her happiness, her wishes, without a qualm."

"My dear," Jonathan said, "please try to control yourself. In these last eight months, I've never felt a greater need for your warmth, your affection. I'm sorry to say that more often than not I've only felt their absence."

He was echoing his friend Dr. Bayley's obnoxious assumption that she should forgive him no matter what he said or did. "Absence," she cried. "You haven't visited my bedroom in two weeks!"

"I haven't felt terribly welcome there. But I hope you still remember how much my visits have meant to us in other years."

"I'm not a bank in which you can deposit your affection and live on the interest."

"I have no intention of doing such a thing."

"You'd better not. Because you're in serious danger of overdrawing your account."

Mere words that followed her metaphor, like lines in a poem, dialogue in a play. They were part of her anger, like a flame running in dry grass. She did not realize that this flame was running on a fuse.

"Jesus Christ!" he roared. He was on his feet, smashing both fists on the table. "Jesus Christ." Silver clattered on the floor, glasses crashed. But the physical carnage was nothing compared to what Cynthia saw. It was the face in the bedroom at the Willard Hotel, the face that had glared at her the night Ben Dall died. The icy eyes, the slitted mouth, the blank rigidity that denied all caring, a death mask of a face. "Nothing in heaven or on earth justifies what you just said. If there is a more patient, more indulgent husband in New York City, I would like to meet him!"

The face seemed to loom larger and larger, filling her with wild anger and fear and loathing that sent words whirling out of her throat, stony words that she flung at the face, wanting only to smash it.

"Just once I'd like to get something more than words or expensive presents that you probably have someone else buy for you. Just once I'd like to see you *sacrifice* something for me—abandon your godalmighty devotion to duty or patriotism or whatever you choose to call your indifference to my feelings—"

For a moment the death-mask face swayed there at the other end of the table. Then it began to fragment. The jaw sagged, the eyes lost their glare, the lips trembled. Jonathan Stapleton slumped in his chair. "All right," he said. "We'll go to Europe."

Cynthia could not believe it. She had won. "I—I'm grateful. Believe me I didn't mean to imply that your feelings for me, or mine for you, are insincere."

"I'm sure you didn't," Jonathan said in a curt toneless voice.

She had won. He was sacrificing his devotion to duty for her. But in a strange, unnerving way, Cynthia also felt she had lost. A new expression was coalescing on Jonathan's face: weary, sullen resignation. She heard Mittie Roosevelt telling her that a wife could moderate her husband's opinions. Was this moderation—or the prelude to new, more catastrophic bitterness?

FOUR

Clay Pendleton stared up at ten thousand enraged strikers and their friends on the ridge that loomed over the Pennsylvania Railroad yards in the center of Pittsburgh. Just ahead of him, moving like sleepwalkers through the paralyzing July heat, some six hundred National Guardsmen from Philadelphia marched toward another five thousand strikers blocking the tracks.

"We could get ourselves killed out here," Pendleton said to Rawdon Stapleton, who was standing beside him in a rumpled white suit.

"Relax," Rawdon said. "Hell will feel like a trip to the North Pole."

Rawdon was enjoying himself. For months he had been predicting that an upheaval was going to shake and perhaps topple President Rutherford B. Hayes. Now it seemed to be happening. Protesting a ten percent cut in their wages, two hundred thousand workers had struck the major railroads of the nation. Scarcely a train was moving between New York and San Francisco. Around them on the twisting miles of interlaced tracks here in Pittsburgh were jammed over two thousand freight cars and locomotives. Water streamed from stranded refrigerator cars packed with meat. From other cars drifted the odor of rotting fruit. Tank cars full of oil and whiskey simmered in the ferocious sun.

The federal government seemed stunned and frightened by the defiant walkout. President Hayes had yet to make a statement. He might have decided it was best to say nothing because there was little he could do. Most of the nation's tiny regular army was still pinned down in the Far West, fighting Indians. State governments had called out their National Guard divisions to break the strike, with very indifferent results. Last night in Baltimore, a regiment of guardsmen had been stoned and dispersed by the enraged populace before they reached their armory. These Philadelphia guardsmen were in Pittsburgh because the local regiments had thrown away their guns and joined the strikers.

Yesterday in New York an exultant Rawdon had telephoned Pendleton and asked him where the *Sun* was sending him. Pendleton had said he had inside information that Pittsburgh was the city where the strike would be most explosive. Rawdon had persuaded James Gordon Bennett, Jr., to assign him to Pittsburgh, too. Pendleton had wondered what Rawdon would say if he told him that the inside information had come from General Jonathan Stapleton.

On the long ride from Philadelphia last night, Pendleton had found himself staring into the darkness trying to decide what he thought about this confusing contradictory man. Now there was no time to think about anything but the sweat pouring down his neck and the physical fear churning in his belly as the column of blue-clad soldiers confronted the solid mass of jeering cursing humanity on the tracks.

From the ridge came howls of encouragement. "Hold the fort! Stand to your post! Don't give an inch to the sons of bitches." Pendleton found himself sympathizing with the soldiers. Twenty-four hours ago they had been peaceful civilians. Now they found themselves surrounded by berserk enemies on a hot grid of railroad tracks in the middle of a strange city.

But the Philadelphians were not intimidated by unarmed strikers. Most were Civil War veterans. So was the general in command, a slim crisp man named Brinton. He barked an order and the column briskly formed a hollow square into which they dragged two weapons that undoubtedly bolstered their confidence: shiny Gatling guns. Mounted on artillery carriages, their eight brass barrels could spew hundreds of bullets a minute at an enemy.

Next to General Brinton stood impassive Alexander Cassatt, vice-president of the Pennsylvania Railroad. "Those tracks have to be cleared," he said in a clanging voice. "We're losing ten thousand dollars a minute."

Beside Pendleton, Rawdon muttered, "There's a walking son of a bitch if I ever saw one."

Calmly, almost casually, General Brinton summoned two of his captains and told them to move their companies down the tracks into the mob with bayonets fixed. The captains barked orders. An instant later, needle-pointed bayonets glinted on the muzzles of 120 muskets. Another order. The guardsmen lowered these murderous weapons and advanced. The howl of the mob deepened to a roar of rage.

A thud and a spray of cinders filled Pendleton's shoes. A brick had landed at his feet. Suddenly the sky was full of dark objects: stones, old shoes, more bricks. A private cried out and toppled into the cinders, one side of his face smashed. A captain staggered and almost fell when a chunk of wood struck him on the back of the head.

The bombardment came from all directions—from the crowd on the tracks, from the ridge above them, from the railyard behind them, where the strikers had taken over a string of loaded coal cars and converted their contents into ammunition.

"Shoot," howled someone. "Shoot, you sons of bitches, why don't you shoot?"

On the ridge Pendleton saw a big man wearing a green shirt standing with legs spread, aiming a pistol. Down on the tracks, a man lunged for the musket barrel of one of the bayonet wielders. The soldier jerked his weapon free and fired into the crowd. An instant later, every soldier in his rank pulled his trigger. A blast of gunfire erupted into the faces of the strikers. With a howl of terror the massive wedge of bodies disintegrated. All around the square, the guardsmen began firing at their tormentors in the coal cars and the spectators on the ridge.

A few dropped flat, but most people on the ridge froze, paralyzed by fear or astonishment as bullets whizzed among them. Then they were engulfed by the mob pounding up from the tracks. Screaming men and women fled up streets and into alleys, crouching, some crawling, to escape the deadly bullets.

"Cease fire!" General Brinton roared, but his men ignored him. The infuriated guardsmen continued to blaze away at the panic-stricken fugitives until Brinton and his officers ran around the square, knocking up their guns.

"My God," Rawdon said. "Do you think they killed anybody?"

"If they didn't, they're the worst shots in the world," Pendleton said.

Pendleton's eyes burned from the cloud of acrid gunsmoke drifting around them in the hot windless air. His ears rang from the crash of guns going off only a foot or two from his head. He was amazed when Brinton, the veteran soldier, turned to Cassatt and said in a perfectly calm voice, "Well—we've cleared your tracks for you."

About twenty yards beyond the square, a striker was sprawled in the cinders, face down. Rawdon ran to the man and turned him over. He had been shot in the chest. His blue workshirt was soaked with blood.

Rawdon waved to Pendleton. "Let's get him to a hospital," he called.

Pendleton was a little uneasy about leaving the protection of the Philadelphians' guns, but he helped Rawdon hoist the man to his feet. In between his gasps he was mumbling something in a thick brogue, "Holy . . . Mother . . . God . . ."

Blood drooled from the man's mouth as they struggled out the railyard gate onto Liberty Street. "Oh . . . boys . . ." he said, and his head lolled.

"I think he's dead," Pendleton said.

"How do you know?" Rawdon snarled. He obviously did not want to believe that his vaunted insurrection killed ordinary people like this man. They struggled up the ridge, half dragging, half carrying their burden. Blood from his oozing wounds smeared the right side of Rawdon's white coat.

"Help me, someone, for the love of God," sobbed a woman in the doorway of a store. In her arms she held a wailing girl about eight years old. The girl's knee had been smashed by a bullet. On the sidewalk a few feet away lay a moaning boy of fourteen, his face shattered, one eye torn out by another bullet. On the next block, a man in a black business suit writhed in the gutter, blood gushing from his throat.

Pendleton's stomach began to revolve. "I'm getting sick," he said. He left Rawdon with the corpse and vomited into some hedges. A moment later Rawdon was beside him, doing the same thing.

Rawdon had lowered their Irishman to rest in the middle of the sloping street. He walked back and knelt on one knee beside him for a moment. "I told you it was going to start somewhere, Pendleton," Rawdon said.

Two contradictory emotions collided inside Pendleton. He was stirred by Rawdon's compassion for the dead Irishman. But his friend's words reminded Pendleton of the daily diet of crow he had been forced to eat when Rawdon turned out to be right about the stolen presidency.

"Let's wait a few hours before we start calling it a revolution," Pendleton said.

"Do you think the people are going to let this happen without demanding revenge?" Rawdon shouted, pointing to the dead and the wounded.

"I don't know—and neither do you," Pendleton said.

Rawdon glowered at Pendleton. Since the stolen election, their friendship had grown precarious. A new complication was Pendleton's emergence as a smoking-hot political reporter, the man who had broken the sensational story of President Hayes's secret deal with the South and with Jay Gould. Rawdon, basking in his friendship with James Gordon Bennett, Jr., had been more than a little nonplussed to find his former court jester from their Princeton days leaping ahead of him.

Pendleton had yet to tell Rawdon that his source was Jonathan Stapleton. There was a reason for his silence, besides his promise to the General. Pendleton had recently concluded that fifty percent of the story, the supposed deal with Gould, was a lie.

They followed a stream of people carrying wounded friends to the gates of a hospital two blocks away. A dozen corpses, including one woman, were stretched on the lawn, surrounded by weeping relatives.

"Haven't you wept enough tears for Ireland's dead?" Rawdon shouted. "Isn't it time you did something about it? Get yourselves guns, wherever you can find them. Steal them. But get them and use them!"

"He's right," thundered a voice from the edge of the crowd. It was the green-shirted man Pendleton had seen firing the pistol on the ridge. "Follow me. I'll show you where to get guns."

With a shout the crowd surged out the hospital gates.

"Rawdon," Pendleton said, "a newspaperman is supposed to report wars and revolutions, not start them."

"Maybe I'm not a newspaperman, Pendleton," Rawdon said. "Maybe I haven't been one since that first day at the *Times*, when that son of a bitch John Reid chopped up my story about the poor Dutchman who shot himself because he couldn't find a job."

Rawdon watched weeping relatives lay beside the other bodies the big Irishman they had left in the street. "How can you stand there and claim to be indifferent to what's been happening in this country?"

"Maybe because it isn't my country," Pendleton said. "Didn't you make that clear to me eight or nine months ago? I'm a man without a country."

"Now is your chance to rejoin it, Pendleton. Make it a different country— and rejoin it."

It was astonishing and a little alarming to hear Rawdon talking this way. He had obviously picked up a lot more revolutionary fervor from the Communists and anarchists who thronged the Lower East Side of New York than Pendleton realized. For a moment, Pendleton saw how it all made sense, if you were a Stapleton with a great-grandfather who helped to win the original Revolution and a grandfather who almost prevented the Civil War and a father who helped to win it.

From the street outside the hospital gates, they watched General Brinton's Philadelphians abandon their defensive square and march toward a red-brick roundhouse a few hundred yards away. The guardsmen vanished into this ready-made fortress, and the vast yards with their twisting lines of locomotives and freight and passenger cars lay there in the setting sun undefended.

Rawdon and Pendleton followed a swelling crowd down Liberty Street, which paralleled the railyards, to the Union Depot. A stupendous mob had gathered in the square before this big soot-stained building. Many people waved axes, picks, crowbars; a few had guns.

"Get Cassatt out here," someone bellowed. "We've got a coffin ready for him."

Another voice howled in Pendleton's ear, "We're going to send every damn Philadelphian home in a box."

A block away, eight of the city's policemen stood helplessly outside a gunshop while the green-shirted man and a half-dozen others passed out rifles and pistols to anyone who extended a hand.

"It looks like revolution to me, Pendleton," Rawdon exulted.

"I still think you're being premature," Pendleton said. "But it's definitely a hell of a story. Let's find a telegraph office."

They discovered a side door to the Union Depot. It was guarded by a frightened-looking railroad employee.

"What's happened to Cassatt?" Pendleton asked.

"I don't know," the man said. "He ain't here. And I ain't gonna be here much longer."

The man told them that the nearest telegraph was in a brick building adjacent to the roundhouse. Pendleton and Rawdon sat down on a waiting-room bench and spent a half hour writing at top speed, by the light of an oil lamp they borrowed from an upstairs office. It was not easy to concentrate with the mob roaring outside. The sound filled the cavernous depot like a continuous crashing chaos; a force that did not need to pause for breath. Superhuman, Pendleton thought. Or inhuman.

They tossed a coin to see who would send the stories. Pendleton lost and began fighting his way back down tumultuous Liberty Street to the telegraph office. A gray-haired operator, looking as nervous as the depot employee, was still on duty. Pendleton got only a glance at the first two sentences of Rawdon's story: "The second American Revolution began on Saturday night in Pittsburgh. Every man in America will have to decide where he stands in relation to it."

Pendleton's lead was far less apocalyptic: "The first bloodshed of the railroad strike was spilled in Pittsburgh on Saturday afternoon. . . ."

It was dark by the time Pendleton returned to Liberty Street. He noticed that the blocks on either side of the Philadelphians' roundhouse were deserted. Three, four, five bullets whining around his ears told him why. He ducked into a doorway and watched a ferocious gun battle erupt between the strikers and the guardsmen. Muskets and pistols banged, bullets thudded into wood, smashed glass.

Taking advantage of a lull in the firing, Pendleton dodged from doorway to doorway until he was out of range and headed back down Liberty Street in search of Rawdon. He noticed that everyone in the crowd around him was carrying something: bags of corn, sacks of wool, cartons of crackers, candies, four or five pairs of shoes. He climbed up on the retaining wall and looked into the railyards. Everywhere, crowds of women and men were breaking open freight cars and looting them.

A block away, a fat man in a buggy was exhorting everyone to return to their homes. No one paid the slightest attention to him. "Who's that?" Pendleton asked a scrawny woman passing him with several yards of satin cloth on her arm.

"That's old McCarthy, the mayor," she said, and let out a Gaelic screech which Pendleton wrote down phonetically and later learned meant "Kiss my ass."

The screecher paused to swig from a bottle of whiskey. Many others in the crowd were doing the same thing. A full moon had risen, filling the streets with lemon light. Up ahead, he heard someone shouting, "Clear the road." The crowd opened and a bizarre procession appeared.

Rawdon Stapleton in his blood-smeared white suit was helping a dozen blue-shirted strikers drag a brass cannon up Liberty Street. Beside him was the green-shirted gunman. Rawdon handed his rope to someone else in the crowd and strolled over to Pendleton. "Come on," he said. "We're going to blast those Philadelphians out of that roundhouse. The Pittsburgh National Guard donated this cannon."

"If the men surrender, we'll just hang the officers," the green-shirted man said, in a thick brogue. "We want to show every National Guard regiment in the country that if they fire on unarmed workers they can expect the same treatment."

"You weren't exactly unarmed, up on the ridge. I saw you aiming a pistol," Pendleton said.

"Who's he?" snarled the green-shirted man.

"A reporter from the *New York Sun*," Rawdon said. "Don't let him worry you. I'll handle him."

The hell you will, Pendleton thought. Obviously, the Stapletons, father and son, both assumed they could get their obedient southern servant to write to order.

A stocky redhead with a slack mouth and a pugnacious jaw rushed up. Rawdon introduced Pendleton to Jack Dougherty, a reporter for the *Pittsburgh Leader*.

"The Associated Press says the strike is spreading beyond the railroads," Dougherty said. "Coal miners have quit all over Pennsylvania. They've had a workers' march in Chicago, another one in St. Louis calling for a general strike."

Rawdon threw his arm around Pendleton's shoulders. "It's Lexington and the fall of the Bastille all rolled into one fantastic package."

"Did the Americans do this much looting at Lexington?" Pendleton asked, looking around them at the stream of people lugging stolen goods out of the railyards. One man passed them with an entire side of beef on his shoulder.

"They got it comin' to them," Dougherty said. "Whatsa matter with this guy? Ain't he on the side of the people?"

Dougherty was drunk. Hardly a sin for a newspaperman. But Pendleton disliked his simpleminded sneer.

"He's peculiar," Rawdon said. "He doesn't believe in faking it. Except when the price is right."

"What the hell are you talking about?" Pendleton said.

"Never mind," Rawdon said. "Just a rumor I don't believe."

"He wouldn't last five minutes on the *Leader*," Dougherty said. "In this town either you fake it to make the Pennsylvania Railroad look good or you're out of a job."

Ahead of them the roundhouse loomed against the moonlit sky. The small-arms battle was still raging. Cheers erupted from the attackers when they saw the cannon. "Now, boys," roared the green-shirted Irishman, "remember your jobs. Do them as if the devil himself had you by the ass."

"Who is he?" Pendleton asked Rawdon.

"He calls himself Pat. He won't tell me his last name. He says he was a Fenian—an Irish revolutionary. When the British smashed them up in 1870 he escaped to Spain, where he became an anarchist."

Rawdon's expression was triumphant. After months of scoffs from Pendleton, he had actually found a live anarchist starting a revolution. Unlike the followers of Karl Marx, anarchists did not sit around philosophizing while the working class evolved into the revolutionary class. Anarchists preached "propaganda by the deed." They believed an elite, dedicated group, or even a single individual, could trigger a revolution by goading the ruling class into outrageous acts.

Pendleton watched Pat and his crew roll the cannon into the street before the roundhouse. It would take only one or two shots to smash open the wooden gates of the Philadelphians' redoubt. Then they would be exposed to a rush by the liquor-inflamed attackers. But the guardsmen had no intention of letting anyone fire the cannon. The second it appeared, a volley of musket balls hissed around it. One after another, the crew crumpled in the lead hail, leaving only the big Irishman on his feet.

"Come on," he roared, trying to roll the gun into position on his own. Five more men rushed out, inspired by his courage. Another volley cut them down or sent them reeling into the shadows, clutching shattered arms or legs.

Then Pat himself went down. Pendleton heard Rawdon snarl, "Jesus." Rawdon dashed into the flying bullets and dragged the big Irishman back to the shelter of their doorway. Pat had been hit in the shoulder. He was writhing in pain.

"Who'll go out there with me and serve that gun?" Rawdon shouted.

While Pendleton watched with mingled horror and admiration, Rawdon walked into the blazing crossfire. Pendleton suddenly remembered a story that Amos Cummings, the managing editor of the *Sun*, had told him about General Stapleton at the battle of Fredericksburg. He had sat on his horse in an open field, ignoring the musketry of an entire Confederate brigade, refusing to retreat until Cummings' regiment recaptured two cannons they had lost.

Four men joined Rawdon beside the cannon. Another blast of muskets from the roundhouse sent them sprawling beside the bodies of their comrades. "Come on," Rawdon shouted, calling for more volunteers. But there were no more takers. The bodies lying around the cannon had sobered everyone. Rawdon stood there, still ignoring the bullets hissing around him, exhorting, gesticulating.

"Rawdon, for Christ's sake get back here," Pendleton shouted.

Love. Was that what tore those words from Pendleton's throat? *I don't let misfortune happen to people I love*, Rawdon had once said. Pendleton could not remain a wry objective observer watching Rawdon die.

Whether it was the shout or the obvious impossibility of persuading anyone else to join him that made Rawdon retreat, Pendleton never knew. But he turned his back on the blazing muskets and returned to the doorway where Pat the anarchist, now in control of his pain, was having his wound bandaged.

"We'll burn the bastards out," Pat said. He vanished into the darkness, leaving Rawdon in charge of the haphazard band that was shooting at the roundhouse.

Fifteen minutes later, in the eastern end of the yards, a tongue of fire leaped into the night. A blazing freight car rolled toward the roundhouse. But someone had missed a connecting switch. The burning car veered into a machine shop two blocks away. Behind it came a half-dozen other cars that soon created a tremendous conflagration. The very magnitude of the blaze made it impossible to get other cars past it to ignite the Philadelphians' roundhouse.

At the opposite end of the yards, a tremendous explosion sent flames soaring fifty feet into the air. Someone had run a freight car full of oil or whiskey under the train shed behind the Union Depot and set it on fire. Soon the building was a roaring pyre. Both fires rapidly became enormous as more and more cars were fed into the blaze. If they could not get at the guardsmen, the strikers were going to punish the Pennsylvania Railroad.

Showers of sparks fell onto wooden houses along Liberty Street, and for a while it looked as though all Pittsburgh would be in ashes by morning. But the firemen who responded to the blaze were permitted to douse the houses.

Only if they tried to fight the fire in the railyards were their hoses chopped and their safety threatened.

"Dougherty wants me to go across the river and meet the head of the trainmen's union, a fellow named Ammon. He's taken over the Fort Wayne and Chicago Railroad," Rawdon said. "Want to come?"

"Why not?"

It was safer than dodging bullets—and it might be more interesting than watching railroad cars burn. In a half hour they had crossed a suspension bridge to Pittsburgh's sister city, Allegheny. The blazing railyards and houses along Liberty Street cast a lurid glow on the black mass of the ridge. Allegheny's streets were full of people, but no one was looting or shouting revolutionary slogans. They looked more bewildered than angry.

The yards of the Fort Wayne & Chicago Railroad were also crammed with cars. But no one was burning them. Perhaps because forty or fifty men were standing in front of the superintendent's office with muskets on their shoulders or pistols in their belts. Inside, Dougherty introduced them to black-mustached Robert Ammon. Big, muscular, self-assured, he was only in his twenties, but he was clearly no ordinary railroad worker. He told them he had a hundred thousand men in his trainmen's union and every one of them was on strike. The blood just spilled in Pittsburgh guaranteed that they would stay out indefinitely.

"What do your men really want?" Rawdon asked.

"What do you think they should want?"

"Ownership of the railroads?" Rawdon said.

"An interesting phrase," Ammon said. "It's been playing through my mind too. We've been running the Fort Wayne for the past two days, without an executive in sight."

"You'd need a new constitution—and a new President," Rawdon said.

"Two more good ideas," Ammon said.

"Would your men fight for them?"

"I think so," Ammon said. "I think a lot of people out this way would fight for them. If you threw in ownership of the steel mills, the coal mines. How do people feel about that sort of thing in New York?"

"A lot of people feel the same way," Rawdon said.

"There's only one thing we lack," Ammon said. "Money. I've knocked around the world a little, after I got expelled from college. I spent some time in Tsingtao, China, where I got mixed up with a warlord who tried to start a revolution. He ran out of money, and his army disappeared. The same thing happened to me in Guatemala."

"There's a hundred million dollars in the U.S. Subtreasury in New York," Rawdon said. "Would that be enough?"

"More than enough," Ammon said.

Was this how revolutions began? Pendleton wondered. After the Bastille fell, did Robespierre meet Danton and find out that they were in fundamental agreement, what the country needed was a reign of terror? Dougherty, already in awe of New York newspapermen, listened wide-eyed as Rawdon discussed how to deal with the situation in Pittsburgh. He urged Ammon to form a committee of safety. "One of my ancestors, Kemble Stapleton, was chairman of New Jersey's Committee of Safety in 1776 when he was about our age," Rawdon said. "You don't have to worry about political parties, factions. A committee of safety runs things."

Ammon nodded. "I've been thinking the same way. The timing is perfect. Congress isn't in session and with no railroads running they can't get to Washington. That leaves old Rutherfraud pretty much on his own down there. A lot of the big-business cheeses like Tom Scott are in Europe."

Rawdon smiled sardonically, thinking of his father, who had sailed to Europe a month ago. "We'll issue a new Declaration announcing the people's independence from the money kings."

Ammon nodded. "Who's going to write this historic document?"

Rawdon pointed to Pendleton. "There's your man. He's the best writer in the newspaper business. Twice as good as I am."

Pendleton shook his head. "I don't write manifestos."

Rawdon smiled confidently at Pendleton. "Maybe I can change his mind on the way back to New York."

"When do you want to leave?" Ammon said.

"Tomorrow morning," Rawdon said.

"I'll have a special with steam up."

"Good. In the meantime we'll get out a revolutionary edition of the *Leader*."

They returned to Pittsburgh, and Dougherty led them to the *Leader*'s offices, a few blocks from the Union Depot. That building was still ablaze. Most of the railyards also continued to burn, with spectacular explosions from tank cars and locomotives adding to the display. At the *Leader* they discovered that the owner had fled the city along with many other wealthy citizens. The editor in chief refused to have anything to do with a revolutionary edition, but several reporters were willing to help and the printers agreed to work when Rawdon persuaded them it would be a memorial for the murdered strikers.

Pendleton stubbornly insisted his first responsibility was copy for the *Sun*. He spent the next two hours writing over four thousand words describing the looting, the fight around the cannon and the attempt to burn the Philadelphians out of the roundhouse.

"What do you think?" Rawdon said, throwing page proofs of the revolutionary edition on Pendleton's desk.

THE LEXINGTON OF THE LABOR CONFLICT AT HAND, proclaimed the head on the lead story. Among other things it declared:

> There is tyranny in this country worse than anything ever known in Russia, China, or Spain in their most autocratic periods—the tyranny of wealth. The war cry has been raised. The principles that freed our nation from enslavement in 1776 will free labor from the murderous oppression of the monopolists and money kings. . . .

"Rawdon," Pendleton said, "this isn't a game. People are going to believe that stuff."

"Don't you believe it?"

"No. The situation is a lot more complicated. There aren't any money kings in the South. There isn't any money. What about the farmers? Who's oppressing them? There are ten times more farmers in the country than workers—even assuming they're all oppressed."

Rawdon stood with his arms folded, shaking his head.

"What about your father? Is he a murderous money king?"

"Sure. If he'd been the general in command out there, he would have turned those Gatling guns on the strikers. He wouldn't have waited for someone to grab a bayonet."

"I don't believe that."

"I'm beginning to wonder about you, Pendleton. The way you rush to his defense. You make me wonder if a certain dirty rumor about him and you is true."

"What?"

"That he paid you five thousand dollars to smear Gould and Rutherfraud."

"That's a goddamn lie. Who told you that?"

"Gould."

"Jesus. You believe that lying bastard?"

"He doesn't lie any more often than the rest of the people on Wall Street, as far as I can see."

Pendleton writhed, remembering an interview he had had with Jonathan Stapleton the week before he sailed to Europe. Pendleton asked him for proof that there had been a deal between Gould and Hayes. Originally, the General had convinced him by showing Pendleton his 1876 campaign ledger, with a million-dollar contribution from Gould clearly listed.

Instead of giving him a straight answer, the General had described Gould's offer of $30 million to line up votes in Congress to give him control of the Texas Pacific. Jonathan Stapleton had told the most powerful man on Wall Street, in the words of some obscure story by Herman Melville, that he preferred not to go near Jay Gould for any amount of money. This explained why Gould was spreading the word around New York that anyone who did business with Jonathan Stapleton was his enemy. But it did not answer Pendleton's question.

Then the General had run his hand through his white hair and given him a lecture on how impossible it was to predict the twists and turns of history. He began telling Pendleton about the impending railroad strike and predicted Pittsburgh could be the powder keg that might send the whole country up in gunsmoke. Sounding like the man of compassion and patriotism Pendleton had once thought he was, the General had denounced the decision to slash railroad workers' pay for the third time in three years, leaving some families living on ninety cents a day.

"What's Genevieve going to think about you trying to unravel the country?" Pendleton said. "Do you think that's a nice idea to present to your wife when she's six months pregnant? 'Oh incidentally, dear, by the time you have your baby there may not be a country called the United States.' "

"She'll understand. I'll explain it to her. I guarantee you she'll understand —and approve. She has more idealism in her soul than you and I put together."

"I can believe that. If idealism could be made soluble, I doubt if either of us would have enough to fill a jigger. But she also has a brain. She may think this is insanity—as I do."

Outside, dawn was filtering through the smoky air. A reporter rushed into the city room and yelled, "The Philadelphians are coming out!" There was a stampede to the roof of the building to watch the carnage. They got there in time to see the last ranks of the two regiments emerge from the roundhouse onto Liberty Street. The two murderous Gatling guns were at the head of the column.

The Philadelphians headed up Liberty Street toward the heart of the city. Everyone on the roof gloated at their folly. Once they found themselves on the triangle of land between the rivers, with no escape except by bridge or water, they would be trapped. But General Brinton was not as stupid as everyone assumed. About three blocks from the roundhouse, the Philadelphians swung left and marched up the ridge to a broad avenue near the top. Here they swung east and headed out of the city.

Most people fled into their houses as the Philadelphians approached. But as soon as they passed, men began swarming in the rear of the column. Someone had given Rawdon a pair of binoculars and he shouted, "There's Pat." Straining his eyes, Pendleton could make out a green-shirted figure at the head of the pursuers.

"They're firing," Rawdon said.

Puffs of gunsmoke rose from the crowd. Other bushwhackers fired into the column from side streets. Soon there were a half-dozen blue-clad bodies lying in the column's wake. The pursuers rushed on, their numbers growing. Suddenly the Philadelphians opened ranks and the rising sun glinted on the brass tubes of one of the Gatling guns. The guardsmen had managed to pass it through the column without breaking their pace. The men on the roof could hear the faint clatter, they could see the tiny spurts of flame, as the gun's eight barrels stitched death across the would-be avengers with terrifying rapidity. "Oh Christ," Rawdon said.

He handed Pendleton the binoculars and walked away. Pendleton raised the glasses to his eyes. The first thing he saw was Pat the anarchist lying on his back, his chest a ribbon of red. Beside him a dying horse kicked spasmodically. A wounded man was trying to crawl away. He was hit by a blast of metal that knocked him ten feet.

The Philadelphians continued the rest of their retreat unmolested. When they disappeared over the top of one of Pittsburgh's surrounding hills, Rawdon tried to pretend it was a victory. "Now the city belongs to the people," he said to Dougherty.

"Yeah," Dougherty said. He was looking somewhat green. Rawdon slapped him on the back and urged him to get to work on organizing a committee of safety. Turning to Pendleton, Rawdon asked if he was coming back to New York with him.

Pendleton shook his head. "They sent me here to cover Pittsburgh. The story isn't over. I feel obligated to let the rest of the country know how the revolution develops here while you try to export it to New York."

"Don't slander it, Clay. Give it a chance to grow. Believe it or not, there's a shining message somewhere in this thing. Look for it. Tell the people about it."

For a moment, Pendleton's heart bounded into his throat. Part of him wanted to share Rawdon's revolutionary zeal, to defy the older men, the arrogant devious victors like Jonathan Stapleton, who had helped to unleash this upheaval. But the wish collided with Pendleton's determination not to surrender his independence as a reporter. That resolve went beyond the Stapletons, father and son. It was connected to the fading editorial from the *Spartanburg Gazette* that he still carried in his wallet.

From the Allegheny side of the river, Pittsburgh's streets swarmed with people, all reduced to the size of ants. The smoldering railyards and the houses along Liberty Street were toy size now, unreal. Was truth a corollary of distance? Pendleton wondered dazedly. He could tell lies about Pittsburgh now, but not while he stood in its chaotic streets. For the first time the meaning of the word "reporter" was like a hand at his throat.

At the Fort Wayne & Chicago railyards, Robert Ammon was waiting for them. Pendleton handed Rawdon a sealed envelope containing his four-thousand-word story and asked him to deliver it to Amos Cummings. Ammon told Rawdon he would have a freight train with fifty armed men aboard it waiting in the Pennsylvania's railyards in Jersey City for the $100 million from the U.S. Subtreasury's vaults. "We'll highball it out here and then you'll see some organizing," he said.

An engineer in a striped uniform, his kerchief around his neck, appeared in the doorway to inform them that the special was ready to head for New York. With mock seriousness, Ammon requested Rawdon to sign a bill for renting an engine and a tender. Rawdon solemnly charged the $250 to "The Second American Revolution."

Outside in the yard, they passed around a bottle for a farewell toast. "Write that manifesto, Clay," Rawdon said. "Make it shine."

"Send the money," Ammon said.

Rawdon climbed into the locomotive's cab. The engineer opened the throttle. The huge wheels turned, the horizontal drivers thrust, retracted, thrust again. In the rifle pits outside the superintendent's office, strikers waved and raised their muskets. Rawdon waved back.

Maybe he should begin drafting a Declaration, Pendleton thought. Maybe it did not matter that the people had no revolutionary ideas in their heads. The newspapers would supply the ideas. Maybe that was the function of newspapers in a revolution.

Maybe. Meanwhile, he would report what he saw.

FIVE

"What would you do about these damned anarchists, eh General?" asked Roderick Chambers, M.P. Red-faced, with at least three chins, he was a virtual caricature of John Bull. Anarchism was the topic of the hour in all the capitals of Europe. Last week, a Russian grand duke had been assassinated at Monte Carlo. The previous week, another disciple of revolutionary violence had tried to kill the King of Italy.

They were standing in the gilded salon of the American ambassador's residence on the Rue Saint-Honoré in Paris. The ambassador, tall affable George Waters, until recently chairman of the board of the New Haven Railroad, stood beside Jonathan Stapleton. Completing the circle was Tom Scott, the president of the Pennsylvania Railroad.

Before Jonathan Stapleton could answer Chambers, Cynthia joined them. She was wearing a new pale-blue Worth gown decorated with cloth-of-gold arabesques. "Can a woman intrude on this solemn conversation?" she asked.

"Only if you have a solution to the problem of the anarchists," Tom Scott said.

"Oh, I do," Cynthia said. "I think they should all marry. Then they'd blame their wives for everything that's wrong with the world, instead of capitalism."

"The first thing I think we should do," Jonathan Stapleton said, ignoring the smiles that Cynthia's playful reply drew, "is admit that anarchists are symptoms—witnesses, if you will—of a serious problem. When I walk to work through the slums of New York's Lower East Side, I'm appalled by what I see. The slums of Paris and London are, if possible, worse. We've created more misery in this century with our wonderful factories and machines than in the previous two centuries combined."

"It seems to me all we've done is intensify the struggle for existence, General," Tom Scott said. "Allowing Darwin's law of the survival of the fittest to become more obvious. The lion isn't sentimental about the way he rules the jungle. I see no point in growing sentimental about the poor—or the anarchists. I say deal with them the way we handle strikers on the Pennsylvania Railroad."

"Couldn't agree more," huffed Chambers, who owned a huge pottery works in the English Midlands.

"Why, Mr. Scott," Cynthia said, "you sound like several plantation owners I knew in Louisiana before the war. They were always talking about how severe you had to be with the Negro."

"I'm afraid it takes a touch of Simon Legree to run a railroad, Mrs. Stapleton," Scott said.

Ambassador Waters' French butler summoned them to dinner in the oval dining room with its ceiling full of pink-cheeked Cupids and nymphs by Louis XV's court painter, François Boucher. Jonathan sat down at the table fuming at his wife. If Cynthia had been joking, her humor was so oblique Scott had been able to ignore it.

Scott had been the last person Jonathan wanted to see in Europe. A month before they sailed, he had traveled to Philadelphia for the semiannual board meeting of the Pennsylvania Railroad and urged his fellow directors and their president to abandon the plan for a ten percent wage cut. Scott had ridiculed him as an alarmist who was afraid to fight Jay Gould for the Texas Pacific Railroad. A particularly galling accusation when Gould was doing his best to wipe Jonathan Stapleton out of existence on Wall Street.

Nothing had gone right on this trip since they left the dock at Hoboken. Cynthia had been seasick as usual, and he had had to play nursemaid to her.

In London she had insisted on seeing Madeline Terhune, who led them into the high (or low) life of the British upper classes, cheerfully filling them in at parties about the mistresses of a certain duke or the lovers of an even more decadent duchess. Cynthia loved it. At some other time Jonathan might have found it amusing. But he had too much on his mind to enjoy himself. He could not escape the conviction that the United States of America was on the brink of an awful explosion. As often as he told himself that he had made a sacred promise to take Cynthia to Europe, another voice asked him about different promises, equally sacred, if unspoken.

A mustachioed French general named Boulanger asked Ambassador Waters what the American people thought of President Hayes. Was it true that he was in danger of being ousted by the army because of his policy toward the South?

Waters eyed Jonathan and squirmed a bit. He was not a Stalwart Republican. That was why he was enjoying this splendid eighteenth-century mansion. "My General," Waters replied, in French that was not much better than Jonathan's, "the American Army isn't big enough to oust anyone, not even a congressman."

Boulanger listened with astonishment as Waters explained how Congress had dismantled the great army Lincoln had raised to fight the Civil War. "A mistake," General Boulanger said. "At the very least you should have taken Canada from the British." Roderick Chambers glared at Boulanger and made a speech about the French always trying to stir trouble between the United States and England.

Tom Scott, who obviously considered himself more qualified to speak for the country than Ambassador Waters (he ran a much bigger railroad), said there was nothing to worry about. He began extolling Hayes as a "profound statesman" who was achieving "an era of peace" that would enable business to prosper in America as never before.

Riding back through the silent streets to the Hotel Splendide, Jonathan and Cynthia passed the scorched hulk of the Tuileries Palace, destroyed by the riots of the Paris Commune. Cynthia talked about Ambassador Waters' beautiful mansion. "How I'd love to live in a house like that for a few years. If you ever make your peace with President Hayes, don't you think you could get an appointment to Paris—or even to London? You've done far more for the Republican Party than George Waters."

"True," Jonathan said. "But I don't have the slightest desire to spend the prime of my life explaining elementary facts about the United States to idiots like General Boulanger."

"You would have a wife, Mr. Ambassador," Cynthia said, "who has the social skill to keep all such bores away from your door. She would guarantee to keep you happy, officially and unofficially."

She pressed her lips against his cheek. At any other time he would have responded with a kiss. More than once on other visits to Paris they had kissed like young lovers on the way back to their hotel. It usually signaled the start of a memorable evening. But tonight he did not even turn his head.

Cynthia retreated to the other side of the carriage. "I am so looking forward to Venice," she said. "It's my last hope for a good-humored husband."

"What do you mean by that?"

"If you could only hear the sound of your own voice, you'd know the answer."

"I think I've been perfectly good-humored ever since we sailed."

"If you say so, Husband dear."

He fumed in silence for several minutes over that remark. Then Cynthia spoke again in the darkness. "The Scotts are going to Venice. He's charming, don't you think?"

"No, I don't think so," he snapped.

A mistake. It proved she was right about his bad humor. It stirred memories of another nasty contradiction in a carriage in Washington that had led to an evening he would prefer to forget.

"I didn't realize you brought your Stalwart politics across the water."

"It has nothing to do with politics."

He tried to tell her how and why Scott had made a fool of him at the Pennsylvania Railroad board meeting. He made a botch of it. Her answer implied that she found it unconvincing.

"How can I possibly know what to do or say about that sort of thing, when you don't tell me about it?"

"Why should I tell you? Would you find it amusing?"

"I would hope—or wish—that you're joking."

"Were you joking when you told Scott he was right to treat his workers like slaves?"

"Surely you don't think I meant that. I can't believe you didn't hear my sarcasm."

"He didn't."

"I was about to tell him that my father always treated his slaves with humanity—and they worked harder for him than any other blacks in Louisiana. But the butler announced dinner—"

"Let's hope you can correct matters in Venice."

Cynthia said almost nothing while they bathed and prepared for bed. Jonathan lay there, damning Tom Scott as an arrogant swine and himself as a contentious fool for dragging his frustration to Europe with him.

Cynthia slipped into bed beside him. A soft southern breeze flowed through the open window, suggesting—if not actually carrying across the great city—the green fragrance of the Bois de Boulogne and the fertile countryside beyond it. It mingled with another fragrance, Cynthia's Violette de Toulouse perfume.

Her lips were on his mouth this time. "I refuse to let our last night in Paris be spoiled by a silly quarrel over a railroad," she whispered.

Wanting, loving this woman stirred in his flesh, leaped in his mind. Did it matter that she was wrong? It was not a silly quarrel. It was not even a quarrel about a railroad. What did these large facts or ideas have to do with the reality of those lifted breasts, those welcoming arms? For a little while love was separate, entire, a thing that only a fool would deny or refuse.

"There's something I'm going to tell you in Venice," Cynthia whispered as he settled himself to sleep. "Something that I hope will convince you that I love you in a very special way."

"Why not tell me now?"

"No. It has to be in Venice."

The next morning was devoted to packing and paying bills. The packing was chaotic and gave him a headache. The bills were catastrophic, and gave him a worse headache. The prices of everything seemed to have doubled since their last visit. Jonathan's war with Jay Gould, which had cost him a half-million dollars in the last few months, made him acutely cost conscious. He was emotionally unprepared for two bills that Cynthia handed him. One was for a painting of a woman on a balcony by Eduard Manet: price, $5,000. The other was for eighteen dresses from Maison Worth: price, $48,000.

"My God," he gasped. "Couldn't you have done with a little less finery?"

"The styles are changing so drastically," Cynthia said.

He paid for the dresses—what else could he do?—but decided they could not afford the Manet. Cynthia was extremely disappointed. "It's the best thing he's done," she said. "It would look so well in our parlor."

"Next year, if he hasn't sold it."

The disagreement cast a shadow on the afterglow of their last night in Paris. Rolling south in the *wagon-lits*, Cynthia had very little to say. When they sat down in the dining car, he ordered a bottle of Château Lafite and said, "I'm sorry about the Manet." He told her how much money he had lost to Jay Gould, and why. With a little help from the wine, he even admitted lying to Clay Pendleton to sabotage Gould and Rutherford B. Hayes.

"You are really quite wicked," Cynthia said. "I wish you hadn't abused Clay's trust that way, no matter how good you may think the cause."

"I hated to do it," he said. "But I think it helped his career. He's become the best-known political reporter in New York. Newspapers don't care whether or not a story is true, as long as it sells papers."

"But Clay may care."

"Do you think so? As far as I can see, he's a worse cynic than Rawdon."

"Why are you so sure Rawdon is a cynic? It could all be a performance, aimed at infuriating you."

"That's not a cheerful thought, either."

Cynthia told him about a conversation she had had with Rawdon just after Genevieve broke their engagement. Apparently Genevieve had some profound if elusive meaning to Rawdon. She had changed his idea of himself. Jonathan was astonished to discover that Rawdon took himself—or life in general—so seriously.

"That's the first hopeful thing I've heard about him in fifteen years," he said.

"Jonathan—I've never been able to understand your attitude toward Rawdon. There are times when you actually seem to dislike him."

For a moment he was tempted to admit there might be some truth to that charge and blame it on Rawdon's resemblance to Charlie. He had been severe with Rawdon because he was determined to prevent that outburst of amoral wildness from recurring in the Stapleton family. But how do you tell a woman that the grand romance of her life is a fraud? No, there was a limit to frankness, just as there was, thank goodness, a limit to the Château Lafite.

As they dined, they talked of the odd ways that people entered each other's lives, never dreaming of the influence, the meaning they would acquire. It was all so haphazard. "There does seem at times to be a kind of destiny that governs our lives," Cynthia said.

"Whether for good or ill is the question," Jonathan said.

The remark seemed to upset Cynthia. "I'm inclined to favor good at the moment," she said.

"I am, too," Jonathan said.

For a moment he found himself wishing he could offer Cynthia some stronger affirmation. Their souls were touching here, in this brightly lit dining car with its snowy tables and shining silver and glass, sharing and touching as intimately as their bodies had met last night.

He sensed that this woman, his wife, needed some spiritual center to her life. For most women, children supplied this need. His possessiveness, his selfishness, had deprived her of children of her own. He wished he could give her some kind of faith, purpose. But the war had destroyed whatever shreds of belief Ben Dall's rational ridicule of Christianity had left in his soul. The same war had destroyed Cynthia's ability to share his private faith—or hope —in the United States of America. Perhaps before they died he could awaken that piety in her soul—or at least make her understand its power in his soul. For the time being, all he could offer was his companionship on the journey they were sharing.

Companionship? No, that was much too weak a word. He wished he had the ability to say something extravagant, to offer her his devotion, without sounding foolish. He poured the last of the Château Lafite into their glasses. "To us," he said.

The following day, late in the afternoon, after they had changed trains in Milan and stopped for tourists and fuel in Brescia, Verona, Mestre, a stir, a murmur, then a cry ran through their car. Everyone on the right side rushed to the opposite windows as they rounded a huge curve and Venice appeared in the distance at the edge of the green alluvial plain.

"At last," Cynthia murmured, suggesting that she had not entirely abandoned her opinion that it was their only hope of a happy vacation.

They rumbled across the long white railway bridge, looking down into the green depths of the lagoon and ahead at the city as the sunset tinted its ancient stones a delicate rose and filled the cloudless blue sky with more spectacular colors. In a half hour they were on the terrace of the station, three porters behind them grappling with their trunks, a regiment of gondoliers ahead of them crying, *"Barca, signore!"* while across the canal the white dome and porticoed façade of San Simeone Profeta loomed in the fading light.

A hand seized Jonathan's arm. Tom Scott and his wife beamed at him. "Where are you staying, General?" Scott said. "I enjoyed Mrs. Stapleton's company so much last night, I absolutely insist on an encore. We're at the Danieli."

He let Cynthia tell them about the Palazzo Rospigliosi and assure them of an early invitation to dinner. Jonathan was certain Mrs. Scott was about to capture them for dinner that very night when a savior appeared. Out of the mass of gondoliers struggled squat Giorgio, the boatman who was attached to the Palazzo Rospigliosi.

In the twilight shadows, the palaces and churches along the Grand Canal never looked more mysterious, more epochal. They could be travelers from Constantinople arriving in fifteenth-century Venice at the height of its power and glory, to be received by one of the nine hundred families on the golden list. Instead they were greeted by mournful Count Rospigliosi and his wife. The last ten years had not been kind to them. The Count's age—or his dissipation—was showing. Unhealthy dark circles hollowed his eyes. His wife's brightness had faded into a brittle bitter gaiety. Ten years ago they had been cash poor, but their noble blood had sustained their sense of superiority. Now Italy had become a republic where politicians, not noblemen, reigned.

They sipped vermouth in the immense reception room while the servants wrestled the trunks upstairs. The Count's views on Italian politics were doleful. "The government does nothing but boast. Statistics of how many yards of silk, gallons of olive oil, we export. They want to stamp numbers on Italy's soul. They will never succeed. It is the same all over Europe. The people are sick of the modern world, with its statistics and its obsession with trade. There is a counterrevolution coming, an upheaval of the spirit."

"I tell him he's talking drivel," the Contessa said. "The modern world is here to stay."

The Count ignored his impudent wife. "No doubt you're disturbed by the turmoil in America, General?"

"I don't know what you're talking about," Jonathan said.

"The newspapers are full of details today. The city of—what is it called— Pittsway?"

"Pittsburgh!"

"Pittsburgh—has been devoured by flames set by revolutionary workers. They have destroyed millions in property. Similar things seem to be happening in other cities. No doubt your army will deal firmly with the malefactors, as you dealt with the southern rebels."

"You're sure this is happening?" Jonathan asked, hearing his voice drift into the shadows of the huge room.

"Unless the newspapers are making it up, which is always possible." The Count hurled maledictions on journalists. The pilot fish of the monster socialism, he called them. He summoned a servant, who returned with an Italian newspaper. There, on the front page, was the story: L'AMERICA IN FIAMME. America in flames.

He had been right, Jonathan thought numbly. The United States of America was dissolving into a stew of ignorant armies, no different from Mexico. And where was he? Sitting in a fifteenth-century palace in the middle of a city that was nothing more than a gigantic museum. Jesus!

Count Rospigliosi and his wife departed. Fabrizio, the grave gray-haired *maggiordomo* of the palazzo, appeared to ask them what they wanted for dinner. Cynthia conversed with him in fluent Italian while Jonathan stared at the incomprehensible phrases in the newspaper: ". . . *caos per le strade . . . la democrazia in pericolo . . . scatenata la rabbia del popolo . . .*"

"What does it say?" he snarled, thrusting the paper at her as Fabrizio withdrew.

She glanced at it. "Pretty much what the Count described. But they may be exaggerating. Europeans often exaggerate what happens in America. Italians especially."

"Good God," he said, and stalked to the door.

"Where are you going?"

"To try to find an English newspaper."

With numerous gestures and a few scraps of Italian, he managed to convey his desire to Giorgio, who took him to the Piazza di San Marco. The immense square was swarming with tourists of all ages and nationalities, and with Venetians in their Sunday finery. Every language in Europe assailed his ears; the various nationalities sat in front of their respective cafés, *trattorie, birrerie* and, for the Americans, saloons, blissfully chatting and sipping. He followed Giorgio into a shop that seemed to have the newspapers of all nations on the shelves. But the English papers were all three days old and contained nothing about America except yachting and racing news.

More gestures, bits of Italian, and Giorgio finally comprehended that he wanted to go to the cable office. The boatman led him across the square past the looming façade of the Cathedral of San Marco to a shop with a wide glass front. Standing in front of it, with a piece of paper in his hand, was Tom Scott, arguing frantically with an Italian official in a military uniform.

"General," Scott cried. "Do you know anyone with some influence in this godforsaken place? This fellow says the cable office is closed on Sunday and nothing short of an order from the King can open it."

"What's happening?" Jonathan said, barely looking at Scott; his eyes were on the paper in his hand. Scott thrust it at him. "This!"

MOB BURNED RAILYARDS IN PITTSBURGH SATURDAY NIGHT. 2,000 CARS, 260 LOCOMOTIVES, UNION DEPOT, ROUNDHOUSES, MACHINE SHOPS DE-STROYED. ESTIMATED LOSS 5 MILLION. ENTIRE WORKFORCE ON STRIKE, EXCEPT FOR A FEW THOUSAND IN PHILADELPHIA. NATIONAL GUARD REGI-MENTS IN READING, PITTSBURGH, HARRISBURG HAVE JOINED STRIKERS. YOUR INSTRUCTIONS URGENTLY NEEDED.

CASSATT

"Five million dollars," Scott said. He was weeping. "I can't believe it. They've destroyed my railroad. They've destroyed me."

"What are you going to do about it?" Jonathan snarled.

"I'm going to cable the President. Demand that the army, the entire regular army, be sent to Pennsylvania."

"There isn't any army to send, you goddamn fool. They're scattered all over the West. It would take two weeks to get enough of them together to make a decent division. By that time there may not be anything left of Pennsylvania—or the Union. There's only one thing you can do. If I can get this office to open, you've got to cable Cassatt to cancel that wage cut."

Scott was breathing like a man with a heart seizure. "How can you get it open?"

Jonathan dragged Scott to Giorgio's gondola. The boatman poled them to the palazzo where the Rospigliosis were staying as guests. The Count led them to the manager of the cable office, who abandoned his dinner to open for business. While Jonathan stood over him, Scott dictated a cable to Cassatt, rescinding the wage cut. Jonathan joined him in signing a cable to

President Hayes, urging him to commit as much of the regular army as he could muster to stop the mobs. Finally, Jonathan took charge of the line and cabled Police Superintendent Walling in New York: "NEWS OF RIOTS. IS NEW YORK SAFE? CAN I DO ANYTHING?"

The demoralized Scott went back to his hotel. Jonathan paced the cable office for an hour. Then the brass key began clicking and the police superintendent's reply raced beneath the Atlantic Ocean and the Mediterranean Sea.

SITUATION VERY TENSE. URGE GOVERNOR, MAYOR, TO GIVE ME A FREE HAND.

Jonathan composed appropriate cables, reminding the mayor and the governor of the disgraceful way their Democratic predecessors had truckled to the mob during the Draft Riots in 1863. He told them that he was sending copies of the cables to Walling—and to the *New York Times*.

Night had long since fallen by the time Jonathan left the cable office and rode back to the Palazzo Rospigliosi in Giorgio's gondola. Torches flared on the landings of other palazzos along the Grand Canal. The tide was out and weedy slime oozed on the lower steps of the landings and on the usually submerged stones of the ancient buildings. A mixture of raw sewage and stagnant marsh water assailed his nose. The real Venice was not a city floating in a glowing empyrean. But its worshipers avoided thinking about its gross reality. Music, laughter, drifted from the windows of a dozen palazzos.

Similar music had been playing here, other visitors had been laughing, drinking, dancing, during the summer of 1861, when he led his men up Henry House Hill at Bull Run. And during the fall of 1862, when he led them into the inferno of Antietam. Yes, and in the summer of 1863, when they clung to Culp's Hill at Gettysburg under murderous artillery bombardment. And in the spring of 1864, the nightmare spring of the Wilderness and Cold Harbor. In the best of times and the worst of times, Venice was a place where history had ceased to matter. Why had he allowed his wife to make him one of these trivial people?

At the palazzo, Cynthia had dressed for dinner. She was writing notes to their Venetian acquaintances. "Adelaide Pell will probably want us to come to tea tomorrow, so she can begin to arrange things," Cynthia said. "By the end of the week, dear old Cuthbert Plimpton will make you the centerpiece of a dinner, which will include at least two Austrian generals so you can refight the battle of Austerlitz, and a Russian grand duke with outrageous opinions about Waterloo. While I'm left to deal with one of those aging English poets of the Spasmodic School, which he still adores—"

"We're not going anywhere," he snapped. "Except home."

"You can't be serious! You'd let a story in a newspaper ruin—"

"It isn't a story in a newspaper anymore."

He told her of seeing Tom Scott with the cable from Pittsburgh confirming the carnage, of the cable from Walling about the situation in New York.

"Why should we ruin our entire trip—ruin everything—because a riot in Pittsburgh might spread to New York?"

She was close to tears. Jonathan struggled to control his exasperation. "This isn't a riot. It's a revolutionary mob. Didn't you read those stories Rawdon published in the *Herald?* New York is the key to the country. If they lose control there, the Union is gone."

"What can you do about it?" Cynthia said. "Assuming we can get a cabin on the fastest steamship on the Atlantic, we couldn't get home in less than two weeks."

"I know that," he snarled. "But I don't intend to sit here in this slimy stinking museum while my country comes apart."

"That's . . . what you really think of Venice?" Cynthia said. "A slimy stinking museum?"

"That's how it looked and smelled just now on the Grand Canal," he said. "With the tide out."

Maggiordomo Fabrizio announced that dinner was served. They sat down in the huge dining room at opposite ends of a table that was twice the length of their dining table at home. It was not a table—or a room—designed for two people. When the Rospigliosis had been one of the nine hundred families on the golden list, they had dined in ducal splendor, surrounded by retainers, relatives, sycophants, foreign ambassadors. But those Rospigliosis had been in their tombs for the last three hundred years.

Cynthia still looked grief-stricken. Jonathan merely noted the fact, as if she were a Venetian artifact, a carving on a church façade or a painting on a museum wall. His mind, his soul, was in New York.

Police Superintendent Walling was tough enough, shrewd enough to stop the mob if the Democratic governor and mayor let him act. He had honeycombed the Communists, the anarchists, the gangsters of the Lower East Side with informers and spies. Jonathan had warned him about the threat of a railroad strike, and Walling had agreed it could trigger an upheaval in New York. At Jonathan's suggestion he had connected all the police stations and National Guard armories in the city by telegraph. They had even discussed tactics. The Draft Riots had taught them the importance of concentrating police and troops and smashing the main body of the mob the moment it formed.

Suddenly Jonathan was there, he was fourteen years and four thousand miles away from this Venetian dining room, coming down First Avenue in the blazing July sunlight, leading two regiments of exhausted, jittery soldiers who had ridden all night on a train after fighting for three days at Gettysburg. The temperature was close to a hundred. Smoke swirled overhead from burning buildings. On a half-dozen lampposts, dead Negroes dangled.

Running toward them were the shattered survivors of a 150-man detachment he had rushed to the neighborhood two hours earlier. Behind the fugitives came the mob, an immense howling sea, brandishing clubs and bricks and guns. Hundreds more were on the rooftops, and the whine of bullets revealed they were well armed. What had begun as a protest against a manifestly unjust draft law had turned into a revolution.

There was no time to think, no time to do anything but fight. He roared orders that sent the men from his rear regiment charging into the houses to clear the roofs. The front regiment opened ranks, and the three cannons in the center of the column were rushed forward. "Fire!" he had roared, and the blue-black guns belched smoke and flame. Grapeshot ripped through the mob. "Fire!" he roared again, and the foot soldiers added a volley. When the smoke cleared there were hundreds of bodies on the cobblestones, some writhing, a few crawling for shelter.

Worse, it had been infinitely worse, than any battlefield.

"I think you're right," Cynthia said. "I think we should go home."

"What?" Jonathan said dazedly. He stared at a cup of coffee that Maggiordomo Fabrizio had just set in front of him. The meal was over. He could not even remember what he had eaten.

"I'd rather go home than stay with you in Venice this way. It will ruin the good memories."

"I'll cable Cunard tomorrow for reservations," he said.

Cynthia retired to their bedroom almost immediately after dinner. Jonathan wandered moodily through the salons and halls and sitting rooms of the palazzo, staring at the treasures the Rospigliosis had accumulated in their five centuries in Venice.

What was in here? Jonathan pushed open an elaborately carved walnut door. Oh yes, the armory. He lit a wall lamp and gazed at the spoils of fifteenth-century Venetian victories over the Turks. A forest of banners and flags, most of them rotted with mildew and age, drooped from the walls. There were dozens of pasha's tails, shields, guns, mortars, statues and bas reliefs of dead heroes.

Jonathan thought of the war corner in his bedroom with its photographs and captured Confederate flags. Was he doing the same thing, trying to preserve memories, victories, that were destined for oblivion?

No. The blood was too fresh, the wounds too raw to accept that judgment. America was not sinking into the mindless enjoyment of wealth for its own sake that had enervated Venice. There was purpose, meaning, in the dead, in the memories he carried in his heart, meaning imperiled by the madness that had erupted in Pittsburgh.

In the bedroom, the same ornate room they had shared on their honeymoon, Cynthia was already asleep. She had left a lamp burning in the adjacent dressing room. Jonathan slipped under the silk sheets, sure he would be unable to sleep. But he was suddenly deep in a dream.

He was on First Avenue again, fighting the mob. Suddenly, out of the screaming mass of humanity behind the improvised barricade stepped a figure in white, brandishing a sword. It was Charlie. He pointed the sword at Jonathan, on his horse, and shouted, *Let's get the butcher!*

The mob poured over the barricades and raced toward him. Jonathan sat on his horse, stupefied; then he pulled his pistol and aimed it at the figure in white. He pressed the trigger and Charlie leaped high in the air as the bullet struck him in the chest. For a moment all Jonathan could see was the glaring, hate-filled handsome face.

He awoke. It was still dark. A sea wind sighed through Venice, filling the night with the sound of lapping water.

The dream. It was also a memory. There really had been a figure in white who led a charge at the climax of the battle on First Avenue. His appearance had revealed the hand of the Confederate government in the Draft Riots. He had shot him in the same way. Where, how, why had he acquired Charlie's face?

A human sound mingled with the lap of the water. Jonathan raised his head. Through the open French windows he saw a figure on the balcony. It was Cynthia, weeping. For a moment his heart seemed to crack into irreparable pieces. He wanted to spring out of bed and put his arms around her. He wanted to tell her how much he regretted abandoning Venice.

Abandoning the good memories. And the secret. He had almost forgotten it. The secret she had been going to tell him. Had she forgotten it, too? Was it important enough to turn his back on his country?

No. It was probably something sentimental. Something important to her as a woman. If he showed even a trace of remorse now, she might trap him into staying here, while America burned.

The iron general lay there, letting his wife weep.

SIX

"Maisie's gone?"

"She ran away last night."

Genevieve Dall Stapleton sopped sweat from her streaming face with an already damp handkerchief. She was sitting in Mother Aloysius McGovern's office at the House of the Good Shepherd. Walking from Fifth Avenue to the East River in July with the temperature over a hundred would have been exhausting even if she were not six months pregnant. For the past three months she had been coming up here to interview inmates for a book she was trying to write on prostitution in New York. Maisie had been a find, intelligent and seemingly cooperative.

"Two other girls ran away with her. We'll have to lock them in their dormitory if it keeps up. Their pimps, their old lovers, their families, are sending them warnings. The gangs are going to burn this place to the ground. They hate us for taking girls away from them."

"Do you think it could happen?"

"If the mob gets loose? Yes. Were you in the city during the Draft Riots in 1863?"

Genevieve nodded, feeling the child stir against her abdomen, as if it had picked up the revulsion those words aroused in her memory. "I was living on Stuyvesant Square."

"They were going to burn us down then. We were next on the list, after the Colored Orphan Asylum. The troops arrived before they got this far uptown."

"But the city is quiet."

Sister Aloysius pointed to a story in the *New York Times* on her desk, reporting plans for a protest rally in Tompkins Square tonight. "That could be the start of it. I was down at police headquarters this morning to ask my old friend Superintendent Walling for some protection."

"Are they sending you some policemen?"

Mother Aloysius shook her head. "It looks like we'll have to rely on prayer."

It was Tuesday afternoon, July 27th. For two days now, the violence and bloodshed that began in Pittsburgh on Saturday had spread across the nation. The entire state of Pennsylvania west of Philadelphia seemed to be in the hands of strikers and rioters, its police powerless, its National Guard regiments routed or dispersed. In St. Louis, the Workingmen's Party of the United States, better known as the Communists, had issued a manifesto calling on the laboring class to take over the government. Mobs rampaged through the streets of Chicago, routing police and guardsmen. Buffalo was in chaos, and flickers of violence were reported in Newark, Cleveland, Baltimore and a half-dozen other cities.

"Where's your husband?" Mother Aloysius asked.

"In Pittsburgh," Genevieve said.

"I hope he's all right. We'll add a prayer for him."

Mother Aloysius thought the strike was justified. There was no excuse for cutting the railroad workers' salaries so low. She saw too much evidence of the evils poverty encouraged. "My heart went out to those poor strikers when I read about them being shot down, but then I read the story in the *Sun* about the soldiers being bombarded with bricks and logs. It's the railroad kings and their lackeys who deserve hanging."

"I agree," Genevieve said.

"I shouldn't be saying such things, wearing a habit. I was the same way in 'Sixty-three. I sympathized with the poor fellows who were being drafted because they didn't have the money to pay their way out of it. But I changed my mind when the mob started hanging and stabbing innocent Negroes."

"They hanged two Negroes in Stuyvesant Park, right in front of our house," Genevieve said.

Silence. Genevieve sensed they were both recoiling from the gruesome memories of 1863. "How's the book coming?" Mother Aloysius asked.

"Not as fast as my other gestation," Genevieve said, ruefully glancing at her widening midriff.

"It must be a boy, when you're that big at six months. You look very tired. Are you getting enough rest? Why has your husband left you in this hot city?"

"We're trying to live on his salary. He can't afford to set me up at some country hotel. Anyway, I'd be bored. I wanted to keep working on the book."

"I don't think you'll get much from the girls today. They're in such a wild mood. I'm going to send one of the sisters over to Fifth Avenue to find a hack to take you home."

Back in her apartment on Forty-third Street, Genevieve sat at the dining-room table, wearily turning the pages of her manuscript. The book was like a cake that refused to rise. She needed more facts—and no one would give them to her. She had written to the police department, the mayor's office, to clergymen who regularly gave sermons against vice, but no one had any facts. If they had any, they did not want to share them with a woman.

One minister had informed Genevieve that no decent woman should write a book on prostitution. Her husband vociferously concurred in this opinion. Rawdon had told her that he would not permit his wife, the mother of his son—he was certain the child would be a boy—to admit to the world that she had prostitution on her mind.

Genevieve had stubbornly persisted. She had secretly enlisted Clay Pendleton's help. He supplied her with vivid word pictures of Satan's Circus, the garish blocks below Forty-second Street on the West Side where thousands of prostitutes thronged. He sent her bits of information about arrests (rare) and suicides in brothels (frequent). But Clay could only provide random assistance while he rushed off on bigger assignments. There was no hope of finishing the book before she gave birth. Then a new demanding presence would devour what was left of Genevieve's freedom.

Stop. Not for the first time, Genevieve admonished herself to welcome her pregnancy more wholeheartedly. Except for flareups over the book on prostitution, the pregnancy had made Rawdon gentle, tender, considerate. She recalled the delight her mother, Eleanor, Alice Gansevoort, even Cynthia Stapleton, took in pregnant Genevieve. If all these other women thought it was so wonderful, it had to be wonderful. Even Wellcombe, sinking into discouragement in her losing battle with the Boston bar, had written her a letter full of envy and congratulations.

Genevieve shoved the manuscript aside and stared at the headlines of the newspapers she had bought on the way home. Upstate on the Erie and the New York Central, National Guardsmen were fighting pitched battles with strikers. The federal government seemed helpless. The *Sun* carried a grim story describing the arrival of fifty regular-army soldiers in Pittsburgh. They had marched through the ruins of the Pennsylvania Railroad railyard and taken refuge in a federal arsenal. The story was undoubtedly written by Clay Pendleton. It was full of his wicked wit and vivid imagery.

She could find nothing in the *Herald* about Pittsburgh that seemed to have been written by Rawdon. But his style was plainer and more ordinary than Clay's; it was harder to identify. She wondered what he was thinking about this upheaval. He was probably as disgusted by the destruction and looting as Clay obviously was.

Genevieve wished her husband was here with her in New York. With Jonathan Stapleton abroad and her mother and Eleanor and the Gansevoorts vacationing at the shore or the mountains, there was almost no one in the city to whom she could turn if the mob got loose.

The rap of the front-door knocker. A scrawny Western Union messenger greeted her. "Mrs. Stapleton? Telegram for youse."

It was probably from Rawdon. She ripped it open and read:

PLEASE JOIN US IN LONG BRANCH. ALL IS QUIET HERE. AWFUL MEMORIES OF 1863 MAKE IT IMPOSSIBLE FOR ME TO SLEEP, THINKING OF YOU IN NEW YORK IN YOUR DELICATE CONDITION. MOTHER.

Eighteen sixty-three again. She did not want to think about those nightmarish days.

For seventy-two hours Genevieve and her mother and Eleanor had huddled in their house on Stuyvesant Square, watching the mob swirl up and down Second Avenue, murdering policemen and Negroes and routing detachments of soldiers. On the third day, they heard the sound of fifes and saw a mass of blue-clad soldiers marching down Second Avenue. Her mother recognized General Stapleton on a white horse and identified the flag of the Sixth New Jersey. "It's your father's regiment," she had cried.

The column had swung down Fourteenth Street toward the East River. Minutes later, the crash of muskets, the thunder of cannon had shaken their windows. Genevieve would never forget the sound of those guns. She had fled into the back of the house, her hands over her ears, horrified at the possibility of her father being killed only a few blocks away.

An hour later, the guns fell silent and the front bell jangled. She had raced downstairs and flung open the door. Her father stood there, his face, his uniform streaked with gunsmoke and dust, the empty sleeve—he had lost his arm at Chancellorsville the year before—dangling loose. His eyes had been opaque, veiled, as if by an act of the will, to prevent her from knowing the horror they had just seen. She had burst into tears and clung to him for a long time, while he stood there, patting her head, whispering, "There, there, my little girl. It's all right. It's all right now."

Maybe she should flee to Long Branch. There were no railroads running, but she could get a steamboat from the Battery.

Did she really want to scurry off, like a frightened doe? Was that one of the prerequisites—or penalties—of motherhood? You could legitimately act like a timid terrified female because you were protecting your child?

At Long Branch she would have to spend her time with Eleanor and Hal Bradford, who had become a twosome. Rawdon encouraged the match, pouring praise of Eleanor into Hal's usually besotted ears. Her mother did the same thing with Eleanor—not that she needed any encouragement. The mere thought of Hal's millions ignited ecstasy in her blue eyes.

A key turned in the lock. The front door slammed. Rawdon! Thank God.

Perhaps she was learning the hard way that there were times when a husband was a very comforting presence.

"Hello," he said, in a voice that was closer to a croak.

Genevieve could only stare at the bizarre figure slumped against the door-jamb, seemingly almost too weak to stand. Was this unshaven filthy exhausted creature the handsome white-suited bright-eyed reporter who had left her for Pittsburgh three days ago?

Ignoring the dirt and grease, Genevieve flung her arms around him. "I'm so glad to see you. I've been sitting here, wondering what to do."

Rawdon slumped into a kitchen chair. "You'll be all right," he said, in the same unnatural croak.

"What happened to your voice?" she asked.

Rawdon shook his head. "Talking too much," he croaked. "With no sleep. I haven't slept in two—almost three days."

"Darling—that's terrible. No newspaper story in the world is worth that sort of punishment. Did Clay come back from Pittsburgh with you?"

Rawdon shook his head. "Came today—the lying bastard."

Genevieve was baffled. "What do you mean? I read all his stories. I thought they were the best reporting I've seen in years. Did you write any of the stories the *Herald* ran?"

Rawdon shook his head. "I quit the *Herald.* When the goddamn cowards wouldn't run what I wrote. In a few days we'll be telling them what to run."

The conversation was growing more and more unreal. "You quit your job? Just when you started to get stories on the front page? Rawdon—what's happening? How are you going to tell them what to run?"

"Because we'll be running the city. The country."

"Who's we? Rawdon, you're not making any sense."

Rawdon pointed to the story on the front page of the *Herald* about the rally in Tompkins Square. Instead of deploring it like the *Times,* the *Herald* congratulated the mayor for trusting the good judgment of the people.

"Bennett's playing his usual I-love-the-common-man game. He's going to get the surprise of his life tonight. We'll have sixty thousand men at that meeting. Enough to take care of the police and the National Guard, if any of them want to fight. Meanwhile, I'm going to storm the Subtreasury with a thousand picked men. By midnight we'll have a hundred million dollars. Enough to finance two revolutions."

It was all said in the croaking exhausted voice. Genevieve stared into the unshaven dirt-smeared face. Only the green eyes belonged to Rawdon. Even they were glazed with sleeplessness. Unreal, Genevieve thought. Unreal, impossible. Rawdon leading a revolution.

"I can't believe you'd do such a thing," she said. "Tell me it's a joke."

"A joke?" The mouth compressed, the eyes glared. He pointed to the reddish smears on his coat. "You see this? It's the blood of innocent men and women shot down in Pittsburgh by some cold-blooded general like my father. Don't believe what Pendleton wrote. I saw it. The General pointed to the strikers on the tracks and said, 'Get rid of those scum.' And the vice-president of the Pennsylvania Railroad, Cassatt, cheered. I swear to you he cheered when he saw the bodies on the tracks!"

"Why would Clay lie about it?"

"He's been bought. By the railroad. He's always been for sale. I heard the other day my father bought him to write that story about Gould and Rutherfraud. Paid him five thousand dollars."

"I—I can't believe that."

"Doesn't matter," Rawdon croaked. "Listen to me." He took her hands and drew her into a chair opposite him.

"Gen," he said. "It's the shining message. The angel was there, in the middle of that drunken mob in Pittsburgh, speaking to me, telling me that now was the moment, now was the time to make a new declaration of independence live in the hearts and minds of the people. I tried to tell Pendleton, but he didn't understand. Only you can understand. That's why I came home. I had to tell you. I wanted you to know—in case something happens to me tonight. I want you to guard the message—and pass it on to our son."

Rawdon croaked on, telling her what he had been doing since he returned to New York on Sunday. Arguing endlessly with the Marxists, with committees of anarchists, with radical labor leaders, trying to persuade them that the situation had true revolutionary potential if New York seized the leadership of the upheaval. He told her about Robert Ammon, the head of the trainmen's union, waiting in Pittsburgh with a hundred thousand men.

There was no time to weigh justice against injustice, dead strikers against dead soldiers. Genevieve spoke out of memory, out of instinct, out of wish. "Rawdon," she said, "no matter what really happened in Pittsburgh, there is simply no excuse for letting the mob loose in this city. For saying or doing one thing to encourage them."

Rawdon's face was blank with incomprehension. "What the hell are you talking about? It's not a mob. It's the people—the workers, the people who've been starved and humiliated and abused like no Americans in the history of the country, including the slaves. It's the people rising up to claim their right to some happiness."

"Rawdon—I saw them in 1863. They're a mob. I was up at the House of the Good Shepherd this morning. The Whyos, the Dead Rabbits, the Tunnel Rats, all those thugs on the Lower East Side are telling the girls to run away. They're going to burn the place."

"Why the hell should we worry about a bunch of whores?" Rawdon snarled.

"If that's the way you and your fellow revolutionists think, I don't want to have anything to do with your shining message. I don't believe, I will never believe, it justifies unleashing a mob that will rob and rape and murder innocent men, women and children. I saw that mob in action in 1863. I saw my father—and your father—fighting it. I saw the horror on their faces, afterward."

"That was different. We were fighting a civil war, brother against brother. In Pittsburgh no one was hurt by the revolutionists except the capitalists and their lackeys."

"What about those poor soldiers from Philadelphia who were shot in the back as they tried to get out of the city?"

"That's more of Pendleton's lies. They did the shooting. The mowed down fifty, maybe a hundred people with their Gatling guns."

Another rap of the front-door knocker. Rawdon answered it. He came back with a yellow cable in his hand. He read it and handed it to Genevieve.

ENROUTE HOME. URGE YOU TO GET GENEVIEVE OUT OF CITY IMMEDI-
ATELY. KEMBLE MANOR SAFEST PLACE.

FATHER

"Rushing back to rally the troops," Rawdon said. "But he'll be too late. By the time he arrives, there'll be a regiment of revolutionary soldiers waiting for him on the dock to arrest him for treason."

The cable said nothing about rallying troops. Jonathan Stapleton was concerned for her safety. "Rawdon," Genevieve snapped, "you are talking absolute nonsense. I'm beginning to think you're out of your mind."

Rawdon's face went blank again. There was no emotion on it, neither affection nor anger. "Get me something to eat," he rasped.

She fried a steak and some potatoes. She watched him wolf it down. Animal, she thought, with his hairy face, his chomping teeth. Her husband was a berserk feral animal. "Rawdon. You can't do it. I won't be able to bear the thought that I'm married to a man who's trying to destroy this city—this country. My father sacrificed his health, his peace of mind, his life, for this country."

"Why do you think he blew his brains out?" Rawdon snarled. "Because he realized it wasn't worth it. What kind of a country lets Jay Gould and William Vanderbilt and Tom Scott starve people? Who gave them the power? Swine like Rutherfraud B. Hayes, sitting down there in Washington calling himself a peacemaker."

He chomped the last of the steak and gulped the coffee. "It's all coming down, the whole rotten mess is going to come crashing down, President, Constitution, tycoons. Then we'll let the people decide what kind of government they really want."

The telephone tinkled. Rawdon had decided this new invention was worth the outrageous $250 a year they were charging for it. "Answer that," Rawdon said.

"Gen—this is Clay," said a sepulchral voice. All voices sounded sepulchral on this latest wonder of the age. "Is Rawdon there?"

"Yes."

"I want to talk to him."

"It's Clay," she called from the hall.

"Tell him to go to hell."

"He says—to go to hell." Her voice choked with tears.

"I'm coming up."

Back in the kitchen, Rawdon exploded when she told him Clay was on his way to the apartment. "I don't have anything to say to that gutless wonder," he said. "If this revolution fails, he'll be responsible. I've spent half of the past two days refuting his lies. He's defamed the workers of Pittsburgh and their dead. If he wasn't my former closest friend I'd have him killed."

"Rawdon!"

"That's the sort of thing a man does—when he loses his faith in a shining message. When he realizes the person he thought was the guardian of his ideals, the person he's shared his innermost soul with, tells him he's talking absolute nonsense."

He staggered to his feet. "I'm going to sleep. When your favorite reporter arrives, tell him to go away. If you weren't carrying my child I'd tell you to go with him."

He disappeared down the hall. She heard the thud of his body in the bed. Five minutes later, she peered into the room. He had gone to sleep with his grimy blood-smeared suit on. He had not even bothered to take off his shoes. Genevieve washed the dishes and the frying pan and sat there, rereading the stories in the newspapers, trying frantically to find the truth.

A knock. Clay stood there in the dim hall, looking as unshaven and bleary-eyed as Rawdon. His dark suit was a rumpled sooty mess.

"He told me to tell you . . . to go away," Genevieve said.

"Do you concur?"

"No. I need—I need to talk to someone, Clay."

He sat down in the kitchen and gratefully accepted a cup of coffee. He had not had much sleep, either, since he returned from Pittsburgh. His managing editor had rushed him down to the Lower East Side, to find out if a revolutionary uprising was brewing there.

"I walked into Justus Schwab's saloon at First Street and First Avenue. That's the unofficial headquarters of the Communist Party. There's big-bellied Justus himself at the bar, with his drawing of the Paris City Hall going up in smoke behind him—he claims he personally burned it down during the Commune. The place was packed with half—or maybe all—the Communists and anarchists in the city. Who's standing on a bar stool making a speech? My old friend Rawdon Stapleton—he's telling them that everything I wrote about Pittsburgh was a pack of lies. There was no looting, no drunkenness. It was a model revolutionary uprising."

"Did you contradict him?"

"You bet I did. Rawdon called me a capitalist puppet, and they threw me head first into the street. I think I may be finished with the Stapletons. I don't like people who lie to me—or accuse me of telling lies."

This outburst left Genevieve floundering in new confusion, worse ignorance. She knew nothing about a Stapleton—was it the General?—lying to him. It also meant—if she believed him—that Rawdon had lied to her about Pittsburgh.

"You think what happened . . . doesn't justify a revolution?"

"That's not my job, to decide that sort of thing," Clay said in a hard empty voice. "I'm a man without a country. I just report what I see and hear, and let other people decide what it means."

No, Genevieve thought. That attitude was as wrong as Rawdon's berserk idealism. It was going to shrivel Clay's soul. She suddenly glimpsed how bitter, lonely, lost he was in this chaotic American world.

"Why are you here, Clay? If that's what you really feel."

"In spite of the compliments Rawdon's paid me on my reporting, I feel a certain debt to him—and his goddamn father—for the friendship they've shown me in the past. I came directly here from police headquarters, where Superintendent Walling told me just how much he knows about Rawdon's plans for the Subtreasury and what Schwab and his WPUS friends are going to try to do tonight in Tompkins Square. He's got informers inside the WPUS and all the anarchist splinter groups. He had ten undercover men in Schwab's last night when I was arguing with Rawdon."

"That won't stop Rawdon."

"Then he's going to get himself killed. They've got Gatling guns in every door of the Subtreasury."

Genevieve began to weep. She hated herself for it. But she could not deny her helplessness. "Clay—he's said terrible things to me too. This whole thing is so awful. Don't leave me, please. I can't deal with him."

Clay walked into the hall. "Rawdon!" he shouted. "I want to talk to you."

He returned to the kitchen and sat down. In less than a minute, Rawdon glowered in the doorway. "Didn't you tell him to go away?" he croaked at Genevieve.

"She told me, but I refused to go. What are you going to do? Call the police?"

"I'll throw you the hell out of here by the back of the neck," Rawdon rasped.

"Before we get to that, maybe you ought to listen to me," Clay said. "If not for the sake of your own arrogant carcass, then for your wife and her unborn child."

"I begin to sense an atmosphere of collusion here," Rawdon said, glaring at Genevieve.

"I asked Clay to stay and speak to you," Genevieve said, hearing—and hating—the tremor in her voice.

"In other words, you believe him and you don't believe me about what happened in Pittsburgh."

She avoided Rawdon's glare. "I think Pittsburgh is irrelevant. I asked Clay to stay and talk to you about what's happening in New York."

"Pittsburgh isn't irrelevant! If you believed I told you the truth about what happened there, if you believed what I told you about him being a bought-up, sold-out liar, you would have slammed the door in his face."

"Rawdon," Clay said, "before you wreck everything, listen to me."

His voice was as husky, he was as close to tears, as she was, Genevieve realized numbly. Did Rawdon have that much power over him too?

"I'll give you five minutes for auld lang syne, then out you go," Rawdon said, sitting down at the table with his arms folded across his chest.

Curtly, coldly, Clay told Rawdon how much the police knew about his violent scheme and what they intended to do about it. "Walling's got a battle plan all worked out. It'll be martial law and no quarter the minute you try anything. He showed me cables your father sent from Venice to the mayor and the governor, backing him to the hilt."

"Do you really think you can frighten me with the august name of General Stapleton?" Rawdon snarled. "Now that you mention him, Pendleton, did he pay you five thousand dollars to smear Gould and Hayes?"

"No," Clay said.

"How much did Cassatt pay you to tell those lies about Pittsburgh?"

"Not a cent. I didn't tell any lies."

Rawdon turned to Genevieve. "Do you still believe him?"

A deep flush was darkening Clay's haggard face. Was it the sign of a bad conscience? Genevieve did not know. She writhed in a torment of ignorance.

"You son of a bitch," Clay said. "I'll make you an offer. Come down to Tompkins Square with me now. I'm covering the rally. If your Communist friends start anything, I'll join your goddamn revolution. I'll go with you to the Subtreasury. If I survive I'll write your shining manifesto."

"Agreed," Rawdon said.

"Clay—" Genevieve said.

"Don't worry, Gen. Nothing will happen," Clay said. "The Communists are a bunch of sauerkraut-eating windbags. When they see what Walling's got ready for them, they won't say boo."

"Let's go," Rawdon said.

They left her there, left Genevieve, the superfluous, ignorant pregnant female, alternately raging and weeping. Finally she sank into a drained, exhausted calm. She wandered dazedly around her apartment trying to make sense out of what was happening.

She stood at the window, gazing downtown over the darkened roofs, listening for the sound she dreaded: the mindless roar of the mob. But she heard only the hazy murmur of the city at night, punctuated by an occasional crash or clatter or shout. She remained deep in ignorance, as swallowed by it as the city by the darkness. She sat down on the couch and tried to read some poetry. It was impossible. She could not concentrate on anything.

Suddenly Rawdon was standing beside her. She must have fallen asleep on the couch. He had lit a lamp, and the light struck her in the eyes. She raised her hand against the glare. There seemed to be a kind of aureole around his head. It was just the aftereffect of the glare. But she remembered another aureole, a boy-man's face beside a sun-bright pond. Was it all a trick, an accident of the eyes and heart?

"What happened?" she asked.

"Nothing," Rawdon said, his voice only a remnant now, a whispered croak. "Or, as I'm sure you want to hear, everything went exactly as Pendleton said it would happen. Before the meeting started, Police Superintendent Walling dragged Justus Schwab and the other speakers up on a roof where he'd set up a command post. He told them he had a hundred plainclothes detectives in the crowd and if there was any trouble they had orders to make sure the people on the platform were the first casualties. There were six hundred police with clubs ready, surrounding the square. Two blocks away, there were two regiments of National Guard, with Gatling guns and cannon. The speakers expelled a lot of hot air about the rights of the workers. But they made a point of saying the protest should be peaceful. Everyone went home. It's all over."

"Really—over?"

"Really over. My friend Ammon will sit in Pittsburgh for a few more days, waiting for the money that could have changed everything. His men will start thinking about their jobs, about feeding their families, and drift away. The police and the National Guard officers will come out of hiding in Pittsburgh and Chicago and St. Louis and arrest the leaders of the Workingmen's Party. They'll blame the riots on the Communists. Foreigners. Native Americans would never try to burn the country down. Oh no."

Suddenly the mockery vanished from Rawdon's unshaven face. She saw his grief, his enormous disappointment. The exhausted remnant of a voice spoke again: "How could you do that to me, Gen?"

"What did I do?" she asked, simultaneously thinking, *You know.*

"You made a fool of me. You let Pendleton make a fool of me. You didn't care about the shining message."

Rational, Genevieve reminded herself. It was important, it was vital, to remain rational. "Rawdon—the shining message is just a phrase."

"Just a phrase—between you and me?"

A blunder. But she did not know how to retreat, even though the ragged voice ripped at her heart.

"It's the essence of what I dreamt of doing with my life. It's why I needed you. I didn't—I don't have faith in the ideal. I have no faith inside me whatsoever, except what you gave me once. That's what I wanted you to stay home here and protect for me. A phrase? I love you is a phrase. Are you ready to dismiss that too?"

What was she supposed to say? How was she supposed to affirm her love for this man when he had made her powerless and ignorant and mocked her ignorance and then accused her of misusing or abusing a totally imaginary ability to preserve his ideals?

"Rawdon, I am not some supernatural creature. You're talking nonsense again."

Rawdon had advanced halfway across the room toward her. Her words froze him. "I finally see it," he said. "I finally see what a fool I've been about you from the beginning. There isn't any love or any idealism in that shrunken rational soul of yours. You're a sad copy of your mother. The mouth without the looks."

Scalded, seared. Those were the only words that described what these accusations did to Genevieve. She felt as if Rawdon had flung boiling water or hot coals in her face. No love, no idealism, in the soul of Benjamin Dall's daughter? A copy of her mother? How could a man with any pretension to love say such abominable things?

"Maybe I've been a fool about you from the beginning, too!"

My God, that clang in her voice. It was an echo of another metallic sound drifting across the years from Mississippi. Her mother's voice, arguing with her father.

Rawdon's lips compressed. The torn voice whispered from the hairy face again, "Well. We understand each other."

He vanished into the darkness beyond the lamplight.

"Where are you going?" she called.

"To get drunk," he said.

"Rawdon, wait—"

The front door slammed. Genevieve sat there thinking: it was not her fault. She was powerless, ignorant.

But the clang in her voice. It was unmistakable, unforgettable, unforgivable. "Oh Rawdon," sobbed the true woman. "I'm sorry. I'm sorry."

SEVEN

Another wedding!

The younger generation was marrying at a spectacular pace. A month ago, on the first Sunday in March, Cynthia had sat in a less prominent pew in Grace Church watching Alice Gansevoort marry Isaac Mayer. Even though Isaac had converted to the Episcopal Church, Alice's father still opposed the match and had refused to attend the ceremony. But Alice's blond beauty had made it the wedding of the year.

Now Cynthia was sitting in the front pew while another bride came up the aisle. This young woman had Jonathan Stapleton as a substitute father. Eleanor Dall was marrying Hal Bradford. The beefy, beaming groom awaited her at the altar, backed by his smiling best man, Rawdon Stapleton. The contrast between Rawdon and Hal was striking. They looked like Don Giovanni and his vulgar servant Leporello. What irony that trim elegant Lionel Bradford should have such a crude, hulking son.

Not that Hal's looks mattered much. Eventually he would inherit twice, perhaps three times as much money as Rawdon. He would be one of the wealthiest men in New York. Beside Cynthia, Margaret Dall looked beatific enough to ascend into heaven. Was there another woman in New York who had married her two daughters so well?

Across the aisle, Lionel Bradford was not looking very beatific. He had made a strenuous effort to talk his son into marrying Cecilia Schermerhorn's lumpy-faced daughter, Grace. Studying his doleful face, Cynthia felt a twinge of guilt.

Last October Rawdon had persuaded her to enter the fray on Eleanor's behalf. Not that she needed much persuasion to seize the opportunity to even the score with Cecilia Schermerhorn. Cynthia had invited Eleanor to give a musicale—she sang and played the piano beautifully—at Stuyvesant Square to which Mrs. Stapleton invited forty of the best names in New York society. Hal had been dazzled and proposed before the champagne reception ended. Cynthia still relished Katherine Kemble Brown's remark that she had shown people that Wall Street was not the only place where millions of dollars changed hands.

This flicker of exhilaration vanished as Jonathan and Eleanor reached the head of the aisle. He lifted her veil and bent to give her a fatherly kiss. A murmur ran through the pews. With her glowing red hair, her creamy white complexion, her startling figure, Eleanor had become one of the most attractive young women in New York. In the pew behind Cynthia she heard Katherine Kemble Brown whisper, "She's the image of her mother." Cynthia was more interested in the juxtaposition of her husband's gloomy profile and Rawdon's handsome sardonic face. Charlie's face. It stirred painful thoughts of a ruined night in Venice, a confession she would never make.

They had abandoned Venice the next day and raced to London. English newspapers were crammed with stories of burning American cities and predictions of the dissolution of the United States. Jonathan had left her with Madeline Terhune and sailed for New York.

Then the great continent-wide explosion had fizzled. A rally of angry workers that English reporters had predicted would wreck New York went off peacefully. The next day all the railroad tycoons except Jay Gould rescinded their pay cuts and the strikers went back to work. Rioters were arrested, order was restored in other cities.

Suddenly the English reporters were giving all the credit for rescuing peace to the South. If the ex-Confederates had joined the strikers and rioters in the North, the federal government would have collapsed. But not a shot had been fired, not a factory or railroad car burned, below the Mason-Dixon Line. It was, as Cynthia remarked to Madeline Terhune, enough to make you wonder if God was trying to tell Jonathan Stapleton something.

But Jonathan Stapleton was not listening. Instead of the penitence she expected, his first letter insisted that the crisis had been real and only the courage of Police Superintendent Walling had saved New York and the country. The rest of the letter was a denunciation of President Hayes and—of all people—his son Rawdon, whom he accused of encouraging the revolutionists. In a final paragraph, which struck Cynthia as an afterthought, he suggested she come home and spend the rest of the summer with him at Kemble Manor.

She had ignored him. She and Madeline Terhune continued to enjoy the hospitality of various English country houses until the end of September. She had a delightful time fending off seductions by no fewer than three baronets, riding to hounds, and playing opposite Madeline in several dramatic skits. Amateur theatrics were the rage among the English upper classes.

She had come home to find her husband more embroiled than ever in the political war with Rutherford B. Hayes. It now seemed reprehensible to Cynthia, as well as futile. Even the *New York Times*, that bastion of Republicanism, agreed that the President had a perfect right to ignore Senator Conkling's tirades and pursue his policy of reconciling the South—and restoring honesty to the Republican Party.

If proof of Jonathan's futility were needed, it was Theodore Roosevelt's decision to side with the President. Two weeks ago he had accepted Hayes's appointment as collector of federal customs in New York, replacing Senator Conkling's toady, Chester A. Arthur. If people as fair-minded, as honest as Theodore supported honesty and reconciliation, how could Jonathan continue to back someone as crooked as Conkling? The *Herald* had hailed Roosevelt's appointment as a wonderful opportunity to cleanse the "Augean stables" of Republican corruption in the Custom House. Without the millions in graft Conkling and his followers drew from it, the paper predicted the Senator's political demise and the rout of the Stalwarts.

Cynthia watched Eleanor and Hal exchange their wedding vows. Perhaps none of it mattered. Perhaps she should stop mourning the expectations she had taken to Venice. Already her anger had cooled into sullen resentment. Eventually that would dissolve into resignation. She and Jonathan Stapleton would become man and wife again, lovers of sorts, going through the motions of affection year after dreary year.

What awful thoughts to be having at a wedding.

The organ boomed; a beaming Mr. and Mrs. Bradford swept down the aisle. The reception at Delmonico's was a confusing disorderly affair. Rawdon, Clay Pendleton and their fellow Princetonians served Hal Bradford champagne laced with brandy, and he got disgracefully drunk. Lionel Bradford watched the proceedings in a bemused bitter way, never making the slightest attempt to control his son.

Mrs. Dall tried to make light of Hal's drunkenness, but Genevieve almost created a scene. She stormed over to her mother's table and said, "This is what's going to happen to them every day for the rest of their lives!"

Genevieve had not been well since the birth of her son last November. It had been a difficult delivery, and afterward she had sunk into an alarming melancholy. She still looked drawn and nervous, although Mrs. Dall had just finished telling Cynthia that the baby was a dream, he never cried or fussed and was already sleeping most of the night.

Jonathan finally intervened in the mess Rawdon and his friends were making of Hal Bradford. He told Rawdon with some vehemence to take Hal upstairs to one of the private dining rooms and sober him up. By this time the wedding breakfast had been served and most of the guests were dancing.

Cynthia sat down with Eleanor, thinking she would be upset to see her husband in such a deplorable condition. But she was perfectly composed. "Hal has a great many faults," Eleanor said. "But none that can't be corrected."

Cynthia was startled by such unromantic coolness in a bride. She was even more amazed by Eleanor's next remark. "Now that I'm a married woman," she said, "I hope we can be friends. I've always admired you."

"Thank you. I'm always in search of friends."

"I'll need help—advice—in decorating my house. We're going to build on West Fifty-fourth Street. I don't know any woman in New York who can match your taste. In art, in decorating, in clothes."

"I'm sure there are many women who do," Cynthia said. "But I'll be delighted to help. Perhaps you'd like to join the little-theater group I've been organizing. We could use someone your age. We're all a bit ancient to play ingenues."

"I'd be thrilled," Eleanor said. "I've always been fascinated by the theater. I think I might have become an actress if Mother hadn't been appalled by the mere thought of it. To some extent a woman's whole life is a performance, don't you think?"

"Not . . . entirely," Cynthia said. "But I suppose there's some truth to it."

"I think there's a great deal of truth to it. Do you remember the song from *The Black Crook*, 'You Naughty Naughty Men'?"

Cynthia nodded. Eleanor had sung it at her musicale.

"I've always thought that summed up woman's lot. Especially the last verse."

Eleanor sipped her champagne and casually recited it:

> *"But with all your faults we clearly*
> *Love you wicked fellows dearly.*
> *Yes, we dote upon you dearly.*
> *Oh! You naughty naughty men!*

"No woman really believes that. But it's what men want to hear."

"I'm afraid so," Cynthia said, trying to sound offhand. This young woman was as thoroughly cynical about men, as Madeline Terhune.

Rawdon returned to the ballroom and strolled through the dancers toward their table. "There's another reason I feel close to you," Eleanor said.

"Rawdon?"

"He told me about your first marriage to his uncle."

Was Eleanor saying that she was in love with Rawdon the way she assumed Cynthia was still forlornly in love with Charlie Stapleton? Before Cynthia could pursue the topic, Rawdon was leaning over them.

"Your beloved will be all right in an hour or so, Mrs. Bradford," he said. "Pendleton's pouring enough coffee down his gullet to float that Cunarder you're sailing on tomorrow morning. In the meantime let's dance the day away!"

Cynthia watched Rawdon and a beaming Eleanor whirl into a Strauss waltz. For a moment she felt a confusing surge of regret, of yearning for their youthful abandon. On the other side of the room, her husband was talking to Blackwell Brown, Katherine Kemble Brown's cadaverous husband. Both wore solemn frowns.

In the same line of sight, she saw Genevieve Dall sitting at a table, watching her husband dance with Eleanor. It occurred to Cynthia that Rawdon had not danced with her once.

"Shall we imitate them?" Lionel Bradford was leaning over her.

"Why not? Even if we creak a little."

"You've been spending too much time with our mutual friend, Madame Terhune. Age is on her mind, day and night."

There was some truth to that. Madeline did talk a great deal about growing old. "I'm bitterly angry with her," Bradford said. "She never told me you were in England until you were back home under lock and key in Stuyvesant Square."

"You would have come all that way on the mere hope?"

"Nothing induces ardor in a beautiful woman more than a distant husband. I presume the General rushed home to save the republic?"

"Yes."

"For a while I thought it was about to disappear. But I would have willingly let it collapse for a weekend in the west of England with you. A man like me can always find another country. A weekend or a week with a beautiful intelligent woman is much more difficult."

"If you say one more outrageous thing, this dance will end."

They waltzed in silence for a while. Suddenly Bradford began talking in a very different voice. "I think what troubles me most is your ingratitude. Louisiana is free. Your brother and his fellow ex-Confederate are getting rich here in New York. What have I received for my reward? You seduce my son into marrying this red-haired doxy, no doubt on your husband's orders."

"Nothing of the sort. He disapproves of the match as much as you do."

"But not, I'm sure, of the money that Hal brings to it. Money that he or his son Rawdon will now control."

"Jonathan doesn't have the slightest influence over Rawdon. You're not really in touch with how people like the Stapletons think, Lionel. Money is not their first consideration."

"I believe money is everyone's first consideration. But I will freely admit that there are other things in life to which we attach importance. Gratitude is one of them. Another is the truth. Would you tell me why I am still a beggar at my lady's gate?"

"You're not a beggar. You're a friend. A dear friend."

"But I want to be more than that."

"I'm afraid that's impossible."

Bradford stopped dancing. They stood there, while couples swirled around them. In a low intense voice, he said, "I've never paid the slightest attention to that word—'impossible.' " He wheeled and strode across the dance floor, and out of the ballroom.

Bemused, confused, Cynthia sat down with Mittie Roosevelt and Katherine Kemble Brown. It was the first time she had seen Mittie in weeks. She had come to the wedding with Bamie, her older daughter; Theodore was in Washington conferring with the President on the Senate hearings to confirm his nomination for collector of customs. Cynthia began apologizing for being such a poor visitor. Once, she had rarely missed a Tuesday, Mittie's day to receive callers. "I've hurled myself into my theatrical career," she said.

Cynthia thought Mittie looked forlorn. She was a bit too old for the amateur theater group Cynthia had founded and much too shy to perform in public anyway. With Madeline Terhune's help via the mails from London, Cynthia had persuaded Bronson Howard and other playwrights to let them produce scenes from their plays, with the understanding that the proceeds would go to charity. Alva Vanderbilt was one of their most enthusiastic participants. They used the ballroom of her magnificent new house on the corner of Fifth Avenue and Fifty-second Street for their performances.

"I thought your acting in *The Gilded Age* was marvelous," Bamie Roosevelt said.

"I'm not sure I like the idea of women from our best families pretending to be actresses," Katherine Kemble Brown said.

"Now, Katherine," Mittie said, "don't be so old Knickerbockerish. You sound like some of my Roosevelt relatives."

Cynthia turned away to watch the dancers. Blue, yellow, violet, the gowns swirled past. "I wish Theodore were here," she said. "No one but Lionel Bradford's asked me to dance." She wanted to be part of that laughing prancing throng. She wanted a man's arms around her waist.

Mittie placed her hand on Cynthia's arm. "Can I see you tomorrow morning? There's something I'd like to discuss."

"Of course. At eleven?"

Rawdon smiled down at her. "Stepmother. Are you willing to risk your husband's disapproval by dancing with his despised radical older son?"

"My father had a saying, 'All things are sweetened by risk,'" Cynthia replied.

The orchestra struck up a polka. The musicians were definitely playing for the young people. For twenty minutes Rawdon whirled her around the floor, telling her about his revolutionary adventures in Pittsburgh and New York. He made it all sound amusing. He claimed that he pretended to egg the anarchists and Communists on, simply to get a good story. He had explained it all to James Gordon Bennett, Jr., at the *Herald* and they decided it might be better if he avoided politics for a while. He was now covering Wall Street.

The music stopped and Jonathan appeared on the floor to ask if a husband could have at least one dance with his wife. Half an hour later the senior Stapletons were on their way back to Stuyvesant Square in their coach. Jonathan continued to growl about Hal's drinking. He seemed to agree with Genevieve that he was certain to make Eleanor miserable.

"She doesn't particularly love him, anyway," Cynthia said. "She told me as much today."

"My God!" Jonathan said. "You find no fault with that?"

"I find a great deal of fault with it. But I see no reason to blink at the fact that a great many women in this city marry for money and the marriages seem to flourish. Or at least survive."

"I don't give a damn what other people do. Eleanor is almost my daughter. I'm appalled that she could have such a mercenary approach to life."

They were practically snarling at each other. There seemed to be some implication that her failure to rebuke Eleanor made her responsible for the girl's attitude. "She's not *my* daughter," Cynthia said.

The quarrel left Cynthia sleepless for most of the night. She lay in her bed, listening to Jonathan pacing the floor next door. Where did he get his maddening habit of fretting over things beyond his control? Why couldn't he simply accept Eleanor Bradford for what she was, a shrewd cold girl who was determined to travel as far as her looks could carry her? Why couldn't he accept the United States of America as it was, money mad and utterly indifferent to causes and crusades, sick of hearing about the war and its glorious dead?

At 3 A.M. Cynthia finally took two ounces of chloral hydrate and sank into a drugged sleep. She arose at 10 A.M. with barely time to dress for her date with Mittie. She was twenty minutes late when she mounted the familiar stairway at 6 West Fifty-seventh Street, breathing the fragrant odor of lilies and gladiolas in great Chinese porcelain vases on the landings. Mittie was in her usual white muslin. But that was the only usual thing about her southern sister. Mittie's smile was feeble, her face drawn, her eyes red-rimmed.

Cynthia seized her hand and pressed the palm to her lips. "Mittie dearest," she said, "what's wrong?"

Mittie made sure her door was firmly shut, and they sat down. "I couldn't speak frankly to you yesterday with Bamie there. I don't want any of the children to know how worried I am about Theodore. If the ordeal in Washington goes on much longer, he's going to break down."

In anguished, often disconnected sentences, Mittie told Cynthia what was happening. Day after day, at the Senate hearings, Theodore was being subjected to savage humiliation by Roscoe Conkling. President Hayes had nominated Theodore without Conkling's approval. "According to the rules of the Senate, this is something called a breach of privilege," Mittie said. "That means most of the senators feel Conkling is entitled to torment Theodore. No one gave him the slightest hint of this problem before he accepted the nomination."

Again and again Theodore would be summoned to hearings, then told they had been canceled. When hearings were held—perhaps once out of the five times that they were scheduled—Theodore was subjected to incredibly abusive cross-examination. The ordeal was taking a terrific toll on him. He had lost twenty pounds, he was unable to sleep, he was wracked by nausea and agonizing stomach pains.

"I encouraged him to accept the appointment," Mittie said. "I could see how little he has to do, with the children grown. His newsboys and other charities weren't enough to satisfy a man of his energy and intelligence. Also —it was a way of helping President Hayes win independence from Roscoe Conkling and the other enemies of the South in the Senate."

There was the heart of the matter, the reason why Mittie was seeking Cynthia's help. "I would never dream of asking you to involve yourself if I didn't honestly believe Theodore's life was at stake. Your husband is close to Senator Conkling. Would you—could you—intercede with him for Theodore?"

"Of course I will."

"I have no illusion that he can change the Senator's mind about the appointment. I just want him to end the ordeal one way or another."

Mittie began to weep. "All these years since the war, I've never truly loved Theodore. I've tried. But there was a wall between me and my feelings. As though my heart were in a kind of tomb somewhere in my body. This ordeal —the noble way he's borne it—has freed me to feel love for him again. Which only makes it more unbearable."

It was the first time Mittie had ever spoken so frankly to Cynthia about her marriage. Cynthia had a sense of reaching a turning point in her life, of passing from youth to maturity, ending her role as younger sister. "My dearest friend," she said, "if I have any influence with my husband, something will be done, I guarantee it."

Riding home, Cynthia gradually became aware of the contradiction at the heart of that extravagant pledge. There was a potential war lurking between the words "if" and "guarantee." The mere possibility of refusal made Cynthia furious. No matter what Jonathan thought about Theodore Roosevelt and his politics, he had to do something!

That night when Jonathan came home Cynthia was waiting for him in the parlor in a new dinner dress, a dark-red faille. She wore the diamond brooch he had given her shortly after their return from New Orleans in 1876—a reminder of a previous capitulation. He paused in the doorway and looked at her in a puzzled weary way that made her hopes sink.

"I used to think when you stared at me that way, you were undressing me in your mind," she said.

It took him a moment to recover from his surprise. "That's not a sin between married folks," he said, dropping into a wing chair. Cousteau served them sherry and he sank a little deeper into the cushions. "I'm in need of consolation. I lost another hundred thousand dollars to Jay Gould today."

"I'm sure you'll get it back tomorrow," she said.

"I wonder. What would you do if I undertook to fight that monster and lost everything? Would you leave me?"

She sensed he was not entirely joking. For a moment she felt irritated. Was he recalling their acrid exchange about Hal Bradford and Eleanor?

"What about my comfortable little fortune? Would you risk that too?"

"No. I still keep that in a separate account, in your name. If you decided to stay around, you could put me on an allowance and complain when my bills at the Union League Club got too high."

"I don't think I'd enjoy being a virago."

They sipped sherry and she let the conversation wander in various directions. Jonathan fretted over the younger generation's fondness for hard liquor. Today, Clay Pendleton had visited him in his office to interview him about Jay Gould's campaign to drive the Vanderbilts out of Western Union. Although it was only three o'clock in the afternoon, Clay was somewhat drunk. "I used to worry about Rawdon going that way. It happens to so many reporters."

"Husband dear, I wish you'd stop trying to be father to half the country."

"I'm fond of Clay. Those stories he wrote in Pittsburgh stopped that riot from becoming a revolution."

A pause. He sipped his sherry. Then her comment about fatherhood swung his mind in an unexpected direction. "Lately I've wished we had a child. Some of our recent difficulties might never have happened."

"If we'd had a son, I'm sure we'd have fought over my spoiling him."

"I would have been worse with a daughter. I'd have been the most doting idiot of a father the world has ever seen."

"I agree. Beneath your stern exterior, General, you have a heart of mush. When you held your grandson in your arms at the christening, I thought you were going to burst into tears."

He frowned. "I was thinking about what the country would be like when he was my age—if there still is a country."

"For a long time, I thought our love was our child." Cynthia kept her eyes down and toyed with the stem of her wineglass.

"I would hope it still is," Jonathan said. Cynthia could not remember when she had seen him so stirred.

Cousteau announced dinner. As they walked to the dining room, Jonathan slipped his arm around her waist. Would the moment to ask him to help Theodore Roosevelt ever be more propitious? At the table, Cynthia found herself remembering the quarrel about going to Europe that they had had in this candlelit room. The memory somehow poisoned both the idea of reconciliation and the possibility of persuading him to help the Roosevelts.

At ten o'clock they went up the stairs arm in arm, pausing on the landing for a long deep kiss. In the bedroom Cynthia found it was too soon for the soaring, the ecstasy of Italy in happier days. She had to embellish her response with little sighs and cries—for Mittie's sake. There was nothing wrong with it, she told herself. She was blending two loves, for a noble purpose.

When it was over, Jonathan held her in his arms for a long time. "Two months ago, I almost lost hope. I almost abandoned happiness as even a possibility. But I couldn't stop loving you."

"I almost stopped, too," she whispered. "But now . . ."

She let him go, confident that tomorrow she would have the power to ask him anything. But in the morning, at Sunday breakfast in the sunny dining room, she hesitated again. Somehow she could not bear to risk a quarrel in this house now. She began to wish rather desperately that she could avoid the risk entirely. But she decided it was cowardice to hesitate any longer. As they left the table, she sighed dramatically and said, "My husband hasn't taken me for a drive in the park for months."

"Shame on him," Jonathan said.

In a half hour they were heading up Fifth Avenue in their barouche. In the Central Park the carriages literally swarmed. Sleek phaetons driven by fashionable young women competed for the road with sedate victorias containing actresses and ladies of even more questionable virtue. The poorer a woman's reputation, the more conventional was her choice of a carriage.

"I'm afraid Mittie is terribly disturbed about what Theodore is undergoing in Washington," Cynthia said.

"Is she, now? Why did she urge him to stick his head into the lion's mouth?"

"How do you know she did that?"

"Theodore told me. He asked my advice when Hayes offered him the appointment. I told him to refuse it. For the sake of his party—and his country."

"Jonathan—he *accepted* it for those two things. Above all for his country. Like a great many people, he's sick to death of the vicious malodorous politics conducted by Senator Conkling in the name of the Republican Party."

Jay Gould swept past in a high-wheeled victoria, his dumpy wife and several children beside him. He tipped his hat. Jonathan simply glared at him.

"I'm perfectly willing to admit that Senator Conkling has his flaws. But I tend to remember a speech he made after the battle of Chancellorsville, when General Lee had smashed up the Army of the Potomac for the third or fourth time. A lot of people wanted to negotiate peace at any price. Conkling stood up in the House of Representatives and gave those gutless wonders the courage to stay in the fight."

His voice was calm, almost reflective. He seemed removed from her. "I was in the House gallery that day. I thought then that Conkling was a man who cared about this country. I haven't seen him do anything that's changed my mind."

Oliver Cromwell followed the curving drive west toward the Mall. When Cynthia rode alone, she often stopped to stroll on this popular esplanade, or have an ice cream in the nearby casino. The Mall was jammed, mostly with young people. A band played military marches in the pagodalike music pavilion; on the right, the fountains arched streams of white spray toward the blue sky.

Jonathan took Cynthia's hand. "My dear," he said. "Please don't involve yourself in this political quarrel. There's a great deal at stake."

"Jonathan, the politics of the subject don't concern me in the least. My concern is for the husband of my dearest friend, who's being *crucified* for his honesty. I can't believe you won't at least try to help him."

"Theodore Roosevelt is not being crucified. He's being roughed up a little, that's all," Jonathan snapped. "He isn't the first and he won't be the last presidential appointment to get a going over from senators who don't like him."

"Jonathan, his health is being *destroyed.*"

She told him about Theodore's weight loss, his sleeplessness, his stomach pains. Jonathan turned his face away from her as she spoke. For a moment she thought he almost looked pleased.

"If you want my personal opinion, Theodore Roosevelt is a big baby who's never had to make his way in a man's world before. He ran out on the war and he quit a business career to spend most of his time as a sort of substitute mother to his children. Maybe he thought he had to do it because he had a wife who more or less resigned from her post. Now he thinks he can suddenly step on stage as a man of integrity and play the civic hero. I think he deserves a bellyache or two and I can't see any reason why we should worry about him."

"Jonathan! It's bad enough that you're abusing a man who's in torment. But when you slander his wife—my dearest friend . . . If you care about me, if your affection means anything, you will go to Washington and try to stop this dreadful business. If you refuse me—I swear I will never be able to love you again."

"Stop! Stop the carriage!" Jonathan roared. Oliver Cromwell hauled on the reins. The barouche slewed and almost overturned.

Jonathan sprang out of the carriage and pulled off his hat. For a moment she felt confused by the sunlight on his white hair. Old. Her old husband. But with manhood still in his face. Oh. That face, changing now, before her eyes, into the death mask. The slitted mouth, the cold gray impenetrable eyes. Had she created it? Was it her fault? Or was this the real man, emerging from his sentimental disguise again?

"I will not continue this discussion until you withdraw those last words."

"They're my deepest feelings. Beyond my control."

"Oliver," Jonathan said, "take Mrs. Stapleton home. I'm going for a walk."

"Yes sir, General."

Cynthia watched him stride across the green grass and up a small rise to a footpath. His limp seemed worse on the grass. He disappeared around a curve without looking back. She sat there, feeling bereft one moment, enraged the next.

"Shall we go home, Missus?"

"Yes."

For an hour, Cynthia sat in her room, trying to read. She skimmed the society newspaper, *Town Topics,* but the usual litany of scandals and intrigues and parties bored her. She called for the week's papers, and went through them, looking for accounts of Theodore Roosevelt's ordeal. None of the papers had the inner story, and only the *Herald* was sympathetic, lavishing praise on Roosevelt and condemning the senators who were blocking his appointment.

An hour later she heard Jonathan's steps on the stairs. But he did not knock on her door. She bathed and dressed for supper, half hoping a new gown would change her mood, without any real faith in the ritual. Instead of joining her for a sherry and a chat, Jonathan stayed in his room.

They ate the entire dinner in silence. It was a test of will. A half-dozen times, Cynthia had to struggle to suppress furious words. Her hand literally trembled when she picked up her wineglass. Over coffee she began to realize that Jonathan was winning. Silence was a kind of victory for him. If it continued, Theodore Roosevelt would go on suffering.

"I won't be treated this way! I'm not a child, Jonathan."

"If I thought you were, I wouldn't take seriously what you said in the park."

"I can't love a man who flaunts his inhumanity. Who lets politics dictate his response to the suffering of another human being."

An edge of anger entered his voice. "I told you—I won't discuss anything with you when you threaten me that way."

Cynthia welcomed his anger. It made her own fury more permissible. A wave of dark exhilaration flooded her body. No matter what it cost her, she would win this argument.

"I begin to think there's something ugly being concealed here. You need Senator Conkling to pass some bill that will help you in your quarrel with Jay Gould. A party trick that will help you get back that money you've lost. You're perfectly prepared to sacrifice a good man's life for a few hundred thousand dollars."

"You're wrong," Jonathan said, lowering his head, refusing to look at her.

"Perhaps it's a question of honor among thieves. Senator Conkling is privy to certain secrets concerning the theft of the presidency. Are you afraid to cross him, for fear that he might tell embarrassing stories to a newspaper-man?"

"No," he said, his head still lowered, an image of wrath—or guilt.

"Then what is it? Why are you conducting yourself in this cowardly way?"

Abruptly his head came up, but there was no gray fire in his eyes. Only a stony sadness. "Last night, it was all a lie, wasn't it? Even that stuff about our love being our child. It was all part of your little plan."

She was left gasping, bewildered by the pain those words caused. Conscience—where, how had conscience acquired so much power? Legrands were not supposed to have consciences. "It was—nothing of the sort. There might have been some—anticipation of your help. Your loving help. I was—so sure of it."

"You're a miserable liar."

"How can you sit there, saying such monstrous things, and possibly expect me to love you?"

"I obviously don't think you can—or will. I begin to wonder if you've ever loved me. If the whole thing hasn't been a performance from the moment I saw you on those stairs at Bralston."

The words, their implication, flung Cynthia back a dozen years. She was in the ruined garden behind the wrecked house, staring at the smashed sundial. A shrouded figure stood beside it. Destiny, fatality, whatever its name, it had been waiting for her there, all this time. In her husband's eyes, perhaps in her own eyes, she had become a courtesan after all.

"What a fool I've been, flagellating myself, tormenting my conscience for my sins," Jonathan raged. "When everything I thought was sacred between us means so little to you, you'd use it to persuade me to turn my back on what I *am*, what I suffered and persuaded others to suffer in a great cause. Even if you can't accept the cause, I was stupid enough to think you accepted, respected, my devotion to it."

I do. The words struggled in Cynthia's throat. But they could not be spoken. She could not cringe before this cold arrogant Yankee. She could not plead for mercy or understanding in the face of these atrocious insults.

"Instead, in return for a night in your bed, you expect me to throw away my political reputation for a man who never risked a hair of his head for his country and is ready to undo it to keep his wife—who I suspect loathes him as much as she loathes everyone else north of the Mason-Dixon Line—happy."

There it was, the central dogma of his creed, a man who sacrifices anything truly important for a woman is a coward and a fool. It was inextricably mingled with his hatred of the South and its people, still as raw and vicious as when she glimpsed it in Paris a decade ago.

"You despise me, don't you," she said. "In your deepest heart you've always despised me. You loathe everything southern, the South and its people."

"I didn't—I tried not to—but you've taught me I was wrong about that too. I wish you'd get out of my sight. Why don't you finish your dinner in your bedroom?"

"I will not be driven from my own dining room!"

"Your own dining room? Madam, since everything between us will now be on a mercenary basis, let me remind you that this is *my* dining room. You don't own a stick of this furniture, you don't own so much as one of these silver spoons. I paid for them. I paid for that dress you're wearing, the rings on your fingers, the necklace on your throat. Go upstairs and think about that."

"If I dreamt you would ever say such a thing to me, I never would have accepted a single gift from you! I would have worn what I could afford to buy from my own money—"

The face she hated and dreaded was confronting her at the other end of the table again. The death mask, with its slitted mouth, its icy hateful eyes. "Your own money?" the mouth snarled. "You never had a nickel of your own money. Charlie died a hundred thousand dollars in debt. I created that comfortable little fortune out of the delusionary idea that if you chose me freely there'd be some honest affection between us."

The revelation was so stunning, for a moment Cynthia could not breathe, much less think. He had lured her to New York with his Yankee money and overwhelmed her with his fraudulent attentions, all the while laughing to himself about the way he was acquiring this southern piece of goods at a bargain price. It was worse, infinitely worse, than her father's disposal of her to Charles Stapleton. Her heart might have been wounded, but at least she had not been treated like a fool.

To Jonathan, her astonished glare only signaled defiance. "I am ordering you as your husband—go to your room," he roared.

Still she could not move. Neither her mind nor her body could recover from the words she had just heard. Jonathan flung down his napkin and strode toward her. "By God, if you won't go I'll drag you."

He seized her by the arm and pulled her out of her chair. For a moment she dangled in midair in his powerful grip. Then her feet found the floor.

"The spoils of war," she said. "That's all I am, all I've ever been to you, isn't it."

His mouth fell open. He swayed as if she had just run a bayonet through him. "No, never," he gasped.

A guilty conscience speaking, if she had ever heard it. Calmly, deliberately, Cynthia pried his fingers from her arm and walked out of the dining room and up the stairs to the third floor.

Waiting for her in the upper hall was Lucy, her eyes wide with fright. "Mistress, are you hurt?" she whispered. "Did he hit you?"

"No. I'm perfectly all right, Lucy."

Out of the shadows in the rear of the upstairs hall emerged Cleopatra, looking equally terrified. "Let her go get Master Robert," she quavered. "He'll protect you."

"No! Go to your rooms," Cynthia said. "Go this instant."

In her bedroom, Cynthia realized she had not wept a tear. She was too appalled by what had just happened. All she could hear was Jonathan's sneering snarling voice: *Your own money? Your own dining room?* She saw herself in the sky parlor of the Metropolitan Hotel insisting that she pay for the champagne, telling him how much it meant to her, to be independent. She remembered the morning when she lay in her bed, thinking contentedly of the house as hers, her creation. When all he saw was his property, his possessions, bought by his money.

Bought, like his wife. It was all sham, his professions of love, his flattery about her beauty. All Jonathan Stapleton ever wanted from her was what her father got from the quadroons on Rampart Street in New Orleans. And the privilege of displaying her as his wife. Look at me, he said, when they walked into Delmonico's or Grace Church or the Academy of Music, look at me, a shot-up middle-aged wreck with a luscious wife like this. Look what I've brought back from the conquered South.

She had never escaped that shrouded figure in Bralston's garden, Cynthia Legrand had never left that cemetery where she vowed to escape her destiny. All these years, while she struggled to preserve some shreds of affection for this brutal Yankee, he had been living a lie with her. Now he had the outrageous gall to accuse her of hypocrisy.

Cynthia stopped pacing and looked around her. She was in her *bedroom.* Where her mother, where Mittie Roosevelt, where so many other women retreated when love failed or misled them. But she had not retreated here. She had been driven here by force. And she was not going to stay.

Just what she would do or think or feel she was not sure. She only knew that a different Cynthia Legrand Stapleton would leave this room tomorrow morning.

BOOK IV
1880–1890

ONE

"Mr. Edison says that eventually houses will not only be lit by electricity, we'll use it for heat—even for cooking. Isn't that marvelous?" Eleanor Dall Bradford said, busily hemming an infant nightgown.

"Maybe Genevieve can use it to galvanize her maid," Alice Gansevoort Mayer said, swiftly cross-stitching a nightcap.

"She's coming along very well," Genevieve said, struggling with the collar of an adult nightgown.

"That means they haven't sent for the police yet," Eleanor said.

"What in the world are you ladies talking about?" Mittie Roosevelt asked.

They were sitting in the sumptuous front parlor of the Roosevelt mansion on Fifty-seventh Street, sewing garments for indigent patients at New York Orthopedic Hospital. Since Theodore Roosevelt's death two years ago, the hospital had become Mrs. Roosevelt's favorite charity. Her husband had been one of Orthopedic's founders and its staunchest patron. There were a half-dozen other well-born young matrons in the semicircle, including Rosalind King Van Rensselaer, Georgianna Apthorpe Van Wyck and Helen Van Vorst Pell.

"We're discussing my sister's strange fondness for hiring ex-prostitutes as maids," Eleanor said.

"They're from the House of the Good Shepherd," Genevieve said. "They've been rehabilitated."

"The first one she hired stole half her wedding silver," Eleanor continued.

"One place setting," Genevieve said.

"I admire your idealism, but I doubt if I have your courage," Mrs. Roosevelt said, displaying a talent for gentle diplomacy. She obviously doubted Genevieve's sanity.

"They're all Irish," Alice said. "That alone disqualifies them as far as I'm concerned. I've found Germans are by far the best servants."

"Absolutely," Eleanor said. She made a habit of echoing Alice's opinions.

Genevieve defended the Celts. "My mother had Irish maids. With the right kind of supervision, they're excellent workers."

Georgianna Van Wyck agreed—perhaps because her husband's uncle had recently been elected mayor of New York with the help of the Irish vote. She said they had always hired Irish servants. The important thing was to make sure they were devout. Then they did not steal.

"I'm so disappointed my friend Mrs. Stapleton didn't come today," Mrs. Roosevelt said. "She promised me."

"Oh. I meant to tell you," Eleanor said, "Bronson Howard invited her to a rehearsal of his new play."

Alice leaned over and murmured in Genevieve's ear, "I hope that's all he invited her to." There were rumors flying all over New York about Cynthia Stapleton and a half-dozen men—including Lionel Bradford, Eleanor's father-in-law.

"She has so much energy," Mrs. Roosevelt said. "It wears me out, just thinking about her."

She aimed for a light tone, but Genevieve thought she sounded wistful. Cynthia Stapleton had recruited Genevieve and Alice and Eleanor for this charitable enterprise by telling them it was an act of compassion for her dearest friend. She had described Mrs. Roosevelt as distraught by the collapse and death of her husband, a victim of the ferocious war between the Stalwarts and the liberals in the Republican Party. He had died within a month of his humiliating rejection by the Senate for the post of collector of customs.

"Cynthia and the General came to little Charlie's birthday party," Genevieve said. "He almost lost his present when he called her Grandma."

"I don't blame her," Mrs. Roosevelt said, defending her missing friend. "I have no intention of letting any child call me that horrid name for at least twenty years."

"I must confess I never thought of her as very maternal. But she couldn't keep her hands off Laura. She must have held her in her arms for a good hour," Genevieve said.

"Cynthia loves children. My tribe adores her," Mrs. Roosevelt said. "How is your little girl's asthma?"

"She hasn't had an attack in a month now," Genevieve said.

"I sincerely hope you don't have to endure what we went through with young Theodore."

Cynthia and Mrs. Roosevelt had jointly terrorized Genevieve with the story of her older son's struggle with asthma. So far Laura's case had been mild, just a few rasps in the middle of the night, quickly halted by a dose of ipecac to make her vomit and break the seizure.

"I still don't know how Genevieve produced a baby as beautiful as Laura," Eleanor said.

"Rawdon takes all the credit for her," Genevieve said. "He claims she's a pure Stapleton. It's practically redeemed me in his eyes for failing to give him another son."

"This one had better be a girl, or I'm going to lodge an official protest with the Archangel Gabriel," Alice said. She patted her swelling stomach. Two years ago she had given birth to twin boys.

"It's getting to the point where I don't care about the sex. I just want a baby," Eleanor said plaintively. She had had three miscarriages in the past three years.

Putting the last stitch in her nightcap, Alice asked if anyone had seen the illustrations of the aesthetic look, the latest Parisian style, in the current issue of *Harper's Bazaar*. The look featured filmy garments in the style of ancient Greece. Mrs. Roosevelt thought only an actress would dare to wear such dresses in public.

"Your dear friend Mrs. Stapleton wore one to Lionel Bradfords' Twelfth Night Ball," Alice said.

"She comes very close to being an actress, as far as I'm concerned," Helen Pell said. "A very good one, I'll admit."

This launched an intense discussion of amateur theatrics, which had now become the rage in social New York. Eleanor let everyone talk, then announced that Mrs. Stapleton had invited her to play the lead in a forthcoming production of *Shenandoah*.

"If I want to see a play, I'd rather go to a professional production, at one of our theaters," Genevieve said.

This remark was greeted with almost universal disapproval. Genevieve stubbornly insisted that it made no sense for women to be putting on amateur plays in a city that had over forty professional theaters.

"Why does everything have to make *sense?*" Eleanor snapped.

"Our little shows are rather charming and, I think, a harmless diversion," Mrs. Roosevelt said.

There was the heart of the matter. Wealthy, bored society women had to have something to do, so why not perform in plays that were better produced downtown—or sew for the indigent sick, when manufacturers were turning out superior garments by the tens of thousands in factories?

On the mantel, a Dresden porcelain clock tinkled five strokes. Two plump maids appeared bearing trays of cucumber sandwiches, sweetmeats, cakes and a magnificent silver tea service.

Eleanor nibbled a chocolate cookie. "Do you ever hear from your friend Wellcombe?" she asked.

"Now and then," Genevieve said. "She likes California. She's found a woman lawyer who's letting her read for the bar in her office."

"I bet they keep her out of sight," Alice said. "She'd scare most clients away."

For the benefit of the other young matrons, Alice supplied a wry description of Wellcombe's ungainly manner, her dowdy clothes, her habit of "looking down that long Boston nose of hers if you weren't discussing something weighty like the meaning of life or the importance of the vote."

A year ago, after a fruitless attempt to read for the bar in Boston, Wellcombe had come to New York. Genevieve had tried to include her in their social circle, with disastrous results. Alice and Eleanor ridiculed her behind her back and sometimes to her face. The final touch had been a doomed attempt to match her with Clay Pendleton.

"You may all end up laughing out of the other sides of your mouths," Genevieve said. "Did you read in the papers the other day that Congress has authorized women lawyers to argue before the Supreme Court?"

"Who cares, except a few freaks like Wellcombe?" Alice said. "It's not as if we had a shortage of male lawyers. Why in God's name do women want to do things that men are already doing very well?"

There was overwhelming agreement from everyone in the room. Genevieve sat voiceless. Wellcombe's year in New York had almost demoralized both of them. Genevieve had been stunned to discover how vulnerable Wellcombe was to seeing her and Alice with babies in their arms. Wellcombe had grown positively moony over Clay Pendleton—until an awful night when Clay had apparently told her that he had no interest in marrying her or anyone else. Rawdon had found it amusing and had tormented Clay about his "conquest." He had shunned their company for the past six months.

"It seems to me the whole furor over women's rights is going the way of the abolitionists," Mrs. Roosevelt said. "Who has a kind word for them now?"

"*I* certainly don't," Eleanor said, practically daring Genevieve to say something.

For a moment Genevieve felt nothing but disgust, incredible, volcanic disgust—at her sister, at Alice, at their comfortable, smug, contented lives. But it was impossible, unthinkable, to snarl denunciations in Mrs. Roosevelt's elaborate parlor, with some of the most fashionable young women in New York watching her. Not for the first time, Genevieve swallowed her anger, her negative thoughts, and told herself to accept the world the way it was constructed. Three years ago, she had begged her husband to do the same thing, when it had looked as though he was going berserk. Could she do less now, in her woman's sphere?

The tea party began to break up. Alice and Genevieve thanked Mrs. Roosevelt for the delicious little feast, and Eleanor soon joined them in the hall. Outside, a nippy February wind swirled out of the Central Park. Alice urged Genevieve into the Mayer coach. "Rawdon says he'll sue me if you catch another cold," she said.

They jounced downtown over the ubiquitous cobblestones. "I really don't see much point to that sewing circle," Genevieve said.

It was the plainest statement she had made of her discontent. "Gen," Alice said, in the firm calm voice of a mother addressing a wayward child, "that is one of the best charitable activities in the entire city. I've had at least six women our age ask me how they could be invited to join."

"Absolutely," Eleanor said. "Where else can you sit in the same room with a Van Rensselaer, a Pell, a Van Wyck on such an intimate basis?"

Alice and Eleanor seldom stopped thinking—and talking—about social acceptance. Isaac Mayer had built Alice a handsome town house on West Fifty-third Street and together they were waging war on the dragon of anti-Semitism. Eleanor, whose almost identical town house was on West Fifty-fourth Street, was equally anxious about her status. The Bradford name still had a shoddy aura about it. Lionel Bradford's separation from his wife did not make things easier for them.

"How is Rawdon's grandmother?" Eleanor asked.

"Getting worse. There's really no hope," Genevieve said.

"I know it sounds awful, but Hal can barely wait for her to die and leave Rawdon some money. He hopes Rawdon will quit the newspaper business and come down to Wall Street with him."

"I don't think Rawdon is interested in Wall Street," Genevieve said.

"Really? That's all he writes about these days."

"That's his assignment. But his real ambition is to start his own newspaper. I'm quite certain that's what he intends to do, if his grandmother leaves him enough money."

They were on Forty-third Street, which now had two other apartment houses rising above the brownstone fronts. "Don't forget dinner on Thursday," Eleanor said.

"Yes," Genevieve said, without enthusiasm. Did Eleanor ever give a dinner party without inviting them? It was part of her plan to inveigle Rawdon into becoming Hal's partner.

Genevieve climbed the six flights to her apartment, vowing that she would wage war on any connection between Hal Bradford and her husband. Hal had not turned into the drunkard she had predicted, thanks largely to Eleanor's vigilance. But he was still an oaf—a rich, emptyheaded oaf.

In the kitchen, she found Kathleen McGuire, her maid, mashing vegetables for the children's dinner. The room was full of steam and unpleasant odors. Kathleen had obviously washed another load of diapers. "Good afternoon, Mrs. Stapleton," Kathleen said in her cheerful, respectful way. "Mr. Stapleton's home. He's in the nursery."

An unexpected pleasure. She seldom saw her newspaperman before midnight. Genevieve strolled to the nursery. Rawdon had his back to the door, bending over Laura's crib. "Hello," she said.

"Hello," Rawdon said, flicking the word over his shoulder. He went back to shaking a rattle at thirteen-month-old Laura, who was sitting up in her crib.

Genevieve stood there, feeling inexplicable pain. There was nothing wrong with a husband saying hello to his wife that way after four years of marriage. But she could not help remembering the Rawdon of their first married year, the impulsive high-spirited lover who pounced on her with unexpected kisses and hurled declarations of passion at her. That man had vanished in the chaotic days and nights of the summer of 1877.

The year of the riots was ancient history now, virtually forgotten by everyone except a few worriers like General Stapleton. But for Genevieve and Rawdon the great nonevent, the revolution that almost happened, was not so easily dismissed. It had inflicted invisible wounds on the true man and true woman.

After a month of drunken disappointment, Rawdon decided he had come perilously close to making a fool of himself and began to mock his own revolutionary pretensions. He was equally cynical of all other idealisms, from the woman's movement to organized religion to patriotism. Only Genevieve and Clay Pendleton knew what had really happened in Rawdon's soul. Clay had joined her in berating, arguing, pleading with Rawdon to accept the American world as it was.

Rawdon had finally accepted it—on his terms. He had accepted his wife, the betrayer of the shining message, the same way. She was part of the real world, the mother of his son, and now of his daughter. But Genevieve sensed, again and again, that something unspoken had been subtracted from the acceptance. This was one of those moments—when "hello" was flicked at her like a stone.

"Where's Charlie?" she asked.

"I don't know," Rawdon said. "Whining in the parlor, probably."

She rushed into the parlor. Three-year-old Charles Gifford Stapleton II was standing in the corner, his head pressed against the wall. "Darling, what's wrong?" Genevieve asked, leading him over to the couch.

His big luminous eyes, her father's eyes, gazed at her, full of tears. "Papa scared me again. Then he sent me away."

"How did he scare you?"

"He threw me up in the air. He threw me up too high, Mama."

"Go see Kathleen. She'll give you some milk and a cookie."

Genevieve marched back to the nursery. "Rawdon, you must stop frightening that child to death. You'll ruin his nervous system."

Rawdon ignored her and continued to tease Laura with the rattle. The trouble with Charlie had begun at his christening, when General Stapleton had pronounced the baby a Dall. It was obvious enough, from his delicate bone structure, his russet hair, his big gray eyes. Rawdon suddenly wondered why he had named him Charles Gifford Stapleton in memory of his heroic uncle. When Charlie began toddling, Rawdon started playing rough games with him. He whirled him around his head and tossed him up to the ceiling. He was now convinced that the boy lacked courage because he stiffened with fear every time his father picked him up.

"She's wet. You better change her," Rawdon said, and strolled out of the nursery.

When Genevieve caught up with him in the bedroom, he was putting on his evening clothes. "Oh. You won't be home for supper?"

Rawdon shook his head. "Bennett's taking me—actually I'm taking him— to a dinner at Jay Gould's."

"Ugh," Genevieve said.

Rawdon ignored her as totally as he had just ignored her plea for Charlie. She renewed the plea and he wearily consented. "Okay, okay. It's just hard for me to accept that I've got a nancy for a son."

"He's nothing of the sort. He's only three years old. You're being ridiculous, Rawdon."

"He plays with dolls."

"There's nothing wrong with that. You probably played with them, too, at his age."

"Never. I played with toy soldiers. I spent fifty dollars to buy him the best set of toy soldiers in the country for Christmas. He's barely looked at them."

"He's too young. Give him another year or two."

Rawdon struggled with his white bow tie. With a curse, he asked Genevieve's help. As she tied it, standing within an inch of his big male body, she felt a sudden wish for him to put his arms around her. But his hands remained impatiently on his hips.

"Have you talked to your father?" she asked.

"No," he said.

"He called again last night. You should talk to him, Rawdon."

Rawdon said nothing. His expression was grim.

"I don't see why you can't do something."

Rawdon walked to the mirror to adjust his tie.

"It makes me feel so awful thinking of your grandmother dying this way, refusing to see her only living son. You could do something, I'm sure of it. She'd listen to you."

"In the first place, the General's getting exactly what he deserves. In the second place, I can't change her mind. No one can. If she thought I was switching to his side, I'd be out of her will tomorrow."

"It's all so meaningless now—"

"Maybe it is to you. It isn't to her—or to me. If you'd stop and think about it, maybe it isn't so meaningless to the country either. Fanatics like your heroic father and mine killed a million white men to free a lot of ignorant niggers. Maybe they deserve to suffer."

Genevieve felt pain deep in her body. How could Rawdon sneer at her father that way, knowing how he died, how she felt about him? "Rawdon— that's a terrible thing to say."

"It happens to be what most of the people in the country believe, these days."

The real world. Once more Rawdon was pushing it in her face. The America of 1880 with its obsession with money and pleasure and its indifference to moral crusades.

"How was the bandage rolling at Mrs. Roosevelt's?" Rawdon asked, shrugging on his long-tailed black evening coat.

"We don't roll bandages. We sew," Genevieve said. "It was boring, as usual."

"Dr. Beard thinks a little boredom is good for you."

"Dr. Beard could be wrong."

"I don't think so," Rawdon said, strolling to the door.

"Give Charlie a kiss before you go."

"Okay."

Genevieve sat down at her dressing table. On it were a photograph of her father in his uniform, the empty sleeve folded across his chest, and a photograph of her mother, standing before the ruins of the Roman Forum. What irony, that her mother should have put her into the hands of Dr. George Miller Beard, specialist in the nervous diseases of women.

A year ago, just after Laura's birth, her mother had departed for Europe with Katherine Kemble Brown. It had seemed like a lovely idea, these two girlhood friends, neither of whom had made particularly happy marriages, enjoying themselves as grande dames in the capitals of Europe for six months. A cable from Rome exploded this sentimental vision. Margaret Dall was dead. The Roman Campagna was as ridden with malaria as the swamps of Mississippi. The deadly fever had recurred with unparalleled savagery and killed her in a week.

All Genevieve could think of was the hardhearted feelings she had nurtured against her mother for her father's suicide. Day and night, words of forgiveness, of apology, whispered in her head, tormenting her because they would never be spoken now. Laura's recent birth compounded her woe. Rawdon had been blatantly disappointed to find himself the father of a girl when he wanted another boy, a son who would be a true heir, unlike whiny Charlie.

Genevieve collapsed into a melancholy far worse than the one that had followed Charlie's birth. She was unable to sleep and was subject to fits of violent weeping for no discernible reason. Rawdon had sent her to Dr. Beard, author of the popular book *American Nervousness*. Dr. Beard shipped her off to the New Jersey shore for a summer of tranquility and gave her a syrupy medicine which put her to sleep instantly. As an additional prescription he advised her to avoid overstimulation.

"Mama, look. Papa gave me a penny for candy. Can we go buy some?" Charlie asked.

"No. It's almost time for bed."

"I don't want to go to bed!"

More tears in those big pleading eyes, this time in protest against the tyranny of mothers.

"Go play with your soldiers. Go!"

Charlie fled, sobbing. Genevieve sat there, looking at herself in the mirror, feeling miserable. Stop, she told herself. Stop accusing yourself of being a failed daughter, a second-rate mother, a third-rate wife.

In the hall, the telephone tinkled. A moment later Kathleen McGuire called, "For you, Mrs. Stapleton."

"Is there any news from New Jersey?" General Stapleton asked.

"No. I asked Rawdon to call you."

"I'm sure you did."

The General's affection for his two grandchildren had done much to diminish the hostile feelings Genevieve had entertained for him in the aftermath of the stolen presidency. He had regained much of his status as her father's best friend. But there was still an unnerving ambivalence in their relationship. She had not entirely forgiven him for the havoc he had wreaked between her and Rawdon. She sensed that his proud spirit had not forgiven her for the rebuke she had flung in his face on New Year's Day, 1877.

"Do you ever talk to Rawdon about what he's doing on Wall Street?"

"I don't know what you mean."

"Rawdon's practically a paid employee of Jay Gould. He killed your father, you know. I'm surprised you can tolerate it."

"We never discuss Rawdon's work," Genevieve said.

"Maybe you should," the General said, and hung up.

Genevieve stood there with the receiver in her hand, feeling very strange.

She tried to identify the emotion and decided it was humiliation. The humiliation of ignorance. It was the feeling she used to have when Rawdon told her she could never be a reporter and knew nothing about the real world, the feeling that had caused her such torment during the riots of 1877.

Genevieve helped Kathleen McGuire feed the children and put them to bed. She listened to Kathleen chatter about her visit to her family in their Fourth Ward tenement yesterday, her day off. Her father had decided to accept her back in the house, now that she had worked for Mrs. Stapleton for six months. Her older sister was not welcome, because she was still a prostitute. But her father accepted the ten or fifteen dollars she sent him each week. He used the money to get drunk.

After the children were finally bedded down, Genevieve and Kathleen ate a light supper and Genevieve spent an hour teaching Kathleen to read. She was a slow learner, but she was honest and goodhearted, unlike her light-fingered predecessor, Betty O'Brien. Rawdon had been violently opposed to hiring ex-prostitutes as maids. He had eventually yielded because the household was, after all, Genevieve's sphere. His work on Wall Street was his sphere—and he quite logically saw no need to discuss it with her.

Separate spheres: Genevieve could hear Alice Gansevoort praising the idea in midnight debates at Vassar as the best guarantee of a happy marriage. This marvelous theory now entitled her to teach Kathleen McGuire to read and Rawdon to have dinner with Jay Gould.

"Mrs. Stapleton," Kathleen said as they finished the reading lesson, "I cleaned the front closet like youse asked me to do."

"As *you* asked me. Don't say 'youse,' " Genevieve said. She kept trying to convince Kathleen that correct grammar was necessary if she hoped to rise in the world and get a job with a wealthy family.

"Anyway, I found this here box full of papers. What should I do with it?"

The cardboard box was sitting on a nearby end table. Genevieve recognized it instantly. It was the manuscript of her book on prostitution. She had put it aside during the turmoil of 1877. After Charlie's birth she had tried to get back to it, but Rawdon had furiously insisted that she abandon it.

Her poor aborted book. Genevieve riffled through the pages. It had been little more than an embryo, anyway. She had thrust it into the back of the closet and tried to forget it. After Laura's birth, it somehow became even more unwritable. Why did being the mother of a girl increase the need for achieving respectability, social acceptance? If she had learned anything in the last four years, Genevieve thought wearily, it was the existence of two real worlds—one for men, the other for women.

"What should I do with it, ma'am?"

"Throw it away," Genevieve said.

Another tinny tinkle from the telephone in the hall. "A Mr. Pendleton," Kathleen announced.

"Clay. How delightful to hear from you," Genevieve said. "Where have you been hiding?"

"No place in particular. Where can I locate that cynosure of cynicism, the duke of disillusion, your husband?"

She told him. "No decent reporter or newspaper publisher should sit down to dinner with Jay Gould," Clay said.

"I'll tell him that."

"No, better not. I'll never get a job on the *Herald.*"

"Do you really want one?"

"Rawdon says Bennett might make me a high-priced offer. They're looking for someone to do special coverage of the political conventions this summer."

"I'd rather see you go back to work for the *Times.*"

"Why do you think you have to save my lost southern soul? First you try to marry me off to New England incarnate—"

"I wasn't thinking of marriage, Clay. I just thought you were two people, more or less alone in New York . . ."

"Both lonely and homely," Clay said in his wry way. "I've got to admit we were a perfect match. I've been embarrassed to come near you because I treated Wellcombe so badly."

"No you didn't. It was her fault, really. She had an attack of . . . marriageitis. It happens to women."

"At last. I finally understand why you succumbed to that callous lout you married."

He was joking, of course. But for a moment Genevieve felt a clutch of sadness, a strange wordless wish. "Yes," she said. "What's new on the political front?"

"Promise not to tell your husband?"

"Of course."

"I'm about to unveil a story that's going to blow the Democratic Party into about six pieces. A certain prominent Republican whose name you happen to bear has just handed me a batch of telegrams from the files of Western Union that prove the Democrats were trying to steal the election in 1876 just as hard as the Republicans, but the General and his friends got there fastest with the mostest money."

"That's incredible, Clay. You're sure they're authentic?"

"Absolutely. It makes you think differently about his trip to New Orleans four years ago."

"I guess—it might," Genevieve said, unable to explain why new revelations would not undo the damage that trip had done to her and Rawdon.

"But the General still doesn't add up for me. He's totally ruthless, corrupt, a liar, yet he's got this thing about the war as a crusade, a cause that he can't let die. Do you have an explanation?"

Suddenly Genevieve saw a scarred haggard face in their parlor, the morning after her father's suicide. She heard Jonathan Stapleton saying, *He loved this country so much he let it break his heart.* Was her father's idealism alive in Jonathan Stapleton's soul?

"I might have a theory I'll tell you sometime. When Rawdon isn't around."

"If that's an invitation to an affair, I accept."

"Clay. Remember I'm the mother of two children. Respectability has been forced on me. When are you coming to Sunday dinner?"

"You mean I'm really forgiven?"

"You silly man. You were never guilty."

"I'll see you this Sunday."

Genevieve hung up feeling lightheaded. The telephone was a wonderful invention. It cured melancholy housewives by giving bachelors a chance to talk romantic nonsense to them. But it was more than pseudo-romance. She had forgotten how much she missed Clay's habit of discussing politics with her.

Because Genevieve spent Monday afternoon at Mrs. Roosevelt's sewing circle, Tuesday was washday in the Stapleton household. Kathleen did most of the work, but Genevieve had to be there to supervise and lend a hand at feeding the clothes through the wringer. By noon it was almost a hundred degrees in the steam-filled kitchen, with the stove going full blast to boil the water and Kathleen pouring it on the clothes in the scrubbing tubs. Genevieve gave herself a leave of absence to get the mail before fixing lunch for herself, Kathleen and the children.

Downstairs the concierge handed her a letter from Wellcombe. Genevieve tore it open as she began her trek back upstairs.

"I've passed the bar," read the opening sentence of the letter. The rest was details, many of them interesting, about prejudiced and unprejudiced judges and lawyers and the lively state of the woman's movement in the West. Genevieve had devoured all four pages by the time she reached the sixth floor.

She walked into her kitchen feeling as though she had just taken a trip to a distant planet. She stood there in her soapsuds-soaked skirt, staring at Kathleen McGuire's cheerful but oh-so-stupid Irish face. In the distance she could hear Charlie calling, "Mama, Sister's hungry and so am I." His plaintive piping voice was drowned a second later by an angry howl from Laura. When she was hungry she let the world know it.

Genevieve rushed across the kitchen and thrust Wellcombe's letter into the fire of her Sunshine stove. The flames leaped out at her and scorched her hand. Kathleen gasped and rubbed butter on it.

Genevieve had no clear recollection of the next two hours. When she regained a degree of self-possession, she was sitting on a bench in the Central Park. It was a raw cold day and the wind had a cutting edge. She sat there thinking about Vassar, about arguments over rational love and reasonable equality in marriage, about obliterated maiden names and dreams of discovering an unknown star.

Charlie scampered around, bouncing a rubber ball. Laura sat up in her carriage, studying every passing stranger with her father's inquisitive green eyes. Then Charlie was tugging at her sleeve. "Mama, can we go home?" he said. "I'm cold."

His lips were blue. Genevieve was appalled at her carelessness. She realized she had practically fled the apartment and had failed to put a sweater under Charlie's coat. She herself was badly chilled. All because she got a letter from a woman who had passed the bar in California.

Back in the apartment, she fixed hot chocolate for herself and Charlie. Kathleen took charge of Laura and informed her that Rawdon had called. He would not be home for supper. He was going to New Jersey to see his grandmother. Eventually they fed the children and got them to bed. Genevieve ate a hasty supper and gave Kathleen her reading lesson. Then she tried to write a letter to Wellcombe. The congratulations were easy enough, but when she tried to add something personal about her own life all she could offer was an apology for having nothing much to tell.

By ten o'clock Mrs. Rawdon Stapleton was asleep. She dreamed of Vassar. Maria Mitchell was shaking her finger at her in the dome room, accusing her of neglecting the telescope. "Irresponsible," she shrilled, her sausage curls dancing.

A hand was on her shoulder. "Gen," Rawdon said. "Charlie seems to be running a fever."

She was out of bed and running to the nursery. Rawdon followed her, telling how he had heard him calling "Mama" in a hoarse, choked voice as he came in. Charlie lay in his crib staring up at her with those sad sweet eyes. Rawdon was right about the fever. His nightgown was soaked. "I don't feel so good, Mama," he said. His piping little voice was a croak.

"I'll get the doctor," Rawdon said, cranking the telephone.

Ponderous Dr. William Pearsall May arrived within the hour. He used a tongue depressor to peer down Charlie's throat. He listened impassively to Genevieve's story of the chill in Central Park. "He was probably sick before you took him there," Dr. May said. "I'm quite certain it's diphtheria."

"Oh no," Genevieve said.

"There's almost an epidemic in the tenements."

Kathleen McGuire. Was her benevolence about to be rewarded with one of the most deadly diseases of childhood?

"I want you to apply hot towels soaked in mustard to his throat, twenty-four hours a day," Dr. May said. "We must do everything we can to prevent the tissues from swelling. Bathe him in cold water twice a day to break the fever. If he begins to have difficulty breathing, call me immediately."

For the next twenty-four hours, Genevieve and Kathleen took turns applying the hot towels. They bathed poor Charlie's thin trembling body in icy water. But nothing helped. The fever continued to burn, the tissues in the small throat continued to swell. Finally there was a frantic call to Dr. May, an attempt to insert a tube into the tormented lungs—and death. Genevieve watched Dr. May close those plaintive Dall eyes for the last time.

There was a funeral service at Grace Church, the little white coffin in the aisle, the same aisle down which Genevieve had walked to become Mrs. Rawdon Stapleton. The rector said appropriate things, Eleanor and Alice wept, Jonathan Stapleton walked up to Genevieve outside the church and embraced her. "Don't let it break your spirit," he whispered. "We all have to learn to accept losses." He reached out to Rawdon too, but Rawdon turned away.

There were tears on Cynthia Stapleton's face. "He was such a dear little thing," she said as she kissed Genevieve. Was she unfaithful to her husband? Could a woman combine adultery and sympathy for a grieving daughter-in-law? Genevieve had no idea.

Rawdon insisted on burying their son in the family plot in New Jersey, next to the first Charles Gifford Stapleton. Then they stopped at Bowood for a horrible hour with Caroline Stapleton. White hair streaming like a seeress's, she sat up in bed wondering what she had done to deserve such punishment from God. The death of another Charles Gifford Stapleton apparently recalled all the anguish of the loss of the first one. Only Laura consoled her. Rawdon had insisted on bringing the child along; he seemed to want to display her as proof that the Stapletons would continue to flourish. "Make sure, Rawdon, make sure she finds the happiness that was denied to your poor mother and to me," the old woman quavered.

Genevieve was horrified. What kind of happiness could this embittered crone wish Laura? Caroline Stapleton had infected all their lives with her poisonous hatred.

At the end of the day, Genevieve and Rawdon were back in their apartment, facing each other, still married, still parents. Rawdon held Laura on his lap. The resemblance between them was never more striking.

Outnumbered, Genevieve thought. One Dall against two Stapletons. And it had been well established that the Dalls had no staying power. Was it because the Dalls were feminine and the Stapletons, with their will to power, money, fame, were masculine? How did Laura fit into that scheme of things?

"The first thing we're going to do," Rawdon said, "is get rid of that little whore Kathleen McGuire. She brought the infection into the house, I'm sure of it."

"Rawdon—she'll go back to walking the streets. She has a sister—"

"That's her problem. Nobody made her become a whore in the first place. We'll get Alice to find a good clean German maid. And a nurse for Laura, someone who knows how to keep a child warm when she takes her out in the winter."

"The doctor said the chill had nothing to do with it."

"Then we're going to get to work on having another son."

Oh. Of course. Get to work. That was the way a husband saw the business of impregnating his incompetent wife. If she objected to the phrase, Rawdon would tell her he was just being rational.

The next morning, Genevieve told Kathleen she was out of a job. The girl wept and wanted to know what she had done wrong. Genevieve stumbled out an explanation: Mr. Stapleton feared another infection; he wanted a German maid. Kathleen only kept blubbering. "Missus, I done everything you told me. I took a bath every week. I washed my hands. I can't help bein' Irish."

Genevieve gave her twenty-five dollars, a whole month's pay, and an extravagant letter of recommendation. She urged her not to go home—her father would take the money away from her—but to rent a room uptown and visit the employment agencies. Kathleen nodded, but Genevieve could see it was all wasted words.

Genevieve spent the rest of the morning packing Charlie's clothes and toys into a trunk. For a long time she clutched to her breasts the little rag doll he had loved and Rawdon hated. Charlie called it his "other sister."

Oh. Oh. Oh. Don't let it break your spirit, Genevieve. Losses were part of life. Her mother had lost her first two children to typhoid fever. Everyone lost children. Alice had almost lost the twins to scarlet fever last year.

Genevieve shoved the trunk into the back of the hall closet, below the shelf where she had stored her book. That was gone now, her absurd ambition to awaken New York to the evil of prostitution. It was logical—rational—to discard Kathleen McGuire too, the last shred of her idiotic dream of accomplishing something brave and new.

At noon Alice Mayer arrived with Ilsa Kohl, a large, bottle-nosed German girl who barely spoke English. She was a cousin of one of the Mayer maids. She fixed lunch for them, and Alice urged religious resignation, the acceptance of the will of God on Genevieve. Since she married Isaac and persuaded him to convert to Christianity, Alice had been devout. Genevieve nodded and thanked her. But the God who had allowed little Charlie's throat to close was as incomprehensible to her as the one who had allowed her father's finger to curl on the trigger of his army pistol.

Alice departed with a burst of cheerful German to Ilsa, and Genevieve was left to make her way in broken English. It was soon apparent that it would be a silent relationship, the opposite of Kathleen's cheerful chatter. Laura did not seem to like their new maid very much. When Ilsa picked her up she wailed and reached out to her mother as if she were being abducted.

At four o'clock the telephone rang. It was Rawdon. His grandmother had had another stroke and was dying. He was on his way to New Jersey and would probably be there most of the night. Genevieve realized she was not surprised. That was death she had seen on Caroline Stapleton's face yesterday as she asked why God made her suffer such torment. Was there an answer to that question? Was it her refusal to forgive her only surviving son?

Silly. She had just rejected Alice's version of God. But the heart of Genevieve's question was not God; it was forgiveness. Suddenly she began to see Caroline Stapleton's death as a door which would either bar forgiveness from their lives or open it to renewed love. She could not allow her to die in bitter lonely estrangement! It would seal all their fates, stamp unforgiveness into all their hearts.

For two hours she waited, hoped, almost prayed, that Jonathan Stapleton would telephone. But the marvelous invention remained silent. Finally, about six o'clock, she called his home number and told him.

"I'm very grateful," he said. "There's a seven-o'clock train I think I can catch."

He hung up, leaving Genevieve alone with the wish that they could have said much more to each other. She wanted to tell Jonathan Stapleton that she did not believe he should suffer endlessly for his sins no matter how corrupt he had become. She wanted to explain that she hoped his mother's forgiveness would change his relationship with his son.

The more Genevieve thought about her little act of independence, the more important it became. She saw Caroline Stapleton persuading Rawdon with her last breath to forgive his father. This would work a spiritual transformation on the Stapletons which would spill over into her life with Rawdon.

Genevieve spent the rest of the night trying to adjust matters between Ilsa and Laura. The child refused to let the maid feed her. She spat vegetables in her face, and Ilsa almost slapped her. Genevieve struggled to soothe her Stapleton daughter. She was an amazingly imperious little thing, the opposite of her sweet, docile brother.

Asleep, Genevieve dreamed of Kemble Manor. She was on the bluff, Rawdon was taking a photograph of her. At the last moment, she saw that underneath the cloth he was concealing not a camera but a huge revolver. It exploded with a great puff of smoke. She looked down at her white dress. It was spattered with blood.

She awoke. It was dawn. She was alone in the bed. Rawdon must still be in New Jersey. A chilly breeze riffled the lace curtains. Her nose was running. She hoped she was not getting a cold. Laura was liable to catch it. The doctor had warned against colds. They could be deadly for an asthmatic child.

Laura! Why hadn't she awakened for her five-thirty bottle? Genevieve sprang up and rushed to the crib. It was empty. She flung on a robe and dashed into the parlor. A man was standing at the window looking down on the city in the gray light. For a moment Genevieve almost cried out. Then she realized it was Rawdon. He had Laura in his arms.

"She finally died. Grandmother."

"Oh—I'm sorry."

"Why? It would have been better for everybody if she died ten years ago."

"I don't understand."

"I don't expect you to understand it."

He sounded enormously weary, as if a weight had been placed on his shoulders that he did not really want. He roused himself by kissing Laura on the forehead. "She loved this little darling too," he said. "Do you know how much she's worth now, in an unbreakable unrecoverable trust?"

"I can't imagine."

"One million dollars."

"That's—amazing."

"I got the same amount. So did my brother George. But he won't get any of his money until he's thirty. I thought it would take him that long to break away from the General."

He smiled coldly, reflectively. "You should have seen the General's face when he read the clause in the will explaining that the old bitch left us the money to make sure we could enjoy the same independent spirit her son displayed in his youth."

"Your father was there?"

"He arrived about a half hour too late. She died without mentioning his name."

So much for her vision of a deathbed reconciliation. "What . . . are you going to do with all that money?"

"I'm going to use it to make a lot more. We're going to get very rich. If Jay Gould can make a billion dollars in twenty years, I should do it in ten. You're going to have to acquire a few social graces, learn to dress with some style. We'll be moving to a town house."

"I thought you always said—when we talked about inheriting your father's money—that you'd start your own newspaper."

"A waste of time. You can buy your way into almost any paper you need. Most reporters are for sale. Anyway, Gould just bought the *World*."

"You're going to invest with Gould?"

"For the time being. I've done him a lot of favors as a reporter. He likes the way I think."

Genevieve heard Jonathan Stapleton's sepulchral voice on the telephone saying, *Gould killed your father, you know.*

Women's lives, Genevieve thought. They were so different from men's lives. Things happened to women. They never made anything happen, not even babies. They never chose, decided. Time, events just swept over and through them and they were supposed to accept, accept, accept and go on loving everyone, even when they got no love in return.

Rawdon handed Laura to her. "She's wet. You better change her. I'm going to get some sleep."

Genevieve sat there with Laura in her lap, watching the sun rise over the gray metallic-looking East River, tinting the swift water and the brown fronts and black roofs of the metropolis. Downstream, the pylons of the new bridge to Brooklyn loomed like mute armless giants. People said it was going to be the eighth wonder of the world when it was finished, the most magnificent feat of engineering in history. Unquestionably, it was an age of progress. They were rushing toward the future at ever more confident speed. Who was she, a humble passenger, to criticize the engineers?

"Mama," gurgled Laura Kemble Stapleton.

Her little millionairess. What sort of future would she enjoy? Would a million dollars guarantee her happiness, or only make it more difficult to achieve? Genevieve lifted the nightgown and unpinned Laura's wet diaper. She stared, transfixed, at the female cleft, so visible without the hairy disguise of age. It was almost a wound, she thought, a guarantee of vulnerability.

The next sound she heard was Ilsa's guttural voice. *"Mein Gott,* Frau Stapleton. Vy you sitting dere so long? She vet all over dat bootiful chair."

TWO

Clay Pendleton sipped his third—or was it his fourth?—bourbon and gazed at the snowy endowments of Sally Gansevoort, Alice Mayer's younger sister. She had the same honey-blond hair, widely spaced blue eyes and bold sensuous mouth. But Sally was more seductively feminine than Alice. Those endowments, all but visible thanks to the aesthetic look, absorbed Pendleton's imagination. He barely heard Sally as she murmured, "You must lead the most *exciting* life, Mr. Pendleton."

He shook his head. "Reporters only lead exciting lives in novels."

Sally curled her lower lip into a devastatingly skeptical smile. Pendleton was momentarily blinded by enough teeth to equip a whole tribe of cannibals. "You're too modest," Sally sighed.

"Oh I say, Pendleton," Hal Bradford said in his blustery fake English accent. "Forgive me for interrupting the course of true love and all that sort of thing. But Lord Elgin here wanted to meet the most famous reporter in New York."

Lord Elgin was blond, red-cheeked; he looked about fifteen. "This can't be the Lord Elgin who's the current viceroy of India," Pendleton said.

"My father," Lord Elgin said.

"Isn't he amazing," Sally Gansevoort said. "Mr. Pendleton knows *everything.*"

Around them in the Bradfords' parlor swirled the last dinner party of the spring season. The room was crowded with self-assured English aristocrats like Lord Elgin whom the Bradfords met on their frequent journeys to London and equally self-assured sons of Wall Street speculators like Hal. As usual, money was demonstrating its superiority to old blood.

The parlor was decorated in Japonaisme, the latest fashion. Giant red-and-green vases full of willows sat in the corners. Screens featuring vividly snarling tigers loomed in front of the mantel. It was a pleasant place to be, drinking his host's bourbon, flattered by the likes of Lord Elgin and Sally Gansevoort.

There were times when Pendleton almost forgot that he had about a thousand dollars in the bank, barely enough to buy a third of Sally's filmy

gold embroidered gown. His whole bank account might even vanish just to
pay for the golden girdle around her supple waist. Recently his friends had
begun parading beauties like Sally past Pendleton. He was the last bachelor,
the only holdout against marriage and respectability in their set.

Lord Elgin was asking Pendleton how the deuce he had gotten his hands
on those sensational telegrams that had set the U.S.A. on its ear and had half
of Europe buzzing. Until Pendleton produced these documents, everyone
assumed that the Democratic Party and its traduced hero, Samuel Tilden,
were the certain winners of the 1880 presidential sweepstakes. "Did you pay
some scurvy beggar at Western Union for them?" Lord Elgin wanted to
know.

Pendleton shook his head. "A good reporter has friends in high places."

Sally Gansevoort's eyes glowed, thinking of those high places and the fuss
she could make there when she curled that lower lip. She had reportedly
become her father's favorite daughter. Everyone said Jefferson Gansevoort,
Jay Gould's broker, would make sure his lovely Sally had enough money to
outdazzle her Jewish sister. Was he willing to become a kept man? Pendleton
wondered.

Pendleton's eyes momentarily wandered from Sally's endowments and encountered Genevieve Dall Stapleton, sitting on a couch in the distance,
watching him. The voice, the melancholy face of his conscience. She had
recently told him that he was the only man she knew with some ideals—a
hilarious misconception if there ever was one. The poor girl confused idealism with Pendleton's dwindling impulse to tell the truth about this dubious
republic.

Lord Elgin was asking whom he thought the Republicans would nominate
in Chicago. "That's what we all want to know," Hal Bradford said. "Another
four years of Rutherfraud will send the stock market to the bottom of the
East River. But if the Stalwarts can put Grant over you'll see a bull market
that will look like Mount Vesuvius. How about a little advance notice, Pendleton old boy?"

"Sorry, Bradford. He's working for me—if he's working for anybody besides his newspaper," Rawdon Stapleton said, smoothly sliding into the circle.

"I'm glad you stressed the 'if,'" Pendleton said.

Rawdon just smiled. "Isn't he marvelous, Sally?" he said.

"I'm absolutely enthralled," Sally said.

The message was perfectly clear to Pendleton. If he had any hopes of
keeping Sally enthralled as something more than a hired entertainer, he had
better go to work for Rawdon Stapleton—and Jay Gould.

The following day, the famous reporter sat in the office of bearded Whitelaw Reid, owner-editor of the New York *Tribune*. The *Sun* had been reluctant

to publish Pendleton's revelations about the Democrats' midnight telegrams in 1876; the paper was fearful of alienating its mostly Democratic readers. The *Tribune*, eager to shoulder the *Times* aside as the Republican standard bearer in New York, had taken the story—and Pendleton. Reid was a smooth, intelligent man, an ex-reporter who had no illusions about the Republican Party. He told Pendleton the *Tribune* was supporting James G. Blaine, the Senator from Maine, for president. Blaine presented himself as a compromise between the Stalwarts and the liberals.

"I hear he's in Jay Gould's pocket," Pendleton said. This was a bit of information Rawdon had casually mentioned to him.

Reid glared at the famous reporter. "This paper is not one of Mr. Gould's enemies," he snapped. "We consider him a much abused man."

Who has loaned you a hundred thousand dollars. Another piece of information Pendleton picked up from drinking with Rawdon.

Pendleton nodded while Reid explained to him that he, not Clay Pendleton, owned the *Tribune* and he intended to set policy for it. He added that as far as he was concerned, a reporter was only as good as his last story.

So much for the wages of fame.

Three days later, Pendleton watched Senator Roscoe Conkling convert the reporters' table in the center of the immense Chicago convention hall into a speaker's platform. Drawing himself up to the full awesome dimensions of his turkey-gobbler strut, Conkling bellowed:

> *"When asked what state he hails from*
> *Our sole reply shall be*
> *He comes from Appomattox*
> *And its famous apple tree!"*

The Senator was nominating Ulysses S. Grant for a third term as president of the United States. For most of the past four years the military hero had been touring the world, getting stupendous receptions everywhere from London to Tokyo and equally stupendous coverage in American newspapers.

For ten minutes in the sweltering arena men went berserk. Pendleton swigged from a flask of bourbon that had become a permanent part of his newspaperman's equipment and watched the New York delegation, which Senator Conkling controlled as absolutely as any plantation owner ever ruled his slaves. They leaped up on their chairs and howled through megaphones, they rang cowbells, they pounded drums, they blew trumpets. Only one man in the delegation remained seated, his arms folded across his chest: Jonathan Stapleton. As the uproar subsided and Conkling resumed telling the delegates why the nation needed another four years of Grant, Jonathan Stapleton stalked out of the hall.

Pendleton felt irked. It was the same sort of exasperation Genevieve Dall Stapleton stirred when she talked hungrily with him about his latest assignment. Pendleton had begun to think he had better stay a safe distance from Genevieve for several reasons. She had confused his feelings about General Stapleton by portraying him as a man who struggled between the corrupt realism of his political heritage and the idealism that his friendship with her father had infused into his soul. The quintessential American, her father had called him, the thing itself in all its contradictions. The idea made the inside of Pendleton's mouth pucker.

In Pendleton's pocket was another reason why Genevieve Dall Stapleton and her father-in-law irked him: a telegram from Rawdon.

WILL PAY ONE THOUSAND DOLLARS FOR ADVANCE INFORMATION ON NOMI-
NATION OF DARK HORSE. BONUS OF SAME AMOUNT IF YOU CAN ACCU-
RATELY PREDICT IMPACT ON STOCK MARKET.

Rawdon Stapleton was no longer a reporter. He was a Wall Street operator, Jay Gould's left-hand man, working hard to get rich enough to become the right arm of the billion-dollar colossus. It was another reason why Pendleton swigged steadily from his flask. He felt responsible for Rawdon Stapleton's fall from grace. Even though Pendleton still believed there had been only one chance in a thousand of a revolution succeeding in 1877, he felt guilty for failing to stand with Rawdon in its brief moment of possibility.

Pendleton took another swig from his flask and followed Jonathan Stapleton toward the door. Once and for all, he wanted to settle accounts with the General. He wanted to make it clear that he understood just how they had used each other to their mutual advantage on these big stories. Along the way he would also demolish Genevieve's absurd theory about the man's closet idealism.

At first Pendleton had thought that the General had given him the Democratic telegrams to justify his dash to New Orleans in 1876. Once more, Pendleton discovered he had seen only half as far as this calculating man and his slippery political allies. With the blot of 1876 removed (or obscured by a universal downpour of soot), the Stalwarts moved boldly to regain control of the Republican Party. Their candidate, Ulysses S. Grant, thought a third term in the White House was a fine idea. If all the pots and kettles in sight were black, what was wrong with a familiar if particularly sooty one?

The Stalwarts girded their loins for a climactic battle with the Goo-Goos, Mary Janes and soreheads who used the cry of civil-service reform to cloak their cowardly peace-at-any-price policy with the unrepentant South. Equally scorned were the "Half Breeds" led by James G. Blaine, who talked out of both sides of their mouths to keep everybody happy.

Pendleton caught up with Jonathan Stapleton in front of the convention hall. "General," he called. "Congratulations."

"For what?"

"For walking out on Roscoe Conkling."

"I heard it all in his suite. When Conkling's got a speech in him, he talks it at you day and night."

"I'm surprised to see you here. Didn't I read somewhere that you were going to Europe?"

"Mrs. Stapleton went—alone. She's visiting her actress friend, Madeline Terhune, in London."

Pendleton thought the General looked a bit forlorn as he reported his wife's whereabouts. "Care to join me in a toast to bachelorhood?"

They hailed a hack and jounced along the Lake Michigan shore in the hot sunshine. The General asked if he had seen Rawdon and Genevieve lately. Pendleton reported Genevieve did not seem happy with her splendid new town house on West Fifty-fourth Street, her brigade of servants and her wardrobe of expensive dresses.

The General did not seem surprised. "She's her father's daughter," he said. "I thought she could pass some of his ideals along to Rawdon, but it looks as if I was wrong."

"Pretty hard to be an idealist these days, General."

"I know, I know."

Pendleton suddenly remembered a conversation he had had with Genevieve at a party Jay Gould had thrown to launch the Mexican Southern Railroad. She had stared across the room at her husband fawning on the pint-sized tycoon and said, *"Rawdon's definition of a woman's sphere is a world the size of a golfball. I'm doing my best to shrink and shrink until I'm small enough to live inside it."*

Should he tell that to the General? No. The new woman was not an idea his generation could even begin to grasp. He would never comprehend the poignancy of watching one drift into melancholy defeat.

They rode beside Lake Michigan for several blocks. Railroad tracks skirted the water's edge. A freight train clanked past, heading for Chicago's vast slaughterhouses or the immense zinc grain elevators that loomed ahead of them on the shore. "More statistics for the boosters," Jonathan Stapleton said.

Chicagoans loved to tell everyone how many hogs they had slaughtered last year (4,805,000), how many bushels of grain they had shipped (137,624,833). "I met a man last night who told me they'd processed one billion, eight hundred and seventy-eight million, four hundred and ninety-three thousand and ninety-one feet of lumber," Pendleton said.

"Chicago is the boasting capital of the country these days," Jonathan Stapleton said. "It's a funny habit—but I sort of like it. In the East we're always toadying and apologizing to the English." He stared out at the debris-littered shore of the lake for a minute or two. "I've always liked this city. Maybe it's because coming here in 1860 to help nominate Lincoln was the first independent thing I'd ever done."

"Really?" Pendleton said.

"I'd always been a very good boy, growing up. A bit of a mama's boy, if you want the whole truth. I was thirty-three years old and I'd never done a thing my mother and father didn't approve, until I turned Republican and came out here."

Pendleton could only shake his head in amazement. How did a mama's boy become this scarred formidable man?

"I met Lincoln here. That's another reason I like Chicago." The General pointed to a handsome stone house surrounded by a well-tended lawn and several old chestnut trees. "Norman Judd lives there," he said. "He's the attorney for the Chicago and Rock Island Railroad. I went to dinner there with Lincoln during the 1860 convention. We sat on the piazza and the moon came up. Lincoln talked about the old stargazers of Egypt and Babylon. He got into the mystery of the universe, the puzzle of where we've all come from, where we're going. I've never forgotten it."

"Where did he think the United States of America was going?"

"He didn't know any more than you or I. But he thought we had a special destiny. A whole continent, conceived in liberty. I know it sounds like Fourth of July stuff, Clay. But Lincoln believed it."

Pendleton felt the inside of his mouth pucker. This was really ripe, a patriotic sermon from the chief backer of Senator Roscoe Conkling, the most corrupt politician in the country.

"Do you think Lincoln would approve of the Republican Party of 1880?"

The General looked uncomfortable. "I don't know. I don't think anyone ever approves of a political party one hundred percent. I know Lincoln wasn't crazy about the abolitionist wing of the Republican Party in 1860—the madmen who armed John Brown and did everything they could do to egg the South into starting the war. I'm pretty sure he'd deplore these civil-service Goo-Goos who are more worried about whether the postmaster of Dubuque passed an examination than they are about black men getting shot when they try to vote."

It was Pendleton's turn to squirm. He recalled his visit to South Carolina last year for his mother's funeral. After the service he had sat in the office of the *Spartanburg Gazette*, listening to his brother-in-law tell him how the local

National Guard regiment used a certain alley for target practice on Election Day. It happened to be an alley Negroes had to cross to get to the polls. Surprise, the Negro vote was very light.

At the Grand Pacific Hotel drinkers were scarce in the Grand Bar, whose one-hundred-foot-long swath of mahogany was one of the wonders of the Midwest. Most of the potential customers were at the convention hall.

Pendleton ordered a double bourbon. "Second the motion," Jonathan Stapleton said.

"Here's to bachelorhood," Pendleton said, raising his glass. "Are you enjoying it?"

"No, and I don't believe you are, either."

That was too close to the truth for comfort. Pendleton got into the political interview as brutally as possible. "You didn't seem very enthusiastic when Senator Conkling brought on his war cry for General Grant."

Stapleton nodded glumly. "We don't have the votes to nominate the General. I urged a quiet retreat to save Grant the humiliation of a rejection. But you know how politicians are. They're all gamblers at heart. They're going to spend the next ten days taking roll-call votes, hoping for a miracle. But Grant will fall short by about forty votes. We'll have enough to block Blaine and anyone the Goo-Goos put up. The nomination will go to a dark horse. Probably Garfield."

Pendleton gulped his bourbon. Rawdon's telegram acquired a life of its own in his pocket. Jonathan Stapleton had just revealed news that could make Pendleton two thousand dollars—and it would still be a tremendous beat when he sent the story to the *Tribune* twelve hours later, giving Rawdon and Gould time to use the information for their own purposes.

Contemplating his own moral collapse, Pendleton grew even more surly toward his drinking companion. "Frankly, General, I can't understand why or how you can associate with people like the Stalwarts. Half the Grant votes they've managed to accumulate are bought."

Jonathan Stapleton took a hefty gulp of his bourbon. "I don't like to bribe people, Clay. I don't like to kill them, either. But when I had to choose between killing people and seeing the Union destroyed, I decided to kill people." He said this in a perfectly calm, conversational voice. "I killed a lot of people, Clay. Your people, my own people, to save the Union. Bribery seems to be a relatively harmless way of doing it."

"Why is the Union in danger now?"

"You know what's happening in the South. You saw what almost happened in the North in 1877. It could happen again tomorrow. Grant is the one man who's tough enough to stop a revolution if it started again in New York or anyplace else. He's had four years to realize that getting tough is the only way to stop the South from going back to half slave, half free under another name."

"All that sounds terribly noble, General. But do you really believe this is why most Stalwarts want Grant? Don't they all just want four more years of unlimited graft?"

Jonathan Stapleton frowned. Was he troubled by Pendleton's snide tone? "Most of them aren't grafters," he said. "They're politicians. They want to stay in office. There'll be some graft, of course. There'll always be some graft and incompetence. I was appalled by what went on in Washington and New York during the war. One day in 1862 I sat down and asked myself what I was going to do about it. Quit the whole mess because people like Jay Gould and Cornelius Vanderbilt were getting rich in perfect safety? Would it have done any good? Clearly, it would only have done harm. It would have demoralized my men. Everyone would have said I was a fraud, I was just afraid of getting killed. So I swallowed hard and went on fighting."

"Aren't you saying that the end justifies the means? In the name of patriotism or the Union or whatever the hell you want to call it, you can justify *anything?*"

Pendleton ordered another double bourbon. Jonathan Stapleton joined him. The General's frowning face dissolved and reformed again. Was he beginning to realize that Clay Pendleton was no longer his obedient southern servant? But the frown did not expand into a glare. Those ferocious eyes were turned inward. The General was trying to answer his question. The General was searching the crevasses and caves and swamps of his life to tell him the truth.

"That thing about ends and means has often puzzled me. It isn't a good idea for anyone to get into the habit of giving or taking bribes. Or lying. Or killing people. Those things damage the soul. It makes perfect sense if your first priority is individual souls. But what if you've already decided the nation is worth the sacrifice of a thousand—or a million—individual souls? That's what Lincoln decided when we went to war."

Suddenly a different man was confronting Pendleton. Not the meditative philosopher, but a man with a haunted face, clutching the bar, staring down at his knotted hands, his voice choked. "I did things during the war, Clay, that I can never forget. They called me a butcher. In a way they were right. I'd go out after a battle and help the wounded. I paid for special rations for them in the hospitals. I marched with my men, step for step. For only one reason: so they'd die for me. And they did. They died by the thousands. Sometimes like sheep. Sometimes like brave men."

What was happening? Pendleton wondered dazedly. Had time taken a leap, had his mind gone blank for the last two drinks? He did not want to know that so much anguish was bubbling beneath this man's skin.

"I've never admitted this to anyone, Clay. Not even to Rawdon or George. Let's keep it a secret between the two of us."

Sonship. This man was offering him sonship. Here in this alien city where Lincoln was nominated and the war that annihilated everything began. Pendleton found himself answering Jonathan Stapleton with furious emotion; the wry objective reporter had vanished. "Why, General, why? What was the purpose of it all?"

"I asked myself that question more than once during the war, Clay. Then I thought that somehow we'd get moving toward the country we were meant to be, once we got slavery and secession out of our system. Lately I've begun to think we've got something worse—a worship of money for its own sake. But I still haven't entirely lost faith in Lincoln's idea of some sort of destiny we're all struggling toward."

"Jesus Christ," Pendleton said, hearing his own voice, cracked, high, unnatural. "You and Rawdon. You both think there's a shining message somewhere."

"Rawdon . . . believes that?" Jonathan Stapleton said.

"He did—until you took that trip to Louisiana."

What a crazy vicious thing to say. He was really speaking for himself. That's what happened when you got drunk. But Pendleton was not too drunk to see the pain on Jonathan Stapleton's face.

"That was the greatest mistake I ever made, Clay. I'm paying for it. Between my wife and my conscience I'm paying for it."

Pendleton gulped his bourbon. He was overwhelmed by remorse. "Ah hell, General. Maybe it wasn't that bad. What do women know?"

"Too much, Clay. Too damn much."

Pendleton clutched his glass. The Grand Pacific Hotel was starting to pitch and toss like a steamer in a gale. For some reason Pendleton started telling the General about his mother's funeral. How the preacher had praised her as a true daughter of the South because she used to patrol the streets of Spartanburg during the war, asking every able-bodied man she saw why he was not in Virginia fighting with General Lee.

"That's what everybody saw—public woman. In private—different story. Can't tell you how many nights my sister and I'd sit there on our front porch while Mother played the piano in the parlor and sang to herself. Then she'd start to cry. Sister'd cry, too. She remembered my father singing with her—night before he left for Virginia.

"Don't know why, but those tears always made me twist and squirm. It was as if she was accusing me of something—saying there was something wrong with me, as a man, sittin' there lettin' women cry. But there was nothing I could do. Sometimes . . . I wanted to cry, too."

They drained their glasses and ordered another round. The General's face had become a blur. "W'scares me 'bout women, General—how you deal with'm when they cry?"

The General was now as drunk as Pendleton. Slowly, mournfully, he shook his head. "Don' know, Clay. Don' know. Ten years ago—I'd've said let'm cry. Now don' know."

The bar filled up with Stalwarts and Half Breeds and even a few Goo-Goos who were ordering sarsaparilla, of course. On the first ballot Grant had fallen short by forty-eight votes. Chauncey I. Filley, the rotund postmaster of St. Louis, was furious. "General," he roared at Jonathan Stapleton, "do these assholes think we can steal two elections in a *row?*"

In the midst of the chaos stood smiling James G. Blaine. He sidled next to Jonathan Stapleton and said, "Jay Gould told me to be sure to say hello, General."

"Tell him to go fuck himself," Jonathan Stapleton said.

"He wants peace in the Republican Party," Blaine said. "He's willing to pay for it—or make you and Conkling pay for it."

"Tell him to go fuck himself twice. The same to you."

"All we want is peace, General."

"The fucking price is too high, Blaine."

After more of this sort of lofty political discourse, the guardians of the republic retired to their rooms. Pendleton found himself in the elevator with Jonathan Stapleton.

"Haven't drunk this much since the night after Bull Run," the General muttered. He gave his head a mighty shake. "Clay," he said, clapping both big hands on his shoulders, "I'm no good at giving advice to anyone your age. Rawdon's taught me that much. But you've got to make a stand, Clay. Stand for something. Otherwise . . ."

Did he see the exasperation on Pendleton's face? "Okay. Maybe I'm wrong. Forget it. I've got to do it. I—owe it. You don't. Maybe I'm wrong."

Pendleton wanted to snarl, *When I find something to stand for, General, I'll let you know.* Either he was too drunk or he felt sorry for Jonathan Stapleton. Take your pick. He felt sorry for a son of a bitch who had probably killed his father. A son of a bitch who admits he's a son of a bitch! Jesus. When he got to his room, Pendleton kicked the furniture, he denounced Chicago. "Go fuck yourselves," he roared out the window. Then he passed out on the bed.

The next morning, he awoke feeling as if God had cursed him. This did not deter him from going to the nearest telegraph office and wiring Rawdon the inside news on Garfield. Back in his room, he wrote the story, and twelve hours later he wired that to the *Tribune.*

For the next five days, Pendleton drank bourbon and watched the Stalwarts fight for Grant. Through thirty-four ballots, Grant's vote never fell below 302 and never rose above 313. To win, someone had to get 378. Wisconsin, last to vote at the end of the fourth exhausting day, suddenly threw 16 votes to Congressman James Abram Garfield, who had made a flowery speech nominating Senator John Sherman of Ohio, a Goo-Goo favorite. On the next ballot, Garfield had 50 votes. On the thirty-sixth ballot the handsome genial Ohioan had 399.

On Wall Street, meanwhile, the market broke when it became apparent that the bulls' favorite, Grant, could not win. Gould and Rawdon had quietly sold short in a dozen stocks days earlier and made several million. When Garfield, a financial conservative, won the nomination, the market rebounded. Gould and his left-hand man had already gone long in the same stocks and made a few more million. Pendleton got another thousand dollars —the promised bonus.

In the tumultuous bar of the Grand Pacific Hotel on the night of Garfield's nomination, Pendleton sipped bourbon and sidled next to Chauncey I. Filley, who was announcing through the bottom of a full glass of the same liquid that Garfield would not carry three states. But there was one consolation. Three hundred and six Stalwarts had remained faithful to Grant. With a munificence startling for a postmaster, Filley announced plans to have 306 medals struck and distributed to the members of the loyal band. Beneath their faces he would put—what? Filley, who was described by the Goo-Goos at *Harper's Weekly* as "a shining example of the thing to be reformed," lugubriously examined possible mottoes.

"How about 'The Old Guard'?" Jonathan Stapleton said.

Filley's salute would have earned him a reprimand in his army days. It missed his forehead and landed somewhere on the top of his head. "The Old Guard dies," he said, "but never surrenders!"

Later, upstairs in his room, Pendleton conjured the image, not in derision, but in all seriousness (if not sobriety). He began trying to write a feature describing the mentality of men like Jonathan Stapleton. Pendleton titled it *The Honest Stalwart.* In it he planned to point out that among the Old Guard who had died for Napoleon at Waterloo were many men who still believed in the ideals of the French Revolution, in spite of intervening years of disillusion. The same thing was true of the Stalwarts. They too had men of good faith in their ranks, men who still cherished the idealism that had created the Republican Party.

Alas, he never got to write more than a few lines. A telegram from New York ordered him to churn out two thousand words describing Garfield as a combination of Lincoln, Jefferson and Washington. A compassionate, wise, forceful idealist. There was no need to explain what had happened. James G. Blaine and the Half Breeds had made a deal behind the podium with Garfield. They would try to sweet-talk the Goo-Goos and the Stalwarts into singing three-part harmony in the White House.

It was not an easy story to write, with vengeful Stalwarts snarling the truth about Garfield into Pendleton's ears. The famous reporter reminded himself that he was only as good—and as well paid—as his last story. He ground out two thousand fulsome words on Garfield. He ignored Jonathan Stapleton's grim prediction that within a month of Garfield's election James G. Blaine would own him as thoroughly as Jay Gould owned the Union Pacific and James G. Blaine. "We'll be worse off than we were with Hayes," the General said. "At least he was an honest man."

The General's stubborn corrupt patriotism exasperated Pendleton so much he found it impossible to write *The Honest Stalwart.* Instead, he spent most of his time with extreme Stalwarts such as Chauncey I. Filley and his friends, reporting that they were sufficiently mollified by the choice of Chester A. Arthur for vice-president to back Garfield.

Dapper Chet Arthur was Roscoe Conkling's chief lieutenant, the man whom President Hayes had fired as collector of customs to appoint the late abused Theodore Roosevelt. That was a tough one for the Goo-Goos to swallow, but it was the sort of foul-tasting medicine that Blaine and his Half Breeds specialized in calling caviar.

On the night of Arthur's nomination, Pendleton went with celebrating Stalwarts to one of Chicago's better whorehouses and spent a dismaying amount of his ill-gotten gains cavorting with a Norwegian blonde from Minnesota. She reminded him of Sally Gansevoort, except for her smile. It was a whore's smile, stained, scarred with insincerity.

Pendleton could not recall exactly what he did with the Minnesota blonde, but when he took a bath the next day he noticed that his right arm was covered with bite marks. Had they been inflicted on him at his request? After worrying about being devoured by women for most of his life, had he finally asked one of them to do the job? Sally's spectacular bicuspids would, he was sure, be even more decisive.

He stumbled out of the tub, finished the glass of bourbon he had been drinking, and noticed it was getting dark. He must have slept all day. He went over to the desk to confront *The Honest Stalwart.* He stared blearily at the one paragraph he had written so far.

The piece of paper suddenly curled its sides into legs and rose on them, turning into a huge cockroach. *Croton Bug?* it whispered in the voice of Managing Editor John Reid of the *New York Times.* Pendleton backed away from it, across the room to the window. Suddenly the room was full of them, all marching toward him across the red-and-gold carpet.

They waved their long roach legs and preened their bearded faces, each of which had an uncanny resemblance to Ulysses Grant. It was the Old Guard, all 306 of them, coming to devour him. In the center of the formation was tiny Genevieve, with a shepherd's crook in her hand, directing the whole operation. Whimpering, Pendleton climbed up on the windowsill. From the sixth floor of the Grand Pacific Hotel the broad waters of Lake Michigan were visible. Pale stars glinted above them.

The Old Guard waited, preening their beards, honestly puzzled by what he was going to do. Tiny Genevieve seemed to be calling something to him, but her infinitesimal voice was drowned by the thunder of Chicago's traffic. Perhaps she was urging him to get down from the windowsill and let the Old Guard devour him. Perhaps she was telling him to stop trying to outdo Lincoln and solve the mystery of where this absurd American tragicomedy was going. Why not just leap across the tangle of traffic below him into the dark peaceful waters of the lake?

Maybe he could not manage that big a leap. Maybe he might crash into that brewery wagon on the corner of Quincy Street. That would be all right. They could just shovel away what was left of Pendleton the newspaperman with the entrails of the 4,805,000 slaughtered hogs at the Anglo-American Packing Company.

"Clay—what the hell are you doing up there?"

It seemed to be Jonathan Stapleton. A man of his size, at least, with his voice, was standing in the middle of the darkened room.

"I was trying . . . to fix the window," Pendleton said. "It was . . . stuck. It's so damn hot in here."

Pendleton peered into the shadows on the floor. Tiny Genevieve and the Old Guard had vanished. He got down and cautiously recrossed the carpet to the bed.

"Clay," Jonathan Stapleton said, "I'm afraid I made a damn fool of myself the other night. I've been having a lot of . . . personal problems lately. But I wanted to see you again. What I was really trying to do, the other night, was ask your help."

"Help? To do what?"

"Go after Gould. See if we can run that piece of slime out of Wall Street. Before he takes over this party—maybe both parties."

The General began talking about what was wrong with Jay Gould. The power of his amoral example, his perpetual greed, his endless hunger for speculation for its own sake, for profits without the slightest concern for the human beings in the companies he looted and the stockholders he swindled. "He's on his way to becoming that creature out of the Bible, Clay—Leviathan, King of the Proud. If no one stops him, he could corrupt this whole country. I need someone like you, a good reporter, who can dig out Gould's secret allies, expose his swindles. It would be a hell of a job. Almost like fighting a war."

Maybe it was the word "war" that did it. While the General was talking, Pendleton had had a sudden vision of showing him "The Honest Stalwart." Of saying yes, he'd help. Of course he would join the march toward America's special destiny. The word "war" reminded Pendleton of how many men the General had already devoured with his mystical faith in this ridiculous country.

"General," Pendleton said, "in words which you told me that you once used to answer Jay Gould—I prefer not to."

Silence from the tall figure there in the darkness. "I was afraid you'd feel that way. But I had to ask."

"I'm flattered, believe me. But—"

He was not a crusader. He was an ex-mama's boy who only wanted to be a survivor, a shrewd Darwinian. He was a man without a country, a son without a father, who saw no percentage in joining a country where fathers devoured their sons' bodies and souls. His flirtation with the DTs just now had not only taught him he was drinking too much. It had made him resolve that no one, Jonathan Stapleton, Rawdon Stapleton, Sally Gansevoort or Genevieve Dall Stapleton, was going to devour Clay Pendleton.

They shook hands. They promised to see each other in New York. The usual baloney. Pendleton was quite certain that he would not see Jonathan Stapleton again unless Whitelaw Reid told him to get an interview with Jay Gould's foe. An unlikely event.

The door closed and Pendleton was alone in the hot Chicago night. Alone in the center of the United States, in the middle of the continent conceived in liberty. That was the way he wanted it: alone. He had just escaped being devoured. Why was he so miserable?

THREE

"Cynthia, dear?" Jonathan Stapleton's voice floated up the stairs. "Cynthia?"

Cynthia sat on her bed, angrily flipping the pages of the *New York Herald.* It was a stiflingly warm June night. She had left her door open, hoping to catch a cross current of cool air from the darkness. "Yes?" she called with a careful blend of curtness and courtesy.

"Would you come downstairs?"

Oh. She was on the obituary page. Her eyes devoured the small black-bordered notice: "Still sacred to the memory of family and friends, Theodore Roosevelt. Beloved father, husband, citizen."

Four years. Theodore would be dead four years tomorrow. Mittie would be going out to Greenwood Cemetery in Brooklyn to lay flowers on the grave. She should be with her. She should be with her dearest friend. But she had not seen Mittie for two months at least. There was a barrier between them now that friendship—no, call it by its right name, love—could not surmount.

Gathering the fashionable quarter train of her shaded turquoise evening dress, with its shorter, more manageable skirt, Cynthia slowly descended the stairs. The men, a half-dozen of them, were standing in the hall, Jonathan at the forefront of the clump, on his face a smile which only she knew was artificial.

"Senator Conkling refused to leave without seeing you," he said.

Roscoe Conkling emerged from the clump to grin carnivorously at her. "Mrs. Stapleton," he said, kissing her hand, "after wandering for hours across the dismal wastes of politics, I felt I—indeed all of us—were entitled to a glimpse of beauty."

"How lovely to see you, Senator," she said to Theodore Roosevelt's former persecutor.

Even though Cynthia knew that Senator Conkling was not responsible for Theodore's death—intestinal cancer had caused his agonizing stomach pains —it required enormous effort to be polite to this man. She managed it only because politeness was part of the wider subterfuge she was practising on her husband.

"Everyone in Washington is still talking about the uncrowned queen of the inaugural ball," Conkling said.

"Really, Senator. I have no desire to make enemies of Mrs. Garfield and Mrs. Blaine."

Everyone chuckled. Cynthia said hello to Thomas Platt, the quiet, surprisingly shy junior senator from New York, and was introduced to four other Conkling followers with jowls the size of their official titles. The senior Senator held an impromptu caucus and everyone agreed that Mrs. Stapleton was unquestionably the most beautiful woman at President Garfield's inaugural ball. A few more pleasantries and the politicians trudged into the humid night. Mr. and Mrs. Jonathan Stapleton were alone.

"I'm sorry they stayed so long. As I said, it was better to meet here. At a hotel or a restaurant there would have been reporters snooping around."

"I understand," Cynthia said.

"May I serve dinner, madam?" Cousteau asked from the doorway.

"Yes. Immediately," Cynthia said.

They sat down before plates of chilled vichyssoise. "I think they're going to pull it off," Jonathan said. "They say Garfield is shaking in his shoes."

Cynthia knew exactly what he was talking about. The newspapers had almost nothing in them except the latest uproar in the Republican Party. President Garfield, at the behest of his oily Secretary of State, James G. Blaine, had declared war on Senator Conkling and his Stalwart cohorts. The Senator had made a daring riposte. He and his colleague Thomas Platt had resigned and called on the people of New York to reelect them, sending Garfield a Stalwart message that he could not ignore if he hoped to win a second term.

"George wants to go west with Theodore and Elliott Roosevelt this summer. I trust he has your approval."

Jonathan Stapleton concentrated on his vichyssoise. His charming wife had just told him that she did not care what his disgusting friend Senator Conkling was going to pull off. "Yes, of course," he said.

Was he also reminded by that name, Theodore Roosevelt, of the original cause of their malaise? She hoped so. It pleased her, if bitter satisfaction could be called pleasing, to remind him of it.

Two years ago she had persuaded young Theodore Roosevelt to spend the better part of a summer at Oyster Bay tutoring George for his entrance examinations to Harvard. He had passed and incidentally had become a devoted admirer of the gifted older brother, virtually abandoning his friendship with Elliott. With Theodore's encouragement George had become a good student at Harvard.

Bitterness: that was Cynthia's current mode of feeling for her husband. It had replaced the rage of the first year, the scorn of the second year, the regret of the third year of their malaise. She looked down the table at the lowered head of the man whose name she shared, doggedly spooning down his soup, accepting bitterness as his lot. For a moment she wanted to fling the silver at him, smash the crystal, scream, *How could you?*

Last year, when his mother died without a word of reconciliation, Cynthia had watched Jonathan Stapleton suffer. She had never seen him so defenseless, so nakedly exposed to the old woman's malice—and Rawdon's malice. She had heard him on the telephone begging Genevieve to intervene with Rawdon. She heard him pacing the floor of his bedroom night after night. That was when regret had whispered tentatively, hopefully, in Cynthia's heart. But Caroline Stapleton was scarcely in her grave before a new political campaign began, a new orgy of bloody-shirt waving and committees and rallies. General Stapleton had plunged grimly into the melee, leaving his wife to conclude that he was hopeless.

"I saw a notice in the paper of the anniversary of Theodore's death," Jonathan said. "I'll send flowers—for both of us."

"Oh. Good."

"Are you going out to Greenwood with Mittie?"

"No. I'm having lunch with Madeline Terhune."

Silence again, as the fish course was served. Silence was the prevailing pattern at most dinners the Stapletons ate alone. She wondered what Jonathan was thinking; probably about politics or some railroad quarrel with Jay Gould. Cynthia was remembering her first visit to Mittie after Theodore died.

She had poured out her rage at Jonathan, presuming she would meet an even more enraged response. "Oh my dear, control yourself," Mittie had said. "You'll do something awful like divorce him. It will be another burden on my conscience, as bad as Theodore—perhaps worse. And I'll lose you as a friend, just when I need you most."

Both ideas had stunned Cynthia. For the first time she was forced to think realistically about the quarrel. Mittie was telling her some of its potential implications. In New York of 1878, a divorced woman became a nonperson. With two daughters to introduce to society and a small army of frowning ultrarespectable Roosevelt relatives surrounding her, Mittie would never be able to receive the former Mrs. Jonathan Stapleton in her house.

Neither Mittie nor Jonathan Stapleton knew they were dealing with a different Cynthia Legrand—a woman who had emerged from her bedroom to write Lionel Bradford a note: *I've been thinking about that word "impossible." In America I believe in it. But I don't in French. Even though it's spelled the same way. Isn't that strange?*

The fish plates were taken away, the meat course—veal à la Montebello—was served, wine was poured. There were times lately when Cynthia felt that her entire life had become as methodical, as inevitable, as the courses of a dinner in which all the food was familiar.

"I saw your friend Lionel Bradford on Wall Street yesterday. He's given up Paris."

"Oh?"

Cynthia reached for her wineglass. She sipped it without a tremor.

Her husband knew nothing. She was still Mrs. Jonathan Stapleton. Still capable at least in theory of being Mittie's friend, still capable—again in theory—of returning to the Palazzo Rospigliosi someday with the stubborn Yankee at the other end of the dining-room table.

The summer of that first year of their malaise, the year of her rage, she had gone to Europe without Jonathan, supposedly to visit Madeline Terhune. One July night on the Champ-Élysées, they had encountered Lionel Bradford. He had bought them a drink at a nearby café. It was all perfectly respectable. If any American friends happened to be in the cheerful throng of strollers pouring down the avenue, they would only see a gentleman being polite to two gorgeously dressed woman friends. When they parted, Bradford had a key to Cynthia's hotel room in his pocket.

Jonathan Stapleton was looking at her across the silence. Not with suspicion. She could tolerate, she would almost welcome, suspicion. With unconcealed, melancholy longing.

No. The word spoke in Cynthia's mind. It had two meanings, one a cold answer to Jonathan's longing, the other a memory. *No.* That was what she had thought as Lionel Bradford entered her. *No.* She had welcomed him and yet she did not want to forfeit Jonathan Stapleton's love forever—which was what she thought she was doing. She also did not want to lose Mittie's love. Incredible, the guardians of her soul.

No. Yet Cynthia Legrand the courtesan was murmuring, "Oh Lionel, Lionel. Dear Lionel." She let champagne and the scent of fresh roses create a flood of dark exhilaration, a compound of southern fury and the scorned wife's revenge. Swept away, obliterated, that forlorn *no*, like a bluff or an island in the path of the rampaging Mississippi.

Yet remembered now, looking into her husband's melancholy face.

At 1 P.M. on the following day, Cynthia stepped out of a maroon barouche and rejoiced for a moment in the soft June breeze, the blossoming trees in Madison Square Park. Once more she resolved to enjoy herself for the next two hours, in spite of a mostly sleepless night.

Picking up the skirts of her sky-blue walking dress, she crossed the tiny lawn to the doorway of society's shrine, Delmonico's Restaurant. In the flower-filled foyer, Philippe, the diminutive headwaiter, greeted her with his usual smile. As he led her past the café, a masculine voice called her name: "Mrs. Stapleton."

Her brother Robert emerged from a swarm of guzzling males at the bar. He was dressed in his usual flashy style: a flowered blue silk vest, a tie that was a narrow version of the Confederate flag, with an enormous diamond stickpin in it. Beside him, far more conservatively dressed, was Colonel Edgar Calhoun. "What an unexpected pleasure," he said.

His smile was warm, but sad. Sadness descended on Colonel Calhoun every time he saw Mrs. Stapleton. He knew about her and Lionel Bradford. Lionel must have boasted about his Paris conquest to Robert, who told the Colonel. It had made Cynthia angrily determined to avoid any and all indiscretions with Bradford in New York.

"What brings you to this romantic bower?" Robert asked. "Not a tête-à-tête with your husband, surely."

Cynthia glared at him. "I'm seeing my dear friend Madeline Terhune. She's in New York to open a new play. I'm not sure who's escorting us. I believe it's her manager."

Robert grinned. "I think you're in for a surprise."

Edgar Calhoun looked stricken, as if the surprise was anything but amusing to him.

Puzzled, Cynthia followed Philippe into the mirror-lined dining room overlooking Madison Square Park. Most of the diners were women, but at every table sat a requisite male, usually some toady like Ward McAllister, to obey the iron law of respectability laid down by Lorenzo Delmonico. Cynthia paused in the doorway, admiring the silver chandeliers, the frescoed ceiling, the splashing flower-bordered fountain. Beauty, in décor, in paintings, sculpture, music, had become almost a necessity to her. Nothing else really soothed her nerves.

Certain friendships had become equally precious. There sat Madeline Terhune at a corner table, sipping champagne. She was wearing a wide-brimmed Manila Longchamps hat trimmed with a long ostrich plume and a cluster of roses. Over her blue-and-white striped spring walking dress was a pelerine, an elbow-length shawl of black Spanish lace edged in jet. Cynthia kissed her on the cheek and said, "How dramatic. You look prepared to mourn—or celebrate."

"Exactly the mood I'm in," Madeline said.

"Where's our escort?"

"He dashed into the café to check the stock ticker. Here he comes now."

Lionel Bradford stood in the doorway. Cynthia had not seen him in almost nine months. Last summer in Paris, regret had made her an unenthusiastic mistress. Lionel had been equally short-tempered, remote. One night he had announced that he had grown tired of playing her summer lover. He wanted her to divorce her husband and marry him. When she refused, he had announced with more than a little bitterness that he was not returning to New York. Cynthia had made the city "impossible" to him. He had spent the winter in London and Paris, reportedly enjoying the company of several ladies of the demimonde.

"He comes determined to conquer," Madeline said, *sotto voce*, as Bradford walked toward them.

True to her neutrality on matters moral, Madeline had never tried to discourage Cynthia's affair. She had willingly, cheerfully, played the part of the silent conspirator. But Madeline had also never encouraged the liaison. In a hundred small ways, she had reiterated a carefully controlled dislike of the financier.

Her lover, Cynthia thought as Lionel Bradford drew closer. But the word did not fit. Love was alien to this cool arrogant man. She suddenly remembered an incident in Paris that had forced her to confront this disheartening fact.

One night, at the Bal Mabille, still the home of the can-can, they had encountered the Contessa Rospigliosi and her latest lover, a French sculptor. The Contessa had understood the situation at a glance and talked wittily about the Venetian tradition of the *cicisbeo*, the male escort who was originally supposed to guarantee the virtue of a restless wife but had degenerated into a license for a married woman to appear in public with her lover. Back at the Hotel Splendide, Cynthia had evaded Bradford's caresses. She spent a sleepless night, remembering Venice.

In the morning, she had tried to explain her feelings to Bradford. "My dear," he had said, "you're much too intelligent to let your conscience bother you. You should have gone to bed with me last night. By now you would have forgotten the whole thing."

Now she was confronting the man—and the fact—in New York. "Lionel dear," Cynthia said, with her brightest smile. "What a pleasant surprise. What brings you back to our great metropolis, after all your vows to scorn it?"

"You," he said, kissing her on the cheek.

"I thought certain impossibilities were understood—and regretfully accepted."

"I'm here to overcome those impossibilities. For your sake."

He snapped his fingers at a waiter, who filled Cynthia's champagne glass.

"I told you he was determined," Madeline Terhune said.

"Madeline darling. Shut up."

Madeline Terhune flushed. Cynthia had never heard Bradford speak to her in that way before.

They sipped their champagne, and Bradford dropped the subject of impossibilities to tell them what he had been doing in Paris for the last nine months. It explained, at least in part, why he was feeling imperious. Using some of his own and more of Jay Gould's money, he had bought up almost all of Egypt's floating debt. The country was bankrupt, and French and English financiers were selling Egyptian bonds and notes for next to nothing. He had inside information that the British were going to invade Egypt and force them to pay the debts in full. "We should clear a hundred million, at least," Bradford said.

"Don't forget my five percent, Lionel dear," Madeline Terhune said.

Lionel Bradford looked as if he would like to forget Madeline completely, even to make her disappear. "Don't worry," he said.

Another snap of his fingers summoned Philippe, to discuss their first course. Soon the waiters were serving timbales à la Mentana, small, drum-shaped hors d'oeuvres filled with strips of beef tongue and truffles, garnished with Périgueux sauce. Philippe poured a delicate Laville Haut-Brion, and Lionel Bradford turned the conversation to the changes that had occurred in the United States since last they met. A new President sat in Washington, handsome affable James Garfield, giving the Republicans two full decades of control of the White House.

"You'd never know it was a new President, as far as Jonathan Stapleton is concerned," Cynthia said.

She told them about the caucus of Stalwart leaders in her parlor last night, plotting their next move against the harried Garfield.

"I'm afraid your husband and his friends are beyond redemption," Lionel Bradford said. "Jay Gould has decided to destroy them. That's why I'm back in New York. To help you declare your independence of your husband before it's too late."

"How do I manage that?"

"It's a complicated process, like everything a woman does. First she separates her feelings from her husband. Then her body. Finally—her money."

"Who told you about my money?"

"Your brother. He says you have a half-million dollars in your own name. But unprotected—completely at the General's disposal."

"That's more or less correct."

"That money, and your chances of obtaining a great deal more, could vanish tomorrow."

"Really, Lionel," Madeline Terhune said, undaunted by Bradford's hostility. "This is better than most of the plays on the boards. I should be taking notes."

Bradford continued to speak only to Cynthia. "Your friend may find it amusing, but I don't. Jay Gould is the wealthiest, most powerful man in the civilized world at this moment. He's going to bankrupt your husband."

Cynthia struggled to remain calm. Was Lionel Bradford speaking out of a genuine wish to protect her—or out of his earlier wish to possess her and set her up as a symbol of his cold defiance of conventional morality? She had learned a good deal about this man in the past four years. He had been born in poverty somewhere in Central Europe, one of those border districts such as the Rhineland where there was no loyalty to any country. He had risen by "making himself useful to the rich," but in his heart he despised the old money and old blood that still ruled most of Europe.

Bradford had carried this hatred with him to the United States. Men like Jonathan Stapleton, with family traditions and stern ideas about duty and responsibility and patriotism, aroused his animosity to an extraordinary degree.

Philippe interrupted them to suggest plovers *à la* Parny as their main course. Soon six little birds arrived in a circular dish with a carved rice foundation. They had been baked beneath layers of fresh mushrooms and finely chopped truffles, then basted with clarified butter. For the wine Philippe chose a fruity Clos de Vougeot.

As they relished this delight with properly ladylike gusto, Madeline told them the denouement of her year-long affair with Lord Randolph Churchill. Once she had gotten from him the secret plans for Egypt that Lionel Bradford found so helpful, she grew bored. But a gradual collapse was turned into a hasty exit when his American wife began having a very public affair of her own. "It's given me the idea for my new play, *Retaliation.*"

"Careful, dear," Lionel Bradford said. "You don't want to reveal your predilections too publicly."

"Why not?" Madeline said. "You don't conceal yours."

Philippe interrupted them again. It was time for dessert, a course for which he had felt no need to consult them. He presented one of Delmonico's supreme creations, *plombières à la Montesquieu.* In pear-shaped molds slices of preserved pineapples and melon were macerated in kirsch and frozen in ice cream. They were served within a ring of little cakes known as *bouchées.*

Madeline nibbled a *bouchée* and smiled mockingly at Lionel Bradford. "Cynthia is perfectly aware that I maintain 'love' is a word that should be scoured from a mature woman's mind. It's another name for slavery, humiliation, despair."

No, whispered in Cynthia's mind, a refusal to abandon faith or hope in love's possibility. She did not agree with Madeline that two women could love each other enough to make them indifferent to masculine love. That solution, if Madeline with her endless succession of lovers was any example, left Cynthia too close to the destiny her father had decreed for her. She still believed in the possibility of a transcendent transforming love, even if she had failed to find it.

Bradford consumed a *bouchée* and smiled at Madeline. "I agree that love is an absurd idea, of course. But there happens to exist an excellent substitute."

"What is it, dear Lionel? Tell us poor ignorant females," Madeline said.

"Eros," Lionel Bradford said, "desire and its fulfillment. Take those *plombières.* If both of you refused to let me have any, it would whet my desire. It would make me desperate for a taste of them. Always, the deepest, most intense desire is for the forbidden, the seemingly impossible."

His eyes met Cynthia's as he uttered this last significant word. "Think about it for a moment," he said. "It explains a great deal. Why ordinary, sanctified marriage, for instance, inevitably ends in misery. Desire for the attainable, for the convenient, for the permitted simply doesn't last. It always ends in boredom, apathy, or hatred. But a marriage which defied convention in the name of Eros would be a different matter."

Madeline dipped her spoon into the *plombières* and held it out to Bradford. "You can have a taste—but that's all, Lionel," she said.

"We Iagos are inured to contempt," Bradford said. "But we're also devotees of the law of progress. We believe that small pleasures lead inevitably to greater ones."

His tongue curled slowly, carefully around the tip of Madeline's spoon, licking away all trace of the dessert. Cynthia found herself fascinated by the supple authority of that tongue until it retreated behind those hard confident lips. *Animal,* whispered in Cynthia's mind. She remembered that tongue exploring her mouth, in Paris. Would it stir deeper darker exhilaration here in New York, where the danger of the forbidden was more acute?

Lionel Bradford let the creamy blend of tastes in *plombières à la Montesquieu* linger in his mouth for a moment, and then he began speaking only to Cynthia. Madeline Terhune virtually ceased to exist. "A block from here, there's a room filled with roses. A bottle of Moët et Chandon stands chilling on the bureau. You know I can guarantee a blend of taste and touch there infinitely more pleasing than anything served on a cold spoon.

"But now there's something else, something more daring than mere infidelity. A blend of pleasure and ambition that we were both born to consummate. I want you to play a part in this war that's beginning between your husband and Gould. You can do more than free Louisiana this time. You can rescue the entire South. If we destroy your husband, it will send a message to all the other backers of the Stalwarts: Waving the bloody shirt will cost you money; Mr. Gould doesn't like it."

Destiny. That shrouded figure in Bralston's garden. Was this the part that Cynthia Legrand had always been fated to play? But where did Mittie Roosevelt's guardian love, memories of a morning in Venice, whispers of *my dearest friend,* fit into the scheme? *Croce e delizia al cor.* The heart was missing from this story. It was all cold brain, fitfully warmed by protection and pity, illuminated by flickering revenge that no longer cast heat. Cynthia hesitated, her eyes drifting from Lionel Bradford's commanding gaze to Madeline Terhune's suddenly somber face, her black lace pelerine. Now she knew why Madeline was poised between celebration and mourning.

A ripple, then a surge of sound, swept the room. What was it? Her brother Robert rushed toward them, his eyes bulging, his mouth slack. "Someone just shot the President!" he said.

"Shot the—?" Lionel Bradford gasped.

"In Washington, D.C.—in Union Station in Washington, D.C. He said he was a Stalwart. He shot him to make Chet Arthur president."

Bradford looked frightened. "Do you think it's a coup d'état?"

"I doubt it. The Stalwarts ain't that crazy."

"Then our chief worry is the stock market." Bradford put his hand on Cynthia's arm. "My dear, forgive me. There are millions at stake. I must get downtown immediately."

He and Robert fled, leaving Cynthia staring after them in bewilderment.

Madeline Terhune dipped another spoonful of their dessert. "Now you know how much *plombières à la Legrand* are worth in the scale of things," she said, and slid the spoon into her red mouth.

Half the tables in the room had emptied. Other diners peered anxiously out the windows, as if they thought a revolution might come boiling across Madison Square Park at any moment. Through the confusion strode a tall, calm, resolute figure.

"Ladies," Colonel Edgar Calhoun said, with a mock bow. "You seem to have been left without that essential thing, an escort. May I join you?"

"By all means," Cynthia said. She introduced him to Madeline Terhune. "What do you make of this dreadful news?" she asked.

"I'd say it's the last shot of the war. From now on, Americans north and south will concentrate on making money."

When they finished their coffee Colonel Calhoun insisted on escorting them home—in Madeline's case, to her hotel. "It's just possible that the news about the President may encourage some riffraff to take to the streets," he said in his offhand but remarkably serene way.

As Madeline kissed Cynthia goodbye at the hotel she whispered in her ear, "Lionel bet me five hundred dollars he'd get you to that room with the champagne and roses. I thought for a while he was going to win."

They rode down Fifth Avenue in the barouche. The streets were rather deserted, but the city seemed calm. Colonel Calhoun smiled at her from the opposite seat. "I didn't wish poor Garfield any harm, but it's an ill wind and all that sort of thing."

"Yes," Cynthia said, still somewhat dazed by Madeline's farewell.

"I never thought of myself as born under a lucky star," Calhoun continued. "Rather the opposite. In fact, I'd made a rather dangerous resolution. I wasn't going to let that scum Bradford touch you again, no matter what it cost me. I was going to cane him on the steps of Delmonico's if necessary. All he wants is your money."

"How—do you know?" Cynthia asked.

They had turned down Seventeenth Street. On the corner of Fourth Avenue a newsboy was howling, "Garfield plugged by a Stalwart!"

"He and Robert are very close. They talk freely and assume my agreement."

"President moidered!" screamed another newsboy.

"I love you," Edgar Calhoun said as they rode steadily toward Stuyvesant Square. "What you choose to do or not to do about it is your decision. I can't help but feel that a kind of destiny brought us together—and still controls us."

Did he know the power of that word destiny in Cynthia Legrand's soul?

But he was proposing a different meaning for it. A destiny that did not exclude love, that insisted on it.

They were in Stuyvesant Square now. The green park was full of bright sunlight. She was forty-one years old. Could love happen again to a heart corroded by bitterness and age? Once she had said insincerely to Jonathan that their love was their child. Now she wanted to say it sincerely to this man.

"We've all been . . . damaged by our lost cause, by the ravages of foe— and friend. But I want to believe, I do believe, there's still the possibility of pure affection."

"I believe it, too," Cynthia said.

The barouche stopped in front of 217 East Seventeenth Street. Colonel Calhoun helped her to the sidewalk. "You must give me time," Cynthia said.

"Of course."

She offered her white-gloved hand. A watching neighbor, if anyone in sedate Stuyvesant Square was interested in such things, might have noticed he held the hand to his lips for a half second longer than decorum dictated.

"Goodbye," Cynthia said. "For now."

FOUR

Jonathan Stapleton sat at his desk, which was piled with annual reports for the Hannibal, St. Louis & St. Joseph Railroad. A man should know everything about a railroad when he had a million dollars invested in it. Especially when Jay Gould was trying to wreck the investment.

But Jonathan was not studying an annual report. He was staring at a letter which contained a message composed of words clipped from newspapers.

DEAR General *you* have an UN*FAITHFUL* WIFE

Watch her CLOSELY you will SEE the signs

your FRIEND

There was a clatter of feet in the hall. George Munsey, his chief clerk, burst into his office, his face twisted with grief. "General. The President is dead. The papers are putting out a special on it."

Jonathan nodded. "Send the telegram to his widow."

The telegram of condolence had been written weeks ago. But James Garfield had lingered, fighting desperately for life, all through the summer.

"It's terrible, isn't it?" George Munsey said, tears in his eyes. "I feel as though I've lost my best friend."

"It's terrible, Munsey. No doubt about it."

One of the cleverest, most charming political hypocrites of the era was dead. During the war Garfield had called Lincoln a second-rate Illinois lawyer and after his death lauded him as one of the few great rulers. He had posed as a fearless foe of corruption and then dashed to New Orleans to help steal the election of 1876. He had abused Grant while he was president and then said no man had carried away greater fame from the White House. He had mortgaged his presidency to Jay Gould and James G. Blaine before he took the oath of office.

But Jonathan Stapleton could not say any of this to George Munsey. President James Garfield was beyond reproach now, a certified martyr to good government. A myth had been created and other men, other causes, had been ruined.

Munsey departed and Jonathan Stapleton sat quietly for a moment, mournfully remembering the day last June when his political world had collapsed. He had been on his way uptown to the Fifth Avenue Hotel to set up a campaign office for Roscoe Conkling's and Tom Platt's reelection to the Senate. Suddenly there were newsboys screaming on every corner that a Stalwart had shot the President. A halfwit who boasted he had done it for the good of the party and the country.

Jonathan remembered Clay Pendleton interviewing him the next day, with the *Tribune*'s story on the desk between them. MURDERED BY THE SPOILS SYSTEM, the head declared. Every paper in the country agreed with this standard smear that the liberals and the Half Breeds had fastened on the Stalwarts. As if they did not hand out jobs to their hungry followers whenever they got the chance. Clay's questions had been crisply professional. Did he think the Stalwarts were finished? (Yes.) Did he think civil-service reform was now inevitable? (No.) But Clay's eyes asked a deeper question: Is this country an evil joke?

What did those memories have to do with the erratic, explosive message in his hand? Nothing—and everything.

"Mr. Apthorpe to see you."

Delancey Apthorpe rushed into the office. His cavalryman's mustaches still bristled even though they were growing gray. "Jonathan. I think we better get the hell out of the Hannibal and St. Joe."

"Why?"

"Gould's little man, Gansevoort, is warning everyone that the Leviathan is going short in it, and he has the Missouri state legislature in his pocket."

"That isn't true. I've got a man out there in St. Louis, Chauncey I. Filley, who guarantees me it can't happen, because he's got the legislature in *his* pocket."

"They may be, but the *World* is running a story about the railroad's floating debt and Christ knows what else. It's going to stampede people out of the stock."

"I'll have to talk to Mayer first."

"I wouldn't be surprised if he's uptown right now making a deal with his fellow Hebrew."

"Gould isn't Jewish," Jonathan snapped.

He had always detested this tendency to persecute and denigrate immigrant Americans. His father, as befitted a Democratic politician, had regularly denounced it. For once, Jonathan had agreed with him. America was big enough, strong enough, to welcome anyone who came to her shores.

"Are you sure?" Delancey said. "The original name was Gold."

"Ben Dall knew his family in Massachusetts. The Dalls came from the same county. The Goulds—or Golds—arrived two or three ships after the *Mayflower.*"

Jay Gould was not explainable by the supposedly sinister talents of the Jewish race. Jay Gould was America's problem, a symptom of something gone awry in America's soul.

"Come along with me to Mayer's."

In ten minutes they were in the offices of Mayer Brothers on Worth Street. The Mayers had begun as cotton brokers, hence their location in the heart of the textile district. Adolph Mayer, bald as an egg, almost as wide as he was tall, held out a stubby hand. "General. I was about to waddle down to your office for the same reason I suspect has brought you here."

"The Hannibal and St. Joe."

"Exactly."

Jonathan had met Adolph Mayer when he had come to a regatta to watch his son Isaac row with Rawdon's crew at Princeton. The Mayers were looking for someone who could advise them on investing in railroads. Jonathan was looking for someone who would give him advice on how to make Principia Mills profitable. They had begun a mutually satisfying relationship.

"I think it's time to fight him, Mayer."

"I'd love to do it. If for no other reason than to repay some of the insults his man Gansevoort throws around town about the Mayers. He's never forgiven his daughter for marrying Isaac. But Gould's bigger than ever. With Western Union and now the Metropolitan Street Railways . . ."

"We have an old saying in this country, 'The bigger they come, the harder they fall.' Gould never has a cent of cash to spare. This move with the Hannibal and St. Joe—it's a partridge flutter, Mayer."

The female partridge lured predators away from her young by fluttering her wings. On Wall Street the unwary investor lunged for the flutter of a promising stock certificate. Mayer had no difficulty with the slang, but he clearly had doubts about challenging Jay Gould.

"I think we can corner it and beat Gould out of four or five million. But that would only be round one. Or the first harpoon—take your choice. We'd have to stay in this thing to the finish."

"Who have you got with us? We couldn't do it alone."

Jonathan took a piece of paper out of his pocket. It had ten names on it, all people who had lost at least a million dollars to Gould over the past five years. They were a mixed bag—western speculators, conservative Bostonians, some old New York money. "There's about fifty million on that list," Jonathan said. "I haven't talked to any of them. I wanted you with me first. Not for your charm, Mayer, but for your European banking connections. I'm good for ten or twelve million at the City Bank if I put Principia Mills up for security."

"I'll come aboard," Mayer said. "What's the name of the enterprise?"

"The Gould Exterminating Company."

Delancey Apthorpe had sat silently throughout the conversation. Outside on Worth Street, he said, "Do you need an eleventh man on that team?"

"You do enough, buying and selling for me. You've got five children to support."

"The other day Gansevoort was in my office offering me a piece of this Egyptian swindle Gould says he's going to pull off. They want to spread the paper around the Street. His condition was an absolute end to doing any further business with you. I told him to shove it all the way up the Nile to Khartoum."

Jonathan Stapleton held out his hand. "We could use a good cavalryman."

Delancey went off to buy another two million dollars' worth of Hannibal & St. Joseph stock. Jonathan Stapleton headed uptown. In the Fifth Avenue Hotel, an elevator took him up to Roscoe Conkling's room. The ex-Senator sat in an easy chair, staring out the window. He was fifty-one years old. For fifteen years he had been one of the most powerful politicians in the country. Now he was finished. A lot of things were finished.

"You've heard the news?" Jonathan said.

"Garfield's dead?" Conkling said.

"Yes."

"That settles it."

"Arthur will do nothing?"

"He'll be a caretaker. A caretaker to a grave. What else can he do?"

The Vice-President, Chester A. Arthur, was best known for his good manners and stylish clothes, in particular his vanilla-cream trousers and white beaver hats.

"At least he'll get rid of Blaine."

"Of course. But otherwise he'll do nothing. He's a fine administrator. Things will run all right. They just won't go anywhere."

This politician, with his theatrical haircut and arrogant strut, had tried to swim against the moral indifference that was engulfing the American people as they marched carelessly into the future. Jonathan Stapleton knew he was a flawed hero, overbearing, conceited, thin-skinned. But he had supported him with money and advice (usually ignored) and friendship because there was no one else with the courage to tell the people that the cause for which men like Lincoln and Ben Dall had given their lives was being betrayed. Now the battle was lost, the dead slept forgotten in their graves. The Old Guard was in the dust, the eagle of the blue chained to the grubby earth once more.

He would not permit this slumped figure, awash with memories, regrets, loneliness, to become his mirror image. "What are you going to do?" he asked Conkling.

"I don't know," Conkling said.

"Open a law office. I need a good lawyer. A fighter. Do you have any money in the bank?"

"About a thousand dollars."

Jonathan handed him a check for five thousand dollars. "You'll make that much in a month before long. I won't be able to afford you."

Roscoe Conkling managed a smile. "You're a real friend, General. Who are we going to fight?"

"Jay Gould."

Conkling thought about it. He would love to attack the man who was backing his archenemy, James G. Blaine. But he was awed by assaulting a billion dollars. "How the hell can we do it?"

"The same way Lincoln beat Jeff Davis. By grabbing a leg here and a tail there and an ear or anything else that's sticking out. It's going to be a gutter fight. But it won't be boring."

Conkling shrugged. "What the hell have I got to lose?"

On the way to the elevator a woman in a sky-blue dress came around the corner of the corridor. She was a brunette, tall, full-breasted, with a wide-brimmed flowered hat. A dark veil hid her features. As she swept past him, Jonathan inhaled a breath of her perfume. Violette de Toulouse. Was

Cynthia walking down the corridor of another hotel or an assignation house at this very moment?

Watch her CLOSELY you will SEE **the** signs

It was not the first time he had wondered if Cynthia had been unfaithful to him. He had loathed the idea of her associating with Madeline Terhune. But he had told himself it was all part of the struggle for power that had erupted between them. The mere fact that she associated with such a notorious woman was proof that she was not being unfaithful—she was only threatening him. Which made it all the more imperative for him to play the cool, worldly New York husband who assumed his worldly New York wife could be trusted. *Jesus.*

At home, Cynthia was in the hall, talking on the telephone. She looked marvelous. Her hair was swept up, revealing her delicately shaped ears, her lovely neck. "I must say goodbye," she said. "My lord and master has just come home."

She turned to him, smiling, sweetly, sadly. "You've heard the news?" she said. "The President's dead."

"Yes."

"My poor husband," she said.

The words rang false. "Why do you say that?" he asked. "You know I haven't shed any tears for him."

Cynthia shrugged and strolled into the parlor. "Doesn't this mean the Stalwarts are finished?"

"More or less."

"Doesn't that upset you?"

"I'll survive."

Cousteau served sherry. They sat down in the parlor. Jonathan studied his elusive wife. He had long since abandoned that declaration of indifference that he had issued in their quarrel over Theodore Roosevelt. He had tried to tear her out of his feelings and found that it was impossible. But Cynthia had proven dismayingly indifferent to the signals he attempted to send, suggesting they negotiate peace. Remarks such as the one she had just made about Garfield left him feeling that the word "husband" had become a legal instead of a personal term in Mrs. Stapleton's vocabulary.

That status was evident in his increasingly rare visits to Cynthia's bedroom. Her reaction to his lovemaking was ominously different from the feelings she had displayed in the quarrel over his venture to Louisiana. In the worst of that bad time, he had sensed a suppressed affection, a wild tangle of disappointment and rage and conflicted loyalties. Now he often had the feeling that she was thinking of someone or something else.

Watch her CLOSELY you will SEE the Signs

Who had sent him that maddening message? He would probably never find out. "Where are we going to dinner tonight?" he asked, to break the awkward silence.

"I *told* you yesterday. Mittie Roosevelt is giving a ball for young Theodore and his wife."

That was not good news. He was still convinced that every time Cynthia saw Mittie or one of her other southern acquaintants, such as Alva Vanderbilt, she came home determined to continue fighting the war.

"Mittie says young Theodore can hardly wait to meet you again. He adores military men."

"I'm not a military man."

Cynthia found that amusing. "Have you been court-martialed and forgotten to tell me?"

"I'm a civilian who became a soldier by necessity. Four years in uniform out of fifty-four doesn't make a military man."

"By all means explain that to young Theodore. I hope you'll be polite to him. George wouldn't be doing nearly so well at Harvard if it weren't for him."

"Of course I'll be polite to him."

Snap and snarl. That was the way the conversation went these days in the Stapleton household. Was that one of the signs?

The Roosevelt mansion on Fifty-seventh Street was alive with fresh flowers; they must have cost several thousand dollars. When Mittie Roosevelt entertained, she went at it on an Astor or Vanderbilt scale. But she did not have the income to sustain it. Theodore Roosevelt's estate had been small, reflecting his early retirement from business. Jonathan wondered if Mittie's preference for splendid parties was a way of denying to the watching world any responsibility for her husband's death.

Was it also the reason she made such a fuss over Jonathan Stapleton? He was one of those who knew the real story. "General," Mittie said. "I swear to goodness you grow more like a noble Roman every time I see you."

"Which one, Mittie dear?" Cynthia said. "Boring old Julius Caesar, who was always suspecting the worst of his wife? Or someone more entertaining, like Mark Anthony?"

"Only you can decide that, my dear," Mittie said.

An excellent orchestra played lively polkas and waltzes for the guests, who were predominantly young. After a single obligatory waltz with Cynthia, he retired to the sidelines and let the good dancers take charge of his wife—something they were always eager to do. He sat down with Katherine Kemble Brown. If she had sent him the mystery message, she declined to add any further hints. Instead she harangued him for a half hour on Oscar Wilde, the Anglo-Irish poet who was prancing around the country in knee britches, proclaiming the importance of art for art's sake, whatever that meant. Katherine was convinced he was a degenerate.

Across the room he saw his daughter-in-law Genevieve sitting alone. She looked wan. He suddenly remembered her telephone call on the day Garfield was shot. She had said that she hoped a mere housewife could offer him condolences—and let him know she admired what he and the Stalwarts had been trying to do.

He escaped Katherine Kemble Brown and sat down next to Genevieve. "Why aren't you dancing?" he said. "You're too young to behave like an old married lady."

"No one's asked me," she said.

"Where's your husband?"

"Working. I sometimes think he divorced me to marry Jay Gould but he's been too busy to mention it."

The thought of Rawdon working with Jay Gould reduced Jonathan to silence.

"Have you heard that we're going to Egypt?" Genevieve asked.

"No."

"Rawdon thought a trip would do me good. I've been so mopy and nervous lately. He and Hal Bradford are going to Cairo to represent Jay Gould and Hal's father in negotiations with the Egyptian government about their public debt."

For a moment he was tempted to tell her what he had heard about Gould's dirty plan to make a killing on the Egyptian-debt crisis. But he decided there was no point in burdening this woman with any more responsibility for Rawdon. The failure of that idea was visible in Genevieve's toneless voice and defeated eyes. "I hope you enjoy yourself while they haggle," he said.

"I think I will," Genevieve said, her eyes brightening. For a moment she looked like her old self. "Clay Pendleton's coming. Rawdon thinks there's a good chance of him doing a story that will make him famous—an exposé of the slave trade. It's still in business in Sudan. And the Egyptians, the British, do nothing about it."

"Fascinating. How's my granddaughter? I hope you're not taking her to that disease-ridden part of the world."

"No. We're leaving her with the Mayers. She's in perfect health except for her asthma. We're still hoping she'll outgrow it the way Rawdon did."

The band was playing a dreamy waltz. Perhaps he could manage another dance without spoiling Cynthia's evening. He looked for her gleaming dark hair in the circling dancers and instead found Alva Vanderbilt dancing with her pudgy, bored-looking husband. "Whenever I see William Kissam Vanderbilt," Jonathan said, "I remember a prophecy your father made to me— that the North was going to produce a moneyed class with the same vices as the southern aristocracy."

A mistake. The brightness had vanished from Genevieve's eyes. "I think of him whenever we visit Gould," she said. "The man is a monster. I almost believe he's incapable of feeling anything."

"Before I'm through with him he may be feeling pain," Jonathan said, his eyes again on the circling dancers.

He finally found Cynthia on the other side of the room, talking to a tall dark-haired man with a flowing black mustache: Edgar Calhoun. Cynthia had invited him to dinner once or twice in recent years. At least the fellow was polite, unlike her obnoxious brother Robert.

As he stood up, even more determined to ask for another dance, Mittie Roosevelt's butler announced that midnight supper was being served. Jonathan found himself sitting next to young Theodore. Cynthia was far down the table, sitting between Calhoun and Lionel Bradford. Theodore drawled excitedly in his ear about his interest in the Civil War.

Except for his affected Harvard accent, young Roosevelt's sentiment seemed genuine, and he reinforced it by talking almost exclusively to Jonathan. At the other end of the table, Mittie Roosevelt was regaling her guests with plantation stories, told in impeccable darky dialect. Alva Vanderbilt added a few city tales from her girlhood days in Mobile. Edgar Calhoun urged Cynthia to contribute some of her bayou tales, and she told several in the Louisiana patois that was even funnier than the Negro talk of Georgia.

Normally Jonathan listened to these stories with only mild annoyance. They were popular everywhere, in magazines and on the stage. They enabled people to stop taking the Negro seriously; at best he was picturesque; at worst, and most people inclined to the worst, he was a joke. But today, with Garfield's death and the extinction of the cause that had cost him so much, Jonathan could not resist turning to Theodore Roosevelt and asking him if he had ever met Frederick Douglass.

"The Negro writer? No."

"I'll always remember him at the White House after Lincoln's second inauguration. This young lady's father was with me."

He smiled across the table at Genevieve, who had sat opposite them, silent, barely conversing with anyone throughout the dinner.

"Douglass walked in with an invitation in his hand and two policemen tried to throw him out. Colonel Dall stopped them and I found Lincoln and told him what was happening. Colonel Dall escorted Douglass into the East Room. There were about two thousand people jammed in there. Lincoln fought his way over to Douglass, and in a voice you could hear on the other side of the room he asked him what he thought of his inaugural address. He said there wasn't a man in Washington whose opinion he valued more. Douglass said, 'Mr. Lincoln, it was a sacred effort.' "

"Fascinating," Theodore Roosevelt said.

Jonathan looked around and realized that he had stopped all conversation at the table. Everyone was confronting him with either frowns or puzzled stares. Cynthia was among the frowners. So be it. He could not help one last gasp of defiance to the smooth-smiling victors.

An alarming sound drew his attention to Genevieve. His daughter-in-law was weeping—steadily, convulsively. "My dear," he said. "I had no idea that would upset you."

She shook her head and fled from the room. Alice Mayer and Eleanor Bradford followed her. "She was . . . very close to her father," Jonathan murmured.

"I know how she feels," Theodore Roosevelt said. "There are times when someone tells me a story about my father that they think will make me feel proud or consoled, and I can hardly bear it."

It was amazing how painful Jonathan found those words. Would either of his sons ever feel that way about him? Not likely. He had sacrificed their affection for the grim dictates of duty. For a weird moment he heard himself reading a poem: *I slept and dreamt that life was beauty. I woke and found that it was duty.* His mother beamed at him, never dreaming that duty would eventually break her heart—and his own.

Maybe he had sacrificed enough to this iron god. Perhaps it was time to try to regain some affection from those he loved, if it was not too late. He would begin with his wife. He would thrust that vicious letter out of his mind and visit Cynthia in her bedroom later tonight. He would ask her to stop blaming him for what he had done and said on behalf of the dead. He would tell her that the cause was ruined but he did not blame her—or the South. He would ask her to join him in a new beginning, a reaffirmation of their love outside the tangle of hatred and hopes in which history had enmeshed them.

The orchestra began playing in the ballroom. Most of the young people resumed dancing. Alice Roosevelt reclaimed her husband and led him away, vainly protesting that he and General Stapleton were about to discuss Gettysburg. The table was soon almost empty. But Cynthia remained seated tête-à-tête between Edgar Calhoun and Lionel Bradford. Calhoun whispered something in her ear. His mustache almost brushed her neck. She laughed and said, "Colonel, that's *extraordinary*."

The southern voice was no longer soothing. Before Jonathan knew it, he was standing over her. "Perhaps it's time we old folks went home," he said.

Slowly, mockingly, Cynthia looked up at him. Her face, still without a wrinkle, her bold green eyes, her ripe mouth told him that he had committed another blunder. She was not one of the old folks. The small smile on Calhoun's face seemed to say the same thing.

"The party's only beginning, Jonathan," she said.

"We'll be glad to see Mrs. Stapleton home when she decides to leave, General," Lionel Bradford said.

"Of course," Calhoun said.

Watch her CLOSELY you will SEE the signs

But he did not want to see them. He did not want to find out that one of these men was now or had been her lover. Nor did he want to take the risk of trying to explain himself. He did not want Cynthia to throw a defiant answer in his face. He did not want to confront the loss of this woman's love forever. Perhaps it was cowardly, perhaps it was wisdom—he only knew that instinct told him to retreat into the ritual politeness of a worldly New York marriage again.

"That's very kind of you gentlemen. I'll see you in the morning, Cynthia."

"Good night, Husband dear."

FIVE

In the glaring African sun, Souakin, the chief Red Sea port of the eastern Sudan, was not one of the world's most attractive places. On its single main square were three dilapidated brownish concrete buildings with numerous patches on their walls. One was the Egyptian governor's residence; opposite it was the customhouse. In between was a guardhouse manned by a half-dozen slovenly Egyptian soldiers. The rest of the town was a random collection of houses of white coral and huts of reeds and palm leaves. On the quay there was not a trace of the ordinary boxes and bales of commerce. Only one commodity seemed to be exported from Souakin: ivory. Glistening in the sun were stacks of elephant tusks.

Clay Pendleton joined Genevieve on the hot deck. "Nine tons," he said, gesturing to the tusks. "Five hundred elephants bit the dust to keep the piano manufacturers and corset-makers of the world going. Doesn't that make you feel proud of being part of an advanced civilization?"

"If we can accomplish what we've come here to do I'll feel—better," Genevieve said.

"Sure," Clay said. He lit a small black cigar and stared at the elephant tusks.

Genevieve felt a peculiar pang of disappointment. It was not the first time Clay had let their conversation lapse. She had looked forward to this trip, not only because it was a noble adventure but because Clay had agreed to come with them. These days he was the only man, in fact the only person, whose company she genuinely enjoyed.

Grunting and gasping, Hal Bradford joined them on the deck to blink into the tropic glare. He had gotten drunk again last night, downing brandy with the ship's officers until 2 or 3 A.M. They had kept everyone awake with their shouts and songs. Genevieve had accepted Hal and her sister Eleanor as traveling companions because Clay was coming along and the purpose of the trip was so exciting. She had even swallowed Hal as Rawdon's business partner. It was part of her new philosophy of acceptance.

"I hope we don't have to spend more than twelve hours in this pesthole," Hal said.

"As soon as we haggle them down to a decent price per camel, we'll be on our way."

The speaker was their guide, Michael Hanrahan, a spare dour Irishman they had hired in Cairo. He had made at least two dozen forays into East Africa, traveling up the Nile to Khartoum and beyond it into unmapped darkness, where primitive tribesmen still worshiped rocks and trees and ate their enemies.

He rubbed his aching temples. "I'm swearing off brandy until we get back to civilization. It's too strong to drink in this confounded heat."

"You'll keep that resolution whether you like it or not, your lordship," Hanrahan said, using the nickname he had given Hal for his fake English accent. "Mr. Stapleton has decided to leave all the liquor aboard the ship, at Mrs. Bradford's request."

"That damn woman," Hal muttered.

He and Eleanor were barely speaking. On the voyage across the Atlantic, Eleanor had told Genevieve why. After her fourth miscarriage, Eleanor had consulted a specialist. She discovered that her husband had infected her with gonorrhea. Because it had been untreated for over three years, there was grave doubt that she would ever be able to have children. She had yet to allow Hal back into her bed, which did not help his drinking.

Rawdon joined them on deck and began discussing the game they hoped to hunt. "We're depending on you, Hanrahan. We know our way around the Dakotas, but this kind of shooting is new to us."

Hunting was the ostensible purpose of their expedition. Neither the Egyptians nor their Turkish masters in Cairo would have allowed them into the Sudan if they had blatantly announced the real goal of this part of their journey. Genevieve studied the deserted streets of Souakin and the empty desert beyond it. Somewhere in those wastes, or perhaps in one of these opaque windowless houses, was evidence of the evil her father had given his life to destroy: slavery. They were here to expose and extirpate its last roots. Clay was going to write the story, which might make him as famous as Henry Stanley's foray to Africa to find lost Dr. Livingston had made that reporter fifteen years ago.

Except for Hal's drinking, Genevieve had enjoyed the trip tremendously so far. Rawdon had proposed it to her more as a cure than as an adventure. Both he and Dr. Beard were becoming alarmed by her bouts of melancholy. From the day they sailed, she had had no need for Dr. Beard's soothing syrup to sleep at night. She seemed to have left her indigo in New York.

Genevieve had been fascinated by Cairo, with its dilapidated Saracen fortresses, its pretentious modern palaces, its miles of winding alleys full of compacted humanity, living in poverty that was worse than anything she had ever seen in America's slums. They rode out to Giza and gazed on even more formidable monuments to history's long slow march—the Sphinx and the Great Pyramid, built by monarchs who had reigned five thousand years ago.

Genevieve found something implacable and chilling about the pyramid's weathered intensity. Rawdon was inclined to dismiss it. "Not much bigger than the Western Union Building," he said.

At Shepheard's Hotel, they were surprised to find America's recent history confronting them. At one end of the veranda a rather homely woman in her late thirties seemed to be holding court. She was surrounded by a dozen Americans around the same age. Others paid their respects to her and departed. Rawdon asked one of the departing courtiers, a sandy-haired young man wearing a dark-blue uniform with a red sash, the name of the lady.

"Miss Mary Lee," he said. "General Lee's daughter."

He explained that there was a sizable number of ex-Confederate officers serving in the Egyptian Army. He himself held the rank of colonel. Rawdon introduced himself and the rest of their party. The southerner began quizzing them about the contemporary United States. He was obviously yearning to go home and soon told them why. Egypt was bankrupt, thanks to a fifteen-year spending spree by the previous Khedive, Ismail the Magnificent. The British wanted seven percent interest on their loans and were thinking of using their army to collect it. "They're lookin' for an excuse to take over the country, but gold ain't good enough," he said in his North Carolina drawl.

"We're here to prevent that from happening," Rawdon said.

"Exactly," Hal said, and explained to the southerner that his father was one of several international financiers who had loaned large sums to the Egyptians. He and Rawdon had come to Cairo to negotiate a peaceful settlement.

After a week in Cairo, Rawdon and Hal had returned to Shepheard's Hotel to announce that the business side of their visit was over. They devoted the next hour to abusing the Egyptians as liars and cheats who refused to pay their debts. If ever there were people who deserved to have their surreptitious encouragement of the slave trade exposed, it was the bloated muftis and viziers of Cairo. The next day they had loaded their food and equipment on this small coastal steamer and sailed through the Suez Canal and down the Red Sea to Souakin.

It took several hours to unload their cargo. Along with a small arsenal of rifles and shotguns, there was a lavish supply of food and gadgetry, bought in London by Hal Bradford and Rawdon to guarantee luxury in the desert. They pitched their tents on the sand outside Souakin, and Hanrahan began negotiating for eighty camels.

Meanwhile, the Americans explored the town. For a guide Rawdon commandeered the local British consul, a small balding man named Brewster. Rawdon casually asked him if he ever saw any evidence of the slave trade. The consul pointed to a dozen blacks squatting in the yard of a fairly imposing coral house. "There's our local dealer," he said.

Genevieve was frozen by the Englishman's casual tone. Most of the Negroes were children and adolescent girls. They were not chained, but they looked half starved and wore incredibly filthy clothes.

"Does he sell them here?" she asked.

"No," Consul Brewster said. "Some dark night they'll be thrown aboard a boat and taken to Arabia."

"Can't you stop them?"

"I have no such authority," Brewster said.

"Let's buy them all and set them free," Genevieve said to Rawdon.

"It would do no good whatsoever," Brewster said. "There's no way they could get back across the desert to their tribes. They'd simply be recaptured and sold again."

That night, dining on tinned beef and native bread called dhurra, Genevieve puzzled over why the British newspapers had not reported the existence of such a visible evil. "Reasons of state, that sort of thing, I imagine," Hal Bradford said. "Her Majesty's government doesn't want to get the wogs' backs up. The beggars are talking about repudiating their loans, you know, and setting up as an independent republic."

Genevieve found the presence of the slaves only a few hundred yards from their camp almost unbearable. She begged Rawdon to buy at least one. "We could take her back to New York as proof."

Rawdon hesitated, almost persuaded. But Eleanor intervened. "Don't be ridiculous, Gen. Haven't Father's idiotic ideas about slavery caused us enough grief?"

"I agree with Eleanor," Hal said. "Try some of this native beer. It isn't half bad."

Not for the first time, Genevieve found the Bradfords loathsome. She got up and walked into the desert and looked up at the night sky. At the tip of the handle of the Little Dipper, she found the North Star. The ancient Egyptians believed its fixed position, its unwavering glow meant it was a guide to the realm of eternity. She reminded herself that its light had begun the journey to earth when the Pharaoh's slaves were building the Great Pyramid. The perturbations of her tiny soul did not matter in the vast wheel of time and history.

When she returned to their camp, she found Michael Hanrahan lecturing Hal Bradford for drinking native beer. "It's the royal route to dysentery, which kills more white men out here than fever or native ambushes."

"Oh stuff," Hal said. "I've drunk worse than this in the Dakotas."

"I'm glad to hear it," Hanrahan said. "Just take care not to get chilled when the sun goes down. I hope the ladies will pay special heed to this advice. A chill can bring on dysentery in an hour. It's a very unpleasant disease, I assure you."

That was the end of native beer. Eleanor insisted on Hal running what was left of the keg into the sand. He took this rather badly, and sometime after dark wandered into Souakin. When he did not come back by midnight, Eleanor woke up Rawdon and Clay and begged them to look for him. They found Hal in a cellar beneath the customhouse, drinking native beer in huge quantities with the ship's crew. He was half carried, half dragged back to his tent and left to the punishment of Eleanor's tongue.

The next morning, after a one-hour lesson in camel riding, they began their march across 260 miles of desert to Kassala, a town on the Abyssinian border where the hunting was supposed to be excellent—and the slave trade brisk.

The camel drivers screamed at each other, the camels bellowed and groaned. The caravan's headman, a tall white-robed sheik named Moussa, laid his kurbash, a whip made of hippopotamus hide, on man and beast indiscriminately. The Americans hung on for their lives. The men, used to riding with stirrups, were more disoriented than Eleanor and Genevieve, who did not find riding with one's legs tucked under much different from riding sidesaddle.

About four o'clock Moussa called a halt for the day. Hal declared he was sure that several of his vertebrae were dislocated. Eleanor laughed nastily. "Just what you deserve for ruining my night's sleep."

As the camel drivers unpacked the tents, a desert rainstorm came lashing out of nowhere. The sky seemed to go from cloudless blue to ugly gray in less than sixty seconds. The natives struggled to raise the tents in the rain and wind while the whites huddled under ponchos. Stung by Eleanor's rebuke, Hal Bradford dashed into the rain to help with the tents. He speeded the process considerably, although he was thoroughly soaked by the icy rain.

Night fell with the usual rapidity in the desert, and the temperature fell with it. Ignoring his wet clothes, Hal continued to supervise unpacking Eleanor's bed and other articles needed to make her comfortable. By the time he sat down with them to supper he was shivering violently.

In the morning, Genevieve noticed that Hal looked pale. He said he had been sick most of the night. He blamed it on the tinned beef they had eaten for supper. On the march he complained of a fierce thirst, and after drinking dry his *zanzimeer*, the four-quart leather bottle strapped to his saddle, he bought some water from a camel driver. It had a grayish soupy look, but he drank it anyway, refusing Genevieve's offer to share her supply.

By the time they pitched camp at 6 P.M., Hal was very ill. Michael Hanrahan felt his forehead, discussed his symptoms, and summoned Rawdon, Clay and Genevieve to a conference at a discreet distance from the tents.

"Your friend has dysentery," he said. "It can get damn serious."

Rawdon asked if there was a cure. Hanrahan shook his head. He would give him some pills, but the real cure was rest and nourishing food. How Hal was going to get any rest on a desert journey, where the day's march was a minimum of ten hours, Hanrahan did not say. Before they began, he had explained that this grueling pace was a necessity lest the entire expedition run out of water.

Around noon the next day, Hal toppled off his camel and lay semiconscious in the sand. They rigged up a litter with an awning of palm leaves to keep off the sun and slung it across his camel. Hanrahan pushed on until 10 P.M., hoping to find a water hole. Clay told Rawdon that this was much too long a journey for their sick friend. He urged shorter marches, or a day of rest. Genevieve concurred.

"What do you two Good Samaritans propose to do if we run out of water?" Rawdon snapped. "Pray for a miracle?"

"I agree with Rawdon," Eleanor said. "Hal brought this whole mess on himself. There's no reason why we should risk our lives for him."

That night, about an hour after they went to bed, Genevieve heard someone fumbling at the entrance of their tent. She woke Rawdon, who sat up with a pistol in his hand. They both thought it was one of the camel drivers looking for something to steal.

"Who's there?" Rawdon called.

"There's bloody millions at stake," Hal Bradford said.

Genevieve untied the flaps, and Hal stumbled into the tent. "Bloody millions here, if we get the story right. We've got to find a few more wogs in chains, Rawdie. Then we'll be home free. Old Pendleton won't have to fake too much. Him and his goddamn delicate conscience. We should have stayed in Cairo and let him come down here to puke his guts out. But it'll be worth it, you'll see. Bloody millions we'll clear. It'll be the making of us, Rawdie. Me, anyway. Father will stop treating me like a pimple on his ass—"

"What in the world is he talking about?" Genevieve said.

"It's none of your business. Forget you heard it," Rawdon said. He hustled Hal back to his tent.

Genevieve suddenly remembered the ex-Confederate soldier in Cairo, telling them that the British were looking for an excuse to invade Egypt. In their camp at Souakin, Hal Bradford had talked with an insider's assurance about the failure of British newspapers to expose the slave trade. Had the British and American financiers, the Bradfords and the Goulds among them, decided it would be more effective if the exposé came from an American newspaper? The British public was hypersensitive to criticism from their former subjects. Were the financiers hoping to use slavery as an excuse to seize Egypt and collect their loans?

Had Rawdon become that corrupt? Was he coolly trying to start a war to collect Lionel Bradford's and Jay Gould's money? Would he deceive his best friend and his wife when he knew how much the subject meant to her? No. She could not accept that much uncaring.

For the next three days, they marched from before dawn until after dusk. Hal drifted in and out of delirium, shouting about his bloody millions. Genevieve wondered if Clay Pendleton was beginning to puzzle over that phrase. But Clay said nothing to Rawdon, except a mild reproof over their grueling pace. Rawdon curtly told him they were dangerously short of water.

In the ferocious sun, Rawdon's skin acquired a bronzed coloring; his lips swelled and cracked, giving an ugly twist to his mouth. Dimly at first, then with mounting dread, Genevieve began to sense malevolence in Rawdon's silence, his relentless pace.

Eleanor tried to soothe her own conscience and reassure Hal by telling him that he would be fine as soon as they got out of the desert's heat. But another day ended with them still surrounded by sun-scorched sand. Hal spent the night in maniacal delirium, talking to his father, his mother, planning the construction of a mansion on upper Fifth Avenue, a palace in England. "Bloody millions," he shouted.

Another fifteen-hour march brought them within sight of the stupendous highlands of Abyssinia. The following day they left the desert behind them at last and traveled through a countryside full of luxuriant vegetation—dhoum palms, tamarisk trees, huge mimosa bushes. About seven o'clock, just after darkness fell, they heard the roar of a lion only a few dozen feet off the trail. It was a terrifying sound.

They camped outside Kassala in the darkness. Hal was delirious all night. Genevieve and Eleanor took turns sitting with him. For a while he seemed to think he was in a rowing shell. He kept crying, "Raise the stroke," and then laughing in a strange nasty way. Then his father seemed to command him out of the darkness and he was back to raving about bloody millions again.

In the morning they found themselves confronting a walled town, with a remarkable mountain, a block of smooth granite, rising thirty-five hundred feet behind it. Goats grazed in nearby fields. Somewhere beyond a line of mimosa bushes, chickens clucked.

Michael Hanrahan appeared with a hatful of eggs and a goatskin of milk. He mixed these with brandy and told Genevieve and Eleanor to feed the mixture to Hal every half hour.

Rawdon's interest in Hal's condition was minimal. He seemed far more perturbed when Clay wryly remarked that he hoped they would find more than a dozen slaves in Kassala. Rawdon ordered Hanrahan to lead them into the gloomy-looking town and introduce them to people who could help them. Genevieve and Eleanor were left to nurse the patient.

Genevieve had worked the last shift and had had no sleep since 4 A.M. She handed the eggnog to Eleanor and threw herself down on the cot in her tent. She lay there, reproaching herself for her suspicions. Rawdon had probably saved Hal's life by escaping the desert as quickly as possible. Whatever Hal meant by his bloody millions, she could not believe Clay was involved in any sordid scheme.

As she drifted into sleep, a hand seized her shoulder, stirring memories of another hand in the night. Genevieve sprang up, violently frightened.

It was Eleanor, clutching the bowl of eggnog. "Hal can't swallow any of this," she said. "He seems to be having trouble getting his breath."

Genevieve rushed to the Bradfords' tent. Hal's eyes were rolling back, the pupils vanishing. He kept bending his body upward off the bed. "Bloody millions," he muttered.

Genevieve sent Sheik Moussa, their caravan leader, running into Kassala in search of Rawdon and Clay and Michael Hanrahan. By the time they arrived, Hal's breath was ratchety, his eyes closed; spasms shook his body.

Hanrahan knelt beside him, his thumb on his wrist. "No pulse worth mentioning," he said. "I'm afraid he's sinking fast."

Eleanor flung herself on her knees beside the bed. "Oh my poor dear boy," she cried. "I'll never forgive myself."

Hal lingered until midnight. Around the perimeter of their camp, instead of roaring lions, the weird half-laugh half-bark of the hyena now echoed, filling the darkness with brainless mockery. Rawdon finally got out a shotgun and discharged both barrels at them, permitting Hal to die in relative peace. Eleanor wept and clutched his cold hand to her bosom. It was an affecting tableau, for those who did not know the true story.

The next morning they buried Hal in a decent coffin, which Hanrahan obtained from a Greek merchant named Mosconas. Eleanor clung to Rawdon's arm and almost fainted on the trek to a garden inside the town where three other Christians were buried. Mr. Mosconas promised that a cross made of ebony would be placed on the grave.

As they walked back to their tents, Genevieve heard Hanrahan telling Clay that Mosconas had promised to give them a very full account of the slave trade as it was practiced in Kassala. The local sheiks raided into Abyssinia for many of their captives. They got others from tribes who raided the equatorial region to the south of the Sudan. It was not a very big business anymore. But he hoped it would give him enough facts for his story. "Good," Clay said.

"Probate the will . . . ," Rawdon said to Eleanor.

For the first time Genevieve realized that her sister was now the sole proprietor of a great deal of money.

With the help of a little laudanum from Hanrahan's medical kit, Eleanor slept most of the day. Clay went off to Kassala again to see Mr. Mosconas. Hanrahan and Rawdon went hunting for lions and returned about five o'clock. Rawdon said he was tired and vanished into their tent for a nap. Genevieve offered Hanrahan a cup of tea. He talked about his growing disillusion with Africa. The British were rapidly absorbing it into their empire. He had come out here to escape them.

"At least that will mean the end of the slave trade, won't it?" Genevieve said.

"Will it?" Hanrahan said. "They could end it now, with a few patrol boats in the Red Sea."

Pendleton returned around six o'clock. Mr. Mosconas, on the promise that his identity would be concealed, had given him plenty of information about the slave trade.

"We'll leave for the coast tomorrow," Rawdon said. "It's vital for us to get to Cairo and cable lawyers in New York and London to start probating Hal's will. If his father finds out about his death first, he'll loot his estate."

Rawdon and Hanrahan went off to organize the camel drivers for tomorrow's march. Genevieve looked into Clay's haggard face. His lips were cracked and swollen, too. They resembled Rawdon's ugly expression. Suddenly Genevieve could not suppress the question. She had to know. "Clay," she said, "is this whole thing with the slave trade a sham? Is it just an excuse to give the British a chance to take over the country?"

"Of course," Clay said. "I thought you knew all about it. I'm getting five percent of the profits. These days, if you work with the right people, reporting can be a lucrative business."

Genevieve felt something stop inside her. Some mechanism connected to the word hope. She went into her tent and stretched out on her cot like a corpse on a bier.

The next thing she knew, Rawdon was standing over her. "You're not going to let Hal's death bring on a bout of indigo, I hope."

Something about the way he displaced "I hope" stirred a flicker of opposition. "Why should it?"

"Who knows what brings them on? I don't pretend to understand the female mind."

Eleanor joined them for dinner. Her eyes were red, her face streaked with tears. Rawdon kissed her gently on the cheek. "How are you feeling?" he asked.

"I still can't believe it."

Rawdon sat her down in one of the camp chairs and took her hand. "Genevieve's as upset as you are," he said. "We're all upset."

After supper, Eleanor returned to her tent. In the Stapleton's tent, Rawdon rummaged in one of their trunks and walked toward Genevieve with a bottle in his hand. It was Dr. Beard's soothing syrup.

"Take a double dose now," he said.

"No," she said. "I don't need it, Rawdon."

"I insist," he said, pouring it into a glass. In another moment the sickeningly sweet stuff was in her hand. "Drink it," he said.

She swallowed it, gagging. "That's a good girl," Rawdon said. "Now let's lie down." He led her over to the cot and forced her to stretch out on it. He stood there for a moment, smiling sadly down at her. "When will you face the truth about the female nervous system, Gen? You should have taken a dose of this on your own and slept during the day, instead of debating ethics with Pendleton."

"There's nothing wrong with the female nervous system."

"Dr. Beard says there is. I'll show you the passage in his book when we get back to New York."

Her objection to the slur on her nervous system was a fragment of Genevieve Dall, the once confident Vassar graduate, who had been replaced by

Mrs. Rawdon Stapleton. That forlorn creature was thinking in the recesses of what passed for her mind, *Debating ethics with Pendleton. Clay told him.*

Rawdon's face was blurring. The double dose was taking rapid effect. "Do you ever think about the shining message, Rawdon?" Genevieve asked.

But Rawdon was gone. She must have closed her eyes and he thought she was asleep. She got up, feeling extremely dizzy, and stumbled to the door of the tent. A glance at the sky told her she was wrong. She had been asleep. The moon had set and the morning star was blazing in the east.

"Rawdon?" Genevieve said.

His bed was empty. She was alone in the tent.

She knew where Rawdon was. She knew where her no longer loving husband was. Rawdon was with Eleanor.

No, wait. He might be drinking with Clay and Hanrahan. If she went outside, she would probably find them sitting under a boabob tree.

A lion roared in the darkness. Genevieve began to tremble. Rawdon was with Eleanor. She was certain of it. As certain as she was of the existence of that roaring lion. And the fact, the indubitable, unavoidable fact that this was the final step in the disappearance of Genevieve Dall. The lion roared again. Suddenly Genevieve knew exactly what she should do.

She put on her white skirt and blouse and walked carefully to the fence of prickly mimosa bushes the camel drivers had constructed around their tents to keep the lions out. After a five-minute search she found the gate and walked slowly, steadily toward the riverbank, where at least one, perhaps two lions were roaring. It would be painful, but it would be quick. There would be no ugly afterthoughts for Laura to agonize over. Her mother had gone to Africa and been killed by a lion. No hint of anything more complicated.

The river glinted in the starlight. She thought of the bodies of the prostitutes they fished out of the East and Hudson rivers each night. Women's lives, women's fate. Disappearance was their inevitable lot. It was infinitely easier than endurance. The lions roared again. There was no need to worry about anything now but physical fear.

"Gen!"

Someone was running toward her along the riverbank.

"Gen!"

Closer now. She recognized the voice. It was Clay. The lions roared spectacularly. But they seemed to be retreating. Perhaps they were frightened by the noise Clay made crashing through the scrub brush.

"What the hell are you trying to do?" Clay gasped.

He had her by the arm. He had a shotgun in his other hand.

"Let the lions have me, Clay. It will simplify everything. Eleanor's always loved Rawdon. They're perfectly matched."

"You're talking like a damn fool. You're not a fool, Gen."

"Didn't you just treat me like one? Did you really think I knew the reason we came here?"

"I'm not going to write the story. I was lying there in my tent, deciding not to write it, when Moussa came in and told me you were down here. I was going to tell you—in the morning."

For you. Genevieve heard the unspoken words. Clay was not going to write the story, he was going to pass up the chance to make fifty or a hundred thousand dollars, for her. It should change something, it should start the hope mechanism moving again. But it was too late. It could not change Rawdon being with Eleanor.

"Genevieve! Where the hell are you?"

It was Rawdon, crashing through the brush with Sheik Moussa and a half-dozen camel drivers behind him, armed with spears.

"Over here," Clay called.

In a moment, Rawdon and his band surrounded them. "Have you gone crazy, Gen?"

"Not quite."

Rawdon's hand fastened on Genevieve's arm with a jailor's grip. "Come on," he said. "We're leaving in two hours."

They started back toward the tents. "Rawdon," Clay said. "I'm not going to write the story."

"What the hell are you talking about?"

"I'm not going to write it. I prefer not to."

Rawdon handed Genevieve over to Sheik Moussa and fell back a half-dozen steps to walk with Clay. Genevieve could still hear everything they said. It was obvious that Rawdon did not particularly care.

"Are you annoyed because I beat you to Eleanor? I had the inside track, Pendleton. She's always been crazy about me. Besides, you wouldn't know what to do with ten million dollars and I do."

"I'm sure of that."

"Be sensible. I'll give you twenty percent of the Egyptian profits."

"I told you. I prefer not to."

"What the hell does that mean?"

"It's something your father said to Gould one time."

"What the hell does he have to do with us? He's a penny-ante player, Pendleton. I'm worth twice as much as he is already. He can't see beyond the borders of his own stupid country. We're playing for the control of the world."

They walked in silence for a dozen steps. A hyena barked in the distance. Rawdon echoed his malicious laugh. "I know what's eating you. It's Genevieve. I've been right about you and her all along. Do you want to console her, Pendleton? You can start tomorrow night."

"No, thanks. I don't intend to salve your conscience."

"The hell with my conscience. I want you to find out what I've been putting up with. It's like kissing a wax dummy. . . ."

Genevieve listened to Rawdon Stapleton abuse his wife. He would pack her up with the rest of the baggage and take her back to New York. There it would be more difficult to disappear. Perhaps she could wander down to the Lower East Side and find the New York version of a lion: some member of the Whyos or the Tunnel Rats who would be glad to dispose of Mrs. Rawdon Stapleton for the price of the jewelry she was wearing. She would watch and wait for the opportunity. In the meantime she would try to tell Clay she was grateful for his sacrifice. Even if it was too late.

SIX

A new year—a new love—a new life.

The words had been whispering themselves in Cynthia Legrand Stapleton's mind for a month now. Outside, an icy January wind punished the stripped trees of Stuyvesant Square. Winter was an external fact. But love created its own unique warmth. Cynthia smiled at the splendidly gowned woman in the full-length bedroom mirror. She was dressed as a sixteenth-century Venetian noblewoman, her dark hair in a gleaming, heart-shaped silhouette, her maroon taffeta gown featuring a magnificent fan-shaped pleated collar and corded puff sleeves. A beauty patch adorned one subtly rouged cheek. Raising her gold-fringed Frangipani gloves to her lips, she inhaled their perfume. An augury of happiness?

A few feet away, on the other side of the bedroom wall, her husband sulked in his room. Jonathan Stapleton had excluded himself from this night of southern triumph at the Vanderbilt mansion. He preferred to sit home with his stockholders' reports, his mad impossible schemes to drive Jay Gould out of Wall Street.

No. That was unfair. He did not prefer to sit home. He had offered to come with her if she permitted him to wear evening clothes instead of a costume. She had told him to stay home.

There. She had precisely measured the exact extent of her infidelity, the precise size of the burden her conscience would have to carry. She was strong enough—love was strong enough—to bear it. Love was strong enough to bare a great many things, she thought, playing with the word. For nine months now, Cynthia Legrand Stapleton had felt strong enough to play with anything—shocking words, daring assignations, men's feelings. Love was power!

"Oh, Mistress, you look so beautiful," Lucy said, after circling her to make sure every pleat and fold and bow was in place. "Cleo would love to see you."

"All right," Cynthia said.

She followed Lucy up the stairs to the servants' floor. Poor old Cleo was completely crippled by arthritis now. She never left her bed. She was slipping away, day by day, almost Cynthia's last link to Bralston. Her mother had died in her sleep last summer, while Cynthia was in Europe.

"Oh?"

She had thrust open Cleo's door to find Jonathan Stapleton sitting beside her bed. "I thought Cleo would like to see my costume."

"We both would," Jonathan said.

"Oh, that's just gorgeous," Cleo croaked. "I was just tellin' the General how you used to come down to the quarter on your birthday to show us your new dress. She only got one new dress a year in them days."

"That's a tradition she left in Louisiana," Jonathan said, smiling ruefully.

"Oh General, ain't it worth the money, to see her so beautiful?" Cleo asked.

"Yes," Jonathan said.

"I suspect my character is being impugned," Cynthia said. "But I don't have time to defend it."

Jonathan kissed her on the cheek. "You look magnificent."

Why did his compliment irk her? It was part of the burden. So was his visit to Cleo. It was the sort of thing Jonathan Stapleton did without thinking about it. He had an incurable sense of responsibility. He had spent endless hours arranging for the care of his mother's ancient servants after she died. He fretted over the way George was turning into a pompous Harvard swell, over Clay Pendleton's lonely unmarried state, over his daughter-in-law Genevieve's melancholy. He was polite to his cold aloof wife. It undoubtedly had something to do with the way his mother had raised him. It had nothing to do with love.

At 660 Fifth Avenue, spectators crowded the sidewalks, behind a wall of policemen. The Vanderbilts' vestibule was a wonderland of roses. Klunder, society's florist, had outdone himself. Here were vases of dark-crimson Jacqueminot and deep-pink Gloire de Paris; there was an urn of pale Baronne de Rothschild. Upstairs, the supper room was transformed into a tropical forest; profusions of orchids hung from palm trees.

Alva and her closest friend, the Cuban heiress Consuelo Yznaga, known as Lady Mandeville since she had married a titled Englishman, received in the dining hall. Alva too had drawn the inspiration for her gown from Venice, as portrayed in the paintings of Cabanel. Her underskirt of white and yellow brocade shaded from the deepest orange to the lightest canary. Her train of blue satin was almost lost in embroidery of gold and Roman red. Past her streamed a phantasmagoria of Americans transformed for the night into magical creatures. Mrs. Pierre Lorillard's electrified Worth gown turned her into a phoenix; she scattered tinsel ashes and sparks. Mrs. Paran Stevens was Queen Elizabeth. Alva's sisters-in-law were especially spectacular: one was a Bo-Peep in antique brocade, another had quilted her pale-blue satin skirt with diamonds.

There was scarcely a woman who did not deserve the word "magnificent"; but the men were another matter. They all tended to look hangdog and a trifle ridiculous. Willie K., as Alva's paunchy husband was called, looked especially silly in yellow silk tights and a black velvet cloak embroidered with gold, copied from a portrait of the Duc de Guise. Only one man had the soldierly bearing and natural dignity to carry off the assumption of noble identity for the evening. She found him waiting for her in the ballroom wearing the red-and-blue uniform of a Venetian officer.

"Isn't it marvelous?" Cynthia said as Edgar Calhoun kissed her hand.

"It's all the Mardi Gras of the century rolled into one," he said.

"Perhaps only southerners know how to enjoy such flights of fancy. These Yankee men all look like condemned prisoners."

"Whenever you grow bored, let me know. I have a room waiting in the usual place, filled with the usual roses."

In the gold-embroidered toga of a Roman emperor, Lionel Bradford seemed to materialize beside them. He gestured to the lavishly decorated room, the costumed figures. "Louis Napoleon with all the wealth of France at his disposal never came close to this. I can't understand why those starving thousands on the Lower East Side let us get away with it."

"My husband had very similar sentiments," Cynthia said drily. "He called the whole affair extravagant nonsense."

"But I'm here, indulging in the nonsense. Because I understand the *raison d'être* of this extravaganza. It's not to glorify a regime. It's to pay tribute to the power of the American woman. Only a fool would try to oppose that power. Don't you agree, Colonel?"

"Absolutely."

"May I ask Mrs. Stapleton for a dance?"

"I will leave that to her discretion, sir."

Bradford opened his arms. Why not? Cynthia thought. There were times when Edgar's jealousy of Bradford grew alarming.

"Did you advise him on his costume?" Bradford asked as they glided onto the floor in a lively waltz.

"He asked me what I was wearing. I suppose he chose a Venetian style for that reason."

"He looks ready to play Cassio."

Cassio was the handsome stupid drunkard who became Iago's unwitting tool in the ruin of Desdemona. But real life had turned the drama in another direction. Cassio had ruined Iago as far as Cynthia was concerned. The deeper her love for Edgar Calhoun became, the more nakedly Bradford revealed the real motive for his return to New York.

"Have you considered my offer?" he asked.

"Yes. I'm not interested."

"Not even if we increase it to a million dollars? A million dollars in your own name in a bank in Paris. Beyond your husband's reach. Independent for the rest of your life. All you have to do—"

"I'm not interested."

All she had to do was pretend to rediscover her love for Jonathan Stapleton. To lure him into telling her the names of his secret partners in the struggle with Gould, to flatter him into boasting about his plans. Ironic that Cynthia Legrand was finally being given an opportunity to play the courtesan on a stage larger than her father's most extravagant dreams—and she was refusing the opportunity in the name of love.

Without the strength, the power of Edgar Calhoun's love, she was certain she would have succumbed to the dark exhilaration Bradford stirred in her. She listened to him now preaching another chapter in the gospel of eros. "Don't allow my candor on this point to cast a shadow on my desire for you. I remain confident of your imminent boredom with Cassio. Then the deception, the triumph, the money, will add new dimensions to our pleasure. Money is the most powerful aphrodisiac in the world. The second most powerful is revenge."

"You don't understand love, Lionel. You refuse to admit its existence."

"I never thought of you as a stupid woman. Don't force me to change my mind."

He left her to make her way back to Edgar, who was glowering on the edge of the dance floor. "I saw no reason why you had to dance with him," he muttered.

"It looks less suspicious, Edgar dear. People are watching us all the time. If I dance only with you, we run far worse risks."

"Ah!"

He wanted to defy, ignore risks. He wanted to be as daring, as reckless as they had been in London last summer under Madeline Terhune's benevolent protection. But Cynthia had insisted on caution, subterfuge, in New York. She had gotten a thorough education in the divorce law of New York State from Lionel Bradford. If her husband caught her *in flagrante delicto*, he could throw her into the street without a penny. He could—and undoubtedly would—keep her comfortable little fortune.

There were other reasons, sentimental but powerful. George's career at Harvard, where social status was as important as scholarship, would be damaged if his parents had a scandalous divorce. There were her friendships with Mittie Roosevelt, Alva Vanderbilt, who would be unable to receive her in their homes.

On the dance floor, Alva Vanderbilt's sister began leading four couples in an Opéra Bouffe Quadrille. In the center of the group she caught a glimpse of Eleanor Bradford's blazing red hair. Opposite her bowed Rawdon Stapleton in the costume of an Elizabethan courtier. Rawdon was the widowed Mrs. Bradford's constant escort these days, causing more than a few tongues to wag. Genevieve had apparently returned from Egypt in such a state of nervous exhaustion she was virtually housebound.

Edgar Calhoun handed champagne to her from the tray of a passing waiter. "Mrs. Vanderbilt wants you to join her for a descent on Mrs. Astor and her sister-in-law."

Alva wanted to savor every last drop of her triumph. She was the most willful woman Cynthia had ever encountered. She obviously despised her pudgy stupid husband and was determined to find her happiness in social power, in the splendor and fame Vanderbilt money could create. This ball was the climax of her campaign to supplant Mrs. Astor as the ruler of New York society.

On the other side of the ballroom, Alva greeted her with a cheerful kiss and led her to a table in the corner, where Caroline Astor sat with her lumpy sister-in-law, Cecilia Schermerhorn. "I know you both want to see this vision out of Shakespeare's Venice," Alva said. "In case you don't recognize her, it's my dear friend, Mrs. Stapleton."

"How very nice to see you," Mrs. Astor murmured, her expression suggesting that a dentist or a surgeon was doing awful things to her.

"Yes," muttered Cecilia Schermerhorn through equally clenched teeth. "How are you, my dear?"

"Oh look. The Star Quadrille," Alva said.

The timing could not have been more exquisite. Mrs. Astor's daughter Carrie was performing the intricate steps of a dance she and her friends had rehearsed for weeks. On New Year's Day, that effeminate fraud Ward McAllister had mentioned it to Cynthia in the course of his duty visit. Mrs. Stapleton had expressed her sympathy for poor Carrie; she was rehearsing a dance that would never be performed at Mrs. Vanderbilt's costume ball. Mrs. Vanderbilt had never met Mrs. Astor or any member of her family.

A week later, Cynthia was at 660 Fifth Avenue helping Alva go over the immense guest list one last time before mailing out the invitations. They were at work in the two-story paneled dining hall when Alva's butler arrived with a calling card on a silver tray. They looked at it for a moment and Alva gave a whoop—a veritable rebel yell—of triumph. There was the sublime scrolled legend that guaranteed one's social standing in New York: *Mrs. Astor*. Rushing to the front windows, they saw the coupé with the driver and footman in blue livery leaving the curb.

Now here stood Mrs. Stapleton, savoring sweet revenge for her exclusion from the Patriarchs. She gazed into the lined empty faces of Caroline Astor and her sister-in-law, and a voice whispered in Cynthia's mind, *Did it really matter?*

Turning, Cynthia confronted Edgar Calhoun's mournful face. She saw that for him she and Alva Vanderbilt had just enacted the triumph of Mrs. Jonathan Stapleton. He loved Cynthia Legrand.

For the rest of the evening, Cynthia danced exclusively with Edgar, refusing invitations from a half-dozen other men. It was dangerous, but a wild mixture of defiance and disillusion impelled her to take risks.

Two or three times, Rawdon Stapleton's handsome face appeared in the whirling dancers, reminding her of Charlie and dreams of southern glory. Upstairs in the supper room, Katherine Kemble Brown seized her arm. "You are being very indiscreet, my dear," she whispered.

Cynthia smiled and plucked another glass of champagne from a passing tray. "To happiness," she said.

At 3 A.M. she and Edgar rode downtown in a closed hack, kissing, fondling. But their indifference to the world around them was jarred by the atmosphere of the assignation house. In the afternoon, when they usually visited the double brownstone on West Twenty-sixth Street, it had been as quiet and sedate as a wayside inn. Now it echoed with drunken screams and shouts. By night the proprietors had an entirely different clientele. Burly men in checked vests reeled past them in the hall. One bruiser reached out to lift Cynthia's veil. "Whattya afraid of, girlie?" he chortled. "Everybody's a good sport here."

Edgar shoved him half the length of the hall and whipped a sword out of his cane. "How would you like this down your filthy mouth?" he snarled. The man hastily retreated into his room.

In their room, Edgar locked the door and leaned against it, his head back. On the dresser, a dozen roses were wilting in the steam heat. A bottle of champagne stood in a bucket whose ice had long since melted. "It's all right, it's all right," Cynthia whispered, kissing him.

In ten minutes they were in bed, he was murmuring, "Princess, oh my princess," against her throat. The miraculous sense of recapturing something lost, precious, soared through Cynthia's body again. She was Jeannie, embracing long-dead Jeff Forsyth, she was the Cynthia Legrand who refused her father's dark summons, she was woman proving the possibility of pure affection, declaring love's power to redeem, ennoble, purify.

When it was over, they lay in a cocoon of pure feeling for a long time. Unfortunately it was penetrated by the crashes and shouts and thuds that echoed from nearby rooms.

"There's only one thing for us to do," Edgar said. "Go home."

For a moment Cynthia was astonished. Was he suggesting that they drive to Stuyvesant Square and confront Jonathan Stapleton with the fact of their love?

"I can never hope to keep you happy in the midst of that Yankee splendor we danced in tonight. I don't have the knack of making that kind of money. But if a deal on a certain railroad stock comes through, I'll have enough to buy back my family plantation on the Cane River. That's where we belong, Princess, where our love can grow deep and strong, where it can sink roots into the land we fought for."

"Yuh-huh-huh-huh!" Drunken laughter from the floor above them. Was it God chuckling at Cynthia Legrand?

"Darling, it's—impossible," Cynthia said.

Cynthia Legrand was naked in his arms. Was that Mrs. Jonathan Stapleton speaking? Or some other woman, a shadowy figure who existed between these two opposites? She did not know. She was too bewildered, appalled, that Edgar Calhoun could misread her so completely.

"What do you mean, impossible? There's no other way," he said.

How could she tell him that she was no longer a southern woman, that Louisiana was no longer home to her? She could only evade the truth. "I have too many . . . obligations here in New York."

"To whom?"

Cynthia said nothing. She wondered why she had chosen that word "obligations."

"To your husband?"

No, Cynthia thought mournfully. Not to her husband. But to the woman who bore his name. To Mrs. Jonathan Stapleton, the woman who had made New York her home. She was as real as—perhaps more real than—Cynthia Legrand.

Her silence stirred Edgar's anger and fear. "How can you go back to him now?"

Amazing, the difference a single word makes. If Edgar had said, "How could you go back to him?" he would have made her feel guilty. "Can" left her wandering in a void of questions. Did he mean that she was beyond hope of redemption? Was he warning her that he or Lionel Bradford would not permit it?

"Going back is a somewhat misplaced phrase. I'm still married to him."

"Jesus Christ!"

Edgar sprang out of the bed and pried open the champagne bottle. He drank off one, two, three glasses without offering her a sip.

"For God's sake don't get drunk like the rest of the people in this dreadful place," Cynthia said.

He drank another glass. "Are you going back to your husband?"

"No. That's impossible, too."

"Then what in Christ do you propose we do? Go on meeting in places like this?"

"Yuh-huh-huh-huh-huh," laughed God, above them.

"I don't know. I asked you once to give me time. I'm afraid I must ask you again."

He finished the champagne and flung the glass across the room and began making love to her again. She did not like it. She saw it for what it was, a statement of ownership, as clear—and not as kind—as Jonathan's visits to her bedroom in Stuyvesant Square.

He was so sad, so desperate, Cynthia answered his kisses. But her mind was alive with more than pure feeling. She was thinking about her love for Edgar. She had seen it as a force that would help him find a place in the present and the future, a place she could share with him. But Edgar remained mired in the past, like a handsome steamboat on a mudflat. For him, far more than for Jonathan, the world had all but ended in 1865. The flourish of arms that redeemed Louisiana was only an afterpiece to the tragic drama of the lost cause.

There was an emptiness, a netherworld of gray pain at the center of Edgar's soul. Her redneck brother-in-law, who had made a business of the war and risen from the bottom of the social heap, had distorted Cynthia's appreciation of what defeat had done to the South's true soldiers. She began to see how much of her love had been a response to this pain—a passionate pity.

Worst of all, her love had not changed Edgar any more than it had changed Jonathan. Edgar remained devoted to her in a narrow clinging way that was the opposite of her hope for him. She wanted him to perform splendid daring deeds on Wall Street or in Congress and write Cynthia Legrand secret letters telling her she was responsible for his newfound greatness. But she never—she saw it so clearly now—she never intended to surrender that other self, Mrs. Jonathan Stapleton.

Meanwhile, Edgar was proclaiming his ownership of her, with the same insistent male hands and hungry lips her husband had used when love between them was still that mysterious compound of *croce* and *delizia*. Before love expired. Oh. Edgar was there, in her body now, telling her that she was irremediably southern, as yielding as delta earth and as steamy as an August night in the lee of the levee. Her body was saying yes, but her mind was saying no.

Not southern. Not northern. Just a woman. A bewildered, uncertain woman.

"Oh my princess, my princess," Edgar whispered. "Forgive me. I'm just so miserable in this city without you."

The words stirred pity, but it was combined with an unsettling image of a husband who never let her out of his sight. Even in the good days of their marriage, Jonathan had been too busy with his railroads and his politics to monopolize her. She shuddered at the thought of being marooned on a plantation with a man who adored her. Was adoration another aphrodisiac, another substitute for love?

"I know," she lied. "I feel the same way."

It was 5 A.M. when Cynthia tiptoed up the stairs to her bedroom in Stuyvesant Square. She took a double dose of chloral hydrate and slept into the following afternoon. Awake, her first thought was: Tuesday. Mittie's day to receive callers. Since Cynthia began her affair with Edgar Calhoun, she had returned to seeing Mittie rather regularly. Odd, the way Lionel Bradford had made it almost impossible for her to face her dearest friend. Mittie somehow underscored the authenticity of the love she had felt for Edgar—love she still felt, even if she saw it was pitiful in the deepest sense of the word.

A half-dozen women were chatting in Mittie's parlor when Cynthia arrived. She noticed an odd lapse in the conversation when she walked in. But when she kissed Mittie and was invited to sit down on the couch next to her, the chatter resumed. Everyone was talking about the Vanderbilt ball, of course. There were exhaustive discussions of gowns and gossip.

Eventually, the other callers departed and Mittie and Cynthia were alone. "Katherine Kemble Brown called me on the telephone today," Mittie said. "She urged me to speak to you about Edgar Calhoun. She said your conduct with him last night was extremely indiscreet. Everyone at the ball was talking about it."

"Oh Mittie."

Cynthia poured out the whole story, beginning with Bradford, concealing nothing. In the end she sat there, dazed; her body felt insubstantial; it reminded her of the first stage of recovery from breakbone fever.

"A long time ago I urged you to find a way to forgive your husband," Mittie said. "I can only repeat the advice."

No. The memory of Jonathan Stapleton's never-retracted insults and revelations rose between her and that possibility. Then there was Edgar. "I feel . . . responsible for him."

"I think you should overcome that feeling. He's a grown man, who must assume responsibility for himself."

That was easy to say. Mittie did not have to face the sadness in Edgar Calhoun's eyes. "Do I still have your love?" Cynthia asked. "I think I've been more afraid of losing that than . . . my respectability."

"You'll always have that," Mittie said. "You have Katherine's love, too. Even Alva Vanderbilt, who I don't think is much given to loving people, adores you. That's why we all fret over your—unhappiness." Trust Mittie to use a gentle word.

At home, Cynthia sat for a long time before her dressing table trying to organize her thoughts. Was Edgar Calhoun her responsibility? Was it her destiny, a perfect punishment for her sins, to end her days on Cane River's faded forlorn Côte Joyeuse, welcoming her sister Jeannie and her smirking spitting husband to dinner?

A tremendous racket in the hall broke her dismal reverie. Under Jonathan's supervision, workmen were hacking out the glass of the oval window on the landing of the stairs. "What in the world are you doing?" Cynthia demanded.

"Installing a new window," he said. "It's by a young artist named Saint-Gaudens I met at the Century Club. He does remarkable work in stained glass."

Jonathan ordered one of the workmen to bring the new window upstairs. "I planned to give it to you as a Christmas present. But you can't hurry the artistic process."

The husky Irish workmen carefully set the oval of glass down against the wall. "It will look a lot better when the sunlight is behind it," Jonathan said.

"Oh," Cynthia said. "Oh Jonathan."

It was a view of the weathered red Palazzo Rospigliosi, with a dark-blue Grand Canal flowing past it and the white dome of the Salute in the distance, all beneath a cerulean sky.

"I know we can't go back there again," Jonathan said. "I know that's my fault. But I'd like to think we can both treasure the memory."

"It's lovely," Cynthia said.

She fled back to her room. Did he know? Was he torturing her?

At dinner, Jonathan said nothing about the Palazzo Rospigliosi. He seemed as cool, as blunt, as husbandlike, as ever. "I'm afraid your brother and his friends lost a good deal of money on Wall Street today," he said. "I'd prefer you to hear it from me than from him or someone else. I didn't do it intentionally. I have nothing against him. But he's always swum in Gould's wake. He and a lot of other people. Today we knocked the stuffings out of one of Gould's pet projects, the Mexican Southern Railroad. The stock dropped forty points. We've taught a lot of people that Gould doesn't translate into gold."

"I wish I understood your determination to war with that man," Cynthia said.

"I wish you understood a lot of things about me," he said, and went on spooning down his soup.

On the following Monday, Cynthia told Oliver she would not need the coach, ignored his usual protests and struggled up to Third Avenue in an icy wind to take a hack to the assignation house. Edgar was in the room, waiting for her. The champagne was open and the bottle was half empty. There were no roses.

Before she could unpin her veil, he snarled, "Did you tell your husband about my investment in the Mexican Southern?"

"How could I?" Cynthia said. "You never even told me the name."

"He and his friends hammered that stock to nothing, while Gould just sat on the sidelines. I lost every cent I had in the bank. Everything I saved in the last five years."

"Oh Edgar."

"Is that all you've got to say? I'm convinced he went after that stock because I was in it. He caught on to us from the way you acted at the Vanderbilt ball."

She almost told him he was talking nonsense. "I don't think that's true, Edgar. It was Gould he was after."

"Maybe it's just as well. Maybe this will make you see you have to do what Bradford suggested a long time ago—separate from him and take your money with you."

"Edgar—I don't have to do anything. I don't like being told what to do."

He sat there on the edge of the bed in his gray trousers and undershirt, his head bowed. It took her a minute to realize he was silently weeping. "Oh princess," he whispered. "I'm so miserable. I'm acting like a swine, but I can't help it. I'm so miserable."

Slowly, mournfully, Cynthia undressed. She sat down beside him and kissed him and told him she forgave him. It was appallingly similar to married love with a difficult husband.

By 5 P.M. she was back home in Stuyvesant Square, deep in a warm fragrant bath. She always bathed after meeting Edgar. Did she think the water washed away her sin? Tonight she wanted to cleanse memory, not conscience. But all the Violette de Toulouse soap powder in her cabinet would not remove the stain Edgar Calhoun had left on her feelings today.

That night, she and Jonathan went to dinner at General Grant's new town house on Sixty-sixth Street. It was a splendid party, even if the guests included Jay Gould and his dumpy wife. General Grant sat Cynthia on his right and reiterated his weakness for southern women. Cynthia struggled to respond with her usual wit, but she felt detached, outside the whole glittering affair.

Before dinner, Grant had summoned Jonathan and Gould to a conference in the corner of the parlor. The ex-President was the titular head of the Mexican Southern Railroad and he was trying to negotiate a truce between the two contestants before the warfare drove the company into bankruptcy. If the way Gould glared at Jonathan during dinner meant anything, the peace conference had failed.

Over dessert, Mark Twain held forth in his standard comic style about his recent lecture tour of the hinterlands. Everyone laughed at the expected moments, but Cynthia did not find the stories very funny. Most of them involved some sort of insult to witless uneducated people. There was something cruel, almost feral, about this writer with his jovial mustaches and his cynical smile and his appetite for adulation.

Riding home in the coach, Cynthia found that Jonathan felt the same way about Mark Twain's performance. "That fellow repels me—and he's so damn successful. I kept thinking of Melville forgotten on Twenty-sixth Street, with five times the talent of that mountebank. The world is so damned unfair."

"I agree. I enjoy Twain's books, but I find his public personality repulsive."

Silence for a block.

"I can't remember when we've agreed on anything so thoroughly," Cynthia said.

"Is it a sign of a change in the weather?"

"What do you mean?"

"When a quarrel lasts as long as ours has, it almost becomes part of the atmosphere."

"Yes," she said.

"Perhaps, if we thought of it as the weather, we might stop worrying about who was responsible for it."

"An interesting idea," she said. "Except that even the weather is memorable when it grows exceptionally ugly."

"True," he said.

Cynthia again wondered if he was playing cat and mouse with her. She was tempted to explode his clever philosophy of reconciliation by telling him about Edgar Calhoun. *You're too late with your subtle attempts to make me feel contrite, forgiving. Give me my money and let us part amicably.* She imagined her next meeting with Edgar, offering herself and the money.

But it was not her money. Could she live for the rest of her life on Jonathan Stapleton's money, in the arms of another man?

"That looks like trouble."

Jonathan pointed to a police wagon outside their house. Had they been robbed? Was he embarked on some new political scheme that was going to bring more rocks crashing through their windows?

In the center hall, Cousteau greeted them, a frown on his intelligent tan face. "Young Mrs. Stapleton's in the parlor with a policeman. He has orders to guard her until you arrive."

In the parlor, Genevieve sat on the couch beneath the portrait of Jonathan in his general's uniform. She looked ghastly. Her hair hung lankly down one side of her face. She was wearing a soiled brown dress.

The policeman, a tall, good-looking young Irishman, practically came to attention when he saw Jonathan. "This was the only address she'd give us, General. So the captain told me to take her here."

"Begin at the beginning," Jonathan said. "Where did you find Mrs. Stapleton?"

"On the Bowery, sir," the policeman replied, looking more and more embarrassed. "She was—well—soliciting, sir. She was walking up to strangers and—offering herself. For five dollars. With the little girl standing right there, watching her."

While the officer was laboring through this astonishing explanation, Genevieve sat silently, her head down, like a condemned felon. Now her head came up, and she glared at them. "I wanted to show Laura the truth about women in this city. The way men can buy them. I wanted to make sure she never sold herself that way. Then I was going to take her home and go down to the East River and become one of the half-dozen women they fish out of the harbor every night."

Jonathan looked as though he might collapse. The policeman sighed and shook his head. "It's all she'd tell us, sir."

"Where's her daughter?" Cynthia asked. "Where's Laura?"

"I took her upstairs, madam. She's asleep in Mr. George's bed," Cousteau said.

Genevieve began to weep. "I know what you're going to do," she said to Jonathan. "You're going to send me away someplace. You're going to say my mind is gone. But I was only trying to tell Laura the truth."

"Oh my dear dear girl," Jonathan said. He tried to take her hand, but she pulled it free and turned frantically to Cynthia.

"Don't let Rawdon have Laura. He'll turn her into a prostitute. He'll raise her as a female animal. I want her to become a woman. I've heard awful rumors about you. But you've been a good mother to George. Laura needs a mother who'll raise her as a woman—but she needs someone to love her first. Eleanor hates her. She'll make her the most degraded female in history. Don't let that happen, please!"

Cynthia did not know how to begin to reply to this frantic monologue. She let Jonathan take charge of the situation.

"Of course Cynthia will love Laura," he said. "So will I. Until you're well again. Whatever's happened between you and Rawdon—"

Genevieve shook her head. "Everything's happened between me and Rawdon. First it was you. Then it was Jay Gould. Then it was Clay Pendleton. Now it's Eleanor." She began to laugh hysterically. "Sometimes I think everything that's ever happened in the world is between me and Rawdon."

"Would you go upstairs and make sure Laura's all right?" Jonathan said to Cynthia.

In George's bedroom, five-year-old Laura was asleep, her hair a splash of blackness on the pillow. Cynthia sank down on the bed beside her, dazed by what had just transpired in the parlor.

In about a half hour, Cynthia heard Rawdon's voice downstairs. In another half hour the front door slammed and Jonathan's footsteps slowly mounted the stairs. No marching step tonight. In a moment he was standing beside her looking down on the sleeping child. "She's going to stay with us. Rawdon made no attempt to deny what Genevieve said about him and Eleanor. I told him he isn't fit to be a father."

"Do you think Genevieve's curable?"

"I hope so. I saw her father collapse that way during the war. A long rest, some help from a good doctor, and Ben came back—for a while. Let's hope Genevieve can make a more complete recovery."

Laura whimpered and put her thumb into her mouth. Jonathan fondled the tousled little dark head. "One thing we can do—is make sure this little creature has a better chance for happiness. Can you give her the love she needs?"

Can—you—give—her—love?

The words split apart and swirled in the dim gaslight above the bed. For a moment Cynthia felt nothing but rage. Then she realized Jonathan was not asking her to love him. His question was really a sad admission of his failure at love—a failure she had taught him to recognize in their years of wintry married weather.

This sleeping child had nothing to do with their ugly quarrel over the fortunes and spoils of war. Was she an opportunity to begin again? Could they both love her in the name of a future that banished the past with its dead hopes and hates?

Can—you—give—her—love?

"I'll try," Cynthia said.

SEVEN

Light crept slowly across the broad meadow that ran down to the Hudson. Mrs. Rawdon Stapleton watched the brown grass, the gunmetal river, begin to glow. She was always awake to welcome the dawn at Grandview Sanitarium. Soon, in the distance, she could see the humps of the Shawangunk Mountains. She was back in the Hudson River Valley, only ten or twenty miles from Poughkeepsie and Vassar.

All the patients in the Grandview Sanitarium were women. Dr. George Miller Beard, author of *American Nervousness,* had built it as a refuge for those difficult females who had read his book and failed to follow his advice.

Genevieve looked around her room. It contained a brass bed, a dresser and one chair. Nothing else. No pictures on the walls, no night table with a reading lamp, no pens or pencils or paper, no books.

Books were forbidden in Grandview Sanitarium. Books and magazines and newspapers were all part of the frantic American world that produced extreme nervous exhaustion in women.

There was a knock and the door was opened by a maid with a ring of keys on her belt. She put a tray of food on the bed and departed. Genevieve studied the contents. Bread pudding soaked in cream, eggs benedict of sorts, a great mound of butter and a half loaf of bread, and a full glass of thick, creamy milk.

Lunch would be an omelet, full of bubbling yellow cheese, a salad with a great mound of cottage cheese, a dish of ice cream, more milk. Dairy products were part of the treatment. Dairy products added pounds to the emaciated frames of nervously exhausted women. The goal was bovinity. Genevieve was sure that in a week or two or three, she would begin to moo.

A knock on the door. Enter Dr. Beard, smiling. He was a tall scholarly man with a pince-nez poised on his Roman nose. He always carried a yellow pad and kept a supply of pencils in the breast pocket of his long white coat. Genevieve stared at the pencils, as a thirsty desert traveler might eye a water bottle.

"Good morning, Genevieve," Dr. Beard said. "How are you feeling today?"

"No better, no worse."

"You didn't eat very much of your breakfast."

"I didn't eat any of it."

"You must eat, Genevieve. You must give your body the strength it needs to deal with your exhausted nerves."

Genevieve gave Dr. Beard a defiant glare. She was sick of this unctuous know-it-all who was trying to turn her brain into cream cheese.

"Now, Genevieve," Dr. Beard said. "You don't want to force us to resort to extreme measures."

Genevieve's resistance crumbled. Dr. Beard had described these extreme measures in some detail. One was called local treatment. It consisted of coating her genital organs with a caustic that burned away the "superfluous tissue" that might be causing her mental disturbance. If this failed, amputation of the clitoris would be the next step. If that failed, removal of the ovaries would be on the agenda. It was all perfectly logical. Unruly stallions became docile when gelded. Berserk women would become calm and obedient when similarly neutered.

"As you know, Genevieve, I dislike these extreme measures. I believe that with rest and a nourishing diet, and a *cooperative* spirit, most women can be restored to their husbands."

"Yes, Doctor."

Genevieve wondered if Dr. Beard ever noticed the remarkable way a mention of extreme measures produced a cooperative spirit in his patients.

"Eat your breakfast, Genevieve. Then we'll discuss what makes a woman happy—and unhappy."

Dr. Beard sat there, writing on his yellow pad while she crammed the bread pudding, gooey eggs and several slices of well-buttered bread down her throat, followed by the entire glass of milk. There. Wasn't Genevieve a good girl?

Yes, Genevieve was a very good girl. Dr. Beard smiled and said so. Now for philosophy.

"We are all limited beings, Genevieve."

"Yes, Doctor."

"Women have particular limitations, just as men."

"Yes, Doctor."

"Women have great gifts, given to them by the God of nature, as do men."

"Yes, Doctor."

"We must balance our gifts and our limitations. That, Genevieve, is happiness."

"Yes, Doctor."

"What is man's greatest gift?"

"To—work twenty-four hours a day? Fight wars?"

Genevieve waited, breathless, to see if Dr. Beard noticed her sarcasm. If he did, he smiled and forgave it. "Exactly. To strive, Genevieve, to contest with other men for mastery in the world. But that's not woman's gift."

"No?"

"Woman's gift is to *nurture*. How do we know this, Genevieve?"

"I don't know."

"Of course you do. You're a mother. You've seen your little daughter reach out her arms to you. You've seen her suckle at your breasts."

"Yes, Doctor."

"Nature tells us the truth, Genevieve. Nothing but the truth. Without the mother's nurture, the infant would die. Without her spiritual nurture, the child would never know love. It would grow up a monster."

For a moment tears choked Genevieve's throat. Was that going to be Laura's fate?

"Without the wife's spiritual nurture, Genevieve, a man can also become a monster. It's the woman's gift, her power, to soften, to refresh the striving spirit of the male, to console him in failure, to restrain him in success."

"Yes, Doctor."

"Why are you frowning, Genevieve?"

"Isn't nurture another word for love, Doctor?"

"Love is only part of it. The nurturing wife creates a nurturing world for her weary husband. A house full of beauty and peace. A family of obedient, devoted children. Meals that are both bountiful and pleasing."

"But love is the center of it. Without love the rest doesn't make much sense, does it?"

"Of course love is the center, Genevieve," Dr. Beard said somewhat testily.

Dr. Beard departed, leaving Genevieve to meditate on this philosophy. Love was supposed to be at the center of so many things. Genevieve began to list all the places in her life where love had been absent.

Love between mother and daughter.

Love between sister and sister.

Love between husband and wife.

Love between father and daughter.

Tears trickled down Genevieve's face. This was the primary failure, the one she should put at the head of the list, if she had the courage to face it. This was the truth that made her writhe in her bed in the middle of the night and now in the middle of the day.

Benjamin Dall had never loved her. He loved no one and nothing except his own arrogant New England soul, pioneering the empyrean in pursuit of the ideal.

Hate him, Genevieve told herself. That was the first step to salvation. Hate Benjamin Dall for putting that gun to his head, for turning his back on your love and arrogantly preferring death to the failure of his glorious male ideals.

Oh. It was not good enough. She had to write it down. She had to think through the implications of this decision to hate instead of love. To hate them all, including her corrupt noble contradictory father-in-law, who had tried to use her as a poultice on his son's spiritual sores.

Genevieve wept for an hour or two. Dr. Beard said this was perfectly normal. He even said it was a good sign. Tears were part of the nurturing process. Tears softened the harsh striving nature of men. Neurasthenic women had to learn how to weep.

That was what she was: a neurasthenic woman. From the Latin *neuro,* nerves, and the Greek *a,* without, *sthenos,* strength. A woman with weak nerves. How did a woman who knew Latin and Greek end up with weak nerves? According to Dr. Beard, she had probably strained her nerves at Vassar. Dr. Beard was not opposed to education for women. But he was very opposed to overeducation. Women's nerves could not handle it. Especially the nerves of neurasthenic women.

Genevieve sat in her barren room and thought about Rawdon in bed with Eleanor, and Alice Mayer presiding at yet another triumphant dinner party, glorying in the satisfactions of her woman's sphere, and Elizabeth Wellcombe practicing law in distant San Francisco, and Clay Pendleton refusing to write the story about slavery in Egypt. The British had taunted the Egyptians into starting a war with them and seized the country anyway, and Rawdon and Jay Gould and Lionel Bradford got richer than ever, proving once more the futility of noble gestures—

Stop. She tried to put something else in her mind. Dr. Beard's words about nurturing women and striving men were all she could find. If she had a book, any book, she could escape this circular maze in which she was trapped. She groped for poetry she had memorized as a girl. *Maud,* by Alfred Lord Tennyson. She and Alice Gansevoort had once recited it in a school play. Alternating sections. Alice had chosen the lyric parts. *A voice by the cedar tree. Come into the Garden, Maud.* Genevieve had taken the grim stanzas, where the desperate lover appraises the mercenary era in which they were living.

> Sooner or later I too may passively take
>   the print
> Of the golden age—why not? I have neither
>   hope nor trust;
> May make my heart as a millstone, set my
>   face as a flint.
> Cheat and be cheated and die: who knows?
>   We are ashes and dust.

There was advice from the greatest poet of the century. Perhaps Genevieve should lie flat and take the print of the age. She should flatly lie and pretend to be the most devoted, the most nurturing female on the continent of North America. It was either pretend or be buried here, forever.

Pretend, pretend, she told herself again and again for the next several days. Or longer. It could have been weeks. Time ceased to exist in the long empty days at Grandview Sanitarium. Time consisted of two visits from Dr. Beard, morning and evening. Genevieve tried to track time by the phases of the moon, the movement of the North Star. But most of her energy was consumed in remembering to pretend. Pretend and you can decide later what you believe, she told herself.

But she never surrendered, never forgot her hate. That was her polestar.

Dr. Beard of course saw only improvement. He saw a woman who said yes doctor with ever increasing fervor. One day, when the moon was new, he announced that Genevieve might begin to receive visitors. First, naturally, would be her husband, Rawdon. For the next several days, Genevieve was in agony. Would she be able to pretend?

A nurse brought her downstairs to a sunny side porch and sat her in a rocking chair. A few minutes later, Rawdon came up the steps and walked toward her. "Gen," he said, kissing her on the cheek. "It's so good to see you looking so healthy. I've just had a long talk with Dr. Beard. He says you've improved faster than any other patient in the place."

"I feel much better," she said.

"Do you want to come home?"

"Yes, of course I want to come home, Rawdon. I realize what I was doing wrong. I was trying to achieve things that were incompatible with being a good wife."

How was that for pretending? Not a word about hating you, not a word about Eleanor. Rawdon's eyes betrayed his dismay. "I think we were both at fault," he said. "But I'm certainly pleased to hear that you realized you've made some mistakes. In a month or two, I hope we can begin talking to Dr. Beard about when you can come home."

A month or two. Genevieve saw how easily that could stretch into a month or three or four or six. Could she survive that long without succumbing to Dr. Beard?

They talked about Laura. She was thriving at her grandparents' house. "Cynthia's already bought her a wardrobe that will keep a personal maid busy ten hours a day. I haven't seen my stepmother so happy in years. I hear she's even given up being wicked."

"How nice."

They discussed Alice Mayer, who was about to give birth to her fourth child. She was quarreling with her Jewish in-laws. Isaac had withdrawn from the family firm and was operating independently. Rawdon was hoping he could persuade Gould to let him into their charmed circle. Ironically, Gould was rather hostile to Jews, perhaps because he was often suspected of being one.

"And how is Eleanor?"

She could not resist testing his pretense, even though it almost wrecked her own. But Rawdon did not flinch. "She's better. She hardly mentions Hal anymore."

Genevieve nodded and smiled as Rawdon reported the tears of concern that Eleanor expended on her. Genevieve said she could hardly wait to come home and see her dear sister. Rawdon glanced at his watch. He had reached the half hour Dr. Beard had allotted him. Was there anyone she would like to see? All her old friends were eager to visit.

"Clay Pendleton."

"I don't see much of him anymore. He's working for a fellow named Pulitzer, who's bought the *World* and turned it into a disgusting sheet—full of stories about rapes and murders. Why do you want to see him?"

"I want to thank him for saving my life—when I wandered down to the river that night in Kassala."

Genevieve could see Rawdon's mind considering the alternatives. According to Dr. Beard's theory of the neurasthenic woman, Clay Pendleton was not a good candidate for a visitor. He would talk about politics and newspapers and overstimulate her. On the other hand, he was a perfect candidate as far as Rawdon was concerned. A little overstimulation might give his wife a relapse and enable him to keep her in Grandview for another twelve months.

Rawdon said he would discuss Clay with Dr. Beard. For the rest of the week, her smiling keeper told her how pleased he was by the way she had behaved with her husband. As a reward, Dr. Beard announced she could have visitors again next Sunday.

Genevieve almost wept with relief when Clay Pendleton joined her on the sunny porch, alone. "Gen," he said, and kissed her cheek. "Rawdon couldn't make it. He and Gould are involved in some major negotiations. I'm so pleased you asked to see me. I wrote you a half-dozen letters up here but they were all returned."

"Tell me what you're doing with this fellow Pulitzer. Rawdon says he's horrible. I don't believe him."

Clay looked uncomfortable. "He's out to build the *World* into the biggest newspaper in America. He plays up some pretty lurid stories on the front page—the sort of stuff papers usually bury in the back. But he's got ideals too, Gen." Clay pulled a page of newsprint out of his pocket. "Here's how he described the *World*'s policy in his first editorial."

Genevieve glanced through a long paragraph which called for a dozen major reforms in American life, from a tax on excessive corporate profits to an income tax to an end to vote buying. The *World* declared itself to be the voice of the people, declaring war on America's irresponsible rich, who were living like Russian grand dukes, absorbed in racehorses, yachts and women.

"I've gotten Pulitzer together with General Stapleton," Clay continued. "Pulitzer's backing him in his fight with Gould. It could make a tremendous difference. The General didn't have a paper behind him."

He began describing in his wry witty way the first meeting between the bearded electric Pulitzer and wary dignified Jonathan Stapleton. "The General found it hard to believe that someone only twenty years in the country could understand it so well."

It was marvelous to see Clay so full of enthusiasm and hope. Listening to him, Genevieve almost forgot why she had asked him to come. She remembered it with a violent start when Clay looked at his watch and remarked that their half hour was almost up. "Clay," she said. "I need some pencils and paper. I need them more than I've ever needed anything in my life."

"Don't they have them here?"

She told him in rapid but not (she hoped) berserk terms the course of her treatment. "Pencil and paper, Clay, so I can talk to myself. A journal. Where I can start to locate the truth."

He took two pencils and a small yellow-covered notebook out of his pocket. "Take these. Will you need more?"

"Yes. The next time you come bring a lot more."

Dr. Beard strolled around the corner of the porch, his broadest, most cheerful smile on his face. "Well, Mrs. Stapleton," he said. "It looks like you've proved your husband wrong in his fears about a newspaperman over-stimulating you. I had confidence in you."

"I was just telling Mr. Pendleton how glad I am that I never went into newspaper work. I would have strained my nerves beyond all hope of recovery."

"Undoubtedly," Dr. Beard said.

Clay's eyes reflected amazement, but his experience as a newspaperman kept his face expressionless.

Dr. Beard patted Genevieve's hand. "Mrs. Stapleton has learned the hard way that there's a price for all our pleasures. When she goes home, there'll be a limit to how much she can do, and she'll accept it, won't you?"

"Yes, Doctor," Genevieve said.

Back in her room, Genevieve took out Clay's notebook and pencils, which she had concealed in an inner pocket of her skirt. With a wildly beating heart, she wrote *Genevieve Dall Genevieve Dall Genevieve Dall Genevieve Dall Genevieve Dall* until the page was filled with her name. For an hour, she sat there staring at it, letting the truth sink into her barren mind. Genevieve Dall had not disappeared. Here was visible proof.

She tore out the page and put it under her pillow. On the next page she wrote: "Antiope's Story."

It was Mrs. Rawdon Stapleton who was going to disappear.

EIGHT

Jonathan Stapleton tiptoed down the hall to his wife's door. He listened for a moment and heard Cynthia weeping.

Small footsteps pattered on the stairs. Bounding toward him came Laura Kemble Stapleton in a green velvet dress, her silken dark hair flying behind her. "Where's Sweetheart?" she asked.

"She's not feeling well," he said. "You can have breakfast with me."

"I want to have it in bed with Sweetheart. That's more fun."

"I'm jealous," he said, picking her up for a hug. "Insanely jealous that you love her more than me."

She kissed him. "Oh, don't worry, Pa. I love you *almost* as much."

Sweetheart and Darling were the only names Cynthia and Laura ever used for each other. It was Cynthia's way of steering around that intolerable word Grandmother. She had also translated him to Pa, although at fifty-five he could hardly complain if someone called him Grandfather.

There were times when Jonathan found it hard to believe the transformation Laura had wrought in their lives. From the day she arrived, the temperature of the whole house seemed to rise. There was a constant exchange of kisses, a remarkably free use of the word "love." Cynthia was always singing, teasing, making up comic word games with her. Each night there was a recital of the impudent impish things Laura had done or said. The child was a kind of conduit, an almost magical creature, slowly restoring affection between them.

Anxiety over Laura's asthma attacks intensified their feelings. The seizures struck with mysterious, shattering suddenness. Laura would go to bed, apparently in perfect health. At midnight Cynthia would be rapping on his door. He would stumble out of bed and they would begin the complicated and awful series of remedies that medical science had devised to break the seizures. While the little body strained for breath, the green eyes, Rawdon's eyes, gazed at him, seeming to ask why, why. He would lower her into the icy bathwater, or force some vile substance such as nicotine down her throat, wondering if she would blame him, hate him. But the next day Laura would be brimming with playful affection, as if the ordeal had never taken place.

The child had been asthma free for almost two months now. She seemed perfectly content with seeing her father once or twice a week. She never asked for her mother. She seemed to have put her out of her mind, by an act of will. During a recent visit, Rawdon had told Cynthia he doubted if Genevieve would ever be able to resume the strain of motherhood. Exactly what that portended for Laura's future Jonathan was not sure.

Then came the blow—the reason why Cynthia wept behind the closed door. A month ago, she had been eagerly awaiting the birth of Mittie Roosevelt's first grandchild. Young Theodore's lovely blond wife, Alice, was the mother-to-be. One day Cynthia remarked that Mittie was not well. The next day the doctor was summoned and the news was worse. She had typhoid fever. A few days later, Alice gave birth to a baby girl. That night, Mittie died, and the young mother died of complications of childbirth a few hours later.

Cynthia was desolated. Jonathan was amazed by the depth of her grief. "Mittie was my sister!" she cried, when Jonathan, fearing for her health, tried to console her. He could only nod and hold her hand, feeling as if he were standing on the shore of a mystic inland sea on which men were forbidden to voyage.

Now, with this small bundle of femininity in his arms, Jonathan decided to rely more on intuition than on logic. He knocked on Cynthia's door. She was sitting up in bed, in a pale-pink nightdress. Her eyes were red.

"This imperious creature insists on having breakfast with you."

"Oh Sweetheart, why are you so sad?" Laura said. "I haven't been bad yet at all today."

"It has nothing to do with you, darling," Cynthia said, opening her arms to her.

"Cleo says I'm bad all the time, she says the other servants tell her I'm the most terrible child they've ever seen."

"That's just Cleo's way. She used to say the same thing to me down in Louisiana when I was your age. She likes to scold."

He deposited Laura in Cynthia's lap. "I was hoping that the worst was over," he said.

"I thought it was. But I dreamt of her last night. We were on a steamboat together. She looked so happy."

"Perhaps she is."

"I'd like to go up the Cane River on a steamboat someday," Laura said.

"We will, darling, we will," Cynthia said.

Laura snuggled into the pillow. "Tell me a Cane River story, please."

"I will—in a moment. Will you be home for dinner, Pa?"

"No. I'm seeing Clay Pendleton. We're going to begin the big battle."

"I should have known you'd grow bored with being a husband and father."

"Nothing of the sort. I wish I could quit the whole business and go to Europe with both of you for a year. But I've made promises, commitments, to these men—"

"I know, I know. I'm only teasing you," Cynthia said.

He kissed both his women and left them together in the big bed, dark heads together, while Cynthia drawled one of her elaborate dialect tales about "strange doin's" along the Cane River. Love, he thought, taking a last look at them from the door. It was amazing the way a man resolved to banish it from his life, only to find it ambushing him in a totally unexpected way.

Two hours later, Jonathan sat in his Wall Street office confronting a dozen grim-eyed men with clenched jaws. The Jay Gould Exterminating Company was in executive session.

"California" Kane, with his buckskin coat, his western boots and string tie, sat next to Delancey Apthorpe, the stylish quintessence of old New York money. Beside him was fleshy Adolph Mayer and beside him lean Nathaniel Appleton, Jr., who spoke for Boston's bankers. Next to them was short wiry Addison Barnes and bulky Charles Wertheimer, two of the wildest plungers on Wall Street, men who would bet on anything, from a racehorse to a wheat future.

By now they had acquired a thorough dossier on the Leviathan's operations. Clay Pendleton had quit the *Tribune* and spent a year investigating Gould for them. They knew all his allies, the major ones such as Russell Sage and Lionel Bradford and the minor but still potent ones such as Rawdon Stapleton. They knew his American, English, French, Dutch, German bankers. Above all they knew Gould's repertoire of dirty tricks, from espionage to slander to blackmail.

For two years they had confined themselves to hit-and-run attacks— "bleeding the monster," Jonathan Stapleton called it. They had cost Gould ten or fifteen million dollars in battles such as the corner Jonathan Stapleton had executed in the Hannibal & St. Joseph's railroad stock, the bear raid on the Mexican Southern Railroad. These were hardly fatal wounds to a man with a billion dollars in assets. But they had shattered the myth of Gould's invincibility.

Simultaneously, they had attacked Gould's corrupt relationships with politicians. When Theodore Roosevelt was elected to the New York State Assembly, Jonathan had urged him to investigate the connection between Gould and Judge T. R. Westbrook, whose habit of hearing cases in Gould's office had enabled the Leviathan to swallow New York's elevated railways. Assailing Gould as a "malefactor of great wealth," Roosevelt had forced Westbrook to resign.

Unfortunately, they had lost young Roosevelt as an ally. Demoralized by the death of his wife and mother, he had retreated west to become a rancher.

But Roscoe Conkling was still a formidable ally. Using his extensive connections in Congress, he had inspired an investigation of Gould's manipulation of the Union Pacific Railroad. The Senate committee turned up so much dirt, Gould was forced to relinquish control of the line, and Charles Francis Adams, unimpeachable descendant of two U.S. Presidents, was called in to run the company.

These successes were encouraging. Evidence of Gould's pain was his sale of the *New York World* to Joseph Pulitzer last year for a mere half-million dollars. It indicated a growing need for cash. Bankers were no longer eager to loan Gould money. Jonathan estimated that the Leviathan would have to raise $25 million in the next six months to maintain the prices of the stocks in which he was committed.

Calmly, almost casually, Jonathan issued their battle orders. "Let me caution you about one thing," he added. "Women. Remember how Gould used them to run the Vanderbilts out of Western Union."

"I'm goin' to trade in my buckskin for a monk's robe, General," California Kane said.

Later, alone in his office, thinking of these men sauntering up Wall Street to their offices, Jonathan could not escape the image that had haunted his mind since the beginning of this business—the hunt for the great whale that Herman Melville had converted into an American parable. He had persuaded these men to step into the financial equivalent of cockleshell boats to battle a creature of immense size and ferocity. Before it was over, some of them would be smashed, destroyed.

He was convinced that they were attacking a creature that was connected in some dark and immense way to evil. Although he no longer believed in a God of redemption and divine grace, Jonathan had no doubt that evil was a force, a dark energy, flowing through his American world. He had never doubted it from the day he faced that howling mob on First Avenue in the summer of 1863. The concentrated malevolence of the sound and the sight, its power to destroy the Union and everything that word connoted—order, peace, happiness—never left him.

What was the connection between that memory and that little girl running down the hall toward him, her dark curls flying? Was it a wish to somehow prevent her from being wounded by the blind malevolence loose in history? He knew this might be impossible. Genevieve, lost in a nightmare of grief, Cynthia, weeping for her southern sister, told him that hard truth. Yet it was all of them, the women he loved, who gave this grapple in the gutter some value. In a mysterious way, they were at the heart of the peace, the order, the happiness he dreamed of achieving.

At the end of the day Jonathan strode up Broadway to Park Row and the shabby three-story building that housed the *New York World*. As he walked into the third-floor city room, a high-pitched voice was cursing at someone with an obscene variety and inventiveness he had not heard since he left the army.

Clay Pendleton sauntered up to him. "Hello, General," he said. "Mr. Pulitzer will be with you in a minute or two. He's busy issuing a gentle reprimand to one of the editors."

"Does he talk that way to you?"

"He talks that way to everybody when he gets excited."

"How often does he get excited?"

"He's always excited."

Jonathan hoped he was not hearing more of the disillusion Clay had displayed in Chicago. He had yet to understand why Clay had suddenly sent him a cable from Cairo two years ago, asking, "IS IT TOO LATE TO GET INTO THE FIGHT?" He was reassured when Clay added, "He's one of a kind, General. You love him and hate him in the same breath."

A huge red-faced man came rushing out of Pulitzer's office and plunged down the stairs. Pulitzer appeared a moment later, hair and beard bristling in all directions. "Accuracy," he shouted to the scribbling reporters in the city room. "Accuracy!"

Then, apparently going from frenzy to calm in a blink of his myopic eyes, he turned to Jonathan and held out his hand with a cheerful smile. "Hello, General. What can I do for you?"

"I have some news that will interest you. Can this fellow join us?"

"Of course." Pulitzer beamed at Clay. "He's one of the few truly imaginative people on this staff. Most of them think it's merely a matter of finding the news, when at least half the time a great newspaper creates it."

"What's the *World*'s circulation now?"

"A hundred and thirty-four thousand. We've passed the *Herald*. Only the *Sun* is ahead of us."

It was an amazing performance. Pulitzer had added over a hundred thousand to the *World*'s circulation in a year.

Thus far, the paper had backed the Gould Exterminating Company's limited forays. Now Jonathan asked if Pulitzer was ready to put the *World* behind them for all-out war.

Pulitzer leaped to his feet, arms flailing. "You've got the *World*'s support, General. But will you support the *World* in another matter?"

"What's that?"

"I want to make the next President a Democrat."

Jonathan glanced at Clay. Was there the trace of a smile on his lips?

"I know your feeling for the Republican Party, General," Pulitzer said. "I know what you've done on its behalf. But it's time for the country to return to a two-party system. It's time to make the Democrats feel they're part of the republic. What's more important, your party has been bought by Gould and his cronies. They're going to nominate James G. Blaine. If he wins, Gould will own the country."

"The General could give us even more help if he stayed Republican and told us what's happening from the inside," Clay Pendleton said.

Pulitzer beamed.

Jonathan wondered if somewhere Senator George Stapleton was smiling. He took a deep breath and held out his hand to Pulitzer. "If Blaine gets the nomination, it's a deal."

At dinner, Jonathan handed Clay a packet of information on the current state of Gould's finances. "This is page-one stuff, General," Clay said.

"Can you help me on another matter?" Jonathan said. "Where can I find Rawdon? I want to talk to him, tonight."

"He's almost always at the Hoffman House Bar."

An hour later they walked into the unofficial headquarters of New York's Democratic Party. Famous faces were everywhere: Tony Pastor, the swarthy impresario; John L. Sullivan, the barrel-chested heavyweight champion of the world; "Honest John" Kelly, the stumpy boss of Tammany Hall. Above the bar, a huge mural proclaimed the beauty of the undraped female body on a scale perhaps best described as Barnumesque.

"There's Rawdon," Clay said.

He was standing in a semicircle of listeners around a man at the bar, who turned out to be Robert Legrand. He was entrancing his audience with the story of another successful shakedown. "So the bozo says to her, 'Father will disinherit me.' And she says, 'Then there's only one way to compensate me for my *ruined* reputation.' "

For a moment Jonathan was fascinated to see before his eyes confirmation of what Clay had described in his reports of Gould's blackmailing operations. Standing beside Robert were some of the key players in his game. Colonel William D'Alton Mann, with his grandfatherly white mustaches and long old-fashioned frock coat, was crucial. The threat of having his escapades published in Mann's newspaper, *Town Topics,* had persuaded more than one New York scion to pry open the family bank account by forging his father's name on a check or two.

Robert Legrand was the man behind the stories of "southern adventuresses" that regularly broke in the New York papers. With Robert's help, Gould had acquired a half-dozen affidavits from women Robert had sent to

Willie K. Vanderbilt, William Vanderbilt's salacious son. The documents had persuaded the Vanderbilts to abandon Western Union to Gould without a fight.

"General," Rawdon said, when Jonathan touched his arm, "don't you realize this is enemy territory? Do you think that scandal-sheet salesman you've got with you can guarantee your safety?"

They retreated to a less populated part of the long bar. "I shouldn't even be telling you this," Jonathan said. "Maybe it's having Laura in the house for the past six months. My partners and I are going to work on Gould. I'd like you with me—in the biggest fight of my life."

Rawdon sipped a brandy. "This isn't even subtle," he said. "Right now I'm worth twenty million dollars. Four times what you're worth. Of course you'd love to have me on your side."

"You've seen Gould—"

"I've seen Gould—and I've seen you in action, General. I'll take Gould. He doesn't have any pretensions to morality. He's in it for the money, for the power, the pleasure of being the richest man in the world. That's what I'm in it for, too." Rawdon picked up his brandy and stalked back to the circle around Robert Legrand.

"I could have told you he was going to say that, General," Clay said.

"I had to ask him," Jonathan said.

Near the door, a figure reeled in front of them. "General," the man said thickly, "how's—Mrs. Stapleton?"

It was Edgar Calhoun. He was drunk. "Fine," Jonathan snapped.

"Good. Please give'r m'regards. Fellow southerners, that sort of thing."

"I will."

"He's been drunk for the last six months," Clay said as they walked out onto Fifth Avenue. "I hear he lost his shirt in the Mexican Southern."

Two days later, on the front page of the *World*, Clay portrayed Jay Gould's empire as a shambles, riven by debt and speculation. The next day, Jonathan Stapleton sold ten thousand shares of Western Union, which he had quietly accumulated over the previous year. The price of this stock, the keystone of Gould's empire, dove ten points. Simultaneously, Roscoe Conkling went into New York State Supreme Court to demand a grand-jury investigation of Gould's manipulation of New York's elevated railways, on behalf of a half-dozen stockholders who claimed he had swindled them. Adolph Mayer began disposing of the bonds he held in several Gould railways in the West, implying that the lines were on the verge of bankruptcy.

Nathan Appleton suddenly revealed himself as a major buyer of Missouri Pacific stock. He denounced Gould for letting the railroad dwindle to "two streaks of rust in the desert" and began dumping his stock on the market. Gould spent $5 million in a single day trying to keep the Missouri's price up.

Meanwhile, California Kane was driving up the price of gold with huge purchases, at the precise moment that Gould was short for over $4 million.

They knew exactly what the Leviathan was doing, they even knew what he was thinking, thanks to their espionage system. Delancey Apthorpe had Gould's runner, Danny Callahan, locked in a top-floor room at the Metropolitan Hotel, drinking champagne and feasting on his favorite food, Welsh rarebit. His look-alike cousin, Billy McGuire, was bringing all Gould's orders and much of his correspondence to Apthorpe first before delivering them to the bankers and brokers for whom they were intended. When Gould, trying to trap one of his persecutors, went short in Missouri Pacific, Jonathan Stapleton came into the market and protected Nathan Appleton, driving the price of the stock up instead of letting it fall, costing Gould another $30 million.

These wild gyrations created immense turbulence in Wall Street. Soon the violent waters were scattered with the financial equivalent of men and boats. One of the victims was Charles Wertheimer, caught short for over $4 million in another Gould railroad, the Denver Pacific. By pouring in borrowed money from a dozen sources, Gould was able to maintain absolute control of the stock for a week. After losing a million trying to help, Jonathan regretfully informed Wertheimer they would have to abandon him. The big German went on a two-day bender. When friends finally found him in a downtown hotel, he was raving at Gould, pounding the wall until his fists were bloody.

They got even a few days later when Rawdon Stapleton, obviously acting on Gould's behalf, tried to create a bull movement in Western Union. The *World* ran a story on how much money Gould had looted from the company since he took it over, and Jonathan summoned Adolph Mayer to join him in a bear attack that drove the stock down another twenty points, costing Rawdon at least $5 million.

Frantically trying to recoup, Rawdon plunged into the gold market, where Gould had reigned as monarch since 1869. California Kane was waiting for him. Borrowing $5 million from other members of the GEC, he battered Rawdon's bear movement to a catastrophic standstill. A desperate Rawdon tried to settle for fifty cents on the dollar. Kane told him to pay or go to jail.

At the end of the week, Jefferson Gansevoort appeared in Jonathan's office. The once arrogant spokesman for Jay Gould was wild-eyed, trembling. Gould had lured him—as he had probably lured Rawdon—into the gold market to extricate himself, and Gansevoort had lost everything. He asked Jonathan to intercede with California Kane for him—and Rawdon.

"Tell my son I gave him a chance to be on the right side in this war two weeks ago. As for you, those lies you told Ben Dall in 1869 have come home to roost."

"I have no regret for anything we did to that abolitionist bastard," Gansevoort snarled.

Gansevoort filed for bankruptcy and fled to Jersey City, a favorite refuge of broken speculators. That night, Cynthia told Jonathan that Rawdon was spreading the story of his merciless father all over New York, blaming him not only for his own losses, but for the ruin of a man with five daughters.

He told her about his invitation to Rawdon—and what Gansevoort had said about Ben Dall. Cynthia sighed and shook her head. For a moment Jonathan's taut nerves almost snapped. Then he realized that there was nothing to prevent him from explaining himself. No inherited loyalties, no southern sister stood between them. He sat down and for a half hour told her why he was trying to drive Jay Gould out of Wall Street. At the end he took her hand and said, "Now I must swear you to secrecy. If any of my partners ever thought they had an idealist lurking among them, they'd take to the boats and never return."

"I'm so pleased that you told me," Cynthia said.

In her bed that night they reached a new realm of feeling. It was more than forgiveness. He felt Cynthia's wish to give him a spiritual sustenance she had never offered before. It was the kind of love he had assumed his first wife would give him when he came home from the battlefield. Now a southern voice was whispering, "I'm so proud of you. So proud to have a husband who *dares.*" Not for the first time, Jonathan concluded life was a totally confusing business.

On Wall Street the all-fronts offensive continued. The interest rates for call money—cash needed to support stocks bought on margin—soared to over 100 percent. A murderous price, even for a Leviathan. Bankruptcy notices began blooming in the *New York Times.* In the *World* Clay Pendleton lashed Gould with exposés of his looting of the Missouri Pacific. He trumpeted the discovery of a hitherto unknown "floating debt" of ten million that Gould had left behind in the Union Pacific. Western Union's stock sagged lower when the *World* published ferocious evidence of the company's inefficiency.

On Monday morning, May 10, the word went up and down Wall Street that the brokerage firm of Grant and Ward had failed with debts of $17 million and assets not worth mentioning. Ulysses Grant had unwisely loaned his name to Frederick Ward, "the young Napoleon of Wall Street," in the same foolish way that he had let Gould use him as a figurehead to sell stock in the Mexican Southern Railroad.

An hour after Grant and Ward went under, the Marine National Bank closed its doors. Old James Fish had loaned the glib Ward $10 million. From the wreckage emerged news of a devastating blow to another young Napoleon. Rawdon had put most of Eleanor Bradford's money into the bank earlier in the week, to use in the war. Now it was gone.

Stocks plunged in a wave of frantic selling. By noon, the streets of the financial district were jammed with men and women trying to get their money out of tottering banks and brokerage houses. That afternoon the Mexican Southern Railroad declared bankruptcy. This was the first of Gould's enterprises to crumble.

The Leviathan was bleeding from a dozen major wounds. Some members of the Gould Exterminating Company thought they had done enough; perhaps they ought to settle with the beast and count their millions. Instead, Jonathan ordered bear raids across the whole front. Every Gould stock was sold short, to the staggering sum of $45 million, almost every cent of the combined assets of the GEC. This order caused severe dissension in the ranks. Selling short was the riskiest move a man could make on Wall Street. If the stock's price did not fall, he would suffer disastrous losses; he might even have to file for bankruptcy or go to prison.

On Wednesday, May 25, Jonathan got to his office at 7 A.M., his usual arrival time these days, to find Delancey Apthorpe waiting for him. "Gould's gone," Delancey said. "I just got a report from the detective we've had watching him. He went aboard his yacht at four A.M. and sailed for God knows where."

"He's trying to rattle us," Jonathan said. "He thinks we'll be ready to settle when he comes back in a week. Meanwhile we'll have reporters and brokers worrying us about whether we can make good on those short sales. There's only one thing to do. We'll disappear, too."

"Where?" Delancey asked.

"We'll go down to Kemble Manor and enjoy ourselves. We could all use a vacation."

He left Apthorpe to spread the word among the GEC and caught a hack to Stuyvesant Square. He permitted Laura to scold him for not coming home in time to kiss her good night for "one whole week." She was very annoyed with him, and so was Sweetheart.

This turned out to be an exaggeration. Cynthia greeted him with a kiss on the cheek and eagerly asked him for news. "I feel the way women felt during the war. Totally superfluous," she said.

"You know that isn't true," he said.

Cynthia blushed. "You *know* what I mean," she said.

"I'm here to ask if you'd consider playing hostess to a dozen worn-out brokers, bankers and speculators. We're going to Kemble Manor for a council of war. I'd like to make it as pleasant as possible. We may have serious reasons to quarrel. I'd prefer not to have them disgruntled over the food and drink— and lack of good company."

"When are you leaving?"

"This afternoon."

"Jonathan Stapleton, are you insane? Do you expect me to plan menus, arrange for servants, food, to be transported to that godforsaken house, pack my clothes and look presentable, in a matter of four or five hours?"

"We'll make you an honorary member of the Gould Exterminating Company," Jonathan said.

"I prefer a better bargain. For every week we delay past the first of June in dubious battle with Mr. Gould, I want an extra month in Venice."

"Done," he said.

"You realize that if you delay six months, you'll owe me two years?"

He smiled. "For some reason the prospect doesn't frighten me in the least."

"Can I come?" Laura asked. "I'll be very good in Venice, Sweetheart."

The child's voice was subdued. She seemed to sense she was being excluded by the current of feeling that was flowing between him and Cynthia.

"No need to worry about Venice for a long while," Cynthia said. "We're going someplace even more exciting. Kemble Manor. You'll love it. We can go swimming and sailing. . . ."

At 2 P.M. he greeted Cynthia on the platform beside their private railroad car in the Pennsylvania Railroad station in Jersey City. She was wearing a mauve traveling dress with a series of small bows down the front. Every dark curl on her forehead was precisely in place beneath a flowery bonnet. Laura was dressed in an identical outfit. Inside the car this influx of femininity cast an instant glow over the group of tense exhausted men who sat smoking cigars or gulping dark glasses of liquor from the bar.

Everyone chuckled when Cynthia introduced Laura as "General Stapleton's granddaughter—and mine by adoption." California Kane, who had previously been close to punching Delancey Apthorpe for wanting to push Gould to the limit, was entranced by the child. He sat her on his lap and asked her if she liked ice cream. When the expected answer was given, there turned out to be none on the train. Kane rushed into the station to buy a quart of chocolate and a quart of vanilla—enough to feed ten six-year-olds. Addison Barnes revealed he was an amateur magician—not a bad hobby for a Wall Street speculator. He fascinated Laura by seeming to draw coins and cards out of thin air.

Meanwhile, they steamed south through the green fields of New Jersey, Gould and the $45 million they were risking to destroy him temporarily forgotten. At Kemble Manor there were more distractions. Cynthia presided over a supper that was worthy of Delmonico's. She had brought their entire New York household staff with her.

But Gould could not be kept at bay indefinitely. After Cynthia withdrew and the table was cleared for port and cigars, the debate on what to do next resumed. "If everything goes the way we hope it will—down," California Kane said, "we'll run Gould off Wall Street. But if he can keep even a third of his stocks up, some of us are going to lose big chunks of our shirts."

"That's why we have an agreement to pool our losses," Jonathan said.

The jittery discussion only underscored for Jonathan the wisdom of this retreat to Kemble Manor. In New York they would have been the prey of every rumor. Reporters, friends, wives, mistresses, would have whispered ruin in their ears, and he would have been unable to counter it.

Jonathan was certain that tomorrow they would hear from Gould. Flanks streaming blood, the Leviathan would surface one last time. Did he himself have the will, the courage, to face him, with everything at risk, and drive home the final thrust?

Yes. Then Ben Dall would rest in peace. One death would have a purpose, even if all the others were sliding away into the oblivion of history. He would have expiated part of the obscenity he committed in Louisiana in 1876.

Abner Littlejohn, Kemble Manor's one-armed caretaker, woke him in the dawn with a series of excited knocks. "General," he said, gesturing toward the window. "There's one hell of a big ship offshore."

There were still patches of fog floating low on the water. Among them loomed a gleaming white yacht at least two hundred feet long. Its upper deck was flush—unbroken except for the three masts and a long deckhouse. It was Gould's *Atalanta.*

As Jonathan watched, a whaleboat was lowered and a twelve-man crew took the oars. Down a companionway came a figure in white. Jonathan focused his field glasses on him. It was Lionel Bradford. The crew stroked methodically to the dock, where the old Stapleton schooner, the black-hulled *Principia,* was tied up.

"Tell Mr. Bradford I'll have breakfast with him," Jonathan said.

He shaved and dressed in casual clothes. Downstairs Bradford chatted with Cynthia.

"Good morning," Jonathan said. "We've been expecting you."

Bradford nodded. "I told Gould he was wasting his time trying to scare you with his disappearing act."

"If you need me for anything, Jonathan, I'll be upstairs," Cynthia said.

"No—stay. There's no reason for you to withdraw." He wanted Cynthia to share the triumph.

"I agree with you, General," Bradford said. "In fact, Mrs. Stapleton may supply an ingredient that's been missing in this drama since it began— compassion."

"For you or for Gould?"

"For Gould. He's a dying man, General. The strain of this ordeal has fatally weakened his lungs."

"All of us are dying of something, Bradford."

"He's also a desperate man."

They sat down at the dining-room table. Bradford unfolded a document and spread it in front of Jonathan. It was an assignment of all the personal property held by Jay Gould—his Fifth Avenue house, his estate in Westchester County, his yacht—to his wife and children.

"I take it from this that he's threatening to declare bankruptcy."

Bradford nodded. "With practically every piece of stock he owns committed to cover outstanding loans, it will be the crash to end all crashes. Western Union, the Missouri Pacific, the Metropolitan Street Railways will all go. He'll take your son Rawdon down with him, of course. Rawdon's only remaining assets are in companies Gould owns. He'll probably take you and your friends down, too. Every share of stock in his various companies that you've promised to deliver for your short sales will be worthless. That will only be the beginning of the chaos. At least a hundred banks will go under."

"But you'll survive?"

"I've made it a rule never to invest more than fifty percent of my capital in one country. Survival has been my chief preoccupation for a long time, General. That and the enjoyment of life's pleasures. A pity you aren't more inclined that way."

His eyes flickered in Cynthia's direction. "I've never understood the strange moral passions of some Americans."

"They have a certain grandeur, Mr. Bradford," Cynthia said.

"Believe it or not I found a certain grandeur in Mr. Gould too," Bradford said. "The scale of his ambitions was beyond the range of ordinary mortals. Would you be willing to come out to the ship, General? He's afraid to come ashore and face certain members of your group, such as California Kane, who threw him down a stairway the last time they met."

"I'll guarantee his physical safety."

"General, he's a very sick man."

"All right," Jonathan said.

He joined Bradford in the whaleboat. In five minutes they were crossing the parquet deck of the *Atalanta* to the main cabin. Gould sat at a mahogany desk; more mahogany paneled the walls and ceiling. The draperies, the hangings of the bed, the furniture were all covered with gold-threaded tapestry cloth. "Hello, Stapleton," he said.

"Hello."

"Say hello to your son."

Rawdon was sitting in a chair on the other side of the room, a strange smile on his face. Jonathan nodded to him.

Bradford sat down in a chair beside Rawdon. They were obviously going to let Gould do the talking.

"I hope by now Bradford has made it clear that if we don't settle it's bankruptcy and we all go under. Now that we can talk more frankly, I'd like to explain my terms."

"None of us will go bankrupt, Gould. We may lose a lot of money, but we won't go bankrupt. We're not interested in your terms."

"Maybe these will pique your interest."

From his desk, Gould took a folder and handed it to Jonathan. He glanced into it. There were about a half-dozen letters on blue stationery, with a gold "MT" at the top. Madeline Terhune? The handwriting was Cynthia's. The first letter began: *Dearest Rebel: Oh to be out of England now that you're not here. London is a bore without you, day and night—especially the latter.* . . .

"Where did you get these?"

"Bradford picked them up from your wife's brother a week or two ago. We didn't ask how he extracted them from the southern hero to whom they're addressed—Colonel Calhoun."

Rawdon's smile was no longer strange.

"If you don't want to see them published in *Town Topics*," Gould said, "you'd better persuade your colleagues to settle, on my terms."

"What are your terms?"

"I want an immediate two-million-five-hundred-thousand-dollar loan to prevent bankruptcy. I want a written promise that your group will absolutely cease further attacks on me. I want a statement from you, apologizing for disrupting the financial community with your mindless vendetta."

"Go to hell," Jonathan said. He flung the folder of letters in Gould's face and strode onto the *Atalanta*'s deck.

Bradford was on his heels. "I hate to insist on such a disagreeable alternative, General," he said, "fond as I am of your wife. But we're serious about publishing those letters in *Town Topics*. Colonel Mann is practically salivating to get his hands on them."

"When I told him to go to hell, Bradford, I included you."

Jonathan was barely conscious of where he was until he found himself standing on Kemble Manor's dock. Up the steep steps he toiled to the bluff. On the lawn, the first person he saw was Cynthia, in a yellow-and-black dress. She had never looked more beautiful. A voice cried within him, *Love*. How in God's name had he let love draw and quarter him this way?

"What news?" Cynthia said.

"Bad," he snapped.

In the house, he assembled his fellow members of the GEC and told them Gould's terms. "I recommend their absolute rejection," he said.

To his dismay, more than half the group disagreed with him. The bankers, led by Adolph Mayer, seemed to agree with Bradford that a Gould collapse would be the crash to end all crashes. Mayer maintained they had never envisioned Gould's complete destruction. They had merely wanted to shrink him to the size of an ordinary millionaire and convince him that his style of speculation and company looting would not be tolerated by honest men.

As they argued, telegrams began to arrive, relayed from Jonathan's office. The first was from J. P. Morgan, the next from William H. Vanderbilt. The Grand Central crowd, as they were called, did not relish the idea of their stocks taking another dive. Each recommended a reasonable settlement with Gould. Around noon, a telegram arrived from Washington: "PRESIDENT FEARS SEVERE SOCIAL UNREST IF GOULD GOES UNDER. CONKLING."

"Maybe we should settle," said Addison Barnes, who had previously voted for Gould's destruction.

"I still say drive him to the wall," Jonathan growled.

He knew he was talking like a madman. Those letters in that folder had unhinged him. Adolph Mayer urged a compromise. They would offer Gould the money but dismiss his other two terms. Instead, they would insist on Gould putting up fifty thousand shares of Western Union stock for security with an option for them to buy the stock—which would give them control of the company—if he resumed speculating.

"He wanted to put us out of business. Let's put him out," Mayer said.

"Let him stew out there for twenty-four hours and then make that offer," Delancey Apthorpe said. "He's obviously desperate for money."

The vote was unanimous. Jonathan wearily accepted the opinion. For the rest of the day he wandered the grounds and the beach, avoiding Cynthia. She entertained their guests with her usual skill, organizing a croquet game on the lawn, a sail aboard *Principia*. Dinner was another feast, and unavoidable torture for him, watching her at the other end of the table teasing Addison Barnes for his pursuit of Lillian Russell, Broadway's latest musical-comedy star, charming and amusing everyone while he sat in silence.

In bed he stared into the moonlit darkness, thinking of his exaltation the other night when Cynthia had whispered her pride in his daring. He had been right the first time when he told her on that bitter night in 1878 that it had all been a performance since the moment on the stairs at Bralston.

Suddenly he could not bear the humiliation. He knew why men murdered unfaithful wives. He walked into Cynthia's room and stood beside her bed. He would kill her and leave no explanation. He would simply walk into the sea. Gould and Bradford and Rawdon would be disgraced for all time when the truth got out—as it eventually would.

My God. In the moonlight, he saw not one but two dark heads on the pillows. Laura was sleeping with Cynthia.

He reeled back to his bed and lay there sleepless until morning. At 7 A.M.

Lionel Bradford was on the dock, implying that no one had slept very well aboard the *Atalanta* either.

"General," Bradford said. "We must have that money today—or a half-dozen banks will foreclose on Gould."

"We have a counteroffer," he said.

His mind, his body, was dross. Perhaps it made him sound more ruthless as he delivered their alternative terms to Gould in his cloth-of-gold tapestried cabin. Rawdon glowered in the corner, no longer smiling.

"I accept," Gould said. "My doctors have told me I have to retire from everything except a caretaker role in Western Union, if I hope to live another year."

Back in Kemble Manor, Jonathan found his partners at breakfast. "Gould accepts our terms," he said.

Cynthia clapped her hands. "Is it time to celebrate?"

"Not quite. But be sure the champagne is on ice."

Amazing. He could still talk to her in a natural voice.

"What kind of hostess do you think I am? It's been there since we arrived."

In an hour he was back aboard the *Atalanta* with a letter of credit for $2.5 million and a contract stipulating that Gould would retire from active trading on Wall Street. Gould handed over his option for fifty thousand shares of Western Union.

"Now for a last piece of business," Gould said. "What are you willing to pay for these, General?" He held up the folder containing Cynthia's letters.

"What are you asking?"

"How much did these cost you?" Gould asked, turning to Bradford.

"A hundred thousand."

"I'd suggest a half million as a fair price. Maybe it will help you see how speculation drives up the prices of things. You've been persecuting me because I like to speculate. In the long run my approach will do more for the country than old-fashioned ideas like responsibility to the workers."

Jonathan wrote out a check. As Gould took it in his hand, he began to cough. Jonathan sat there watching him clutch a white handkerchief to his mouth. Slowly but perceptibly, the handkerchief turned red. Bradford had told the truth. The Leviathan was dying.

Jonathan looked past Gould at Rawdon. He had a sneer on his handsome face. Not a hint, an iota of sympathy. Evil, Jonathan thought, with a shudder. Its tentacles had enveloped his son. Why did he think he could escape injury in close grapple with it?

Once more, he barely remembered crossing the *Atalanta*'s deck to the waiting whaleboat. Still clutching the folder, he found himself on Kemble Manor's dock again. Out on the water, smoke poured from *Atalanta*'s funnel.

She was getting under way. Jonathan thought of Ahab's death in *Moby-Dick*, the curling line around his throat, hurtling him into the blood-flecked sea in the wake of the maimed leviathan. In this real world, the hero did not die so spectacularly. Instead of his life, it was his happiness that was ripped from his body and dragged forever beyond his reach in the fathomless depths.

The rest of the day was torture. He had to smile and drink champagne all the way back to New York. Cynthia was never in higher spirits. She kissed every member of the Gould Exterminating Company and vowed that henceforth they would assemble for dinner on the thirtieth of May every year to celebrate their victory. In Stuyvesant Square, she told Laura that Pa was now the most famous man in America, and he would have to be kissed a dozen times a day to keep him happy.

Not until Laura had gone to bed did he give Cynthia the letters. "I paid Gould a half-million dollars for these," he said. "Bradford bought them from your brother."

She had only to glance at them. "Is there anything I can say?" she asked.

He shook his head. "For the time being, while Laura stays with us, you can live here. I think with a little management we can avoid seeing each other most of the time. After Laura goes back to her parents, we'll have to make other arrangements."

Tears streamed down Cynthia's face. "Jonathan, please listen to me. It's true, I loved him for a while. But I stopped seeing him months ago. Laura was part of the reason. But it was you—the return of my feelings for you. That was the most important reason."

"A superb performance," he said. "No wonder they call you the best amateur actress in New York."

"I'll make you believe me," Cynthia said. "Somehow, someday, I'll make you believe I still love you."

"We'll both have to live a long time," Jonathan Stapleton said.

NINE

"Pendleton! Send a wire to the Washington bureau. Tell them to make sure the President got my message about appointing Jonathan Stapleton to the Civil Service Commission."

"Yes, Mr. Pulitzer."

"I met this new boss of Tammany, Croker, at a dinner party the other night, and I didn't like the smell of him. Investigate him. Send a wire to the governor and tell him to have nothing to do with the fellow until we decide he's all right. Tell the mayor the same thing."

"Yes, Mr. Pulitzer."

"Now let's go over this Bangs murder story again. You did a nice job of condensing it for today's edition. But we can get at least three more stories out of it."

"Yes, Mr. Pulitzer."

It was 2 A.M. Pendleton had been working since noon—fourteen hours. Yesterday he had worked eighteen hours. He had no idea how long Joseph Pulitzer had been working. The man was incredible. He was trying to run the federal government and the governments of the state and city of New York and simultaneously publish with passionate attention to every detail the biggest newspaper in America.

In the city room, suave, mustachioed Managing Editor John Cockerill smiled at him. "Keeps you busy, doesn't he?" Behind Cockerill's smile was a mounting rage. Pendleton's official title was city editor, the man who assigned reporters to stories. But Pulitzer liked to play people off against each other. He was treating Pendleton more like the managing editor these days.

Pendleton stared blearily at his notes. It was typical Pulitzer—equal time for reform of the Democratic Party and the federal civil service and the mystery of why Harold Bangs slashed his bride to death on his wedding night and then committed suicide. There were times when this unstable combination of sensational gore and crusading politics threatened Pendleton's sanity. But working for Pulitzer was still the most exciting experience of his life.

Nine months ago, Grover Cleveland had become president of the United States—the first Democrat elected in twenty-four years. He had won New York State and the White House by a wispy 1,149 votes. Without Pulitzer and the *World*, he never would have done it.

The Republican candidate was Jay Gould's favorite politician, James G. Blaine. In the weeks before the election, the *World* ran a series of columns aimed at Republican readers, linking this oily charmboy to payoffs and deals with corporations seeking government favors. The columns were signed "Stalwart." The author, with some help from Pendleton, was Jonathan Stapleton. The series alone undoubtedly changed more than 575 minds—all that was needed for Grover Cleveland to carry New York.

Jonathan was not the only Republican to turn his back on Blaine, subtly or openly. Even the *New York Times* broke with the party it had helped to found. In Pendleton's numerous meetings with the General, he found him strangely morose. At first Pendleton thought it was political pain—the wrench of abandoning the Republican Party. But he soon noticed that the General was living alone in Stuyvesant Square. When Pendleton inquired for Mrs. Stapleton and Laura, he was told that they had decided to spend the winter in the south of France, in the hope that the sunshine would improve Laura's asthma.

Rawdon soon told Pendleton the real story. He of course had no sympathy whatsoever for his father. Perhaps this explained the extraordinary amount of energy Pendleton put into trying to revive Jonathan Stapleton's morale. After the presidential election, he seemed adrift. Pendleton invented excuses to visit him. He lured him out of the house to political dinners. He urged him to resume a role in the Republican Party, which had broken into squabbling factions. But the General seemed to have lost interest in politics—and business.

On Wall Street, buccaneers such as Gould were being replaced by legalized pirates such as John D. Rockefeller, who organized all the companies in an industry into a monopoly called a trust. They then rigged prices and swindled the public in perfect safety. The *World* was attacking them, and Pendleton urged the General to get into the fight. He shook his head. He claimed he had no interest in becoming a full-time crusader, a public scold. In his perplexity, Pendleton urged Pulitzer to sponsor their stranded Stalwart as a member of the new Civil Service Commission. Perhaps a presidential summons would lift him out of his lethargy.

"Pendleton!" Pulitzer was in front of his desk. "I almost forgot the campaign for the Statue of Liberty. I want a comprehensive plan on my desk tomorrow morning. This is your baby, start to finish. Write an editorial kicking every rich tightwad in New York in the ass. Call on the people to pay for it in nickels and dimes. Prove we don't need the rich."

"Yes, Mr. Pulitzer."

For eight years the Statue of Liberty had been lying around Paris in twenty or thirty pieces, waiting for New Yorkers to undergo a seizure of patriotism and come up with the cash for a pedestal. Pulitzer had decided it was a perfect project for the *World*. All Pendleton had to do was figure out how to fit it into his fourteen-hour day.

A half hour later, Pendleton walked into the Hoffman House bar in search of a little relaxation. The crowd was beginning to thin out. Standing at the bar was Isaac Mayer, who was winning a reputation—and several million dollars—on Wall Street as an ingenious organizer of trusts. After Pendleton ascertained that Alice and the four children were well, their conversation turned, as usual, to Rawdon Stapleton.

Isaac sighed. "I tried to bring him into the last trust I organized, the cordage industry thing that your employer Mr. Pulitzer attacked so viciously last week. But no one wants to have anything to do with him. It's the Gould connection."

"Does he had any money left?"

"Not much. He's lost a million in the last year, trying to play a lone hand. I'm afraid he's going to have to imitate Gould and go into retirement for a while."

"How's Genevieve?"

Isaac sighed. "Alice visits her as often as she can. But the new baby keeps her tied down."

"I haven't been up there myself for two or three weeks," Pendleton said. "Pulitzer's been dragging me into the office on Sundays to keep him company."

Excuses, excuses. Their eyes, their voices, betrayed their guilt. No one seemed to know what to do or say about Genevieve. She had come home from Grandview Sanitarium nine months ago, escorted by a large German nurse. For a while, Pendleton had been a frequent visitor. He encouraged her determination to lose the extra pounds she had gained at Grandview on their dairy diet. He enjoyed talking to her about the *World*'s crusades—and Pulitzer's assumption that everyone should eat, drink and sleep the news, as he did. Genevieve seemed to enjoy it too.

After one particularly lively visit, Pendleton got a telephone call from Rawdon, warning him that he was "overstimulating" Genevieve. Henceforth he was ordered to keep the conversation banal. Rather than insult Genevieve's intelligence, he had stopped visiting her, a decision which made him surprisingly morose.

"Rawdon's still diddling Eleanor," Isaac said. "It's gotten pretty notorious. People have seen him going into her house at all hours of the night. Alice finally had to tell Eleanor last week that their friendship was over. We've run into enough problems trying to make a match for Sally, without adding a scandal."

Sally Gansevoort had been living with the Mayers since her father's financial collapse. Alice was trying to marry her to a New York scion with enough wealth to be unbothered by Sally's poverty. The effort had aroused the specter that Alice and Isaac had defied, and were apparently still defying—anti-Semitism. A number of promising bachelors who were more than willing to enjoy the pleasures of their dining room had become extremely evasive when exposed to Sally's charms. Isaac thought it was their reluctance to have a Jewish brother-in-law.

Pendleton thought Isaac was too sensitive on the subject. Tonight he reiterated this opinion.

"I wish I agreed with you," Isaac said. "But I've been hearing things on Wall Street that make me pretty uneasy. Lionel Bradford has been telling

people General Stapleton was just a figurehead in the fight with Gould. My
father was the brains of the operation. Gould's telling everyone the Jews are
going to fill the vacuum he's left."

"What have we here, an embryo reunion of Princeton 'Seventy-six?'" Rawdon Stapleton said.

"Hello, Cap," Isaac said.

"How's the young Napoleon of the trusts?" Rawdon said. "I'd pay the
reporters not to call me that, if you want my advice. It didn't bring me or
Fred Ward anything but bad luck."

"Your luck will change any day now," Isaac said.

"Sure," Rawdon said, and ordered a brandy he obviously did not need.

For those who knew him in his Princeton days, when he was the magical
leader of the crew, the man whose friendship seemed to add stature to those
to whom he deigned to proffer it, the last year had left cruel marks on
Rawdon. He was no longer the golden scion who seemed destined to rule his
generation. Failure subtracted more than money from a man in Darwinian
America. It thinned his smile, shadowed his eyes, turned opinions once delivered with resounding certainty into unconvincing bravado. In what had now
become known as the Panic of '84, Rawdon had lost $18 million of his own
money and $8 million belonging to a woman who had trusted him. That was
enough failure to last most men a lifetime.

Isaac began trying to explain why his partners had not welcomed Rawdon
into the consortium that created the National Cordage Company.

"Never mind, never mind," Rawdon said. "I'd like you to answer a tougher
question. Why has Alice stopped calling on Eleanor?"

"Rawdon—I had nothing to do with it. That's strictly between the
women."

"Maybe it's time you stopped letting Alice make the rules, Ike. You think
all that blond hair and blue eyes will turn you into an American. As if this
goddamn hypocritical country was worth joining in the first place. One of
these days you're going to find out you should have stayed Jewish—"

"I better be getting home," Isaac said.

Head down, Isaac hurried out the door. Rawdon watched him, his mouth a
bitter slash. "Young Napoleon," he said. "When are they going to start
calling you something like that, scribbler?"

"I'm satisfied with city editor," Pendleton said.

Rawdon unfolded his copy of tomorrow's *World.* "How do you put up with
heads like this, Pendleton?" he asked, pointing to BACHELOR BANGS' BRIDAL
NIGHT!

"That's a hell of a story. Murder and suicide," Pendleton said.

"Or these." Rawdon pointed to PIERCED HIS WIFE'S EYES. MADDENED BY
MARRIAGE. BAPTIZED IN BLOOD.

"They sell papers," Pendleton said. "We're over two hundred thousand daily now."

In better days, Pendleton would have admitted that some of Pulitzer's headlines made him retch. You could admit the truth to a friend. But Rawdon Stapleton was no longer a friend. He was not quite an enemy either. Undeniably, Pendleton's feelings about Rawdon remained complicated. As complicated as his feelings about Genevieve.

Rawdon began telling him that the *World* was the cheapest, most sickening newspaper in New York. Pendleton drank his bourbon and swallowed the abuse for a while. "Have you ever read the editorial page?" he said. "You might catch a glimpse of a shining message there. It gets on the front page too." He pointed to a head, MURDER BY NEGLECT. "That's about Kate Sweeney, who drowned in her Lower East Side cellar yesterday when the sewer that ran under her tenement overflowed. It's going to be the opening gun in a campaign for more and better sanitary inspectors."

"Is that your answer to the problems of our time, Pendleton? More and better sanitary inspectors?"

"I don't think there is an answer to the problems of our time," Pendleton said.

"We could have put out a better paper, Pendleton."

"We didn't try."

"You mean I didn't." Rawdon brooded on the gigantic nude above the bar for a moment. "I'm sorry, if that's worth anything to you."

Pendleton felt an inner tremor. The power of friendship was still there. "I'm sorry, too," he said. "Sometimes working for Pulitzer is like working for John Reid with a steam engine up his ass."

Rawdon laughed. "How is that old Croton Croaker?" Rawdon asked.

"He's drunk most of the time these days. The *Times* is falling apart. When they refused to back Blaine, they lost the Republican Party faithful to the *Tribune.* Reid blames it all on Pulitzer for electing a Democratic President. It's really your father's fault. He talked Reid into it."

"How's that old bastard?"

"He's all right. Pretty lonely but all right."

Rawdon's flicker of camaraderie vanished. "He deserves a lot worse than loneliness. So does your friend Pulitzer. He's going to get it, too, one of these days."

"What do you mean?"

"We'd rather have it come as a surprise. Gould's still worth thirty or forty million dollars. That gives him a lot of leverage with a lot of people. Bradford likes to even scores, too. He's about the only man I admire these days."

"Give me one reason."

"He's got an international point of view. If Gould had listened to him more often, no one could have touched him. Bradford was always telling him to invest more of his money abroad. But Gould wanted to be the king of America."

Rawdon gulped his brandy, a little drunk now, unable to conceal his bitterness. "The Exterminating Company broke Gould's nerve, not his health. He should have gone bankrupt and taken the whole rotten system down with him."

It was interesting how a ruined financier could sound a lot like a disappointed revolutionist.

"How's Genevieve?" Pendleton asked.

"I don't know. Most of the time she just stares at me. We've got nothing to say to each other."

"She misses Laura. Why don't you bring her home?"

Rawdon angrily shook his head. "I'm never going to let her near that child again. I'd rather have my stepmother raise her. Even if she ruins her morals, at least she'll give her some style."

Rawdon finished his brandy and smacked it on the bar for emphasis. "Genevieve's a loon, Pendleton. Why can't you get that through your head?"

"Don't you feel any responsibility for it?"

"Responsible? Sure I'm responsible. But I don't feel any twinges of guilt for it. My marriage to that bitch was a struggle for survival, Pendleton. She thought she could rationalize me into a nice subservient husband. She was playing my father's game, from the start. But she found out all those ideas floating around in her educated head didn't make any difference in the bedroom. She couldn't handle defeat, Pendleton. That's why she's gone bats."

"Jesus Christ, Rawdon! That woman loved you. She tried with all her heart and soul to love you."

Rawdon laughed sardonically. "She still loves me. That's another reason she's gone bats. I've shown her that a man is stronger than a woman in every way. She can't stand it."

Rawdon began comparing Eleanor to Genevieve. There was no struggle for superiority with Eleanor. She adored him. She forgave him no matter what he did—even losing her money. She had sacrificed her reputation for him.

"If she's so goddamn wonderful why don't you divorce Genevieve and marry her?" Pendleton said.

"You'd like that, wouldn't you, Pendleton. You'd be right there, hat in hand, waiting to take charge of Genevieve. My father would leave you a million or two in his will if you did that. But you're not going to get the chance."

"I'm beginning to think this friendship is over," Pendleton said.

"It's been over for a long time. Let's make it official."

Pendleton trudged home to his bachelor bed on Bleecker Street tormented by his helplessness. He kept remembering Genevieve Dall Stapleton at her typewriter in Mrs. Wilbour's parlor, the confident mouth with the erotic vulnerable upper lip, the gray eyes with their moody depths. A woman—a woman he loved—was being destroyed, and there was nothing he could do about it.

The next morning at the *World*, Pendleton found another version of the new woman seated beside his desk. Plain was the word for Elizabeth Ann Cochrane, better known as Nelly Bly. She had no discernible figure. In repose her face had a blank waiflike quality. This was undoubtedly part of her talent for assuming a hundred different disguises. There were times when Pendleton wondered if being a reporter was also a disguise, right down to the pseudonym.

Nelly was proving, too late for poor Genevieve, that women had a place on a newspaper. Pendleton had urged Pulitzer to hire Nelly when she appeared in the city room one day and showed them some of the stories she had done for a Pittsburgh paper. He had won the imaginative award of the week for concocting the idea of using Nelly as a secret agent, getting her committed to various public institutions such as the insane asylum on Blackwell's Island and then exposing the horrifying conditions that prevailed there.

Nelly was grateful to Pendleton and had hinted several times that she would like to prove it. But he kept her at arm's length. Briskly, he ordered her to interview Harold Bangs's mother. And the late Mrs. Bangs's grieving friends. Nelly pouted and asked why he had not given her any more secret-agent assignments. Those were the jobs she loved.

"The readers are bored with exposés," Pendleton said. "Let's give them a little art. Find a ballet company and enroll as a dancer. Give us the inside story on what they go through—their low pay, their love lives."

"Do you have one?" Nelly asked, giving him her biggest smile. She was almost pretty when she smiled.

"A love life? You'd have more fun with Harold Bangs. Get going. I want good stuff from his mother for the first edition."

Fourteen hours later, Pendleton was still at his desk, struggling to complete the editorial and prospectus for the Statue of Liberty campaign, which were supposed to have been on Pulitzer's desk ten hours ago. It had been a wild day. A lawyer shot by a beautiful client in his office, a woman attacked by a drunken Irishman on a Third Avenue elevated train, a blast from the mayor of New York, telling Pulitzer to keep his nose out of City Hall.

A cry of anguish burst from Pulitzer's office. Pendleton rushed to the door, fearing the worst. Everyone from his wife to his doctor had been warning Pulitzer against overwork.

He was sitting at the littered desk, his pince-nez dangling from one ear as if he had just been struck in the face. "Look," he said. "Look what those sons of bitches at the *Sun* are publishing tomorrow."

The *Sun*'s editorial was a savage, totally hypocritical attack on Pulitzer as a Jew whose "unholy ambition to lord it over the people and dictate to the politicians" was threatening to arouse a wave of anti-Semitism in New York. There was only one solution: Pulitzer would have to go. He had been driven out of St. Louis "for polluting the civic atmosphere" of that city. For the good of New York, its newspapers and its people, he should "move on!"

There were tears on Pulitzer's face. "This will start it again," he whispered. "It was one of the reasons I left St. Louis." He slumped in the chair. "When I courted my wife, I didn't tell her I was half Jewish. I thought, I really thought, that in America it wouldn't matter. But when you make enemies . . ."

Enemies. Pendleton suddenly remembered Rawdon telling him that Gould and Bradford were going to even the score with Pulitzer. Pendleton turned a team of reporters loose on the story and they soon turned up the evidence he wanted: The *Sun* had borrowed several hundred thousand dollars from Jay Gould to buy new printing presses. Pendleton published the story and backed it with a ferocious editorial flaying the *Sun*'s ethics and motives. The paper had been badly hurt by the *World*'s rise and was as hungry for revenge as Gould and Bradford.

The *Sun* made no attempt to answer Pendleton. Instead, it simply reprinted the editorial, with a double-leaded head: MOVE ON, PULITZER!

The next day, Pulitzer did not come to the office, an unprecedented event. Jonathan Stapleton telephoned Pendleton. "I've been trying to reach your boss," he said. "Would you tell Mr. Pulitzer that the *Sun* doesn't speak for the decent people of New York?"

"I will. I can't understand why more people haven't spoken out."

"I'll try to organize something. Have you seen Genevieve lately?"

"No."

"I was up to see her the other day. She's in terrible shape. Pay her a visit, if you can."

Back in the *World*'s city room, Nelly Bly was camped at his desk. "There's no story in ballet dancing," she said. "They practically threw me out on the street. I'm too old. I told them I was twenty-three and they said I should have come around when I was six."

Pendleton had almost forgotten that he had given Nelly her ballet assignment. "Try a different approach. Drop the disguise routine. Tell them who you are and how much publicity they'll get. We're not looking for an exposé."

Nelly looked dubious. "I feel like such an ugly duckling with those women."

"Make that part of the story."

The next day, Pulitzer was back in a frenzy that transcended anything Pendleton had ever seen. He announced he was starting an evening paper and was going to put Pendleton in charge of it. It would sell for one cent and put the *Evening Sun*, launched the previous year, out of business in a month. He fired off a telegram to President Cleveland, demanding his support for the candidate of Pulitzer's choice in a forthcoming election for district attorney in New York. Simultaneously, so it seemed, he managed to excoriate Cockerill, Pendleton and half the reporters on the paper for yesterday's edition, published without his supervision.

Pendleton tried to pile planning the *Evening World* on top of the Statue of Liberty campaign and the routine chaos of the newsroom with Pulitzer on the rampage every day. He was soon sleeping about four hours a night. Occasionally General Stapleton's plea for Genevieve drifted through his overburdened mind. But all he could see was Rawdon's triumphant sneer in the Hoffman House bar. Why torment himself, and possibly Genevieve, with impossible thoughts about love? Besides, how could he take responsibility for a woman who was on the edge of another mental breakdown? He was married to the *New York World.*

Yet Pendleton found himself repeatedly swept by a yearning for a caring presence in his life. The streetwalkers on Broadway, with their patently fake smiles, no longer aroused him. Trudging home about ten days after the *Sun*'s anti-Semitic smear drove Pulitzer berserk, Pendleton ignored the whores calling to him from almost every doorway. Up the stairs to his fourth-floor rooms he toiled. Somewhere a church clock bonged 4 A.M.

A figure stood in the shadows by his door. He reached for the derringer that he carried on his hip, like most men who traveled around New York at night.

"Don't move," he said. "I've got a gun."

"It's me, Clay. Genevieve."

Never did heart leap higher than Pendleton's at that moment. Or plunge lower as he considered the best and the worst reasons for this apparition.

He hurried her into his sloppy sitting room and hastily drew the portiere across the archway to the bedroom, concealing his unmade bed. The gas lamp popped and he studied her anxiously. She seemed perfectly calm. She had lost most of the weight she had gained at Grandview Sanitarium. Her face had regained its fine-boned clarity. She was wearing a plain brown dress and a cloak. In her hand was a large particolored portmanteau.

"Are you going on a trip?" he asked.

"I'm going to California, Clay. If you'll loan me the money."

"What—why? Who's in California?"

"Some women who care about me. One in particular."

"Elizabeth Wellcombe?"

"Yes."

The gray-blue eyes confronted him. They were more desperate than mournful now. Was it the desperation of mania? Was he dealing with another episode of looniness?

"I've been trying to find the strength, the courage, for months. I was going to ask you to help me a half-dozen times. But I could see the way you looked at me—you'd say no."

"Why should I change my mind now?"

"Rawdon's moving to Havana to invest Lionel Bradford's money for him down there. He's taking Eleanor with him. He's going to put me back in an asylum."

"Good Christ."

"You've got to help me, Clay. There's no one else. General Stapleton's just as bad as Rawdon. He thinks my mind is gone. It isn't. My mind is all right, Clay. It's as good as it's ever been. Here's the proof."

From her portmanteau she drew a sheaf of papers—a manuscript. On the first page was the title: "Antiope's Story."

"Read it," she said. "If you won't give me the money when you finish it, I'll go home quietly."

In those words Pendleton heard a flash of the Genevieve Dall who had fascinated him ten years ago. "Get some sleep," he said.

While Genevieve dozed on his double bed, Pendleton read *Antiope's Story*. They were all in it under different names: Rawdon, Eleanor, Alice, Genevieve's mother, her father, the General. Some of it was narrative, but much of it was philosophy, a brilliant, thoroughly radical explanation of how Genevieve Dall had lost her identity, her soul, and why her experience had relevance for women everywhere.

The book began with a recollection of a joking conversation Genevieve had had with Pendleton and Rawdon about the Greek myth of Theseus and the Amazon Queen, Antiope, whom the hero subdues and marries. Taking the myth seriously, Genevieve speculated on how a Greek warrior would have broken the spirit of a fierce, independent woman ruler. This would have been necessary because in ancient Greece, as in modern America, wives were excluded from politics and business and kept at home, virtually prisoners under guard.

Genevieve then translated the myth into American marriage, using her own story. The central image was the phenomenon popular at Vassar in her student days: smashing. But Genevieve extended this idea to the shattering of the woman's sense of self. Sometimes this was done early, by a father. Or begun by him, with the husband finishing the process. Sometimes the husband performed the entire task. If the woman was poor or unlucky, the smasher was often the pimp. The theory was wide enough to include the submissive daughter, the passive wife and the enslaved whore.

But men were not the only smashers. There were women collaborators in the process: mothers, sisters, friends. Here Genevieve wrote a searing assault in which Alice Mayer, her sister Eleanor and her mother were virtually flayed. The rage made Pendleton wince. He winced even more at succeeding pages, in which male collaborators, men who pretended to admire independent women, yet were not willing to offend their fellow men by doing much for them, were handled almost as roughly.

As theory, *Antiope's Story* was brilliant—and chilling. It included everything in women's experience except love. Antiope had apparently not yet discovered how her reassembled self dealt with that phenomenon. But the book—it was about fifty thousand words—conclusively demonstrated that Genevieve Dall had not lost her mind. Whatever was wrong with her nervous system, her mind was still a strong supple beautiful thing.

Pendleton stared at the sleeping woman in his bed, wondering if he had the power to reawaken her belief in love. He had spent his life keeping women at arm's length. How could he hope to heal someone as wounded—and still as formidable—as this woman?

Suddenly Genevieve's eyes were open. "Well?" she said.

"You've got the money."

"Oh Clay." Tears streamed down her cheeks. "You've been such a friend."

"If you stayed in New York you might find out there are people here who are ready to be—more than friends."

Slowly, mournfully, Genevieve shook her head. "No. It can never be, Clay. There'll never be anything between me and a man again. Isn't that clear from the book? I destroyed that part of myself. I used the space to resurrect Genevieve Dall. She's not a complete woman, Clay. But she's free. Whether she can stay free is something I have to find out in California."

Pendleton went to his bank and withdrew five hundred dollars. He bought a transcontinental ticket at the Union Pacific Railroad office for $132 and gave Genevieve the balance of the cash. They took a hack to Grand Central Station, where a train to Chicago was waiting to carry her on the first third of her journey.

"You'll come back," he said. "I know you will. There'll be a job for you at the *World.*"

"No, Clay, please," she said with terrific vehemence. "Don't wait for me. Don't!"

The next weeks were the most barren time in Pendleton's life. A strange indifference insulated him from Pulitzer's increasing frenzy as the *Sun,* day after day, kept up its cruel barrage: MOVE ON, PULITZER! Around him, people quit in disgust, unable to endure Pulitzer's rages. Pendleton worked on, putting out a daily paper, planning an evening paper.

He could not decide which was more disheartening, his growing dislike of Pulitzer or his disgust with the silence that prevailed in New York, the intellectual and financial capital of the land of the free and the home of the brave, permitting the *Sun* to flaunt its anti-Semitism. Finally came the night when Pendleton heard his name being snarled from Pulitzer's office. He trudged to the door, wondering if he was going to be told to send a telegram to God to reform the universe.

Pulitzer was sitting at his desk staring at the proofs for tomorrow's paper. "What the hell's the matter with the electricity, Pendleton? Call that bastard Edison and tell him we're not getting any light."

The *World* had naturally subscribed to the latest wonder of the age, Thomas Edison's power station, which was illuminating several dozen downtown buildings. One of Edison's 100-candlepower bulbs was burning brightly above Pulitzer's desk.

"There's nothing wrong with the light," Pendleton said.

"The hell you say. I can't see the proofs."

Pulitzer slumped in his chair.

"I can barely see you."

"I'll take you home."

At the four-story mansion on East Fifty-fifth Street, a frantic Mrs. Pulitzer called the doctor. Pendleton waited in the foyer until the physician came downstairs. He was a walrus-mustached old crustacean who did not waste words. "How good a newspaperman are you?" he said.

"You better ask Mr. Pulitzer that one."

"You better be damn good, because you're not going to be able to ask Mr. Pulitzer anything for a long time. I've ordered him to be confined to a dark room for the next six weeks, and then to take a six-month trip around the world."

"Do you read the *Sun?*"

"I know what you're thinking. It may come true—the Wandering Jew. But I hope not, if he takes a genuine rest."

"Do you think that's possible?" Pendleton asked.

"Do you?"

"No."

Pendleton rode back to Bleecker Street along the empty avenues. He slept for three or four hours and went to work. At the *World*, the news of Pulitzer's collapse had already arrived. Managing Editor Cockerill greeted Pendleton with an edict. "We've decided you've got enough to do on the city desk, Clay. We're taking the *Evening World* away from you and giving it to some people we're hiring away from the *Evening Sun.*"

Pendleton saw the future, the infighting and backstabbing that would become endemic on the *World* in Pulitzer's absence. What to do, but do your job? It was still Darwinian America.

On the following Sunday morning, Nelly Bly telephoned him in his rooms. She was writing her ballet story and wanted some advice. She appeared in a dark-red velvet dress totally unlike anything she had ever worn to the city room. The advice she wanted turned out to be exceedingly trivial—which anecdote should be the lead for the story. They had coffee, and Clay complimented her on her dress. Nelly beamed. "It cost me a week's salary. But it was worth it. I feel like a woman."

She hesitated, and the rest of it came in a rush of words. "I haven't felt like a woman for a long time. Maybe never. I grew up in a family with eight brothers and no father. My mother never paid any attention to me. I never thought of myself as a woman until I started hanging around with those ballet dancers. A woman reporter, yes, but not a *woman*. Do you know what I mean, Clay?"

"I think so," he said.

"You've been so good to me, Clay. Almost like a father. But I want to be more than a daughter to you."

He had not bothered to draw the portiere. His bed was all too visible beneath the eaves. Consolation, Pendleton wondered? Or was it a wish to touch, explore, some version of the new woman, now that he had lost the one he had really wanted?

It took only a few minutes to undress. The consummation took much longer, because it was Nelly's first time. She was terrified and when it was over she wept in his arms for a half hour. Then she rubbed her small breasts against him and whispered, "In the office, I'll still be Nelly Bly. But here I just want to be your Lizzie Ann. Your darling little girl."

The words chilled Pendleton. Had he been right about Nelly? Was the new woman as nervy reporter just another disguise? Was she going to cling and simper as much as the women who had haunted his youth? Maybe he just wanted a new woman with more understanding and sympathy in her gray-blue eyes. But she had just put a continent between them.

TEN

On the crowded main deck of the Inman Line's new steamship, S.S. *City of New York*, Senator Jonathan Stapleton bent his ramrod back and kissed his wife on the cheek. "Goodbye, my dear," he said.

Grave, Cynthia thought, as cold as the grave. Their manners were perfectly correct, as befitted the pseudo-parents of a watching ten-year-old daughter-granddaughter. Once Jonathan had accused her of being an actress, pretending a love for him that she had never felt. Now he had become a superb actor, concealing his loathing for his wife behind grave cold formality.

Senator Stapleton gave Laura a kiss and a hug that made her squeal with pleasure. He slipped a ten-dollar gold piece into her hand. "For candy," he said.

Standing beside his father, George Stapleton smiled his approval. He had just given his niece a similar hug. "Goodbye, Mother," he said, and kissed Cynthia with far more warmth than his father had just displayed.

Beside George stood an impassive Rawdon Stapleton and his new wife, Eleanor. In contrast to his father's and brother's standard black business outfits, Rawdon wore the white suit and wide-brimmed Panama hat of the Cuban aristocrat. With his dark hair, his skin deeply tanned by the tropic sun, he looked the part.

Last year Rawdon had divorced Genevieve on the grounds of desertion and married Eleanor in Havana. He seemed to be prospering down there, investing money funneled to him by Lionel Bradford and other financiers. Now he was on his way to Europe with Bradford to persuade their backers to put still more cash into their enterprises.

"You've got to spend next summer at Kemble Manor," George said to Cynthia. "That's where I can really toughen Laura up."

A bachelor vainly pursuing a reluctant Virginia belle, George had made a pet out of Laura. To his credit, he had not simply spoiled her. Recalling that his friend Theodore Roosevelt had defeated his childhood asthma with vigorous exercise, George had enlisted Theodore and together they had worked out a regimen of dumbbell lifting and medicine-ball pitching and horseback riding that had carried Laura through the winter with only one asthma attack.

"Your mother doesn't like Kemble Manor," Jonathan snapped. "Besides, I want that Paris doctor to examine Laura. He's the world's leading expert on asthma. And these summers in Florence have given her a wonderful education in art."

"Yes," Cynthia said, wearily endorsing these lies.

Laura was the excuse for another four-month separation from Jonathan, the disguise for their ruined marriage. Ironically, saying goodbye to the child was agony for him. Laura flung her arms around his waist and said she was going to miss him. "Not half as much as I'm going to miss you," he said.

Laura was the only person for whom Jonathan was able to express affection. He had nothing to say to Rawdon. He was quarreling with George over his choice of a wife. As far as Cynthia could see, Clay Pendleton was the only other human being for whom her husband had a cordial word, and that could be explained by politics.

Having no wife or children to distract him, Jonathan had accepted his Pulitzer-sponsored appointment to the new Civil Service Commission and toiled at the job with a dogged persistence that had impressed politicians of all stripes. Never mind that he did not particularly believe in civil-service reform. Nor the irony that he was now laboring for the cause that Theodore Roosevelt, Sr., had died trying to launch. Nor the double irony that Theodore Roosevelt, Jr., had been appointed one of his fellow commissioners.

When the Republican Party triumphed at the polls in 1888, electing a President and governors and state legislatures everywhere, and the term of one of New York's senators coincidentally expired, Jonathan Stapleton suddenly became the choice of both wings of the party to fill the vacancy. The New York *World* helped more than a little. An editorial no doubt written or inspired by Clay Pendleton urged the sterling qualities of the candidate on the Albany legislature.

Naturally, Jonathan accepted the legislature's summons. It was an even better excuse to bury himself in Washington for months at a time, avoiding the necessity of living with his wife.

The stewards were striding up and down the deck, beating their brass gongs. "All ashore that's going ashore," they shouted. Soon the huffing tugs were pulling the big liner away from the dock. Cynthia waved mechanically to the tall white-haired man with the scarred face standing on the pier staring up at them. Was he suffering, or were the old wounds simply inflicting a kind of pathetic makeup on that face? Beside her she noticed that Laura was crying.

"I'm going to miss Pa and George so much," Laura said.

"Listen," Rawdon said, crouching beside her. "You and I and Aunt Eleanor are going to have a great time together."

Laura nodded perfunctorily, but she did not stop crying. She did not have much confidence in a father she had seen only a half-dozen times in the past five years. As for Eleanor, she had already gotten such an icy response from her attempts to befriend Laura during the past week in New York, she did not even try to intervene.

From midriver, the figures on the pier were a blur. There was only New York's brown and gray immensity, wreathed in a haze of factory smoke. Another farewell had been accomplished. Cynthia remembered the first year she and Laura had sailed to Europe. Crushed with regret, guilt, she had felt the exile was a kind of death. She had even hoped it would be a real death. Europe was full of diseases. Rome's malaria would demolish her, the way it had killed Margaret Dall. Or typhoid fever would take her in a night, as Mittie had died. But nine months of wandering from clinics to spas to sunny seacoasts had failed to produce the wished-for immolation. Instead, as contrition dwindled, she began struggling with far more dangerous emotions.

Everyone rushed to the opposite side of the ship to get a close look at the Statue of Liberty. Jonathan Stapleton had been among the select all-male audience who sat at the feet of the stupendous copper-sheathed figure when President Chester A. Arthur dedicated it three years ago. Even then Cynthia had been inclined to side with the feminists who circled the island in a ship, shouting through megaphones that the whole thing was a fraud, portraying a woman as a symbol of freedom when American women were still their husbands' slaves.

Now she gazed up at the statue's blank face and struggled for calm. She was theoretically free. As free as Genevieve Dall in California. There was nothing to stop her from taking a lover. Or pocketing her comfortable little fortune and obtaining a divorce and a new husband, like Eleanor Dall.

"How tall is she?" Laura asked, peering up at the Statue of Liberty.

"I don't know."

"Does she have a name?"

"No."

"It's a fake," Rawdon said, "like everything else in the United States of America."

"What do you mean?" Laura said, rubbing the tears from her eyes. He had gotten her attention.

"The whole country is a fake. The Declaration of Independence, the Constitution, the Statue of Liberty all promise Americans they're going to be free and happy. When they're all slaves to a few misers who control the money."

"Rawdon—she's much too young for those sorts of ideas," Cynthia said.

"Can an outsider join this Stapleton ménage?"

Lionel Bradford doffed his gray top hat. Only at the last moment had Rawdon told Cynthia he was sailing with them. She made no response to Bradford's greeting, even though it was addressed to her. She did not intend to let this man think there was even a remote possibility of resuming their friendship, much less anything beyond friendship.

Rawdon and Eleanor greeted him effusively. Eleanor called him "Father," as if she were still married to Hal. He kissed her on the cheek and told her how lovely she looked—a polite lie. Eleanor was getting fat.

"How is this charming little creature?" Bradford asked, patting Laura on the head.

"Blossoming," Rawdon said, smiling at his daughter. "Isn't it obvious?"

"Why don't you take a walk around the main deck?" Cynthia said. "Remember, we must exercise every day. We can't lose the ground we've gained."

"All right," Laura said sulkily, and strode away, swinging her arms in the style George Stapleton and Theodore Roosevelt had prescribed for her.

"What an extraordinarily beautiful child," Bradford said.

With this obeisance to sentiment, Bradford turned to Rawdon and began telling him that he had received cables from their financial partners in London, Paris and Hamburg assuring them of a cordial welcome. "Money hasn't been so plentiful since the early seventies," Bradford said. "The bankers are practically begging people to take it off their hands."

"That's what I like to hear," Rawdon said.

They began talking about investment possibilities in other countries in Central America, particularly Colombia, which controlled the Isthmus of Panama. Bradford said he had lost a great deal of money in the recent attempt by the French to build a canal across the isthmus, but he was still convinced that a waterway would be built by someone. When that happened, the value of their investments in Cuba and elsewhere in the Caribbean would soar.

"No doubt you're planning to see our mutual friend in London and do your best to comfort her?"

Bradford was talking about Madeline Terhune. "Why does she need comforting?" Cynthia asked.

"Her new play was a disaster. She was practically booed off the stage. I'm afraid her career is over."

Cynthia saw the triumph in Bradford's eyes. He had forced her to speak to him. He added some details of Madeline's failure. The play was a tired rehash of *Retaliation* and other earlier hits. She had played a woman ludicrously younger than her real age. "Not something you have to worry about," he said. "If I may be permitted a little gallantry—"

"Thank you," Cynthia said icily.

Rawdon's smile was sardonic. Eleanor's eyes were wide. She obviously knew Lionel Bradford was still pursuing Mrs. Stapleton.

In Paris, during Cynthia's first year in Europe, she had received a long letter from Bradford, apologizing for the purchase of her love letters and claiming he would have bought them from Robert and given them to her if he had not been involved in the struggle between Jonathan and Gould. He had the effrontery to argue that this abuse of her reputation was mild compared to the damage the letters could have done to her if they had fallen into other hands.

Cynthia had ignored the letter. But Bradford had continued to pursue her. She never knew when a charming Italian or a witty Frenchman at a dinner party would suddenly turn serious and say, "Lionel Bradford is waiting in Capri" (or Cannes or Rapallo) "and I am prepared to escort you there." Bradford wanted her to feel that she was never beyond the reach of his mind, his power.

Cynthia began to wonder if it was only a matter of time before she succumbed. It had nothing to do with Bradford's irresistibility. It was the slow erosion of that defiant vow to Jonathan. As the years of unforgiveness lengthened, resentment began raging in her soul below the contrition. She began to anticipate the moment when she would lie down with Lionel Bradford or some other man and say to him, "Do anything you please." While in her mind she composed a letter to Jonathan Stapleton, telling him exactly what she had done, exactly why he could now despise her forever.

Lately the rage was extinguished only by chloral hydrate each night and soothed by Balm of Gilead by day and occasionally eluded by a popular new drink, Vin Mariani, wine laced with cocaine, which lifted her into moments of her old exhilaration.

Cynthia found herself wishing she had kept Laura beside her. That innocent face, those inquisitive green eyes guarded her soul.

Bradford was telling Eleanor that his wife was seriously ill in London. He needed to give some thought to the future of his daughter, Hal's younger sister, Eleanor's childhood playmate from Kemble Manor days. "She's going to inherit a good deal of money and I don't want some penniless British aristocrat to get his hands on it. I want her to marry an American with a fortune that doubles hers, at the minimum."

"Capital idea," Rawdon said, grinning wolfishly.

Cynthia felt dismay creep through her flesh. Dismay and a kind of fear, to see what time had done to Rawdon. The bold indignation of his youth, which sometimes used to arouse her sympathy, had become a snide craftiness.

Laura was back, breathing hard. "I walked around the whole ship," she said. "It's big. A sailor told me it's a half mile round."

"Let's go below and get ready for dinner."

In their beige-and-gold stateroom, they found Lucy unpacking their steamer trunks. She was Cynthia's last link with Louisiana. Cleopatra had died last year. They talked about the size and luxury of the *City of New York,* which was now plowing the swells of the Atlantic. The motion was barely noticeable in the 10,000-ton vessel. Cynthia compared it to the pitching and tossing of the stubby little 3,000-ton Cunarder in which she had made her first crossing on her honeymoon twenty-three years ago.

She started telling Lucy and Laura how seasick she had been, and memory came in a devastating rush: Jonathan sitting beside her bunk, feeding her beef broth or warm milk, barely leaving the cabin lest she need him.

Tears, she was engulfed by tears. Lucy was dismayed. Laura thought she understood. She put her arms around Cynthia as she sat on the bed, wiping her eyes. "You don't want to go, either," she said. "I promise I'll do my exercises every day. This will be the last year we have to go."

"No, no, darling," Cynthia said. "It has nothing to do with you."

"Here, Mistress, take some of your wine," Lucy said, holding out a glass of Vin Mariani.

An hour later, in the *City of New York*'s opulent dining saloon, which featured an arch of stained glass, blending topaz, turquoise and amethyst, a brigade of waiters served no fewer than fourteen main dishes under identical silver covers. Feeding passengers on the Atlantic had become a contest in gluttony between the steamship lines. Cynthia ate little of the overabundance, and Eleanor, considering her growing avoirdupois, too much.

Rawdon asked Laura if she had read her mother's book, *Antiope's Story.* Laura pouted and shook her head. "Pa said I was too young. I begged Cynthia to bring a copy with her to Europe, but she wouldn't do it."

"Next year," Cynthia said.

Antiope's Story had been published in New York six months ago. It had created a mild stir for the fury of its indictment of male oppression. Cynthia had been far more concerned by the book's impact on the Stapletons. Anyone who knew the real names of the characters in the story was bound to be titillated. She had written Genevieve a very stiff letter, pointing out the difficulty the book was certain to cause Laura when she became old enough to enter New York society.

Rawdon began telling Laura the book was a lie from the first page to the last. "If you read it," he said, "I hope you'll talk to me about it. I'll explain every one of the lies."

Laura was looking confused and unhappy. Cynthia had told her *Antiope's Story* was an interesting and serious book, which would help her understand herself as a woman when she was old enough to read it. Partly in self-defense, Cynthia found herself arguing with Rawdon. "I wish Genevieve hadn't published the book," she said, "but there's a good deal of truth in it about men's attitudes toward women."

"I thought so, too," Lionel Bradford said. "The new woman is going to require a drastic revision in men's thinking to deal with her."

Laura listened, wide-eyed. She had only a few hazy memories of her mother. None of what she was hearing jibed with the melancholy, listless woman she recalled.

Dinner was almost over. Bounding up to Laura's chair came Georgianna Livingston, Katherine Kemble Brown's granddaughter, with whom they had shared several previous crossings. Her imperious grandmother had converted her into a traveling companion. Georgianna's streaming blond hair made her look as if she had just stepped out of an illustration for *Alice in Wonderland*. She and Laura embraced and raced off to explore the ship. Cynthia immediately urged a moratorium on further discussions of Genevieve. "I think Laura should be allowed to make up her own mind about her mother," she said. "All you'll do now is make her ill."

Rawdon looked sullenly unconvinced. It was almost frightening to see the intensity of his dislike of Genevieve. "She's made it impossible for me and Eleanor to come back to New York."

"I left calling cards with at least two dozen people last week," Eleanor said disconsolately. "I didn't get a single response."

"It's time someone challenged the reign of hypocrisy that we call society," Lionel Bradford said.

Cynthia ignored him and tried to reassure Eleanor. "In a year or two you may have no difficulty. Divorce is becoming so common. People have short memories about books like *Antiope's Story*."

"I don't," Rawdon said.

"A Stapleton trait, I'm afraid," Cynthia said. For a moment she was shaken by the bitterness in her own voice.

"Life is too short for long memories," Lionel Bradford said. "We should never allow mental quirks or legal trivialities to prevent us from enjoying the pleasures of this world."

"Shall we apply your philosophy in the smoking saloon?" Rawdon said. "I find a deck of cards one of the few things I enjoy these days."

"A good idea," Bradford said. "The ladies have probably heard enough philosophy to last them the rest of the voyage."

"Don't bet too much," Eleanor said to Rawdon.

"Don't worry," Rawdon said. "I'm feeling lucky. Even Bradford here better play it safe."

"I always do," Bradford said.

Outside the saloon, stewards bundled Cynthia and Eleanor in blankets and they stretched out in deck chairs to inhale the marvelously pure sea air. The dark starlit Atlantic hissed and foamed around them.

Eleanor began telling Cynthia how desperately she wanted to give Rawdon a son. Their lack of a child was the only flaw in their happiness, Eleanor declared. They had a wonderful life in Havana. Rawdon was by far the richest man in Cuba, which was not saying a great deal, because most of the wealthy landowners had abandoned the island after the devastating decades of revolutionary warfare. But it was an agreeable life. Rawdon was generous with his money. He liked to see her dress well. Their life was one continuous round of dinner parties.

As Eleanor's monologue continued, wisps of unhappiness appeared amid her glowing testimonial. There were times when Rawdon gambled away money belonging to his foreign backers and sank into a bitter gloom that frightened her. So far he had managed to win the money back or invent a plausible excuse for the loss. But she had no regrets. "I'm married to the only man I've ever loved. That's more than most women can say."

As Cynthia descended the companionway, clutching the train of her dinner dress, she felt vaguely ill. A pain gnawed beneath her left breast. Was Eleanor reawakening the regret she once felt at the death of Charlie Stapleton and the lost splendors of the purple dream?

In her stateroom she found a note slipped under the door.

My dear Cynthia:

   I am in B12. I hope we can dine together a few times before we dock. Of course I can't associate with your stepson and his spurious wife. I'm sure you understand that. I hope Laura can join us. She's such a charming child.

                                        Katherine Kemble Brown

There it was, the hypocritical public morality that permitted her to live the lie of being Mrs. Jonathan Stapleton while Eleanor Dall, who had married the man she loved, was ostracized. Was Lionel Bradford right? Was society and its sanctimonious insistence on respectability a corrupt lie that should be attacked, destroyed? There was still enough rebel spirit left in Cynthia's soul to respond to the idea.

Laura burst into the room, her hair wild, her face bathed in perspiration. "We *ran* around the deck twice. I beat Georgianna by a mile! Mrs. Brown was furious at us. She said ladies never ran. It was undignified. I don't know how Georgianna puts up with her."

"I'm more worried about you getting a chill. Get into your nightclothes," Cynthia said.

A half hour later, Cynthia sat on Laura's bed and listened to her prayers. "Dear God, please bless Pa and George and Father and Cynthia. Keep us all happy and healthy and make sure this ship doesn't sink because I can't swim."

"Why did you leave out your mother and Aunt Eleanor?"

The angelic face confronted her. "Because I don't like them."

"That's not the point. When you're talking to God you should try to overcome those feelings. Your mother and Eleanor need God's help just as we all do."

"Do you think He really helps people?"

"Of course I do," Cynthia said.

"Why won't He cure my asthma? I've asked Him again and again."

"It is getting better, little by little. God helps those who help themselves."

For a moment Cynthia was appalled by her own hypocrisy. She did not believe a word of this perfunctory testimonial to God. All her own feelings were swirling in the opposite direction, away from forgiveness and submissive faith in divine or human authority. If a being such as God existed and He was directing her life, He was making a botch of it.

"God bless my mother and aunt," Laura said in mock pious voice, and let Cynthia kiss her good night without returning the embrace.

Cynthia took some chloral hydrate and soon joined Laura in slumber. She awoke in the middle of the night with an incredible thirst which no amount of water seemed to quench. In the morning she felt appallingly listless. She barely had the strength to drag herself up the companionways to the dining saloon. There she found Rawdon in a celebratory mood. His luck at cards had been fantastic and he was giving Laura credit for it. He gave her five ten-dollar gold pieces, one for each hundred dollars he had won.

Rawdon bet Laura another ten-dollar gold piece that he could beat her around the main deck running backward. Cynthia retreated to a deck chair and was soon joined by Katherine Kemble Brown, who reluctantly permitted her granddaughter to pursue Rawdon and Laura around the deck.

"Laura is turning into a tomboy," Katherine said. "She's much too pretty for that."

"I'm sure she'll outgrow it. I was always climbing trees and falling into muddy ponds when I was her age."

"You grew up on a plantation, where such activity was tolerated. These are city children. They should have city manners."

Katherine pondered the heaving Atlantic for a few minutes. Then, with her usual bluntness, she got to the real reason why she wanted to talk to Cynthia. "There's something very wrong between you and Jonathan, isn't there?"

"Yes."

"Rumors have been floating around for years. Does it have anything to do with some letters you wrote to a certain southern colonel that this fellow Bradford sent to Jonathan?"

"Yes."

"I'm going to do my best to bar that man from every decent house in New York." Katherine Kemble Brown stared out at the ocean again. "Jonathan can't forgive you. He's his mother's son, in spite of everything."

"And I can't forgive him. I can't forgive him for so many things." She began listing all the reasons she could not forgive Jonathan Stapleton. It was staggering, the bitterness that poured out of her soul.

"You're absolutely justified," Katherine Kemble Brown said.

For some reason, that was not the answer Cynthia wanted to hear. It left her trapped, smothering in this scorpion's web of rage she had woven around herself.

"And unjustified at the same time. He's a man, my dear. They go on determined to get their own way, putting politics and money before all other considerations, and then wonder why they're dry dead husks that no woman can love."

"I refuse to accept that idea—that love is our responsibility. You seem to have gotten on very well without it."

There was a long silence. "Did it ever occur to you, my dear, that I'm one of those husks? I've gotten my own way on practically everything I have ever confronted in this life. My husband can't wait to get me on a ship to Europe each year at this time so he can concentrate on his bank. My daughters dislike me. Only this grandchild is temporarily fond of me because I spoil her."

Laura came racing toward them. "I beat Father by two miles. Even Georgianna beat him. He bumped into ten or twelve people trying to run backwards. He was so funny! He kept explaining to everyone that he was trying to turn things around so he could go back to being ten years old again and marry one of us when we got to be eighteen."

"Thank God the laws of nature prohibit some ideas," Katherine Kemble Brown said.

Rawdon strolled up to them, holding Georgianna's hand. "Hello, Mrs. Brown," he said.

"How do you do, Mr. Stapleton," Katherine said. "Georgianna, come with me. It's time for your nap."

"I haven't taken a nap in years!" Georgianna cried.

"You're taking one now. You look exhausted. Too much strenuous exercise."

Katherine Kemble Brown stumped away—she now relied on a cane to support her enormous weight—with her protesting granddaughter.

"You have the nicest friends, Stepmother," Rawdon said.

"She's too old to change her ways," Cynthia said.

"So am I," Rawdon said.

Dropping the subject, Rawdon announced that Lionel Bradford was a friend of the ship's captain and they were all invited to visit the bridge. Cynthia declined to struggle up a half-dozen ladders and companionways and let Laura go skipping off with her father.

Rawdon was obviously captivating his daughter. The sight of Laura gazing up at that handsome male face was a preview of the future. It would not be long before she began looking that way at a handsome stranger. Where, how, could she avoid becoming a woman even more dismaying than Katherine Kemble Brown's dry husk, a creature who had gotten neither her way nor her love?

Day by day, Laura's fascination with her father increased. Eleanor barely came out of her cabin. Rawdon said she was seasick, but Cynthia suspected she was pained by the triumph of her present and future rival. This was, after all, Genevieve's daughter.

Each day Rawdon invented a new, sillier race for them to run. He and Laura explored the ship together, from the bridge to the bowels where be-grimed seating stokers shoveled tons of coal into the huge furnaces. Each night, Rawdon's winnings in the smoking saloon soared. Laura soon exulted over fifty ten-dollar gold pieces.

Cynthia's listlessness, her vague nausea continued, without quite blossoming into seasickness. She allowed Katherine Kemble Brown to take virtual possession of her and surrendered Laura to Rawdon. Katherine at least kept Lionel Bradford at bay. Her glares stopped him from coming within twenty feet of their deck chairs. But Cynthia ended the voyage feeling more spiritually adrift than when she had started.

In grimy, gloomy Liverpool, Mrs. Brown and Georgianna transferred directly to a Channel steamer which took them to France. Cynthia succumbed to Lionel Bradford's offer to get them through customs without the usual maddening searches. Since Irish-Americans began exploding bombs in London in the early 1880s, American visitors to England had their trunks, their hatboxes, even their purses opened by grim customs inspectors.

Bradford made good on his promise. Less than a half hour after they landed, he led Cynthia and Laura and Rawdon and Eleanor to a comfortable compartment on the London express.

As the train pulled out, Bradford began talking about Ibsen, the Norwe-gian playwright who had been shocking Europe for the past decade. "What a shame Madeline's past her zenith," he said. "She'd have made a marvelous Hedda Gabler. It's a perfect part for you, Cynthia."

Cynthia had read the play, which no producer had yet dared to stage in the United States or England. "Do you see yourself as Judge Brack?" she asked. Brack was the man who drove Hedda to suicide.

"Perhaps," he said, "but exercising my license to rewrite scripts, I would never let Hedda destroy herself. I think Ibsen showed his moralistic Norwegian provincialism in that ending. Women are much too valuable."

He smiled at Laura. "Take this charming creature," he said. "In ten years she'll be capable of changing the destiny of a great fortune—perhaps of a nation. Women only need a little management to accomplish the most marvelous things in this world."

"You must teach me that art, Bradford," Rawdon said, smiling at his daughter, who was sitting in a corner, counting the gold pieces in her lap.

Riding through the sedate English countryside in the rain, feeling as though her flesh were made of dough, Cynthia was suddenly shockingly aware of evil. It was all around them in this rocking compartment. There was evil in Lionel Bradford's suave silken voice, evil in Rawdon's possessive smile.

"All it takes is some skill as an actress—and management," Lionel Bradford said. "In many ways, I think the new woman may have even more potential than the old one. She'll be less vulnerable to sentiment, traditional attachments."

His eyes roved Cynthia's face. "Beauty is essential, of course."

"I like the way you're always thinking ahead," Rawdon said.

Evil, Cynthia thought. Rawdon had become Bradford's pupil. That meant both she and Laura were threatened by this formless shapeless presence whispering between the casual phrases, the fond glances.

It was dusk when they arrived in London. As they left Charing Cross Station, the bells of St. Paul's pealed across the city. For some reason, they stirred resistance in Cynthia's flaccid flesh. She declined any further help from Rawdon and Lionel Bradford and hailed a hansom cab.

"Will you be staying long in London?" Bradford asked.

"It depends on how Madeline is feeling. We were planning to go to her house in Surrey for a week. I don't like to expose Laura to this awful air."

London's soot-filled fog was gathering around them. Already carriages and pedestrians were blurs a half block away.

"If you stay in town, I'd like to take her up to Cambridge this Saturday. A fellow on the ship told me they're rowing against Harvard," Rawdon said.

"No," Cynthia said. "We definitely won't stay here another five days."

"Why can't I go?" Laura whined.

"I trust Eleanor and I are welcome in Italy," Rawdon said. "If we have time to get down there."

"Of course," Cynthia said.

"Oh please come, Father," Laura said. "You can help me buy a painting. That's what I'm going to do with my lucky gold pieces."

"Give dear Madeline my best regards," Lionel Bradford said. "Tell her I hope to visit her soon."

The housekeeper who greeted them at the door of Madeline Terhune's town house was the same plump Irishwoman, Hannah Kelly. But she no longer wore the placid face of a contented servant. "Oh Mrs. Stapleton," she said, "I think it would be better if you took rooms in a hotel."

Leaving Laura with Mrs. Kelly, Cynthia went upstairs to Madeline Terhune's green-draped bedroom. There she found a ghastly caricature of the once beautiful woman who had lured rich and famous men of power in London and New York. Flesh had vanished from her body; her hair was no longer fiery red, seemingly immune to time. She had stopped dyeing it. On the night table stood a half-empty bottle of Irish whiskey.

She splashed some liquor into the glass. "Welcome to the wake," she said. "Would you like some?"

Cynthia shook her head.

"You heard about it, no doubt?" Madeline said. "I'm sure dear Lionel told you on the ship coming over."

"Yes."

"They booed me. They laughed at me. When the program clearly stated I was playing a woman of forty. The critics said I looked like her mother."

"There'll be other parts."

Madeline shook her head. "I've never played supporting parts and I never will." She drank half the tumbler of whiskey and gestured to a dozen leatherbound books beside her bed. "I've been reading my diaries, trying to decide who my favorite lover was—and my least favorite."

"What a marvelous idea," Cynthia said. "It could be the opening chapter of your memoirs."

"The least favorite is easy—Lionel Bradford," Madeline said. "Going to bed with him was my closest contact with the reptile world. Did you find something cold—almost scaly—in his touch?"

"I—I don't remember," Cynthia said.

"The favorite—that's the really difficult part. They were all repellent in one way or another." Madeline asked Cynthia to hand her a box of photographs and began examining the features and recalling the flaws of a half-dozen prominent names in English politics and commerce. "I blackmailed a good many of them, you know," she said. "That's something I learned from Lionel. He taught me the finer points of the art."

For a moment her face was suffused with hatred. "That's how he got his start, you know. Pimping for the rich. Then blackmailing them."

She shoved the box aside and began looking through stage photographs of her various roles. "I never really had any confidence in myself as an actress. Lionel predicted I'd starve, when I broke with him and went on the stage. I was never able to scour that prediction out of my mind, no matter how hard I tried. That's why I always chose plays that created a sensation—and lovers who did the same thing. But I got back a pound of flesh for almost every touch, every kiss. Retaliation. That's the heart of it, my dear."

Cynthia was too appalled to speak. She was watching a woman she liked, a woman she had admired, groping through the remnants of her life in search of some sort of spiritual consolation. And finding only hatred, retaliation, as her legacy. This was far worse than Katherine Kemble Brown's dry husk.

"You don't agree. I can see it on your face," Madeline said. "Has your husband forgiven you for your sins?"

Cynthia shook her head.

"Well, keep your hands on your money," Madeline said. "That's the important thing. Money is the only thing that really matters in the long run. Where would I be now without my money?"

She looked around the splendid room, with its objets d'art from Italy, its Dutch and Italian paintings and inlaid Renaissance Revival furniture.

"Yes," Cynthia said. "Where would you be."

Cynthia retreated to the Grovesnor Hotel. Laura was in a sullen mood. She wanted to know why they could not go to the Metropole, the huge beehive on Trafalgar Square where Rawdon and Eleanor were staying.

In bed, not even chloral hydrate could silence those farewell words from Madeline Terhune. *Money is the only thing that matters in the long run.* Simultaneously she saw Lionel Bradford and Rawdon gazing at Laura, agreeing that there was no limit to the marvelous things a beautiful woman could accomplish in this world.

Escape, flight, were in Cynthia's mind when she awoke in the morning. She rushed to Thomas Cook and revised her travel plans, skipping the visit to the asthma specialist in Paris. Laura was now in an ugly mood. She had been hoping she could talk Cynthia into letting her stay in London and go to the Cambridge races with Rawdon. Cynthia ignored her, hoping Italy would work its magic on her too.

In the hills above Florence, the Villa Ristori and its owner, gray-haired Contessa Beatrice Rospigliosi, awaited her. The Contessa was a startlingly different woman from the bitter, blasé pleasure seeker Cynthia had met in Venice and Paris. Since her husband's death a decade ago, she had become religious. A priest came to the villa two or three times a week to say mass in the chapel. She had sold off most of the family's property to launch her two sons in business in Milan, keeping only the villa and the palazzo in Venice, which she rented to support herself. She lived in one wing of the villa, giving Cynthia two thirds of the place.

Cynthia sank onto a chaise longue and looked down on Giotto's bell tower soaring into the golden sunlight beside the multihued cathedral. In her years of exile, this had been the nearest thing to a refuge she had found. The Contessa had become a discreet friend. She had long since undoubtedly noticed the absence of General Stapleton, but she did not ask prying questions. She shared with Cynthia an enthusiasm for the art of fifteenth-century Florence, particularly for Botticelli, the master of the melancholy of beauty, the limitations of human love.

Laura announced she was the proud possessor of five hundred dollars in gold coins and said she wanted to buy a good painting with the money. The Contessa said she would enlist Bernard Berenson, the ebullient Boston-bred scholar-aesthete who lived in a nearby villa, to help them find a masterpiece.

"We have to wait until my father visits me," Laura said, casting a defiant glare at Cynthia. "He wants to help me pick it out."

In the hour of conversation Cynthia drank a half-dozen glasses of iced coffee. She remarked on the persistence of the thirst that had begun on the ship. When they rose from their chairs the landscape suddenly whirled. She was assailed by an appalling weakness.

The Contessa caught her arm. "Are you all right, my dear?" she asked anxiously.

"The trip was very tiring," Cynthia said.

That night Laura declined to say her prayers when she went to bed. Cynthia was too weary to argue with her. At 2 A.M. Lucy awoke Cynthia from her chloral-hydrate slumber. "Miss Laura's got the asthma real bad."

Cynthia could hear the strangulating wheeze as she rushed to Laura's room. The rest of the night was devoted to walking the floor, forcing Laura to smoke vile jimsonweed cigarettes, the latest remedy. It was dawn before they broke the seizure. Cynthia stumbled into bed, blaming herself for not stopping in Paris to consult the specialist.

The next night repeated the scenario. Cynthia grew more and more convinced that Laura was protesting her separation from her father. Frequently —but not always—her asthma attacks coincided with a disappointment.

The following day, Cynthia was near collapse. Contessa Rospigliosi insisted on taking charge. She put Cynthia to bed and pinned a medal of her favorite saint, Saint Teresa of Ávila, to her pillow. "Isn't Laura the one who needs the prayers?" Cynthia murmured.

"She's been in my prayers—you've both been in my prayers, for a long time," the Contessa said.

"Why?"

"I pray for all my friends," she said. "But I also believe in medical science. I wish you would have a physical examination, my dear Mrs. Stapleton. I had a sister who suffered similar problems—the constant thirst, the extreme exhaustion . . ."

A young English doctor practicing among the expatriates in Florence listened to Cynthia's heart, tested her eyesight, analyzed her urine—and informed her that she was suffering from diabetes. Fortunately, it was not a serious case. If she stayed on the low-starch, no-sweets diet he gave her—which eliminated most of her favorite foods—she would remain in perfect health and even lose weight. "One more very important thing," he added in his offhand English way as he packed his black bag. "At all costs avoid worry and emotional strain."

The Contessa cheered Cynthia somewhat by telling her that her younger sister was healthier and thinner now than she was when her diabetes was diagnosed five years ago. "If it goes on this way, diabetes may become as fashionable as consumption was in my youth," she said. "After Verdi wrote *La Traviata,* everyone I knew grew languid and coughed by the hour. It was guaranteed to attract a lover."

Laura's asthma had vanished. Cynthia was now the only patient. After another day in bed, the Contessa suggested an excursion to a village church where Bernard Berenson had recently discovered a hitherto unidentified painting by Fra Angelico. They rode through the sunswept countryside of the Val di Nievole, considered by connoisseurs the loveliest landscape in Italy. Fields of golden wheat alternated with green pastures and hillsides of gray olive trees.

It was noon by the time they reached the village with its single street lined with identical whitewashed stone houses. In the church, the unshaven pastor kissed the Contessa's hand and expelled a half-dozen *bella*s over Laura's beauty as he led them to the painting on a wall to the right of the altar. It was a variation of Angelico's *The Coronation of the Virgin.* The sky had the same heavenly blue, the same exquisite delicate sweetness was on the faces.

The church bells began bonging in the tower above them. The pastor explained to the Contessa that he was preaching a novena to the women of the village and urged them to stay for benediction. "Do you mind?" the Contessa asked. "It won't take long."

About forty women in peasant black straggled into the church. Cynthia and Laura sat beside the Contessa in the first row as the pastor harangued his flock on being faithful wives and good mothers. He told them it was their duty to give at least one child to the church, preferably two, a son and a daughter. Then he donned a green, gold-trimmed chasuble and began the service of benediction. The women sang the Latin hymns, and two unkempt altar boys in dirty cassocks swung censers full of incense. Finally the priest raised the white host in its gold monstrance for them to worship.

Cynthia gazed at the white disk surrounded by its sunburst of gold rays, and suddenly a voice was whispering, *A child of this world.* She was back forty years in the Convent of the Sacred Heart at College Point on the Mississippi, gazing at another monstrance, feeling her heart fill with wordless longing. Then she was in the office of the mother superior listening to her father say that he had sent her to the convent to make sure that she would never be bothered by religion. Next she stood beside him in the dome of the St. Charles Hotel in New Orleans and he was asking her to choose between the world and her soul. While downstairs, Charles Gifford Stapleton waited for her.

Smashed. Those were the primary moments when her self was smashed like the women in *Antiope's Story.* Suddenly there was nothing in Cynthia's soul but hate. Not for Jonathan Stapleton but for her father. Hate without the sentimental pity that had confused her mind when he died in stoic despair in 1866.

Users, abusers, exploiters of women. That was the Legrand tradition.

The Lionel Bradford tradition.

Perhaps—God forbid—the Rawdon Stapleton tradition.

Evil. Now she knew why she had been able to sense it without giving it a name. She was one of the victims. The evil was still loose in her soul. She had seen another face of the evil in Madeline Terhune's bedroom. The despair such use and abuse roots in the souls of women.

My God. My God.

Cynthia rode back toward Florence in a daze. Beside a shaded brook they stopped to picnic on green salad and cold chicken. The Contessa deplored the priest's sermon. "When I hear such things, I understand why my husband thought the Church was a kind of monster that was always threatening to devour him in conspiracy with certain women such as his mother—and me."

"Yet you're still religious?"

The Contessa handed Laura a pitcher and asked her to get them some cold water from the brook. "At first I took a lover every time he took a mistress. But my hatred of him only intensified. Now I see that he could not help himself. He was a typical Italian man. After ten years of prayer, I can pity him."

That night, after Laura went to bed, Cynthia walked down the silent halls of the villa to the end of the opposite wing and entered the chapel. It was dark, except for a single red-glassed candle burning before the tabernacle. She sat there in the silence, thinking of what she had discovered in her mind and heart today. She thought of what the Contessa had revealed about her marriage. She was trying to help her. She saw a woman groping from chloral hydrate to Balm of Gilead to Vin Mariani each day and now facing another burden: illness.

Could her American soul find spiritual strength where the Contessa had found it? The memory of that moment in the convent of the Sacred Heart's chapel gave Cynthia hope. What was it she had felt that day? A sense of communion with a power beyond the narrow reach of the body. A presence that filled the mind and heart with sweetness, love. Was it here in this chapel too, behind that flickering red candle?

The Contessa Rospigliosi sat down beside her. "How do you pray?" Cynthia said. "I've never really tried it."

"It is a little like making love. You give yourself to God. You wait for Him to enter you. Often He chooses not to come. It can be somewhat humiliating."

"I'm used to that. After so many years of a husband who . . ."

"Yes," the Contessa said, making it clear how much she knew.

For the next week, Cynthia spent the hours before midnight in the chapel, waiting for the presence. Gradually she found her hatred for her father diminishing. She began to pity him again in a new, more clear-minded way. She saw that he was driven by his sense of being a Creole, a man apart. Like most Creoles, the Legrands never lost their bitter resentment against the Americans, who bought Louisiana, their country, as if it were a piece of goods in a store and marched into New Orleans with their troops and their flag, expecting their money to buy submission, even admiration, from their new subjects.

Victor Conté Legrand had seen the futility of Creole isolation in American-owned Louisiana. He had married an American. But in his proud heart he had never abandoned his secret resentment. That was the source of his passionate commitment to secession, a southern confederacy in which Louisiana would be the leader and guide on the world stage. That febrile dream was worth the sacrifice of a dozen daughters' souls.

My God, my God, how history obsesses the heart as well as the mind.

Perhaps all of them had been used by history. All of them were spinning, writhing, whirling in history's grip, like the dancers in the tarantella. Charlie Stapleton, her brother Robert, poor pathetic, drunken Edgar Calhoun, they were all among the used. Was Jonathan Stapleton? Perhaps among the most abused?

The next day brought a letter from Jonathan, carefully addressed to Cynthia and Laura. It informed them that everyone at Stuyvesant Square was well. In Washington the Senate spent most of its time wrangling about the tariff, a subject he was sure they would find as boring as he did. Then came the close, "Love from a lonely grandfather," inadvertently—or deliberately—excluding his wife from his affection. That night there was no presence, there was only rage and resentment in the silent chapel.

The next day brought a telegram from Rawdon. He was on his way to Florence. Laura's excitement was intense. Rawdon and Eleanor arrived the next morning. Eleanor was looking fatter than ever after two weeks of feasting in London and Paris. Laura flung herself into Rawdon's arms and they went off with the Contessa to collect Bernard Berenson and hunt for her masterpiece.

They returned with a copy of Uccello's greatest work, *Saint George and the Dragon*, done by one of the master's pupils. It was a delightful painting. Saint George sat on his horse, thrusting his lance into the throat of a very small but fierce dragon. Behind the horse, hands folded in prayer, was the lady the knight was serving.

"It's a parable of American life," Cynthia said. "Except that most wives spend more time shopping than praying."

"How true," Rawdon said.

That night at dinner all Rawdon talked about was Cuba. He and Bradford had raised enough money to buy another million acres of land. They planned to build the biggest sugar factory on the island. They were hiring geologists to explore for minerals. They were planning to double the trackage of the island's only railroad, which they already owned. Other countries in Central and South America were ready for similar development. He saw Havana as the financial headquarters of a vast network of investments in mines and plantations and factories from Mexico to Argentina.

"Someday," Rawdon said, talking exclusively to Laura now, "you'll come down to Havana and live in a palace. The richest men from South America and North America will be there to do business with your father. A dozen of them will fall in love with you. Maybe you'll marry one of them and persuade him to join us in building an empire your children will inherit."

Never. The word blazed in Cynthia's mind. It was her father's purple dream, reborn on New York's Wall Street and London's Lombard Street and the Paris Bourse. It was enough to give her shivery thoughts about reincarnation, listening to Charlie's double sitting here talking about palaces and money-eyed marriages.

"Laura," Cynthia said. "It's past your bedtime. You've had a very tiring day."

Laura seemed to sense exactly what Cynthia was doing. She gave her father an extravagant embrace and departed without even kissing Cynthia good night.

"I'm worn out, too," Eleanor said. "Are you coming to bed soon, Rawdon?"

"No," he said curtly. "There's something I want to talk to Cynthia about."

He sipped his wine and waited until his wife and daughter left the room. "Lionel Bradford's in Venice," he said. "He's waiting for you at the Grand Hotel. We can take Laura with us to Rome. We'll bring her back in a week and no one will be the wiser."

For the tiniest moment, remembering Jonathan's letter, Cynthia wavered. But the hours she had spent opening herself to the presence in the villa chapel were now part of her life. "Tell Mr. Bradford that if he sends me one more of these messages, I'll tell my husband. He'll deal with him in rather direct fashion the next time he comes to New York."

"I don't understand what's happening to you, Stepmother," Rawdon said. "Bradford loves you, as much as he's capable of loving anyone. Are you telling me you're still in love with your oversized icicle of a husband? George says he barely speaks to you from one end of the year to the next."

"Rawdon—a woman does not have to be in love with someone else to despise a man as loathsome as Lionel Bradford. The more I listen to you, the more I think you're turning into a copy of him. I wouldn't worry about that sad fact too much if it didn't involve Laura. Do what you please in Havana. But don't drag her into your purple schemes."

"Why should I let you turn her into your version of the American woman, the one who spends most of her time shopping?"

"I'm not turning her into anything. I don't want you to try it, either."

"She's my daughter," Rawdon said.

"That doesn't mean you own her! You spent years complaining that your father wanted to own you."

Rawdon glared at her. She knew what he was thinking. *It's not the same thing. She's a female.* But he did not quite have nerve to say it. A small victory for someone. Cynthia Stapleton? Genevieve Dall? Incredible to discover that at this moment she could be one in spirit with a woman she had once thought she despised.

Rawdon stalked out of the dining room. Cynthia finished her sugarless coffee and retreated to the villa chapel. She sat there before the flickering sanctuary lamp, struggling to open her mind and heart to the presence. Gradually, she began to realize that something extraordinary had just happened. In that final rejection of Lionel Bradford and the bitter exchange with Rawdon she had become an independent woman.

An independent loveless woman. Perhaps a necessary step. An agonizing but necessary step.

But she did not want to live without love for the rest of her life. She did not want to end her days as a dry husk. Across four thousand miles her spirit reached out to her husband, yearning for the words of forgiveness he withheld. The presence, the presence, surged like a tidal sea in her soul, encompassing Laura and Jonathan and George. But Jonathan was at the center of it. He was the test of her challenge to the destiny her father had tried to impose on her. Until she heard loving words from her husband's lips again her life would be a failure.

Would the presence sustain her while she waited? Or would it prove to be no more than a flickering Italian candle that a cold American wind would snuff out?

She did not know. She did not know.

ELEVEN

"With health and work and happy love, a woman's life is complete. Will a man's life be less so? Of course not. This is the reason why the vote for women is so important. I believe it can and will lead to a world in which happiness can not only be pursued but be achieved by every American!"

The audience applauded. Genevieve Dall, one of the West's best-known lecturers on women's rights, bowed and smiled from the stage of Denver's Broadway Theater. As the applause subsided, a woman about Genevieve's age arose in the front row. "You're the author of *Antiope's Story?*" she asked.

"Yes."

"How can you hold yourself up as a model for other women? You admit you abandoned your daughter and your husband to live in California. What would happen to this country if other women started imitating your immoral example?"

A roar of approval and a burst of applause supported these words. The speaker was an anti-suffragist—part of a rapidly growing group of women who actively opposed the vote.

Genevieve struggled to explain that the psychological principles, the insights of *Antiope's Story* were the important point, not the personal example. "What I did was necessary for my survival," she said. "I wrote the book to help other women before they reached the brink of desperation. Now I'm campaigning for women's right to vote because I believe this is the first step to a redeemed social order in this country."

The suffragists in the audience applauded vigorously. The anti-suffragist was not impressed. "A redeemed social order! You want to destroy the sacred place American women have won in the hearts of their men! You want to destroy respect, love, motherhood!"

Another roar of approval and burst of applause backed this assault. Genevieve defended herself. The argument raged for another half hour. Genevieve left the stage feeling exhausted and dismayed. It was her first encounter with the "anti-suffs," as the newspapers called them, and she had found them more vituperative and hostile than most men.

In the lobby of the theater, as a group of young suffragists rushed to congratulate her, a florid-faced man with a mouthful of yellow teeth stepped between them. "Kennedy of the *News*," he said. "What happened in Massachusetts?"

"We lost."

"How do you explain the low turnout of women voters?"

"It's a conservative state."

"What are you talking about? Four times as many men voted in favor of it as women."

Kennedy looked like a beery oaf but he had a reporter's head for facts. The recent referendum in Massachusetts had been a disastrous defeat for the woman suffrage movement. Only 23,000 women had voted in favor of it. Twice as many women had voted against it. The majority did not bother to vote at all.

"Obviously, we have to educate women as well as men," Genevieve said.

While her subdued supporters watched dolefully, Kennedy asked her what she thought of the "hair-pulling match" she had just fought with the anti-suffs. It was all too obvious how Kennedy was going to write his story. Like most papers, the Denver *News* ridiculed woman suffrage.

Lunch at the Hotel Metropole with the president of the Denver Women's Club and her inner circle was not much more encouraging than the interview with Kennedy. There was a referendum on woman suffrage on Colorado's ballot this year. The Women's Club was campaigning hard for it, but they had found most Colorado women apathetic or hostile. If the referendum won, the votes would come from male members of the new Populist Party, which was looking for as many new voters as it could find to support its struggle for survival against Democrats and Republicans.

"It's a stunner," Genevieve said. "But I think we had better face the truth. Most women don't want the vote. The antis have convinced them that it isn't worth the price they may have to pay."

She briskly dismissed this "phantom fear" that men would refuse to love and honor women if they achieved equality. She was Genevieve Dall, spokeswoman for an embattled cause. But deep in her mind the ghost of Mrs. Rawdon Stapleton asked ironic questions.

Three days later, Genevieve Dall lay on her back on a sidewalk in downtown San Francisco. Around her stood a circle of curious pedestrians. A policeman knelt beside her and sniffed her lips. The stale whiskey on his breath almost made her vomit. "She ain't drunk," the lawman said.

Genevieve kept her eyes closed. Voices swirled around her.

"Not bad lookin'."

"Just off one of them Panama steamers, I bet. Probably got typhoid."

"Might just be hungry. They come here without a cent left over from the fare."

"Oughta quarantine everybody—from trains and boats."

"Or send'm straight to the Barbary Coast. She'd do pretty good down there. Make ten, maybe twenty a night."

An ambulance clopped to the curb. Two burly attendants lifted Genevieve onto a stretcher. In a moment she was jolting toward the City Receiving Hospital. One of the attendants, a swarthy unshaven man with uneven teeth, sat beside her. He slipped his hand under her dress. She felt it moving up her thigh.

"Where am I?" she said. "What's happening?"

"I'm takin' y'pulse," the attendant said, grinning. He did not withdraw his hand.

Genevieve sat up and angrily pushed him away. "I'm a respectable woman," she said.

"My name's Fred," the man said. "Where you from?"

"New York."

"Got any money?"

"A little."

"Gimmy five, if you want to get treated right at the hospital. If me and Harry give you thumbs down you ain't even gonna get fed."

Genevieve began to weep. "I'm all alone in this city . . ."

"Gimmy five."

She gave him five dollars. It did not improve her treatment at the hospital. Fred and Harry carried her into a small room on a deserted corridor and told her to take off her clothes.

"Why?"

"We gotta examine you."

When she protested, Fred held her down and Harry undressed her. Their examination consisted of squeezing her breasts and trying to thrust a finger up her vagina.

"I want to see a doctor!" she screamed, kicking Fred in the chest and lashing out at Harry with a free arm.

A white-coated man with a stubble of beard swayed in the doorway. "What the hell's going on, boys?"

"Examinin' this bimbo, Doc. We think she's got the syph," Harry said.

"I fainted on the street. These men are abusing me!"

"Now, now. They're just doing their jobs." The doctor smiled drunkenly. The liquor on his breath was overpowering. He ran his hands up Genevieve's belly. "Pretty nice piece. Give her an enema. That'll clean everything out."

Two hours later, Genevieve stumbled out of a taxi in front of a dilapidated building on Montgomery Street and toiled up three flights of stairs. The chaos of the *San Francisco Examiner*'s city room assailed her. For a moment all she could hear was Rawdon Stapleton saying, "Reporters live in the city's sewers." She walked unsteadily past the clacking typewriters and cursing reporters and copyboys to the desk where a tall cadaverous man wearing a monocle sat, snarling orders.

"Is it as bad as we heard?" Managing Editor Sam Chamberlain asked in an almost civilized voice.

"Worse. A lot worse," Genevieve said. She began telling him what they had done to her at the hospital.

"Jesus Jumping Christ," Chamberlain roared. "The Chief's got to hear this."

In another moment she was telling the story to a big boyish-faced man in an office at the rear of the city room. William Randolph Hearst grew more and more excited. "Tear up the goddamn front page," he shouted at Chamberlain in his odd high-pitched voice. "This will sell an extra twenty thousand copies."

It was after eight o'clock when Genevieve trudged up another three flights of stairs to her apartment in the Mission District of San Francisco. She threw a copy of the afternoon's *Examiner* on the blue couch. WORSE THAN RAPE, boomed the double-leaded head reporting what the City Receiving Hospital did to women who happened to faint on the streets of San Francisco.

Genevieve tried to shove the images of Fred and Harry and the drunken doctor out of her mind. She had something more important and far more pleasant to absorb her. A letter from Clay Pendleton. The first one in months. For a while, he had written to her regularly, determined to keep in touch with her, ignoring her failure to answer him at first. Over the past eighteen months, since he became managing editor of the *New York World*, his letters had regrettably dwindled. This one made Genevieve realize how much she missed them.

Life at the *World* had not changed. Pulitzer was still wandering the globe in search of a cure for his shattered nervous system, meanwhile driving everyone at the paper insane with an endless stream of telegrams and cables and letters full of orders, criticisms and exhortations. Occasionally he showed up in New York, triggering total uproar.

Clay described a luncheon he had recently had with his employer and Senator Jonathan Stapleton. The Senator had lamented Pulitzer's failure to support a bill some ex-Stalwart Republicans had introduced last year, requiring the federal government to use force to protect the voting rights of Negroes in the South. Clay sided with the Senator, and Pulitzer had begun excoriating his managing editor with all the obscenities in his vocabulary.

Jonathan Stapleton had rebuked Pulitzer, and Clay was sure he was about to be fired. To his amazement, Pulitzer had apologized.

That led to several paragraphs on the Stapletons. The General and Cynthia were still estranged. Rawdon had recently come to New York, full of boasts about the growing prosperity of his Caribbean Investment Company. But Rawdon was being outdistanced as a financier by his younger brother, George. With the help of Isaac Mayer, George had emerged as a textile tycoon. He was the president of the National Silk Company, which Isaac had formed from a clutch of independent mills, using the Stapleton company, Principia Mills, as the linchpin.

As for Laura, Clay saw no need to comment on her, since she had so recently visited Genevieve. "She's obviously going to give Consuelo Vanderbilt a run for the title of most beautiful girl in New York. Her grandfather considers her atrociously spoiled—and admits he's fifty percent responsible. Rawdon, incidentally, only talked about two things—how much money he's making, and Laura."

Finally came the familiar, now mostly joking offer of a job on the *New York World*. "Why did I ever mention your name to Willie Hearst? It's becoming the greatest mistake I ever made—and I've made some lulus. Just ask Pulitzer."

Wisps of bay fog were streaming past Genevieve's window as she finished the letter. Hearing from Clay always recalled her journey to San Francisco four years ago. She had sat in the dingy day coach, surrounded by immigrants babbling strange languages, wondering if Dr. Beard was right, if she was a neurasthenic woman and this act of desperation would end in final collapse, incurable mania.

She had staggered into the vile station restaurants to bolt down tinned beef, stale bread and bitter coffee. In growing horror she had stared at the wan faces of the local women, the bored blank expressions of the men, stunned, it seemed, by the vastness, the silence of the West. She became certain that it would swallow her too. Who was she, after all? A woman with a resurrected name, a kind of ghost; the closest thing to no one that a human being could manage this side of nonexistence.

San Francisco had rescued her from the West's immensity. To find this sun-drenched pocket version of New York at the end of her journey had steadied her. Elizabeth Wellcombe and her circle of feminist women had been equally important. They had been loving, patient sisters as Genevieve struggled to regain her sense of self and find new purpose for her life. In sunny Casa Fuller (named for Margaret Fuller, America's pioneer feminist) on top of Telegraph Hill, Wellcombe and her friends published a magazine called *The Unicorn*, financed by a well-to-do widow from Massachusetts. There, one memorable night, Susan B. Anthony had been their house guest.

Listening to this indomitable woman tell the story of her forty-year struggle for the vote, Genevieve had become a totally committed suffragist.

The telephone rang. Elizabeth Wellcombe's voice came over the wire, the Boston accent still intact. "Is that story true? Did that really happen to you?"

"Yes."

"My God, Gen. You don't have to do that sort of thing to make a living."

"I've told you—I like it. Mr. Hearst gave me a bonus of fifty dollars for it."

A mistake. Wellcombe was never impressed by how much money Genevieve was making. Her silence implied there was a hint of prostitution in the boast.

"Aren't you pleased to know those thuggish attendants and that drunken doctor will be out of jobs tomorrow?"

"Of course I am. But I wish some other woman, someone without your reputation in the movement, did the job. Can you imagine what the anti-suffragists will say if they connect you to that story? Don't you get enough abuse now?"

"Wellcombe, once and for all, let me go my own way. I don't want to be a lawyer. I'm as happy with what I'm doing as I can hope to be."

"I wish you'd never published *Antiope's Story*. It's ruined you!"

Outside, the fog was very thick now. Horns bellowed hoarsely on the bay. Genevieve walked around her apartment exhorting herself not to let the fog influence her, to begin cooking supper. She paused in the doorway of the second bedroom. It was decorated in bright primary colors. Stuffed animals sat in corners. On the dresser, on the walls, were at least a dozen photographs of a stunningly beautiful twelve-year-old girl. They all had the same expression: serene, mocking disdain.

Wrong, Genevieve thought. Everything about the room, about her life, was wrong. Let us begin with the room. You decorated it as if you were expecting an eight-year-old—that was about as much as you were willing to admit Laura might have aged since you left New York. Instead this disdainful incredibly self-possessed creature had stepped off the train. Laura had laughed—yes, actually *laughed*—at the room her mother had prepared for her. She seemed to know with uncanny prescience exactly where and why Genevieve had gone wrong.

Wrong. Everything about the visit had been wrong. Cynthia had come with Laura, of course. Genevieve had been braced for more of the hostility her ex-mother-in-law had displayed toward *Antiope's Story*. Instead she had been extremely friendly. California had delighted her. She kept seeing Italy everywhere. But wary Genevieve could not bring herself to trust Cynthia, to accept her as a friend.

Meanwhile, Laura had posed as Miss Sophisticated New York, bored with the West's scenery and sunshine. She had tried to play Cynthia off against

Genevieve, a gambit that Cynthia had carefully sidestepped. There were long monologues about Rawdon and the fortune he was amassing in Havana. At the beginning of the second week, William Randolph Hearst had abruptly canceled Genevieve's vacation to cover the gruesome story of a wife murdered by a jealous husband in Sausalito. She had writhed at the thought of Laura and Cynthia reading the gory prose Hearst loved in murder stories.

All that was left of her hopes of persuading Laura to spend summers with her, perhaps to live with her permanently, were those photographs Genevieve had taken with her new Kodak box camera. Now they reminded her of photographs she had once taken of another face, with the same symmetry, the same perfection of bone and flesh and features.

The real world. Accept the real world, Genevieve.

But the other voice kept whispering, *Wrong.* Health and work and happy love were what Genevieve Dall preached to her woman suffrage audiences. She had health. She had kept her body slim and lithe hiking and camping in the mountains of Big Sur. She had work. But she did not have love. Wellcombe's petulant telephone call was final proof of that dolorous fact.

Sam Chamberlain and other newsmen at the *Examiner* had made more or less obligatory passes at her. Reporters, especially San Francisco reporters, felt they had reputations as bohemians to maintain. She had received probes from other members of the city's bohemia when *Antiope's Story* won her modest fame.

Joaquin Miller, the poet who strode about with a bearskin over his shoulder and declaimed his verses from bluffs in Big Sur, had offered to make her one of his maenads. California's Keats, George Sterling, slim and handsome as Rawdon Stapleton, had been even more insistent. But Genevieve remained true to the bitter vow she had made when she said goodbye to Clay Pendleton. The poets dubbed her "the nun."

Wellcombe's sisterly love was another matter. Until Genevieve realized that it went beyond the sisterly. It did not quite reach the sensuality of Lesbos—but Wellcombe had visions of walking the beach below Cliff House in the twilight hand in hand, of dining à deux in adobe-walled restaurants in Monterey, of possessing Genevieve's love for life. Unfortunately, she also thought love meant directing Genevieve's destiny. She saw herself as the guide, the mentor who had converted Genevieve to feminism. This qualified her to decide where and how Genevieve could make her greatest contribution to the movement.

Wellcombe had been openly dismayed when Genevieve accepted William Randolph Hearst's offer of a job. The young millionaire had spent a year working at the *World* and had returned to California a worshiper of Pulitzer and his right-hand man, Clay Pendleton. Clay's recommendation and a glance at *Antiope's Story* had been enough to convince Hearst that she could become San Francisco's Nelly Bly.

There was some truth to Wellcombe's argument that this sort of reporting was beneath a woman of Genevieve's intelligence and education. She was baffled and hurt when Genevieve said, coldly, calmly, "I want to do it." Wellcombe could not begin to understand the private demons Genevieve Dall was exorcising when she earned bonuses from Hearst and praise from veteran editors like Chamberlain.

Wrong, Genevieve thought, remembering the vituperation of the anti-suffragists. The crusade that gave her life meaning and purpose was sliding into the same muddle of egotism and greedy endorsement of the status quo that disgraced politics as conducted by America's males. Susan B. Anthony and the rest of the pioneers were too old and too disheartened by this new and cruelest twist of history's knife to do anything about it.

The foghorns boomed on the bay, long hoarse squawks that reminded Genevieve of laughing hyenas in another time and place. Skipping supper, she threw herself on her bed without even bothering to undress.

Still sleepless in the dawn, Genevieve looked out on a city swallowed by grayness. She felt the fog inside her body, a kind of anticipation of the grave. Her eyes ached, her brain was a piece of rusty metal, it was an effort to stand erect. She told herself it was a metaphor of real life, the real world. Gray fog crept into every adult soul without warning.

Genevieve bathed and dressed in fresh clothes. She stood for a moment in the doorway of the second bedroom, looking at the photographs. For the first time since Laura and Cynthia returned to New York, Genevieve closed the door. Head erect, the *San Francisco Examiner's* star reporter strode up the city's shrouded hills on her way to work.

Antiope's story was not over.

BOOK V
1893–1900

ONE

"Do you think Father would be upset if I asked Rawdon to be my best man?" George Stapleton asked.

"Possibly. Why on earth would you ask him?" Cynthia said.

"Laura wants me to do it. She hinted very strongly the other day that it would please her tremendously."

"George. That's not a good reason. Laura never stops to think about how much trouble she may cause when she announces what she wants. Do you want Rawdon?"

"Well, no, to be completely frank. I admire the way Rawdon's stood up to Father on some things. But on most matters I think he's all wet. The way he sneers at this country, for instance."

"Whom would you like to ask?"

"Teddy Roosevelt. But he's so busy making headlines these days . . ."

After six years in Washington as a Civil Service commissioner, Theodore had returned to New York to become a police commissioner under a Republican mayor. He was turning the department upside down with midnight inspection tours and ruthless prosecution of corrupt officers. The newspapers were giving him columns of publicity.

"I'm sure Theodore would be delighted to be your best man," Cynthia said. "He's very fond of you. In the past year you've been a true friend to him —and Elliott."

A few months ago, New Yorkers had opened their newspapers and had been shocked to read that Theodore Roosevelt was trying to have his younger brother Elliott committed to an asylum as a lunatic. Cynthia was as dismayed, if not surprised, as everyone else. Over the past five years, George had told her something about Elliott's descent into alcoholism. As Elliott's drink-

ing increased and his behavior became more and more bizarre, Theodore
tried to intervene in his brusque headlong way. Elliott had responded with
vituperative rages that forced Theodore to turn to George as an intermediary.

"Nell's drinking himself to death. I can't figure it out," George said.
"When he's drunk he despises Theodore. The next day he'll spend an hour
telling me how much he admires him. It's the same way with his wife and
kids. When he was drunk he threatened to kill them. Now he'd give a year of
his life to be able to see them. But his wife won't go near him anymore."

"It's hard to believe, but you can love and hate someone at the same
time," Cynthia said.

George's eyes searched her face for a moment. He obviously knew she was
speaking from experience. "I've tried to get Nell to come see you. I think you
might be able to help him."

"I'd love to see him. But I'm not sure what I can do to help him. I'm
afraid Elliott has lost hope. It's very hard to regain it."

Was she in that perilous condition, too? Cynthia wondered. In recent
months, as George discussed his coming marriage, she had been tormented
by an almost unbearable sadness. She seldom slept more than three hours a
night. She was haunted by memories of her wedding to Jonathan and the
following years of happiness. Lost, irretrievably lost happiness.

Stop. Self-pity was not going to do her or George any good. "Friendship's
not the only reason Theodore will be glad to be your best man. I'm sure he's
also impressed with your emergence as a Wall Street tycoon," she said.

George smiled. "Sometimes I can't quite believe how much money I'm
worth these days," he said. "I have to call Isaac Mayer on the phone to
confirm it."

"What's your stock selling at now?"

"It went over a hundred again today. But I'm not sure how long it will stay
there. The market has had a base case of the jitters since the Democrats took
over the White House again."

Last November Grover Cleveland, defeated in 1888, had performed the
unprecedented feat of recapturing the presidency. Senator Stapleton had
startled his wife and family by announcing he was secretly pleased. He
thought Cleveland would make a far better president than the do-nothing
dullard from Ohio, Benjamin Harrison, whom the Republicans had elected in
1888. In private, Jonathan frequently denounced his own party for living in a
"moral vacuum," interested only in winning elections. He had almost resigned from the Senate when the Republicans, with majorities in both
houses, failed to pass a single piece of legislation to protect the South's
Negroes from midnight violence.

George consulted his watch. "I better get over to Jersey City to meet
Anne's train. Do you expect the Senator to be here for dinner?"

"If Congress adjourns on time."

"I hope they drag their collective feet. I'd like you and Anne to get to know each other a little better. I hope you don't mind taking charge of her. I really can't spare much time from the office with the market behaving so oddly."

"I don't mind in the least. I'm looking forward to it."

A half hour after George departed, the sound of a key unlocking the front door interrupted Cynthia's perusal of the *New York Herald*. Senator Stapleton frowned in the doorway.

"Hello," he said.

"Hello. How are you?"

"As well as a man with a bad stomach can be after three months of eating in hotel restaurants. How are you?"

"Fine. The doctor says I'm the healthiest diabetic in New York. Some of my friends are hoping to catch the disease to help them keep their figures."

A ghost of a smile drifted across the Senator's gaunt weary face. He had lost weight. His digestion grew worse with each passing year. How would she feel if he died without forgiving her? If he barred her from his deathbed, the way his mother had barred him?

When someone loses hope it's hard to regain it.

How much longer could she go on hoping this cold remote man would say the words of forgiveness she wanted to hear? His continuing refusal had driven her into the Catholic Church in spite of grave reservations about some of its doctrines, such as the supposed infallibility of the Pope. She had tried to substitute the forgiveness of God, through the priest in the confessional, the host at the communion rail, as food for her soul. But she knew her motive was flawed by her hunger for Jonathan's forgiveness. That was why she seldom went to Sunday mass, although she blamed her lapses on the incredible boredom of the average sermon.

"What has Congress accomplished lately?"

"Damn little. As you no doubt read in the papers, we spent most of our time arguing about whether to annex the Hawaiian Islands and then dropped the subject, giving the Germans or the British a perfect excuse to grab them if they're interested."

"I'd love to visit Hawaii. The papers make it sound more beautiful than Italy."

He ignored the reference to past happiness and sat down on the edge of a wing chair, suggesting that only sheer willpower kept him in the room with her. "We should have repealed the Sherman silver purchase act," he said. "We should have given the country the sound money it needs to avert a panic."

He might have been reciting from a newspaper editorial or a political speech. "I'm afraid my poor female head is incapable of grasping this argument over gold and silver coinage," Cynthia said.

"A lot of male heads can't grasp it, either. It comes down to this. The rest of the world is on the gold standard. For the last two years, thanks to harebrained western Democrats like William Jennings Bryan, the United States has backed its paper money with both silver and gold. As a result, no one wants to do business with us. Foreign investors are pulling their money out. I'm worried about the stock market. I hope George is, too."

"He does seem concerned."

"Not concerned enough to curtail plans for that supper at Delmonico's, I bet."

After his wedding in Virginia, George was planning to bring his bride to New York for an elaborate party at Delmonico's to meet the many friends that Anne Lee Randolph's family, in their comparative poverty, could not invite to the ceremony. The following day the newlyweds were leaving for a three-month honeymoon in Europe.

"Jonathan, I read in the paper the other day that George is worth ten million dollars. Surely he can spend a few thousand to make himself and his bride happy. He's lived very frugally as a bachelor, compared to most young men his age."

"I suppose you're right. But that ten million isn't real money. It could vanish overnight."

They had quarreled rather nastily over George's decision to form the National Silk Company with Isaac Mayer's help. Jonathan had had a dozen objections—it was too risky, it smacked of an illegal trust. Cynthia thought the real reason for his hostility was his lack of confidence—and something deeper, a lack of sympathy, of understanding, in his relationship with his younger son.

Cynthia was enormously proud of George's accomplishments as president of Principia Mills. He had converted the company to silk production and doubled the profits in six years. At the same time, in her admittedly prejudiced opinion, he had become an attractive, admirable young man. Unlike his father and older brother, he was an idealist who saw the best in people, who looked to the future with hearty optimism.

"Really, Jonathan. Will you never stop trying to tear George down?"

"I'm not tearing him down. I'm only trying to inject a little realism into him."

"I sometimes think you won't be happy until you turn him into Rawdon."

That was too cruel. Cynthia saw the pain on his face. She almost regretted her ability to say things that reduced Jonathan to muttering incoherence. He did not know how to deal with a wife who was also an independent woman.

Fortunately another Stapleton spun the front-door lock. Laura peered into the parlor, simultaneously flinging aside her blue school cloak. At sixteen she was already one of the most beautiful young women of her generation. Her years of exercise had given her a broad-shouldered confident body; from her father she had inherited a faultless face and a natural hauteur. She was a virtual personification of the emerging feminine style of the 1890s as drawn by the illustrator Charles Dana Gibson.

"Welcome home, Senator," she said, leaning over Jonathan to give him a quick kiss. "Have you heard the news?"

"I've done all the talking since I arrived. I haven't heard a thing."

"The famous Genevieve Dall's coming back to New York. William Randolph Hearst is buying the *New York Journal* and he's hired her to work on it."

"We were too busy discussing the gold standard for me to tell him," Cynthia said.

"Ye gods, what a romantic couple," Laura said. "Are you going to let Mother in the house, Pa?"

"Of course I'm going to let her in the house. Why shouldn't I?" Jonathan said.

"Didn't she insult you and humiliate you publicly in *Antiope's Story?*"

"It was mild criticism compared to some of the things other people have said about me in my time."

Laura grimaced. "I suppose that means I've got to see her and be nice to her."

"It means exactly that," Jonathan said.

"If I had any money, if those stupid lawyers hadn't deprived me of my inheritance until I'm twenty-one years old, I'd leave here tomorrow and go to —Havana!"

She stormed out of the room. Jonathan Stapleton struggled to his feet. "What a lovely homecoming," he said, and trudged upstairs.

Cynthia let her head fall back against the antimacassar. Avoid worry and emotional strain, the English doctor in Florence, and all subsequent doctors, had told her. Why did she stay here, letting these maddening Stapletons make her ill? She was the one who should take her money and go someplace far far away—Hawaii, Tahiti.

Two hours later, Cynthia sat at the dinner table trying to cope with three Stapletons and another highly emotional young woman—Anne Lee Randolph. Tall and willowy, with a cascade of blond hair, Anne emanated feminine fragility and delicacy. Previous meetings with her had been brief: dinner, the night George graduated from Harvard (Anne was his roommate's sister), a lunch in Washington two years ago. But these encounters had been enough for Jonathan to give George a lecture urging him to choose a wife who shared a similar background. George had rather tartly pointed out he had not followed his own maxim, and Senator Stapleton had retired into sullen but still hostile silence.

Jonathan surprised Cynthia by beginning the dinner with a gesture of conciliation. He raised his wineglass and said, "To another southern beauty. I'm glad to see that the South continues the tradition."

"Thank you, Father," George said, after they drank the toast. "I would like to salute a southern woman whose beauty still deserves admiration." He raised his glass to Cynthia.

"Dear George," she said. "I suppose people do admire ruins—Pompeii, for instance."

There was a pause. Anne Lee Randolph watched Jonathan Stapleton begin to drink his mock-turtle soup. "My goodness, Senator. You mean you're *not* going to respond to your wife's remark? I suppose it's a perfect example of the difference between the North and the South. In Virginia, a woman couldn't *say* such a thing without her husband—and a dozen other men—contradicting her. Especially someone like Mrs. Stapleton, who still retains so *much* of her youthful beauty."

"I think Mrs. Stapleton knows I'm well aware of that," Jonathan muttered.

"Fortunately George doesn't share your Yankee taciturnity," Anne Lee continued in her artless way. "Maybe it's the result of having a southern stepmother. You should see the *extravagance* of his letters. Even my mama, who's probably had more compliments paid to her than any woman in the entire South, thought they were *extreme.*"

"Why not," Cynthia said. "He's extremely in love with you."

"Oh I know," Anne said, as if this was something inevitable like rainfall in the spring. "But the crucial thing, the doubt I had to resolve, was in regard to George's ideals. I found it hard to believe that a Yankee could have any."

"Why?" Jonathan growled.

"Yankees spend so much of their time fretting over the ugly mercenary details of life, like profits," Anne said. "But Georgie convinced me that your family was different, Senator. He pointed out your tradition of public service. But the main thing has been George's enthusiasm for the Knights of the Golden Purpose. I suppose he's told you about them?"

"Not a word," Jonathan said. "What are they, George?"

"They're mostly men about my age, Father. We meet once a month to discuss how to implement American ideals—to raise the moral tone of business and politics."

"Have they given you any advice on how to get the Japanese to stop raising the price of raw silk?" Jonathan asked. "That must be doing a lot of damage to the National Silk Company's profits."

"Oh they'd never get involved in anything so mercenary," Anne said. "But they have heartily approved George's plans to improve America's public architecture."

"Oh?" Jonathan said.

"That is the ideal George and I share, Senator. As you know, Thomas Jefferson was my great-great-grandfather, and architecture—good taste—is more or less in my *blood*. Each year George is going to devote ten percent of the ten million dollars in profits he's making to hire Richard Morris Hunt and other architects to lecture in various cities around the nation on the latest developments in their art. And of course we'll hire one of them, perhaps Stanford White, to design our house on upper Fifth Avenue—"

"Ah," Jonathan said. "I'm getting an education, just listening to you."

"I've been meaning to discuss some of this with you, Father," George said. "But you've been so involved in Congress . . ."

"Of course. What do you think of the stock market these days, George? Or does making ten million dollars a year enable you to ignore such mundane matters?"

"I'm worried, like a lot of other people. But I think things will settle down, once everyone realizes President Cleveland is still his steady, sensible, conservative self."

"Marvelous. Do you join him on your knees each night, praying for William Jennings Bryan to disappear?"

"I heard some awful news about your friend Elliott Roosevelt today, George," Laura said, obviously trying to come to her uncle's rescue.

"What?"

"My friend Georgianna Livingston says Elliott's wife is dying and she refuses to see him or any other Roosevelt."

"How awful," Cynthia said.

A pause. Would Jonathan deplore the idea of carrying unforgiveness to the grave? He was certainly qualified to comment on the pain of such an experience. Or would he at least be reminded that George could do worse things than join the Knights of the Golden Purpose?

"I always knew Elliott would go sour. His mother spoiled him," Jonathan growled.

"That's not true!" Cynthia said, her affection for Mittie combining with disappointment to create perfect fury.

"I agree with Mother," George said. "It's a good deal more complicated."

"Sending you to St. Paul's was the best thing anyone ever did for you, George. It got you out of this house and away from Elliott."

"I wish I could agree, Father. But from my viewpoint, what changed my life was the summer Mother arranged for me to spend on Long Island, being tutored by Theodore. That was where I found the older brother I needed."

"Why didn't Elliott feel the same way about him?" Laura asked.

"He did, sometimes. But his father tended to favor Teddy. That made Elliott feel left out. I felt the same way about you and Rawdon for a long time, Father," George said.

"Why, in God's name? All I ever did was quarrel with Rawdon."

"I used to wish you'd do the same thing with me. It was better than being ignored."

Guilt was practically visible on Jonathan's face. But he declined to admit it. "Well—eventually a man has to grow up and realize it doesn't matter what his father or mother thought of him."

"I couldn't agree more, Father," George said, giving Anne a quick, triumphant smile. She had obviously encouraged him to act on that principle.

"Did you ever fight in the Shenandoah Valley during the war, Senator?" Anne Lee Randolph asked.

"No."

"Oh I am so glad. Let me tell you why."

With a vigor and indignation that made it sound as if it had happened yesterday, Anne told them how raiding Yankee cavalry had wantonly burned her grandfather's house in 1864, destroying, among many other keepsakes, several hundred of Thomas Jefferson's letters. "Poor Grandpa begged them to let him rescue his papers, but they only *scorned* him when he mentioned Great-Grandfather Jefferson. They said he was nothing but a slave driver and repeated that monstrous story about him seducing his female slaves. Later we heard that General Sheridan had ordered the house destroyed. Do you think that's true, Senator?"

"No."

"Well, I'm still glad you never fought in the Shenandoah Valley. I would hate to have to tell my children that their grandfather burned down my grandfather's house and destroyed letters that might have changed our understanding of American history."

"I would hope by the time your children are old enough to hear it, that kind of story will be forgotten," Jonathan said.

"I hope so, too," Cynthia said.

Anne looked baffled by Cynthia's agreement. George consulted his watch and suggested that he and Anne had better skip dessert. He had tickets to a new play by David Belasco. The remaining Stapletons listened to Anne's liquid accent as George hurried her into the May night.

Laura popped a fresh strawberry into her mouth. "She's a bit of an idiot. But I can see why George loves her."

"Why?" Jonathan said. "Enlighten me from the depths of your feminine wisdom."

"She's ethereal. That's what men want in women these days. They adore creatures like Consuelo Vanderbilt, who look as though a high wind will blow them away. It's why I'm doomed to remain single."

"Oh bosh. Finish those strawberries and get upstairs and do your homework," Cynthia said.

Jonathan made no attempt to resume the conversation after Laura departed. "Anne's so incredibly southern," Cynthia said. "It's almost as if she were playing a part."

"She's a walking talking example of how the South has turned in on itself," Jonathan said. "I hear that sort of guff from southern senators all the time. I'm not sure I want to hear it at my dinner table."

He shoved aside his strawberries and began taking a half-dozen different pills for his digestion.

"Be patient with her, Jonathan. I was rather defensive about being southern when I first came to New York. When she sees how little the war means to most people, she'll change."

"You had the advantage of intelligence."

"I'm really rather touched by their idealism," Cynthia said. "They're looking for things to admire in American life. They want to contribute something to the country."

"From a mansion on upper Fifth Avenue. I get the feeling that's as important to Miss Randolph as the gospel of beauty and good taste according to Thomas Jefferson."

"Jonathan—that's cruel. Anne didn't leap into George's arms like your typical fortune hunter. They love each other. Maybe it's not the way we did. But it's genuine."

"I'll take your word for it," he said. "Will you excuse me?"

Cynthia sat alone at the table, hearing for the second time what she had just said. *The way we did.* She had spoken of their love in the past tense and her husband had coldly accepted it. For a moment she felt panicky; she groped for some words of prayer, for a memory that put her in touch with happiness. But nothing came.

Anne Lee Randolph had come to New York to shop for her trousseau. George had asked Cynthia to guide her through the dressmaker–department-store maze. Over the next few days, Cynthia began to think Jonathan might be right about Anne's social ambitions. Her figure was made to order for the new hourglass look and she adored the velvets, satins and lush silks that were doubling the prices of evening gowns and tea dresses. She had obviously inherited her great-great-grandfather Thomas Jefferson's fondness for the best things in life, a trait that had left him bankrupt in his old age.

On the third or fourth day of their shopping, they were coming out of Arnold Constable when Cynthia heard a newsboy howling, "Hey, get a *Woild* extra. Wall Street's fallin' apart."

She gave him two cents for the paper and read it on the way downtown. The head on the lead story read:

PANIC!
NATIONAL CORDAGE COMPANY COLLAPSES
THREE BANKS FAIL
BROKERS SUSPENDING

"What does it mean?" Anne asked.

"It's not good news."

At six o'clock, Jonathan telephoned to say that he and George would not be home for supper. Midnight had just finished booming in St. George's Church when they finally arrived.

"What's happening?" Cynthia asked. "It can't be as bad as those dreadful expressions on your faces."

"We could be bankrupt tomorrow. That's what's happening," Jonathan said.

"Father—it's not that bad yet."

"I can smell disaster in the air. Tomorrow you're going to see the worst panic since 'Seventy-three. In those days we only had to worry about overcapitalized railroads. Now we have these marvelous paper empires called trusts that are going to come down on our heads."

"I predict our stockholders will stand fast, Father," George said.

"You're dreaming, George. You've been dreaming from the start. You and your friend Isaac Mayer have bought up a collection of companies with more debts than assets. You don't have a single large investor in the picture except Mayer, and he's so committed in other trusts he won't have enough cash to pay his heating bills. I wish to God Adolph Mayer were still alive. European bankers trusted him. I'm sure they won't lend Isaac a nickel."

"We'll be first on his list, Father. He may have to let other people go down, but he won't turn his back on the Stapletons."

"George, I'm not impressed by your faith in human nature any more than I am by your choice of a wife."

George retreated upstairs. He never argued with his father.

"Is it necessary to wound the boy that way, Jonathan?" Cynthia said.

"You can get out of my sight, too," he snarled. "You're as much to blame. You talked me into giving him and his Virginia social climber a chance to make ten million so you could introduce them into society the way you introduced Eleanor Dall. Probably with the same results."

For a moment Cynthia could feel nothing but the old hatred surging in her soul. "I never said one word to you about George's ambitions! I only asked you to give him a hearing!"

"You didn't have to say anything. I knew what you wanted. What you've always wanted. To turn me into a simpering weak-kneed fool."

"I never wanted to change you into anything. I only wanted to stop you from becoming a man without compassion or consideration for anyone or anything—above all for his wife."

She left him fuming in the parlor. In the dawn she awoke to hear him pacing up and down in his room. Was it possible—could they lose everything? Cynthia tried to imagine what it would be like. Would they have to beg in the streets, stand in bread lines?

At breakfast she discovered Anne and Laura absorbed in the newspapers. The *World* shrieked panic. The other papers were not much better. Laura said Jonathan and George had drunk hasty cups of coffee and rushed downtown. She was wildly excited. "I heard what Pa was saying last night. Are we really going bankrupt? I hope we do. It would be a fascinating experience."

Anne Lee Randolph was looking very uneasy. "Isn't she exaggerating?" she asked Cynthia.

"I hope so."

Cynthia and Anne departed for another day of shopping. The stores were ominously deserted. But Delmonico's dining room was as full of handsome men and pretty women in stylish dresses as it ever was—and apparently would be until the end of time. Alva Vanderbilt waved from a nearby table, and returned to an intense conversation with swarthy Oliver Belmont. Alva had shown her rebel spirit—and sent fashionable New York reeling—by divorcing Willie K. Vanderbilt for "repeated infidelities." Oliver Belmont had recently divorced his wife. There was no doubt that he and Alva would soon marry. They planned to live in France most of the time to escape petty snubs and slights.

Next to the almost-Belmonts sat Lionel Bradford with a pretty auburn-haired girl—probably an actress, although her subdued tan walking dress did not look very theatrical. Bradford glanced across the dining room at Cynthia, the impenetrable eyes momentarily aglow, the feral smile in place. Except for lines of age on his throat, he remained immune to time. But he had abandoned his pursuit of her.

George Stapleton had been supposed to meet them at 1 P.M. He did not appear until 1:30, and his manner was not reassuring. He was pale and his hand trembled as he drank his champagne. In response to Cynthia's questions, he would only say that the situation was "not encouraging." Stocks were plummeting. Foreign banks were calling in all their loans. The shares of Rawdon's Caribbean Investment Company, which was heavily dependent on European money, were turning into wastepaper. Isaac Mayer had received a cable from Rawdon, begging him for a loan of a million dollars.

Anne chattered about the marvelous buys Cynthia and she had discovered at Tiffany's in new Chinese export porcelain. Cynthia wondered why she could not see the desperation in George's eyes. Halfway through lunch, the headwaiter summoned him to the telephone. He returned enormously agitated and said he had to go back downtown immediately. "We've had some very bad news," he said.

Anne looked bewildered as George rushed off. "Is Laura right? Are they losing all their money?"

Cynthia did not like the use of "they"—as if George and his father were strangers. "A good deal more than money is at stake, Anne," she said. "You must know how much his success means to George—as a man."

"Cynthia? Who is this lovely blond creature?"

Cynthia introduced Anne to Lionel Bradford. He in turn introduced them to the girl in the walking dress, whom he playfully called his "English daughter," Cornelia. Her mother had died last year. He had brought her to New York to introduce her to American society. "Unfortunately, I seem to have made some enemies who are persecuting me through her. Your friend Katherine Kemble Brown, for instance. I can't remember what I've ever done to offend her."

"Perhaps you should examine your conscience again," Cynthia said.

Bradford's eyes hardened. He told his daughter to wait for him in his carriage and sat down at Cynthia's table. "I could be very helpful to your stepson Rawdon if you spoke to Katherine Kemble Brown on Cornelia's behalf," he said.

Since their encounter in Florence, Cynthia did not feel she owed Rawdon anything. They had become antagonists, struggling for Laura's allegiance. She saw no need to explain this to Bradford. Better to let him know once and for all her opinion of him. "If I thought you were really interested in your daughter's happiness, Lionel," Cynthia said, "I might try to do something. But I know you're only going to try to sell her to the highest bidder."

Bradford muttered something about an impossible woman and strode out of the restaurant.

"Who is he?" Anne Lee Randolph asked.

"A denizen of upper Fifth Avenue," Cynthia said.

At 5 P.M. Cynthia sent Oliver Cromwell over to Union Square to buy the evening papers. The whole front page of the *World* was devoted to the chaos on Wall Street. There were drawings of an immense mob in front of the Stock Exchange, stories of frantic people pounding on the doors of closed banks. THE CRASH TO END ALL CRASHES, the headlines shrilled.

"What does it all mean?" Anne Lee Randolph asked. In Virginia, the cows would go on giving milk, the wheat and corn would continue to grow. It was hard for a country girl to grasp any connection between her life and events on a narrow stony street at the bottom of Manhattan Island.

Cynthia left Anne reading the papers and walked across Stuyvesant Square to St. George's Church. She knelt in the shadowy silence and prayed for George and Jonathan, for Rawdon and Eleanor in Havana. She shuddered to think of what the loss of a second fortune would do to Rawdon. She prayed for Anne—and for herself. She struggled to open her heart to the presence, to ask God for strength and wisdom. But she found the path clogged with images of evil, chaos, fear.

Back home, the first sound she heard was a woman sobbing. In the parlor, Anne Lee Randolph sat on the couch, her eyes streaming. Beside her sat George, looking as though he had just been mortally wounded. Jonathan Stapleton paced up and down the Aubusson rug.

"What's happened?" Cynthia asked.

"Isaac Mayer's gone under," George said. "He owes at least forty million dollars. No one can find him. He's probably in Canada."

"It's an old story," Jonathan said. "Isaac used the same stock to guarantee a half-dozen different loans. Including his stock in the National Silk Company."

"It was the coup de grace," George muttered. "We might have held on . . ."

"General—what's going to happen to George?" Anne asked. "Will he go to jail with Isaac Mayer?"

"Get her out of here," Jonathan snarled. "She's done enough damage. I have something very important to discuss with your mother."

"What damage have I done?" Anne cried.

"You filled George's head with idealistic cotton wool which was even worse than the sawdust that was in there already."

Anne fled, sobbing. George followed her. "Is it necessary to reduce us all to absolute misery, Jonathan?" Cynthia asked.

"Why not?" he snarled. "That's where we're all going. Where the whole country is going. Why not get a preview of it? Do you know how much money we lost today?"

Cynthia shook her head.

"Eleven million dollars. That includes the million in cash that I threw into the cauldron to try to support the National Silk Company's stock. The company went bankrupt at four o'clock. Principia Mills—the one thing we owned that was real, besides this house and our property in New Jersey—is now owned by the City Bank. Somewhere, I wonder if Jay Gould is laughing."

Gould had died two years ago, reportedly with a stock ticker tape running through his hand. Jonathan kept pacing, not looking at her. She could see he was in agony, but he would not let her touch him.

"I think we can buy back the mills, for about a million in cash. But the only money we've got left in this world belongs to you."

"Is it enough?" Cynthia said. "I barely look at those statements Delancey Apthorpe sends me."

"It's well over a million dollars."

He was as far away from her as he could get now, in the bay window, overlooking Stuyvesant Square. "I can understand why you might want to say no. You could take this money and go to Europe and try to forget me—forget the whole Stapleton tribe."

"Why should I want to do that?"

"Have we done anything but make you miserable?"

"You've made me happy—and unhappy. I'm afraid I've done the same thing to you."

"But I don't deserve any compassion because I have none. Isn't that it? You don't need me, now that you have your prayers and your saints."

"Don't need you, Jonathan Stapleton? If I could tell you how often a touch of your hand, your lips, would have saved me a night of misery."

She stood there in the fading light, trembling. As she expected, her words made no impression on that glaring tormented face. Why not tell him the whole truth? "I'm much too spoiled, too much a creature of this world to get more than an occasional flicker of consolation from God, under any circumstances. But your refusal to forgive me has made it almost impossible for me to feel any contrition for my . . . sins. That cuts me off from God—as well as from you."

"Do you think I haven't—a hundred times—wanted to say something? But it was . . . impossible. It was death—something died inside me when I saw those letters."

The words were flung from his mouth like chunks of stone or metal. They stood there in the rubble of their love.

"You can have the money," Cynthia said. "As long as you understand it has nothing to do with us. It's for George's sake, and Laura's if her inheritance is involved in this debacle."

He took a packet of papers out of his pocket. "Sign these," he said in a flat empty voice.

She signed them and he rushed out of the house without touching her, without even saying "Thank you." If she had been alone Cynthia would have sat down and wept. But duty, responsibility, those iron Stapleton words, did not give her time to mourn the final loss of hope.

Upstairs, she knocked on George's door. "Come in," he said.

He was stretched on his bed, like a corpse on a bier. "Where's Anne?" Cynthia asked.

"I don't know. In her room, I suppose."

"What are you and she going to do?"

"I don't know. Nothing, I suppose. What can I do now?"

Cynthia went down the hall to Anne's room. Anne sat on her bed, sobbing. Laura stood in the doorway.

"I told her she should go home," Laura said. "The Senator will be twice as impossible, now that he's lost his money."

"Go to your room," Cynthia said, shoving Laura into the hall. She sat down on the bed and put her arm around Anne. "Don't blame George for his father. He's a completely different man."

"I know that. But why didn't he speak up on my behalf? Why did he let him humiliate me that way?"

"Because George has just suffered a far worse humiliation."

"How could he do that to his own son?"

"Not by his father, dear girl. His father only added a minor laceration or two. The serious wound was inflicted by the world, Anne. This American world. You don't know how hard and cruel it can be. The men protect us from it—or think they do. But if you live with a man long enough you'll see the scars. You may also acquire a few. I'm afraid it's part of becoming a woman."

Anne had stopped weeping. For a moment Cynthia wondered if she was giving her the right advice. Would she be more honest if she told this girl to pack her bag and flee this tribe of contumacious Yankees? No. She was part of them now. She had just proven it by signing away her independence.

"George is going to need a great deal of love to heal that wound. If he lost you—I don't think he could bear it."

"He's not going to lose me. I love him," Anne said. "The money—the money was never that important to me."

Anne's inner struggle was painfully visible as she said these words. Cynthia wondered if they were entirely true. But the affirmation had been made. "Go tell him that now."

Downstairs, Cynthia asked Cousteau to serve cold suppers to all of them in their rooms. It was not a good night for family conversations. She heard Anne's footsteps go down the hall to George's room. An old-fashioned chaperone might have grown uneasy about how much time she spent there. But Cynthia quietly rejoiced.

She sat in her room struggling to pray for Anne and George—and for Jonathan. It was easy to envision prayer helping to open the hearts of young lovers. But her husband was another matter. Could anything penetrate the soul of a man who had encased himself in unforgiving metal?

About ten o'clock she heard Jonathan's footsteps on the stairs. They were slow, weary. Did that mean the news was bad? He knocked on her door. "Come in," she said.

"We've got them," he said. "The bank's given us a line of credit to start buying raw silk as an independent mill. We can be back in business tomorrow morning. If there's any business to be done. I shudder to think what this collapse is going to do to the country."

"Forget about the country for a while," Cynthia said. "There's something else you have to do here."

"What?"

"Tell George you want him to become the president of Principia Mills again. Show him you haven't lost confidence in him."

For a moment she saw nothing but the old familiar glare.

"Do it, Jonathan. If you don't want him to end up like Elliott Roosevelt."

Fifteen minutes later, Jonathan returned to the open door of her room. "His Virginia charmer is sticking with him. When I told her they'd have to live in New Jersey to save the cost of a plant manager, she didn't say a word. That's more devotion than I gave her credit for."

"I think the correct word is love, Jonathan," Cynthia said.

She expected the word to send him fleeing down the hall to his war corner. But he stood his ground in the doorway. "May I come in?"

"Of course."

He closed the door behind him and walked slowly around the bedroom, studying the religious paintings on the walls. He ended up in the far corner, by the window. He still seemed to feel a need to distance himself from her.

"I have a proposition for you. As an actress, would you consider playing a wife who pretends to love a fool who drove a woman out of his life and then refused to forgive her when she stopped loving him?"

"I'm not an actress anymore, Jonathan."

"Then—there's no hope?" he said staring gloomily at Uccello's painting of Saint Francis.

"Oh, there's always hope. I often dream I'm in Venice and my husband is putting his arms around me and saying—"

Two strides and he was holding her, whispering the words she had waited almost a decade to hear. "Oh my love my love my love."

TWO

Genevieve Dall stood at the window of her sixth-floor room in the Belvedere Hotel, overlooking Union Square. Below her, several thousand people swarmed in front of the equestrian statue of George Washington on the edge of the park, listening to a bearded orator harangue them on the evils of capitalism. Insane, Genevieve thought, the United States of America was going insane.

As a thinking woman, Genevieve had participated in the growing criticism of the American industrial system that had swirled around her in San Francisco. She had applauded when the Socialist Henry George had migrated from the bay city to run for mayor of New York in 1886, losing by a whisper to a conservative Democrat. She often had kind words to say from speakers' platforms on behalf of the new Populist Party, which was winning numerous elections in the West by calling for a drastic overhaul of American society.

As a feminist who was fighting for a change in the status quo that many people regarded as more drastic than anything being proposed by the political and economic reformers, Genevieve welcomed the socialists and populists as theoretical allies, even when many of them showed no sympathy for the woman's movement. But she was unprepared for the violent men and women that the Panic of 1893 unleashed on the country.

When William Randolph Hearst asked her to join him in his invasion of New York, Genevieve had requested two weeks off to speak on behalf of woman's rights in a dozen midwestern and eastern cities. She had no idea that she was exposing herself to shrill shrieking combat. Everywhere the anti-suffragists assaulted her with a ferocity that verged on the hysterical. Their numbers had grown ominously since Genevieve's first encounter with them in Denver, four years ago. It did not take her long to understand why.

On the outskirts of every city, Genevieve saw huge camps of unemployed men living in shacks and packing cases. Long lines of hungry men, women and children stood before soup kitchens set up by churches. On street corners, agitators roared radical solutions that made the West's populists seem like timid souls. Anarchists shouted for guerrilla war against the upper classes, like the one they had been waging against the crowned heads of Europe.

Communists bellowed that the economic collapse proved Karl Marx was right, the downfall of capitalism was inevitable. In this overheated atmosphere, it was easy to lump suffragists with other extremists who were trying to revolutionize America.

From another window, Genevieve looked downtown at Manhattan's amazing skyline. Scarcely one of the enormous office buildings that now filled the horizon had been there when she left New York seven years ago. By far the most eye-catching of the new stone and steel towers was the eleven-story red sandstone home of the New York *World,* with its gleaming gold dome. She wondered uneasily what Clay Pendleton would think of her, returning to New York with William Randolph Hearst to declare war on the *World.* She wished Hearst did not see the *World* as his natural rival. It was the old story of the young disciple deciding he could outdo the aging master. She wished she and Clay were not caught in the middle of the battlefield.

Genevieve wondered what they all thought of her, now that *Antiope's Story* was six years in the past. She had never heard a word from Alice Mayer since it was published. In a recent letter Laura had told her about the Mayers' devastating fall. She often saw Alice's twins, Adolph and Jeff, at Junior Assembly balls. Isaac Mayer had lost $50 million in the panic and had almost gone to jail for stock fraud. Only Senator Stapleton's intervention had rescued him. From a château on upper Fifth Avenue the Mayers had plunged to a small house in Chelsea.

Rawdon too had been ruined by the panic. His Caribbean Investment Company had collapsed. He was back in New York, working for a group of businessmen who had formed a Cuban-American League to protest Spanish restrictions on trade between the United States and Cuba. She wondered what he would be like now, after losing a second fortune. She remembered all too vividly the awful effect of losing so many millions in the Gould collapse of 1884. When he was drunk he accused her of putting a curse on him. He had called her a witch, an evil spirit. There were times when she had been sure that he was going to murder her. She wondered if Eleanor was bearing the brunt of this second disappointment.

As Genevieve left the Belvedere and started to cross Broadway, a brass band came umpah-pahing into Union Square. For a moment she wondered if she had lost track of some public holiday. Then she read the banner being carried by a half-dozen men in the rear rank: BUY THE NEW YORK JOURNAL. William Randolph Hearst was letting New York know he was in town.

For some reason, that made Genevieve feel a little more confident as she walked the next six blocks to the familiar brownstone house on Stuyvesant Square. Cynthia Stapleton welcomed her in the parlor. She was still an attractive woman, without a sign of gray in her curled, gleaming hair. Her rose-colored dress was emphatically in fashion, with its gored straight skirt, long-waisted bodice and balloon sleeves.

"I'm so *delighted* to see you," she said. "So pleased that you're back in New York."

Cousteau, his tan skin now crowned by a shock of white hair, was summoned and asked to serve tea. They sat down and Cynthia admired Genevieve's straight-rimmed straw hat and mannish gray suit and tie. "Do you realize how much you're in fashion?" she said. "I saw a photograph of the Archduchess Stephanie of Austria the other day, wearing almost exactly the same outfit."

"It's nice to know someone is listening to our campaign for sensible clothes."

"Someone! I think the whole country is listening. But I don't think you're entirely fair to women my age. For us a corset is a *necessity.*"

Genevieve smiled ruefully. "I may soon find that out from experience. I was forty last week."

"I doubt if you'll ever have to worry about your figure. I think you're more attractive now than you were when you married Rawdon. I hope you're going to give some New York men a chance to do more than admire you from a distance. Jonathan is convinced that you're the real reason why Clay Pendleton is still a bachelor, no matter how often Clay blames it on Pulitzer and his eighty-hour weeks."

Genevieve was surprised to discover how much pleasure those words stirred in her. "Do you see Clay often?"

"He comes to dinner whenever Jonathan's in town. Lest my previous remark go to your head, I'm sorry to report they spend most of their time discussing how to save the country."

"I'm glad someone is discussing it."

Genevieve told Cynthia about the unrest she had seen and heard on her trip east, including, almost as an afterthought, the anti-suffragists' attacks on her.

"It must be very painful for you—to discover that women are becoming your chief opponents."

"It is," Genevieve said.

What a relief it was to be able to confess this pain, to escape being Genevieve Dall, official spokesman and public figure, for a few minutes. She talked frankly about the disarray in the women's movement—the disagreements over tactics and goals, their perpetual financial problems. "We don't have enough money to run a genuine political campaign for the vote," she sighed. "We all have to support ourselves."

"What you need are a few wealthy women backers," Cynthia said.

"We're not likely to find them as long as everyone in the upper class considers us wild-eyed radicals," Genevieve said.

"Not all of us feel that way," Cynthia said. "I wish I could contribute much more than I do—but most of my money is tied up in Principia Mills at the moment."

Genevieve was too astonished to do more than murmur that she was delighted to know Cynthia was a supporter. She asked about the other members of the family. George was happily married and living in New Jersey, Senator Stapleton was in Washington. "I wish I could be with him," Cynthia said, "but I don't want to take Laura away from the friends she's made in New York. She needs some sense of permanence, of home, in her life."

"Yes. How . . . is she?" Genevieve asked as Cousteau placed the tea service in front of Cynthia.

"As well as can be expected—now that her father is living in New York and she sees him constantly."

"What do you mean?"

"I'm afraid Rawdon encourages her already defiant temperament. She also runs around with a group of sophisticated young ladies who all see themselves as Mademoiselle New York. Do you know that magazine?"

Genevieve shook her head. Cynthia asked Cousteau to bring them a copy of *M'lle New York* from Laura's bedroom. Genevieve flipped through the pages. They were full of illustrations in the decadent style of the English magazine *The Yellowbook*. All the men and women had heavy-lidded eyes and weary mouths, and struck poses of extravagant languor. In *M'lle New York* the women were more jaded than the men. They read Verlaine and the other French poets of fashionable despair and flirted with anarchism. Their ambition was to try everything, from free love to revolution, even though they expected to be disappointed by each experience.

Genevieve remembered her own youth, reading *Revolution* and other feminist publications that had shocked her mother. But those magazines had been a call to battle, they had challenged the reader with a vision of a better future. This magazine offered nothing but the consolation of sensuality.

"Why don't you bar this trash from the house?"

"She'd only read it in someone else's house and take it more seriously. Really, Genevieve. You moralists are all alike. Jonathan said the same thing."

Genevieve shook her head. "You can't allow a sixteen-year-old to read this sort of thing without challenging her."

Cynthia handed Genevieve a cup of tea. "That's precisely why I said I was glad you were back in New York. You told me a long time ago you wanted her raised as a woman, not a female. From *Antiope's Story* I would gather that meant you didn't want her spirit broken. Well, it's intact. Very much intact. That's the problem."

Was Cynthia laughing at her? Was she implying that the famous feminist's theories, when applied to her own daughter, had produced a monster?

"Please don't think I'm complaining. I love Laura very much. Having her here has meant a great deal to me and Jonathan. But I've never had any talent as a disciplinarian."

Surprised by Cynthia's honesty, Genevieve again dropped her public personality. "I know it's probably too late—I don't deserve any affection from her. But I'd like to try to establish some feeling between us."

"You will. I'm sure of it. She's really quite intrigued by you, even though she purports to be critical. You'll have to give her time. She still sides with Rawdon in your quarrel."

"I want to convince her that the quarrel is over as far as I'm concerned."

"I hope you're not looking for any sort of reconciliation with him," Cynthia said, with surprising sharpness.

"Just a truce."

"I'm not even sure that's possible." Cynthia hesitated, as if she was tempted to say more. "I don't want to be an alarmist, but this uproar Rawdon is trying to start about Cuba worries me. It's already having an effect on Laura."

An uproar over Cuba? Genevieve did not know what Cynthia was talking about. In California, Cuba and its problems were as remote as Corsica or Hungary.

Before she could ask a question, the front door slammed. There was a swirl of feminine voices in the hall. Laura paused in the parlor doorway like a confident actress savoring her entrance to the fullest.

"My famous mother," she cried, and rushed across the room to embrace Genevieve.

It was much too extravagant. Giggling in the doorway was the audience for whom the gesture was intended.

"Mother, I'd like you to meet my two dearest friends. They're completely decadent, but you're a woman of the world who's no doubt had scads of lovers in California and won't hold that against them."

They were obviously schoolgirls, but they affected the swaybacked languorous slouch of the world-weary women in *M'lle New York*. Gloria Atwood was a tall brittle-boned brunette, Ruth Kinsolving was blond and voracious-looking beneath her languor.

"They wanted to meet someone who'd actually spoken to Susan B. Anthony," Laura continued. "It's almost as historic as knowing George Washington."

"Miss Anthony isn't *that* old," Genevieve said.

Laura urged her to tell them about William Randolph Hearst. Was it true that he had a different mistress for each day of the week?

"He has a mistress, Tessie Powers, to whom he's remarkably faithful. His mother won't let him marry her, and Mrs. Hearst holds the purse strings."

"He's been squiring the Willson sisters around town," Laura said.

"Who are they?"

Eyes rolled. Anyone who did not recognize the Willson sisters was close to hopeless. "They're in *The Girl from Paris* at the Herald Square," Gloria Atwood said. "Two of the Merry Maidens."

"A dance group," Cynthia explained.

"Millicent Willson's only sixteen," Laura said.

"She's the one he's after," Ruth Kinsolving said.

"Maybe you should introduce me to Mr. Hearst, Mother," Laura said. "I wouldn't mind marrying a hundred million dollars."

"I don't find this conversation particularly amusing," Genevieve said. "Mr. Hearst's private life is his own business."

Laura's green eyes gleamed with satisfaction. She had provoked a rebuke. "Oh Mother, I'm *so* sorry," she said. "I'm only trying to be lighthearted so you won't worry about me. I have to spend most of my days with these boring creatures, discussing America's puerile art and literature, which leaves us enormously *triste*. Do you mind if we smoke?"

"Yes," Cynthia said. "I told you—seventeen is much too young for that habit."

All three rolled their eyes and slouched in unison. They could now be exasperated with both older generations.

"What we really want to talk about, Mother, is virginity," Laura said. "We think its value is exaggerated. At the next convention of the American Woman Suffrage Association, we want you to introduce a resolution calling for its abolition."

"I'll take that under advisement," Genevieve said, while Gloria and Ruth giggled. Cynthia suggested it might be time for them to go home, and they departed. She went off to write some letters and left Genevieve and Laura alone.

"Are you really as disillusioned with everything as you seem to be?" Genevieve asked.

"Oh, I don't know. Does it matter?" Laura said, throwing herself flamboyantly on the couch.

"It matters a great deal to me."

"But you and I are *different*, Mother," Laura said. "You lack a sense of beauty. That's what attracts me. Beautiful things, beautiful people. I see that as woman's primary role in life—cultivating, encouraging, creating beauty. Not fighting for the right to vote on the tariff or the free coinage of silver—all the boring idiotic things men quarrel about."

"I suppose that means my letters are boring. All that news and comment on the women's movement."

For a moment they faced each other, mother and daughter, woman and woman. "Yes," Laura said.

Bide your time, Cynthia had advised. But Genevieve found herself incapable of controlling her anger. "Since we're being so frank, let me tell you what I think of you. Judging from present appearances, I would say you are a deplorably spoiled, possibly immoral creature, who has been allowed to have her own way for so long you can't imagine there's anyone or anything that doesn't exist for your satisfaction. Along with working to support myself, I've traveled five thousand miles a year telling women in the West and Midwest that they can be independent, they can earn their own self-respect. What do I find when I visit my daughter? A woman whose only interest, aside from some vague ideas about beauty, is to find a husband worth a hundred million dollars."

"You don't have the slightest idea why I said that! You couldn't even begin to comprehend it!"

"Perhaps not. Would you mind at least trying to explain it?"

"Do you know what a *mano negro* is?"

"No."

"It's Spanish for anarchist. I'm going to be a *mano negro* among the rich. And convert my husband to the cause."

"That strikes me as an absolutely dreadful way to select a husband."

"That's exactly what Father predicted you'd say. You hate the idea of men and women working—and loving—together to create a better world. That's why you turned your back on Father when he needed you most."

Genevieve was speechless. Rawdon had told Laura about the shining message. Did it mean anything to him now? Or was it simply a device to sow hatred in Laura's soul? She struggled to defend herself.

"I don't hate the idea of men and women working and loving together. That's the fundamental principle of the woman's movement—working with and loving each other as equals."

"Men and women aren't equal and they never will be. When you try to force that idea down people's throats, they end up hating each other, like you and Father. Then men like Father lose faith in women and marry idiots like Eleanor."

Genevieve was staggered by this child-woman's capacity to hurt her. "I don't hate your father," she stammered. "I—I wish him well."

"Can a mere male interrupt this feminine reunion?"

Rawdon stood in the doorway in a tan suit, a small cigar in his hand. He was almost alarmingly thin. But it was the face that held Genevieve's attention. It had not aged at all. If anything, the loss of flesh had restored the magical image of the boy-man she had loved at Kemble Manor.

Genevieve was dazed and confounded by the sight. She had expected to meet a man embittered by frustration and disappointment. Something, someone, had restored him, or somehow defended him from these losses. Was it Eleanor? Or some inner vision that had escaped her?

He bent over Laura and kissed her on the lips. "How are you, my lady?" he said.

"Perfectly fine," she whispered. No mock affection, pretended adoration, here.

"May I offer the motheress the same gesture of peace?"

"Of course," Genevieve said. She turned her head, and his lips only brushed her cheek. But a tremor ran through her body.

"What were we talking about?" Rawdon said, sitting down on the couch beside Laura.

"The woman's movement," Laura said.

Rawdon threw up his hands like a man fending off a blow. "I plead not guilty and demand a change of venue," he said. "Can't we discuss something less likely to lead to violence?"

"I don't think we have anything more to say about it," Laura said, glaring at Genevieve.

"Good. I've gone out of the way to avoid the subject with this willful creature," he said, casually putting his arm around Laura's shoulder. "A declaration of independence would give her a license to break every heart in New York."

"Except yours," Laura said.

"No, mine too. Every woman I've ever known has broken my heart, one way or the other. Why should you be the exception?"

"You know perfectly well why," Laura said, the long lashes down, her face a sullen cloud. The ferocity of her devotion made Genevieve cringe.

"Why don't you go upstairs and do your homework for a while," Rawdon said. "Your mother and I have some things to discuss that will only bore you."

Laura gave Rawdon a coquettish kiss on the cheek and obeyed him.

"Isn't she marvelous?" Rawdon said when they were alone. "She's going to be the most spectacular female of her age."

The word "female" gnawed at Genevieve's nerves. "I think she's spoiled."

"Oh, you would. But that's going to be part of her attraction for some very rich young man."

"Rawdon—that's an absolutely abominable idea. Don't you care about her?"

"Of course I care. I'm encouraging her to choose the way of life that's best suited to her nature. Anyone that beautiful is destined to marry a rich man. But I've given her a reason for doing it, beyond a life of endless shopping sprees."

"You mean that nonsense about being a *mano negro* among the rich? Turning her husband into an anarchist?"

"Try 'revolutionary' instead of 'anarchist.' That may not bother you so much. You're a revolutionary in your pedestrian rational way."

"Rawdon—I'm afraid you'll have to fill me in on a few things. How did Jay Gould's favorite follower turn into an anarchist?"

Rawdon leaned back in his chair, a bitter smile on his face. "Do you think you're the only one who can rethink his life? The only one who can look back and see the moment when he let someone betray him into abandoning the person he was meant to be? Once I got the money out of my system down in Havana, I was able to start listening to people who've given some serious thought to the meaning of revolution."

He began a veritable oration on the Cuban yearning for freedom and justice. Genevieve cut him short. "I know absolutely nothing about Cuba. But I do know something about a woman's happiness. Reducing your daughter to a tool in a revolutionary struggle, however praiseworthy, is not a good idea."

"Does drafting her into the woman's movement make better sense? You and your fellow manhaters couldn't stand the thought of a woman who attracts men."

I am not a manhater. The women's movement does not hate men. The furious replies crowded in her throat. But Genevieve saw she was in no position to argue with Rawdon. "I don't think either of us should try to inflict our ideas on her. I've tried to avoid it."

"Oh sure you have," Rawdon said. "*Antiope's Story* was a wonderful way of avoiding it."

"That book was written by a woman struggling for her existence, Rawdon. Couldn't you see that?"

"It was *published* by a cold-eyed killer," Rawdon said. "Someone who was out to annihilate me in the eyes of my daughter, my father, my friends. But it didn't work with Laura. It actually gave me an opportunity to talk to her about my inner self—to share things with her that most fathers never tell their daughters."

"Rawdon," Genevieve said, "I'm willing to admit everything you claim about *Antiope's Story*—if you agree to a truce between us. An absolute stop to trying to influence Laura, one way or the other."

Rawdon fell back on the couch, his arms folded on his chest. "I'm not sure I can trust you."

"Give me a chance to prove I don't bear a grudge against you. If you want to know the truth, there are times when I feel regret—deep regret—about the summer of 1877. When I see what's happening in this country now, I wonder if it would be any worse off if something revolutionary had been tried then."

The smile on Rawdon's face sent a shiver of fear through Genevieve. It was almost triumphant. Did he think this confession gave him power over her? Could he be right?

"Okay," Rawdon said. "I agree to a truce." He popped a sweetmeat from the tea tray into his mouth. "What do you think of William Randolph Hearst?"

"I like him, personally. He's a tremendously generous boss."

"Has Mommy Hearst really given him seven million dollars to spend here in New York?"

"That's what he told us in San Francisco. I don't suppose it's a secret."

"Is he sincere about being on the side of the people against the predators of great wealth, as he calls them?"

"Yes. He proved it in California. He fought the railroad tycoons—Collis Huntington, Leland Stanford—who act as if they own the state. He'll do the same thing here, I'm sure of it."

"Do you think I could talk to him about Cuba? Frankly, we could use a little publicity. I sold myself to this Cuban-American League as a man who could get them space in New York newspapers, but so far I haven't had much luck. Eleanor is pregnant, after all these years. If I lose this job I'll be reduced to borrowing money from my brother George or my father."

Eleanor is pregnant. In spite of so many years of knowing that Rawdon and her sister were husband and wife, the words still caused pain.

"I'll speak to him about it," Genevieve said.

"I'd love to see Hearst cut Pulitzer and his faithful servant Pendleton down to size," Rawdon said. "They've become insufferably arrogant. You should hear the way Clay sneers at the *Journal* and everyone who works for it."

"He's going to get the surprise of his life," Genevieve said.

The next day, in the chaotic city room of the *New York Journal*, William Randolph Hearst greeted Genevieve with an exuberant smile. "Isn't this a great way to lose a hundred thousand dollars a month?" he said.

He beckoned her into a small office off the city room. There the smile vanished. In spite of the parades and the boasts about the *Journal*'s rising circulation, things were not going well. The mostly western editors and reporters he had brought with him from San Francisco were lost in New York. "I was about to hire a couple of private detectives to shanghai you off the lecture circuit. You're going to have to give me all your time and attention for a while."

Genevieve nodded. "I'm afraid I'm not very useful to the movement any-more," she said. She told him about the abuse she had taken on her trip to New York.

"Susan B. Anthony's loss is my gain," Hearst said. He had no real convic-tions about woman's rights. As far as Genevieve could see, he had no real convictions about anything. He attacked the rich, he supported the woman's movement because it excited people and that helped sell newspapers. "We need some women's stories—stuff that will appeal to young working girls. Have you got any ideas?"

"Prostitution. How women are lured into it. You never let me go after it in San Francisco. It's even worse here, and I know where to get the facts."

"Sounds good," Hearst said. "There aren't any girls here who might em-barrass me by telling stories about my father."

It was not easy to get Hearst's attention. While she had it, Genevieve asked him if he would see Rawdon on behalf of the Cuban-American League. Hearst winced. "He sent me a letter the other day. There's only about twenty thousand Cubans in New York and half of them can't read English. I don't see what's in it for us."

Genevieve plunged into the prostitution story. Mother Aloysius, now a crusty septuagenarian, was still in charge of the House of the Good Shep-herd. The situation had not changed an iota from the 1870s, she avowed. Prostitution had only gotten bigger—and more ethnically diversified.

But Genevieve had changed. As she prowled the streets of the Tenderloin, the new name for the old Satan's Circus district on the West Side below Times Square, trying to make friends with wary prostitutes, interviewing nervous policemen and surly politicians, she felt a diminution of her crusad-ing spirit, a loss of hope. The numbers of these smashed ruined women were so overwhelming, their stories so disheartening. She was forced to face how feeble her noble ideals, her brave speeches were in the struggle with the real world. No one in the Tenderloin had ever heard of *Antiope's Story* and its clever analysis of women's fate. Wisps of gray fog began to creep through Genevieve's mind and body.

Rawdon did not help by telephoning her and sarcastically suggesting she had no intention of getting him an interview with William Randolph Hearst. Nor did a venture to Chelsea help. Genevieve visited Alice Mayer hoping to heal the breach between them.

Alice sat in her shabby living room in a dirty calico housedress and served tea in chipped cups and complained about her health. "The ordeal," as she called the Mayers' financial collapse, had affected her heart, her digestion. She was still preoccupied with money and status, not in her old proud exul-tant way but with the bitter obsession of loss. Genevieve listened to a litany of people who had failed to help them because Isaac was Jewish, to the brutal details of the way creditors had seized their yacht, their horses and carriages, their mansion.

Suddenly Alice was weeping. "Isaac blames me. He says I turned him against his family, his people. He—hates me—and this country. He's talking about going back to Germany."

"Oh Alice . . ." Instinctively Genevieve reached out to take Alice's hand. Alice withdrew it as if her touch was poisonous. "How does rational love deal with something like that? Can you tell me, Antiope? What does the new woman have to say?"

"This isn't the new woman who came to see you. It's your old friend—who wants to help if she can."

"You didn't come here to help. You came to gloat. You're one of the radicals who turned European investors against America. You're just like your father, ready to destroy this country to push your fanatical ideas down people's throats. But there's one thing you can't take away from me. I have four children who love me. That's more than you can say."

Genevieve was not in the best of moods when she answered a telephone call at the *Journal* and a secretary asked her if she would hold on for the managing editor of the *New York World*, Clay Pendleton. It took him at least two minutes to come on the line.

"How are you?" he said. "I'm sorry I didn't greet you with a brass band. But your boss seems to have hired every one in town."

"Circulation is up a hundred thousand," she said. "Maybe you ought to try it."

"Hey—I'm calling Genevieve Dall, not the Queen of the Amazons. How about dinner?"

He made a date to meet her in Delmonico's on Beaver Street and kept her waiting a half hour. "Sorry," he said, sliding into the banquette and kissing her on the cheek. "Pulitzer telephoned as I was walking out the door."

"Why didn't you keep walking?"

"Where? Over to see Willie the Wunderkind? He's called me three times already. He's trying to hire editors and reporters all over town. It doesn't say much for his confidence in his staff."

"You could do worse. He's a very considerate boss."

"But where's the brain? He's just a cheap imitation of Pulitzer."

"Really, Clay. That's my paper, my boss you're talking about."

Clay ordered a drink and muttered something about not being used to dining with Amazons. Before she could tell him she was getting tired of that designation, he began deploring Rawdon's Cuban-American League. He told her that Lionel Bradford was threatening to sue Rawdon because he had siphoned a lot of money from the defunct Caribbean Investment Company into the league. Clay claimed it was really a front group which was buying weapons and ammunition for a revolutionary army that was planning to invade Cuba.

"Personally, I think Rawdon plans to set himself up as the dictator of Cuba or the power behind the scene if the revolution succeeds. He wants to own the whole damn island."

"What if you found out he was sincere?"

"I'd be the most surprised newspaperman in the country."

"I think you're being grossly unfair to him, Clay."

It was appalling, the chill those words inflicted on the rest of the evening. Clay retreated to talking journalist to journalist, which inevitably led to more boasting about the size and power of the *World* and his confidence that they were going to demolish Hearst and the *Journal.*

Back in her room at the Belvedere, Genevieve stood at the window looking down at deserted Union Square. Suddenly the streetlights began to blur. She was weeping. What was wrong with her? What had she expected to happen? Did she think that a man whom she had ignored for seven years had actually waited for her? The managing editor of the *World* had his pick of the most beautiful women in New York. Clay was probably in bed with one of them now, laughing about his crazy go-round with this female icicle, Genevieve Dall, the famous Amazon.

The next day, Rawdon invited her to an "indignation meeting" that Cuban exiles were staging in the auditorium of Cooper Union. The audience was about fifty percent American. Genevieve sat in the front row with Rawdon while orators shouted abuse of Spain in both English and Spanish. The climax of the evening was a speech by a small slim man with blazing eyes, whom Rawdon identified as José Martí, the leader of the exiles. He spoke in both languages. His English speech was an earnest plea for American support, quoting statistics to prove Spain's exploitation of Cuba, citing the help that America had given revolutionary leaders such as Hungary's Kossuth and Italy's Garibaldi.

Martí's Spanish speech was totally different. It was an ecstatic sermon, snatches of which Rawdon translated for Genevieve. Eyes closed, almost chanting his words, Martí offered his fellow Cubans a vision of a nation in which love and trust would be the principles of government, in which every citizen would have a voice in his destiny. The impact on the Cubans was incredible. They leaped to their feet, tears streaming down their faces, shouting revolutionary slogans.

"Now maybe you understand why I want to help these people," Rawdon said.

Afterward, they joined Martí and his followers at La Liga, a school for revolutionaries that he ran in a building on Bleecker Street. Rawdon introduced Genevieve to the Cuban leader, and Martí asked Rawdon a question in Spanish. Rawdon responded in the same language and smiled at Genevieve. "He wants to know if you're on our side. I told him you were just beginning to discover the truth about the Monster."

Martí took her hand and spoke with the intense, almost ecstatic self-confidence of a man who has discovered an ability to mesmerize audiences. "As a reporter, you are in the front lines of this struggle. We depend utterly on changing public opinion about Cuba. Only we few who have lived in the Monster's lair with open eyes know what is at stake—the freedom not only of Cuba but of all of Spanish America. Only an independent Cuba can prevent the Monster from devouring the rest of the New World."

It took Genevieve a moment to realize that the Monster was the United States of America. She nodded, although she was not ready to use that anarchist term to describe her country. She was trapped by the words she had spoken to Rawdon in the Stapleton parlor, by her promise to prove to him— and to Laura—that she was not his enemy.

That evening, Genevieve marched into Hearst's office and gave him a preview of the prostitution story as it was building up. Then she told Hearst what she had seen and heard at the indignation meeting and renewed her plea for Rawdon.

"You going soft on this guy again?" Hearst said. "I thought he made your life miserable once."

"Nothing of the sort," Genevieve said. "It's a good cause, that's all. It deserves a little help."

Hearst was still dubious. But he wanted to keep one of his best reporters happy. "Okay," he said. "Tell him to drop by around midnight."

Hearst and Rawdon both strolled into the *Journal*'s deserted city room at twelve-thirty. Hearst had two brunette beauties in tow. He introduced Genevieve and Rawdon to Anita and Millicent Willson. Tessie Powers had apparently failed to make the transition to New York. Millicent Willson was more regal as well as more beautiful than blond, good-natured Tessie.

Hearst explained that he had to put the paper to bed. Rawdon asked if he could join him. "Why not?" Hearst said, and left Genevieve in charge of the Willsons.

"Oh look," Millicent said. "Willie's put up the picture of Napoleon."

On the wall behind Hearst's desk was a portrait of the French emperor gazing across a tumultuous battlefield. "He's buying statues and books and pictures of him all the time," Anita Willson said.

Genevieve had not even noticed the portrait. There had been an odd resurgence of interest in Napoleon in recent years. Dozens of novels and history books had been published, most of them glorifying him as a supreme military genius. The portrait made her realize how little she really knew about William Randolph Hearst's inner life.

Moments later, Rawdon and Hearst returned to the office. "Genevieve," Hearst said, "why didn't you tell me this guy was an ex-newspaperman? Now I know why you divorced him."

Hearst sat down behind his desk. "Okay," the Californian said with a skeptical smile, "tell me why I should get worked up about Cuba."

Rawdon lit one of his small cigars. "There's going to be a revolution in Cuba," he said. "A revolution that William Randolph Hearst can inspire and support. A revolution that can make him a hero to the American people and raise the *Journal*'s circulation to a million copies a day when the United States declares war on Spain."

Hearst sat there, still with a smile on his broad face. But it was no longer skeptical; it was a smile of fascination, beguilement. It occurred to Genevieve that these two men had a great deal in common. Both were born rich, both had a tendency to grandiose dreams.

"Genevieve," Hearst said, "why don't you show Millie and Anita around the paper while Mr. Stapleton and I have a talk."

THREE

As usual, sleep eluded Clay Pendleton in the bedroom Joseph Pulitzer had outfitted for the managing editor of the *World* on the floor below the golden dome. Pendleton lay there while images, worries, memories swirled through his overtired mind.

Image: Lionel Bradford opening a thick white envelope in his suite in the Hotel Splendide in Paris. An explosion blows off two thirds of his face.

Worry: Another random triumph for anarchism? Or did it have something to do with Bradford's offer to tell Pendleton how Rawdon Stapleton had swindled him and a lot of other capitalists to finance the Cuban revolution that was burning down or blowing up the plantations and factories and railroads they thought they owned?

Memory: Erma Jane Hogg, secretary to the editor of the *Sunday World*, standing in the doorway of his office, saying, "Mr. Pendleton—they're gone."

Pendleton bolted downstairs to the floor where Morrill Goddard and his staff produced the hundred-page extravaganza known as the *Sunday World*. Erma Jane Hogg had told the truth. The place was empty. Abandoned.

Typewriters sat on the desks beside half-written stories. William Randolph Hearst had stolen the most profitable Sunday paper in the country, the publication that produced more than half of the million dollars Joseph Pulitzer banked last year.

Image: Joseph Pulitzer with his blank eyes drilling through Pendleton like the death rays that science fiction writers imagined in the *Sunday World*. He is wearing a bloodstained apron. In his hand he waves a large cleaver. A berserk butcher, he screams at Pendleton, "You fucking idiot!"

Worry: What if nightmares, like other dreams, sometimes came true?

Image: Genevieve Dall, in the revealing outfit of a fourth-century B.C. Amazon, is stretched out on two shoved-together desks in a city room. Above her, wearing surgeon's gowns, hover Rawdon Stapleton and a grinning William Randolph Hearst. In Rawdon's hand is a scalpel. Hearst lifts Genevieve's mane of chestnut hair, revealing her delicate ears. They are going to amputate them. Genevieve does not say a word. All Pendleton can see is submission in her gray eyes.

Worry: Was he going crazy?

Pendleton sat up in bed, his heart pounding, his nightshirt soaked with sweat. Pulitzer expected the managing editor of the *World* to sleep—or try to sleep—in this monk's cell at least four nights a week. Otherwise he could not expect to be managing editor for very long. That was all right with Pendleton. After four years of cohabiting with Nelly Bly, he had decided that sleeping alone was not such a bad idea.

For Nelly, Pendleton had been job insurance. The clinging, lovable little Lizzie he had seen in the first installment had vanished almost as quickly as one of the disguises Nelly assumed for her stories. Ironically, she turned out to be good for Pendleton's career too. In 1889, he came up with the ultimate invented story for Nelly. He sent her racing around the globe by steamship, train, rickshaw and sampan to see if she could beat the 80-day record of Jules Verne's fictional hero. Nelly did it in seventy-two days, six hours and eleven minutes, jumping the *World*'s circulation 100,000 copies with story after sensational story. It had made Nelly internationally famous. An ecstatic Pulitzer made Pendleton his managing editor.

Thereafter, with job insurance no longer necessary, only sentiment kept them together for a while, a sort of mutual fondling of the sort someone might give a rabbit's foot that had worked. As a celebrity, Nelly attracted the attention of a lot of other men. She showed what really interested her by marrying a seventy-two-year-old millionaire and quitting the newspaper business.

Pendleton changed his nightshirt, pulled on his pants and lit a Sweet Caporal cigarette. He wandered across the empty city room and up the stairs to the dome. A long way down, he thought, staring at the hydra-headed monster known as New York, blinking its million and one eyes into the darkness.

The empty Sunday editorial room had been the beginning of the madness. Hearst had already hired away the *World*'s political cartoonist and a half-dozen other talented people. Pulitzer had done the same sort of pirating from the *Herald* and other papers when he came to New York thirteen years ago, but no one except Willie Hearst had ever had the gall, or the money, to buccaneer an entire staff—twenty people, and the editor in chief.

It was also the beginning of the phrase that made Pendleton writhe: yellow journalism. Wrapped around the outside of the *Sunday World* was a cartoon feature called "The Yellow Kid." The cartoonist had jumped to Hearst with the rest of the staff, but the *World* hired a new artist and continued the cartoon. With both papers drenched in the same color, it did not take long for someone on the *Herald* to invent the loathsome term.

Genevieve Dall's indifference to the term had been the final step in their depressing decline from friendship tinged with the hope of something deeper to cool, almost antagonistic indifference. For a while Pendleton could not decide whether they were victims of the war between Pulitzer and Hearst or of the war between men and women that Genevieve also seemed to be fighting.

Like everyone else at the *World*, including Pulitzer, Pendleton had totally underestimated William Randolph Hearst. The Californian's readiness to spend $7 million transcended ordinary imagination. It was over the border-line of sanity.

Like any reasonably red-blooded American male, Pendleton was irked by Genevieve's determination to prove that she and the rest of the Hearst crew could outslug the mighty Pulitzer dreadnought in its home waters. Her accomplishments over the next few months did little to soothe Pendleton's nerves. She published a series of sensational articles on the connections between New York's prostitutes and Tammany politicians and policemen. The Irish gangs of the seventies had been replaced by Jewish "cadets" who lured young women into prostitution with seduction and flattery and drugs. Public outrage was stupendous. While cops and politicians scurried for cover, Hearst gleefully fired off ten thousand dollars' worth of fireworks on the Battery and posed as a defender of the working woman's embattled virtue.

"Now do you believe me?" Miss Dall had asked in her cheeriest, most Amazonian tone the next time they had dinner.

What made Pendleton's pain exquisite was the quiet radiance that the restored Genevieve Dall emanated in these first few meetings. The potential woman he had glimpsed in their youth had been achieved, at least to Pendleton's longing eyes. She moved with a confident grace, she wore her suits and dresses with carefree style, adding a rose to a mannish coat, a flowery hat to a plain white shirtwaist and black skirt. That erotic mouth could go from stern to tender in a blink of those gray-blue eyes.

But the Darwinian struggle for survival made all this irrelevant. "We have not yet begun to fight," muttered Captain Pendleton, grimly lashing himself to his shattered mainmast. Dinners with Miss Dall became infrequent as Pendleton maneuvered his dreadnought to fire broadside after broadside into the upstart Hearstlings. But no matter how many direct hits he scored, no matter how many times Pulitzer declared the battle won, the Croesus from California slapped another million dollars across the damage and sailed blithely on, using ammunition that grew more and more yellow until both sides were covered with that repulsive color.

On that point, Hearst never showed the slightest remorse. Far from writhing at the term yellow journalist, Hearst glorified in it as proof that he was a man of the people. He even organized a transcontinental "yellow fellow" bicycle race in which all the contestants wore the color.

No matter how splotched they became, for a while Admiral Pulitzer and Captain Pendleton kept the *World* on course. The presidential campaign of 1896 had been—Pendleton thought—the ultimate test. Pulitzer detested the Democratic candidate, William Jennings Bryan, and his crackpot ideas about creating cheap dollars with the free coinage of silver. Hearst backed Bryan and threatened to become the voice of the Democratic Party in New York— something that was bound to cost the *World* readers. Pulitzer never wavered. The *World* refused to back either candidate, and in one brilliant editorial after another, many of them written by Pulitzer personally, the paper tried to educate the nation on the danger of Bryan's brainless crusade. Pulitzer proved that he cared more about the country than he cared about circulation or the Democratic Party.

Bryan lost by 500,000 votes and the republic was saved from disaster once more. On Election Day, Hearst's *New York Journal* printed 956,921 copies of the morning edition and 437,401 of the evening edition. The *World* printed a few thousand more—but it was evident that Hearst had made an enormous gain.

As the uproar over Bryan subsided and William McKinley's Republican administration took office, Hearst unlimbered the secret weapon Rawdon Stapleton had been developing for him. Cuba rose in revolt against the Spaniards, and the struggle of the heroic rebels was flung in the faces of newspaper readers with a demand for U.S. assistance. The very first battle gave Hearst an instant hero. The Cubans' charismatic leader José Martí got a bullet in the head, aborting Pendleton's plan to expose him as a two-faced liar who whispered adulation into the ears of his American backers and told his Cuban followers the *gringos* were capitalist swine.

At first no one on the *World*—or any other newspaper—grasped the ruthlessness of Hearst's approach. They sent reporters to Havana to cover this minor war with no special expectations. Failed uprisings were almost as common in Cuba as hurricanes. Only when one lurid story after another with *faked* visible in every line leaped from the *Journal*'s presses did Hearst's fervent support for a free Cuba make sudden, sickening sense.

As these yellow fictions sent the *Journal*'s circulation soaring, Pendleton had yet another dinner date with Genevieve Dall. When he began denouncing Rawdon and her employer as a pair of liars, Genevieve shook her head and began telling him how completely Rawdon had captured Laura's devotion with this crusade. Pendleton could only stare in disbelief at the defeat on Genevieve Dall's face. Guilt, remorse, were consuming her Amazonian soul. It was demoralizing—and infuriating. "What about the truth?" he said, pounding the table.

All she could do was shake her head. She did not care about the one thing that still mattered to him, the only source of satisfaction in his lonely life. Pendleton let Pulitzer make the money and the reporters get the glory; his satisfaction was those truth-telling broadsides that his dreadnought could fire into the faces of that baffling entity, the American people. He had become Jonathan Stapleton's son, the lonely realist, stained by commerce and compromise, consoled by a private vision of duty.

But Genevieve Dall did not care about Pendleton's shining message. She did not share his detestation of that leprous American newspaper tradition of faking it. Antiope was still a woman, tormented by the fear that she was a failure at love.

Pendleton scoffed at the idea that Rawdon was sincere. He insisted that the whole thing was a performance, designed to put Rawdon back in Havana as king of his little capitalist hill again. Even if he was sincere, anarchism was an idiotic creed, a bizarre compound of love for humanity in the abstract and class hatred which permitted the true believer to kill and maim the innocent as well as the guilty. He cited recent European examples, among them the murderous bomb blast in a Paris railroad café that left over fifty dead. But Genevieve was not listening. She could only talk about Laura, her fanatic enthusiasm for her father's cause, her refusal to tolerate anyone who disagreed with him. That was when Pendleton glimpsed Genevieve's new vulnerability to Rawdon.

There was nothing he could do about it. He was too busy trying to save his job. He was, at the bottom, too disappointed in her failure to care about the truth. He decided to stop seeing her. The whole thing was too complicated anyway. Every time they met, he risked one of the innumerable informers on the *World* telling Pulitzer that Pendleton was communicating with the enemy.

Pendleton turned on one of Mr. Edison's magic bulbs and opened an atlas to a map of Cuba. The long narrow island dangled off the tip of Florida like a piece of bait in the blue Caribbean. He thought about the mocking letters Rawdon sent him, urging him to switch to Hearst before it was too late. He thought about the things the *World* should be doing, such as trying to connect the murder of Lionel Bradford to Rawdon and the Cuban-American League.

Or printing some intelligent reporting on Spain to help people understand her determination to keep Cuba.

Or investigating the local brigands of Tammany Hall, who had just seized control of newly created Greater New York, a bizarre unworkable oh-so-plunderable megalopolis that included Brooklyn, the Bronx, Queens and Staten Island.

Instead, all the wealth, the intelligence, the power of the greatest newspaper in the United States was being absorbed by a sputtering revolution on this trivial leftover piece of Spain's lost empire.

The next morning at breakfast in a hash house near the *World*, Pendleton paged through a copy of the late city edition. Beside it, he studied a copy of Hearst's *Journal*, comparing the coverage of every story. He knew that Pulitzer would be doing the same thing on his estate in Florida later in the day, and Pendleton had to be ready to defend himself.

Basically, there was only one story these days. DOES OUR FLAG PROTECT WOMEN? howled the *Journal* headline, in five-inch type—a Hearst innovation.

SPANISH BUTCHER UNARMED PRISONERS, boomed the *World* in the same size type.

The *Journal* story included a half-page sketch by Frederic Remington, portraying three naked women surrounded by leering Spanish officers. The story told how three innocent Cuban maidens had been pursued aboard the American ship *Olivette*, brutally stripped on the open deck while the crew watched helplessly, and searched with sadistic intensity to make sure they were not carrying rebel dispatches to New York.

The *World* lead told how the Spaniards had executed fifty Cuban rebel prisoners. It described how one man's arms and legs had been hacked off by Spanish sabers and formed into a crude version of the Cuban five-pointed star. The story was replete with gouged eyes, chopped-out tongues and missing ears. Unfortunately it was only a pale imitation of a slaughter the *Journal* had described a week ago. No matter how hard the *World*'s reporters tried, they could not compete with Rawdon Stapleton and the brigade of fictioneers he had trained to perfection in the severed-ear school of journalism.

Peering over his shoulder, Pendleton's waitress expressed the outrage of the average reader. "If I was a man, I'd volunteer to fight them Spaniards. They're monsters," she said.

"If I was a man I'd do the same thing," Pendleton said. "Unfortunately I'm only a newspaper editor."

Whitney Branch, the *World*'s boyish city editor, sat down at the table. "It looks like we lose another round," he said, gesturing to the papers.

It was common knowledge that Branch was after Pendleton's job. "I'll bet a month's salary that stuff about the nude search never happened," Pendleton growled.

Branch shrugged, implying that Pendleton's argument was irrelevant. He and Branch had argued violently over Cuba. When Rawdon and his fictioneers began filling the *Journal* with faked gore, Pendleton had ordered the *World*'s man in Cuba to refute the stories. Branch had recommended recalling this veteran correspondent with his archaic ideas about telling the truth and replacing him with a half-dozen reporters who understood "the ideals of the Cuban revolution." He announced he was an expert on this subject and had been educating a circle of followers at the city desk in the small hours of the morning, when ordinary newspapermen were either asleep or out drinking and whoring.

When the *Journal*'s circulation began to soar, the other four members of the *World*'s general staff, who shared power more or less equally with Pendleton, became violently concerned for their jobs and backed Branch. Pendleton was forced to ship some of Branch's experts in revolutionary warfare to Havana. They were soon sending dispatches containing such epiphanies as "blood on the roadsides, blood in the fields, blood on the doorsteps, blood, blood, blood!"

Pendleton waited for an explosion of reproof from Pulitzer, the man who once put ACCURACY in large signs all over the *World*'s city room. Not a word was heard from the wanderer in his yacht *Liberty*. The message was unmistakable. Accuracy had been replaced by circulation in the Pulitzer canon.

Upstairs beneath the golden dome, Pendleton wondered if it was time to try an end run on Branch. It might be impossible to refute Hearst's lies in Havana, where stories depended on unidentified eyewitnesses who disappeared back into the bush. Catching the yellow fellow in a whopper here in New York, with other papers ready and eager to confirm the deception, might do some real damage—and prove that truth was not irrelevant after all.

A barked order worthy of John Reid brought blond Helen Blair, Nelly Bly's current replacement, to his office. "The *Olivette*, the ship with those three violated Cuban virgins aboard, should be arriving sometime today. Hire a tug and meet her off Ambrose Light. Find out what really happened to them."

Blair looked puzzled.

"What's wrong?" Pendleton snapped.

"Isn't it a good story?"

"It's a great story. But I don't think it's true."

Blair's frown suggested she too thought Pendleton's interest in the truth was irrelevant. She had her own reasons. The *Olivette* story was the sort of thing a woman could have covered far better than a man. She began telling him about a discussion of Cuba they had had last night at the Women's Press Club. The women reporters—there were now at least a dozen in the city— criticized the male coverage of the war as too exclusively military.

"I wish you'd send me to Havana. Hearst is sending Genevieve Dall."

"What?" Pendleton said. He had been translating a coded telegram from Pulitzer demanding to know why profits were down.

"Hearst is sending Genevieve Dall to Cuba. We passed a resolution at the press club, congratulating him. It's about time we had a woman war correspondent. Would you consider sending me?"

"I'll take it up with Mr. Pulitzer. In the meantime, hire that tug and get me the facts on this story."

Pendleton spent most of the day in tense conferences with his fellow *World* executives, discussing news policy, promotion, story ideas and finances. The telegram from Pulitzer had everyone puffing Sweet Caporals at a record pace.

Back in the office his secretary handed Pendleton another telegram. This one was from Washington.

OUTRAGED OVER WORLD'S CONTINUED FAILURE TO TELL AMERICAN PEO-PLE THE TRUTH ABOUT CUBAN WAR. THE SPANISH ARE CLEARLY WINNING. WHY ARE YOU LETTING HEARST MAKE YOU THE TAIL TO HIS YELLOW KITE?

Pendleton sighed. He got this sort of message from Senator Stapleton almost as often as he got coded threats from Pulitzer. The Senator was a fierce foe of the prowar party that was gaining strength every day in America. He made speeches in the Senate exposing Hearst and Pulitzer atrocity stories as lies.

As the Senator saw it, no one could expect the Spaniards to negotiate with the rebels as long as they had guns in their hands. Lincoln had inflexibly maintained the same principle in the war with the South. Once peace was restored, the United States could urge compassion and generosity on Spain. Of course, the Spanish Captain General, Valeriano Weyler, was bringing peace to Cuba the same way that Grant and Sherman had pacified the South —by shooting rebels wherever he found them. He had recently killed a Cuban general and driven his army into ragtag flight. There was mounting evidence that the revolt might end the way previous Cuban revolutions had ended—in a sad fizzle.

About 10 P.M., Whitney Branch stuck his head in the door. "Hot news.

The Youngstown Chamber of Commerce has struck a blow at the cruel Spaniards by voting to boycott the Spanish onion."

"Page one, definitely," Pendleton said.

They went down to the composing room and began laying out the paper. Sylvester Scovel, the *World*'s star reporter in Cuba, had gotten himself arrested by the Spaniards for trying to sneak out of Havana to find a live rebel soldier. Scovel had smuggled a letter from his prison cell, and this was the lead story. It reeked of the usual gore. The sound of breaking bones was heard in the night. The screams of the tortured and dying resounded all day.

"Maybe he should change his name to Shovel," Pendleton said.

"It's good stuff," Branch said.

Pendleton bit his tongue. Branch was one of the *World*'s most diligent informers. Any remark deemed detrimental or hostile to prevailing policy was certain to reach Pulitzer if it was spoken within range of the city editor's eager ears.

About eleven o'clock the assistant city editor, Carl Newman, appeared with a story not yet set in type. "Blair's had an interview with those three doxies on the *Olivette*. She showed them the *Journal* sketch and they were outraged. They said it didn't happen that way at all. They were searched by three policewomen in a cabin, and they didn't take off all their clothes even there."

"Let's make it the lead," Pendleton said.

"And drop Scovel?" Branch said.

"He'll still be the second lead."

"But he's our story."

"Let's lead with the truth for once," Pendleton said.

The silence was instantaneous—and ominous. But Pendleton, survivor of thirteen years with Pulitzer, was not listening. He scribbled a headline: THE UNCLOTHED WOMEN SEARCHED BY MEN WAS AN INVENTION OF A NEW YORK NEWSPAPER. It was not a *World* headline. It belonged in the *Times* or the *Tribune*. No one said a word against it. Pendleton should at least have written a headline Pulitzer would approve, such as NUDE SEARCH OF FRANTIC CUBAN FEMALES A FRAUD. The combination of the news about Genevieve Dall and the telegram from Jonathan Stapleton had disrupted the delicate mechanism of survival in Pendleton's psyche.

The following day, editors from the *Tribune* and the *Times* shook Pendleton's hand and congratulated him in the Hoffman House bar. The *Journal* had been full of resolutions from a half-dozen congressmen and senators, demanding explanations and retaliation for the supposed insult to the American flag and female virtue aboard the *Olivette*.

Hearst's face should have been red. But it went right on being yellow. Without even apologizing to the befuddled politicians, the following day the

Journal's headlines roared another atrocity: A Cuban dentist named Ricardo Ruiz, a naturalized American citizen who had been arrested for robbing a train, had been found dead in his cell. The Spanish warden said he had committed suicide. The *Journal* screamed the Spaniards were now murdering Americans.

The next day Pendleton got a telegram from Pulitzer informing him that the *Journal*'s press run with the sketch of the three stripped Cuban women on the front page had been a record—over a million copies. "WHY BOTHER TO CORRECT HEARST'S LIES AND MAKE THE WORLD THE TAIL TO THE JOURNAL'S KITE? THE WORLD SHOULD LEAD LEAD LEAD." The telegram was signed "SEDENTARY," which meant that an immediate reply was expected. Pendleton telegraphed: "SEMAPHORE," which meant that he understood the message.

That afternoon a baffling story arrived on the Atlantic cable from Madrid. The Prime Minister of Spain had been assassinated by an anarchist. No one could decide whether it meant anything. For one thing, the anarchist was an Italian. Was it just another crazy assault on the ruling class by the believers in propaganda by the deed? Or was there some connection to the situation in Cuba? Once more Pendleton silently cursed their ignorance of Spanish politics.

As Pendleton debated with his fellow editors, who were inclined to play the assassination down, his secretary told him he had a telephone call from Washington. "Clay?" Jonathan Stapleton said. "I've got some important news. The new Spanish Prime Minister will be a liberal. He's going to recall General Weyler and try to work out a compromise with the Cubans. They're going to give them autonomy, their own government, everything short of independence. Now is the time for the *World* to about-face and back this thing. It's the last chance for peace."

"You better talk to Pulitzer about that, General. I can't make that kind of decision."

"You can influence it, Clay. See if you can line up the other top men. I'll wire Pulitzer tonight."

"What's the mood in Congress?"

"The Senate is just about evenly divided. The House is hungry for war and isn't likely to change its mind. But President McKinley is determined to avoid war. He's sending me to Spain as a special envoy to see if we can work out a deal."

"Jesus Christ, General, that's our lead story."

"Don't make me sound like a glory hound, Clay. I didn't call you for any personal publicity."

Pendleton sighed. The man was incredible. "Don't worry."

Pendleton ordered the first page torn apart to make the peace initiative the lead. He pushed James Creelman, another of the *World*'s Havana fictioneers, to the bottom of the page although the story had more than the usual quota of severed ears. The peace mission caught the *Journal* still roaring about the death of Dr. Ruiz. But Hearst recovered in time to comment on it in the late-city edition, showering the President and the Senator with terrific abuse.

Meanwhile, Pendleton convened a meeting of the *World*'s executives and proposed a change of policy. He wanted them to sign a statement recommending that Pulitzer back the new Spanish government and peace. There was no enthusiasm whatsoever for the idea. Whitney Branch predicted that the switch would cost them fifty thousand copies a day. As they argued, a reporter stuck his head in the door of the dome room to tell them that Pulitzer's yacht, *Liberty,* had been sighted off Ambrose Light.

Pendleton went back to his office and dictated a letter to Pulitzer, recommending the change in policy. He made it clear that no one else in the top echelon agreed with him. "The aberration is mine and mine alone. But I think we owe it to ourselves and perhaps to the country," he said.

He had just signed the letter when his secretary handed him an envelope. In it was a card with an undoubtedly private phone number and a one-line scrawl: "Mr. Hearst would be pleased if you would call him." It was Pendleton's fifth or sixth invitation.

Pendleton telephoned the *New York Journal* and asked for Genevieve Dall. He got the assistant city editor, who said she was out on an assignment. He left his name. Four hours later, while he was conferring with Whitney Branch on how to deal with the latest blood-soaked special from one of his revolutionary reporters, Genevieve called back. Branch's big decidedly unsevered ears quivered when he heard her name.

"I hear you're going to Cuba," Pendleton said.

"Yes," she said. "I'm leaving tomorrow."

"Who's idea was it?"

"Mr. Hearst's."

"You're sure it wasn't Rawdon's?"

"Perhaps. Does it matter?"

"I don't think you should go anywhere near that damn island."

"Why not?"

"Do you really like the idea of having Rawdon for your boss?"

"That's my worry, isn't it?"

She was telling him that this outburst of solicitude was both unwelcome and insulting—and she was right. Having devoted most of the past year to maneuvering his dreadnought and fighting off Whitney Branch's creeping mutiny, he had lost the ability to speak as a friend.

"Let's have dinner tonight," he said. "Maybe I can explain myself."

"I can't. I'm having dinner with Cynthia and Laura."

"Well, bon voyage. I hope you prove you can lie like a man."

"I'm not going to tell any lies. I intend to make that very clear."

"Good luck."

The next day, from his window in the dome, Pendleton could see the sleek *Liberty* at anchor off the Seventy-second Street yacht basin in the Hudson. Around 3 P.M., one of Pulitzer's secretaries called. The Great Man wanted to see Pendleton in one hour.

In the main stateroom, the walls draped with dark-green damask to protect the owner's nerves against external and internal noises, there were no pleasantries. Pulitzer waved a letter at him. "I got this screed from Stapleton," he said. "No doubt you put him up to it."

"No one puts General Stapleton up to things. You know that, Mr. Pulitzer."

"How does he talk so knowingly of *World* policy?"

"He reads the paper, Mr. Pulitzer."

"And you're his echo, is that it?"

"You know that isn't true, Mr. Pulitzer."

"I know you're trying to take my paper away from me, Pendleton. You call unauthorized meetings of the staff and try to convince them to change our policy. How do I know you're not secretly working for Hearst? That would be the ultimate trick, wouldn't it?"

"If you think that's true, Mr. Pulitzer, why don't you just fire me and get it over with?"

"I don't think it's true. I pride myself on judging character, Pendleton. I want to find out what's happened to you. You've always been the brightest, the most dependable of my editors. Is it this Dall doxie? Has she unscrewed your brain and turned you into a Hearst fink? I know all about you, Pendleton. I have a file of reports on you from your colleagues that's at least a foot thick by now. What's eating you?"

"I don't know, Mr. Pulitzer. You'll have to tell me sometime."

"You replied 'Semaphore' in your last telegram. You know what I want. What I have *ordered*. Why aren't you doing it?"

Pulitzer was shouting now. At any moment the rage would begin. First the sarcasm, then the rage, the expletives.

"Because I think it's wrong, Mr. Pulitzer. Wrong for the *World*. Wrong for the country."

The obscenities, allegations about the morals of Pendleton's mother, the mongrel status of his father, his resemblance to various parts of the anatomy not mentioned in polite society, thudded off the soundproofed walls. "You think it's wrong to refuse to let that ignoramus from California destroy me, wrong to fight for my paper's survival? Now I know what's eating you, Pendleton. I see what you've struggled to keep secret all these years. You're a coward."

Pulitzer was erupting, but the earthquake was in Pendleton's soul. The self he had struggled to construct since he confronted Jonathan Stapleton the honest Stalwart in Chicago in 1880 was buried in the ruins. Good riddance, said the secret rebel, the ghost of young Pendleton, as he looked on, triumphantly uncaring.

"You fucking son of a bitch," he said in a conversational tone. "I'll show you who's a coward."

"Get off my ship. Get off my paper," Pulitzer screamed.

Pendleton left Pulitzer gasping, a doctor giving him an injection. Stepping off the gig at the Seventy-second Street dock, he put his hand into his pocket and found Hearst's card. Perfect, he thought. The timing was perfect.

There was one more ritual to perform. He opened the flap in his wallet containing his father's last editorial. He had not touched it in years. It fell out in a dozen crumbling pieces.

He threw them up in the air and watched the icy north wind whirl them down the stony indifferent streets of New York.

FOUR

"War with Spain will increase the business and earnings of every American railroad! It will increase the output of every American factory! It will stimulate every branch of industry and domestic commerce! Every certificate that represents a share in any American business enterprise will be worth more money than it is today!"

Cynthia Stapleton sat in the gallery of the U.S. Senate and listened to Senator Howard Thurston of Nebraska bellow sentiments that would guarantee him a front page in the *New York Journal.* Thurston had recently returned from a sojourn in Cuba as a "commissioner." He and four other members of Congress had been given this title by Hearst, who had of course paid all their expenses.

A few desks away, Senator Jonathan Stapleton kept raising his hand to get the attention of Garrett Hobart, the porcine Vice-President of the United States. Hobart ignored him and recognized another senator, who rose to declare that war with Spain would pit the divine right of kings against the divine right of man. Such a war would be a blessing to the world!

Finally, Garrett Hobart could no longer avoid recognizing Senator Stapleton. Jonathan conceded the courage of the Cuban rebels and deplored Spain's sorry record of exploitation in Cuba. But there was a limit to his sympathy. The rebels had started the war without any expectation of winning it—they had never put more than 25,000 men into the field—on the assumption that they could stampede the American people into rescuing them. Everything pointed to a conspiracy between the rebels and the yellow journalists.

Spain was now in the process of giving Cuba the same dominion status that the British had given Canada. It was the duty of every responsible citizen to support this peaceful solution. "I don't want to see American soldiers die to help William Randolph Hearst sell newspapers," Jonathan thundered.

Cynthia felt a rush of pride and affection for her combative Yankee husband. This was the formidable man she had loved when they married, the daring man who fought Jay Gould. Now he was ignoring the abuse he received from Hearst and Pulitzer to speak out for sanity and peace.

Cynthia and many of the listeners in the gallery applauded as Jonathan sat down. Vice-President Hobart rapped his gavel and called for order. On Cynthia's right, a stocky young man with a drooping mustache whispered into her ear, "You've got to talk to him. You're the only person who can change his mind."

Theodore Roosevelt had been arguing with Senator Stapleton ever since he arrived in Washington to become assistant secretary of the navy. He was baffled by Jonathan's opposition to intervention in Cuba.

"I have no influence over him in political matters," Cynthia said.

Theodore looked skeptical, perhaps remembering his mother's influence over his father. On her right, Laura whispered, "For someone who pretends to be religious, you're a shameless liar."

Laura was wearing a green cashmere dress with militaristic black ruchings of mousseline de soie on the blouse. Practically everything she wore had a military motif these days. Beside her, holding her hand in a most possessive way, was Winthrop Astor Chapman, heir to one of the branches of the Astor fortune. He was a darkly handsome daredevil who looked and acted enough like Rawdon Stapleton to be his younger brother. If the Cuban revolution ended in victory, Cynthia feared, Laura planned to marry Winty and place him and his ten-million-dollar inheritance at Rawdon's service in Havana. The purple dream was alive and alarmingly well—more powerful than it had been in the days when Rawdon was a capitalist.

A former Confederate brigadier named Taylor, the Senator from Louisiana, won the floor. He began deriding Jonathan's speech. On the opposite side of the visitors' gallery, a burly bearded man applauded him. Robert

Legrand stared defiantly across the chamber at his sister. He was running a Washington publicity office for the Cuban-American League. The Louisiana lottery had collapsed in a swirl of scandals several years ago and Robert had been reduced to living by his wits—or his women. No doubt he had brought some of his adventuresses with him to the capital.

Cynthia found herself trembling inwardly, her heart pounding. She suggested they adjourn for lunch and let the senators join them after they had finished insulting each other. Jonathan had reserved a table for them in the Senate dining room. The younger generation sipped champagne and Cynthia drank Apollinaris water while Theodore Roosevelt repeated a number of arguments he had tried on Jonathan at their dinner table recently.

"We should intervene in Cuba immediately! The country needs a war. It will take people's minds off this perpetual rot about low wages, Wall Street bankers, calls for revolution. A war will give young men a chance to escape the confounded mercenary spirit that pervades everything these days."

Winty Chapman vehemently agreed. Like George Stapleton, he was an admirer of Theodore Roosevelt. Winty (and George) had hunted bears and buffalo with him in the West and supported his attempts, largely futile, to reform New York politics.

"The explanation is quite simple," Laura said. "My father is fighting for Cuban independence. That makes it impossible for the Senator to support it."

"It's not that simple, Laura dear," Cynthia said.

"Oh—your opinion doesn't count. You're in love with him, for some ridiculous reason."

The senators arrived. Theodore had invited bearded Henry Cabot Lodge of Massachusetts, a rather frosty patrician whose wife was one of the most charming hostesses in Washington. They had met at several dinner tables, and Lodge greeted Cynthia cordially. The waiter took their orders, and Theodore got down to the business of the luncheon.

"Do you feel free to share the particulars of your mission to Spain with us, General?"

"I'm afraid that's out of the question," Jonathan said. "It's a very delicate approach, which would be destroyed instantly by newspaper publicity."

"Am I correct in deducing that you hope to acquire Cuba peacefully?" Lodge asked.

"You might be," Jonathan said.

"But Cuba isn't the real prize, General," Theodore said. "It's the Philippines."

"The Philippines?" Jonathan was genuinely amazed.

"Yesterday I sent orders to Admiral George Dewey at Hong Kong to have our Far Eastern Squadron ready to go to sea on an hour's notice. He can take the Philippines five minutes after he arrives in Manila Harbor. The Spanish have nothing out there but a lot of old wooden hulks."

"Those islands will enable us to challenge the British and Germans in China, General," Henry Cabot Lodge said.

"Why in God's name do we want to do that?" Jonathan said.

"Don't you think it's time America took her place among the great powers, General?" Theodore asked.

"No question about it. I've supported all the President's bills for a strong navy, an expanded army."

"Now that we've got the navy at least, why shouldn't we use it?" Theodore asked.

"Because peace is always preferable to war, as long as our survival as a nation isn't threatened."

"It isn't simply power we're after, General," Senator Lodge said. "Theodore and I want to see our moral force play a part in Asia, Africa, South America."

"We think we can fuse power and idealism," Theodore said. "We can do more for the black and brown and yellow people of this world than any of the old empires."

"I wish I could believe that," Jonathan said. "But I can't—as long as we let four or five million Negro Americans languish in the South without the right to vote or go to a decent school."

Theodore began a labored explanation of the necessity of allowing that "reprehensible condition" to exist for a few more years. National unity in the face of a hostile world was more important. Jonathan listened, stony-faced, while Theodore talked himself into a corner.

Henry Cabot Lodge sighed, suggesting he never had much confidence in Theodore's ability to change Senator Stapleton's mind. Turning to Cynthia, he asked if she was going to Madrid with her husband.

"He's done everything in his power to frighten me out of a winter voyage across the Atlantic. But I'm still on the passenger list."

"I'd much rather go to Havana," Laura said.

"She wants to ship out as my chief boatswain's mate," Winty Chapman said. The look he got from Jonathan made him hastily add, "I wouldn't dream of letting her do it, Senator."

"She's coming to Europe with us," Jonathan growled.

Laura glowered. Cynthia prayed that Jonathan would let the matter drop. Getting Laura far away from Winty Chapman was a necessary first step to persuading her that he would make an inferior husband. Cynthia was not at all sure it would work. Distance might even lend enchantment to Winty, who had thus far done nothing with his life—he was almost thirty—but wander the world in search of adventure. He had already made two daring trips to Cuba smuggling rifles and ammunition to the rebels. He was in Washington to meet with a certain naval officer on Theodore's staff who was going to supply him with surplus weapons from a government arsenal.

One of Senator Lodge's secretaries rushed up to him with a copy of the *New York Journal.* Hearst regularly shipped his paper to Washington to influence members of Congress. DYNAMITE ATTEMPT ON OUR FLAG, boomed the headline. The story told how officials of the U.S. consulate in Havana had discovered a time bomb in the basement strong enough to demolish the building.

"What do you think of that Spanish dirty work, General?" Theodore asked.

"Why would the Spanish do such a thing when they're trying to negotiate with us?" the more cautious Lodge asked.

"They wouldn't do such a thing. But there are men in Havana who'd do it and let the Spanish take the blame," Jonathan said.

"Why can't you at least admit that the rebels are men of honor, Pa?" Laura asked.

"I don't have any confidence in the honor of people who have demonstrated such a total indifference to the truth," Jonathan said.

"I will not sit here and listen to you insult my father," Laura cried. She sprang up and strode out of the dining room.

"Winty," Theodore Roosevelt said, "if you're serious about making that girl your responsibility for life, I admire your courage."

Jonathan decided the news from Cuba required him to return to the Senate for the afternoon. Cynthia and Winty Chapman searched the Capitol for Laura and found not a trace of her. He went off to his clandestine weapons conference and Cynthia went home to their rented house in Georgetown to continue packing for the trip to Europe. About four o'clock Laura wandered into the bedroom.

"Where did you go?"

"I walked to the top of the Washington Monument and down again. I feel much better." She had acquired a fondness for these physical feats to prove she had cured her asthma.

"I'll tell Theodore Roosevelt. He takes all the credit for making you a healthy woman." Cynthia paused, trying to judge whether Laura was in the mood for a serious conversation. "I gather from something Theodore said that Winty Chapman wants to marry you."

"Yes. But he doesn't dare ask the General while he's running guns to Cuba."

"Do you want to marry him?"

"Why not?" she said, and sprawled on the bed.

"Laura dear—marriage is the most serious decision of a woman's life. It's not a casual matter."

"I still say why not?" she said. "What's wrong with Winty?"

"Not a great deal. He's charming, good-looking and rich. But I don't think he's terribly intelligent. Brains have never been plentiful among the Astors."

"I've got enough brains for both of us."

"But what about happiness? As a man grows older and his physical charm declines, his intelligence and his disposition become crucial."

"You took a lover or two. That's exactly what I'll do, if necessary."

Cynthia seized Laura by the wrist and jerked her to a sitting position. There were limits to how much impudence she had to swallow in the name of independent womanhood. "I have never said one word to you about that topic and I never shall. I can only urge you not to believe gossip about me—or think that any woman, any serious woman, takes a lover to relieve her boredom."

Cynthia went back to her packing. Laura sat there rubbing her wrist. "You're still treating me like a child. I'm an adult, Cynthia dear. I could give myself to Winty Chapman this afternoon, and there's nothing you could do to stop me. Unfortunately, he'd be shocked into utter disillusion if I suggested it."

She picked up a pair of lacy underdrawers and dropped them into a suitcase. "I have to let him do something heroic in Cuba first. Then I'll succumb to his charms and say, 'Yes, I'll marry you.' By that time the war will be over and I'll tell him there's only one place I want to live—Havana. It will be marvelous to live in a country where my husband and my father are both heroes."

"What about you?" Cynthia said. "You seem to see yourself as nothing more than a reflection of their glory."

"I'll love them both—I'll be the link between them," Laura said.

"You still see yourself as the lady in the painting of Saint George and the Dragon, don't you?"

"I do not. I'm not the praying type."

"I'm not talking about prayers. I mean standing on the sidelines, a spectator while the men perform the daring deeds. Your mother thinks women can do more than pray—or applaud. I'm inclined to agree with her."

"Then talk Pa into letting me go to Cuba with Winty. I know as much about handling a sloop as he does."

Cynthia groped for an answer. "I'll be all alone in Madrid. Jonathan will spend all his time with Spanish officials."

Laura's lip was curling derisively. Cynthia hastily decided to let Jonathan bear the brunt of the blame. "You know your grandfather would never say yes."

Two days later, they sailed on the Inman Line's *City of New York.* Cynthia soon discovered why Jonathan worried about winter on the Atlantic. She had assumed that a modern steamship could plow serenely through the biggest waves. But not even the most heroic engineers could build a vessel to match the gray foaming mountains of the Atlantic in February.

Before the first day was over, Cynthia was violently seasick. She was not alone. Jonathan and Laura reported the dining room deserted. For eight nightmare days, the plunging, pitching, rolling, tossing continued, and so did her retching. When she stumbled off the ship at Liverpool, she was so weak she had to cling to Jonathan's arm.

By the time they reached rainy chilly Paris, after another buffeting on the Channel steamer, Cynthia had acquired a bad cold to complete her misery. She crept into the first available bed at the Hotel Crillon. "I'll rest here for a week and join you in Madrid," she said.

"Out of the question," Jonathan said. "Madrid has the worst winter weather of any capital in Europe. I want you to stay here until you feel completely well again. On April first, head for Italy. I'll join you there—in Venice, if you're in agreement."

He sat down on the bed and took her hand as he said these last words. Cynthia felt a tremor of love pass through her weary body. They had not returned to Venice since their reconciliation. In the beginning, both feared that the bad memories might triumph over the good. Then the struggle against the war had engulfed them in politics again.

"Venice, by all means," she said. "I was going to suggest it. But I don't see why that bars me from Madrid. I think I could be helpful there."

"I'm sure you could, but I won't let you risk it. I've had a terrible premonition about this Cuba thing. Something ugly and dark is loose in this affair—something more evil than I've ever felt before."

She held his hand to her heart, frightened by the gloom on his face. "It's Rawdon."

"Yes," he said. "The thought of him down there in Havana telling those lies—turning the country war crazy. Now Clay Pendleton's joined him. It's like a disease, infecting our best minds. Young Roosevelt . . ."

"It's Genevieve I worry about," Cynthia said. "I begged her not to go down there. But she said she couldn't refuse. She was afraid Laura would throw it in her face for the rest of her life. She's still so vulnerable, Jonathan."

"I thought she was the complete Amazon," he said. He blamed some of Laura's rebelliousness on Genevieve.

Cynthia could not conceal her exasperation. "There are times, General, when you are quite impenetrable."

"I plead guilty, as usual," he said morosely. "If I live to be a hundred and twenty, I'll never understand women."

"We don't always understand ourselves."

They kissed and he walked to the gilded door. "Jonathan," Cynthia said. "Promise me something. No matter what happens, be patient with Laura. Patient—and kind."

"I'll try."

She lay there wondering why she felt such a strange urgency about that message. She was not really ill. Just exhausted and half starved. A few good Parisian meals and she would be trotting through the Louvre with Laura, dashing around to see old friends such as Alva Belmont. But after a week of cautious eating and deep dreamless sleeping, she still felt miserable. Her cold clung to her. The weather continued to be abominable.

Winty Chapman had given Laura the name of a half-dozen friends in Paris. She was gone most of the day, returning only to dress for dinner and tell Cynthia about some duke or baron whom she had met at lunch or tea.

Jonathan's letters from Madrid were brief and uninformative. He explained in the first one that he could not say much, because he was afraid they might be read by the secret agents of several governments interested in the crisis, or by an ambitious newspaper reporter. But he sounded hopeful. The Queen Regent, María Cristina, had taken a liking to him and invited him to her apartments for private talks. The majority of the Spanish cabinet wanted peace.

Toward the end of the second week, Cynthia was still gasping and choking with her cold, when she received a telephone call from Alva Belmont. She had met Laura at a party and was dismayed to hear that Cynthia was bedridden. She wanted to see her and bring half the doctors of Paris with her to effect an instant cure. Cynthia persuaded her to come without the doctors, and in a half hour Alva was beside her bed, as beautiful and as full of energy as ever.

"How is Oliver?" Cynthia asked, inquiring about Alva's second husband.

"All right. When our horses win."

Alva talked for a while about the huge amounts of money the Vanderbilts and the Belmonts and other wealthy Americans were spending to breed horses that were beginning to win prizes at Ascot and Longchamps. Unfortunately, Alva's former husband, Willie K. Vanderbilt, was having much better luck at finding the right thoroughbreds.

"How is the General?" Alva asked.

Cynthia told her what Jonathan was doing in Madrid. Alva gave her a curious look, a mixture of rueful affection and something close to dislike. "I wonder if you know how many women envy you," she said. "Having a man who's doing something more important than putting stallions to stud."

It was a glimpse—Alva would never give anyone more than a glimpse—of unhappiness. It was hard to believe. Here was a woman who had won every battle she had ever fought, including the unprecedented feat of making a powerful husband pay publicly for his infidelity. But Alva was admitting, quietly, sadly, to her southern older sister that the battles had all been trivial, the victories more or less empty, because she had never married a serious man.

"Why don't you find an interest of your own, beyond putting stallions to stud?" Cynthia said. "Have you ever thought of the woman's movement? I suspect it would appeal to your rebellious nature."

Alva only laughed and changed the subject. She wondered if the cure for Cynthia's malaise might well be a trip in her newest possession, a Mercedes Benz touring car that would take them spinning through the Paris countryside at an incredible thirty miles an hour. Everyone was buying automobiles. As soon as the sun began shining again, she would call Cynthia and set a date.

Alas, the sun refused to shine. Even when her cold finally departed, Cynthia still felt alarmingly weak. She decided that there was only one cure for her flaccid spirits and ailing flesh: Italy. Ignoring Laura's groans at the thought of leaving Paris, she telegraphed Contessa Rospigliosi and learned that the palazzo was available. She struggled into a corset and traveling clothes and took the Orient Express to Venice.

They arrived on a sunny March day; Cynthia had never seen the sky so blue. But the benevolent weather, the white curve of the dome of Santa Maria della Salute, failed to revive her. She crept into bed again, and an alarmed Contessa Rospigliosi called a doctor—a Frenchman this time. After his examination, he told Cynthia that she would have to stay in bed for at least two or three weeks and gave her the strictest diet yet. Cold baths—as cold as she could stand—and daily massages were also in the regimen.

"What's the matter with me?" she asked the Contessa as she drew the covers around her.

"The doctor says your diabetes has gotten unexpectedly worse," she said. "You must rest and eat with great care."

"That's all I've been doing for two weeks."

"You must continue."

The Contessa took charge of Laura. She was soon enjoying the flattery of a half-dozen young Italian aristocrats. In the morning, after Cynthia recovered from her icy bath, they spent an hour or two together. They talked about Genevieve and Rawdon, about Winty Chapman and the war. Most of the time Cynthia avoided arguments. She let Laura argue with herself as she puzzled over her mother and father's failed marriage, and the larger puzzle of men and women and love. Cynthia cautiously volunteered some information about her own life and discovered that it was received with fascination. Before she quite realized it, she was talking frankly about her marriage to Charlie Stapleton and her father's purple dream.

"Marrying Charlie was the worst mistake of my life," she said.

"Why?" Laura asked truculently. "Did you blame your father because he died in Cuba?"

"I did for a while. I was only nineteen and I was as violently in love with my father as you are. It was a terrible shock to discover he could be so wrong. But what I came to regret was the way I confused my own feelings—marrying someone I didn't really love."

"I don't intend to let my feelings get confused by any man," Laura said. "Including my husband."

That reckless answer almost made Cynthia weep. A moment later she was assailed by overwhelming nausea. Laura helped her to the bathroom, where she vomited her breakfast. "What is wrong with me?" she asked as Laura helped her back to bed.

Each day, Laura went down to St. Mark's Square and bought English newspapers to keep up with the latest events in Cuba and the United States. She also got letters from Winty Chapman and other friends, but she said very little to Cynthia about them. As far as Cynthia could gather from her vague remarks, the situation in Cuba remained a stalemate, with the rebels still hoping the Americans would rescue them.

One day, Cynthia asked Laura the date. She was startled to learn that March was almost over. Jonathan might be arriving any day. "I should begin planning some dinner parties. We'll have to hire some more servants . . ."

Laura suddenly turned away, as if she wanted to hide the expression on her face. She fled from the room. A moment later Contessa Rospigliosi was at Cynthia's bedside. "My dear friend," she whispered. "You must no longer think of dinner parties. Think of the Holy Spirit, of God's presence that you discovered in Florence. He will be with you on the journey you will soon begin."

She was dying? No, it was ridiculous. She was very weak, she had had a horrible crossing of the Atlantic, and the vile winter weather of Paris had not given her a chance to recuperate. She was not, she could not be dying when so much was about to happen. When Jonathan was about to become what he had always yearned to be—a peacemaker. In her secret heart she believed it was her prayers that had awakened this wish in his soul.

"Do you want me to send for your husband?"

"No. There's too much at stake in Madrid. But I want to live until he comes. Pray for that, my friend. Let us both pray for it."

The Contessa was weeping, objecting. "I don't want to see you suffer. My sister died last year. It was a hard death."

"Help me anyway. Against your better judgment. There is one more sad foolish thing I have to tell him."

FIVE

In her bedroom in the Hotel Inglaterra, Genevieve Dall awoke with the first stroke of Havana's bells. It was not, as in other cities, a richly timbred peal, signifying hope and faith descending from the sky. In Havana the bells sounded as if men were battering them with clubs.

Genevieve flung some water in her face and looked out at Havana's harbor. A dozen ships, including three black-hulled Spanish men-of-war and the stubby white American battleship U.S.S. *Maine,* sat motionless on the opaque water. She sighed and picked up several sheets of paper on the gilt-trimmed white desk beside the window. Lighting a gas lamp—electricity had not yet reached hotels and private houses in Havana—she read the opening lines of her story.

Ten days ago, on Feb. 5, 1898, a company of Spanish troops invaded the tiny hamlet of Hildago, in Oriente Province. Before they left, 24 hours later, they would add a new chapter to Spanish brutality in Cuba. . . .

Genevieve threw the pages back on the desk and paced the shabby red carpet. She was sure the squat young Cuban woman who had told her the story yesterday was lying. With her had been Rawdon Stapleton and his Cuban shadow, a lean, intense young man named Carlos. He was Rawdon's contact with the rebels in the bush. Genevieve disliked his perpetually sardonic expression, the snide way he spoke in Spanish to Rawdon about "los Americanos." Carlos was a devotee of the fallen leader, José Martí, and he had inherited from him a pervasive contempt for the United States of America.

But Genevieve could not disprove the story. Oriente Province was hundreds of miles from Havana. It would take weeks to reach it and return to the capital. If she made the journey without being raped or murdered, what would she have to show for it? William Randolph Hearst would not be elated to have one of his reporters prove that the Cuban rebels and their spokesman, Rawdon Stapleton, were liars.

She stared at the story, feeling helplessness rise within her. *Gray fog,* whispered the ominous voice. Here in Havana's perpetual sunshine, her old nemesis from San Francisco had begun to haunt her again.

Genevieve had arrived in Havana vowing she would write nothing but the truth. It was the only response to Clay Pendleton's obnoxious sneer about proving she could lie like a man. She had scarcely settled in her room at the Inglaterra when Clay arrived in Havana, as an employee of William Randolph Hearst. He had switched sides and Hearst had appointed him bureau chief in Cuba. He needed someone to coordinate the dozen reporters and sketch artists covering the war for the *Journal* and to make sure visiting senators, congressmen and other influential Hearst "commissioners" were properly entertained.

Clay had convened a meeting of the Hearst group and told them that the public was beginning to grow bored with severed ears. He suggested severing other parts of the anatomy in future stories. They should also stop laying on the gore like house painters. It was time to bring some artistry to their fakery. Henceforth they should limit themselves to one lie to a paragraph. Rawdon had sat in the back of the room smiling.

Genevieve was appalled and bewildered by Clay's moral collapse. Still she vowed to go her own way, to find her own stories, all of them true. She had avoided the military side of the situation and concentrated on Cuban women's reaction to the revolution. She was soon convinced that the rebels no longer represented a majority of the Cuban people, who were sick of the war and ready to accept Spain's offer of autonomy.

Last week, Rawdon had smuggled a message from rebel headquarters rejecting Spain's peace terms. The *Journal* had backed the rebels' intransigence, but a coded message from Hearst demanded dramatic evidence that the Spanish offer was a sham. This was why Genevieve was sitting in her room, staring at the unwritten atrocity story from Oriente Province. Rawdon had decided that it would be more convincing if it was written by a woman. Clay, smiling ghoulishly, had concurred. "Make them sob," he had told her.

Genevieve looked at her watch. She had been sitting at the desk for an hour without writing a line. She dressed and went downstairs for breakfast. At a round table in the sunny dining room sat Clay, Rawdon, Sylvester Scovel of the *World* and the American consul in Havana, Fitzhugh Lee. A former Confederate general, Lee was at first glance a plump, good-natured white-haired paterfamilias. Only when he opened his mouth did his startling views on Cuba and Spain become apparent.

Clay was wearing a rumpled white suit without a tie. His hair was disheveled and he needed a shave. He had been drinking steadily for weeks and looked it. Rawdon, on the other hand, was crisp and cheerful in a fresh tan shirt, jodhpurs and jungle boots, a more or less standard outfit for correspondents.

"Have you finished the Hildago story?" Rawdon asked as Genevieve sat down.

She shook her head. "I've barely started it," she said.

"Join us in a morning eye-opener," Clay said, raising a brown rum punch. "We've got something to celebrate. We've chased the Spanish ambassador out of Washington."

Rawdon smiled expansively. Fitzhugh Lee raised his rum punch to him. "Congratulations," he said.

"We couldn't have done it without Miss Dall," Rawdon said.

Hatchet-faced Sylvester Scovel cocked an inquiring eye at Genevieve. Like many men, he was sure women reporters used sex to get their stories.

"I was only a courier," Genevieve said. "The ambassador's really resigned?"

Pendleton fished a copy of the *Journal* out of a leather case. After a cautious look around the empty dining room, he flashed a headline: THE WORST INSULT TO THE UNITED STATES IN ITS HISTORY.

The Spanish ambassador had made the mistake of writing a private letter to a pro-government editor in Havana, in which he unburdened all his frustrations with American politicians and newspapers. A rebel sympathizer had stolen it from the editor's files and given it to Rawdon. He passed it to Genevieve, only hours before the Spanish police ransacked his room. With agents watching every male Hearst reporter, she slipped out of Havana and got the letter to a dispatch boat that she met on a dark beach near Matanzas. In forty-eight hours it was on the front page of the *Journal*, and the Spanish ambassador was now persona non grata to most Americans.

"The day is not far off, children, when this island will be our fortieth state," Fitzhugh Lee said. "That bomb we found in the consulate cellar last month—it's a sign of the dons' desperation."

"No question," Rawdon said.

From the start of the revolution, Fitzhugh Lee had disregarded all the laws and regulations of the diplomatic corps in regard to neutrality in a foreign war. He did his utmost to protect Cuban rebels who had become U.S. citizens while in exile, and bombarded the state department with criticisms of the Spaniards and demands for protection of American lives and property in Havana. Thanks to him, the battleship *Maine* was sitting in the harbor, supposedly restraining Spanish vengeance.

General Lee orated on the reason he wanted to see an American army land on Cuba's shores and join the rebels in battle against the despicable Spaniards. "Southerners and northerners fighting side by side for the cause that united them in 1776—independence from a foreign despot. It will put the War between the States behind us, boys."

"No doubt about it, General," Rawdon said.

Sylvester Scovel and Lee went off to see an American citizen who had just been released from the Cabañas prison and had horror stories to tell. "Let's get down to business," Rawdon said. "I suspect Miss Dall here doesn't approve of the story Teresa Céspedes gave her yesterday."

"I don't believe it."

"Carlos dragged that woman up and down the Sierra Maestre mountains for five days to get her here. We need the story for several reasons—to show people that the war is still going on, to give the Congress something new to howl about—"

"I don't like taking dictation," Genevieve said. "I want to see what I report."

Rawdon pushed back his chair. "Give her an order, Pendleton."

"What's one more lie at this point?" Clay said.

"It may not matter to history, but it matters to me," Genevieve said.

"Then maybe you better get out of here."

Rawdon shook his head impatiently. "Pendleton is trying to tell you that even he finally recognizes newspapers have become weapons in the revolutionary struggle. If you don't like it, you should go back to wasting your time on woman's rights."

Before Genevieve could answer either of them, they were interrupted by Frederic Remington, who asked Clay in exasperated tones if anything was happening anywhere. The artist was getting $150 a week from Hearst to cover a war that seemed nonexistent. "I sent Hearst a cable yesterday, telling him I wanted to go home. Here's what I got back."

He flourished a yellow Western Union cable: "YOU FURNISH THE PICTURES, WE'LL FURNISH THE WAR."

"That's exactly what we intend to do," Rawdon said. He began telling Remington about the massacre in the village of Hildago.

"Now, that's the sort of stuff I'm looking for," Remington chortled.

"Miss Dall—or some other reporter—is writing the story," Rawdon said. "Why don't we go see Miss Céspedes now so you can get started on the sketches." He strode off, his arm around Remington's shoulder, leaving Genevieve alone with Clay.

"I mean it, Gen," Clay said softly. "Get out of here. Before you start drinking these." He drained his second rum punch.

"What in God's name is happening to you?"

"Never mind—you're not really interested, are you?"

"How can I be when we've barely exchanged a personal word since I came back from California?"

Clay drained his drink. "It's pretty hard to get personal with the Queen of the Amazons. That's all I saw in New York—a steely-eyed creature who bragged about making me look silly."

"What choice did I have? The Clay Pendleton I knew, the one who made me laugh, who made me feel that he cared about me, wasn't there."

"That character got used up by Pulitzer while you were becoming a superwoman in California."

"A superwoman? You wouldn't say that if you read my diary, Clay. I could use a friend. I don't have one here—or anywhere else, these days, since I've more or less abandoned the women's movement."

Clay ordered another rum punch. "Forget about the Céspedes story. I'll get someone else to write it. But Hearst will be on my back. You haven't sent anything for a week."

"I'm working on something."

She left Clay in the middle of the empty dining room and hurried up the Prado, Havana's broad palm-lined boulevard, into the twisting streets of the Angel District. In the narrow lane of San Juan de Dios, she knocked on a door studded with large nailheads. A nervously smiling mulatto woman welcomed her into a parlor furnished with massive cedarwood chairs. The leather seats and backs had grown withered and dry with age, and rips were numerous. A wax candle burned before a statue of the Virgin in the dim corner.

Isabel Álvarez had been the mistress of a Spanish captain who had been killed in action in Santiago Province. He had written letters to her, describing the savage war conducted there by both sides. Her sister was a maid at the Hotel Inglaterra and she had told Genevieve about the letters.

Isabel Álvarez served Genevieve a *panale*, a meringuelike wafer of egg and sugar, which was dissolved in a glass of water. She brought the letters down from her bedroom. They were tied in a large blue ribbon. "Please understand that he was a man of honor," she said. "He believed above all in doing his duty. But with me he was very generous, gentle, kind. He left me enough money to buy this house."

The Spanish captain's name was Castro. Genevieve sat in the parlor of the small house on San Juan de Dios and read about ambushes in the night, summary executions in the dawn, hideous wounds exposed to the glaring tropic sun. Isabel Álvarez had sown doubts about the wisdom of the war Spain was fighting. They multiplied as his men died of wounds and yellow fever. For a while his loathing for the rebels and their cruelty to neutral civilians overcame his doubts. "If they want to turn Cuba into a desert," he wrote in one raging passage, "we will oblige them!" But he became more and more disconsolate about what the slaughter was doing to his soul. "Will you drive me from your door on San Juan de Dios? I would not blame you. I am afraid your eyes, your sweet innocent eyes, will condemn me to hell."

Those were his last words. Genevieve looked into Isabel Álvarez's innocent eyes and said, "I'll give you a hundred dollars for these letters."

"What will you do with them?"

"I'll publish them in a newspaper in New York. But there won't be any mention of your name."

"You promise that faithfully? The authorities might become angry . . ."

"I promise faithfully. I'll bring the money tomorrow."

"No. I—I must think about it. I loved him."

"A hundred dollars is all I can pay."

"I *loved* him," she said.

There it was again, that demoralizing word. "I'm sorry," Genevieve said. "I'll come back again tomorrow."

She stumbled back down the Prado in the tropic sunshine. Gray fog crept through her mind and body. She did not want to think about Captain Castro's wounded soul, or her own empty soul. Clay Pendleton waved to her from a table in the Louvre Café on the Parque Isabelle, Havana's central square. Another empty soul.

Genevieve went back to her room and lay on her bed. Isabel Álvarez's sister, María, who lacked her innocent eyes, knocked on the door and asked her about the letters. Genevieve told her they were excellent and she hoped to buy them. María Álvarez wanted to know how much; Genevieve waved her out the door, sick of the whole business. Sick of Havana and lies and the truth, which might be worse than lies.

She could not hide in her room indefinitely. That night she emerged to join the other reporters for their usual apéritif at the Louvre. They sat and watched the *paseo*, the annual evening parade of Havana's best people along the Prado. Everyone was dressed in stylish clothes. The boots and shoulder straps of the officers gleamed. She told Clay about Captain Castro's letters, and he authorized her to pay five hundred dollars for them if necessary. Properly edited, they could make marvelous reading for the *Journal.*

Rawdon joined them, still in the open-collared shirt and jodhpurs he had worn at breakfast. As usual, Carlos was beside him. Clay got involved with Frederic Remington about some drawings of the imaginary massacre in Oriente. "Gen," Rawdon said. "You've got to write that story. The police arrested Teresa Céspedes. Her father is one of General García's lieutenants. She risked her life to come into Havana to tell it to you. Even if it isn't true, won't that change your mind?"

Her hand lay on the table, inert, like the rest of her. Rawdon placed his hand on top of it. Carlos watched, his sardonic smile glittering. "I know I've barely spoken to you since you arrived," Rawdon said. "I've been waiting—hoping for a sign that you care about what I'm trying to do down here. This —this story would be a sign . . ."

I loved him, Isabel Álvarez had said. As if money, newspapers, the Cuban cause were all quite possibly irrelevant beside that fact. Rawdon's voice purred in her ear.

"For my sake—and Clay's sake. Hearst would be very upset if he knew how drunk Clay got every day. How much of his work I'm really doing. He needs a story like this, Gen. The whole situation is getting very precarious. The Cubans are on the brink of collapse. Carlos just came back from Santiago Province. The rebels don't have two thousand soldiers left there. The Spanish have forty thousand. If this revolution fails, if the Americans don't intervene, Hearst is going to look like a fool. He won't have kind thoughts for the people who put him in that position."

"All right," she said. "I'll do it."

Back in her room after dinner, Genevieve was terrified by her submission. Rawdon was exercising his old power over her. Perhaps the lies would be so loathsome she would be too sickened to surrender any more of herself to that devious voice, that charismatic face. She sat there hoping for the worst, writing Teresa Céspedes' story about disemboweled children and women with amputated breasts and a Spanish captain exultantly dipping his hands in their blood.

It did not work. Lying did not protect her. Each day in the following week, as Havana festooned itself for Carnival—ignoring the stalemated war—Rawdon became more tender, more considerate. Genevieve returned to Isabel Álvarez on the street of San Juan de Dios and was told that the letters were not for sale after all. She offered five hundred dollars, and Isabel's innocent eyes glazed with pain. But she still said no.

For some absurd reason, that seemed to make Rawdon all the more difficult for Genevieve to resist. He began talking to her about what he was really doing in Cuba. He kept mentioning exaltation and wanting to share it with her. Not the childish exaltation they had known at Kemble Manor or the quickly evaporated exaltation of their marriage, but exaltation that transcended the body, ennobled it, purified it.

Clay Pendleton drank rum punches and edited their lying copy and watched Genevieve's gradual disintegration. Clay's laugh grew more and more hollow, his smile became a ghastly parody of his old sly humor. She did not care. She did not care about anything but this exaltation that Rawdon told her would unite her with him and Laura. It was infinitely superior to that bourgeois emotion, love.

On the night that Carnival began, Clay joined them at the Louvre and they watched the Prado fill with celebrants. Everyone wore a bizarre, vaguely medieval costume and a grotesque mask. Guitars strummed, the warm night was full of friendly shouts and songs.

Sick of sweet *panales*, Genevieve announced that she wanted a real drink. Rawdon recommended tequila, Mexico's favorite beverage. The salt on the rim of the glass, the bitter lemon flavoring, suited her mood. It was time she learned to drink if she was going to be truly equal to these exalted male bastards.

From the harbor drifted a sound that pierced the racket of Carnival. The bugler on the battleship *Maine* was sounding taps. The plaintive notes stirred melancholy in Genevieve. They reminded her of her father's funeral. She suddenly saw the bugler in blue, Jonathan Stapleton standing beside her mother. It was all *inevitable*. She had never had a chance to escape Rawdon Stapleton. Why had she spent ten years trying?

"Pick out a few stars for us, Gen," Pendleton said.

"I'm not sure if I remember one from another," she said. "There's Orion," she said, "and the Pleiades."

"Whatever became of that old-maid astronomer Maria Mitchell?" Rawdon said.

"She died in 1889."

"For all the wrongs I supposedly wreaked on you, Gen, at least I saved you from that fate."

"Being an old maid?"

"An old-maid astronomer."

She realized that Clay had asked her to star-gaze with malicious intent. He knew it would arouse Rawdon's animosity. The pathetic persistence of Clay's affection baffled her. Why didn't he hate her? Wasn't that the inevitable progress of unrequited or abused love? From adoration to vexation to hate?

Now Rawdon was telling her that there was another stage that transformed everything. Exaltation without the need for sweetness or joy. Somehow she would have to explain that to Clay. She wanted to explain that her surrender was not a cowardly or craven thing. It was her fate.

Out of the night came a tremendous explosion, followed by a spout of flame. The sound of tinkling glass followed it as windows broke all over Havana. Every street light in the city went out, as if snuffed by a giant hand. A fierce fire was blazing in the middle of the harbor, casting a glow over the hulls of nearby ships. From the center of the blaze spouted innumerable red, white and blue streaks—exploding rockets not unlike the ones William Randolph Hearst used to advertise the *Journal* with fireworks displays on the Battery in New York.

"Jesus Christ, what ship is it?" Clay asked.

"I think it's the *Maine*," Rawdon said.

"Let's get to it," Clay said. They leaped from their seats and piled into a *volante*, one of Havana's open carriages. Clay thrust a gold coin into the man's hand and told him to ride for the waterfront. They clattered through the darkened streets, which rapidly emptied of people.

The customhouse gate was besieged by a shouting crowd. "Officers from the *Maine*," Clay roared, and Rawdon translated it into Spanish. The guards let them through, but stopped Genevieve. "Wife of an officer," Rawdon shouted. That got her through.

At the end of a wharf they found Colonel José Paglieri, head of the Havana police force, getting into a launch. They jumped in with him and chugged into the bay. In five minutes they were only a hundred yards from the *Maine*. Exploding ammunition whizzed through the air over their heads. By the glow of the flames they could see great masses of twisted and bent iron plates and beams thrown up by a terrific explosion amidship. A half-dozen boats rowed by Spanish sailors were circling the wreck, dragging Americans out of the water. Pendleton and Rawdon hauled one white-clothed figure aboard the launch. Blood oozed from his mouth. They propped him against a bulkhead and asked him what had happened.

"She just blew up," he said. "She just blew up."

"Are there many dead?" Clay asked.

"Everybody below decks. They never had a chance. She just blew up and sank," the sailor said. His head fell back. He was unconscious and probably dying.

"This is the devil's work," Colonel Paglieri said.

"A Spanish devil, Colonel?" Rawdon said.

"Is that what you're going to tell your newspapers? I think it was a Cuban —or even an American devil."

He began shouting at Rawdon. "Yes, my friend. That dynamite bomb found in the basement of your consulate was made from explosives manufactured in America. Last week we learned that the man you pretend is your interpreter, the fellow named Carlos, is an expert at assembling such devices. Where is he?"

"I have no idea," Rawdon said. "He went off to visit his family in Santiago last week and never came back. I thought you might have assassinated him."

"There is assassination," Colonel Paglieri shouted, pointing toward the burning wreck. "The assassination of Spain's honor. Why would we do such a thing, when we have eaten shit to avoid a war with you?"

By now the launch was back at the dock. Clay and Rawdon carried the wounded sailor ashore. Other boats were unloading more wounded men on either side of them. The wharf was a chaos of wild-eyed Spanish soldiers and officers, bewildered nurses and doctors, American and British reporters trying to hire boats to get out to the *Maine*. Rawdon found a carriage and they galloped for the *Journal*'s office.

They rushed upstairs and Rawdon began writing the story. Clay gave Genevieve a list of the eleven other Hearst correspondents in Havana and told her to get them out of beds or bars or brothels and over to the office immediately. She managed to find six of them. Clay ordered one to locate the captain of the *Maine* if he was still alive and interview him, another to interview surviving *Maine* crewmen, a third to get a statement from Captain Ramos Blanco, the new Spanish commander in Cuba. By the time everyone was deployed, Rawdon had finished writing the story.

Clay read it and shook his head. "The censor will never let this go through."

Rawdon smiled. "I've been saving this for an emergency." He handed Clay a cable blank which already had the censor's stamp of approval on it.

"Copy it on this, will you, Gen?" Clay said, handing it to her.

"Get Remington in here to make a drawing," Rawdon said. "It should have a huge hole in the forward section of the ship, where the mine went off."

While they discussed these details, Genevieve copied Rawdon's story onto the cable blank.

> The United States battleship *Maine* was blown up in Havana Harbor shortly before 10 o'clock this evening.
>
> Many of those on the *Maine* were killed and many more were injured. The injured do not know what caused the explosion. But it is widely believed here in Havana that the Spaniards arranged to have the *Maine* anchored over one of their harbor mines. If this can be proved, the brutal nature of the Spaniards will be shown by the fact that they waited to spring the mine until after all the men had retired for the night.

"Put Clay's name on it," Rawdon said. "I want him to get credit for the story of the century. He'll have a job with Hearst for life."

Genevieve handed the copy to Clay. He took it downstairs to the cable office to make sure it went out immediately. Genevieve sat there in the dim gaslit office, staring at Rawdon. Tequila, chaos, horror were blurring her brain.

Clay came back, sat down at his desk and took a bottle of rum out of a drawer, filled a water glass almost to the top, and sat back in his chair.

"I think you'll get your war now," he said, sipping his drink.

"I wouldn't be surprised," Rawdon said.

"Did you do it?" Clay asked. His voice was perfectly casual. He might have been asking Rawdon if he had enjoyed his dinner.

"I was sitting in the Louvre beside you," Rawdon said. "How could I have done it?"

"You arranged it. Or you let Carlos and his friends arrange it."

"It's none of your business, Clay."

"I know it. But I'm a reporter. Or I was, once. I like to know the truth."

"How many times have I told you, that kind of truth is irrelevant."

"I know it's stupid of me—and at the moment it sounds idiotic—but I still don't agree with you." Clay slapped his glass on the desk and frowned at Genevieve. "What the hell are we doing, sitting here discussing ethics when the story of the century is in our laps? Miss Dall, get over to the hospital and come back with something that will make women and red-blooded American men cry their eyes out."

She left Rawdon sitting opposite Clay, his arms folded on his chest. Was it possible? Rawdon was responsible for those dazed bleeding men she saw being dragged out of the harbor? Rawdon? The boy-man who told her that his dream was to leave one noble thought behind him? Rawdon, the idealist of 1877 who wanted them to risk everything to regain America's shining message?

At the entrance to the hospital, she was halted by a cordon of Spanish soldiers. A lanky young man with an aquiline nose and a tawny mustache calmly informed the soldiers that she was a reporter. They opened ranks and let her in. She thanked Stephen Crane. He was one of the few correspondents in Havana who accepted her presence without hostility. Last year, he and his wife had covered the Greek–Turkish War together and she had filed several dispatches.

"It's not pretty in there," Crane said.

"I'll manage," Genevieve said.

"It's starting a war at the wrong end—seeing the wounded. You should see a battle first."

Crane avoided emotion when he talked about war. His novel about the Civil War, *The Red Badge of Courage*, had been a huge success. It more or less forced him to assume an expert's role, although he had written it before he ever saw a battle.

"I'll go with you," Crane said. "I can probably use another look."

He led her down a corridor into a long narrow ward. In the first bed, a man with a huge bandage around his head shouted, "Bread! Get me a piece of bread."

"A marine," Crane said. "Got a hunk of the deck plate in his head. He'll be gone before morning."

A nurse spread gelatin on the blackened eyes of another man, who moaned and begged someone to tell him where he was, what had happened. "He's seen his last sunrise," Crane whispered.

In the next bed a petty officer was sobbing. Genevieve asked him if she could help him. "Tell them to let me die," he said.

"Both legs are gone—one above the knee," Crane whispered.

A few feet away from the blind man two sailors sat up in their beds smoking cigarettes, laughing at a joke one of them had just told. The joker had his arm in a sling, the other had a patch bandage on his neck. Crane introduced them as "the two luckiest lugs in the U.S. Navy." They grinned cheerfully and one of them held up a rabbit's foot.

"It's the only thing worth remembering about a war," Crane said as they continued down the ward. "How people act under fire—or just after it."

There was no laughter in the next half-dozen beds. Men writhed in pain or lay inert, heads, bodies swathed in bandages. "Don't miss the eyes," Crane said. "You'll never see anything like the eyes of a wounded man. The mind is trying to escape from the body."

Genevieve whirled, struggling to control a wild mixture of anger and revulsion. "I—appreciate your help, Mr. Crane. But this is not what I came here to do. I'm not a novelist."

Crane looked vaguely apologetic and left her there. She spent the next hour talking to a dozen wounded men. A few described the nightmare minutes aboard the *Maine* after the explosion: seawater cascading over the dead and the living, men clawing their way up narrow ladders, choking in acrid smoke, screaming as flames roared down the corridors. But most of them gave her messages for wives and mothers, they clung to her hand and sobbed. She was more than a reporter to them. She was home, peace, safety, comfort: a woman.

Genevieve sat on a bench in the hospital's entry room and wrote the story. No matter who was guilty or innocent, the words she had just heard, the suffering she had seen, were real. When she finished it, she found a *volante* at the gate and clattered through the dark empty streets of Havana to the *Journal* office. She found Clay still sitting at his desk. Rawdon was gone. She handed Clay the story.

"Good stuff," he said. "Page one."

The familiar words of acceptance had a strange effect on her. She remembered Clay's exchange with Rawdon about who was responsible for the explosion. She realized she had been using the hospital assignment to escape the truth.

"Clay?" Genevieve said. "What should we do?"

"I told you once. Get out of here before he smashes you again. Now it may be too late."

"What are you going to do?"

"Me? What can I do? I'm just a yellow fellow. You still stand for something. I never have. I just had this pathetic desire to tell the truth about various matters to the indifferent citizens of the United States of America."

He drank some rum. "Rawdon's waiting for you. Back at the hotel."

"How do you know?"

"I have an unfortunate gift for reading his mind."

In her darkened hotel room, she groped for the gas lamp. It popped, flared, and she saw Rawdon sitting by the window.

"How was the hospital?" he asked.

"Horrible," she said.

"Tell me about it."

She told him in grisly detail. He listened somberly. "Did you write it that well?" he asked.

She nodded.

"Now you know why I need you, Gen. I need someone who understands, who'll forgive me for those sailors."

"Understand what, Rawdon? What can possibly justify that—that horror?"

"The future," Rawdon said. "The future of peace and equality and kindness and generosity that will emerge from the revolution their deaths will help to create."

"I don't even know what you're talking about."

"I know. That's my fault. I want to confess my sins against you tonight, Gen. I neglected your mind. I wanted to preserve that marvelous innocence I saw when we first loved each other. But I wasn't a revolutionist then. I was that despicable thing called a reformer. I saw myself entangled with the miserable details of politics and commerce, smeared by their slime, needing your innocence like a mountain pool, a waterfall of grace, to cleanse me. Only after you left me, and I got the money out of my system and then I met men like José Martí and began to see the endless stupidity, the pointlessness of reform, when I started to read and think about revolution on a world scale, when I shed my provincial American ideas and saw the future that I could help create—only then did I realize how much I needed you in this new way."

"What—what is this future?" Genevieve said. She had never seen anything like the intensity of emotion that was suffusing Rawdon's face.

"The future that this miserable wreck of a century has been heaving and groaning to give birth to for decades. It will begin with a revolution that overthrows the authority of the bayonet and the nightstick and it will end with the abolition of the state, with the people as the owners and administrators of the oil, the coal, the factories, the railroads, all the things that the millionaires use to exploit and destroy human happiness."

"What has this got to do with the *Maine*—with those dead and wounded sailors?"

"Here in Cuba is where the revolution is going to begin. We've started with the Spanish because they're the weakest link in the chain. A war with

America will wreck them. Spain happens to be the country where anarchism has made the most progress. A revolutionary situation will emerge from the war. Cuba meanwhile will be the revolution's bridge to South America."

Genevieve was sitting on the bed. Rawdon was still in the chair, leaning toward her, thrusting his whole body into his words. "It's global, Gen. The beginning of a movement that will eventually change the whole world. Nationalities mean nothing in the struggle. You remember the Spanish Prime Minister, Canovas, who was assassinated by that Italian anarchist, just as General Weyler was on the brink of victory here? That was managed by the Cuban agent in Paris. We got rid of Lionel Bradford when he found out how much money I'd stolen from him to finance this revolution. There'll be a lot more deaths among the power gods before we're through with them.

"I can see from the expression on your face that you don't like it. It offends your childish American idealism. That's because you haven't thought things through, Gen. You haven't asked yourself to do more than expose the conditions of those women who work twelve hours a day in New York's sweatshops. And those women who lie on their backs in the parlor houses of New York and take thirty visitors a night. I want to confess my sins against them too, my indifference. I see now they're all part of the wretched of the earth.

"You've been denying your rage against their real oppressors, Gen. You've been channeling it into pleas for the vote, as if votes ever changed anything. Only guns and bayonets and dynamite change things, Gen. Your father knew that. He knew it was the only way to defeat the slave system in the South. I'm telling you it's the only way to defeat the slave system in the North, the same system that's fastened its grip on England, France, Italy, Germany, Russia."

He was on his feet now, only an arm's length away from her. "Join me, Gen. I need you. It isn't easy to face the things we've done, the lies, the dead men and women and children. It won't be easy. But together we can share the pain—and the exaltation. There isn't another woman—there never will be another woman—who can share that with me."

His hand was reaching out to her, his face aglow. Once she had assumed that the being who brought the shining message was an angel of light. Now she saw it was an angel of darkness from the beginning. Never did the depths of Rawdon's green eyes seem more forbidding—or more inviting. She could plunge into them and find alien brightness, a kind of happiness. She was sure of it.

But a voice, an infinitesimal voice, said no. It had something to do with the truth, and with Clay Pendleton sitting there in the darkened office above the whirring clicking cable that connected them to the roaring presses of New York's newspapers. Clay sadly stubbornly saying, "I still don't agree with you," when Rawdon told him the truth was irrelevant. It had something to do with the way she felt when she wrote lies about massacres that never happened and heroic revolutionary acts that never took place. It had something to do with kneeling beside the beds of the maimed and mangled sailors of the U.S.S. *Maine* knowing that they talked to her as a woman, that they were grateful for her woman's presence, her mere mute presence, and its power to soothe their pain.

All the somethings, swelling swelling to a single whispered word: "No."

No, Rawdon, I love you, but it's wrong. That was what she almost said. Instead she whispered, "It's evil, Rawdon. Evil."

"Evil is not acting, not risking, not believing, Gen. Evil is where we were. Where you still are. Let me take you where I am. Into the light, Gen. The light of tomorrow. The light of the twentieth century."

She shook her head. She was not capable of more than this possibly final act of resistance. If he touched her, she would surrender. Genevieve Dall would be smashed finally and forever. Spiritual and physical surrender would be simultaneous, absolute, incomparable.

Yes, incomparable. Exaltation was what her soul had been yearning to experience since birth. Her New England soul, inherited from her father, the Puritan spirit yearning for transcendent righteousness, perfect blindness, even annihilation in the brightness. She would belong to Rawdon, to this angel of darkness who spoke in the cadences of light, forever. All he had to do was touch her lips with his murderous mouth.

Instead, Rawdon's hand came whirling out of the shadows, striking her in the face. Genevieve hurtled across the room and crashed into a dresser. "You fucking bitch!" Rawdon snarled.

Both hands were whirling now. Terrific slaps drove Genevieve across the room again. Rawdon followed her, never more than an arm's length away, never missing with a single swing, adding a snarl to every blow.

A final smash crumpled her against the wall. He clutched her blouse with one hand and lifted her to meet another series of slaps, backhand, forehand. "I—ought—to—kill—you—now," he said, punctuating each word with a blow.

One last tremendous smash drove Genevieve down the wall into the corner. She curled into a fetal ball, her mind and body a blur of pain.

"You're as responsible for those drowned sailors as I am. Do you know that?" Rawdon said.

Genevieve saw death looming above her unless she answered him. "Yes," she said. "I know it."

A lie. Or was it the truth? The terrible twisted truth?

Genevieve lay there for at least an hour after Rawdon stalked out of the room. She stumbled to the washbasin to bathe her battered face. Out in the harbor, searchlights from the Spanish cruiser *Alfonso XII* played on the hulk of the *Maine*, which had settled into the mud of Havana Harbor. Flames still guttered here and there through the ripped steel plates.

She heard Clay's voice: *Get out of here.* There was no longer any doubt about the wisdom of that advice.

But there was something else Clay had said. Something that echoed in her dazed mind with enormous poignance. *You still stand for something.* No matter what had happened—or failed to happen—between them since she returned from California, he was the one who had helped her survive. She owed him the hand of friendship he had once extended to her.

In ten minutes she was back in the shadowy room above the cable office on Obispo Street. Clay still sat at his desk. The bottle of rum was almost empty. Genevieve poured the rest of it into the sink. "You were right," she said. "He tried to smash me—figuratively and literally."

"I was sure you'd be in bed with him by now," Clay said.

The light was too poor for him to see the bruises on her face. She decided not to show them to him. He might feel impelled to try something heroic. "Clay—I think we should both get out of here," Genevieve said.

"Noble of you. But I've got no place to go."

"Let's worry about that later. Let's get back to the United States and tell the truth about the *Maine*."

Clay drunkenly shook his head. "No evidence. Hearst'd smear us as Spanish agents, Christ knows what else. Ruin you 'specially. Smear the whole woman's movement—unpatriotic."

"Come with me anyway."

Clay shook his head again. "Going to stick with the story. Old newspaperman's instinct. All be leaving soon anyway."

"The war will start?"

"Can't miss."

"I want to tell you something. Are you too drunk to remember it?"

"Depends on how important it is."

"You are not, and never will be, a yellow fellow."

"I'll remember that."

SIX

Esta sí que es calle calle,
Calle de valor y miedo.
Quiero entrar y no me dejan,
Quiero salir y no puedo.

Jonathan Stapleton had heard the song before. The guitarist who sang it in the twilight outside the southern entrance of the royal palace may or may not have appreciated the irony of the words, which Práxedes Sagasta, the quizzical Prime Minister of Spain, had translated for him.

Oh what a street, what a street,
A street of valor and fear.
I want to get in and am barred,
I want to get out and I can't.

"It is a very Spanish song," Sagasta had said, with a grimace. His fringe of gray beard, his mane of gray hair, his melancholy manner seemed more appropriate to a failed poet than to a politician. The Prime Minister had told him the song was a nice summary of Spanish politics. Those who are out of office wait hungrily for power. Those who are in office look desperately for some way to exit with honor. They called Sagasta the smiling pessimist. Canovas, the assassinated Prime Minister whom he replaced, was known as the stern pessimist. In Spanish politics, there were no optimists.

Jonathan mounted the grand staircase with its alternating black and white steps, each a single slab of marble, and trudged down gilded corridors past salons aglow with fresco paintings by the great artists of other centuries. Finally he reached the Hall of the Ambassadors, an immense room with five marble balconies.

Crimson velvet bordered with gold covered the walls. Overhead hung rock-crystal chandeliers, beneath a ceiling painted by Tiepolo. This was the room in which Imperial Spain had received the homage of the nations of the world in its years of glory. More than a vestige of that proud tradition was visible in the regal face of the woman who sat on the room's silver throne guarded by crouching lions of the same precious metal: María Cristina, Queen of Spain.

"Good evening, your majesty," Jonathan said in his atrocious French, and performed the required bow.

"Good evening, Senator," the Queen replied, with a small smile.

Beside the queen, the Marqués de Lema also smiled. The elegant aristocrat had told Jonathan that the Queen found his bow amusing. She said it looked as though his American spine might crack at the necessity of bending before royalty.

The Queen asked if Cynthia's health had improved.

"A great deal," he said. "I had a note from my granddaughter yesterday."

The Queen had given Jonathan a relic of the true cross to send to Cynthia to speed her recovery. Her illness was a nagging worry. For several weeks she had dictated brief letters to Laura and signed them in her usual scrawl. The last two letters had come from Laura, reporting steady improvement.

"I wanted to see you personally, Senator," Queen María Cristina said, "because I thought you should know how much I appreciate America's generosity in this awful crisis. Alas, I must tell you I have conferred with the head of every political party in Spain, and offered to support whoever would form a government and accept your proposal. I have not found one man with the courage to do it."

Jonathan thought the Queen leaned rather hard on the word *homme*. For more than ten years, she had ruled Spain as its constitutional monarch while her son, Alfonso XIII, grew to manhood. She, a woman and an outsider, an Austrian, was willing to risk her son's crown and her hard-earned popularity with the Spanish people for peace. But her politicians remained paralyzed by ambition and self-preservation.

Two days ago, Jonathan had played the last card in his diplomatic hand. He had sat down with Spain's Foreign Minister in his ornate office on the Plaza Oriente and informed him that President McKinley was prepared to pay Spain $300 million for Cuba. To speed the process through the Cortes, Spain's parliament, $6 million would be available to the mediators at once. He had almost gagged on the last part of it, because it stirred memories of Louisiana in 1876. But everyone in the State Department had assured him that it was absolutely necessary. Nothing could be accomplished in Spanish politics without money.

Later in the day, he had repeated the $6 million inducement to the Marqués de Lema. The Marqués had laughed and said, "Very American, that." Now the Queen was telling him that no one was willing to undertake the task. The politicians who traded Cuba for peace might be $6 million richer, but they would be ruined men. Spain's honor, a crucial presence in the street of valor and fear, was now at stake. The insults of Hearst's *Journal* and Pulitzer's *World* had been reprinted in the Spanish newspapers. Only last night there had been a huge demonstration in the Plaza Oriente calling for war against the obnoxious *gringos.*

"It is the affair of the *Maine,*" the Queen said. "It has everyone in torment."

Jonathan Stapleton nodded. He had thoughts about the *Maine* that he could not share with anyone. For the last month, everything revolved around the question of who or what had sunk the ship and killed 266 American sailors. The Madrid papers reported the vicious accusations thundered by Hearst and Pulitzer. THE WARSHIP MAINE WAS SPLIT IN TWO BY AN ENEMY'S SECRET INFERNAL MACHINE, was one Hearst headline. Both the *World* and the *Journal* published a fake cable supposedly from the captain of the *Maine,* saying that the explosion was not an accident.

While Spanish authorities were giving the *Maine*'s dead an elaborate state funeral in Havana and the Spanish government was expressing its condolences to the American embassy in Madrid, the *Journal*'s headline was: HAVANA POPULACE INSULTS THE MEMORY OF THE MAINE VICTIMS. In the same issue, Hearst published a sketch showing how wires from a mine beneath the *Maine* ran to the Havana shore, where a Spanish officer supposedly detonated it.

"In the present atmosphere," the Marqués de Lema was explaining in English that he had learned at Sandhurst, the British military academy, "we are deeply afraid that any agreement reached between the United States and Spain would so outrage our army, there would be a *golpe* from the right, which would destroy the constitution and the dynasty. Her Majesty's courage —and her desire for peace—is really alarming to those who love her and believe her son is Spain's one hope for order."

Jonathan nodded again. He had been given a crash course in Spanish history by a half-dozen Spanish politicians. The country had never recovered from the wrecking job done on it by Napoleon. For sixty years Spain had been tormented by a series of civil wars as the government reeled from autocratic kings and queens to military dictators to a republic to the present system, a constitutional monarchy with the crown as the focus of order, respect, loyalty.

Jonathan had explained this attitude in a long methodical cable to President McKinley. As he wrote it, he wondered if the President would ask himself whether peace with Spain was worth the collapse of the Republican Party. Hearst's repetition of the cry REMEMBER THE MAINE had whipped the country into such a frenzy, any politician—and McKinley was first and last a politician—might shudder at opposing it.

The Queen went over a long list of politicians whom she had consulted.

Finally, after a night of prayer, she had turned to her last hope. She had conferred with the papal nuncio and discovered that Pope Leo XIII was prepared to act as a mediator. "At his recommendation, I am prepared to proclaim an immediate suspension of hostilities in Cuba for six months, and the submission of the fate of the island to his arbitration. You may tell your President in the strictest confidence that I have already reconciled myself to the separation of Cuba from Spain."

"We ask only one small gesture on your part to satisfy the honor of Spain," the Marqués de Lema added. "You have concentrated your battle fleet at Key West. We ask you to withdraw the fleet to a more distant port, as an indication of your confidence in our sincerity."

The Queen gave Jonathan a copy of the proposed proclamation. "It will go to my government tonight," Jonathan said.

Back at the embassy, he and Ambassador Stewart Woodford toiled over the cable. The President was due to place a message on Cuba before Congress in a few days. They decided not to mention the problem of the fleet at Key West and concentrated on the heart of the matter, the Queen's offer to suspend hostilities.

"What do you think our chances are?" Jonathan asked as an attaché rushed the message to the cable office.

"It's a long shot," Woodford said. He was a veteran politician, a former Roscoe Conkling lieutenant and ex-chairman of the New York Republican Party. Woodford thought the recent announcement by William Jennings Bryan that the time had come for intervention in Cuba was particularly ominous. Bryan and his silver-coinage crackpots still controlled the Democratic Party machinery and he was very likely to be renominated in 1900.

Jonathan said good night and walked through the dark chilly streets of Madrid toward his hotel. An occasional pedestrian passed him, muffled to the eyes in his cloak. He was glad he had not brought Cynthia with him. Not even Spaniards bared their throats to the bitter air of Spain's capital.

Instead of carrying him to his hotel on the Calle Mayor, his feet led him into the twisting streets of the old Moorish section of the city. In a few minutes he was sitting in the back of the little parish Church of St. Andrew, where Queen Isabella had prayed for the success of Columbus' voyage. He had come here a dozen times at night, after Queen María Cristina told him she felt it was the most sacred church in Spain. He stared at the white altar, with its banks of blazing candles and its one flickering red lamp in the center, before the tabernacle.

He found himself wishing he could accept Cynthia's faith in a caring presence that gave comfort and guidance to the soul. Tonight all he could do was accept history, to concede its dark inevitability—and simultaneously throw a kind of defiance into its gloomy face. He admired that gallant young

Queen struggling to extricate peace from the politicians. She reminded him of Genevieve, his lost daughter; the severe proud way she held her head and met your eyes as she spoke. Perhaps there was more importance to the struggle for women's equality than he had been willing to concede.

He sat there in the church where a woman had prayed for the stupendous drama that began with that four-hundred-year-old voyage of the Italian navigator, and thought of Cynthia waiting for him in Venice. The last five years had done more than restore her to the center of his private life. She had become his political confederate in this struggle for peace. She had given innumerable dinner parties and receptions aimed at increasing his influence in the Senate. Part of the alarm he felt in Paris had been a guilty awareness that she had risked her health for this difficult, now possibly lost cause. For a moment, staring at the hypnotic tabernacle light, he almost found a prayer on his lips, a plea to let them have a few more years of happiness.

Back in the hotel, he slept well until dawn; then he awoke thrashing out of a dream that he had had a half-dozen times since the madness over Cuba had begun. He was back on the battlefield at Cold Harbor, looking out at the Confederate entrenchments and the thousands of dead men in blue lying in the cleared ground in front of them. He turned and snarled an order for another attack. He thought he was talking to Ben Dall. But the face that emerged from the battle smoke was Rawdon's. There was a blast of musketry, and Jonathan woke up trembling. The last time he had the dream, the face in the smoke had been George's.

At the embassy, he saw from a glance at Woodford's face that the news was bad. The ambassador handed him McKinley's reply.

THE PRESIDENT HIGHLY APPRECIATES THE QUEEN'S DESIRE FOR PEACE. HE CANNOT ASSUME TO INFLUENCE THE ACTION OF THE AMERICAN CONGRESS BEYOND A DISCHARGE OF HIS CONSTITUTIONAL DUTY IN TRANSMITTING THE WHOLE MATTER TO THEM WITH SUCH RECOMMENDATIONS AS HE DEEMS NECESSARY AND EXPEDIENT.

"He's throwing in the sponge," Jonathan said.

Woodford nodded. They both knew that a President did not merely transmit matters to Congress like some powerless figurehead. He was the master of Congress when he chose to be.

"You've done your best, General," Woodford said.

Jonathan sat there shaking his head, thinking of the faces in the battle smoke. Woodford was saying something to him about another telegram. Bad news never comes singly, he was saying. What in God's name was he talking about? There was a telegram in his hand. A telegram from Venice. He opened it and stared at the words: "CYNTHIA DYING PLEASE COME IF POSSIBLE LAURA."

"I'll take the President's message to the Queen," Woodford said.

By noon Jonathan was on a train to Paris. He got there at midnight and had to wait until the next morning to find a train to Italy. He read James Gordon Bennett Jr.'s *Paris Herald* while the *wagon-lits* rolled south through the green center of France. It had the complete story of the President's message to Congress. To salve his conscience, McKinley stopped short of calling for war with Spain. He talked about our duty to humanity, our duty to rescue the Cuban people from their suffering. At the very end, as an afterthought, he mentioned that the Spanish had offered to proclaim a cease-fire.

It was abominable! The House of Representatives, that repository of popular idiocy, had promptly voted for war by 310 to 6. But the Senate had barely consented, 42 to 35. Jonathan writhed. Was this mission to Spain a fraud, designed to get him out of the country? A change of four Senators' votes and there would have been peace. He and Cynthia might have been able to change four minds.

He took out the telegram from Laura. *Come if possible.* Did she really think he might wire back that the salvation of the United States of America required him to let his wife die alone? Those words illuminated his whole sorry record as a husband and father.

Now he understood all those letters dictated to Laura. Cynthia had been dying for the last two months. But she would not let Laura send for him. A long time ago, she had told him that she would prove she loved him. She had proved it not once but twice. She had given him her money. Now she had sacrificed their last two months together to his ruinous devotion to the United States of America.

Land of milk and honey, whispered the consoling voice from another time. Did it mean anything to an America that seemed to be eluding the founders' dreams, Lincoln's hopes? Jonathan Stapleton did not know. All he could do was acknowledge its presence—and his pain.

SEVEN

In the Palazzo Rospigliosi on the Grand Canal in Venice, a great stillness seemed to be engulfing the world. Cynthia lay in her canopied bed, knowing that death was prowling through the room with the dawn's gray light. The Contessa had done her best. She had hired doctors who tinkered with Mrs. Stapleton's diet and nurses who massaged her and bathed and fed her. She had prayed beside her bed and in the chapel of the palace. But the great world, the march of history in which Jonathan was so fatally enmeshed, was not going to release him to satisfy women's wishes or prayers.

A few minutes ago a round-faced priest in a brown cassock stood beside her bed and asked Cynthia if she was sorry for her sins. She nodded and he anointed her hands and her feet with holy oils and placed the sacred host on her tongue. She could not swallow it. She could not seem to swallow anything, either bread or water.

Then Laura stood beside the Contessa and they were both weeping. She reached out her hand to touch Laura's prism of a face, so perfectly beautiful, Charlie's face, in the golden haze of the moonlight at Bralston, and Rawdon's face, calling her *wicked stepmother*. She wanted to tell her how simple life was, if you *loved*, that was the only test, to love a serious man seriously, even if you failed. To attempt it, in spite of knowing that in his world, so dark with blunderous history, love was not the main thing, love was always at risk.

Her reach somehow failed. Laura's face withdrew into a shimmering distance. Something magical was happening. Cynthia rose in the stillness, as if her body was composed of air. She looked down on them now, at weeping Laura and the sorrowful Contessa and the sleeping woman on the bed. So much gray in her hair. What would her friends think if they found out that she had been dyeing it for years?

Pounding footsteps in the hall. Jonathan burst into the room. He embraced Laura and sank down beside the woman on the bed. He had come after all. He had abandoned the United States of America for her sake. There was some conversation with the Contessa. They seemed to think she was still in her body. Oh, this was delicious. But sad. Jonathan was weeping. "I've only begun to love her," he said. "Really love her."

Cynthia left him there and wandered the white-and-gold halls of the palazzo, remembering the happy hours they had spent there in other days. Above all, that marvelous summer of 1867, their honeymoon summer, when the whole world seemed to belong to them, to await their pleasure. In particular she paused in the master bedroom, where they had looked out on the Grand Canal on their first golden morning in Venice and she had whispered, *My dearest friend.*

Suddenly the most extraordinary sight appeared through the mist on the canal. A huge white steamboat moving without a sound or the sign of a ripple on the water. It was for her. It was the steamboat of her dreams at Bralston, coming to carry her away to a destiny beyond the stars. She hurried back to the bedroom where she had died and kissed Jonathan's cheek. "Goodbye," she whispered. "Goodbye, my dearest friend."

Magically, such was the power of the spirit, she moved along the halls to the palazzo's great doors, which opened at a wave of her hand. Down the steps she went to the edge of the canal as the steamboat arrived, docking expertly, without a sound of bells, a hoot of the whistle, in spite of the thick dawn mist.

She was sure there would be friends aboard. She expected to see her mother, Jeff Forsyth, her brother Lancombe, perhaps Blind Tom the fiddler, and her father at the wheel in the pilothouse. And Mittie Roosevelt in a shimmering white gown. But there was no one.

Still she was not in the least afraid. She would meet them all at the end of the voyage. Jonathan would be there, too, when it ended beyond the stars.

Cynthia looked up and saw in the window of the palazzo his scarred face, blank with desolation. She realized she had left without revealing the secret she had waited to tell him.

"I never loved Charlie. I never loved anyone but you," she called.

Somehow he seemed to hear her. His face softened. He began to weep again. That was the last thing she saw, Jonathan's scarred grieving face, dwindling, dwindling, as the great paddlewheels silently churned the dark water and she rode down the canal past fog-shrouded palaces and churches to the sea.

EIGHT

Nipping bourbon from a flask, Clay Pendleton stood beside William Randolph Hearst on the heaving deck of the steamship *Sylvia*. They were watching hundreds of small boats unloading American soldiers from thirty-two transports off the southern coast of Cuba. The boats, mostly navy cutters, maneuvered through heavy surf to land the men on a rocky beach, beyond which lay a rim of barren gray hills. The June heat was stifling, even on the water. Around them, a half-dozen men snapped photographs, and one cranked a moving-picture camera.

From a Darwinian point of view, Pendleton was riding high. He had just produced near ecstasy in his employer by pulling off a hoax on Pulitzer and the *World* that left all New York guffawing. Pendleton had invented a foreign volunteer, Colonel Reflipe W. Thenuz, and a story of how he had died fighting heroically beside the Cuban rebels in a recent battle. When the *World* republished the story with embellishments, the *Journal* revealed that the Colonel's name was a rearrangement of: "We pilfer the news."

Hearst studied the coast through field glasses. "See that blockhouse on the plateau above the beach?" he said. "Let's put an American flag up there. It's got a flagstaff waiting for it."

"I'll send Marshall," Pendleton said.

They signaled a *Journal* cutter—there were ten of them roving through the fleet off the beach—and Pendleton scribbled out the order to the correspondent on shore.

"How's Stapleton coming with his report?" Hearst asked. "I want to present it to General Shafter."

In the main cabin, Pendleton found Rawdon writing at a table covered with recent copies of the *Journal*, all with the top-of-the-page blurb, HOW DO YOU LIKE THE JOURNAL'S WAR?

"The Commander in Chief wants to know if you've finished your report."

"It's right here," Rawdon said, pointing to a sheaf of papers on which he had been working since dawn. "This," he added, folding the page and putting it into an envelope, "is a letter to Laura. Give it to her if I get killed."

"What if *I* get killed?"

"Editors don't get killed."

"I'm not an editor anymore. The Commander in Chief's demoted me to butler. But I've persuaded him to let me earn my outrageous salary by doing some reporting."

"About time."

Rawdon handed him the letter and lit a cigarette. He tilted his chair against the swaying bulkhead and closed his eyes. His face was gray, his khaki knickers gashed and torn, his tan shirt smeared with mud. They had picked him up on a point of land only nine miles from the harbor of Santiago, shivering with some tropical fever. He had obtained from his Cuban compatriots a good estimate of the number of Spanish soldiers in the Santiago garrison, the location of their main fortifications, and the disposition of the Spanish fleet in the harbor. It was Rawdon's third venture into Cuba since the war began in April.

"No message for Eleanor or your son?" Pendleton said, putting the letter into his pocket.

"You deliver it. You're better at noble bullshit that I am, Pendleton."

"He's a cute little kid," Pendleton said. He had seen the boy, now almost two years old, at Cynthia Stapleton's funeral in New York. He had been puzzled by Rawdon's indifference to him in contrast to his near-obsession with his daughter.

"He's not my son," Rawdon said, head back, his eyes still closed. "He's Eleanor's insurance policy—and my private joke on the General. He's the illegitimate son of Eleanor's ex-cook. We faked Eleanor's pregnancy when I went to Cuba to make sure that the old bastard would support her if I got killed." He took a long drag on his cigarette. "It was the best way to get her off my mind."

Pendleton nodded. He had stopped arguing with Rawdon. He was along as a Darwinian observer, nothing more. He told himself he was motivated only by a desire to keep eating regularly—although he was not averse to a little revenge on Pulitzer. Every once in a while an inner voice disagreed. He heard Genevieve Dall saying: *you are not a yellow fellow.* But it was a voice crying in a yellow wilderness.

Besides, Genevieve was no longer a newspaperwoman. She had quit Hearst and become a full-time woman's-rights crusader.

A tremendous racket drew them out on deck. In obedience to Hearst's order, one of the *Journal*'s reporters had raised the American flag on the abandoned blockhouse overlooking the beach. The men ashore and in the small boats and on the transports and warships were cheering, and all the ships' whistles were joining in the salute.

"Patriotism," Rawdon said.

There was an edge of emotion in his voice that his sarcasm did not entirely obliterate. The two months they had spent in Tampa while the War Department organized an army to invade Cuba had been a difficult experience for Rawdon. He had discovered two generations of Americans behind him: officers in their thirties like his brother George and Theodore Roosevelt, and boys of eighteen and twenty in the ranks, all aflame with patriotic idealism.

It was stunning to discover how totally the younger men had swallowed the lies Hearst had told them about the Spaniards. It was almost demoralizing to hear them shout, "Remember the *Maine!*"

"Isn't this marvelous?" Hearst said, gesturing like an impresario to the patriotic uproar. "Be sure and get a story from the reporter who raised the flag, Pendleton. I want it in New York for tomorrow morning's edition."

Hearst was wearing a white linen suit and a flowery tie and a panama hat. He might have been strolling down Fifth Avenue. The contrast between him and Rawdon's battered condition was stark. "You look pretty done in, Stapleton," he said. "Is the report ready?"

"Yes," Rawdon said. He had been barely civil to Hearst since the publisher arrived on the scene with his flotilla of dispatch boats and his army of reporters and photographers. Hearst's ebullience seemed to grate on Rawdon's nerves. Perhaps it had something to do with the way Hearst talked and talked about the *Maine.* He was in the process of raising money for a monument to the 266 dead sailors.

In the cabin Hearst read Rawdon's report of the whereabouts and strength of the Cuban army led by General Calixto García. He was operating west of Santiago; the Americans were landing to the east. Hearst spread a map of Cuba on the table and began planning a pincer movement on the Spanish garrison. Rawdon pointed to the figures in his report. García claimed he had five thousand men, but Rawdon thought the truth was closer to two thousand. "Most of them are so weak from hunger they can't do any real fighting."

"We'll get them food. How much would a week's rations for two thousand men cost, Pendleton?"

"I'll find out, Mr. Hearst," Pendleton said.

"Can't you see the story?" Hearst said, beaming. " 'The *Journal's* Food Fuels Cuban Freedom Fighters.' "

"I think the most we can do is persuade García to block Spanish reinforcements to Santiago when we attack," Rawdon said.

"Good idea," Hearst said, enjoying himself hugely. He really did consider it his war, and he was determined to tell the admirals and the generals how to win it. Shortly after 1 P.M. they boarded a launch and rode through the fleet to the transport U.S.S. *Seguranca* to confer with the army's commander in chief, Brigadier General William E. Shafter. Hearst blithely greeted him as if

he were on the *Journal* staff and handed him Rawdon's report of his recon-
naissance of Santiago.

Shafter was not a reassuring sight to those who wanted to believe that
America's victory in Cuba would be swift and certain. The General was sixty-
three years old and virtually spherical—he weighed over three hundred
pounds. He spoke—and moved—with mastodonlike slowness.

Hearst briskly demanded that Shafter tell them his plan for the campaign.
The General, seeming to recognize the presence of a superior power, did so.
The main Spanish fleet was in Santiago Harbor. His orders were to capture
the city and force the fleet either to surrender or to run for the open sea,
where the American fleet would attack and destroy it with the same dispatch
that Admiral George Dewey had displayed in annihilating the Spanish squadron in Manila Bay two months ago.

Hearst pointed to Rawdon's estimate of the Santiago garrison at well over
twenty thousand men. Shafter had only seventeen thousand. Hearst wanted
to know if the General thought his army was big enough. If not, the *Journal*
would immediately demand reinforcements for him.

"Stapleton here says Spanish morale is high. They blame us for preventing
them from beating the Cubans and they can't wait to get a whack at us."

"Stapleton?" General Shafter said, "Jonathan Stapleton's son?"

Rawdon nodded.

"I served with your father in the big war. I wish they'd sent him down here
for this campaign. But someone has to train the volunteers."

At his wife's funeral, Jonathan Stapleton had told Pendleton he still considered the war a travesty. But he had succumbed to the President's plea and
resigned from the Senate to accept a commission as a major general. This
helped to balance several commissions given to former Confederate generals,
including Fitzhugh Lee, Rawdon's consular collaborator in Havana.

Shafter assured Hearst that he had complete confidence in the men under
his command, especially the regulars. Almost all of America's tiny regular
army was in the expedition. Hearst frowned. He told Shafter not to favor
regulars over volunteers. The *Journal* wanted to see the volunteers have an
equal share in the victory. He did not explain to General Shafter that this
would help sell papers. There was no need for a commander in chief to
explain everything to his subordinates.

When they returned to the *Sylvia*, Hearst beckoned Pendleton into his
private cabin. It was decorated with another large portrait of Napoleon, not
unlike the one in his office at the *Journal*. A bust of the Emperor sat on a
shelf.

"I'm shocked by Shafter," Hearst said. "I want you to start a new file. Call
it presidential reforms. We'll put into it the things I intend to change when I

become president. Number one on the list will be a rule that no general over the age of sixty can command an army."

"Yes, Mr. Hearst," Pendleton said.

A week later, the American army began its advance up the Camino Real to Santiago in a pelting rainstorm. In ten minutes the King's Highway became a bog of sucking mud that pulled the boots off men's feet. Pendleton and Rawdon marched with Theodore Roosevelt's Rough Riders, officially known as the First Volunteer Cavalry. Hearst had decided to make this mostly New York regiment the heroes of the battle. With their heavy sprinkling of famous names, the Rough Riders were guaranteed circulation builders.

When it finally stopped raining, the woods emitted billows of fetid air that threatened the marching men with asphyxiation. The temperature continued to hover around one hundred. The men were wearing woolen winter uniforms—the only ones the army in its rush to war could find in its warehouses. Dozens of marchers collapsed from heat prostration. The rear of the column was soon littered with blanket rolls, canteens, haversacks of rations, which Cuban soldiers eagerly appropriated.

By this time the Americans had written off the Cubans as allies. They were too few in number—and Rawdon's report of their semi-starved condition proved to be all too accurate. Stephen Crane, with his fondness for savage truths, wrote that eating, not fighting, was the Cuban soldier's chief interest.

Far to the rear, General Shafter was lying in a hammock, sweating and shaking with malaria, to which age had added a bad case of gout in his left foot. He had handed his subordinates a battle plan that was so simple everyone in the army knew it. Half the Americans were going to attack the fortified village of El Caney, on one flank of Santiago's defenses, then join the other half to assault the trenches on San Juan Hill, overlooking the city.

On July 1, the army camped in the jungle, close enough to the Spanish positions to prepare for battle. The reporters sat around the campfire with Roosevelt and his officers, listening to them discuss the skirmish they had fought at Las Guásimas just after they landed in Cuba. They had lost over fifty men and discovered a number of dismaying things about the Spanish army. The enemy were crack shots and were equipped with German-made Mauser rifles, which used smokeless powder, enabling them to remain almost invisible in the jungle. The Americans had thirty-year-old Springfields, which emitted a blast of smoke with every shot, making the shooter an instant target.

In spite of the lessons of Las Guásimas, Roosevelt and some of his captains were still not convinced that an officer should take cover under fire. Rawdon vehemently reiterated the lecture he had given them at Las Guásimas, "Anyone who doesn't keep his head and his ass as close to the ground as possible is a goddamn idiot," he snarled.

"Before Las Guásimas, I didn't agree with you," Captain George Stapleton said. "But that fracas changed my mind." George had been one of the first to volunteer when Roosevelt announced he was raising the regiment.

Captain Bucky O'Neil, one of the Rough Riders' swaggering westerners, scoffed. Rawdon suggested his brain was made of buffalo chips, and O'Neil drew a bowie knife and dared him to repeat it. Wiser if not calmer heads separated them. Rawdon left the volunteers to their debate and withdrew to a distant palm tree. Pendleton joined him and offered to split a bottle of Hearst's rum he had stuffed in his haversack for emergencies.

"Asshole idealists," Rawdon snarled, gulping the liquor straight.

"Is there something on your mind—or conscience?" Pendleton asked.

"I don't want to see George get killed. Believe it or not, Pendleton, I've always been fond of that dumb bastard."

They drank in silence for a while. When the bottle was half empty, Pendleton asked a question that had been on his mind since he came to Cuba. "As one old oarsman to another, are you on the level about being a revolutionary?"

In the moonlight, Pendleton thought he saw craftiness on Rawdon's face. But he was not sure. "What the hell do you care?" Rawdon said.

"I'm interested. It's part of the story."

"Are you planning to write about me, Pendleton?"

"Maybe. Maybe I'd just like to know the truth."

"Jesus Christ. You're still bugged by that word. I guess you're never going to stop trying to be a good boy, are you, Pendleton?"

"I guess not."

Rawdon took a long gulp of rum. "The answer is yes, Pendleton. This time I'm not going to let anybody turn me back. Not you with your bullshit about the truth or Genevieve with her goddamn bloodless rationalism or Eleanor with her pathetic whimpers. After we win here Laura and I are going to take Winty Chapman's money and go to Mexico. That's the real prize, and it's ripe for revolution. Whoever grabs that country can take the rest of South America in a walk. We're going to organize a new international, based on American ideas, independent of those German and Russian assholes who worship Karl Marx. The earth belongs to the living. Do you know who wrote that beautiful anarchistic idea, Pendleton?"

"Thomas Jefferson. But James Madison told him it was idiotic and he dropped it."

"Fuck you and your know-it-all realism, Pendleton. I hope you marry Genevieve. She'll cut off your balls and wear them for a charm bracelet."

Pendleton chose silence. When he saw the bruises on Genevieve's face in Havana, he had come close to going after Rawdon with a gun. They had not mentioned her name since she left them.

Rawdon drank and brooded for a moment. "I almost had her that night—when the *Maine* . . ." He could not seem to find a word to describe what had happened to the *Maine.* "I almost had her the way I've always wanted her."

"Old friend, you should have known that nobody can change Antiope's mind. That's her kingdom."

"Old friend." Rawdon was slurring his words. It was the first time Pendleton had seen him get drunk since he arrived in Cuba. "I sometimes think you've been more of an enemy than a friend for a long time, Pendleton."

"I think 'enemy' is a little strong. People hate their enemies. My feelings have been closer to those emotions they say are necessary to a successful tragedy. Pity and fear."

"That's interesting," Rawdon said. "Pity and fear sum up what I've felt about you since 1876. Pity for your pusillanimous soul, fear that I might succumb to it. What would you call that state of mind, Pendleton?"

"Loath. I believe the dictionary defines that word as unwilling, reluctant, disinclined. Add an *e* and you get 'loathe.' I've tried, but I've never quite managed to add the *e.*"

"I like that, Pendleton. That's where I am, too. Loath."

They started to laugh. They laughed and laughed until out of the darkness flew an army boot and a curse. "Why don't you dumb bastards go to sleep? We've got a war to fight," snarled the voice of the American soldier.

The next day began with the boom of artillery far off on the American right flank—the opening of the attack on the fortified town of El Caney. A few minutes later, more cannons crashed a few hundred yards behind them, on a ridge known as El Pozo. A cloud of white smoke hovered over the foot soldiers. Almost instantly Spanish shells came hissing through the acrid haze. The Rough Riders hastily sought shelter in the jungle at the base of the hill.

An hour and a half later, the infantry began their advance up the Camino Real again. It was the only road to Santiago, and the Spaniards knew it. They had hundreds of snipers in the trees along the route and soon the air was thick with the feline whine of Mauser bullets. Ahead of the Rough Riders marched a brigade of regulars. The side of the road soon became populated with their dead and wounded. Where the road crossed San Juan Creek, the jungle ended and Mauser bullets poured down in sheets from the Spanish trenches on the heights.

"It's a goddamn massacre," Rawdon said.

That was no exaggeration. There were dozens of dead bodies floating in the creek. Dozens more lay along the bank. For a moment the Rough Riders halted, milled, then dove for cover as the Mausers went to work on them. Roosevelt rode among them, cursing furiously, shouting that they had to cross the creek. Simultaneously, the army supplied them with another nightmare. Over their heads appeared a yellow observation balloon, towed by a half-dozen men. It was exactly what the Spanish artillery needed to identify the whereabouts of the column. Soon shells were gouging the muddy earth all around them.

One of the officers in the gondola of the balloon threw down a message. George Stapleton crawled into the bullet-swept center of the Camino Real and brought it back to Roosevelt. It told them that there was another crossing of the creek, five hundred yards to the left. Roosevelt roared orders to the regiment, and they headed for it as the balloon, riddled by Spanish bullets, came whirling down, practically on top of them.

They crossed the creek and crawled into the high grass along the bank while Spaniards on a small hill just in front of them poured bullets into their ranks. For the next two hours the Rough Riders lay there taking fearful punishment. Anyone who did more than raise his head risked instant death. Even Roosevelt got off his horse and took cover in the grass. Only one officer, the western daredevil Captain Bucky O'Neil, stayed on his feet. Pendleton, flat in the grass a few yards away, watched while a sergeant pleaded with him to get down. O'Neil coolly lit a cigarette and said, "The Spanish bullet hasn't been made that will kill me." A second later, a bullet struck him in the mouth and went out the back of his head.

The Rough Riders grew more and more frantic. "Show us somebody to fight," they shouted to their officers. "For God's sake don't keep us here to be shot without giving us a show."

George Stapleton crawled to Roosevelt and offered to take a message back to Shafter, asking for orders to attack. Roosevelt scrawled it, and George disappeared into the grass. He came back in an hour to report that the road behind them was jammed with regiments still trying to get into position, and with walking wounded, deserters, men who had broken under fire. There was no sign of General Shafter anywhere.

A moment later, a lieutenant colonel rode up and shouted, "Forward, forward! Support the regulars." He pointed up the hill to the right, where lines of blue-clad soldiers, many of them black cavalrymen of the Ninth and Tenth Regiments, were advancing in long irregular lines. Roosevelt leaped on his horse and spurred it into the grass ahead of the Rough Riders, his sword in his hand. Not a man rose to follow him into the whining swarms of bullets.

"Are you afraid to stand up? Look at me—on horseback!" he roared. A man stood up a foot away from him and was shot dead.

Out of the sword grass a dozen feet away rose Captain George Stapleton. "H Company is with you, Colonel," he shouted. A bullet knocked off his hat. He ignored it and turned to his men. "On your feet," he said. "We're going up." Sixty men obeyed him. Seconds later the entire regiment was standing in the deadly firestorm.

"Charge!" Roosevelt howled, and spurred his horse up the hill. The Rough Riders soon blended with the regulars, and the long blue line went up the slope in a tenuous, wavering but somehow irresistible way, ignoring men who pitched forward or toppled backward into the grass, closing ranks where a half-dozen men were swept away by a burst of Spanish fire.

"My God, they're fantastic," Rawdon shouted. "Let's go, Pendleton."

He pulled the pistol out of Captain Bucky O'Neil's holster and started up the hill. Forgotten were all his words of caution about the deadly aim of Spanish marksmen. He was an American, Jonathan Stapleton's son, joining his brother and his fellow Americans in a moment of historic glory.

Rawdon had gone only a step when the bullet hit him in the heart. Pendleton felt the *chug* in his own flesh. Rawdon tried to ignore it. He took one, two more steps but a third was impossible. He twisted sideways as he fell, so Pendleton, when he knelt beside him, looked into his face.

"Clay," Rawdon said. "Help me up—I want—"

Then he was gone, spinning into the darkness like the meteor he had always been, leaving behind him the seared lives of those he had touched in his plunge past earth.

Ignoring the headlines being made on the heights above him, Pendleton picked up Rawdon's body and struggled back down the trail. It was crowded with wounded men; some were being carried on litters, others were hobbling along on their own. Around them hissed bullets from Spanish snipers, cutting down wounded and helpers. Pendleton finally reached an aid station a mile back in the woods. Hundreds of men were lying on the ground. A frantic young doctor rushed up to him. "Where's he hit?"

"In the heart," Pendleton said.

"What the hell do you expect us to do for him?" The doctor rushed off to examine other new arrivals.

Pendleton laid Rawdon on the ground at the edge of the clearing and knelt down beside him. For some reason he could not bear the thought of leaving him. He sat there remembering a voice saying, *I don't let misfortune befall people I love.* A reaching hand, a different voice saying, *Give me that telegram.* A figure in white kneeling before a dead Irishman in a Pittsburgh street. Another voice saying, *There's a shining message in it somewhere.*

One of the wounded spread out on the grass around the aid station started singing, "My country 'tis of thee . . ." Other voices joined him. Soon the quavering, mostly off-key sound of pain-filled patriotism competed in the humid jungle air with the thunder and crackle of cannons and rifles.

Then people were shouting reports of victory. They had captured San Juan Hill. But the Spanish were still full of fight, blistering the crest with artillery and rifle fire.

A big hand fell on Pendleton's shoulder. He looked up at William Randolph Hearst's excited face. "El Caney was fantastic. We captured a Spanish flag for the *Journal*. Who's this? Stapleton? It looks like he's run out of luck. Get this story to a dispatch boat as fast as possible."

Hearst thrust a sheaf of notepaper at Pendleton. He ignored it.

"How did Roosevelt do?"

"He was fantastic. He's a presidential candidate. Guaranteed."

"Marvelous. Did you get a statement from him?"

"No."

"Have you written anything, for Christ's sake?"

"You write it. Just put a sword in your hand and imagine how you'd feel riding uphill into about ten thousand bullets."

"I'm paying you to write it."

"I prefer not to."

"What the hell's the matter with you?" Hearst shrilled. "You've seen dead men before."

"I loved him," Pendleton said.

"That's no excuse for not filing the story of the goddamn century!"

"I prefer not to," Pendleton said.

NINE

Major General Jonathan Stapleton sat at his desk in the ramshackle headquarters in the middle of the training camp near Cold Harbor, Virginia, where sixty thousand Americans from the North and the South were learning to be soldiers. He was reading with an expert's eyes the details of the attack on San Juan Heights and El Caney. They were outposts, nothing more. About seven hundred Spanish soldiers had inflicted over twelve hundred casualties on the attacking Americans—almost ten percent of their effective strength. The Americans were now clinging to these outposts under artillery and small-arms fire, trying to decide what to do next. An attack on the main defenses of Santiago would undoubtedly cost them another five thousand men—and might very well fail.

It would be a miracle if Captain George Stapleton survived. He had seen his type of naïve idealist die by the hundreds in the Civil War. He had tried to talk to him before he left for Cuba, to tell him that an officer had to lead by example, but that did not mean he had to get killed doing it. George barely listened. He was determined to live up to the sort of brainless courage his wife expected of him.

On his desk was a frantic query from the Secretary of War: "ARMY IN CUBA IN DANGER OF COLLAPSE. MALARIA, YELLOW FEVER, DYSENTERY TAKING TERRIBLE TOLL. CAN YOU SUPPLY 20,000 REPLACEMENTS IMMEDIATELY?" The splendid little war Theodore Roosevelt and his friends had wanted to inspire a renewal of patriotism might yet end in a humiliating disaster.

"Idiocy," Jonathan Stapleton growled, glaring at the misleading headlines in the *New York Journal* and other papers, trumpeting that the Americans had won a glorious victory.

"Did you call me, General?" asked his aide, a young West Point graduate named Jefferson Davis King. He had a thick Georgia drawl.

"Have we got that report on which regiments we can send to Cuba?"

"Not yet, sir. General Taylor says they all want to go. It's impossible to get a decent estimate of their readiness from the officers."

"Tell Taylor to pick them by lot, in that case."

"Yes, sir. The review will be starting in fifteen minutes, General."

"I know. Is my horse ready?"

King hustled out to the parade ground. A moment later a private with a Signal Corps patch on his shoulder stuck his head warily into the office. "General Stapleton?" he said. "Got a telegram for you."

He handed Jonathan the yellow Western Union envelope. Jonathan gazed at it for a full minute before opening it. George was dead. What else could it be? All the love he had failed to give him pounded in Jonathan's veins. Finally, he cut it open and read: "RAWDON KILLED JULY 1 ON SAN JUAN HILL. DEEPEST SYMPATHY. CLAY PENDLETON."

Rawdon.

No. He was the indestructible one, the son who had tried to slay him, the father. The son he had been forced to slay in his heart a thousand times, who rose again and again with his furious refusal to obey, to understand, to forgive.

The boy on the rocking horse, with the prince's arrogant stare. That boy still sat on his desk, here in the middle of another battlefield, where Americans had once slaughtered each other in record numbers. He picked up the photograph and held it against his heart.

The accuser, the one who had whispered "Butcher" within the walls of his own house, who had joined his mother and grandmother in trying to destroy the meaning of his war, to strip the dead of their sacred purpose. Dead now, in another war. Was there any meaning to it?

Perhaps this pain paid the price of those savage words, *Father, you're talking like a fool.* Now he was one with that grieving father, he could reach into the darkness and ask his forgiveness too. He could even ask the same gift from his mother. He could see, he could almost feel, the anguish history had inflicted on her, the guilt she felt at Charlie's death, her wild wish to give it meaning.

Rawdon. Rawdon. Rawdon.

Captain King returned with a cheerful smile on his freckled face. "All set, General. I got Swaney Sue, the big brown mare, for you. I know you like to ride Mars, but that stallion will never stand still for a whole review."

"Good," he said.

He left the telegram on his desk and went out and mounted Swaney Sue. With King beside him, he rode across the parade ground to the line of field officers waiting on horseback in front of the massed regiments in blue.

General Taylor, his white beard trimmed to make him resemble his old Confederate commander, Robert E. Lee, nudged his horse out of the line and saluted. "Sir," he said. "The Seventh Corps is ready for inspection and review."

"Thank you, General," Jonathan said, returning the salute.

With Taylor beside him, Jonathan rode slowly past every regiment. He stopped in front of the Twenty-first Ohio and asked the short stocky lieutenant colonel, "Do you think your men are ready to go to Cuba?"

"Yes, sir," the colonel replied.

"If we don't go we're goin' to write our congressman," someone yelled from the rear ranks.

General Stapleton asked the same question of the Fourteenth Alabama. The lieutenant colonel, a tall austere-looking man, whirled and asked the whole regiment to answer. "Yes, sir!" they roared, and added a rebel yell.

"I wish we could send them all," Taylor said. "Did I tell you that I've requested permission to go with them?"

"You may begin the review, General," Jonathan said.

He sat there on his horse as the band played "The Star-Spangled Banner" and Old Glory fluttered in the massed colors beside him. Line after line of blue-clad soldiers swung by to salute the General and the flag. The bands played a mixture of southern and northern songs, "Tenting Tonight," "Aura Lea," "The Battle Hymn of the Republic." At their first review the bandmaster had nervously asked Jonathan if it was all right to play "Dixie." "Certainly," he had replied. "As long as you play 'The Battle Cry of Freedom' right after it."

Maybe there was some purpose to it all, Jonathan mused, staring at the young faces. Here he was, sitting beside an ex-Confederate general, reviewing troops from almost every state in the Union. That was a step, a very tiny step in the right direction. But he still did not believe it had required a war to make it. Nor was it, in his lonely opinion, the larger step America needed to take. There was not a single black soldier in those ranks. He had written a furious letter to the Secretary of War, denouncing the policy of refusing black volunteers. He had not received a reply.

A fat man rushed out of the headquarters building and ran along the edge of the parade ground. He was a Signal Corps major. He puffed up to Jonathan and gasped, "General! The news just came over the wire. They've sunk the whole Spanish fleet off Cuba. They tried to make a run for it and we've sunk every damn one of them."

Jonathan turned to Brigadier General Taylor. "Why don't you tell the news to the troops? You're better at making speeches than I am."

When the review ended and the men were in the ranks again, Taylor announced the naval victory in spreadeagle style. Jonathan listened to the apostrophes to glory and heroism and the answering cheers and thought of Rawdon in the sword grass on San Juan Hill. Genevieve had tried to explain why Rawdon had wanted the war, but Jonathan had found it incomprehensible that his son could allow his mind to be consumed by foreign ideas about a world revolution.

Back in headquarters, Captain King and his staff were waiting for him. King had found the telegram. They murmured condolences, shook his hand. He thanked them in a calm, mechanical way. A part of his inner self, where his emotions lived, seemed amputated. It was the way he had always imagined dying would feel. Only after the staff departed and he was alone did Jonathan realize that his life was not over. There were other human beings who required his care.

He dreaded how Laura would react to Rawdon's death. He was certain her grief would be extravagant. He remembered, not without pain, her reaction to Cynthia's death. Outside the bedroom, he had turned to Laura and said, with nothing but grief and regret in his mind, "Now you're the only person in the world who loves me."

Her response had been chilling. "Of course I love you, Pa," she had said. "But not the way I loved her."

Genevieve, who was living at the house on Stuyvesant Square, might also be a problem. A half-dozen times she had talked about Rawdon in a way that made him suspect she knew something much more terrible than Rawdon's descent into anarchism, but could not bring herself to tell him.

He decided to return to New York immediately. The naval victory made the end of the war a certainty. He handed over the command of the camp to General Taylor and told Captain King to get him a seat on the first northbound train. It occurred to him as he packed that Eleanor and her scrawny son, who had no resemblance to any Stapleton or Dall in his memory, would now become the family's responsibility.

As he was about to leave for the depot, Captain King handed him a package that had just arrived from New York. It was a copy of the *New York Journal* for July 3rd. Bordered in black was the story of Rawdon's death, described in feverish prose as an act of supreme heroism. With it was a letter from Pulitzer.

> MY DEAR GENERAL:
>
> Please accept my deepest sympathy for your loss. Let me take this opportunity to tell you how much I regretted the necessity of attacking you in the *World* for your views on the war. It was a time of excess in all directions, in which the *World* committed perhaps more than its share of sins. May I still call you my friend?

Jonathan Stapleton scribbled a telegram and told Captain King to send it to Pulitzer: "IF YOU WANT TO PROVE YOU ARE MY FRIEND—AND STOP YOUR NEWSPAPER FROM TURNING INTO YELLOW TRASH—HIRE CLAY PENDLETON BACK FROM HEARST." Then he boarded the train to New York to console his grieving women.

TEN

Genevieve lay in Cynthia Stapleton's bed listening to her daughter sob. Laura was in her room, across the hall. It was a month since Genevieve had returned from a planning session for the forty-ninth congress of the American Woman Suffrage Association and found Laura with the July 3rd edition of the *World* clutched to her breasts, rocking back and forth on the edge of the couch in the darkened parlor.

For Genevieve the news had been like a blow in the face—one last smash out of the darkness. Although she embraced Laura and tried to find comforting words, the image that crowded her mind was Rawdon in her room in the Hotel Inglaterra, going from exaltation to murderous hatred in a breath. A dozen times since she returned to New York Genevieve had awakened trembling from a dream in which he was trying to batter down the door to get at her again. Now he was gone: the male figure against whom she had struggled for most of her life.

For a time, Eleanor's hysteria had vied with Laura's agony. But she had been soothed by a trip to Europe at Jonathan Stapleton's expense. Genevieve was left to cope with Laura. As her grief persisted, it became like a dark thing in the night, threatening her own stability. No one seemed able to console Laura, neither her grandfather nor her mother nor her fiancé. Winthrop Astor Chapman visited her every day. He emptied flower shops, he took her for rides in his Stanley Steamer, the latest favorite in the growing craze for automobiles. He feasted her at Delmonico's. Still her gloom persisted.

More than once, Genevieve was tempted to tell Laura the truth about her father. But Clay Pendleton had complicated this problem by convincing Genevieve that the whole truth—Rawdon's role in the destruction of the *Maine*—might kill General Stapleton. Clay had added a further complication by giving Laura a letter from Rawdon that she refused to show anyone. Genevieve was sure it was an attempt to possess her soul from beyond the grave.

Clay had quit Hearst and come home from Cuba without a job. He said that he was talking to several newspapers, including the *New York Times*, which was rapidly reviving under a new publisher. Last week he had talked of going back to South Carolina and starting a crusading paper there. Living dangerously, he called it.

He was obviously trying to elicit a response from Genevieve Dall. She had none to give him. Her inability to console Laura confirmed her inner emptiness. She decided that she was incapable of giving affection to anyone. With a stoicism worthy of Jonathan Stapleton in his grimmest iron-general phase, she abandoned all hope of a personal life.

Her confrontation with Rawdon had sent her back into the woman's movement, not as a public speaker but as a politician working behind the scenes. She was involved in a nerve-shredding struggle to regroup and restructure the suffrage organization, to get rid of failed tactics and aging leaders. Genevieve wanted to give meaning and substance to her refusal to join Rawdon's dark idealism. She wanted to prove to herself—and the rest of the world—that there was another choice, another path to peace and justice. And women would lead the way.

Still Laura sobbed. Suddenly it was more than Genevieve could bear. She would tell Laura the truth about Rawdon. She would make her stop mourning her murderous father.

She sprang out of bed, fumbled for her robe. The city murmured outside the open windows in the August heat. She heard her footsteps thud in the silent house. She was in the hall, her hand on the knob of Laura's door.

"Don't—"

It was Jonathan Stapleton in the darkness at the other end of the hall. A click and the electric light came on. He was spectral, the gaunt face above the dark-blue military robe.

"I want to tell her. I've got a right to tell her—she's not the only one who's ever lost a father."

The words seemed to burst from the center of her body as if they were ripped by an invisible hand. They were an evasion of the ugly truth she wanted to tell her daughter and shrank from telling this man. But they inflicted pain on Jonathan Stapleton's scarred face.

"I tried to make up for it," he said.

"Why? Why did you feel so responsible for my father's death? He dragged you into the war."

"I loved him," he said. "But I failed him—failed that love—when I turned on him during the Draft Riots. I looked down First Avenue at the men—and women and children—we'd just slaughtered, and I said to him, 'Ben, the price of freeing your niggers is too high.' I wounded him, wounded the love between us, in the deepest most terrible way."

Laura continued to sob. Genevieve stood there in the sweltering darkness of New York in August trying to connect that threatening word, love, to the twisted threads of history in which they were entangled. She remembered the blazing day in July of 1863 when her father had come home from killing men and women in the streets of New York. Now she knew what she had seen on his face that day—it had been not only the horror of the war in the heart of the city, it had also been the death of love, the only love that meant anything in Ben Dall's transcendental soul. *Jonathan Stapleton, the quintessential American, the thing itself in all its contradictions.*

"That was what the message meant—the one he left for you?"

"Yes. He turned it back on me. He was telling me that the price of peace —of ordinary happiness—was too high. Let's not inflict that sort of wound on Laura. Let her find happiness on her own terms."

Genevieve stood here, her hands still frozen on the doorknob, wondering if Jonathan Stapleton knew the whole truth about Rawdon. She sensed that he suspected it. She also sensed that he did not want to have it confirmed.

"Laura wants to love you, Gen. But she's afraid of you. She can't be the woman you've become. A pillar of fire. Give her time to become a woman in her own way."

Genevieve withdrew her hand from Laura's door. The real sufferer, the one who needed forgiveness which only she could offer in Ben Dall's name, was standing there in the dimness at the other end of the hall. She walked toward Jonathan Stapleton, thinking how simple it would be to put her arms around him and whisper, *Father.*

But it was impossible; the mere idea froze her in midstride. "Maybe you're right," she said.

Genevieve retreated to Cynthia's bedroom and spent the rest of the night staring into the darkness, absorbing what Jonathan Stapleton had just told her, letting its meaning permeate her flesh.

At breakfast, Laura informed them that she was not going to marry Winthrop Astor Chapman. "I'm probably not going to marry anyone," she said. "If I ever do, he won't be an American. I'm disgusted with the United States of America and its miserable politics, its cheap newspapers, its utter indifference to art and beauty. I want to move to Florence and study art under Bernard Berenson while I decide what to do with my life. I assume you'll loan me the money, Pa. I'll pay it back next year, when I finally get my inheritance from your mother's estate."

It was too much. Genevieve had succumbed to silence about Rawdon. But she was not going to allow her daughter to become a mere aesthete. She was about to begin a lecture on the importance of struggle, caring for others, ideals, when a masculine hand seized her wrist under the table. "I hope you'll at least let your family come visit you. Or are you sick of us too?" Jonathan Stapleton said.

"Refugees will always be welcome," Laura said.

It was outrageous, that iron grip insisting on her silence. Suddenly a voice whispered, *You moralists are all alike.* It was Cynthia, telling Genevieve Dall how much she resembled this man sitting next to her.

"I hope—I can be among the visitors," Genevieve said.

The sullen hostility on Laura's face wavered and broke, "Of course, Mother. No one would be more welcome."

It was a beginning.

Later in the day, Genevieve was working on a speech she was planning to give at the suffrage convention when Cousteau informed her that Mr. Pendleton was downstairs. She greeted him with a wary smile. He looked in much better spirits. "Pulitzer wants me to come back. He wants me to help him bleach the yellow journalism out of the *World.*"

"Do you think he means it?"

"There's only one way to find out. How would you like to join me in the great experiment?"

"I'm too involved in this reorganization of the suffrage movement—I've decided that I can't be a reporter and a crusader at the same time."

"I meant join *me,* not the *New York World.* I need someone around to remind me twice a day that I'm not a yellow fellow."

"I have to stand for something first, Clay."

"You can do both. We'll stand together." He took her hands. "Gen, I've loved you from a distance long enough."

Here was the answer to the loneliness Laura was inflicting on her, to her sense of failure as a loving woman. "Oh Clay. I want to try it. But I'm so afraid I'll fail again. My mind says yes. I've loved you too for a long time. But my heart is—still mute. What if it never learns to speak?"

He drew her to him for a long, gentle kiss. "I know how you feel, Gen. We're both mourning Rawdon. I don't know how long it will last. But I'm willing to wait."

"What if it's forever?" she said.

"That's a little longer than I'd like. I'll give you until the next century."

"That's only a year and a half away."

"No kidding."

The next day, Clay invited her to a staff meeting in the *World*'s city room. "Politicians invite their wives to their inaugurations. Why can't I invite you to my resurrection?" he said.

Whitney Branch, the new managing editor, announced Clay's return to the paper as editor of the editorial page. Everyone understood that Clay was again one of the paper's top men, with as much influence as the managing editor—perhaps more. Branch cleared his throat and said the real purpose of the meeting was to announce some changes in the *World*'s policy. Mr. Pendleton had a message to deliver from Mr. Pulitzer.

Clay spoke in his quiet matter-of-fact voice, still with a trace of a southern accent. "It's time for the *World* to become a normal newspaper again. I think I can say it is Mr. Pulitzer's desire that no one in any capacity, high or low, great or small, should ever do anything as a member of the staff of the *World* which he would not do or believe in doing as a man—or woman. Be just as clever as you can. Be more energetic and enterprising than any other reporter if you can—but, above all, be truthful."

It was all done so calmly, so casually, with none of the histrionics that other men might have brought to the occasion, it took Genevieve a moment to realize that she was witnessing a turning point in the history of American journalism. But she was far more concerned with its meaning in Clay's life, and her own. She stared at Clay's rugged squarish face with the bulldog jaw and wry skeptic's smile and thought, *I want to love this man.*

He was Rawdon's opposite in almost every way. Was that why love was suddenly possible? No, it was a gift she wanted to offer Clay for his own sake, a compound of knowledge and gratitude and admiration that had been gathering force in her soul for a long time.

Somehow it seemed right, fitting, that this time love should occur in the most unlikely place, the bare ugly city room, with its acrid smell of paste and printer's ink, before two dozen tough-eyed reporters, those denizens of the city's sewers, sitting on their littered desks while the blaring beeping rumbling sounds of the great metropolis drifted through the open window. Beyond question, this was love in the real world.

Between love as wish, as a spiritual reality, and love as flesh there still remained the no man's land of Genevieve's self-doubt. She begged Clay to be patient, she tried to show him in a hundred ways that love was real, a fact in her voice, her eyes, in the slow steady growth of her yearning for his arms around her.

Meanwhile she borrowed money from him to travel across the continent trying to persuade suffragists to support a new strategy that she had evolved in long midnight discussions with Clay. She wanted to mix political guile with feminism's crusading spirit—to downplay the call for equal rights for the time being and concentrate on getting the vote as the all-important first step.

In the fall of 1899, Genevieve sailed to Europe to forge links with woman suffrage movements there. In Paris she received a note from Alva Vanderbilt Belmont inviting her to tea. Mrs. Belmont amazed Genevieve by announcing that she was interested in the suffrage movement. A few months before her death, Cynthia Stapleton had dared her to get involved in it. The idea had been gnawing at her mind ever since. What could she do?

Genevieve began telling her about their desperate need for a national headquarters and the money to run it. "Take a floor in a New York office building and send me the rent bills," Mrs. Belmont said. "I want to help a little with other expenses too." Whereupon she handed Genevieve a check for $200,000.

In Italy, Genevieve stopped in Florence to see Laura. They spent a tense four days together, which virtually annihilated Genevieve's exultation over Mrs. Belmont's generosity. Laura constantly substituted lectures on art for conversation. They at least avoided arguments—which might be considered another step forward. But they did not come close to achieving the communion for which Genevieve longed. Only once, when they were looking at Uccello's painting *Saint George and the Dragon* in the Pitti Palace did Laura drop her guard.

"Guess who I ran into, looking at this very picture. Dolph Mayer. He and his twin brother are working for their banker cousins in Hamburg. Supporting the whole family, I gather. His parents are pretty much broken down, physically and mentally."

"How sad," Genevieve said.

"Dolph is the only intelligent male of my acquaintance. I was delighted to find he shares my low opinion of our native country. I showed him Father's last letter. He said it was the most beautiful thing he's ever read."

"Someday—I'd like to see that letter."

Laura shook her head. "We'd only argue about it."

Genevieve sailed home full of forlorn thoughts about her failed personal life. Clay met her on the dock with an armful of yellow roses. He kissed her and she found herself kissing him fervently in return.

"I used those letters you sent me on the way militarism is spreading through Europe as background for a half-dozen editorials," Clay said as they rode uptown. "Pulitzer said they were the best stuff we've published in a year."

"He's been behaving himself?"

"No worse than usual."

He congratulated her on Mrs. Belmont's generosity, which she had also told him about by mail, and again urged her to let him publish something on it. Genevieve demurred; she did not want to embarrass their only patron.

"How's Laura?"

"She's all right," Genevieve said. "But—I couldn't get close to her. I'm beginning to think I never will."

With a last inner tremor, she let Laura go. She accepted the reality of the distance between them. "I can't live her life for her."

"Amen," Clay said, taking her hand. "Have you given any thought to living your own life?"

She retreated to the opposite side of the hack. She wanted to speak as Genevieve Dall, uninfluenced by masculine arms around her. "Maybe I had to go away for a month to realize how much I need you, Clay. If you're still willing to risk me—"

His kiss stopped this attempt to issue a final warning.

The next day Genevieve went over to New Jersey to give Jonathan Stapleton a report on Laura. Shortly after peace was signed with Spain, he had resigned his general's commission, sold his house on Stuyvesant Square and returned to his native state. He said New York was too full of memories of Cynthia.

Genevieve found him in Bowood's garden, arranging toy soldiers in battle formation for his grandson Paul, George Stapleton's oldest child. The General pointed to a mass of tiny figures in gray. "That's the southern army over there," he said. "Ninety thousand of them."

"Why are you filling his head with that stuff?" she asked.

Little Paul looked over his shoulder. For a moment Genevieve was speechless. It was Rawdon. The same chiseled symmetrical face. But the eyes were gray—the General's eyes.

"You haven't met this fellow," Jonathan said, hauling him up on his hip. He was about two years old. "Say hello to Aunt Genevieve."

Paul said hello and scampered away. Jonathan watched him go. "You saw the resemblance," he said.

"Yes."

"He's like him in other ways too. Very headstrong. I'll see if I can modify that." He averted his eyes, as if he expected a rebuke. "Don't worry. I won't overdo it."

Genevieve smiled. The man was indomitable. Still trying to mold sons and daughters, no matter how often they eluded his paternal grasp.

Sunshine filled the air around them; it glowed on the green boxwood hedges that some Stapleton had planted a hundred years ago.

"How do you like this weather?" the General said, taking out a big meerschaum pipe and stuffing it with tobacco. "Saint Martin's summer, they used to call it in Revolutionary days. It reminds me of a poem Melville wrote about the peace he felt in his old age, with a pipe and his memories. He called it a Saint Martin's summer of the mind."

"I wish I could get the whole world to smoke that brand of tobacco," Genevieve said.

In the midst of a struggle for an embattled cause, she found strength in this old man's contentment. He had faltered, he had made mistakes, some of his most cherished hopes and quests had failed, but in his soul was the consolation that he had given the best of himself to the challenges of his time. Above all he had loved—sometimes crudely, sometimes angrily, often in sorrow—but still loved those few who had gained entrance to his guarded heart. Perhaps that was the most important thing about him, the largest of his many meanings for her.

She told him about Laura. She did not mention the sense of failure and loss she had confessed to Clay. She talked about the way Laura was pursued by swarms of Italian, French and English painters and sculptors but kept them all at arm's length. "Only one man seems to have penetrated her antiromantic armor," she said. "Dolph Mayer. They seem to enjoy seeing themselves as fellow exiles from America."

"She always liked him," the General said. "His middle name is Rawdon."

"I think you miss her much more than I do," Genevieve said. "Why don't you pay her a visit?"

"The less she sees of me the better," he said. "Besides—I couldn't bear Italy without Cynthia."

"I have something else to tell you," Genevieve said. "I'm going to marry Clay Pendleton."

A smile transformed his scarred face. He opened his arms and drew her to him for an enormously powerful squeeze. "That makes me the happiest father in America," he said.

Father. The word spiraled through Genevieve's mind like a wandering comet. Then, obeying no law of astronomy that she knew, it suddenly became a fixed star. It spoke in the center of her body, and for the first time there was no pain. She surrendered the last and deepest hurt, the failure of that primary love. She gave her lost father to history's grief and accepted this man's long wishful need to heal the wound.

"I really came to thank you for everything. For Laura. For Clay. Even for Rawdon," she said.

"No," he said. "I'm the grateful one. To have this gift of love from you, after all these years. When I don't deserve it. When I think of how I inflicted the Stapletons' woes on you—and Cynthia."

"They were honorable wounds," Genevieve said.

Two hours later, Genevieve rode up Manhattan Island on the Sixth Avenue elevated to Clay's apartment in the Navarro Flats on Fifty-ninth Street. A marvelous sense of newness stirred in her as the elevator rose to the ninth floor. At the door, she heard Clay inside, picking out "Sweet Genevieve" on his mandolin. Her finger paused on the white bell and she saw the future and the past bathed in the glowing present.

She had thought she could rule the future by abolishing the past. She had thought history could be dismissed. Now she knew that it was from the past that sweetness came, the blessed sweetness of forgiving and being forgiven. It was a new and better exaltation than the trumpet call of the ideal.

In a few months she would join Clay in the golden dome of the *World*, looking down on the great metropolis as it celebrated the new century. Husband and wife, they would stand there, side by side, knowing that there was no hope of changing it from the City of Man to the City of God overnight. They would not surrender to Rawdon's evil will, the voice of Cain, demanding perfect justice from the fathers. But they would not abandon his youthful dream of a shining message in America's destiny. Rawdon was not excluded from the forgiveness ripening within her now.

POSTSCRIPT

According to a handwritten note on the title page, this manuscript was found among the papers of Clay Pendleton, who died in the sinking of the steamship *Lusitania* in 1915. From internal evidence it would seem that it was largely written by Mr. Pendleton with considerable additions from his wife, Genevieve, who died in 1925. For obvious reasons it could not be published while some of the principals were still alive. It was placed in a vault at Bowood along with other papers of the Stapleton family, which are now being published under grants from the Principia Foundation. Among earlier volumes are *Rulers of the City* and *Promises to Keep*, which tell the story of some of the twentieth-century Stapletons, and *Dreams of Glory* and *Liberty Tavern*, which deal with the Stapletons of the Revolutionary War era.

antiope – queen of the amazons!